THE LATINO READER

Books by Harold Augenbraum

Latinos in English

Growing Up Latino: Memoirs and Stories
Co-edited with Ilan Stavans

Books by Margarite Fernández Olmos

Sobre la literatura puertorriqueña de aquí y de allá: aproximaciones feministas

Pleasure in the Word: Erotic Writing by Latin American Women
Co-edited with Lizabeth Paravisini-Gebert

Remaking a Lost Harmony: Short Stories from the Hispanic Caribbean
Co-edited with Lizabeth Paravisini-Gebert

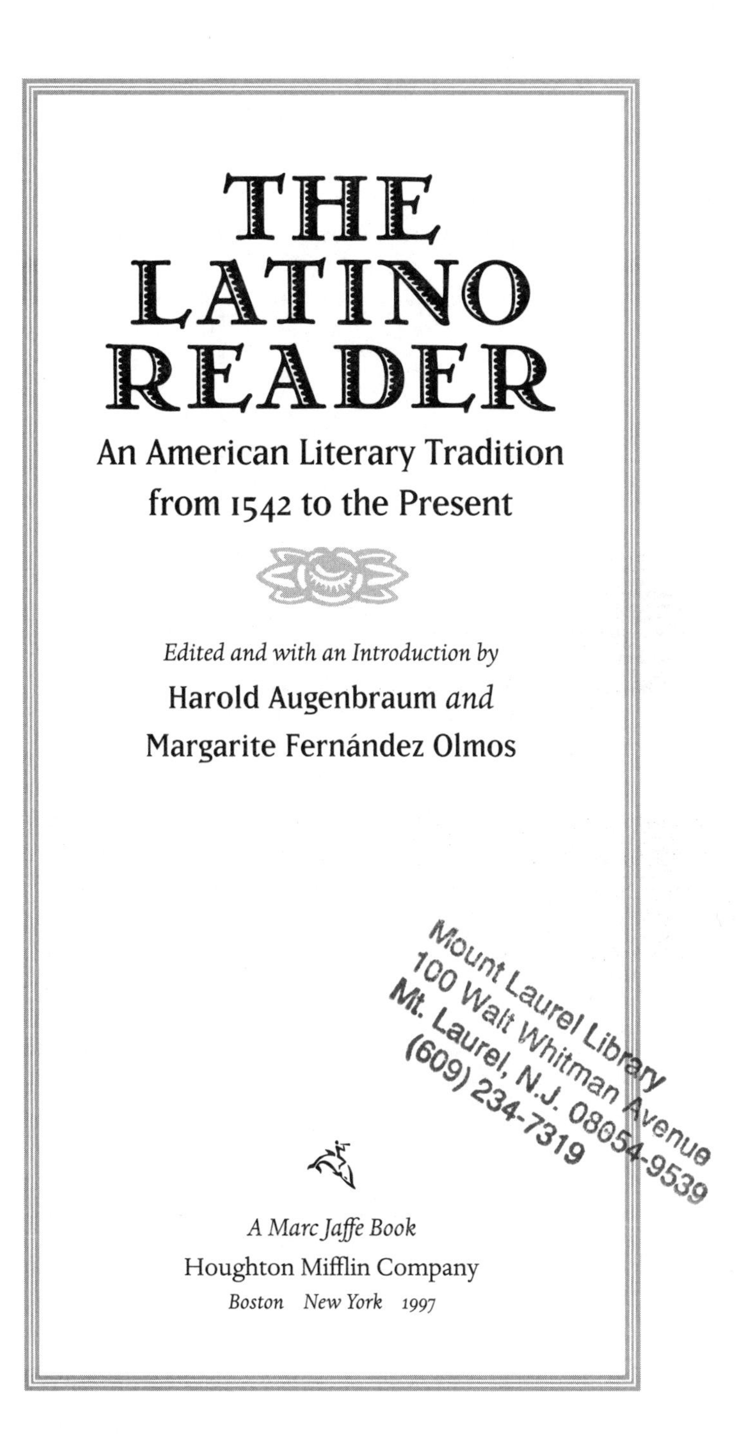

THE LATINO READER

An American Literary Tradition from 1542 to the Present

Edited and with an Introduction by

Harold Augenbraum *and*

Margarite Fernández Olmos

A Marc Jaffe Book
Houghton Mifflin Company
Boston New York 1997

Kaen 16.00

To my mother, Virginia Fernández, and
my daughter, Gabriela Carmen Olmos Fernández,
U.S. *boricua / quisqueyana* / Latina. What's in a name?

— M.F.O.

To Audrey

— H.A.

For information about this and other Houghton Mifflin trade and reference
books and multimedia products, visit The Bookstore at Houghton Mifflin
on the World Wide Web at http://www.hmco.com/trade/.

Library of Congress Cataloging-in-Publication Data
The Latino reader : an American literary tradition from 1542 to the present /
edited and with an introduction by Harold Augenbraum and Margarite
Fernández Olmos.
p. cm.
"A Marc Jaffe Book."
Includes bibliographical references and index.
ISBN 0-395-76529-3 — ISBN 0-395-76528-5 (pbk.)
1. American literature — Hispanic American authors. 2. Spanish American
literature — Exiled authors — Translations into English. 3. Hispanic Americans
— Literary collections.
I. Augenbraum, Harold. II. Fernández Olmos, Margarite.
PS508.H57L4 1997
810.8'0868 — DC20 96-42277 CIP

Printed in the United States of America

QUM 10 9 8 7 6 5 4 3 2 1

Book design by Melodie Wertelet

Credits begin on page 504

CONTENTS

Part II ~ Prelude *63*

Part III ~ Latino United States *137*

INTRODUCTION
An American Literary Tradition

Contemporary writing about Latino culture in the United States is rife with geographic and topographical metaphors. Calls for a "cognitive remapping of cultural terrain" and "(de)construction of psychic borders and historical bridges" combine with insistent demands for a "deterritorialization of the mainstream" in order to eliminate "psychic dislocations and the cultural marginalization of those on the periphery." Such metaphors are not exclusive to Latino reality, but they are entirely appropriate. Indeed, one can say that Latinos are linked, directly or indirectly, to their precursors, the early Hispanic explorers in the southeastern and southwestern United States, in having to chart a course through a treacherous and often bewildering landscape. For contemporary Latino authors, however, the frontier is the literary culture of the United States, where they have been struggling to gain their rightful place.

Geography has always played a major role in the formulation of Latino history in this country. From the Hispanic soldiers and missionaries in the former Spanish territories, to the *hispanos, californios,* and Mexicans in lands invaded and later occupied by Anglo Americans before and after the Mexican-American War, to the Caribbean (im)migrants affected by U.S. political and economic incursions, the destinies of Latino peoples have been intricately linked to imperial territorial expansion and the vagaries of geopolitics. But the geographical metaphor also extends to those who dare to synthesize or define U.S. Latino culture: they may discover that they are on shaky ground.

Given the recent critical recognition and widespread popularity of Latino writers both in the United States and internationally, a historical anthology seemed timely and necessary. In fact, we were amazed to discover that no such collection existed. We quickly discovered why. Any attempt to consolidate the culture of such a diverse group of people under the single rubric of "Latino" is problematic in several important areas, revealing more differences than similarities, more questions to be considered than issues resolved.

Although loosely united by a common heritage as native Spanish speakers or their descendants, the numerous Latino groups in the United States are as ethnically, racially, and socioeconomically heterogeneous as the more precise names many prefer: *mexicanos, puertorriqueños, cubanos, dominicanos, salvadoreños, colombianos,* and so on. Each Latino subgroup represents not only a distinct culture and geographic area of the Americas but also a specific history vis-à-vis the United States. (Using the term "Latino" and the more official "Hispanic" to describe the culture of this population is also problematic. "Hispanic" is rejected by many authors as too reductive in its association with Spain and Spanish culture, thereby ignoring the indigenous and/or African heritage of many Latin American and Caribbean peoples. "Latino" is perceived as a more useful, if still unsatisfactory, label, as it is based more neutrally on an identity shared through the use of Romance languages. For Gustavo Pérez Firmat, neither choice is valid. "My trouble is," he writes, "that I don't see myself as Latino, but as Cuban — *cubano, cubiche, cubanazo, criollo.* To tell the truth, the Latino is a statistical fiction. Part hype and part hypothesis, the Latino exists principally for the purposes of politicians, ideologues, salsa singers, and Americans of non-Hispanic descent." "Chicano" and "Nuyorican," which are more recent, are occasionally interchangeable with "Mexican American" and "mainland Puerto Rican," although "Chicano" in particular reflects a political expression of ethnic pride. We have given preference to "Latino" until a more precise term emerges.)

A native population with deep historical roots in this country, Mexican Americans have the longest U.S. Latino heritage, dating at least from the 1848 Treaty of Guadalupe Hidalgo, which ceded a third of Mexico's territory to the United States and transformed more than 80,000 Mexicans into residents of this country. As the playwright and filmmaker Luis Valdez's oft-cited remark appropriately recalls, "We did not come to the United States at all. The United States came to us." Rooted in Spanish colonialism, the residents of these areas had to adapt not only to a foreign force with differing political practices but also cultural habits that clashed with several centuries of Hispanic, Roman Catholic, communitarian, and patriarchal tradition. The frontier or border culture that emerged initially had the predominant role of preserving heritage and memory (real or imagined); in time the cultural conflicts with the larger U.S. society would grow increasingly complex, as would the twentieth-century Mexican-American/Chicano literary response.

Puerto Ricans and Cubans, the other two major Latino subgroups, which had strong cultural ties to Spain and Africa, began to make their presence felt in the United States in the late nineteenth and early twentieth centuries through the political exile communities in New York City and South Florida. The great waves of Caribbean (im)migration to the United States, however, occurred after World War II: Puerto Rican migrants (having been U.S. citizens since 1917) came in great numbers in the late 1940s, while Cuban exiles first arrived in the years immediately following the triumph of the Cuban Revolution in 1959, with repeated sporadic waves in the decades following.

The more recent arrival of people from the Dominican Republic and Central and South America is part of an ever-increasing diaspora from Latin America and the Caribbean. According to 1995 Census Bureau figures, Hispanics comprise 10.2 percent of the total U.S. population; at present rates of growth, Hispanic peoples will make up one quarter of the population by the year 2050. Such projections indicate that the United States is undergoing one of the most profound demographic shifts in its ethnic and racial makeup since the late nineteenth century, thereby creating a multicultural society of unparalleled diversity. By the middle of the next century, the descendants of white Europeans, who have defined U.S. national culture for most of the country's existence, will be in the minority. The future is clear: "Without fully realizing it," noted Martha Farnsworth Riche in *Time* magazine, "we have left the time when the nonwhite, non-Western part of our population could be expected to assimilate to the dominant majority. In the future, the white, Western majority will have to do some assimilation of its own."

~~~
~~~

In his book *Chicano Narrative,* Ramón Saldívar observed that from the perspective of the dominant culture, Mexican Americans, along with other so-called minority groups, "helped define Anglo America by serving as its contrasting personality, idea, and experience." What often goes unrecognized is the extent and the depth of the influence of Latino culture on American literary culture, within which it has existed not only as a contrast but as a long and authentic parallel tradition.

As recent studies in cultural history have shown, art and literature helped to build both empire and nation; colonial discourse not only created and described the American "Other" for a European audience but was itself a form of social and political practice, as it forged the new reality it set out to conquer. In this context the writings of early Hispanic explorers and missionaries in areas that are now part of the United States should be considered a component of U.S. literary tradition.

Recent anthologies of American literature have recognized the works of such figures as Alvar Núñez Cabeza de Vaca and Gaspar Pérez de Villagrá, as well as the oral tradition of tales and poetry from the northern provinces of Nueva España (later Mexico and the American Southwest) as reflections of the first European writings produced on this continent. Clearly the legacy of these years of Spanish rule goes much further than the renaming of the topography with the Hispanic names that survive on U.S. road maps.

According to recent scholarship by Juan Bruce-Novoa, Luis Leal, Ramon A. Gutiérrez, and María Herrera-Sobek, among others, this early literature laid the foundation for Chicano literature. As European explorers reinvented the Americas and the indigenous populations they encountered, shaping them to the models they had brought from the Old World, they represented these peoples as inferior brutes and savages in order to rationalize European political domination and cultural hegemony. This process of ethnic marginalization was later repeated by Anglo-American colonizers with the conquered Mexicans in 1848 and with the U.S. Latino population throughout the twentieth century. As Herrera-Sobek wrote:

> The conquered Mexican-American population became a voiceless entity, frequently described by the terms invisible and silent minority. Denied their history, their literature, their

> language, and their culture, Mexican Americans' artistic expressions were marginalized and ignored by the mainstream Euroamerican community. And although Chicanos resisted colonization and oppression, as is evident in court records throughout the Southwest and as narrated in resistance corridos, or ballads, such as the "Ballad of Gregorio Cortez," it was not until the 1960s that this ethnic group began to reassert itself into the national consciousness.

But beyond these considerations there is the important symbolic function of a figure such as Cabeza de Vaca. *The Account* (1542) describes his shipwreck and adventures in the Southeast and Southwest as a captive of the Indians and his subsequent transformation into a faith healer in order to save his life. Cabeza de Vaca's metamorphosis into a being neither European nor Indian, a cultural hybrid created by the American experience, converts the explorer into a symbolic precursor of the Chicano/a. Not entirely identified with either Mexican or Anglo society, the Chicano/a, like Cabeza de Vaca, undergoes a cultural adaptation and transformation that makes him or her the ideal New World American. S/he can change her/himself to fit the situation and celebrate that change — in other words, s/he can make a virtue of necessity.

Although important Chicano critics acknowledge that these early works comprise the foundation of Chicano literature and as such can claim an important role in American literature in general, others disagree. The question always arises, do these early works represent the Spanish literary tradition or Spanish-American letters? Are the works a part of Mexican literature or U.S. literary culture? Perhaps all works prior to 1848 should be identified, as Ray Padilla has suggested, as "pre-Chicano Aztlanese materials," referring to the legendary land of Aztlán in the southwestern United States where the Aztec peoples are said to have originated. If indeed there is truth in the adage that "America creates Americans," then early Hispanic writing is a truly original product; with its fantastic tales of cities of gold and stories of fabulous potential for wealth and power for all who dared to make the attempt, this tradition may be considered the source of the mythical American Dream.

In the late nineteenth century, a young Cuban poet who had suffered imprisonment and exile for his revolutionary ideas settled in the United States. From 1881 to 1895, José Martí inspired others to organize for the second war of Cuban independence from Spain. Among his many activities he founded the Cuban Revolutionary Party as well as La Liga (the League), a society for the advancement of Cuban Blacks; he lectured in New York and South Florida; and he devised a revolutionary code that insisted on unity for the Americas, tying Cuba's freedom with that of the rest of the hemisphere.

During his exile years in New York, Cuba's most beloved patriot also wrote incessantly. He published articles and letters in Latin American and U.S. periodicals as well as his great literary works, which are considered the preeminent expressions of Cuban national literature. Among these are his *Versos sencillos* (*Simple Verses,* 1891) and the famous and powerful essay "Nuestra America" ("Our America," 1891). Martí's writings enlarged Latin America's understanding of the United States through his appreciation of such authors as Mark Twain, Walt Whitman, Henry W. Longfellow, and Ralph Waldo Emerson; his numerous translations, including Helen Hunt Jackson's novel *Ramona* (1884), with its cast of wooden Mexican Americans; and his articles and essays on American society and political culture. His letters, in impeccable English, to U.S. newspapers demonstrate a keen awareness of North American attitudes toward its neighbors to the south, and his defense of Cubans and other groups against ethnic attacks in the American press unfortunately retain a canny relevance today, more than one hundred years after their first appearance.

Martí's writings distinguished between his America — Latin America, "Our America," "Mother America" — and Anglo-Saxon America, "the Other America." He ruefully observed that the Latin American republics had fought against Spain for political independence only to have their economic sovereignty compromised by new imperial powers. His essay "Our America" warns Latin America of the threat of U.S. imperialism, a danger that could be checked only by more enlightened attitudes in both the United States and Latin America.

> Perhaps Our America is running another risk that does not come from itself but from the difference in origins, methods, and interests between the two halves of the continent, and the time is near at hand when an enterprising and vigorous people who scorn or ignore Our America will even so approach it and

> demand a close relationship. . . . The pressing need of Our America is to show itself as it is, one in spirit and intent, swift conqueror of a suffocating past, stained only by the enriching blood drawn from hands that struggle to clear away the ruins, and from the scars left upon us by our masters. The scorn of our formidable neighbor who does not know us is Our America's greatest danger. And since the day of the visit is near, it is imperative that our neighbor know us, and soon, so that it will not scorn us. Through ignorance it might even come to lay hands on us. Once it does know us, it will remove its hands out of respect. One must have faith in the best men and distrust the worst. One must allow the best to be shown so that it reveals and prevails over the worst. Nations should have a pillory for whoever stirs up useless hates, and another for whoever fails to tell them the truth in time. [Translated by Elinor Randall]

Of course, the "day of the visit" came sooner than even Martí had predicted: as a result of the Spanish Cuban American War, by the end of 1898 Cuba had gained its independence but remained under the political and economic influence of the United States for decades to follow, and Puerto Rico became a U.S. territory, having been acquired as war booty after the Spanish defeat. Mexico, Central America, and the Caribbean also felt the scorn of their powerful neighbor; repeated invasions and military occupations of the area set the stage for the massive immigrations of these peoples to the United States as the century progressed.

Edna Acosta-Belén and other scholars in the growing discipline of Latino studies have referred to Martí's "contemporary resonance," in terms not only of his political foresight but of his continental vision of Latin America. Martí's affirmation of the non-Western elements and hybrid cultural configurations of the Americas was a call to "decolonize" the mythologies that Latin Americans had held about themselves. How could the hemisphere be understood without the Indian and the African as well as the European? Martí's appeal to end monocultural definitions of ethnicity and nationality and to build cultural bridges is the basis of contemporary postmodern and postcolonial writing, articulated by such writers as Gloria Anzaldúa and Cherríe Moraga. What Martí could not have foreseen, however, was the extent to which the very categories of "Our America" and the "Other America" would be blurred in the late twentieth century by the massive movement of peoples from south to north and by precisely the more enlightened, encompassing vision he had championed.

The Latino panethnic consciousness that scholars now elaborate in their research is what *The Latino Reader* proposes to illuminate. Our survey of this cultural legacy will, we hope, challenge conventional interpretations of literary tradition and undermine some of the "truisms" that used to inform American literary histories. The questions of nationality and of the relationship of literature to national identity are keys to understanding contemporary Latino authors. According to critic Jean Franco, these writers no longer have to choose between assimilation and national identity but can fashion "original personalities." Once denigrated as being neither "de aquí ni de allá," not from here or from there, Latino writers have converted that status from a liability to an advantage. They can refer to their origins without being, in Franco's words, "imprisoned in nationality. . . . Latino artists and performers are now the vanguard voices in the American context, members of a global border culture no longer confined to the U.S./Mexican border."

These aesthetic options have been enthusiastically embraced by contemporary Latino artists. But, as *The Latino Reader* will demonstrate, the celebration of cultural syncretism, the fusion and convergence of traditions, are not really new phenomena: they have been a mobilizing element of Latino culture all along and an integral component of the American literary tradition.

One of the thorniest problems of compiling an anthology like *The Latino Reader,* apart from selecting a few texts from the many that merit inclusion, is responding to legitimate concerns that the compilers are attempting to present as a cohesive literary tradition works by authors who, for the most part and until fairly recently, were unaware of each other's literary production. The argument is certainly valid. Critics and editors have always been susceptible to this criticism; any attempt to formulate cultural consensus has inherent shortcomings.

Americanists, however, have traditionally made a virtue of literary revisionism. Robert E. Spiller declared in the classic *Literary History of the United States* (1948) that "each generation should produce at least one literary history of the United States, for each generation must define the past in its own terms," echoing Ralph Waldo Emerson's earlier call in *The American Scholar* (1837): "Each age must write its own books; or rather, each generation for the next succeeding. The books of an older period will not fit this." Creating consensus in the United States after the Vietnam War, the Cold War, and the movements for civil rights, women's rights, minority-group rights, and gay rights is, however, an increasingly formidable task. Indeed, as Sacvan Bercovitch has noted in *American Literary History*, "Consensus of all sorts has broken down. . . . It was the achievement of the Spiller *History* to consolidate a powerful literary-historical movement. It will be the task of the present generation to reconstruct American literary history by making a virtue of dissensus." Recent books have begun to recognize the need for a reconceptualization of American literary discourse. In the 1988 edition of the *Columbia Literary History of the United States,* the editors did not attempt to tell a "single, unified story" with a "coherent narrative," conceding that it was no longer "possible, or desirable, to formulate an image of continuity when diversity of literary materials and a wide variety of critical voices are, in fact, the distinctive features of national literature. The research and criticism of the last thirty years had revealed that the history of the literature of the United States is not one story but many different stories."

The Latino Reader articulates one of those stories: that of the Latino culture, which has made a substantial contribution to the American literary heritage. Given that the complex process of cultural transmission has never been satisfactorily explained, we have taken as our philosophical point of departure T. S. Eliot's perception: "A common inheritance and a common cause unite artists consciously or unconsciously. . . . Between the true artists of any time there is, I believe, an unconscious community." Despite the thematic, aesthetic, and political diversity of Latino literary culture, a common historical subtext permeates this multivocal and even multilingual literature.

Although anthologists' choices are always to some degree personal, our editorial decisions have relied on the views of scholars and researchers who have developed a critical Latino discourse based on emblematic texts and/or authors. Therefore works deemed to have had a strong impact on the evolution of Latino letters appear alongside writings that we ourselves have recovered, in several cases making them accessible for the first time in English translation. Likewise, some authors not traditionally perceived of as Latino, such as William Carlos Williams, whose Spanish-American roots and influences have only recently come to light, are presented along with writers who may not identify themselves as Latino, preferring Chicano, Nuyorican, or Cuban to the broader term.

The uneven aesthetic quality of the texts reflects various stages in the development of Latino literature; nonetheless, all of these works have played a formative role in that evolution. We hope that by presenting a broad historical panorama of this dynamic literary culture, *The Latino Reader* will encourage discussion and afford the reader an opportunity to trace the various threads that define the Latino tradition.

The anthology is organized broadly into three parts — Encounters, Prelude, and Latino United States — each with a brief introduction providing historical and thematic context. The divisions are not definitive but are simply useful points of departure. The works, presented chronologically according to their approximate date of publication, cover the broadest possible range; regretfully, limitations of space have obliged us to exclude many worthwhile texts. Part III focuses on U.S. Latino authors; Latin American authors who reside in the United States but whose works have not yet had a major impact on the U.S. Latino tradition are a subject for future study. Though an important topic of debate, these writers fall outside the purview of this anthology.

Naturally, no single collection can represent the totality of such a fertile experience as the Latino tradition. *The Latino Reader* is a starting point in the attempt to articulate a long neglected literary history and reclaim a previously dismissed body of writing. It has been said that the search for an authentic "America" entails a cultural remapping and renaming that will ultimately benefit not only Latinos and other minority groups but the entire society. For Latino artists, however, the search for America has been and continues to be less concerned with the ultimate destination than with the pleasures and perils of the journey.

EDITORS' NOTE

The date given for each work is that of its publication in final form, usually in book format. In those cases in which publication was delayed, we have given the approximate date of composition. For the dramas, we have included the date of the first production. In bilingual poems with Spanish titles we have retained the original title. For books that were originally written in Spanish, the titles of published translations in English are given in italics; unpublished English titles are in roman.

The editors would like to thank José B. Fernández, Monica Espinosa, and Ilan Stavans for their advice and assistance and Marc Jaffe for his unflagging enthusiasm for this project and others in Latino letters. Our thanks also to the Wolfe Institute for the Humanities at Brooklyn College, Julio Marzán, Lizabeth Paravisini-Gebert, Aileen Schmidt, Mindy Keskinen and Peg Anderson at Houghton Mifflin, the staff of the Brooklyn College Gideonse Library, particularly Robert Litwin, and the staff of the Mercantile Library of New York for their invaluable help. And a special thanks to our families for their tolerance and encouragement.

This anthology would not have been possible without the extraordinary dedication of Nicolás Kanellos and the staff, advisers, and scholars of the Recovering the U.S. Hispanic Literary Heritage Project at the University of Houston. The project provided funds for translations of heretofore untranslated texts and new translations of texts whose older translations needed to be updated. But the true value of the project has been as a standard setter (and bearer) for every scholar and editor working on the history of U.S. Latino letters.

Part I

ENCOUNTERS

When Christopher Columbus sailed for Asia and encountered what would later become known as the Americas, the Iberian Peninsula had recently reached the end of a significant transformation. In the eighth century, Moorish kings from North Africa had invaded the peninsula, where they established a formidable civilization. For the following seven centuries, monarchs of the several Christian Iberian kingdoms had attempted to drive the Muslims back across the Strait of Gibraltar, an effort called La Reconquista. They waged, in effect, a holy war to recapture the lands they believed belonged to them by divine right. Finally, in 1492, a few years after the marriage of Ferdinand of Aragon and Isabella of Castile had created a powerful military bloc, the same year as Columbus's voyage and Spain's expulsion of the Jews, the Christian Iberians ousted the last of the Moorish rulers from the stronghold of Granada. With this victory, *los reyes católicos,* the Catholic kings, as they were called, created modern Spain.

Each time Christian kings had expanded the territories under their control, they had sent priests to convert the infidels (in Spanish, *los infieles,* those without faith). Over the many centuries of warfare, this political and military tactic had evolved into a pattern. In Spain in the late fifteenth century, the Crown saw religious homogeneity as an aid to the consolidation of territory and allowed the Inquisition, led by the infamous Tomás de Torquemada, to wield a terrible power against the defeated Muslims and the other major minority, the Jews. The interdependence of politics and religion was an important tenet of various Spanish governments not only in the New World but also on the peninsula, well into the eighth decade of the twentieth century.

In the early sixteenth century, when the Spaniards began their conquest of America, they translated this pattern for use in their new territories. Each marauding army of impoverished nobles and soldiers of fortune was accompanied by missionaries, priests, and lay brothers, whose task was to convert *los infieles* and thereby secure the loyalty of the local population. In contrast to the attitudes toward the Indians in the British- and Puritan-dominated North, the Spanish encouraged religious conversion of the indigenous peoples and miscegenation as a way of furthering their colonial objectives. This was a direct parallel to the forced conversions of the Moors during the latter stages of La Reconquista, although in defense of the missionaries, it must be added that *their* main objectives were pastoral and apostolic.

The early conquerors, missionaries, and colonists often used the imagery of Spanish history in the art and literature they produced in the Americas. New Spain was, in a sense, a part of old Spain, and the indigenous people little different, it was thought, from the Moors. A late-sixteenth-century drama of unknown authorship, *Los moros y cristianos* (The Moors and the Christians), which is performed in Santa Cruz, New Mexico, to this day, was to a great extent meant to intimidate the American Moors. The early-seventeenth-century statue of the Virgin Mary, dubbed by the colonists "La Conquistadora," reflected the Creole belief that the Virgin herself aided in the conquest of the heathen (the statue can still be seen in the Cathedral of St. Francis in Santa Fe, New Mexico).

Over time, however, an American form of literary expression gradually emerged. Although the themes of the late-eighteenth-century drama *Los comanches* are similar to those of *Los moros y cristianos,* its characters, settings, and action are drawn from American history. Its story, of the defeat of the Comanche chief Cuerno Verde (Green Horn) by the Christian colonial forces of Don Carlos Fernández, closely parallels that of the earlier drama. This defeat, however, was recent and local, with few images or situations borrowed from Spanish history or legend. (Early in the drama a Spanish castle appears in the background as a symbol of the invading colonists.)

The origins of what we call Latino culture and literature today lie in the encounter between the Spanish sensibility and that of the native peoples. On this basis one can argue that Latino literature begins with *La relación (The Account),* Cabeza de Vaca's chronicle of eight years among the Amerindians, for the writer, experiencing the clash of the two cultures, undergoes a change in his world-view. But the Latino writer, though he leaves one culture behind, never fully becomes part of the culture he encounters. He is thus left in between, an intercultural being.

The body of literature created by people in this intercultural situation is often not all that literary. Yet the notion of encounter is basic to the tradition of Latino literature. Much Spanish colonial literature in what was to become the United States shares certain specific elements. Singly, these characteristics may not separate Latino literature from that of other Spanish colonial regions, but as a group these elements have had a profound and unique effect.

First, Latino literature was written by men, which was not always the case in other Spanish colonies. Though women often accompanied military and colonial expeditions, they apparently did not write, or at least their writings have not survived. At the end of the colonial period, it has been speculated, regional writings by women, especially articles, recipes, and letters to newspapers, may have been published throughout the colonies. One hopes they will be uncovered by further research.

Second, these writers were not literary specialists; many had little writing talent at all. While some of their work shows sophistication, much of it is crude, particularly in comparison with the colonial writings of other administrative regions of the Americas, such as that of Sor Juana Inés de la Cruz and Bernardo de Valbuena in Mexico. Some colonial works were patterned after Spanish epic poetry (Fray Alonso de Escobedo's *La florida,* for example), but most are dry accounts of daily movements through hostile territory, discussions of the establishment of missions, and descriptions of natural surroundings. One exception is *La florida del Inca* by Garcilaso de la Vega, half-Spanish and half-Incan, who also wrote a fascinating history of Peru and made translations of love poetry. Garcilaso's account of the ill-fated (a phrase often associated with the *conquistadores*) expedition of Hernando de Soto is an exciting history that includes respectful descriptions of the Amerindians.

Third, the cultures that produced these literatures lay on the margins of the Spanish colonial world. Unlike the administrative centers of Mexico, Lima, and La Habana, which were built on the ruins of highly advanced civilizations or had regular and direct contact with the home country, the northern frontier of New Spain was established among the loosely integrated indigenous populations of the colonial edges. Not until the nineteenth century, which brought political independence to other colonies and a nationalism that meant migration, exile, and occupation, did the writers of this northern area achieve the sophistication of their southern brethren or their northern British cousins.

Fourth, as noted earlier, much Spanish colonial literature is based in the conflict between cultures. Even so, it is not a monolithic tradition. It runs the gamut from fascinating accounts of personal change to religious poetry and drama to exciting historical chronicles that in some spots are as thrilling as adventure stories.

Fifth, there exists today very little, if any, written literature in the languages of the indigenous peoples of the colonial period. Though there was an oral tradition, the written literature and its cultural legacy originate in the Spanish language and a predominantly Spanish and/or Creole viewpoint. An irony is that the struggle to validate works written in languages spoken by a minority of inhabitants continues today, as literature composed in Spanish now must fight for publication and shelf space in the contemporary United States.

During the colonial period the chronicles of the *conquistadores,* regional poetry, and biography set the stage for the writing of the national (and hemispheric) periods that followed. The relation to Spain and Spanish history provided continuity in a new environment. But by the close of the eighteenth century, it was clear that the Spanish empire in the Americas was ending, as the monarchy came under extraordinary pressures at home. The motives for writing would change as the indigenous culture reemerged in the literature, presaging an American revitalization.

Alvar Núñez Cabeza de Vaca was born in Jerez de la Frontera, Spain, around 1490, the fourth son of a prominent family. Cabeza de Vaca was a successful soldier in the service of King Carlos V on various military expeditions in the Mediterranean. His name (in English, Cow's Head) originated with a thirteenth-century ancestor, a shepherd, who marked a secret pass through the mountains for King Sancho of Navarre with a cow's skull, which enabled Sancho to defeat the Moors in a decisive battle.

La relación (*The Account*) is widely considered to be the first example of Latino literature growing out of the experience of the territories that would later make up the United States. Cabeza de Vaca was the official treasurer, who reported to the king, for the 1527 expedition of Pánfilo de Narváez, a short-lived, disastrous trip that began in Cuba and ended, for all but four survivors, several months later in shipwrecks along the Florida coast. Cabeza de Vaca and three fellow *conquistadores,* now turned explorers, made their way westward, believing that their only chance of survival was to find the Christian settlements in the Southwest. Their journey lasted eight years and included stints as slaves (their clothes were taken away to keep them from escaping) and as faith healers. When Cabeza de Vaca and his companions finally encountered Christians, their physical appearance was so changed that the Spanish horsemen had difficulty believing their story.

Cabeza de Vaca himself later returned to Spain, where his tales (the first version of *The Account* was published in 1542, a second in 1555) won him an appointment as governor of Paraguay in 1542. He remained in that position for only two years. Scholars have speculated that because he had spent a great deal of time with the Amerindians of the north, the Spaniards in Paraguay thought he was too sympathetic to the native peoples. He is believed to have died in Seville, Spain, sometime between 1556 and 1564. The following passages are from the 1555 text.

from **The Account**

Which Tells When the Fleet Sailed, and of the Officers and People Who Went with It

On the seventeenth day of the month of June of 1527, Governor Pánfilo de Narváez departed from the port of San Lúcar de Barrameda by authority and order of Your Majesty to conquer and govern the provinces which lie on the mainland from the River of Palms to Cape Florida. The fleet that he took consisted of five ships in which went six hundred men, more or less. The officers that he took — for they ought to be mentioned — were those named here: Cabeza de Vaca as treasurer and Provost Marshal; Alonso Enríquez, purser;

Alonso de Solís as Your Majesty's Factor and Inspector; and a friar of the Order of St. Francis named Juan Suárez, as Commissary, along with four other friars of the same order.

We arrived at the island of Santo Domingo, where we remained nearly forty-five days provisioning ourselves with necessary supplies, especially horses. Here more than 140 men deserted our fleet, wanting to remain there because of the proposals and promises made to them by the people of that land. From there we departed and sailed to Santiago, a port on the island of Cuba, where during our stay of a few days the Governor supplied himself with men, arms and horses.

While there it happened that a gentleman named Vasco Porcalle, resident of the town of Trinidad on the same island, offered the Governor certain provisions he had in Trinidad, one hundred leagues from the aforementioned port of Santiago. The Governor departed for Trinidad with the entire fleet. But having gone half the distance and having reached a port called Cape Santa Cruz, it seemed to him that the fleet should wait there and send a ship to bring the provisions. For this purpose he sent a certain Captain Pantoja there with his ship and to be on the safe side, he ordered me to go with him. And the Governor remained with four ships, since he had bought another vessel on the island of Santo Domingo.

When we arrived at the port of Trinidad with these two ships, Captain Pantoja went with Vasco Porcalle into the town, one league away, to obtain the provisions. I remained on board with the pilots, who told us that we ought to leave that place as rapidly as possible, for it was a very poor harbor and many ships were lost in it. And because what happened to us there was very noteworthy, it seemed appropriate to the purpose and aim of my account of this journey to tell about it here.

The following morning there were bad signs in the weather. It began to rain and the seas were getting so rough that I gave permission for the people on board to go ashore. They nevertheless saw how bad the weather was, and since the town was one league away, many returned to the ship rather than expose themselves to the rain and cold.

Meanwhile a canoe came from the town bringing me a letter from a resident urging me to go there, saying that he would give me whatever provisions were available and necessary. I declined his offer, saying that I could not leave the ships.

At midday the canoe returned with another letter requesting the same thing with great insistence. A horse for me to ride was brought to the shore. I gave the same answer as before, saying that I could not leave the ships. But the pilots and the people begged me very much to go so that I might hasten the transfer of provisions as much as possible, so that we could leave there, since they greatly feared that the ships would be lost if they remained there for long. For this reason I decided to go to the town. But first I made arrangements with and ordered the pilots to save the people and the horses when the south wind blew, and to beach the ships if they found themselves in danger, for winds from that direction wreck many vessels. Then I left. I wanted some people to accompany me, but they did not wish to leave, saying that it was too rainy and cold and the town was too far, but that the following day, which was Sunday, they would leave with God's help to hear mass.

An hour after I departed the sea began to be very stormy and the north wind blew so strongly that not even the skiffs dared go toward land, nor could they beach the ships because of headwinds. They remained there that day and Sunday until nightfall with great difficulty because of the swirling winds and the heavy rainfall. At that time the rain and the storm began to increase so much that it was just as strong in the town as on the sea, for all the houses and churches were blown down, and it became necessary for us to go about in groups of seven or eight men locking our arms together so that we could keep the wind from blowing us away. And we feared being amidst the trees as much as the houses, for they too were being blown down and we could have been killed beneath them. In this storm and danger we went about all night without finding a place nor a spot where we might be safe for half an hour.

While we were going about we heard all night long, especially from the middle of the night onward, a great uproar and noise of voices, and a great sound of little bells and of flutes and tambourines and other instruments that went on until morning, when the storm ceased. Never in these parts had such a fearsome thing been seen. I gathered evidence of it and sent the testimony to Your Majesty.

Monday morning we went down to the port and did not find the ships. We saw their buoys in the water, from which we realized that they had been lost, and we went along the coast to see if we could find signs of them. Since we found nothing, we went into the woods, and a quarter of a league into them we found one of the ship's boats in some trees. Ten leagues from there we found the bodies of two persons from my ship, and certain box covers, and the bodies were so disfigured from having struck the rocks that they could not be recognized. A cloak and a quilt torn to shreds were also found, but nothing else appeared.

Sixty people and twenty horses perished on the ships. Those who had gone ashore the day the ships arrived, who must have numbered up to thirty, were the sole survivors of those who had come on both vessels. Thus, we endured several days with great hardship and need, for the provisions and sustenance that were in the town were lost, along with some livestock. It was pitiful to see the condition the land was left in, with fallen trees, the woods stripped bare, all without leaves or grass.

We stayed there until the fifth of November, when the Governor arrived with his four ships, which also had weathered the great storm but had survived because they had found safe harbor in time. The people he brought in them and those he found there were so terrified of what had happened that they feared setting sail again in winter, and they pleaded with the Governor to spend the season there. And he acceded to their wishes and those of the residents and wintered there. He put me in charge of the ships and the people, so that I could go with them to spend the winter in the port of Xagua, twelve leagues away, where I remained until the twentieth day of the month of February. . . .

How We Left Aute

The following day we left Aute and marched all day until we got to where I had been. The march was extremely difficult because we did not even have sufficient horses to carry the sick nor did we know how to cure them. It was very pitiful and painful to see the affliction and want that was on us. When we arrived we saw that there was little we could do to continue onward, because there was no place to pass through. Besides, even if there had been a good passage, our men could not have gone on because most of them were sick, and there were too few able-bodied men. I will not talk about this at great length here, since each person can imagine what we went through in this land that was so strange and so bad and so totally lacking in resources either for staying or for leaving. We nevertheless never lost confidence in the idea that God our Lord would provide the surest relief.

Something else happened that made our situation worse still: the majority of the cavalrymen began to leave secretly, thinking that they could save themselves. They abandoned the Governor and the sick men who were totally weak and helpless. But among them there were many noble and well-bred men who did not wish to see this happen without reporting it to the Governor and to Your Majesty's officers. Since we decried their objectives and set before them what a bad time this was to desert their captain and the sick and weak men, and especially to leave Your Majesty's service, they agreed to stay and share everything without abandoning one another.

When the Governor saw this, he called them all and one by one requested their advice for leaving that awful country and seeking some help, for there was none to be found in it. Since a third of the men were quite sick and with every passing hour more were succumbing to illness, we were certain that we would all get sick and die, and the situation was made more serious by the place we were in. Seeing all these and many other obstacles and suggesting many solutions, we all agreed on one, very difficult to carry out. It was to build boats in which we could leave. It seemed impossible to everyone because we did not know how to build them and had no tools, iron, forge, oakum, pitch, rigging, or any of the many things needed for it, and we especially lacked someone to provide expertise. Worst of all, there would be nothing to eat while the vessels were being built nor skilled men to do the job. Considering all this, we decided to think about it at greater length, and the discussion ceased that day. Each man commended the situation to God our Lord, asking him to lead it so that he would be best served.

The following day God willed for one of the men to come forth saying that he would make some flues from wood and several bellows from deerskins. Since we were in such a situation that anything that had the appearance of relief seemed good to us, we said that it should be done. And we agreed that we would make nails, saws, axes and the other necessary tools out of our stirrups, spurs, crossbows and other iron items we had, since we had such a great need for this. To relieve our lack of food while we were doing this, we decided that four forays to Aute were needed, with all the men and horses that could go. We also said that on the third day we should slaughter one of the horses to divide it among the sick and those who were working on the small boats. The forays were made with as many men and horses as possible, which yielded about four hundred *fanegas* of corn, although not without struggles and fights with the Indians. We had many palmettos gathered to use their fiber and covering, twisting it and preparing it to use it instead of oakum for the boats. The sole carpenter in our company had begun constructing the boats. We worked so diligently that we began on August 4th and had finished five boats by September 20th. Each one measured twenty-two cubits, and was caulked with the palmetto fibers. We caulked them with a kind of pitch from resin, made by a Greek named Don Theodoro from some pine trees and the palmetto fiber. From the horses' tails and manes we made rope and rigging; out of our shirts we made sails; and from some junipers near there we made oars, which we thought were necessary. And that land to which we had been brought by our sins was such that it was very difficult to find stones for ballast and anchors. Nowhere in it had we seen any. We skinned the legs of the horses in one piece and cured the hides to make skins for carrying water.

Twice during this time, while some of our men were gathering shellfish in the coves and inlets of the sea, the Indians attacked and killed ten of them within sight of our camp, but we could not go to their aid. We found them shot right through with arrows. Although some of them had good armor, it was not enough to withstand the arrows that they shoot with such skill and strength, as I said above.

According to the sworn statement of our pilots, we had traveled about 280 leagues from the bay we called La Cruz to this point. In all this land we did not see any mountains nor did we hear of any at all. Before we set sail — not counting those killed by Indians — more than forty of our men had died of illness and hunger.

By the twenty-second of September we had eaten all but one of the horses. That day we embarked in this order: forty-nine men went in the Governor's boat; in another that he gave to the Purser and the Commissary went an equal number; the third he gave to Captain Alonso del Castillo and to Andrés Dorantes with forty-eight men; another to two captains named Téllez and Peñalosa with forty-seven men; he gave the last one to the Inspector and to me with forty-nine men. After we loaded provisions and clothing, there was no more than one *xeme* above the water line. Besides this, we were squeezed in so tightly that we could not move. So great was our hardship that it forced us to venture out in this manner and to go out into such rough seas, without having anyone with us who knew the art of navigation. . . .

How the Indians Left Us

After I had been with the Christians for six months waiting to carry out our plan, the Indians went to gather prickly pears, that grew about thirty leagues from there. When we were about to flee, the Indians we were with fought among themselves over a woman, hitting one another with fists and sticks and striking one another on the head. They were so angry that each one took his lodge and went off by himself, making it necessary for us Christians who were there to leave also. In no way were we able to come together until the following year.

During this time my life was miserable because I was so hungry and so mistreated by the Indians. I tried to escape from my masters three times, but each time they went after me intending to kill me. God our Lord through his great mercy protected and sheltered me from them. When prickly pear season came again, we came together in the same place, since we had already plotted and picked the day we were to escape. On that day the Indians left us and each one of us went his own way. I told my companions that I would wait for them in the prickly pear fields until the time of the full moon. That day was the first of September and the first day of the new moon. I told them that if they did not appear at the time we agreed upon, I would go away without them. So we left, each with his own Indians. I was with mine until the thirteenth day of the moon, and I had decided to flee to other Indians once the moon was full.

On the thirteenth day of the month, Andrés Dorantes and Estebanico came to where I was and told me how Castillo was nearby with other Indians called the Anagados. They told me that they had had great difficulties and had gotten lost and that on the following day our Indians had moved towards where Castillo was. They were going to join the others and become friends, since they had been at war until then. In this manner we found Castillo.

The whole time that we ate the prickly pears we were thirsty. To quench our thirst we drank prickly pear juice. We squeezed the juice into a hole we made in the ground, and when it was filled we drank until we were satisfied. The juice is sweet and has the color of syrup. The Indians do it this way because they have no vessels. There are many kinds of prickly pears, some of them very good, although they all seemed good to me, since my hunger never allowed me the luxury of being selective or thinking about which were better. The great majority of these people drink rain water collected in various places. Although there are rivers, the people do not settle in one place, since they do not have any known or reliable sources of water. Throughout this country there are very large and beautiful pasturelands, with good grazing for cattle, and I think that it would be a very fruitful land if it were cultivated and inhabited by civilized people. We did not see any mountains the entire time we were there. Those Indians told us that there were others further away towards the coast called the Camones, who had killed all the men that came in Peñalosa and Téllez's boat. They said that the men were so weak that, while they were being killed, they did not fight back, and so the Indians finished them off. They showed us their clothing and weapons and told us their boat was stranded there. This is the fifth boat and the one that had not yet been accounted for. We have already told how the Governor's boat was carried out to sea. The one with the Purser and the friars had been seen stranded on the coast, and Esquivel told how they met their end. We have already mentioned the two boats Castillo, Dorantes and I were in, and how they sank near the Isle of Misfortune. . . .

How They Brought Other Sick People to Us the Following Day

The following morning many Indians gathered there, bringing five sick persons who were crippled and in a very poor condition, looking for Castillo to heal them. Each one of the sick persons offered his bow and arrows, which he accepted. At sunset he made the sign of the cross on them and commended them to God our Lord, and we all asked God, as best we could, to restore their health, since He knew that that was the only way for those people to help us, so that we might escape from such a miserable life. And God was so merciful that the following morning they all awakened well and healthy. They went away as strong as if they had never been sick. This caused great astonishment among them and caused us to thank our Lord heartily for showing us his kindness ever more fully and giving us the sure hope that He was going to free us and bring us to a place where we could serve Him. For myself I can say that I always had hope in his mercy and knew that He would bring me out of captivity, and I always said this to my companions.

Once the Indians had left with their cured companions, we left for another place where some others were eating prickly pears. These are called the Cutalches and Malicones, which are also the names of other languages. With them were others called the Coayos and the Susolas, and from another place some called the Atayos, who were at war with the Susolas. The Atayos and the Susolas fired arrows at each other every day. Throughout the land the only thing people talked about was the marvelous deeds that God our Lord worked through us, and people came from many places asking us to cure them. After two days some Susolas came to us and asked Castillo to go cure a wounded man and other sick people, saying that among them was a man about to die. Castillo was a timid physician, especially when the cases were frightful and dangerous. He thought that his sins would sometimes prevent a successful healing. The Indians told me to go heal them, because they liked me and remembered that I had cured them at the place where we gathered nuts and they had given us nuts and hides. This had happened when I came to join the Christians. So I was obligated to go with them. Dorantes and Estebanico went with me.

When I neared their huts, I saw that the sick man whom we were supposed to heal was dead, because there were many people weeping around him and his lodge was dismantled, a sign that its owner was dead. When I got to the Indian, I saw that his eyes were turned. He had no pulse and it seemed to me that he showed all the signs of being dead. Dorantes said the same thing. I removed a mat that covered him, and as best I could I beseeched our Lord to be pleased to grant him health and to grant health to all who needed it. After I made the sign of the cross over him and breathed on him many times, they brought his bow to me along with a basketful of ground prickly pears. Then they took me to cure many others who had sleeping sickness. They gave me two other baskets of prickly pears, which I gave to the Indians who had come with me. Having done this, we returned to our dwellings. Our Indians, to whom I had given the prickly pears, remained there and returned that night. They said that the man who was dead and whom I had healed in their presence had gotten up well and walked and eaten and spoken to them, and that all the people we had healed had gotten well and were very happy. This caused great wonder and awe, and nothing else was spoken about in the entire land.

Our fame spread throughout the area, and all the Indians who heard about it came looking for us to that we could cure them and bless their children. When the Cutalchiches, the people who were with our Indians, had to leave for their homeland, they offered us all the prickly pears they had stored for their journey, without keeping any. They gave us flints up to a palm and a half long, which they use for cutting and which they highly prize. They asked us to remember them and to pray to God for their good health, and we promised them that we would. With this they left as the happiest people in the world, after giving us the best things they had.

We remained with those Avavares Indians for eight months, keeping track of the time by the phases of the moon. During all this time, people came from many places seeking us, saying that we were truly children of the sun. Up to this time Dorantes and the black man had not performed any healings, but we all became healers because so many people insisted, although I was the boldest and the most daring in undertaking any cure. We never treated anyone who did not say he was cured. They were so confident that our cures would heal them that they believed that none of them would die as long as we were there.

These Indians, and the ones we encountered before, told us a very strange thing which they reckoned had happened about fifteen or sixteen years earlier. They said that a man whom they called "Evil Thing" wandered that land. He had a small body and a beard, but they never were able to see his face. When he came to the house where they were, their hair stood on end and they trembled. Then there appeared at the entrance to the house a burning firebrand. Then he entered and took whomever he wanted and stabbed him three times in the side with a very sharp flint, as wide as a hand

and two palms long. He would stick his hands in through the wounds and pull out their guts, and cut a piece of gut about a palm in length, which he would throw onto the embers. Then he would cut his victim three times in the arm, the second cut at the spot where people are bled. He would pull the arm out of its socket and shortly thereafter reset it. Finally he would place his hands on the wounds which they said suddenly healed. They told us that he often appeared among them when they were dancing, sometimes dressed as a woman and other times as a man. Whenever he wanted, he would take a *buhio* or a dwelling and lift it high. After a while he would let it drop with a great blow. They also told us that they offered him food many times but he never ate. They asked him where he came from and where he lived; he showed them an opening in the ground and said that his house was there below. We laughed a lot and made fun of these things that they told us. When they saw that we did not believe them, they brought many of the people who claimed he had taken them and showed us the marks of the stabbings in those places, just as they had said. We told them that he was evil, and, as best as we could, gave them to understand that, if they believed in God our Lord and became Christians as we were, they would no longer fear him, nor would he dare come to do those things to them. We assured them that as long as we were in their land he would not dare to appear. They were greatly relieved by this and lost much of their fear.

These Indians told us that they had seen the Asturian and Figueroa on the coast with other Indians, the ones that we called Indians of the Figs. None of these peoples reckoned time by the sun or the moon, nor did they keep track of the month or the year. But they do understand and know about the different seasons when fruits ripen or fish die. They are very skilled and practiced in knowing when stars appear. We were always treated well by these people, although we had to dig for our food and carry our share of water and firewood. Their dwellings and foods are like those of the previous groups we encountered, although they suffer more hunger because they have no corn, acorns or nuts. We always walked around nude with them, covering ourselves at night with deerskins. We were very hungry for six of the eight months we spent with them. Another thing they lack is fish. At the end of this time, the prickly pears were beginning to ripen.

We left without being noticed, for others were further ahead called the Maliacones. They were a day's journey from there. The black man and I reached them, and after three days I sent him to bring Castillo and Dorantes. When they arrived, we all departed with the Indians, who were going to eat some small fruits that grow on trees, their only food for ten or twelve days while waiting for the prickly pears. There they joined other Indians called the Arbadaos, whom we noticed were very sick, emaciated and swollen, such that we were very astonished. The Indians with whom we had come returned the same way they had come, but we told them that we wanted to stay with these others, which saddened them. So we stayed in the wilderness with those others near their dwellings. When they saw us, they got together after having talked among themselves, and each one of them took one of us by the hand and led us to their dwellings. With these people we suffered greater hunger than with the others, because the only thing we ate all day was two handfuls of that fruit. It was so green and had so much milky juice that it burned our mouths. There was little water and it made anyone who ate it very thirsty. Since we were so hungry we bought two dogs from them, trading for them some nets, a hide that I used as a cover and some other things.

I've already mentioned that we went naked all this time. Since we were not used to this, we shed our skins twice a year like serpents. The sun and the air caused very large sores on our chests and backs, which caused much pain because of the great loads we had to carry, the weight of which caused the ropes to cut our arms. The country is very rugged and overgrown. We often gathered firewood in the woods, and by the time we carried it out, we were scratched and bleeding in many places, since the thorns and thickets we brushed against cut any skin they touched. Many times the gathering of firewood cost me a great deal of blood and then I could not carry it or drag it out. When I was afflicted in this way, my only comfort and consolation was to think about the suffering of our redeemer Jesus Christ and the blood he shed for me, and to consider how much greater was the torment he suffered from the thorns than what I was suffering at that time.

I traded with these Indians, in bows and arrows and nets and made combs for them. We made mats, which they need very much. Even though they know how to make them, they do not want to be occupied in doing other things because they have to search for food instead. When they work on them, they suffer a great deal from hunger. At other times they would tell me to scrape and soften skins. I was never better off than the days they gave me skins to scrape, because I would scrape them very well and eat the scrapings, which was enough to sustain me for two or three days. It also happened that when these people, or the ones we were with before, gave us a piece of meat, we ate it raw, because if we tried to roast it, the first Indian that came by would take it and eat it. We thought that we should not risk losing the piece of meat. Besides, we were in no condition to take the trouble to eat it roasted, since we could better digest it raw. Such was the life we led there. What little food we had we earned from the trinkets we made with our own hands.

[1542/1555]

Translation of *La relación* by Martin A. Favata and José B. Fernández

Inca, Garcilaso de la Vega, is the pen name of the first mestizo writer of the Americas, Gómez Suárez de Figueroa, who was born in Cuzco, Peru, in 1539. His father was the Spanish captain Garcilaso de la Vega Vargas, and his mother was Chimpu Ocllo, niece of the emperor Tupac Yupanqui and hence an Incan princess. At the age of about twenty, just after the death of his father, Garcilaso left Peru for Spain, never to return. Among his major literary works were the translation of *Diálogos de Amor* (love poetry written in Italian by the Portuguese Judah Abarbanel), and the *Comentarios Reales (Royal Commentaries)*, an extraordinary history of Peru and an homage to his Incan forebears.

La florida del Inca is an adventurous account of the expedition led by Hernando de Soto from Cuba to the west coast of Florida and then west of the Mississippi River, between 1538 and 1542. It is perhaps the first great epic of the Americas, written by a highly literate author with dual sympathies. Composed six decades after the expedition itself, it is based on published accounts by three participants in the expedition, including the official chronicler, the Hidalgo de Elvas, and probably on interviews with Gonzalo Silvestre, a soldier in de Soto's brigade. Garcilaso de la Vega himself never set foot on the mainland of North America.

Garcilaso's account is marked by respect for the native peoples de Soto encountered. He never forgets that both the natives and the Spanish acted brutally toward each other, but he also includes anecdotes about Amerindian dignity, bravery, and integrity. The following excerpt describes one Indian taking on four Spaniards. It also gives the reader a clue to Garcilaso's informant, as Silvestre appears in a heroic moment.

According to a plaque later placed in the Chapel of the Souls of Purgatory, Garcilaso de la Vega died in Córdoba, Spain, on April 22, 1616, within hours of the death in Madrid of Miguel de Cervantes, whose masterwork, *Don Quijote,* was published in the same year as the Inca's *Florida*.

from **Florida**

A Fight between a Tula Indian and Four Spaniards, Three of Whom Were on Foot and One on Horseback

Since the facts of history demand that we narrate the brave deeds of the Indians as well as those of the Spaniards, and that we not do injury to either race by recounting the valiant achievements of one while omitting those of the other, but instead tell all things as they occurred and in their proper time and place, it will be well for us to describe here a strange and singular feat performed by a Tula Indian shortly after the battle to which we have referred. But we beg that our listeners not be offended because we relate this incident in such detail, for since it happened as it did, it is necessary to record it thus.

It was on an occasion when some of those Spaniards who boasted of being more valiant than others had scattered out in pairs over the field of battle and, as was their custom, were examining the dead and taking note of grave wounds inflicted by powerful arms. This they always did when some great and much disputed struggle had taken place. Now a native of Medellín named Gaspar Caro had fought that night on horseback, and however it may have been, whether by the Indians knocking him off or by his falling off of his own accord, he lost his saddle, and his horse fled through the fields away from the conflict. This soldier then borrowed the horse of a friend to go in search of his own, and when he had found it, returned, driving the animal in front of him. Thus he came to where four other soldiers were examining the dead and wounded, and one of these men, Francisco de Salazar, a native of Castilla la Vieja, proceeded to mount the riderless steed in order to demonstrate his fine horsemanship, of which he was proud.

At this point, a native of Seville named Juan de Carranza, who was one of the three unmounted soldiers, cried out, "Indians! Indians!" His reason for doing so was that he had seen an Indian rise from behind some bushes and then conceal himself again. Believing that there were many Indians and not bothering to investigate further, the two men who were mounted rode out at a gallop in opposite directions for the purpose of cutting off others who might appear. Juan de Carranza, who had discovered the infidel, rushed to where he was hidden in the bushes, and he was followed quickly by one of his two companions, but the other, not having seen more than a single foe, came after them only by degrees.

Now when the barbarian perceived that he was cut off on all sides by both horsemen and foot soldiers, and that escape was no longer possible, he hastened out from the bushes to receive Juan de Carranza. In his hands he bore a battle-ax, which had been his portion of the sack and loot acquired that dawn from our archers. It had belonged to Juan Páez, and as the property of a captain of crossbowmen, possessed both a keen edge and a well-planed and polished shaft more than three feet in length. Clasping his weapon in both hands, the Indian struck Juan de Carranza with such force as to knock half his shield to the ground and badly wound his arm. So tormented was this Spaniard, both by the pain from the wound and the force of the blow, that he had no further strength to harm his assailant, who now turned upon a second Spaniard standing nearby and proceeded to deal him a blow equal in force to the one he had bestowed upon Carranza. For he split this man's shield into two parts and wounded him seriously on the arm, leaving him like his companion, incapacitated for fighting. This soldier was Diego de Godoy, a native of Medellín.

Presently Francisco de Salazar, he who had mounted Gaspar Caro's horse, perceived that these two Spaniards had been sorely wounded, and he attacked their assailant with extreme fury, but the Indian to escape being trampled took refuge under an adjacent live oak. Not being able to ride his horse beneath this tree, Francisco de Salazar passed to one side of it and without dismounting made some very sad thrusts, none of which reached their mark. Meanwhile the infidel was finding it impossible to swing his ax effectively because of the branches, and he came out from beneath the tree to station himself to the left of the cavalier. Then lifting his weapon in both hands, he struck the horse across the shoulder and with the iron hook of the ax laid the animal open from the withers to the knee, thus rendering it incapable of stirring.

At this point another Spaniard approached, coming on foot and not making any more haste since it appeared to him that two unmounted Spaniards and one on horseback were sufficient for a single Indian. He was Gonzalo Silvestre, a native of Herrera de Alcántara. When the Indian saw him close by, he came forward to receive him with the utmost ferocity and savagery, having mustered new courage and strength with the three such triumphant blows he had bestowed. Seizing his ax in both hands, he now delivered a blow which would have achieved the same result as his first two had not Gonzalo Silvestre advanced more cautiously than the others so as to be able to step aside when the blow fell. Thus the ax merely grazed his shield without striking it and then because of its great force continued on to the ground. At that the Spaniard gave a backstroke from above to below and on reaching the Indian with his sword slashed him from the forehead down across the whole of his face and in the chest, and he even wounded his left hand in such a manner as to sever it completely at the wrist. Finding himself minus one of his hands and thus unable to swing his ax with both as he wished, the infidel placed the shaft of his weapon over the stump of his mutilated arm and lunged forward desperately in an attempt to wound his opponent with a sudden thrust in the face. But Gonzalo Silvestre turned the ax aside with his shield and then putting his sword beneath his shield gave his enemy a backhand slash through the waist. Because of the Indian's little or no protection of arms or clothing, or even of bones which the body might possess in that region, and moreover because of the good strength of Silvestre, everything was severed with such speed and keenness of the sword that after it had passed through him, the Indian remained standing and said to the Spaniard: "Peace be with you." These words uttered, he fell dead, severed in twain.

At this moment Gaspar Caro arrived, it being his horse that Francisco de Salazar had brought to the fight. When he saw the condition of the animal, he took it without uttering a word, guarding his anger so as to express it elsewhere. And now that he had rescued his mount he led it to the Governor and said: "In order that Your Lordship may be aware of the wretchedness of some of the soldiers of his army, even though they boast of their valor, and that you may perceive at the same time the ferocity and bravery of the natives of the province of Tula, I would have you know that one of these Indians with three blows of an ax has incapacitated for fighting two Spaniards on foot and another on horseback, and that he would have succeeded in destroying them had not Gonzalo Silvestre arrived in time to give them assistance. For with the first slash of his sword, that cavalier opened the face and chest of this Indian and cut off one of his hands; and with the second, he severed his body at the waist."

The Governor and those present marveled at the valor and dexterity of the Indian and likewise at the good arm of Gonzalo Silvestre. And since Gaspar Caro, in his rage at the mishap to his horse, was requesting that the first three Spaniards be branded as knaves and cowards, the Governor, in an effort to restore their honor, for indeed they were gallant men and worthy of any good deed whatsoever, told this soldier that he should lay aside his wrath and regard his companions as victims of fortune, which shows itself variable in nothing more than in the events of war, favoring one today and another tomorrow; that he should make haste to treat his horse, which in his own opinion would not die since its wound was not deep; and that being amazed at this story and believing it only right that many be able to bear witness to matters so heroic as these, he himself wished to go and behold with his own eyes what had happened. With these words, the Governor did go out in the company of many people to see the dead Indian and the heroic feats he had accomplished; and on learning from the wounded Spaniards themselves the particulars of what we have told, both he and all those who were listening were amazed anew. [1605]

Translation of *La florida del Ynca* by
John Grier Varner and Jeannette Johnson Varner

Gaspar Pérez de Villagrá was born in Puebla de los Angeles, New Spain, probably in 1555 (several dates have been given, but this is the most reliable). He graduated from the University of Salamanca in Spain and returned to New Spain at about the age of twenty-five. When, at age forty-three, he signed on to accompany Juan de Oñate for the conquest and colonization of New Mexico, he was described as of medium stature and gray-bearded. In 1596, two years before the expedition, Oñate appointed Villagrá *procurador general* (chief supply officer); he was also later appointed *juez asesor* (assistant to the head missionary).

Villagrá's *History of New Mexico,* one of the earliest epic poems composed in New Spain, is written in 12,000 eleven-syllable lines of rhyming verse. During the past 350 years, it has been judged again and again to be an extraordinary chronicle of the Oñate expedition. Villagrá's bravery and other personal qualities made him an excellent eyewitness, and fellow soldiers often chose him to accompany them on dangerous and important missions. Nineteenth- and early-twentieth-century critics were quick to point out that Villagrá wrote very poor poetry (some went so far as to say that it was a shame that he didn't compose the *History* in prose), but recent reassessments have been kinder. The culminating event in the epic is the battle of Acoma peñol (Acoma Rock), which has the power of the declamatory literature popular at the time. Villagrá relates the Acoma Indians' flamboyant speeches, which most likely he embellished. The following excerpt is the final canto of the poem.

In about 1604, Villagrá returned to Mexico, where he was made mayor of the town of Guanacevi; about 1610 he returned to Spain. Several years later, having been found guilty of crimes committed during the colonization of New Mexico (he had cut off the heads of two deserters and let two others go without reason), he was banished from New Mexico for six years. Later rehabilitated, he died at sea during a voyage to Guatemala, where he was to assume the post of mayor of Zapotitlán.

from The History of New Mexico

How the fortress of Acoma continued to burn and how Zutacapán was found dead from a great wound, and of other events which happened until the news of the victory was carried to the Governor, and of the deaths of Tempal and Cotumbo.

Being fatigued by this our toilsome voyage,
Let us now leave the holy, unconquered
Standard of Christ, which we had set up there.
Hold back your tears for they do leave
Your souls grieving and afflicted,
And you, most holy Philip, who have been
Listening to my rude muse thus attentively,
I beg you to tire not, for I have come
And arrived now upon the promised spot.
Trusting, great lord, unto the excellence
Of your great greatness, that, as the father
Of all the toilsome exercise of war,
You will open a pleasant door for me,
With which immense encouragement strengthened
I spread sail to the wind and thus return
Unto the fearful fire, whose flames,
Trembling with power and spitting forth
Live coals and embers and ashes,
Did rapidly consume the tall houses.
Behold, lord, there, the lofty roofs,
The walls, the rooms, the high garrets
Which, open at a thousand points, do break
And suddenly crumble into pieces
And bury, both in living fire and earth,
Their miserable neighbors, that nothing
Remains that is not burnt up and consumed.
Behold the many corpses, also, lord,
Who from the lofty summit of the wall
Have hurled themselves down in desperation
And, smashed and broken there among the rocks,
Lie there in pieces and in small fragments.
Likewise upon the hard ground there do lie

Barbarian men and women who, burning,
Lament, together with their little babes,
Their miserable misfortune and sad fate.
The Sergeant, at this spectacle of death
Being moved with pity and with lofty zeal,
As in the storm and the great hurricane
A great and skillful pilot goes about,
Leaping everywhere with energy,
Ordering mariners and passengers
With many shouts, so that they all
Come to his aid with an impetuous haste
And help the weak and tiny ship, attacked
By the sea's mighty force and by the wind
Driven among a thousand watery mountains,
So he, strengthening Chumpo and a few
More savages who did desire peace,
Doth shout out promises and assure them
The lives of all if they will but abstain
From the horrid destruction and harsh death
Which these wretches were causing for themselves.
Hardly had the poor old man well noted
The words of that ardent young man when he,
Shouting aloud together with the few
Barbarians who were there to help him,
Tries to persuade and recommend to all,
Making the strongest efforts with his signs
And most paternal gestures that they stop
And not give themselves to such sorry deaths,
Because their lives are promised them all,
And he assures them of noble treatment
Without a shade of doubt or suspicion,
Deceit, trickery, or double-dealing.
As after lightning stroke we all have seen
Everyone in suspense, insecure,
In color like the dead, their fearful hearts
Beating like hammers at the breast,
So they, all timid, all in suspicion,
Some from one side, from the other some,
Come creeping out with laggard steps

To see if they are safe, the destruction
Caused by the now ended struggle.
So, many came, few at a time,
Alert, fearful, and right timid,
With furtive steps, yet taking care
Lest they should step upon the bloodless corpse
Of some dear friend or faithful protector
Of those poor walls which now were stained
And bathed all over with their blood.
Thus, trembling and sad and afflicted,
Surrounded as they were on every side
By the pale hue of death and death itself,
They made approach. And the Castilian band
Beheld them all caressing with much joy
All their neighbors and saw them give
Sure and great signs of their content
At seeing them saved and removed
From that cruel slaughter they undertook.
As we see downcast and humbled
The high-uplifted heads of wheat when lashed
By gust on gust, ever stronger,
Of mighty winds which go plowing
Its spiky heads into great rippling waves
And bend them to the ground and beat them down,
So, conquered, humbled, and disarmed,
More than six hundred surrendered
And in one plaza, with all their children
And all their women, they did put themselves
Into the Sergeant's hands and were at peace,
Moved by the good Chumpo, who had given
A promise of safety and life to all,
Without whose aid I doubt, nay, I'm sure,
That great, laborious Numantia,
E'en when most unfortunate and lost,
Would have been no more desert and empty
Than this poor fort now surrendered.
All being now quite pacified
And truce now made without suspicion
Of any armed turmoil or uprising,

Agreements signed and to be signed
And all on both sides well appeased,
Suddenly the barbarian women, mad,
As we see suddenly falling and breaking up,
Coming on us to our astonishment,
A terrible and mighty tower
But recently erected, placed, and set,
And with a terrible fear all our blood
Flows back upon our hearts and we grow pale,
So, lord, immense and powerful,
Raising a fearful cry, they all set off,
And all crowding, as the peasants
Do crowd together round a hockey ball
And all do try with curving sticks
To give it greater impulse with their strength,
So we did see them, gathered in a knot,
With sticks and blows of stones smashing
A miserable body. So at once
We all set out for their squadron
To see was it a Spaniard and avenge
So treacherous and excessive a deed.
And when they saw us then, all out of breath
And all excited, did cry out to us:
"Ye valiant and generous men,
If to have given ourselves into your hands
Deserves that you give us some satisfaction,
Then let us finish what we have commenced.
Here Zutacapán lies stretched out
And thanks to the Castilian who has made
Such soul be snatched from such a wound.
He caused the deaths which we have dealt
To your unfortunate companions.
He sowed discord and disturbance
Among all those poor creatures who
Are lying lifeless on this ground."
And gazing now upon their dead
And then upon the traitor, all, raging,
As on the chopping block skilled cooks
Do mince up meat and sunder it,

So, in their rage they all gathered around
And left him battered into small pieces;
Happy and satisfied at this their deed,
Returned unto their former peaceful state.
And we, lord, never could find out
Whose was the arm that with one mighty cut
Had shorn through five of his ribs at one time.
As we most anxiously and greedily
Do seek, after a battle has been won,
Some great and famous man from whom we hope
To get great ransom, finding him hidden,
And thus soulless, madly, out of our wits,
We go to seek for him and examine
All of the conquered and eagerly fix
Our gaze attentively to find that man,
So these barbarians, attentive, with their mouths
Open and eyes that never moved
An eyelid, were then seen by us
To look at us in fear, astonishment.
And hardly would some soldier appear
Who had by chance been absent from the group
When all of them, as flies to honey crowd,
Would instantly run and crowd around him
And look into his face attentively.
Seeing the great care which they took
Not to leave anyone aside
Whom they should not well note and scrutinize,
'Twas necessary to ask for what mark,
What sign or what cause they did gaze
Thus anxiously and thirstily on us.
Giving authority to Chumpo, that for all
He might reply, the old man said to us:
"These sons of mine seek a Castilian
Who, being in the battle, always rode
Upon a great white horse and has
A great long beard, both white and thick,
And a bald head, is tall and wears
A terrible and broad and mighty sword
With which he has stricken us all to earth,

A man extremely valiant. And also
My people seek, as well, a beauteous maid,
More beautiful than the sun or the heavens.
They ask where these may be, where they have gone."
The Spanish leader then, hearing these things,
Being moved, perhaps, by He who could
Make that doubt clear, also help us
And protect us in similar affairs,
Like to a taper or a torch whose light
Makes our sight clear and cleaves the veil
Of blind darkness, so he, shining,
Said to the grateful old Chumpo:
"Reply to these your children, noble sire,
That they should not tire or fatigue themselves
Nor should they try to seek these more,
For they have now returned to Heaven,
Where they do keep their dwelling, nor leave it
Except to come to our aid and defense
When we are injured or one dares,
As those men dared, to slaughter ours
With such atrocious and such cruel deaths,
Those few poor Spaniards who did climb
To the height of this fortress heedlessly.
Let them watch what they do, and not repeat
A second time of that their work begun."
The Trojan had not ended, had not drawn
The rein of silence with more vivid force,
When to the famous queen he did relate
The tale of Troy and of its misfortunes,
As Zaldívar had here, for he left them
Astonished and silent, so they spoke not
Another word nor muttered, whereat he
Did say: "Immense Lord, since we won
This great victory on the very day
Of the Sacred Vessel, the saint that this land
Had as a Patron, we do comprehend,
Did then come with the Virgin to guard us."
There are things hidden that are not
Clear to me, lord, for I have always been

And am a sad and despised trifling worm.
And so, lord, I return to my leader,
Who is dispatching, in the hottest haste,
The purveyor Zubía to carry
The famous, joyous news of victory
Unto our General, who had been
Informed of it upon the very day
That it had been won by these forces
By an old Indian woman within her ring.
And as he was waiting for certain news,
The purveyor being upon the way,
By chance Tempal and poor Cotumbo, destitute,
Riding a terrible storm without sails,
Having now escaped out of the fortalice,
Did happen to cross his path and, seeing
The blow that the rigor of harsh fate had struck
After so much misfortune, covering themselves,
The two did feign, behind a mask of peace,
Like astute pirates, that they were natives
From far within the land and that they had
Been robbed by some who came fleeing
From the great rock. And thus, most timidly,
They asked with much grieving that they be given
Something by which their fierce hunger might be
Alleviated so they might not die.
At this the Spaniard had them seized
Not to err in the juncture, for, once lost,
It might detract from a great soldier,
And so they were taken and, arriving
And having then delivered the message,
He had them placed and locked in a kiva.
And, having now with much pleasure received
The news, the General was then informed
By certain noble, friendly barbarians
That those prisoners whom he had shut up
Inside the kiva and retained in custody
Were of the bravest and most valiant
That Acoma could show and they had raised
The outbreak to its highest point and roused

The peaceful fortress that was now destroyed.
At this, the two barbarians, enraged,
Seeing themselves discovered, did destroy
The ladder of the kiva and, grown strong,
With clubs and blows of rocks they prevented
The entrance of anyone for three days,
So well they did defend and keep themselves.
And seeing that they must needs surrender
Through the hunger and the raging thirst they felt,
They then laid down their arms and said:
"Castilians, if you are not content
As yet, though you have drunk up all
The generous blood that, succulent,
Your tireless bravery has already had,
And only this bit that is left to us
Will satisfy you, then give us
Two blunt knives, one for each, that we
May here appease your throats for you,
Taking our lives ourselves, for it is right
That no one may say, to stain us,
That two such warriors placed themselves
In hands so infamous and vile
As are your hands, which we despise."
At this the General was told
By all of his barbarian friends
That if he gave them pardon he would put
All of the land in a mind to revolt.
As he had done in vain all that
Could have been done to see them surrendered
And added to the bosom of the Church,
He ordered that they be refused the knives
For greater safety, and that they be given
Two long, strong halters, well and truly made.
And throwing these inside, they looked at them
With eyes bloodshot and pressing tight
Their lips and their strong teeth,
Their sides swollen, their nostrils wide,
Absorbed, deaf, dumb, they did remain.
And being thus in quiet for a time,

Throwing off fear and despising
All of your army and your mighty sword,
Never was seen thus to give up
His neck unto the running noose
A man who, being tired of this life,
Desired to leave this life swiftly and soon,
As we saw these barbarians who, at once,
Loosing their badly tangled hair,
Took the two nooses and, setting
The same upon their necks and knotting them,
They came out of the kiva, and casting
Their glance over the camp, which wondered much
At their courage and sympathized with them,
They halted it and centered it upon
Some lofty poplar trees that were well grown
And were, by some evil chance, near.
And hardly had they noted them when they
Informed us instantly they wished
To hang themselves and die upon those trees.
And, giving them an open hand in all,
The great and choking knots, hard drawn,
There they examined, and, dragging
Their halters behind them, they went
From the Castilian camp, worn out,
Accompanied by the barbarian folk.
Not the strong brothers of Carthage
Who, running rapidly, increased
The boundaries to their own dole, did thus
Give themselves up unto dark death,
Allowing themselves to be buried though alive,
As these barbarians, who, arriving
At the foot of those tree trunks, lifted up
Their gaze unto the top and, instantly,
Like skillful cabin boys who run lightly
Upon the masts and yards and high tops,
Climbed the poplars to a great height,
And then, testing the branches, appeared as
Their own hangmen; and having tied the ropes,
Looking upon us all, they said to us:

"Soldiers, take note that hanging here
From these strong tree trunks we leave you
Our miserable bodies as spoils
Of the illustrious victory you won.
Over those wretched ones who are
Rotting amid their weltering blood,
The sepulcher they chose since infamous
Fortune chose so to pursue us
With powerful hand and end our days.
You will remain joyful for we now close
The doors of life and take our leave,
And freely leave to you our lands.
Sleep sure and safe because no one
Ever returned with news about the road,
Uncertain and laborious, we now take,
But yet of one thing we do assure you:
That if we can return for our vengeance,
Castilian mothers shall not bear,
Barbarian either, throughout all the world,
Sons more unfortunate than all of you."
Thus raving, angry, all heedless,
Together they both leapt out into space,
And now their eyes, turned back, displayed the whites,
Their joints were all loosened and slack,
As were their mighty thews and sides.
Spurting out foam they discovered
Their hidden tongues, now all swollen
And tightly clenched between their teeth.
And, as may two separate and free vessels,
Lower their broad main sails and bridle up
The mighty banks of oars and all at once
The foaming prows do come to rest
And all is calm, so, together,
Calm, without motion, they remain
And there give up the breath of life.
And at this harsh and severe pass,
Leaving them hanging, I must now
Bring silence to this harsh canto.
And if your famous Majesty

Should wish to see the end of this story
I beg upon my knees that you will wait
And pardon me, also, if I delay,
For 'tis a thing difficult for the pen
To lose all shyness instantly,
Having to serve you with the lance. [1610]

Translation by Miguel Encinias, Alfred Rodríguez, and Joseph P. Sánchez

Fray Mathias Sáenz de San Antonio, a friar of the Franciscan order in Zacatecas, Mexico, was part of the 1716 expedition that helped consolidate the northeastern Texas frontier for the viceroyalty of New Spain in response to the establishment in 1715 of French settlements near Spanish territory. Brother Mathias was a trusted companion of the missionary leader Father Espinosa, author of the *Chrónica apostólica,* a historical account of the founding of missions in New Spain, who employed Sáenz to carry official reports to the viceroy, the Marqués de Valero.

The missionary movement was an endeavor of great passion among Spanish priests. Junípero Serra in California, Antonio Margil in Texas, and Eusebio Kino in Arizona played important roles in the Spanish colonial settlements. Because little funding accompanied their extraordinary efforts, many of the friars would write to the king for assistance in their cause; *Lord, If the Shepherd* is an example of such a letter. Along with an intriguing portrait of Texas as a veritable paradise awaiting only assistance from King Philip V of Spain, the letter gives an interesting portrait of the missionary, who aside from his pastoral duties is a business agent, international spy, and investigator of corruption. Because little infrastructure existed on the margins of the empire, Spanish missionaries were expected to fulfill all these functions.

Apart from its value as a historical document, *Lord, If the Shepherd* is a stunning literary work, full of witty metaphors and persuasive arguments. Like many official writings of the time, it used punctuation sparingly, with some sentences running to more than two hundred words, with independent and dependent clauses separated only by commas. The following translation brings it into conformity with modern style.

Lord, If the Shepherd Does Not Hear

Lord,
If the shepherd does not hear the sheep's complaint, if the father does not hear his children's cries, if the Lord does not heed his vassals' lament, he will not feel a loving duty to fill these needs. As Saint Bernard said in the vernacular, if the eyes do not see, the heart does not break.

Today urgent needs are placed before the royal and pious Catholic Majesties, needs of the inhabitants of the newly conquered New Philippines in the Province of Texas, in the time of capable government of the Marqués de Valero in New Spain, so that Your Majesty, as Shepherd, may hear them, as Father, may give encouragement, and, as King and Lord by right, may protect them and provide for them. Understand, Your Majesty, that in their need they come to you with the love and the gratitude that Your Majesty has for this assistance.

So that Your Majesty will better understand the core of these difficulties, I should first set before you, for your Royal consideration, what the Province is, its location, and who its inhabitants are, in a few words, but so that you may acquire an understanding of it.

For a hundred years before 1716, we did not gain even an inch of land in these territories. Then Divine Providence decided that, at great risk, with twenty-five men, forty fellow brothers from the Apostolic College of Our Lady of Guadalupe and Zacatecas, and five other brothers from Santa Cruz de Querétaro, with great travail we make our way three hundred leagues, from the last Christian Garrison into said Province of Texas, in the hills of whose district innumerable Barbarian Nations live. In that selfsame Texas we established six Missions that exist to this day, the last one within sight of a French Garrison. Upon becoming aware of it, I went to scout its perimeter, so that the French could not advance until I could notify the Crown.

This Province, my Lord, is so rich in minerals that every mound is a treasure-trove. It is so lush with flowers and plants, rivers and springs, that it is a paradise. It is so fertile in fruits, that it is a wonder. In fact, everything one puts into it, it returns a hundredfold or more. It is overrun with wild fruit, such as grapes, plums, pomegranates, medlars, walnuts and chestnuts, and many other fruits in abundance. It includes indigo plants, and diverse medicines, and substantial foodstuffs. The meadows are wondrous for all manner of meat, turkey, pigeon, and other birds, of which there are a great many. The rivers and springs are rich with many different kinds of succulent fish. Its inhabitants are Barbaric Gentiles, idol-worshippers, without discipline nor government, whose houses are little shacks and a few caves. They often move in search of the wild fruits and roots they live on and to hunt the bear, deer, wild boar, and buffalo on which they survive. They go naked from head to toe. They wear animal skins to stave off the rigors of winter, but their clothing has no style. They live on no more than what the natural world of animals has given them. Nevertheless, they are by nature docile and well disposed to the Spanish, who treat them well, because with the Spanish they feel protected and defended against their enemies.

These lands are situated at about 32 degrees north. The climate is healthy, similar to that of Castile. From the center of the Province, looking north, one can see New Mexico at a distance of 300 leagues, prudently speaking; to the south is the Province of Tampico, at more or less 200 leagues; toward the east, one finds the Port of Santa Maria de Galvez, which is on the edge of Central Mexico. Its neighbor is the Port of Movila [Mobile], which the French occupy and which stretches 200 or more leagues, from the Nachittoos border, next to our Texas, to the aforementioned Movila, whose district the French have settled with small towns and Garrisons, and whose capital is New Orleans, on the Palisade River, which empties into the sea there. This river is very lush, being composed of the Missouri, Mississippi, and Red Rivers, all of which are large. To the Northeast are the English and the Picaroons [pirates], with whom we have not wanted to have any contact because of the opposition of these nations and their Indian friends to us. To the west is the Kingdom of New León, whose border we crossed to come here. The Barbarian Nations, who occupy these areas, are innumerable and many.

Now that we have given you a brief picture of the Province, its location, and inhabitants, I place before the pious eyes of Your Majesty the needs of your new children and vassals, which they offer to you, as Shepherd, Father, King, and Lord, for remedy and assistance.

First, they need financial support and doctrinal guidance. For this they need settlers of Christian habits, and workers like Galicians or

[Canary] Islanders, who will teach them, inspire them, and stimulate them to the beneficial use of the land, the making of houses and cloth, and other tasks that comprise a well-ordered Republic, for which the Creoles of America are no good. The Creoles are, for the most part, feeble workers, some because of their constitution. Some are lazy, others are idlers because their land is so fertile and abundant. The rest are no good because of habits born of similar principles. Because the Infidels are rough and uncultured, they receive the Holy Faith and Christian Doctrine through their eyes more than their ears. They need upstanding models if they are to follow this Doctrine and the Holy Sacrifice of the Mass and acquire obedience and reverence to priests and evangelical ministers, as the primitives of those other territories have had. In this way Christianity will succeed here, as it has done there.

If this is provided, the lost and scattered sheep of Christ will gather together in life's needed pasture, rejecting the death grip in which the devil blindly holds them. In such company they will be able to defend themselves and secure themselves against this enemy, by whose hand they live a divided existence. When they have such peace, they will be able to free themselves from sudden, warlike assaults when they gather together at differing times and places, only to die like ants, with the devil reaping an abundant harvest. It is a shame that Catholic hearts cannot respond to such feelings of so many souls lost, a situation so different from that of the most precious blood of our Redeemer, whose representative is Your Majesty, to whom, as a pious Father, these wretched people, these forsaken children, set forth their needs.

To you, their King and Lord, they would like to make clear that the loss of not only these lands and provinces is threatened but that of all the kingdoms of New Spain, in view of the fact that the French, English, and Picaroons come ever nearer. The power of these nations is increased by the addition of a multitude of Indians, who are already skilled in the use of firearms, pikes, broadswords, lances, and half-moons, which have been provided to them in great numbers. If they declare war, there will not be enough strength to resist them, and if, may God forbid, peace cannot be maintained or the European Powers take up arms, any of them could run through our land and reach as far as Mexico as easily as if they were walking through their own homes, since the land is solid and clear, free of obstacles. The 300 men that Your Majesty keeps in the Bay of Espíritu Santo on the San Antonio River and in Texas itself, stationed over a distance of greater than 200 leagues, serve more to maintain your dominions than to defend them in an emergency. This, in particular, is what demands Your Majesty's attention. The French, English, and Picaroons are composed of Huguenots and other heretics who, wherever they go, declare freedom of conscience, a powerful attraction for the peasants, who are able to retain their bad habits and false religions, to which, aided by the devil, they give themselves over voluntarily, their safety satisfied by armed protection. If such a misfortune were to occur, it would be very serious, even cruel. In the heart and the Kingdom of our Mexican Provinces, our Holy Faith is ailing and the palates of most inhabitants are so ill-favored to the sweetness and tenderness of the Laws of Christ that if they become accustomed to this pestilential freedom of conscience they will run breathless to the enemy, who outnumber us. If you take away Your Majesty's faithful, committed vassals, the great body of our people is composed of Negros, Mulattoes, Lobos, Indians, and Mestizos, so much so that for every Spaniard they number five hundred. This, my Lord, weighs heavily upon us. And this fact is so well known to the public that you will not find anyone who has been in these territories who will not support it. As an upstanding witness, the Marqués de Valero can substantiate this. This situation must be attended to without delay and the path to its remedy cleared, before more damage is done. If such a remedy is brought about promptly, it will be easy and not expensive to the Royal House. If well thought out, it can result in increases to Your Majesty's fortunes (as good a reason as any to carry it out). In this way, our Holy Faith will be spread, preserved, and increased in Your Majesty's dominions, as I will hereafter make clear.

If Your Majesty sends, as indeed you should, 500 families, if possible Galicians and Islanders, and distributes 150 of them in the Bay of Espíritu Santo and the outpost at San Antonio, and 250 in appropriate parishes, the free passage of these foreign nations will be impeded. The year after they settle in these areas, 200 soldiers of the 300 Your Majesty currently maintains in Texas, the outpost at San Antonio, and the Bay of Espíritu Santo could be eliminated. The 135 pesos that these 300 soldiers cost per year will be reduced by 90 pesos a year. If you take into account the many subsequent years, the Royal Exchequer will save millions. These eliminated soldiers can stay in the area with the financial support of the settlers. All in all, these lands will continue to flourish, the nation will expand, duties, tributes and other Royal Prerogatives will increase, and Christianity will grow here. We have seen an example of this in the production of fruit and tobacco on the island of Havana, as it has been in all the other provinces of the American Empire, which have supported and continue to support the Spanish peninsula and have enriched all the European powers.

With these grants, my Lord, you will contain these foreign nations. Your Majesty's domains and the Empire of Jesus Christ will expand among many nations, which will seek Spanish protection. Your Majesty will achieve the same glory as his ancestors, from the invincible Carlos V, Hercules I of the New World, until Your Majesty, every one of whom tried to spread Catholic devotion, in the interests of God. Your Majesty's father the King manifested this so clearly in the Golden Charter, which Your Majesty has reiterated during your invaluable and exemplary reign, whose tenderness would melt stone.

Finally, my Lord, what is requested is very little; what it means is great. Not doing this would put everything at risk, because the way such a Monarchy as this is constituted, its preservation is like that of a body, composed of flesh and blood. The blood of this body is that of the mineral veins of the American kingdom. And if, may God forbid, we fail, it will mean complete ruin. In that ruination, and the inexplicable misfortune of such an outrage to God's Faith and the Mansion of Jesus Christ, the devil will take the throne, and our God will be badly served. To this end, my Lord, God has brought me to these vast regions, for Your Majesty's Royal projects, under the protection of the Marqués de Valero, who can testify to and support these truths with more elegant and convincing reasons and who has himself looked into these difficulties.

I must also put forth for Your Majesty's consideration the grave need for spiritual guidance in the things experienced by your vassals in the two kingdoms of New León and New Vizcaya, one of which borders Texas and the other New Mexico. These provinces suffer from a lack of ecclesiastical assistance since their governors overemphasize politics and the military. The governors tend to their own interests, to the detriment of Your Majesty's vassals and to the detriment of both of Your Majesties. In both kingdoms of New León and New Vizcaya, most people die without the Blessed Sacrament of Confirmation, because their bishops never reach most of these kingdoms. This is not the Bishops' fault. The See of Durango and that of Guadalajara to which they belong are more than 350 leagues long and are for the most part uninhabited, without dwellings for 40 or 50 leagues. Much of the time there is danger from hostile, heathen Indians who have threatened many travelers in the past and continue to threaten them today. The Bishops take steps to learn about their parishioners and send inspectors, who are usually young men since they need to be robust. Of these, none can perform confirmations. Many of them, instead of cleansing the ailments and infections of the sheep and dressing them in holy instruction, undress them, and promote these selfsame ailments, by introducing new ailments that I will not mention. In New Mexico and its environs, where until now no Bishop has come, not even an inspector, they live like sheep without a shepherd, even though they have Curates. I do not know what to say on this point because I can only cry over this misery. Plants that never feel the influence of the sun will never bear ripe fruit. Your Catholic Majesty is the firmament of that light, and must provide it.

Added to this, motivated by their own whims and desires, the governors exalt their own power, which they obtain more from their own tyranny than from the Crown or the Papacy and suppress the ecclesiasts and lay brothers more than they should, contrary to the laws of God and Your Majesty. Even the Viceroys of Mexico cannot solve this problem, since their patients are scattered over more than 500 leagues. Nor have these poor people recourse in the courts since they have little means and because those who express their complaints are later strongly oppressed. If someone had the strength to do so, going as far as an Inquiry, he could not win a judgment either, because everyone, to avoid persecution or because of self-interested friendship, bears false witness, contrary to the truth and in behalf of the governors. In such remote regions, someone or other will always supply false testimony. All this is why the land is so little inhabited, because so many of these poor people leave and go elsewhere.

These governors use soldiers to serve their household needs, and sometimes as mail carriers in Your Majesty's service, taking for themselves the money the soldiers are owed, which is the reason that, being few, and busy with these tasks, they don't patrol the borders, nor do they attend to dangerous areas. Because of this, hostile Indians have places to steal livestock and kill ranchers and unforewarned travelers, whose troubles also force them to leave. This, my Lord, is a fact that, even if a trial judge should find out about it, nothing will happen, because of the reasons already mentioned. I have seen this and felt it personally, as I go about these parishes on my apostolic rounds. As your loyal vassal and evangelical minister, I must tell this to Your Majesty, affirming it (as I do affirm) that I am not motivated by anything more than the service to both Majesties and the discharging of my conscience to Your Majesty, as God is my witness.

To this I should add that the soldiers go hungry, half-naked, and many unarmed because the governors and captains collect their salaries and pay them with merchandise from shops they themselves own, at very high prices. The soldiers end up being given what is worth six for twenty, so that two thirds of the soldiers' pay is lost. They go about perennially in debt, their basic needs unmet. What happens is that some of them run away, some because they cannot pay their debts. When others die, those who replace them are often charged with the debts of the dead ones. No one willing to take the position under such conditions, they are left vacant, until these obligations, which are not really due them, are satisfied. With fewer soldiers, the Royal Service becomes less effective.

I have no idea what the solution is for this. But if we go back to the experiences of the past, it seems to me that the best way is for Your Majesty to provide persons of great enthusiasm in the service of God and of souls, and service of Your Majesty, to the Sees of El Parral de New Vizcaya and New Mexico, and the Kingdom of New León, naming apostolic and unselfish men, as those lands have requested, so that they might apply themselves enthusiastically to their work, adapting themselves to the meagerness or mediocrity offered in the current state of these Jurisdictions, and get along decently. And if Your Majesties decide to confer on them the payments the Governors and Military Captains receive today, they will have even more relief, and many other benefits will result. First, because they will look upon their parishioners and the soldiers as do Fathers. The latter will be assisted with charity and will not be tyrannized, because having to assist them with alms for their needs, they will not take the work of these poor people away from them. Second, because they will be in the shadow and company of such Prelates, these lands will be settled, as the See of Durango was settled, which, until a Bishop was installed there, had found itself with the same needs. Third, the Holy Gospel will shine more brightly, Christian Doctrine will be more widely practiced, and the Curates and Judges will find themselves more closely overseen. Fourth, in all cases Your Majesty and the Viceroys of Mexico will have witnesses of great integrity for news and emergencies.

Fifth, and most remarkable, one particular evil will be suppressed, a huge obstacle to the propagation of our Holy Faith. This is that, until now, the Governors and Captains, in the name of patrolling the land, have gone into heathen territory to kidnap children and women in order to give them to their friends, relatives, and colleagues and often to sell them as slaves, contrary to all rights and royal and divine laws. When they commit these atrocities, they injure some people and kill others. The poor, terrified Indians flee from our Holy Faith and, in pain, like lions whose cubs have been taken away, they run wildly through the hills, ridges, and passes, bringing nations together for the purpose of revenge. In such a way they roam the land enraged. With a Bishop, a charitable and zealous Apostolic Governor, these troubles will disappear. The Indians will seek the Bishops out, and with tenderness and affection the Bishops will bestow on them things of little value, like glass beads, coral, ribbons, little mirrors, combs, knives, tobacco leaves, sackcloth, flannel, and other things to which they are drawn like a flock of sheep. All of this my experience with the Indians of Texas has taught me: when beginning to seek them out and to attract them, how to attract them is to find this type of gift, because this is the only powder with which these innocents are defeated, these are the swords and arms for which they give themselves up. It is not much, because, being children of these rocky hills, even such small gifts break their resolve.

If Your Majesty wants more direct and broader notice of proof of these truths, the Marqués de Valero can give it to you. He is aware of it from his time as Governor of Mexico for Your Majesty's father the King, and today he finds himself with paper, minutes, and instruction for the said Bishops, with all the information needed for their elevation, with the reasons for their fitness and how fitting they are. Your Majesty can find out from the aforementioned Marqués about the most prudent resolution. If for a judicious accord it seems appropriate to Your Majesty to inform a Minister of Intelligence in these parts to give me a hearing and put these difficulties before him, I will give him these reasons that, according to God, I will reach. I stand ready to do whatever Your Majesty decides, for the great service that I place in God, the people, and Your Majesty. May you live for many years. [1724]

Translation of *Señor, si el pastor no escucha el queixido de la oveja* by Harold Augenbraum

Los comanches (*The Comanches*) follows the structures of the Spanish popular heroic folk drama but transforms it into a New Mexican folk play. It is thought to be the first secular drama written in the Southwest, a successor to the oft-performed *Los moros y cristianos* (The Moors and the Christians, also known as Jousts of the Moors and the Christians), which was first performed in the region in 1598, the year Juan de Oñate began his forays into New Mexico (see Gaspar Pérez de Villagrá's *History of New Mexico*). These plays were probably meant to intimidate the Amerindians and thus avoid conflict with them; there is a certain irony in the interest of contemporary performers of the drama in continuity with their Hispanic past.

The Comanches probably dates from about 1780, just after the final defeat of the Comanche tribe in that part of the country, since it is assumed that its unknown author wanted to commemorate that victory. However, it was not published until 1822, so it may have been written anytime between those two dates. Around the turn of the century the folklorist Aurelio Espinosa discovered *Los comanches* and transcribed, annotated, and republished it in 1907.

The Comanches were considered to be a fierce tribe, very independent and, hence, a ferocious enemy of the Spanish. Several times in the eighteenth century, Spanish colonial governors sent military expeditions against them, finally prevailing in 1774 and 1779. *Los comanches* celebrates the Spanish victory of 1774 but notes the death of Cuerno Verde (Green Horn), which occurred in 1779.

The Comanches

LIST OF CHARACTERS

CUERNO VERDE (Green Horn) *Chief of Comanches*

DON CARLOS FERNANDEZ *Spanish General-in-Chief*

DON JOSÉ DE LA PEÑA *A Spanish Captain*

EL TENIENTE (The Lieutenant) *A Spanish officer, name not given*

DON SALVADOR RIVERA *A Spanish Captain*

OSO PARDO (Grey Bear) *A Comanche chieftain*

CABEZA NEGRA (Black Head) *A Comanche chieftain*

LOBO BLANCO (White Wolf) *A Comanche chieftain*

ZAPATO CUENTA (Beaded Moccasin) *A Comanche chieftain*

TABACO *A Comanche chieftain*

DON TORIBIO ORTIZ *A Spanish General*

BARRIGA DUCE *A Spanish camp follower*

SCENE — On the Staked Plains of New Mexico

TIME — In the year 1777.

CUERNO VERDE, *Chief of all the Comanches, speaks:*
From the sunrise to the sunset,
From the South to frigid North
Is seen the glitter of my arms
And my trumpet blares go forth,
And alike among all nations
Boldly I make my camp and rest.
Such is the valor, such the bravery
That reigns within my breast.
And my banners are unfurled
To the breeze where none else do
For the most enraged I humble
And the haughtiest I subdue.
Unrestrained and without fetter,
Knowing none who master me,
Like the savage bear and tiger
Wandering unopposed and free,
For there's not a hill or mountain,
Not a stone and not a tree,

But that will not be a witness,
Of the praise they tell of me.
Those who have opposed my progress
Have had reason to regret,
And this proud and haughty Castle
Will also feel my vengeance yet.
Today's sun will see its downfall,
See in ruin its haughty walls,
Though its strength be great and mighty
I'll assault it till it falls.
Well I know they are preparing
To receive my warriors bold.
I have watched their preparations,
And much more I have been told.
Let them ask the many nations
Who have felt my conquering heel,
Let them ask my might and prestige,
Learn the misery they now feel.
Today they find themselves abandoned,
And their homes in ruin see
Let them ask the Caslana nation,
What it is to war with me.
Today their star is dimmed forever,
For from such prestige they fell,
That . . . but why should I repeat,
Facts which everyone knows well.
Everyone except these Christians
And without number though they be,
Today for certain blood will flow —
Blood that means revenge for me.
This recalls to my memory
One of these, though brave and bold,
He left his blood to stain the flowers
On a battle field of old.
Those I've slain are without number
They have slipped my memory now
Without counting all the captives,
Men and women and children. Now
My brave men, valiant redmen,

Let this order go with care,
I, your general, give this edict,
Let everyone his arms prepare.
Prepare we must, and meet them ready,
What general would seek to rest,
With the enemy before him.
Prepare to do your best.
I will never be contented
With a victory half complete.
Don your war paint, sound the war drums,
We must bring them to our feet.
I shall go and seek this general,
This foolhardy, impious man.
Let him meet me in this battle
And survive me if he can.
Who is he, what do they call him,
Whomsoever he may be.
I, Cuerno Verde, challenge him
To come and combat me.

DON CARLOS FERNANDEZ, *the Spanish general, answers the Comanche:*
Bide your time, Oh bloody heathen,
I will come without your call.
Your challenge is not needed
I will meet you one and all.
But first, tell me, who are you,
And whence those idle boasts.
Hearken to these words I utter,
You and your savage host.

CUERNO VERDE, *the Comanche, speaks:*
I am that mighty captain
At whose name men shake with fear.
I am the brave, the bold, the terrible,
This horn which you can see
Green and golden, see it glisten,
All its fame it takes from me.
Today I claim the homage of
Not alone these warriors at my side
But all men proclaim me master,

Through this nation far and wide.
From the sunrise to the sunset
From the South to frigid North,
Caiguas, Quituchis, Indios, Caumpes,
All follow me when I go forth.
Many others without number
There's no need to name them all.
Yield to me their blind allegiance,
And are ready at my call.

DON CARLOS FERNANDEZ, *the Spanish general, answers Cuerno Verde:*
Bide your time, oh bloody heathen,
I will be your master yet.
You will find your spirit broken,
When the Spaniard you have met.
In the land across the waters,
There reigns a prince of right
Who rules the world from pole to pole
Through his power and his might.
Throughout this entire world you see
His power reigns supreme.
Germans, Englishmen, and Turks,
All peoples whomsoever they be
When they hear the name of Spaniard,
Bend and tremble at the knee.
You have never met a worthy foe
Nor do you know the might
Of Catholic arms in battle
You will learn this in this fight.
This is why your idle vauntings,
This is why your spirit bold.
I shall meet you in this battle,
I shall leave you dead and cold.
And if you wish to know who I am,
I shall state that you may know.
This is not my first encounter,
This battle you offer, and so,
Here you find me in your own land
And though I am advanced in years,

Know and note, oh impious stranger,
Carlos Fernandez has no fears.
Your lands I've always invaded,
When it suited me that way.
And now, oh boastful captain,
Go prepare you for the fray.

CUERNO VERDE, *the Comanche chieftain, replies:*
You have said it, without fail,
We shall see who shall prevail.

DON CARLOS FERNANDEZ, *the Spanish general, addresses his men.*
This war again presents to us
An opportunity to show
The valor of your Catholic arms
That all the world may know,
That Spanish arms in battle,
Never yet have left the field
Without honor to their country.
A Spaniard will never yield.
You have heard how this Comanche,
This untutored savage beast
Comes before us with such boasting,
'Tis high time that this should cease.
He addressed me with such vauntings,
Applauded by his savage bands,
Asking who could be this general
Who had dared invade his lands.
Told us of the hosts he'd murdered.
Of the lands he'd filled with fear
And I answered with equal frankness
That his equal he'd find here.
Told him that the Spanish soldier
Knows no rival, knows no peer.
Told him of that mighty nation
At whose name men shake with fear.
But 'tis time to cease this vaunting,
We must hasten to the fray,
You, my captains, speak your counsel,
How we best can win the day.

Let Tomas Madril come forward,
José de la Peña, too,
And Don Salvador Rivera.
Bring your sergeants all with you.
We must all consult together
And decide what we must do.

DON JOSÉ DE LA PEÑA, *a Spanish captain, speaks:*
Oh, my brave and worthy general
Of whose valor we well know,
Plan your battle, give your orders,
We shall follow where you go.
A more worthy, a more just
War than this was never seen.
Let us haste and give them battle,
And exterminate this spleen.
For my heart cries loud for action,
And the issue holds no fear.
With the aid of Virgin Mother,
I see victory is near.
Through her Immaculate Conception,
Born of woman, without sin,
Full of grace and full of mercy,
She will surely help us win.
And besides to help us conquer,
Is that celestial martial band,
With the blessed angel Michael
Who will surely be on hand.
He, the patron of my brave men,
Who are ready for the fray.
Give your orders, we are ready,
This is all I have to say.

EL TENIENTE, *the Lieutenant, speaks:*
The worthy José de la Peña
Has spoken what I would say.
Only one word I have to offer,
Then I am ready for the fray.
Listen, Oh worthy Don Carlos,
My obedience to you I yield.

'Tis a special honor to serve you,
Proof I'll give you on this field.
My will is made, I am ready,
To go forth to battle this day,
To fight for your honor and glory,
Or to perish in the affray.
Well I know I am not worthy,
To serve in such an honored task.
In truth the honored post I have,
Is more than I would ask.
Don Carlos I shall not fail you.
This is all I have to say.
I am ready for the battle.
I shall follow Don José.

DON SALVADOR RIVERA, *a Spanish captain, speaks:*
Señor Don Carlos Fernandez
I have hearkened to what you say.
I am ready with the lieutenant,
With the lieutenant and Don José.
With powder and ball we'll assail them.
We shall make them repent their sins,
And forget their idle boastings.
Faith and valor is what wins.

CUERNO VERDE, *the Comanche chieftain, addresses his war captains:*
Hear, ye lions, all my captains
You, the bravest in the fray.
All prepare your arms of battle
We are out to win the day.
Up and at them with a fury
Let them know whom they assail,
And remember that united
You can never, never fail.
Bear in mind what you have pledged me.
Fight with valor, fight with might.
With the valor of your forebears,
You are battling for the right.
I shall be there with a vengeance.
This is not an idle boast.

You well know me and my mettle.
We shall crush this savage host.

OSO PARDO *(Grey Bear), a Comanche chieftain, speaks:*
I also rise to speak a word.
It is both meet and right,
That the promises given Cuerno Verde,
We should ever keep in sight.
Remember, you are the chosen ones,
Whom your captains called to war.
Yon Spaniards, answer me today
Or be silent forevermore.
What captain from amongst you
Will match this savage bear?
This bear who tames the savage beasts.
Who will assault him in his lair?
The fiercest lion of the wilds
Flees to the forest deep,
When this Grey Bear presents himself,
Now who will dare to leap
And with this Grey Bear match his arms
This day in single battle?
Whence is your courage, whence your might
Come forth and prove your mettle.

DON JOSÉ DE LA PEÑA, *the Spanish captain, speaks:*
This Grey Bear shall be my quarry
This rock shall prove his end.
Rock of valor, rock of prowess,
Tame this savage that he may send
No more idle threats and boastings.
Idle glutton, boastful one,
I shall prove your false feigned courage
On this field e'er we are done.
And the high sun of your glory
Soon will set, your day is o'er
When we meet in mortal combat
That sun for you will rise no more.
Not long ago I met your warriors,
In numbers great they came to fight.

With but a handful of my brave men
I met and put them all to flight.
Valor such will merit boasting
Deeds like these, in days gone by,
Rolando and his twelve immortals
Performed beneath the Spanish sky.
But, you know not whence I speak of,
Of whom I speak or what I say.
Did you know, and having met us,
You would think them here today.

CABEZA NEGRA *(Black Head), another Comanche chieftain, speaks:*
Why this chatter, why this waiting?
Worthier tasks we have to do.
See this sharp and glistening lance point?
It shall pierce their general through.
Pierce that proud and haughty Christian,
Leader of these hosts they say.
Cease this talk and reminiscing,
I have come to kill and slay.
Be there brave men from amongst you,
In your haughty warrior band,
Who would meet Cabeza Negra,
In single combat, hand to hand?

LOBO BLANCO *(White Wolf), another Comanche chieftain, speaks. First he addresses Cabeza Negra.*
Worthy sir, hold back a while yet,
Soon we'll have them in our foils.
I must be the first to meet them,
For my blood within me boils.
Let me first show them my prowess.
Their fury is not new to me.
We have met before in battle,
And I've nothing new to see.
And because we've met in battle,
And I thirst for vengeance too,
Let me be the first to smite them,
With a vengeance they shall rue.
It is time this battle started,

Time we struck them with our might.
We are fighting for our hearthfires,
For our honor and our rights.

ZAPATA CUENTA *(Beaded Moccasin), another Comanche chieftain, addresses Cuerno Verde and his warriors:*
Valiant Redmen, bend your war bows,
With a true unerring eye, that
With each arrow from your bowstrings,
We may see a Spaniard die.
Don your paint and gaudy feathers,
Sound the war drums, take your stand.
Sing of joy and sing of battle,
For the hour is at hand.
I, your captain, will support you,
You will find me at your side.
Zapata Cuenta is your chieftain
And in him you can confide.

TABACO, *a Comanche chieftain and an ambassador seeking peace, speaks:*
Noble Redmen, you have ordered,
That your men be ready all.
And these Christians who seek battle,
Soon will hear your martial call.
Tabaco is also a mighty captain,
With many warriors at his command,
And we recognize no master,
In this broad and mighty land.
Alone, unarmed, and fearing no one,
To Taos I went, among these men,
On a peaceful mission went I,
And we signed a treaty then.
I can say this of the Spaniard,
He respects a worthy foe.
Without fear I went amongst them,
Mingled freely, and you may know,
This is why I cannot join you.
I cannot join this strife today.
I cannot prove a traitor

To the peace I've made to stay.
I go forth to seek the Spaniard,
Urge him to leave and save his life,
For if he persist most surely,
He will perish in this strife.
I shall tell him Cuerno Verde,
With his numerous warrior band,
Have come to meet the Spaniard,
And drive him from this land.
That I come from the Napeiste,
Bringing him these tidings true,
That Oso Pardo and Cabeza Negra,
Are here to give him battle too.
If you choose, go forth to battle,
This is what I have to say.
I will keep the pledge I've made.
I and mine will leave today.

DON TORIBIO ORTIZ, *a Spanish general, speaks:*
I am Don Toribio Ortiz,
And a general's rank I hold.
In the service of my king,
I have grown gray and old.
But my right arm still is potent,
And my step is firm and steady.
Come, a champion from your ranks,
Don Toribio Ortiz is ready.
Cuerno Verde I have heard it,
That you are a valiant foe.
Come you hither, give me battle,
I would let your warriors know,
That to me your strength and valor,
Means but little, when we meet,
I shall smite you with this sharp sword,
And will lay you at my feet.
All my troops, stand at attention,
Let no one seek the fray,
Till I give the word to battle,
We must conquer these today.

Let each lance thrust claim a victim,
Every one of them must yield.
Either crown yourself with glory,
Or leave your bodies on the field.
Our Immaculate Mother Mary,
She shall be our strength and guide,
Send a message of your prowess,
Through this nation far and wide.

DON CARLOS, *the Spanish general, again speaks.*
Your assurances make me happy,
For I know you all are true.
And on many fields of battle,
You've been tested through and through.
Since we all are of one spirit,
And all are eager for the fray,
Form your men in line of battle,
Unleash your war dogs and away,
Sound the trumpets, Santiago!
Holy Virgin! Lend your aid!
Cross through yonder willow thicket,
That is where their camp is made.

CUERNO VERDE, *the Comanche chieftain, speaks to his warriors.*
They advance! They seek the issue,
Meet them with your battle cry.
In their midst I see their general,
Either he or I must die.
Hear their shouts, oh valiant Redmen,
Of the brave Comanche race,
You who've never met your equal,
Here or any other place.
You alone of all the Redmen,
Still defy the Spanish might.
We have clashed with them in battle
And we've put them to the flight.
Wave aloft my lofty banners,
Which have never known defeat.
Up and at them with a fury,
That will sweep them off their feet.

BARRIGA DUCE, *a Spanish camp follower, speaks as he views the battle from afar:*

Let them die, the more the better,
There will be more spoils for me.
Soft tanned skins of elk and beaver,
What a comfort they will be.
Meat of buffalo in abundance,
Everything that one might need,
I will fill my larder plenty,
I have many mouths to feed.
My good wife shall want for nothing,
She shall cook a gorgeous meal.
Oh my comrades, give them plenty,
What a happiness I feel.

The Comanches abandon their camp and Barriga Duce enters.

Ah, at last I've reached their treasure,
There is plenty here indeed.
Sugars, fruits, and meats, and jellies,
What a life these heathens lead.
Everything to tempt the palate,
What a feast, fit for a king.
I shall eat and then I'll gather,
I'll not leave a single thing.
Let them fill themselves with glory,
While I eat with joy and mirth.
With their arms they prove their valor,
My glory is measured by my girth.
And if anyone should doubt this,
Let him measure side by me.
Not with words and idle boasting,
But with proof that all may see.
Give no quarter, comrades, smite them,
Do your duty, have no fear,
Strike them, smite them, without mercy,
I'll attend to what is here.
Santiago! You are with us.
How the battle rages fierce!
See our brave and valiant comrades,

How they cut and thrust and pierce.
Like the autumn leaves they scatter,
It is o'er. They all have fled.
While upon the field of battle
Lies Cuerno Verde, with his dead.

THE END. [ca. 1780]

Translation of *Los comanches* by Gilberto Espinosa

Francisco Palóu was born in Palma de Mallorca in 1723. In 1740, at the Lullian Franciscan Seminary in Palma, he met Junípero Serra (1713–1784), who was to become Palóu's friend and lifelong inspiration. Palóu's biography of Serra is an adoring account of one of California's most important missionaries, who dedicated much of his life to the establishment of missions throughout California, despite a decades-long bout with a crippling leg ailment. That dedication is recognized today in Serra's image on a United States postage stamp, his name on a California state park, portraits painted posthumously, and several commemorative statues. *The History of the Life and Apostolic Work of the Venerable Fray Junípero Serra* tracks the missionary from his birth on the island of Mallorca to his death in California and includes fascinating information on the area's native peoples and the interrelationship of secular and religious authority.

Palóu was one of the more prolific writers of the colonial period of New Spain. Apart from the life of Serra, he produced a major work about the missionary movement called *Noticias de Nuevo California (Historical Memoir of New California)*, written between 1773 and 1783. During that time Serra and Palóu traveled north from Baja California and founded missions at Monterey and San Francisco, among other places.

Palóu died in 1789, five years after Serra and two years after completing the biography.

from The Historic Account of the Life and Apostolic Work of the Venerable Fray Junípero Serra

The Founding of the Second Mission [the First in Alta or Nueva California], That of San Diego, and What Happened in It

That ardent zeal which ever burned and consumed the heart of our Venerable Father Junípero did not permit him to forget the principal object of his coming. And it was this which impelled him, on the second day after the departure of the expedition, to make a beginning toward the preaching of the gospel in this Mission and port of San Diego, which had been discovered since the year 1603, and which had been so named by the Admiral Don Sebastian Vizcaino. He made the service for the foundation of the Mission to consist of High Mass and the other ceremonies, which were also celebrated in the founding of the Mission of San Fernando, on the 16th of July, the day on which we Spaniards celebrate the Triumph of the Most Holy Cross. For he hoped that exactly as through the power of that sacred emblem the Spaniards had gained a great victory over the barbarous Mohammedans, in the year 1212, they might also win a victory by raising the standard of the Holy Cross, and, putting to flight all the army of hell, bring under subjection to the gentle yoke of our Holy Faith all the savage tribes of pagans who inhabited this New California; and besides, he implored the special patronage of the Most Holy Mary, who on this day is honored by the Universal Church under the title of Our Lady of Mount Carmel. Moved by this ardent faith and zeal for the saving of souls, the Venerable Father Junípero raised the standard of the Holy Cross, fixing it in the place which seemed to him most appropriate for the building of the city, within sight of the harbor. The Missionaries in charge were our Venerable Father and Fr. Fernando Parron. The few men who were well enough to be about, in the intervals when not called upon to attend the sick, were kept busy in the construction of little shacks.

As soon as a place had been prepared and dedicated for the provisional church they tried to attract to it with gifts and expressions of affection the pagans who came about; but as they could not understand our language they paid no attention to anything but the receiving of gifts from us, and they took everything with eagerness except food, which on no condition would they touch, so that if any little boy happened to put a piece of sugar in his mouth he would spit it out as if it were poison. They naturally attributed the sickness of our men to the things they ate, as they were things they had never seen. This was, indeed, a singular Divine Providence, for if they had had the same desire for our food which they had for our clothing, the little group of Spaniards in the colony would surely have been left to starve to death.

However great may have been their aversion to our food, no less intense was their desire to possess themselves of our raiment, they going so far as to steal everything of this sort they could lay hands upon. They went to such an extreme that even the sails of the ship were not safe from their hands. One night the men on board found that they had come out in their canoes and were cutting pieces out of one of the sails, and on another occasion cutting up a rope, in order to carry them off. This made it necessary to put a watch of two soldiers on board (taking them from the eight which had been left) and with the fear of these men the vessel was protected. However, this diminished the guard at the Mission and especially on Holy Days when it was necessary for one of the Fathers to go on board to celebrate Mass, taking with him two of the soldiers as an escort in case he should be attacked by any of the pagans.

All these movements they watched most attentively, but were ignorant of the force of our firearms and they had great confidence in the fact that they greatly outnumbered us, and in the virtue of their arrows and wooden sabers which could cut almost like steel, and their other arms, such as war-clubs, with which they could do much damage. So they began to steal things without any sign of fear and when they saw that this was not permitted them they decided to try their fortunes with us, taking all our lives and carrying off the spoils. This they attempted on the 12th and 13th of August, but when they found they were met with resistance they had to retire.

On the 15th of the same month in which is celebrated the Great Festival of the Glorious Assumption of our Queen and Lady of the Heavens, as soon as two of the soldiers had gone with the Rev. Fr. Fernando on board ship to say Mass, leaving only four of the soldiers on shore, just as the Venerable Father President and the Father Viscaino had finished celebrating the Holy Sacrifice in which some of the men had received Communion, a great number of the pagans, all armed for battle, fell upon us and began to steal everything they could find, taking away from the poor patients in the hospital even the sheets that covered them. The corporal raised the cry, "To arms!" and when their enemies saw the soldiers in the act of arming themselves with their leather jackets and shields (a defense easily able to turn aside their arrows), and that at the same time they were taking up their guns they drew off and began to discharge their arrows. At the same time the four soldiers, the carpenter and the blacksmith discharged their weapons with great valor; but the blacksmith excelled them all for without doubt the Holy Communion which he had just received filled him with extraordinary courage and though he had no leather jacket to protect him he went about among the houses and shacks crying out, "Long live the Faith of our Lord Jesus Christ, and let these dogs of enemies die the death," firing at the same time upon the pagans.

The Venerable Father President, with his companion, was at the time within the little house used for a chapel, commending all to God and praying that there might be no death among the men, and also praying to spare the lives of the pagans that they might not die without baptism. The Father Viscaino, wishing to see if the Indians had retired, raised a little way the agave mat which served as a curtain, or door, to the room, but he had scarcely done so when an arrow pierced his hand, and with that he let the curtain fall again and gave himself up to prayer, as did Father Junípero. Though he afterwards was healed of the wound, he always remained crippled in that hand.

The battle continued and the noise of shots mingled with the cries of the pagans. Suddenly the servant called Joseph María, who personally attended on the Fathers, rushed into the little shack, and, falling down at the feet of our Venerable, cried out: "Father, absolve me, for the Indians have killed me." No sooner had he received absolution than he died, as his throat had been pierced by an arrow. The Missionaries kept his death a secret and the pagans never knew of it. From among them several fell and when the rest saw the terrible destruction made by the firearms and the valor of the Christians, they quickly retired with their wounded, without leaving one on the ground in order to prevent us, as they supposed they could, from knowing if any had been killed in the combat. Two of the Christians had been wounded, besides Father Viscaino, one of them a jacketed soldier, an Indian from Old California and the valiant blacksmith, but the wounds were not of great seriousness and all were soon well with the exception of the servant boy, whose death was kept a secret.

From among the pagans, although they kept secret the number of the dead, we knew that quite a number had been wounded, because after a few days they came back seeking for peace, and asking to be doctored, a service which the good surgeon very gladly did them, and they recovered. This charity which they noted in us could not help forcing them to hold us in esteem and the sad experience of their unhappy attempt to rob us filled them with fear and respect for us so that they behaved quite differently than before, for while they continued to visit the Mission with frequency, they did not bring in their arms.

Among those who came frequently was a young Indian of about fifteen years, who got to coming every day and he became accustomed to eat whatever the Fathers gave him, without any fear of consequences. Father Junípero tried to favor him and encourage him to learn our language so as to see if through him he might not bring about the baptism of some of the children. Several days passed and when at last the Indian boy understood somewhat, the Father told him to try to bring to him some little baby, with the consent of its parents, as he would make him a Christian like ourselves by putting a little water on his head, and in that way he would become a child of God and of the Father and a brother to the soldiers (whom they called *Cueres*) who would also give him clothing that he might go about dressed like the Spaniards. With these expressions and others which the zealous Father easily conjured up for the occasion, it seems that the Indian understood and communicated the same to the rest, for within a few days he returned with one of the pagan men (accompanied by many others), who brought in his arms a child and indicated by signs that he was willing to have it baptized. Filled with great joy, our Venerable Father immediately gave him a piece of cloth with which to cover the child, invited the corporal to act as sponsor and the other soldiers to be present in order to duly solemnize this first baptism. The Indians of course were all present. As soon as the Father had finished the ceremonies, and was in the act of pouring out the water of baptism, the pagan snatched away the child and ran away to their village, leaving the Father standing with the shell in his hand. Here it was necessary for him to use all his prudence not to become incensed at the rude act and it was only respect for him which prevented the soldiers from attempting to avenge the profanation, but considering the savagery and ignorance of the poor, miserable creatures it was necessary to overlook the offense.

So great was the sorrow of our Venerable Father at having been frustrated in the baptizing of the child that for many days he went about with his countenance full of the pain and the sorrow he felt, as he attributed the failure to his own sins. Even after the lapse of years, whenever he told the story, he would have to stop to dry the tears which started from his eyes and he would generally end by saying: "Let us thank God that now so many of them have received baptism without the least repugnance." So it was that in that Mission of San Diego the number reached one thousand and forty-six who were baptized, counting children and adults, whose salvation was due to the Apostolic labors of our Venerable President, and among them were many of those same who at the first had tried to take his life.

Very different was the lot of one of the men who had taken an important part in this attack on the Mission. Far from imitating the rest in repentance, he became set in his pagan errors and was one of the principal movers in the mutiny of the year 1775, and of which I shall speak in its place as well as of those others who had a part in the cruel death and martyrdom of the Venerable Fr. Luis Jayme. Having been taken prisoner for his part in this last crime and placed with others in the jail of the garrison, he was there visited by the Venerable Father Junípero, who had come down to that port in August of the year 1776. The Father wished to bring to the prisoners some comfort as well as to convert them to our Holy Faith. The sergeant pointed out to our Father this miserable pagan (he was with the rest in the stocks), saying that he was the same one who had tried, in the year 1769, to take the life of his Reverence and of the others in the first days of the founding of the Mission. Then it was that the ardor and zeal of our Venerable Father overflowed in a flood of exhortation and loving appeal toward this unhappy mortal, begging him to become a Christian and assuring him that in case he did, God our Lord and the King would undoubtedly pardon his crimes. But he was unable to obtain a single word from him, although the other prisoners, greatly moved to tears, begged the servant of God to intercede for them, saying they wanted to become Christians (as indeed they did later). But this unhappy gentile, having committed suicide, was found dead on the morning of the 15th of August (exactly seven years from the date of the attack), it being a cause of great wonderment to all that while at the side of his companions he should be able to put a rope around his neck and hang himself without letting any one among the prisoners know of it and much less the guards. All were astonished not only at the disastrous end of the unhappy man but that it should happen on the day of the Assumption of Our Lady and just seven years from the time he and his companions had tried to kill the Venerable Father Junípero and those who accompanied him, which would have frustrated many great Spiritual Conquests, as we shall see later. [1787]

Translation of *La relación histórica de la vida y apostolicas tareas de Fray Junípero Serra, y de las misiones que fundó en la California Septentrional y nuevos establecimientos de Monterey* by C. S. Williams

Part II

PRELUDE

By the end of the eighteenth century, Spain's dominance in Europe and the Americas had ebbed to the point that it was a second-rate power. Its economy had become increasingly dependent on income from its colonies, whose leaders had become more and more restive. A colonial rebellion in the thirteen British colonies that became the United States of America provided a model for various states to the south.

Spain's crumbling monarchy could offer little hope to American possessions that feared internal slave revolts and outside encroachment from France and the United States along its northern borders. Finally, in 1802, when Napoleon invaded Spain and placed his brother on the Spanish throne, such American leaders as Simón Bolívar and José de San Martín were ready to declare independence.

The implication for the Hispanic population of Spain's northern colonies was enormous. As nationalism became the political dogma of the time, Spanish imperial influence diminished yearly. The United States was thus able to engage in an early form of manifest destiny and begin to take control of former Spanish territories. In 1803 President Thomas Jefferson purchased from the French the territory of Louisiana, much of which had been held by the Spanish before Napoleon's takeover. In 1821, the year Mexico gained its independence, the United States and Spain, after a brief series of skirmishes, signed the Adams-Onis Treaty, which ceded southern Florida to the United States. In 1848, after more than a decade of Anglo migration to Texas and the Southwest and warfare between the United States and Mexico, the Treaty of Guadalupe Hidalgo forced Mexico to cede almost a third of its territory, thereby giving control of Texas, most of present-day New Mexico, Arizona, and

California to the Anglo North. To complete the picture as we see it from the present, in 1898, after the Spanish Cuban American War, Cuba and Puerto Rico (as well as the Philippines) came under U.S. domination. Despite these annexations, the metaphorical gulfs between the Anglo North and the Hispanic South continued.

For Latinos, the price of these geopolitical changes, of the moving of borders and creation of nations, was a cultural break and a sense of discontinuity. To residents of former Spanish colonies, which had over the years become either nationalistic or regionalistic, the United States was an occupying power. Latino culture was more or less kidnapped and sequestered, becoming, in essence, *una cultura secuestrada*. Where nationalism could continue its growth, in particular where geography separated Latino or Latin American culture from the mainland, as in Cuba and Puerto Rico, art and culture could evolve with less Anglo-Puritan interference and only a minor irritation from the English language (though before World War II, two generations of Puerto Rican schoolchildren were educated in English). In the contiguous, formerly Mexican areas, though, valiant attempts were needed to resist Anglo hegemony. The community's need to retain or rebuild a Chicano, Mexican-American, or Latino culture is very much a response to the discontinuity created by this Anglo pressure.

In the nineteenth century U.S. Latino literature became dominated by cultural nationalism in the form of a call for resistance to Anglo pressures, particularly by Cuban and Mexican-American writers (there were few Puerto Ricans in the United States until the Jones Act of 1917 made all Puerto Ricans citizens of the country). As noted in the introduction to Part I, politicians, published writers, and other culture makers of the Americas slowly transferred their focus from Spain to the West. Many began to think of themselves as a breed apart. Bolívar himself called the Latin American *una especie media,* an in-between thing.

As early as the 1820s and until 1898, many Cuban writers, in a colonial rebellion against Spain, wrote passionately from the heart of Cuban nationalism and, through exile, made New York the second city of the Caribbean. José María Heredia's depictions of romantic longing for the natural beauty of Cuba and his literary efforts on behalf of New York's Spanish-speaking community mark the establishment of Latino literature (as opposed to Spanish colonial literature) in the United States. Though Heredia spent less than two years in this country, when he was in his early twenties he not only published his own writings but also edited and published a newspaper in Spanish. Hispanic cultural life in New York, often thought to be a post–World War II phenomenon, has actually existed for over 170 years. In 1858 an extraordinary volume of Cuban exile writing, *El laúd del desterrado* (The Exile's Lute) was published in New York. It brought together more than a dozen poets whose work had been printed in now little-known periodicals. By the time José Martí raised Cuban exile writing to its apogee, within the Spanish-speaking and reading community a literary culture had existed for almost seventy years.

A few years after the Treaty of Guadalupe Hidalgo, Mexican-American literature began to appear, even gaining something of a national audience. Autobiography by Mexican Americans (the term "Chicano" did not come into use until the middle of the twentieth century) began in the 1850s with the 1855 publication of the memoirs of Juan Seguín; later, Frederick Bancroft published a collection of Californian oral histories. In 1885 the first novel acknowledged to have been written by a Mexican American, María Amparo Ruiz de Burton's *The Squatter and the Don,* was published (she had published an earlier novel, but it was anonymous). *The Squatter and the Don* is a melodramatic work that very much reflects Anglo aesthetics of characterization and style.

Just seven years later, however, what has been called by many critics "the first Chicano novel" was published in the very literary state of New Mexico. Eusebio Chacón's *El hijo de la tempestad* (*The Son of the Storm*) appeared first in Santa Fe in 1892. That same year *Tras la tormenta la calma* (The Calm after the Storm) was also published by *El boletín popular.* In Chacón's opinion, Anglo literary aesthetics could not convey the life and society of Mexicans in the United States, so he set about to establish a Mexican-American literary form with a strong relationship to the Mexican novel of the time.

Mexican-American literature was broader than the writings mentioned above. For hundreds of years the Mexican border regions, especially the area that is now New Mexico, enjoyed folk and religious poetry and drama that is only now being appreciated for its elegance. The *corrido,* or border ballad, was popularized during the nineteenth century to spread word of the exploits of such bandits as

Joaquín Murrieta, a Californian Robin Hood, and Gregorio Cortez, a victim of racism and linguistic misunderstanding who became a hero when he held scores of Texas Rangers at bay for weeks.

The picture of nineteenth-century Latino literature will be complete only when the many local and regional publications are recovered, examined, evaluated, and republished. In the late eighteenth and early nineteenth century, changing loyalties and newly created political traditions sowed the seeds for separate cultural entities among Spanish-speaking people, which grew into the multiplicity of Latino cultures in the United States today. Not until the late twentieth century would the question of a pan-Latino culture in the United States and a culture of the Americas be considered in a widespread way. Even then the national cultures created in the last century would often resist assimilation into a larger community.

José María Heredia was born in Santiago de Cuba in 1803, but because of his father's peripatetic life, he spent little of his childhood there. In 1823, a month before his twentieth birthday, after taking part in revolutionary activities, he was forced to flee to the United States. He landed in Boston, but for the following two years he lived in New York, in Connecticut near New Haven, and in Philadelphia, before leaving for Mexico.

Despite the briefness of his stay in the United States, Heredia is a key figure in the establishment of the literary exile community of the 1820s and '30s. During this time he wrote some of his most beautiful poetry, founded a newspaper, and produced an extraordinary diary; his first collection of poetry, *Poesías,* was published in New York in 1925. According to the critic Angel Aparicio Laurencio, Heredia's patriotic poetry "is essentially lyrical and epic: lyrical because he expresses his own feelings; epic because he narrates the political misfortunes and the tyranny suffered by his country."

The poem included here represents Heredia as a poet of nature and landscape, which, along with his leftist politics, is the reason he is often associated with the European Romantics. Heredia's poetry was better known in the United States in the mid-nineteenth century than it is today. Translations of his work appeared under the names of such well-known poets as William Cullen Bryant. Many of those translations poorly serve the beauty of Heredia's fervent verse; if he is to take his place among other nineteenth-century poets who spent time in this country, new translations will be necessary.

Like José Martí, for political reasons José María Heredia spent little of his adult life in his beloved Cuba. He went back there in 1836, but in 1837, he returned to Toluca, Mexico, where he died in 1839.

Niagara

My lyre, give me my lyre,
For inspiration burns in my trembling,
restive soul. Oh, how long it lay hidden
in the mists without its light
shining on my brow. Billowing Niagara,
only your sublime face can restore the divine gift
that the unholy, mocking
hand of sorrow has taken away.

Mighty torrent, be calm, and hush
your terrifying thunder: Lift a bit
the mists that surround you,
let me gaze upon your tranquil face
and with burning zeal fill my soul.
I am worthy of musing upon you: I have always
shunned the common and the mean,
thrilled to the terrific and the sublime.
As the furious hurricane hurled itself upon us,
when lightning's ray touched my brow,
my heart beat with pleasure: I saw the ocean,
lashed by southern storms, rock my bark,
and open its depths beneath my feet: I loved its dangers,
I loved its wrath. But even that fury did not leave
in my soul the deep impression of your grandeur.

You flow softly and majestically, and then,
on the harsh rocks broken,
you pitch forward, violent, enraged,
like destiny, blind and irresistible.

What human voice from this roaring bar
could describe that terrifying face?
When I look upon your
fervid currents, my soul is lost
in wandering thought, and in its flight seeks,
from the dark edge of the highest cliff,
to track the breathtaking sight:
a thousand waves, like thoughts quickly passing,
crash and beat themselves into a fury.
Another thousand, and yet another overtake them,
and then, among the foam and noise, they disappear.

Look! They come . . . they leap! The horrid depths
devour the fallen torrents,
which cross there in a thousand rainbows,
the woods are deafened
and echo that awful sound.
With each great crash, the water
breaks apart against the rocks, and leaps.
A cloud of swirling fog covers the
depths with whirlpools, then rises, and eddies.
An immense pyramid lifts up
into the sky and, over the nearby forests,
frightens a solitary hunter.

But what in you seeks my yearning eye,
with such a restless urging? Why around your
immense cavern do I not see palm trees?
Ah, delicious palms, that, on the plains
of my burning land are born
from the smiling sun, and grow and flourish,
waving softly in the blowing ocean-breeze,
under the purest of blue skies.

The memory, to my dismay,
comes back to me. Your destiny
lacks nothing, O Niagara, you need
no more than the rustic pine
to crown your terrible majesty.
In a frivolous garden, the palm, the myrtle,

and the delicate rosebush
inspire soft pleasures and dull languor.
On you, chance has bestowed
a worthier, more sublime goal.
The free, generous and strong soul
approaches, sees you, is moved,
transcends life's smaller gifts,
and feels uplifted still
at the mere mention of your name.

God, God of Truth! In other climes
I have seen execrable monsters
blaspheme in your holy name,
spread terror and unholy thought,
drown fields in blood and tears,
incite useless wars between brothers
and, frenzied, lay waste to the earth.
I have seen them, and at that sight
my breast burned with grave indignation.
I have seen lying philosophers
dare to question your mysteries, scorn You,
and impiously draw men down
to sorrowful depths of despair.
Because of this, my mind has always sought
You in sublime solitude: now,
it opens wholly to You; it feels your
hand in this surrounding immensity,
and from this deluge
in eternal thunder
your deep voice into my breast descends.

Dread torrent!
How the sight of you overwhelms the spirit
and fills me with terror and admiration!
Whence comes your source? For so many
centuries, who has fed your inexhaustible springs?
What powerful hand
keeps the ocean waters that receive you
from overflowing the earth?

The Lord opened his omnipotent hand,
covered your face with roiling clouds,
gave his voice to your rushing waters
and adorned your brow with his terrible bow.
I watch your waters, which tirelessly flow,
as the long torrent of centuries rolls
into eternity. Thus fly past the flowering days
of a man, and he wakes to sorrow . . . Alas, my
youth has withered, my face wizened, and
a deep, roiling pain furrows my brow
with clouds of sorrow.

Until this day, I had never before felt so deeply
my isolation, my loneliness, a crying lovelessness . . . Can
a passionate and stormy soul be happy without love?
Oh, that a beauty, worthy of me, would love me
and share the wandering thoughts and solitary path
that leads from these depths to the turbulent edge!

How I would love to see her face covered
by a light pallor, become even more beautiful
in her sweet terror, and smile as I hold her
in my loving arms! Such delirious virtue! Ah,
in exile, without country, or love, before me
I see only tears and sorrow.

Powerful Niagara!
Hear my last words: in a few years
the cold tomb will devour your humble
poet. May my verses endure with
your immortal glory! Would that some pious
traveler, upon seeing your face, heave a sigh
to my memory! Thus I, as the sun sinks
into the west, will fly happily to where
the Creator calls me, and, hearing in the clouds
the echoes of my fame, raise a radiant brow. [1824]

Translation of "Niágara" by Harold Augenbraum,
with Margarite Fernández Olmos

Eulalia Pérez's memoir, which she dictated in 1877 to Thomas Savage, an agent of Hubert Howe Bancroft, states: "I do not remember the date of my birth, but I do know that I was fifteen years old when I married Miguel Antonio Guillén, a soldier of the garrison at Loreto Presidio." According to Savage, Pérez was 139 years old in 1877, a person of "uncommon age" who nevertheless had a remarkably fresh memory concerning her long and varied life as a midwife, cook, and supervisor of various shops in the mission at San Gabriel, California. Her memory commences with her early life, when the area was still under Spanish rule, and ends in the 1830s with the secularization of the missions during the Mexican era.

Eulalia Pérez was one of some 40 women out of a total of approximately 150 persons, many of them the formerly powerful patriarchs, whose personal testimonies were recorded during the 1870s as part of a collection commissioned by Bancroft for his work on California history. The documents provide an invaluable source of information on Hispano/Mexicano life before and after the loss of California and much of northern Mexico to the United States after 1848. These often nostalgic recollections of the *californios,* as the residents of the area were called, provide an image that is frequently at odds with the way they are represented in Anglo-American fictional and historical accounts. These people tell of the dispossession of their lands and their livelihoods while attempting to maintain their dignity. Bancroft's project allowed them to present their own vision of their lives and a vanished way of life.

Of the female narrators, many were from prominent families. The few testimonies of working-class women reveal a striking sense of self-reliance and autonomy. Eulalia Pérez's strong personality — and the fact that her brief marriages figured insignificantly in her memoir — has led critic Genaro Padilla to comment that Bancroft's project gave these women a unique and self-affirming opportunity to reconstruct their lives. "There are strikingly discernible moments in each of their narratives when, in the process of reciting, in obligatory tone, the customs and manners Bancroft wanted recited, they discover areas of long evaporated personal experience that amplify the narrational voice of an individual female identity."

An Old Woman Remembers

I, Eulalia Pérez, was born in the Presidio of Loreto in Baja California.

My father's name was Diego Pérez, and he was employed in the Navy Department of said presidio; my mother's name was Antonia Rosalia Cota. Both were pure white.

I do not remember the date of my birth, but I do know that I was fifteen years old when I married Miguel Antonio Guillén, a soldier of the garrison at Loreto Presidio. During the time of my stay at Loreto I had three children — two boys, who died there in infancy, one girl, Petra, who was eleven years old when we moved to San Diego, and another boy, Isidoro, who came with us to this [Alta] California.

I lived eight years in San Diego with my husband, who continued his service in the garrison of the presidio, and I attended women in childbirth.

I had relatives in the vicinity of Los Angeles, and even farther north, and asked my husband repeatedly to take me to see them. My husband did not want to come along, and the commandant of the presidio did not allow me to go, either, because there was no other woman who knew midwifery.

In San Diego everyone seemed to like me very much, and in the most important homes they treated me affectionately. Although I had my own house, they arranged for me to be with those families almost all the time, even including my children.

In 1812 I was in San Juan Capistrano attending Mass in church when a big earthquake occurred, and the tower fell down. I dashed through the sacristy, and in the doorway the people knocked me down and stepped over me. I was pregnant* and could not move. Soon afterwards I returned to San Diego and almost immediately gave birth to my daughter María Antonia, who still lives here in San Gabriel.

After being in San Diego eight years, we came to the Mission of San Gabriel, where my husband had been serving in the guard. In 1814, on the first of October, my daughter María del Rosario was

* If Doña Eulalia was 139 years old when Savage interviewed her, she would have been born in 1738 and thus 74 years old and pregnant at the time of the earthquake! *Trans.*

born, the one who is the wife of Michael White and in whose home I am now living. . . .

When I first came to San Diego the only house in the presidio was that of the commandant and the barracks where the soldiers lived.

There was no church, and Mass was said in a shelter made out of some old walls covered with branches, by the missionary who came from the Mission of San Diego.

The first sturdy house built in San Diego belonged to a certain Sánchez, the father of Don Vicente Sánchez, alcalde of Los Angeles and deputy of the Territorial Council. The house was very small, and everyone went to look at it as though it were a palace. That house was built about a year after I arrived in San Diego.

My last trip to San Diego would have been in the year 1818, when my daughter María del Rosario was four years old. I seem to remember that I was there when the revolutionaries came to California. I recall that they put a stranger in irons and that afterwards they took them off.

Some three years later I came back to San Gabriel. The reason for my return was that the missionary at San Gabriel, Father José Sánchez, wrote to Father Fernando at San Diego — who was his cousin or uncle — asking him to speak to the commandant of the presidio at San Diego requesting him to give my son Isidoro Guillén a guard to escort me here with all my family. The commandant agreed.

When we arrived here Father José Sánchez lodged me and my family temporarily in a small house until work could be found for me. There I was with my five daughters — my son Isidoro Guillén was taken into service as a soldier in the mission guard.

At that time Father Sánchez was between sixty and seventy years of age — a white Spaniard, heavy set, of medium stature — a very good, kind, charitable man. He, as well as his companion Father José María Zalvidea, treated the Indians very well, and the two were much loved by the Spanish-speaking people and by the neophytes and other Indians.

Father Zalvidea was very tall, a little heavy, white; he was a man of advanced age. I heard it said that they summoned Zalvidea to San Juan Capistrano because there was no missionary priest there. Many years later, when Father Antonio Peyri fled from San Luis

Obispo — it was rumored that they were going to kill the priests — I learned that Zalvidea was very sick, and that actually he had been out of his mind ever since they took him away from San Gabriel, for he did not want to abandon the mission. I repeat that the father was afraid, and two Indians came from San Luis Rey to San Juan Capistrano; in a rawhide cart, making him as comfortable as they could, they took him to San Luis, where he died soon after from the grueling hardships he had suffered on the way.

Father Zalvidea was very much attached to his children at the mission, as he called the Indians that he himself had converted to Christianity. He traveled personally, sometimes on horseback and at other times on foot, and crossed mountains until he came to remote Indian settlements, in order to bring them to our religion.

Father Zalvidea introduced many improvements in the Mission of San Gabriel and made it progress a very great deal in every way. Not content with providing abundantly for the neophytes, he planted [fruit] trees in the mountains, far away from the mission, in order that the untamed Indians might have food when they passed by those spots.

When I came to San Gabriel the last time, there were only two women in this part of California who knew how to cook [well]. One was María Luisa Cota, wife of Claudio López, superintendent of the mission; the other was María Ignacia Amador, wife of Francisco Javier Alvarado. She knew how to cook, sew, read and write and take care of the sick. She was a good healer. She did needlework and took care of the church vestments. She taught a few children to read and write in her home, but did not conduct a formal school.

On special holidays, such as the day of our patron saint, Easter, etc., the two women were called upon to prepare the feast and to make the meat dishes, sweets, etc.

The priests wanted to help me out because I was a widow burdened with a family. They looked for some way to give me work without offending the other women. Fathers Sánchez and Zalvidea conferred and decided that they would have first one woman, then the other and finally me, do the cooking, in order to determine who did it best, with the aim of putting the one who surpassed the others in charge of the Indian cooks so as to teach them how to cook. With that idea in mind, the gentlemen who were to decide on the merits of the three dinners were warned ahead of time. One of these gentlemen was Don Ignacio Tenorio, whom they called the Royal Judge, and who came to live and die in the company of Father Sánchez. He was a very old man, and when he went out, wrapped up in a muffler, he walked very slowly with the aid of a cane. His walk consisted only of going from the missionary's house to the church.

The other judges who also were to give their opinions were Don Ignacio Mancisidor, merchant; Don Pedro Narváez, naval official; Sergeant José Antonio Pico — who later became lieutenant, brother of Governor Pío Pico; Don Domingo Romero, who was my assistant when I was housekeeper at the mission; Claudio López, superintendent at the mission; besides the missionaries. These gentlemen, whenever they were at the mission, were accustomed to eat with the missionaries.

On the days agreed upon for the three dinners, they attended. No one told me anything regarding what it was all about, until one day Father Sánchez called me and said, "Look, Eulalia, tomorrow it is your turn to prepare dinner — because María Ignacia and Luisa have already done so. We shall see what kind of a dinner you will give us tomorrow."

The next day I went to prepare the food. I made several kinds of soup, a variety of meat dishes and whatever else happened to pop into my head that I knew how to prepare: The Indian cook, named Tomás, watched me attentively, as the missionary had told him to do.

At dinner time those mentioned came. When the meal was concluded, Father Sánchez asked for their opinions about it, beginning with the eldest, Don Ignacio Tenorio. This gentleman pondered awhile, saying that for many years he had not eaten the way he had eaten that day — that he doubted that they ate any better at the King's table. The others also praised the dinner highly.

Then the missionary called Tomás and asked him which of the three women he liked best — which one of them knew the most about cooking. He answered that I did.

Because of all this, employment was provided for me at the mission. At first they assigned me two Indians so that I could show them how to cook, the one named Tomás and the other called "The Gentile." I taught them so well that I had the satisfaction of seeing them turn out to be very good cooks, perhaps the best in all this part of the country.

The missionaries were very satisfied; this made them think more highly of me. I spent about a year teaching those two Indians. I did not have to do the work, only direct them, because they already had learned a few of the fundamentals.

After this, the missionaries conferred among themselves and agreed to hand over the mission keys to me. This was in 1821, if I remember correctly. I recall that my daughter María del Rosario was seven years old when she became seriously ill and was attended by Father José Sánchez, who took such excellent care of her that finally we could rejoice at not having lost her. At that time I was already the housekeeper.

The duties of the housekeeper were many. In the first place, every day she handed out the rations for the mess hut. To do this she had to count the unmarried women, bachelors, day-laborers, vaqueros — both those with saddles and those who rode bareback. Besides that, she had to hand out daily rations to the heads of households. In short, she was responsible for the distribution of supplies to the Indian population and to the missionaries' kitchen. She was in charge of the key to the clothing storehouse where materials were given out for dresses for the unmarried and married women and children. Then she also had to take care of cutting and making clothes for the men.

Furthermore, she was in charge of cutting and making the vaqueros' outfits, from head to foot — that is, for the vaqueros who rode in saddles. Those who rode bareback received nothing more than their cotton blanket and loin-cloth, while those who rode in saddles were dressed the same way as the Spanish-speaking inhabitants; that is, they were given shirt, vest, jacket, trousers, hat, cowboy boots, shoes and spurs; and a saddle, bridle and lariat for the horse. Besides, each vaquero was given a big silk or cotton handkerchief, and a sash of Chinese silk or Canton crepe, or whatever there happened to be in the storehouse.

They put under my charge everything having to do with clothing. I cut and fitted, and my five daughters sewed up the pieces. When they could not handle everything, the father was told, and then women from the town of Los Angeles were employed, and the father paid them.

Besides this, I had to attend to the soap-house, which was very large, to the wine-presses, and to the olive-crushers that produced oil, which I worked in myself. Under my direction and responsibility, Domingo Romero took care of changing the liquid.

Luis the soap-maker had charge of the soap-house, but I directed everything.

I handled the distribution of leather, calf-skin, chamois, sheepskin, Morocco leather, fine scarlet cloth, nails, thread, silk, etc. — everything having to do with the making of saddles, shoes and what was needed for the belt- and shoe-making shops.

Every week I delivered supplies for the troops and Spanish-speaking servants. These consisted of beans, corn, garbanzos, lentils, candles, soap and lard. To carry out this distribution, they placed at my disposal an Indian servant named Lucio, who was trusted completely by the missionaries.

When it was necessary, some of my daughters did what I could not find the time to do. Generally, the one who was always at my side was my daughter María del Rosario.

After all my daughters were married — the last one was Rita, about 1832 or 1833 — Father Sánchez undertook to persuade me to marry First Lieutenant Juan Mariné, a Spaniard from Catalonia, a widower with family who had served in the artillery. I did not want to get married, but the father told me that Mariné was a very good man — as, in fact, he turned out to be — besides, he had some money, although he never turned his cash-box over to me. I gave in to the father's wishes because I did not have the heart to deny him anything when he had been father and mother to me and to all my family.

I served as housekeeper of the mission for twelve or fourteen years, until about two years after the death of Father José Sánchez, which occurred in this same mission.

A short while before Father Sánchez died, he seemed robust and in good health, in spite of his advanced age. When Captain Barroso came and excited the Indians in all the missions to rebel, telling them that they were no longer neophytes but free men, Indians arrived from San Luis, San Juan and the rest of the missions. They pushed their way into the college, carrying their arms, because it was raining very hard. Outside the mission, guards and patrols made up of the Indians themselves were stationed. They had been taught to shout "Sentinel — on guard!" and "On guard he is!" but they said "Sentinel — open! Open he is!"

On seeing the Indians demoralized, Father Sánchez was very upset. He had to go to Los Angeles to say Mass, because he was accustomed to do so every week or fortnight, I do not remember which. He said to me, "Eulalia, I am going now. You know what the situation is; keep your eyes open and take care of what you can. Do not leave here, neither you nor your daughters." (My daughter María Antonia's husband, named Leonardo Higuera, was in charge of the Rancho de los Cerritos, which belonged to the mission, and María del Rosario's husband, Michael White, was in San Blas.)

The father left for the pueblo, and in front of the guard some Indians surged forward and cut the traces of his coach. He jumped out of the coach, and then the Indians, pushing him rudely, forced him toward his room. He was sad and filled with sorrow because of what the Indians had done and remained in his room for about a week without leaving it. He became ill and never again was his previous self. Blood flowed from his ears, and his head never stopped paining him until he died. He lived perhaps a little more than a month after the affair with the Indians, dying in the month of January, I think it was, of 1833. In that month there was a great flood. The river rose very high and for more than two weeks no one could get from one side to the other. Among our grandchildren was one that they could not bring to the mission for burial for something like two weeks, because of the flood. The same month — a few days after the father's death — Claudio López, who had been superintendent of the mission for something like thirty years, also died.

In the Mission of San Gabriel there was a large number of neophytes. The married ones lived on their rancherías with their small children. There were two divisions for the unmarried ones: one for the women, called the nunnery, and another for the men. They brought girls from the ages of seven, eight or nine years to the nunnery, and they were brought up there. They left to get married. They were under the care of a mother in the nunnery, an Indian. During the time I was at the mission this matron was named Polonia — they called her "Mother Superior." The alcalde was in charge of the unmarried men's division. Every night both divisions were locked up, the keys were delivered to me, and I handed them over to the missionaries.

A blind Indian named Andresillo stood at the door of the nunnery and called out each girl's name, telling her to come in. If any girl was missing at admission time, they looked for her the following day and brought her to the nunnery. Her mother, if she had one, was brought in and punished for having detained her, and the girl was locked up for having been careless in not coming in punctually.

In the morning the girls were let out. First they went to Father Zalvidea's Mass, for he spoke the Indian language; afterwards they went to the mess hut to have breakfast, which sometimes consisted of corn gruel with chocolate, and on holidays with sweets and bread. On other days, ordinarily they had boiled barley and beans and meat. After eating breakfast each girl began the task that had been assigned to her beforehand — sometimes it was at the looms, or unloading, or sewing, or whatever there was to be done.

When they worked at unloading, at eleven o'clock they had to come up to one or two of the carts that carried refreshments out to the Indians working in the fields. This refreshment was made of water with vinegar and sugar, or sometimes with lemon and sugar. I was the one who made up that refreshment and sent it out, so the Indians would not get sick. That is what the missionaries ordered.

All work stopped at eleven, and at twelve o'clock the Indians came to the mess hut to eat barley and beans with meat and vegetables. At one o'clock they returned to their work, which ended for the day at sunset. Then all came to the mess hut to eat supper, which consisted of gruel with meat, sometimes just pure gruel. Each Indian carried his own bowl, and the mess attendant filled it up with the allotted portion. . . .

The Indians were taught the various jobs for which they showed an aptitude. Others worked in the fields, or took care of the horses, cattle, etc. Still others were carters, oxherds, etc.

At the mission, coarse cloth, serapes, and blankets were woven, and saddles, bridles, boots, shoes, and similar things were made. There was a soap-house, and a big carpenter shop as well as a small one, where those who were just beginning to learn carpentry worked; when they had mastered enough they were transferred to the big shop.

Wine and oil, bricks and adobe bricks were also made. Chocolate was manufactured from cocoa, brought in from the outside; and sweets were made. Many of these sweets, made by my own hands, were sent to Spain by Father Sánchez.

There was a teacher in every department, an instructed Indian who was Christianized. A white man headed the looms, but when the Indians were finally skilled, he withdrew.

My daughters and I made the chocolate, oil, sweets, lemonade and other things ourselves. I made plenty of lemonade — it was even bottled and sent to Spain.

The Indians also were taught to pray. A few of the more intelligent ones were taught to read and write. Father Zalvidea taught the Indians to pray in their Indian tongue; some Indians learned music and played instruments and sang at Mass. The sextons and pages who helped with Mass were Indians of the mission.

The punishments that were meted out were the stocks and confinement. When the misdemeanor was serious, the delinquent was taken to the guard, where they tied him to a pipe or a post and gave him twenty-five or more lashes, depending on his crime. Sometimes they put them in the head-stocks; other times they passed a musket from one leg to the other and fastened it there, and also they tied their hands. That punishment, called "The Law of Bayona," was very painful.

But Fathers Sánchez and Zalvidea were always very considerate with the Indians. I would not want to say what others did because they did not live in the mission. . . . [1877]

Translation of "Una vieja y sus recuerdos"
by Ruth Rodríguez and Vivian C. Fisher

María Amparo Ruiz de Burton was born in 1832 in Loreto, Baja California, to a prominent landowning *californio* family. In 1849 she married Henry S. Burton, a captain in the U.S. Army. Their marriage — a *california* and an *anglo,* a Catholic and a Protestant — flouted the conventions of the time. María was thought to be very beautiful, and some have conjectured that she is the subject of the popular song "The Maid of Monterey," which was sung by Mexican War veterans in the early days of the state of California. The memoirist and historian M. G. Vallejo, an old friend of Ruiz de Burton's, once described her as "an erudite and cultured lady, passionate for the honor and traditions of her homeland, a worthy wife, a loving mother, and a loyal friend."

Ruiz de Burton's first book, *Who Would Have Thought It?* published in 1872, was printed with no author's name on the title page (a not uncommon practice at the time). Library catalogues note that it was written by H. S. Burton and Mrs. Henry S. Burton, even though Burton had been posted to the east for ten years before he died in 1869. María Ruiz de Burton died in 1895.

Who Would Have Thought It? and *The Squatter and the Don* are the first known English-language novels by a Latina. The latter book focuses on the struggle by Mexican landowners trapped in the United States by the Treaty of Guadalupe Hidalgo to retain control of their own property. The treaty was supposed to protect the property rights of the Mexican landholders, but in many cases unscrupulous squatters moved in and took over the land. The Mexicans found little help from an unsympathetic U.S. Congress.

Contemporary critics often find *The Squatter and the Don* problematic, since the upper classes on both sides of the question behave (in general) with dignity, while the working classes are portrayed as grasping and unethical. It is, however, an enjoyable, well-written work, if often melodramatic. The following two chapters provide an example of Ruiz de Burton's tone and style, as well as a glimpse of the legal question at the center of the story.

from The Squatter and the Don

Squatter Darrell Reviews the Past

"To be guided by good advice, is to profit by the wisdom of others; to be guided by experience, is to profit by wisdom of our own," said Mrs. Darrell to her husband, in her own sweet, winning way, as they sat alone in the sitting room of their Alameda farm house, having their last talk that evening, while she darned his stockings and sewed buttons on his shirts. The children (so-called, though the majority were grown up) had all retired for the night. Mr. and Mrs. Darrell sat up later, having much to talk about, as he would leave next day for Southern California, intending to locate — somewhere in a desirable neighborhood — a homestead claim.

"Therefore," continued Mrs. Darrell, seeing that her husband smoked his pipe in silence, adding no observations to her own, "let us this time be guided by our own past history, William — our experience. In other words, let us be wise, my husband."

"By way of variety, you mean," said he smiling. "That is, as far as I am concerned, because I own, frankly, that had I been guided by your advice — your wisdom — we would be much better off today. You have a right to reproach me."

"I do not wish to do anything of the kind. I think reproaches seldom do good."

"No use in crying over spilt milk, eh?"

"That is not my idea, either. On the contrary, if by *'milk'* it is meant all or any earthly good whatever, it is the *'spilt milk'* that we should lament. There is no reason to cry for the milk that has not been wasted, the good that is not lost. So let us cry for the *spilt milk,* by all means, if by doing so we learn how to avoid spilling any more. Let us cry for the *spilt milk,* and remember how, and where, and when, and why, we spilt it. Much wisdom is learnt through tears, but none by forgetting our lessons."

"But how can a man learn when he is born a fool?"

"Only an idiot is, truly speaking, a born fool; a fool to such a degree that he cannot act wisely if he will. It is only when *perversity* is added to foolishness, that a being — not an idiot — is utterly a fool. To persist in acting wrongfully, that is the real folly. To reject good counsel, either of one's own good thoughts or the good thoughts of others. But to act foolishly by deciding hastily, by lack of mature reflection, that I should only call a foolish mistake. So, then, if we have been foolish, let us at least utilize our foolishness by drawing from it lessons of wisdom for the future. We cannot conscientiously plead that we are born fools when we see our errors."

Mr. Darrell smilingly bowed, and with a voice much softer than his usual stentorian tones, said:

"I understand, little wife, but I fear that my streak of perversity is a broad one, and has solely been the bane of my life; it has a fatality accompanying it. I have often seen the right way to act, and yet I have gone with my eyes wide open to do the wrong thing. And this, too, not meaning to do harm to any one, nor wishing to be malicious or mean. I don't know what power impelled me. But if you will forgive my past wickedness, I'll try to do better."

"Don't say that. Don't speak of your wickedness, for real wickedness is perversity. You have acted wrongly at times, when you have misapplied your rights and the rights of others, but you have not intentionally done wrong. You are not perverse; don't say that."

"In a few days it will be twenty-four years since we crossed the plains with our three babies, in our caravan of four wagons, followed by our fine horses and choice Durham cows. I firmly believed then, that with my fine stock and my good bank account, and broad government lands, free to all Americans, I should have given you a nice home before I was five years older; that I would have saved money and would be getting more to make us rich before I was old. But see, at the end of twenty-four years, where and how do I find myself? I am still poor, all I have earned is the name of '*Squatter.*' That pretty name (which I hate because you despise it) is what I have earned."

"Don't say that either, William. We will only recommence one of numerous fruitless discussions. We are not poor, because we have enough to live in comfort, and I do not despise the name of Squatter, for it is harmless enough, but I do certainly disapprove of acts done by men because they are squatters, or to become squatters. They have caused much trouble to people who never harmed them."

"They, too, the poor squatters, have suffered as much distress as they have caused, the poor hard-worked toilers."

"That is very true, but I am afraid I shall never be able to see the necessity of any one being a squatter in this blessed country of plentiful broad acres, which a most liberal government gives away for the asking."

"That's exactly it. We aren't squatters. We are '*settlers.*' We take up land that belongs to us, American citizens, by paying the government price for it."

"Whenever you take up government land, yes, you are 'settlers,' but not when you locate claims on land belonging to any one else. In that case, you must accept the epithet of '*Squatter.*'"

Darrell set his teeth so tightly, that he bit a little chip off his pipe. Mrs. Darrell went on as if she had not observed her husband's flash of irritation.

"But I hope we will never more deserve such name; I trust that before you locate any homestead claim in Southern California, you will first inform yourself, very carefully, whether any one has a previous claim. And more specially, I beg of you, do not go on a Mexican grant unless you buy the land from the owner. This I beg of you specially, and must *insist upon it.*"

"And how am I to know who is the owner of a rancho that has been rejected, for instance?"

"If the rancho is still in litigation, don't buy land in it, or if you do, buy title from the original grantee, on fair conditions and clear understanding."

"I don't know whether that can be done in the Alamar rancho, which I am going to see, and I know it has been rejected. But of one thing you can rest assured, that I shall not forget our sad experience in Napa and Sonoma valleys, where — after years of hard toil — I had to abandon our home and lose the earnings of years and years of hard work."

"That is all I ask, William. To remember our experience in Napa and Sonoma. To remember, also, that we are no longer young. We cannot afford to throw away another twenty years of our life; and really and truly, if you again go into a Mexican grant, William, I shall not follow you there willingly. Do not expect it of me; I shall only go if you compel me."

"Compel you!" he exclaimed, laughing. "Compel you, when you know I have obeyed you all my life."

"Oh! no, William, not all your life, for you were well grown before I ever saw you."

"I mean ever since I went to Washington with my mind made up to jump off the train coming back, if you didn't agree to come North to be my commandant."

"I don't think I have been a very strict disciplinarian," she said, smiling. "I think the subaltern has had pretty much his own way."

"Yes, when he thinks he might. But when the commandant pulls the string, by looking sad or offended, then good-by to the spirit and independence of the subaltern."

"One thing I must not forget to ask you," she said, going back to the point of their digression, "and it is, not to believe what those men have been telling you about the Alamar rancho having been finally rejected. You know John Gasbang could never speak the truth, and years have not made him more reliable. As for Miller, Hughes and Mathews, they are dishonest enough, and though not so brazen as Gasbang, they will misrepresent facts to induce you to go with them, for they want you with them."

"I know they do; I see through all that. But I see, too, that San Diego is sure to have a railroad direct to the Eastern States. Lands will increase in value immediately; so I think, myself, I had better take time by the forelock and get a good lot of land in the Alamar grant, which is quite near town."

"But, are you sure it is finally rejected?"

"I saw the book, where the fact is recorded. Isn't that enough?"

"Yes, if there has been no error."

"Always the same cautious Mary Moreneau, who tortured me with her doubts and would not have me until Father White took compassion on me," said he, smiling, looking at her fondly, for his thoughts reverted back to those days when Miss Mary was *afraid* to marry him; but, after all, he won her and brought her all the way from Washington to his New England home.

William Darrell was already a well-to-do young farmer in those days, a bachelor twenty-eight to thirty years of age, sole heir to a flourishing New England farm, and with a good account in a Boston bank, when Miss Mary Moreneau came to New England from Washington to visit her aunt, Mrs. Newton. As Mrs. Newton's husband was William Darrell's uncle, nothing was more natural than for Mary to meet him at his uncle's house. Nobody expected that William would fall in love with her, as he seemed to be proof against Cupid's darts. The marriageable maidens of William's neighborhood had in vain tried to attract the obdurate young farmer, who seemed to enjoy no other society than that of his uncle Newton and his wife.

But Mary came and William surrendered at once. She, however, gave him no encouragement. Her coldness seemed only to inflame his love the more, until Miss Moreneau thought it was best to shorten her visit and return home about the middle of September.

"Why are you to return home so early?" Darrell asked Mary, after Mrs. Newton had informed him of Mary's intention of going.

"Because I think it is best," she answered.

"Why is it best?"

"For several reasons."

"May I be permitted to ask what are those reasons?"

"Certainly. One reason is, that as I came to see my aunt and at the same time to rest and improve my health, and all those objects have been accomplished, I might as well go home. Then, my other aunt, with whom I reside, is not feeling well. She went to spend the summer in Virginia, but writes that her health has not improved much, and she will soon come back to Washington. Then some of my pupils will want to recommence their lessons soon, and I want to have some little time to myself before I begin to work. You know, Mr. Darrell, I teach to support myself."

"Yes, only because you have a notion to do it."

"A notion! Do you think I am rich?"

"No, but there is no need of your working."

"It is a need to me to feel independent. I don't want to be supported by my aunts, while I know how to earn my own living."

"Miss Mary, please, I beg of you, let me have the happiness of taking care of you. Be my wife, I am not a rich man, but I have enough to provide for you."

"Mr. Darrell, you surprise me. I thank you for the compliment you pay me with your honorable offer, but I have no wish to get married."

"Do you reject me, Miss Mary? Tell me one thing; tell me truly, do you care for any one else?"

"No, I care for nobody. I don't want to marry."

"But you will marry some time. If you knew how very miserable you make me, I think you would not have the heart to refuse me."

"You will get over it. I am going soon. Forget me."

Darrell made no answer. He staggered out of the room and did not return until the following week, when Mary had left for Washington, accompanied by Letitia, her colored servant (called Tisha), who was devotedly attached to her.

Darrell had become rather taciturn and less sociable than ever, Mrs. Newton noticed, and since Mary left he seemed to lose flesh and all his spirits, and passed the winter as if life were a burden to him. But when spring came, he brightened up a little, though he felt far from happy. About that time Mrs. Newton had a letter from Mary, saying that she was going to spend vacation in Maryland with her other aunt, and Tisha for her escort.

"She don't come here, because she fears I shall pester her life with my visits. As she knows I can't keep away from her, she keeps away from you. She hates me. I suppose you, too, will take to hating me, by and by," said Darrell, when he heard that Mary was not coming that summer.

"No danger of that, William," Mrs. Newton replied.

"Yes, there is. You ought to hate me for driving her away. I hate myself worse than I hate the devil."

"William, you mustn't feel so. It isn't right."

"I know it. But when did I ever do anything right, I'd like to know? I wish I could hate her as I hate myself, or as she hates me."

"William, she does not hate you."

"How do you know she don't?"

"Because she would have told me. She is very truthful."

"I know it. She gave me my walking papers in a jiffy. I wish I could hate her."

"William, do you promise not to get angry, if I tell you why Mary declined your offer?"

"Say on. You couldn't well make a burning furnace any hotter. I am too mad already."

"Well, I'll tell you. She likes you, but is afraid of you."

"Afraid? afraid?" said he, aghast — "why! that is awful! I, an object of fear, when I worship the ground she treads on! But, how? What have I done? When did I frighten her?"

"At no particular time; but often you gave her the impression that you have a high temper, and she told me, 'If I loved Mr. Darrell better than my life, I wouldn't marry him, for I could never be happy with a man of a violent temper.' Then she spoke, too, of her being a Roman Catholic and you a Protestant."

"But you are a Catholic and uncle is Protestant."

"Certainly, I think the barrier is not insuperable."

"So, my temper frightened her! It is awful!" He mused in silence for a few minutes and then left the room.

About an hour after, he returned dressed for traveling, carrying a satchel in one hand and a tin box under his arm. He put the box on the table, saying:

"Aunt Newton, I am going away for a few days. Please take care of this box until I return or you hear from me. Good-by!" and he hurried away, for he had only barely time to catch the train going to New York.

Darrell was in New York for a few hours. He bought a finer suit of clothes, a very elegant light overcoat, hat and boots, and gloves to match, and thus equipped so elegantly that he hardly recognized himself, as he surveyed his figure in a large mirror of the furnishing store, where he was so metamorphosed, he took the night train for Washington.

It was early on a Sunday morning that Darrell arrived at Washington. He went to a hotel, entered his name, took a room, a bath and a breakfast, and then called a hack to go in search of Mary. He knew that was not an hour for calling, but he had *business* with Mary. His was no friendly visit; it was a matter of life and death with him.

He rang the bell, and presently he heard Tisha's flapping steps coming. "Lud a massa!" she exclaimed, stepping back. But recovering herself, said with true heartiness — "Come in the parlor, please. It is true glad Miss Mary will be to see ye."

"Do you think so, Tisha?" he asked.

"I know it; no thinking about it, neither. She is going to mass; but she'll see you for a little while, anyway."

Opening the parlor door for Darrell to walk in, Tisha ran up stairs to Mary's room.

"Oh Miss Mary!" said she, "guess who is down stairs."

"I couldn't, Tish, being so early and on Sunday, but I heard a man's voice. Is it a gentleman?"

"You bet; ah! please excuse me, I mean sure as I live it is, and no other than Mr. Darrell, from New England."

"Ah!" said Miss Mary, affecting indifference, but her hands trembled as she tied her bonnet strings.

Darrell knew he must appear self-contained and not in the least impetuous, but when he saw those beautiful dark eyes of Mary's he forgot all his pretended calmness.

"Is my aunt well?" Mary began as she came in.

"Yes, yes, everybody is well; don't be alarmed at my coming, I know it must seem strange to you. Two days ago I had no idea of coming to Washington, but Miss Moreneau, your aunt told me you were not coming North this summer, and this news nearly drove me crazy."

"Oh, Mr. Darrell!"

"Wait, don't drive me off yet. Your aunt told me that you refused me because you believed I have a violent temper. Now, I am not going to deny that, but this I am going to say — That I have never violated my word, and never shall, and I make a most solemn oath to you, that if you will marry me you shall never have occasion to be made unhappy or displeased by my quick anger, because you will only have to remind me of this pledge, and I shall curb my temper, if it kills me."

"Mr. Darrell, I believe you are perfectly sincere in what you say, but a strong trait of character is not controlled easily. It is more apt to be uncontrollable."

"For God's sake don't refuse me, I feel I must kill myself if you spurn me. I don't want life without you."

"Don't say that," Mary said, trying to keep calm, but she felt as if being carried away in spite of herself, by the torrent of his impetuosity. She was afraid of him, but she liked him and she liked to be loved in that passionate rebellious way of his; she smiled, adding, "we must postpone this conversation for I must go to church, and it is quite a long walk there."

"The carriage that brought me is at the door, take it, and don't walk, it is quite warm out."

"Will you go with me to church? You see, that is another obstacle; the difference of religions."

"Indeed, that is no obstacle; your religion tells you to pity me."

"We will talk to Father White about that."

"Then Mary, my beloved, will you give me hope?"

"And will you really try to control your anger when you feel it is getting the mastery over you?"

"I will, so help me God," said he, lifting his hand.

"Take care, that is an oath."

"I know it, and mean it," said he, much moved.

They went to church together. After church, Mary had a few moments' conversation with her pastor. She explained everything to him. "Do you love him, my child?" asked the good Father, knowing the human heart only too well. Mary blushed and said — "Yes, Father, I believe I do."

"Very well, send him to see me tomorrow morning."

Darrell had a long talk with Father White, and promised solemnly not to coerce or influence his wife to change her religion, and that should their union be blessed with children, they should be baptized and brought up Catholics.

And his union was blessed. Mary made his New England home a paradise, and eight children, sharing largely their mother's fine qualities, filled to overflowing his cup of happiness.

The Don's View of the Treaty of Guadalupe Hidalgo

If there had been such a thing as communicating by telephone in the days of '72, and there had been those magic wires spanning the distance between William Darrell's house in Alameda County and that of Don Mariano Alamar in San Diego County, with power to transmit the human voice for five hundred miles, a listener at either end would have heard various discussions upon the same subject, differentiated only by circumstances. No magic wires crossed San Francisco bay to bring the sound of voices to San Diego, but the law of necessity made the Squatter and the Don, distant as they were — distant in every way, without reckoning the miles between them — talk quite warmly of the same matter. The point of view was of course different, for how could it be otherwise? Darrell thought himself justified, and *authorized,* to "take up lands," as he had done before. He had had more than half of California's population on his side, and though the *"Squatter's Sovereignty"* was now rather on the wane, and the *"squatter vote"* was no longer the power, still, the squatters would not abdicate, having yet much to say about election times.

But Darrell was no longer the active squatter that he had been. He controlled many votes yet, but in his heart he felt the weight which his wife's sad eyes invariably put there when the talk was of litigating against a Mexican land title.

This time, however, Darrell honestly meant to take no land but what belonged to the United States. His promise to his wife was sincere, yet his coming to Southern California had already brought trouble to the Alamar rancho.

Don Mariano Alamar was silently walking up and down the front piazza of his house at the rancho; his hands listlessly clasped behind and his head slightly bent forward in deep thought. He had pushed away to one side the many armchairs and wicker rockers with which the piazza was furnished. He wanted a long space to walk. That his meditations were far from agreeable, could easily be seen by the compressed lips, slight frown, and sad gaze of his mild and beautiful blue eyes. Sounds of laughter, music and dancing came from the parlor; the young people were entertaining friends from town with their usual gay hospitality, and enjoying themselves heartily. Don Mariano, though already in his fiftieth year, was as fond of dancing as his sons and daughters, and not to see him come in and join the quadrille was so singular that his wife thought she must come out and inquire what could detain him. He was so absorbed in his thoughts that he did not hear her voice calling him — "What keeps you away? Lizzie has been looking for you; she wants you for a partner in the lancers," said Doña Josefa, putting her arm under that of her husband, bending her head forward and turning it up to look into his eyes.

"What is the matter?" she asked, stopping short, thus making her husband come to a sudden halt. "I am sure something has happened. Tell me."

"Nothing, dear wife. Nothing has happened. That is to say, nothing new."

"More squatters?" she asked. Señor Alamar bent his head slightly, in affirmative reply.

"More coming, you mean?"

"Yes, wife; more. Those two friends of squatters Mathews and Hagar, who were here last year to locate claims and went away, did not abandon their claims, but only went away to bring proselytes and their families, and a large invoice of them will arrive on tomorrow's steamer. The worst of it all is, that among the new comers is that terrible and most dangerous squatter William Darrell, who some years ago gave so much trouble to the Spanish people in Napa and Sonoma Counties, by locating claims there. John Gasbang wrote to Hogsden that besides Darrell, there will be six or seven other men bringing their families, so that there will be more rifles for my cattle."

"But, didn't we hear that Darrell was no longer a squatter, that he is rich and living quietly in Alameda?"

"Yes, we heard that, and it is true. He is quite well off, but Gasbang and Miller and Mathews went and told him that my rancho had been rejected, and that it is near enough to town to become valuable, as soon as we have a railroad. Darrell believed it, and is coming to locate here."

"Strange that Darrell should believe such men; I suppose he does not know how low they are."

"He ought to know them, for they were his teamsters when he crossed the plains in '48. That is, Miller, Mathews, Hughes and Hager, were his teamsters, and Gasbang was their cook — the cook for the hired men. Mrs. Darrell had a colored woman who cooked for the Darrell family; she despised Gasbang's cooking as we despise his character, I suppose."

Doña Josefa was silent, and holding on to her husband's arm, took a turn with him up and down the piazza.

"Is it possible that there is no law to protect us; to protect our property; what does your lawyer say about obtaining redress or protection; is there no hope?" she asked, with a sigh.

"Protection for our land, or for our cattle, you mean?"

"For both, as we get it for neither," she said.

"In the matter of our land, we have to wait for the attorney general, at Washington, to decide."

"Lizzie was telling Elvira, yesterday, that her uncle Lawrence is a friend of several influential people in Washington, and that George can get him to interest himself in having your title decided."

"But, as George is to marry my daughter, he would be the last man from whom I would ask a favor."

"What is that I hear about not asking a favor from me?" said George Mechlin, coming out on the piazza with Elvira on his arm, having just finished a waltz — "I am interested to know why you would not ask it."

"You know why, my dear boy. It isn't exactly the thing to bother you with my disagreeable business."

"And why not? And who has a better right? And why should it be a bother to me to help you in any way I can? My father spoke to me about a dismissal of an appeal, and I made a note of it. Let me see, I think I have it in my pocket now," — said George, feeling in his breast pocket for his memorandum book, — "yes, here it is, — 'For uncle to write to the attorney general about dismissing the appeal taken by the squatters in the Alamar grant, against Don Mariano's title, which was approved.' Is that the correct idea? I only made this note to ask you for further particulars."

"You have it exactly. When I give you the number of the case, it is all that you need say to your uncle. What I want is to have the appeal dismissed, of course, but if the attorney general does not see fit to do so, he can, at least, remand back the case for a new trial. Anything rather than this killing suspense. Killing literally, for while we are waiting to have my title settled, the *settlers* (I don't mean to make puns), are killing my cattle by the hundred head, and I cannot stop them."

"But are there no laws to protect property in California?" George asked.

"Yes, some sort of laws, which in my case seem more intended to help the law-breakers than to protect the law-abiding," Don Mariano replied.

"How so? Is there no law to punish the thieves who kill your cattle?"

"There are some enactments so obviously intended to favor one class of citizens against another class, that to call them laws is an insult to law, but such as they are, we must submit to them. By those laws any man can come to my land, for instance, plant ten acres of grain, without any fence, and then catch my cattle which, seeing the green grass without a fence, will go to eat it. Then he puts them in a *'corral'* and makes me pay damages and so much per head for keeping them, and costs of legal proceedings and many other trumped up expenses, until for such little fields of grain I may be obliged to pay thousands of dollars. Or, if the grain fields are large enough to bring more money by keeping the cattle away, then the settler shoots the cattle at any time without the least hesitation, only taking care that no one sees him in the act of firing upon the cattle. He might stand behind a bush or tree and fire, but then he is not seen. No one can swear that they saw him actually kill the cattle, and no jury can convict him, for although the dead animals may be there, lying on the ground shot, still no one saw the settler kill them. And so it is all the time. I must pay damages and expenses of litigation, or my cattle get killed almost every day."

"But this is infamous. Haven't you — the cattle owners — tried to have some law enacted that will protect your property?" George asked. "It seems to me that could be done."

"It could be done, perhaps, if our positions were reversed, and the Spanish people — *'the natives'* — were the planters of the grain fields, and the Americans were the owners of the cattle. But as we, the Spaniards, are the owners of the Spanish — or Mexican — land grants and also the owners of the cattle ranchos, our State legislators will not make any law to protect cattle. They make laws *'to protect agriculture'* (they say proudly), which means to drive to the wall

all owners of cattle ranchos. I am told that at this session of the legislature a law more strict yet will be passed, which will be ostensibly 'to protect agriculture,' but in reality to destroy cattle and ruin the native Californians. The agriculture of this State does not require legislative protection. Such pretext is absurd."

"I thought that the rights of the Spanish people were protected by our treaty with Mexico," George said.

"Mexico did not pay much attention to the future welfare of the children she left to their fate in the hands of a nation which had no sympathies for us," said Doña Josefa, feelingly.

"I remember," calmly said Don Mariano, "that when I first read the text of the treaty of Guadalupe Hidalgo, I felt a bitter resentment against my people; against Mexico, the mother country, who abandoned us — her children — with so slight a provision of obligatory stipulations for protection. But afterwards, upon mature reflection, I saw that Mexico did as much as could have been reasonably expected at the time. In the very preamble of the treaty the spirit of peace and friendship, which animated both nations, was carefully made manifest. That spirit was to be the *foundation* of the relations between the conqueror and conquered. How could Mexico have foreseen then that when scarcely half a dozen years should have elapsed the trusted conquerors would, '*In Congress Assembled*,' pass laws which were to be retroactive upon the defenseless, helpless, conquered people, in order to despoil them? The treaty said that our rights would be the same as those enjoyed by all other American citizens. But, you see, Congress takes very good care not to enact retroactive laws for Americans; laws to take away from American citizens the property which they hold now, already, with a recognized legal title. No, indeed. But they do so quickly enough with us — with us, the Spano-Americans, who were to enjoy equal rights, mind you, according to the treaty of peace. This is what seems to me a breach of faith, which Mexico could neither presuppose nor prevent."

"It is nothing else, I am sorry and ashamed to say," George said. "I never knew much about the treaty with Mexico, but I never imagined we had acted so badly."

"I think but few Americans know or believe to what extent we have been wronged by Congressional action. And truly, I believe that Congress itself did not anticipate the effect of its laws upon us, and how we would be despoiled, we, the conquered people," said Don Mariano, sadly.

"It is the duty of law-givers to foresee the effect of the laws they impose upon people," said Doña Josefa.

"That I don't deny, but I fear that the conquered have always but a weak voice, which nobody hears," said Don Mariano.

"We have had no one to speak for us. By the treaty of Guadalupe Hidalgo the American nation pledged its honor to respect our land titles just the same as Mexico would have done. Unfortunately, however, the discovery of gold brought to California the riff-raff of the world, and with it a horde of land sharks, all possessing the privilege of voting, and most of them coveting our lands, for which they very quickly began to clamor. There was, and still is, plenty of good government land, which any one can take. But no. The forbidden fruit is the sweetest. They do not want government land. They want the land of the Spanish people, because we 'have too much,' they say. So, to win their votes, the votes of the squatters, our representatives in Congress helped to pass laws declaring all lands in California open to preemption, as in Louisiana, for instance. Then, as a coating of whitewash to the stain on the nation's honor, a 'land commission' was established to examine land titles. Because, having pledged the national word to respect our rights, it would be an act of despoliation, besides an open violation of pledged honor, to take the lands without some pretext of a legal process. So then, we became obliged to present our titles before the said land commission to be examined and approved or rejected. While these legal proceedings are going on, the squatters locate their claims and raise crops on our lands, which they convert into money to fight our titles. But don't let me, with my disagreeable subject spoil your dance. Go back to your lancers, and tell Lizzie to excuse me," said Don Mariano.

Lizzie would not excuse him. With the privilege of a future daughter-in-law, she insisted that Don Mariano should be her partner in the lancers, which would be a far pleasanter occupation than to be walking up and down the porch thinking about squatters.

Don Mariano therefore followed Lizzie to their place in the dance. Mercedes sat at the piano to play for them. The other couples took their respective positions.

The well-balanced mind and kindly spirit of Don Mariano soon yielded to the genial influences surrounding him. He would not bring his trouble to mar the pleasure of others. He danced with his children as gaily as the gayest. He insisted that Mr. Mechlin, too, should dance, and this gentleman graciously yielded and led Elvira through a quadrille, protesting that he had not danced for twenty years.

"You have not danced because you were sick, but now you are well. Don't be lazy," said Mrs. Mechlin.

"You would be paying to San Diego climate a very poor compliment by refusing to dance now," George added.

"That is so, Papa. Show us how well you feel," Lizzie said.

"I shall have to dance a hornpipe to do that," Mr. Mechlin answered, laughing.

To understand this remark better, the reader must know that Mr. James Mechlin had come to San Diego, four years previously, a living skeleton, not expected to last another winter. He had lost his health by a too close application to business, and when he sought rest and relaxation his constitution seemed permanently undermined. He tried the climate of Florida. He spent several years in Italy and in the south of France, but he felt no better. At last, believing his malady incurable, he returned to his New York home to die. In New York a friend, who also had been an invalid, but whose health had been restored in Southern California, advised him to try the salubrious air of San Diego. With but little hope, and only to please his family, Mr. Mechlin came to San Diego, and his health improved so rapidly that he made up his mind to buy a country place and make San Diego his home. William Mathews heard of this, and offered to sell his place on what Mr. Mechlin thought very moderate terms. A lawyer was employed to pass upon the title, and on his recommendation the purchase was made. Mr. Mechlin had the Mathews house moved back near the barn, and a new and much larger one built. Mr. Mechlin devoted himself to cultivating trees and flowers, and his health was bettered every day. This was the compensation to his wife and two daughters for exiling themselves from New York; for it was exile to Caroline and Lizzie to give up their fine house in New York City to come and live on a California rancho.

Soon, however, these two young ladies passed their time more pleasantly, after making the acquaintance of the Alamar family, and soon their acquaintance ripened into friendship, to be made closer by the intended marriage of Gabriel — Don Mariano's eldest son — to Lizzie. Shortly after, George — Mr. Mechlin's only son — came on a visit, and when he returned to New York he was already engaged to Elvira, third daughter of Señor Alamar.

Now, George Mechlin was making his second visit to his family. He had found New York so very dull and stupid on his return from California that when Christmas was approaching he told his uncle and aunt — with whom he lived — that he wanted to go and spend Christmas and New Year's Day with his family in California.

"Very well; I wish I could go with you. Give my love to James, and tell him I am delighted at his getting so well," Mr. Lawrence Mechlin said, and George had his leave of absence. Mr. Lawrence Mechlin was president of the bank of which George was cashier, so it was not difficult for him to get the assistant cashier to attend to his duties when he was away, particularly as the assistant cashier himself was George's most devoted friend. George could have only twelve days in California, but to see Elvira for even so short a time he would have traveled a much longer distance.

Mr. James Mechlin affirmed repeatedly that he owed his improved health to the genial society of the Alamar family as much as to the genial climate of San Diego County. Mr. Mechlin, however, was not the only one who had paid the same tribute to that most delightful family, the most charming of which — the majority vote said — was Don Mariano himself. His nobility of character and great kindness of heart were well known to everybody.

The Alamar family was quite patriarchal in size, if the collateral branches be taken into account, for there were many brothers, nephews and nieces. These, however, lived in the adjoining rancho, and yet another branch in Lower California, in Mexico. Don Mariano's own immediate family was composed of his wife and six children, two sons and four daughters.

All of these, as we have seen, were having a dance. The music was furnished by the young ladies themselves, taking their turn at the piano, assisted by Madam Halier (Mercedes' French governess), who was always ready to play for the girls to dance. Besides the Mechlins, there were three or four young gentlemen from town, but there were so many Alamars (brothers, nieces and nephews, besides) that the room seemed quite well filled. Such family gatherings were frequent, making the Alamar house very gay and pleasant.

George Mechlin would have liked to prolong his visit, but he could not. He consoled himself looking forward to the ninth of June, when he would come again to make a visit of two months' duration. On his return East, before renewing his duties at the bank, he went to Washington to see about the dismissal of the appeal. Unfortunately, the attorney general had to absent himself about that time, and the matter being left with the solicitor general, nothing was done. George explained to Don Mariano how the matter was delayed, and his case remained undecided yet for another year longer. [1885]

José Martí, Cuba's most beloved poet and political visionary, was born in 1853 in Havana, Cuba. At the age of sixteen he was arrested by the Spanish colonial authorities for sedition and was sentenced to several months at hard labor. The following year, 1871, he was deported to Spain, and from that point until his return in 1895, when he met his death fighting for Cuba's independence, Martí visited the island for only brief periods.

After completing a law degree in Spain, Martí went to live with his family in Mexico. From 1877 to 1880 he traveled through several countries, lecturing and publishing articles in favor of Cuban independence. In 1881 Martí settled in New York City and, except for short trips to Mexico, Central America, Santo Domingo, and Jamaica, he remained in the United States for the last fourteen years of his life. He spent most of his time in New York, with visits to Tampa and Key West, important Cuban communities and centers for the independence organizing efforts.

Martí appeared to possess boundless energy. In New York he wrote for the leading Latin American newspapers as well as the *New York Sun;* he edited *Patria,* the organ of the Cuban Revolutionary Party, which he organized in 1892, and served as consul for Uruguay and Argentina; in addition he translated books into Spanish, published *La Edad de Oro* (The Golden Age), a journal for children, and wrote essays, articles, plays, a novel, children's stories, and poetry. Collected in *Ismaelillo* (1882) and *Versos sencillos* (*Simple Verses,* 1891), his poetry is considered a precursor of modernism, the first original literary movement in Latin America. His writings fill seventy volumes, and, despite a proliferation of research, much of what he published in South American newspapers remains uncollected.

Simple Verses was the last complete book of poetry that Martí published. Written in the Catskill Mountains of New York, where he had gone to recover his health, these poems are among his most famous, and many have been set to music by contemporary artists (for example, in the popular folk song "Guantanamera"). Deeply personal, they also return to his basic theme of freedom for Cuba and love of country: "I love simplicity and believe in the need to put feelings into plain and sincere forms."

Although Martí's poetry is perhaps his best-known work, his essays and newspaper articles are equally important. His prophetic warning of the danger of Latin America's absorption and exploitation by the United States became an important element of his revolutionary activity. Martí feared that U.S. economic expansion would engulf Cuba and meet with a favorable response from wealthy elements on the island who might welcome U.S. intervention and even annexation. His long experience in the United States, "in the belly of the beast" as he said, was the basis for his letter, "A Vindication of Cuba," in response to an attack on Cuban honor published in the *Philadelphia Manufacturer* in 1889 and endorsed by the New York *Evening Post*. Martí's perceptive observations of American society and his eloquent defense of contrasting cultural values are as relevant today as when they first appeared.

A Vindication of Cuba

To the Editor of *The Evening Post:*

Sir: I beg to be allowed the privilege of referring in your columns to the injurious criticism of the Cubans printed in the *Manufacturer* of Philadelphia, and reproduced in your issue of yesterday.

This is not the occasion to discuss the question of the annexation of Cuba. It is probable that no self-respecting Cuban would like to see his country annexed to a nation where the leaders of opinion share towards him the prejudices excusable only to vulgar jingoism or rampant ignorance. No honest Cuban will stoop to be received as a moral pest for the sake of the usefulness of his land in a community where his ability is denied, his morality insulted, and his character despised. There are some Cubans who, from honorable motives, from an ardent admiration for progress and liberty, from a prescience of their own powers under better political conditions, from an unhappy ignorance of the history and tendency of annexation, would like to see the island annexed to the United States. But those who have fought in war and learned in exile, who have built, by the work of hands and mind, a virtuous home in the heart of an unfriendly community; who by their successful efforts as scientists and merchants, as railroad builders and engineers, as teachers, artists, lawyers, journalists, orators and poets, as men of alert intelligence and uncommon activity, are honored wherever their powers have been called into action and the people are just enough to understand them; those who have raised, with their less prepared elements, a town of workingmen where the United States had previously a few juts in a barren cliff; those, more numerous than the others, do not desire the annexation of Cuba to the United States. They do not need it. They admire this nation, the greatest ever built by liberty, but they dislike the evil conditions that, like worms in the heart, have begun in this mighty republic their work of destruction. They have made of the heroes of this country their own heroes, and look to the success of the American commonwealth as the crowning glory of mankind; but they cannot honestly believe that excessive individualism, reverence for wealth, and the protracted exultation of a terrible victory are preparing the United States to be the typical nation of liberty, where no opinion is to be based in greed, and no triumph or acquisition reached against charity and justice. We love the country of Lincoln as much as we fear the country of Cutting.

We are not the people of destitute vagrants or immoral pigmies that the *Manufacturer* is pleased to picture; nor the country of petty talkers, incapable of action, hostile to hard work, that, in a mass with the other countries of Spanish America, we are by arrogant travellers and writers represented to be. We have suffered impatiently under tyranny; we have fought like men, sometimes like giants, to be freemen; we are passing that period of stormy repose, full of germs of revolt, that naturally follows a period of excessive and unsuccessful action; we have to fight like conquered men against an oppressor who denies us the means of living, and fosters in the beautiful capital visited by the tourist, in the interior of the country, where the prey escapes his grasp — a reign of such corruption as may poison in our veins the strength to secure freedom; we deserve in our misfortune the respect of those who did not help us in our need.

But because our government has systematically allowed after the war the triumph of criminals, the occupation of the cities by the scum of the people, the ostentation of ill-gotten riches by a myriad of Spanish officeholders and their Cuban accomplices, the conversion of the capital into a gambling-den, where the hero and the philosopher walk hungry by the lordly thief of the metropolis; because the healthier farmer, ruined by a war seemingly useless, turns in silence to the plough that he knew well how to exchange for the *machete;* because thousands of exiles, profiting by a period of calm that no human power can quicken until it is naturally exhausted, are practising in the battle of life in the free countries the art of governing themselves and of building a nation; because our half-breeds and city-bred young men are generally of delicate physique, of suave courtesy, and ready words, hiding under the glove that polishes the poem the hand that fells the foe — are we to be considered, as the *Manufacturer* does consider us, an "effeminate" people? These city-bred young men and poorly built half-breeds knew in one day how to rise against a cruel government, to pay either passages to the seat of war with the product of their watches and trinkets, to work their way in exile while their vessels were being kept from them by the country of the free in the interest of the foes of freedom, to obey as soldiers, sleep in the mud, eat roots, fight ten years without salary, conquer foes with the branch of a tree, die — these men of eighteen, these heirs of wealthy estates, these dusky striplings — a death not to be spoken of without uncovering the head. They died like those other men of ours who, with a stroke of the *machete,* can send a head flying, or by a turn of the hands bring a bull to their feet. These "effeminate" Cubans had once courage enough, in the face of a hostile government, to carry on their left arms for a week the mourning for Lincoln.

The Cubans have, according to the *Manufacturer,* "a distaste for exertion," they are "helpless," "idle." These "helpless," "idle" men came here twenty years ago empty-handed, with very few exceptions; fought against the climate; mastered the language; lived by their honest labor, some in affluence, a few in wealth, rarely in misery; they bought or built homes; they raised families and fortunes; they loved luxury, and worked for it; they were not frequently seen in the dark roads of life; proud and self-sustaining, they never feared competition as to intelligence or diligence. Thousands have returned to die in their homes, thousands have remained where, during the hardships of life, they have triumphed, unaided by any help of kindred language, sympathy of race, or community of religion. A handful of Cuban toilers built Key West. The Cubans have made their mark in Panama by their ability as mechanics of the higher trades, as clerks, physicians, and contractors. A Cuban, Cisneros, has greatly advanced the development of railways and river navigation in Colombia. Marquez, another Cuban, gained, with many of his countrymen, the respect of the Peruvians as a merchant of eminent capacity. Cubans are found everywhere, working as farmers, surveyors, engineers, mechanics, teachers, journalists. In Philadelphia the *Manufacturer* has a daily opportunity to see a hundred Cubans, some of them of heroic and powerful build, who live by their work in easy comfort. In New York the Cubans are directors in prominent banks, clerks of recognized ability, physicians with a large practice, engineers of world-wide repute, electricians, journalists, tradesmen, cigarmakers. The poet of Niagara is a Cuban, our Heredia; a Cuban, Menocal, is the projector of the canal of Nicaragua. In Philadelphia itself, as in New York, the college prizes have been more than once awarded to Cubans. The women of these "helpless," "idle" people, with "a distaste for exertion," arrived here from a life of luxury in the heart of the winter; their husbands were in the war, ruined, dead, imprisoned in Spain: the "Señora" went to work; from a slave owner she became a slave, took a seat behind the counter, sang in the churches, worked button-holes by the hundred, sewed for a living, curled feathers, gave her body and soul to duty, withered in work her body. This is the people of "defective morals."

We are "unfitted by nature and experience to discharge the obligations of citizenship in a great and free country." This cannot be justly said of a people who possess, besides the energy that built the first railroad in Spanish dominions and established against the opposition of the Government all the agencies of civilization, a truly remarkable knowledge of the body politic, a tried readiness to adapt itself to its higher forms, and the power rare in tropical countries of nerving their thought and pruning their language. Their passion for liberty, the conscientious study of its best teachings, the nursing of individual character in exile and at home, the lessons of ten years of war and its manifold consequences, and the practical exercise of the duties of citizenship in the free countries of the world, have combined, in spite of all antecedents, to develop in the Cuban a capacity for free government so natural to him that he established it, even to the excess of its practices, in the midst of the war, vied with his elders in the effort to respect the laws of liberty, and snatched the sabre, without fear or consideration, from the hands of every military pretender, however glorious. There seems to be in the Cuban mind a happy faculty of uniting sense with earnestness and moderation with exuberance. Noble teachers have devoted themselves since the beginning of the century to explain by their words and exemplify by their lives the self-restraint and tolerance inseparable from liberty. Those who won the first seats ten years ago at the European universities by singular merit have been proclaimed, at their appearance in the Spanish Parliament, men of subtle thought and powerful speech. The political knowledge of the average Cuban compares well with that of the average American citizen. Absolute freedom from religious intolerance, the love of man for the work he creates by his industry, and theoretical and practical familiarity with the laws and processes of liberty, will enable the Cuban to rebuild his country from the ruins in which he will receive it from his oppressors. It is not to be expected, for the honor of mankind, that the nation that was rocked in freedom, and received for three centuries the best blood of liberty-loving men, will employ the power thus acquired in depriving a less fortunate neighbor of his liberty.

It is, finally, said that "our lack of manly force and of self-respect is demonstrated by the supineness with which we have so long submitted to Spanish oppression, and even our attempts at rebellion have been so pitifully ineffective that they have risen little above the dignity of farce." Never was ignorance of history and character more pitifully displayed than in this wanton assertion. We need to recollect, in order to answer without bitterness, that more than one American bled by our side, in a war that another American was to call a farce. A farce the war that has been by foreign observers compared to an epic, the upheaval of a whole country, the voluntary abandonment of wealth, the abolition of slavery in our first moment of freedom, the burning of our cities by our own hands, the erection of villages and factories in the wild forests, the dressing of our ladies of rank in the textures of the woods, the keeping at bay in ten years of such a life, a powerful enemy, with a loss to him of 200,000 men at the hands of a small army of patriots, with no help but nature! We had no Hessians and no Frenchmen, no Lafayette or Steuben, no monarchical rivals to help us; we had but one neighbor who confessedly "stretched the limits of his power, and acted against the will of the people" to help the foes of those who were fighting for the same Chart of Liberties on which he built his independence. We fell a victim to the very passions which could have caused the downfall of the thirteen States, had they not been cemented by success, while we were enfeebled by procrastination; a procrastination brought about, not from cowardice, but from an abhorrence of blood, which allowed the enemy in the first months of the war to acquire unconquerable advantage, and from a childlike confidence in the certain help of the United States: "They cannot see us dying for liberty at their own doors without raising a hand or saying a word to give to the world a new free country!" They "stretched the limits of their powers in deference to Spain." They did not raise the hand. They did not say the word.

The struggle has not ceased. The exiles do not want to return. The new generation is worthy of its sires. Hundreds of men have died in darkness since the war in the misery of prisons. With life only will this fight for liberty cease among us. And it is the melancholy truth that our efforts would have been, in all probability, successfully renewed, were it not, in some of us, for the unmanly hope of the annexationists of securing liberty without paying its price; and the just fears of others that our dead, our sacred memories, our ruins drenched in blood, would be but the fertilizers of the soil for the benefit of a foreign plant, or the occasion for a sneer from the *Manufacturer* of Philadelphia.

With sincere thanks for the space you have kindly allowed me, I am, sir, yours very respectfully,

José Martí　　120 Front Street, New York, March 23

[1889]

Simple Verses

I

I am an honest man
From where the palms grow;
Before I die I want my soul
To shed its poetry.

I come from everywhere,
To everywhere I'm bound:
An art among the arts,
A mountain among mountains.

I know the unfamiliar names
Of grasses and of flowers,
Of fatal deceptions
And exalted sorrows.

On darkest nights I've seen
Rays of the purest splendor
Raining upon my head
From heavenly beauty.

I've seen wings sprout
From handsome women's shoulders,
Seen butterflies fly out
Of rubbish heaps.

I've seen a man who lives
With a dagger at his side,
Never uttering the name
Of his murderess.

Twice, quick as a wink, I've seen
The soul: once when a poor
Old man succumbed, once when
She said goodby.

Once I shook with anger
At the vineyard's iron gate
When a savage bee attacked
My daughter's forehead.

Once I rejoiced as I
Had never done before,
When the warden, weeping, read
My sentence of death.

I hear a sigh across
The land and sea; it is
No sigh: it is my son
Waking from sleep.

If I am said to take
A jeweler's finest gem,
I take an honest friend,
Put love aside.

I've seen a wounded eagle
Fly to the tranquil blue,
And seen a snake die in its
Hole, of venom.

Well do I know that when
The livid world yields to repose,
The gentle brook will ripple on
In deepest silence.

I've laid a daring hand,
Rigid from joy and horror,
Upon the burnt-out star that fell
Before my door.

My manly heart conceals
The pain it suffers; sons of
A land enslaved live for it
Silently, and die.

All is permanence and beauty,
And all is melody and reason,
And all, like diamonds rather
Than light, is coal.

I know that fools are buried
Splendidly, with floods of tears,

And that no fruit on earth
Is like the graveyard's.

I understand, keep still,
Cast off the versifier's pomp,
And hang my doctoral robes upon
A withered tree.

V

Should you see a hill of foam,
It is my poetry you see;
My poems are mountains
And feather fans.

My poems are daggers
Sprouting blossoms from the hilts;
My poems are fountains
Spraying jets of coral.

My poems are palest green
And flaming scarlet;
A wounded deer that searches for
A refuge in the forest.

My poems please the valiant;
Sincere and brief, my poetry
Is rugged as the steel they use
To forge a sword.

XXXIX

I cultivate white roses
In January as in July
For the honest friend who freely
Offers me his hand.

And for the brute who tears from me
The heart with which I live,
I nurture neither grubs nor thistles,
But cultivate white roses.

[1891]

Translation of *Versos sencillos* by Elinor Randall

Pachín Marín, the pen name of Francisco Gonzalo Marín, was born in 1863 in Arecibo, Puerto Rico. Marín's short life was highly productive, not only in the arts but in the struggle for the independence of Puerto Rico and Cuba. A typesetter by trade, at the age of twenty Marín founded a newspaper, *El Postillón,* in Arecibo; he would spend most of his remaining years, however — from 1887 until his death in 1897 on a Cuban battlefield — in exile in various places, including Santo Domingo, Haiti, Curaçao, Venezuela, Jamaica, Martinique, Colombia, and New York.

In 1891 Marín, like many other prominent Antillean political exiles, settled in New York City. There he worked alongside such figures as José Martí, whose vision of Antillean unity he shared. Marín wrote most of his poetry in New York, publishing it in *Romances* (1892) and *En la arena* (On the Sand, 1898). He also collaborated on the New York separatist newspaper *La Gaceta del Pueblo,* which published the narrative "New York from Within" in 1892.

Romantic, bohemian, intensely passionate, and patriotic, Pachín Marín is one of Puerto Rico's most respected poets. He is also considered a precursor by many U.S. Puerto Rican writers who share many of his views regarding the political status of the island and identify with his often ironic perceptions of the United States from the perspective of a poor immigrant. For the critic Juan Flores, Marín's writings contain "immense prognostic power in view of subsequent historical and literary developments. . . . In a history of Puerto Rican literature in the United States they provide an invaluable antecedent perspective, a prelude of foreboding, even before the fateful events of 1898."

New York from Within: One Aspect of Its Bohemian Life

If you present yourself in this metropolis in the enviable guise of a tourist, and bring, as it is customary, suitcases stuffed with Mexican *soles* or shimmering gold doubloons, things will naturally go very well for you, my amiable reader. But you will not have known New York from within, as it really is, with its grand institutions and prodigious marvels.

To attain an intimate knowledge of this elephant of modern

civilization, you will need to set foot to the ground without a quarter to your name, though you may bring a world of hope in your heart.

Indeed! To arrive in New York, check into a comfortable hotel, go out in an elegant carriage pulled by monumental horses every time an occasion presents itself, visit the theaters, museums, *cafés chantants*, cruise the fast-flowing East River, lulled by the ebb and flow and murmur of the waves, visit Brooklyn Bridge — that frenzy of North American initiative — and the Statue of Liberty — that tour de force of French pride — pay twenty dollars or more to hear La Pattissi sing, as she is doing now, at the Metropolitan Opera House, frequent, in short, the places where elegant people of good taste gather, people who can afford to spend three or four hundred dollars in one evening for the sole pleasure of looking at a dancer's legs, oh!, all that is very agreeable, very delicious, and very . . . singular; but it doesn't give you the exact measure of this city which is, at one and the same time, an emporium of sweeping riches and rendezvous-point for all the penniless souls of America.

The convenient — if you prefer, the reasonable — thing to do, is for you to present yourself at one of the vast New York docks without even a semblance of resources; ready and agile as a student and as hungry as a schoolteacher. You have already realized your most cherished dream; you are overjoyed because since childhood your happiness has centered on great voyages . . . What! You don't speak any English? Are you overwhelmed by the incessant howling of the locomotives, the vertiginous agitation of the factories, and the vista of a million people hurrying past, trampling each other, yet going on their way as if nothing had happened? Well, don't you stop. Let's walk, walk! Here in New York time is sacred, since it is the most genuine representation of money. Don't stand there in perplexed contemplation of an eleven- or twelve-story building whose highest windows seem to look down on you as if mocking your smallness. Time is urgent. Walk hurriedly, as if you had most important business at hand. One must find a friend, a friend or countryman, at all cost. Where? How? Don't you know how? Well, by asking everyone. Come on; try it out on that gigantic policeman looking at you so tenaciously. Throw care to the wind and plunge in. Gentleman, would you be so kind as to point out where I can find a friend . . . How stupid of me! Now I get it, this man can't speak any Spanish . . . You're beginning to grow sad. You see no familiar faces. My

God! you exclaim. I'm a wretch! Some identical incidents read in novels dart past your imagination with the speed of lightning. Jean Valjean, Jean Valjean . . . If the same thing that happened to Jean Valjean were to happen to you . . .

If there is a civilized country capable of astonishing the most indifferent and stoic, the United States, or better yet, New York, is the place.

Its buildings, its portentous architectural works, its elevated railways fantastically crisscrossing through the air, its streets — broad arteries roamed by inexhaustible hordes from all countries of the world — its parks — austerely and aristocratically designed — its steam engines, its powerful journalistic institutions, its treacherously beautiful women, its wonders, all instill, at first sight, a deep malaise in the foreigner, because it occurs to one that these large cities, deafening in their progress, are like the mouth of a horrible monster constantly busy simultaneously swallowing and vomiting human beings; and it is amidst these great noises and grand centers that our soul finds itself increasingly besieged by that horrendous malady called sadness, and assumes the somber character of isolation and silence . . .

For the poor in money but rich in ambition, arriving here in the circumstances outlined above, however, New York is a great house of asylum where all who believe, more or less vigorously, in the virtue and sanctity of work, ultimately find their niche.

Are you very poor? Have you not succeeded yet in finding something in which to invest your talents and energies? Are you feeling the sting of hunger? Are you cold?

Don't distress yourself. Don't despair in any way. Do you see that establishment on the corner whose door continuously opens and closes? Well, it is commonly known here by the name of Lager Beer Hall. Have you been inside? Such cleanliness and tidiness everywhere! Isn't it true that places like these are better decorated than the presidential palaces of our republics? But we shouldn't waste time in useless ramblings, not even in here. Take that table nearby; throw five cents on it; it's a tip in advance; don't go believing anything else. Pay attention now. In the first place, they bring you a big mug of beer, fresh, foamy, poured on smooth glass. Drink it. In this country, beer is a necessity; it fortifies and warms limbs numbed by the cold. But . . . don't be a fool! Take care. Let us, before draining the contents of the glass, eat ham, beef, sausage, cheese, etc. That stuff you gobble down for starters. At least that's what gastronomy calls it. Well! Good heavens! But principles be gone! You must eat it all. Here comes the waiter; this time he's bringing you a succulent soup preceded by its wafting aromas. Eat until you've had your fill: I am your host, you honorable Maecenas . . .

Are you pleased? Yes? Let's not waste time, then, take a toothpick, light this cigarette I'm offering you and . . . onto the street.

"But, sir, didn't you offer to pay the check? We can't leave without paying . . . I am an honest man . . ."

"Come now, blockhead. The sum of what you have gobbled down amounts to five cents. You have already paid . . ."

And after leaving the place, satiated and proud of our find, forgetting the novelistic tortures that made Jean Valjean suffer from such acute hunger, then we recall the real New York, the wise and good New York, hospitable and gay; and we laugh our heads off at the admirers of the Brooklyn Bridge and the Statue of Liberty, of the elevated railway and gigantic buildings, of all the great institutions of this surprising republic, since, never fear, I doubt that there is in this country of inventions and colossal enterprises anything as grand, as portentous, as human as those establishments where for five coppers they feed the hungry and give drink to the thirsty.

Ample reason has my philosopher friend, who, every day, upon returning from heaven-knows-where with an enormous toothpick in his hand, says to me:

"Oh! A Lager Beer Hall is indeed an institution." [1892]

Translation of "Nueva York por dentro: una faz de su vida bohemia" by Lizabeth Paravasini-Gebert

In the Album of an Unknown Woman

I know you not; but know
by a patriotic bond, you are my sister;
by your sculptured beauty, Cytherea;
by your disdain for oppressors, a Cuban.
Concepcion is your name and your name suffices
for me to feel your unseen soul!
Concha is the nacre set by the sea
and shell's soul is a pearl.

For you, I too have no name,
nor does this being disquiet the Universe:
I am what remains, the commonplace: a man!
I am what grieves in the crowd: a poet!

On paper I set my unpolished lines
as a firebrand on a carpet.
Poor page this that was a flash of light
bathed by my poetry, a shadow.

Resign yourself: I am a pilgrim
arrived at the hemicycle of the war,
inquiring of all the path of honor
leading to my native soil.

And till Puerto Rico be free,
or the seething fire consume my estate,
for a rifle, I shall spurn ideas,
for a machete, I shall set aside the pen.

[1892]

Translation of "En el album de una desconocida"
by Theresa Ortiz de Hadjopoulos

Improvisation

I want to die on rustic fields
where my first youth unfolded;
and, setting, the sun may disperse
a flash of golden light on my melancholy brow.

I want to die facing a palm tree,
my face hidden by a glorious wound,
so my soul's mistress, fleeing from me,
terror-stricken, may linger,
seeing how slowly life escapes me.
I want to die on the wild plain
where goats gambol and oxen bellow
and one can hear the thicket thrush . . .
I want to die with royal splendor:
the sun, my torch; my canopy, the heavens!
May pleasure's victim, that coward
who watched his weeping nation, unmoved,
fall on his rose and jasmine couch!
May my youth not last till evening
if it must be spent in odious bondage.

I am the sad and solitary bard
singing the orphanhood of my native soil,
where pallid Equity, put to shame,
dons a veil to hide her face.

I am the cantor challenging the Tempest
and carrying to her the defiant dare,
even to the threshold of her secret mansion.
I am a commoner ruled by a miserable commander!
I am my country's last poet!

I want to sleep where my own may invoke
their liberty; and I may hear vibrate
the martial trumpet when they call to battle . . .
and on my brow let them place a cross;
upon the cross this epitaph, "Free!"

[1892]

Translation of "Improvisación" by Theresa Ortiz de Hadjopoulos

Eusebio Chacón was born in Peñasco, New Mexico, in 1869 and raised in southern Colorado. He received an undergraduate degree from Jesuit Las Vegas College in Las Vegas, New Mexico, in 1887 and a law degree from Notre Dame University in Indiana in 1889. Back in New Mexico, he became a forceful essayist and speaker on behalf of Mexican Americans. He died in 1948.

New Mexico during the nineteenth century appears to have had the most productive and developed Mexican-American literary tradition in the Southwest. Unlike California and Texas, where the large numbers of Anglos overwhelmed the native communities, New Mexico developed at a less disruptive pace. Nevertheless, few examples of fiction from this era have been found, undoubtedly owing to a lack of publishing resources and a stable reading public. Although largely inaccessible since their publication, Eusebio Chacón's two novellas, *El hijo de la tempestad* (*The Son of the Storm*) and *Tras la tormenta la calma* (The Calm after the Storm), both published by *El boletín popular* in Santa Fe in 1892, are the first novels to express a Mexican-American sensibility in contrast to the Anglo-dominated tradition of Chacón's education.

The Son of the Storm is the more highly regarded of the two; it is a romantic, almost gothic, portrait full of determinism. Both novellas are, however, somewhat overwrought dramas infused with local superstitions and motifs. Although they fall short of Chacón's literary aspirations thematically and stylistically, they nonetheless created a different expressive mode. As the critic Francisco Lomelí has noted, they bear many similarities to popular novels of the time in Mexico and other Spanish-speaking countries.

The Son of the Storm

I

On a stormy summer night two individuals, a young man and woman, made their way with some difficulty along the side of a mountain, searching for shelter against the inclement weather. The fury of the wind, the denseness of the rain, the roar of the thunder, and the terrifying flash of the lightning made that evening a night of fear. Amidst the confusion of the elements our nocturnal travelers had strayed from the path and anxiously implored heavenly guidance on such a horrifying night.

Whoever has experienced the drama of a mountain storm, with the din of thunderclaps and the howling torrents of rain, can well imagine the emotions and sad anxiety that overwhelmed, in such a sad situation, those two hearts. That of the man, the woman's husband, beat with uncommon violence in his search to find some spot in which to shelter his companion, who was weak and sick, soon to give birth. After many hours of suffering they finally found the desired refuge at the foot of an imposing and magnificent wall of rock, and were barely inside one of its numerous caves when the woman began to feel ill; in less than an hour, suffering agonizing pains, she gave birth to a beautiful son and then ceased to exist.

The rains thundered and the lightning slithered a sinister blaze through the clouds. In the midst of that dreadful din could be heard the last "ay" of she who was on her way to heaven accompanied by the first wail of he who was coming into the world. Wailing was heard as well from an anguished husband, who lamented his widowhood and celebrated his fatherhood with the same cry. On the hard ground of the cave lay the body of the woman who had just become a mother, with the rays of lightning serving as her funeral crown.

At last daybreak arrived. Not one cloud was left in the sky, and the sun rose, gilding the grand mountain peaks with its rays. Everywhere one looked, the birds warbled and the dewdrops shone on the flowers like a rain of fiery pearls. Nature awoke filled with a thousand charms as if the previous night had not slept in the arms of a hurricane. However, in the midst of that universal delight, a man cried on his knees in a cave at the foot of a dead woman and a tender infant cried, struggling in vain to nurse from her stiff breasts.

As soon as the day had arrived, the ranchers turned to their daily chores; at the foot of the hillsides they scattered their cattle, followed by the shepherds and their dogs. The cow herder returned to his cows, and the simple laborer set out for the fields humming some ballad, brandishing his cutting scythe at the air. At this early hour it so happened that a gypsy fortuneteller passed by the ranch, as slovenly as any of her race, but skillful in her trade and knowledgeable in the arts of singing and dancing. Accompanying her was a foul-looking monkey, a *vihuela* guitar, and a parcel of rags in which, according to her, she carried all her worldly goods.

Arriving at the first door she whispered some strange words into the ear of the monkey, and unwinding the vihuela from around her neck, began to play it and sing the following verses:

I know who was born at the wrong time,
At the flash of the lightning ray,
I know who died in labor
In the middle of the storm.
There was a young gentleman
Who fell in love with a young maid,
The young man became a widower,
An orphan the young child.

The turtledove leaves its nest,
And the pearl its shell,
In order to be free again
After having been enslaved.

He who killed his mother
When he was born during the storm,
What won't he do when he is grown?
What won't he do when he is a man?

The milk that he drinks
Will be that of witches,
Because he killed his mother
In the middle of the storm.

In the forest he will find
Her who will give him nurture,
The forests will be his homeland
His refuge will be the mountains.

On a night of terror,
A night without stars,
Was born he who will be called
The Son of the Storm.

Woe to those who give him refuge,
Pity those who are pious and wish
To shelter under their roof
Him who was born in the darkness of night.

When she had arrived at this point, a multitude of men, women, boys and girls, young and old, had congregated around the gypsy, and in silence, with their mouths agape, contemplated her talents and watched her dance with the monkey. The monkey, doing leaps and pirouettes, and she, freeing her gracious contours into the air, barely protected by a tattered tunic, presented a contrast never before seen in that remote spot; the voice of the fortuneteller awoke a thousand echoes in the nearby mountains. The gypsy was pretty, although disheveled and dirty; but that did not put her at any disadvantage when it came to entertaining ranchers, who in those times were not very given to cleanliness themselves — although it is true that among the mob there were some who would flatter strange women, at the risk of creating a jealous wife or losing a lover. The dogs barked their fear of the monkey; the ranchers applauded; the vihuela grew louder; the ranchers whispered; the monkey leaped, and the gypsy continued:

> I tell of good fortune,
> I know of love and its riches,
> I sing, my girl, of the future
> with the strum of my vihuela.
>
> I know whom you must marry,
> I know the fate that awaits you,
> I read the stars up in the heavens
> and inside the veil of clouds.

As she spoke of divinations, a half dozen voices interrupted the gypsy, asking her to tell them their future.

"Tell me my fortune. Tell mine! Will I be rich?" asked one.

"Tell me if I should marry," jumped in an oft-times-refused bachelor.

"Will I reach old age?" sighed a fifty-year-old spinster.

"Will I one day be a widower?" cried out an old dandy with a jealous wife.

"Tell us! Tell!" they all shouted, crowding over each other with true rancher enthusiasm.

In this manner, they all clamored around the gypsy so as to be the first to hear her response, though for more than a few the enthusiasm to know their good fortune cooled down when she announced the bad news: that which is good comes at a cost, and if they wanted to know their luck they'd have to pay her well for it. Their resources were scarce, but there were always some whose curiosity would overcome them, and in a short time the gypsy had collected a herd of goats and pigs, a mountain of grain, and a henhouse worth of chickens. Of the grain she took little, as she had nowhere to raise it, converting it into more portable merchandise. Good luck had favored this descendant of Mohammed, as it favors all the adventurous who are well known for what they do; and so in an hour the cunning gypsy had reaped the profits of what represented many days' toil for a rancher. As she was leaving, she turned to whisper something in the ear of the monkey. As light as thought, it spurred on the cattle like a clever little boy, and, in the middle of the confusion of the departing procession, from time to time a song could be heard:

> The turtledove leaves its nest,
> And the pearl its shell,
> In order to be free again
> After having been enslaved.

II

The gypsy had barely been lost from view when a man carrying his newborn son in his arms arrived at the same door where she had been dancing a few moments earlier, asking for shelter for himself and his child. He was the traveler of the previous night and was coming to leave his precious orphan with some charitable person while he returned for the body of the mother to give her burial. He asked for refuge but was denied; he asked in the name of charity who would give his son some food, but only received a negative reply and an exclamation of horror. Filled with superstition, the people remembered the fortuneteller and her song, and the poor orphan found neither shelter nor sustenance: "Woe to those who give him refuge." The phrase was still fresh in the minds of the ranchers. So in this state the sad father had to leave that thankless place, knocking from door to door without an offer of succor. Muttering a curse, he set out for the same forest in which a few minutes earlier the gypsy had hid herself with her monkey, her profits, and her vihuela.

After walking for a short time he found her sitting on the trunk of a fallen tree and addressed her with tears in his eyes: "Good woman, I am carrying my orphan son who since his birth last night has not touched food. In the name of what you hold dearest, let him suckle from your breast while I return to the mountains for his mother whom I left behind, now dead."

"Ah," murmured the gypsy. Flashing her eyes, she took the little one in her arms. She gave him her breast, and two large tears rolled down her cheeks. A memory of the past crossed her mind: years ago another had fed her too, in the same way, and that is why she now wandered as a nomad through the world.

The father went off, silent and pensive; the gypsy stayed with the orphan, and with each moment she took more of a liking to him. She spoke softly to him and whispered a thousand endearments. Crazy with emotion, she felt a new impulse in her heart and in her delirium she forgot the monkey, the vihuela, the goats, and the pigs, and when the sun began to set on the horizon, she fell profoundly asleep rocking the baby, dreaming of faraway lands with palaces of marble where everything was youth and flowers.

The next morning the boy's father did not return. Some unexpected event had detained him, and the gypsy began to feel hungry and thirsty. She prepared to light a fire to toast some foodstuffs for breakfast when an eighty-year-old woman appeared before her. Bent over, with a nasal, hollow voice, she walked with slow steps, helping herself along with a staff fashioned in the manner of a walking stick, shaped like a broom on the uppermost tip. The gypsy was startled a bit to suddenly discover herself with such a strange visitor, but then, recovering her natural aplomb, she continued making the fire and singing, in a low voice, a song in some strange language. The old woman approached and, describing an imaginary circle over her with the point of her staff, said these words:

"Daughter of the desert sands. My days on earth are numbered. Destiny calls me and heed I must; but before I go I want you to allow me to see the face of this child; then I will return to follow my path."

"Who are you?" asked the gypsy.

"I am she who comes and goes."

"What is your name? From where do you come? And with what right do you ask to see the face of this infant?"

"My name is Shadow of Light; I come from Time, and my right to see this infant is written thus."

Mysterious replies for sure, and calculated to awaken a thousand suspicions in the mind of the gypsy, who, feigning the need to collect wood for the fire, walked away a distance and whistled for the monkey to approach her. She whispered something in its ear. The monkey's hair stood on end; it grunted, and from its eyes emerged what appeared to be two tears of red flame.

The gypsy returned to her fire and then it was she who spoke to the old woman with a proud and provocative tone. "Return, old woman, to the road from which you have come. The Shadow of Light will not see the child who was born in the storm."

"But it is essential," argued the old woman. "That which is written must be obeyed."

"Do you care to take some breakfast?" asked the gypsy, changing suddenly her tone and the direction of the conversation.

"No. The Shadow of Light does not eat as the daughters of the desert do."

"So what does she eat then?"

"The heart of those who are born in the middle of the night when Hecate makes love with the spirit of the hurricane, in the midst of the lightning bolts — that is what is written."

The gypsy then understood that the woman must be a sorceress and that she wished to see the face of the baby so that she could extract his heart and leave, savoring the dish whose very name inspires fear. And that indeed is how it was: realizing that she was dealing with another sorceress, the old witch threw herself over the child who lay asleep on his back, about to claw open his chest with her long fingernails. Then the sky darkened. A groan was heard from the center of the earth, a bolt of lightning snaked through the darkness, and in the place of the monkey that had leaped onto the old woman, the fallen angel appeared. It drove in its claws, and with a rapid movement overcame her. The old woman found herself face to face with the devil and, fighting to free herself, shouted: "Let me go, Lucifer; you do not wish to go against that which is written."

"It was also written," the devil responded without letting her go, "that the Shadow of Light should not feed upon the heart of the Son of the Storm."

"What? Isn't it a sacred law in Hades that all who are born when Hecate makes love with the spirit of the hurricane must die? And that his heart will be food for the witches? I claim my prey, Satan!"

"It is also law that what is written must be carried out."

"And this child must not die?"

"No."

"I demand my prey, Satan!" shrieked the old woman in a cavernous voice. "And if you don't give him to me I shall curse you once again from the bottom of my cursed soul! Let me go, Satan!"

"Calm down, old woman, calm down. If it is a law that all those who are born when Hecate makes love with the spirit of the hurricane must die, there is also in the laws of Hell another that says: If he who is thus born feeds from the breast of a sorceress, he will not die; but rather he will live to be the scourge of many peoples and the terror of humanity. Destiny will fulfill itself. What is written must be carried out."

"But I do not know this law; and it is unjust that a child who will be a calamity when he grows should live."

"In Hell there is no justice, only that which is made by the Lord of San Miguel. I delight in humanity's disasters; villains are the ministers of my fury, and of my revenge."

"Satan, I curse you!" howled the old woman. She reached with one arm to where the child lay sleeping, and dug one of her fingernails into his chest with such rancor that he cried out and the blood gushed from the wound.

The devil let out a burst of laughter. The old woman fell dead at his feet, and the earth opened up, swallowing her.

It was midday. On the neighboring hillsides countless cattle were grazing, and the shouting of shepherds and barking of dogs could be heard. The gypsy played her vihuela, the child slept doubled over by the pain of his wound, and the devil resumed his disguise of a monkey, sitting sullen and angry a short distance away, licking its snout and throwing off poisonous stares from its eyes.

III

Many years passed. The gypsy no longer played her vihuela nor told fortunes throughout the villages. The bloom of youth had fled her face, replaced by deep wrinkles. Her voice was no longer sonorous as in other times. The monkey, now decrepit and bent over, stayed with her in the darkest corner of the cave in which they lived and every day became more sullen and surly. The Son of the Storm was now the leader of bandits that terrorized the countrysides and destroyed the towns, committing heinous crimes with a satanic cruelty. Like any enemy of the law, he had run for the hills, making them the target of a band of assassins and thieves, whose pleasure consisted of scavenging and fighting. The same cave where he was born and where his mother died was the entrance to a labyrinth of subterranean passages where he and his men had their quarters. There they kept their stolen treasures, and there, in horrible slavery, moaned the many men and women who had been taken during their campaigns. There, in short, was where the gypsy and her inseparable monkey lived in eternal partnership, she being both Madonna and housewife as the stepmother of the Son of the Storm. Pity on him who failed to respect and obey her!

One delightful morning in May, the Son of the Storm was strolling on horseback in a spirited trot by the bottom of a ravine, with twenty of his armed men following him on their magnificent steeds. Not long out on the road wound a small creek, and to the right and left rugged hills rose up. The road left to travel was long and monotonous, and the men were beginning to grow impatient when they heard a chorus of harmonious voices. They stopped their horses at their leader's signal and listened for a moment. The voices came from a small woods situated to the left, farther than one hundred yards away; evidently those who were singing were not only men because among the voices could be heard two or three female tones. The robbers turned to listen and, making their calculations, began to prepare to attack, whipped up by their ferocious desire for combat and for the treasure and the slaves they thought to acquire — so accustomed were they to victory, as no one till then had defeated them. With a shout that resounded throughout the hills, they began their move toward the singers in the woods. Their attack was not so sudden, however, as not to give time for the others to prepare their defense. The song broke off and in its place came the confused rush of running footsteps; when the robbers appeared, they were received with an abundant fire of rifle shots. That was a surprise for the Son of the Storm. What had happened? How could it be that when they at most imagined an encounter with a party of unprepared travelers they should instead have delivered themselves to the continuous, perfectly aimed fire of a well-organized defense?

The Son of the Storm apprehended the situation with a single glance. The local governments had offered a great bounty for his head, and for years he had been persecuted mercilessly by their troops, facing them often but always emerging victorious. This now was an enormous blow for the Son of the Storm. His own avarice had led him to a precipice and, unawares, he found himself face to face with an infantry corps. With his first discharge he attempted a right-handed maneuver in order to be able to attack his enemies while preserving his own position, but he found himself flanked by another corps of troops that immediately opened fire on him, with fatal results. Four of his men fell mortally wounded. It was unavoidable: there was no choice but to fight. With a fierce cry, they charged the enemy, and the battle became bloody and gruesome. The curses, the shouting, the neighing of the horses, the moans of the dying, mixed with the shots and the crashing of swords, creating an ill-fated din that reverberated through the neighboring hills. The women who had accompanied the troops as part of the plot to entrap the horrible bandit dispersed like a flock of doves at the sight of a hawk. The battle intensified: one by one the bandits fell, as their leader fought like a lion. His horse had died and he himself was in pain from a gunshot wound in the arm. Seven of his men were left, all fighting with desperation. The troops closed in on them and there was nowhere to run: three more bandits fell and then another and another and then only two were left in addition to the leader. Like imprisoned eagles, the three fierce partners advanced toward the captain of one of the companies and, killing him and several others, leaped up with a blood-curdling curse, saving themselves by climbing up the rocky cliffs and losing themselves among the scrub. In vain the troops searched for them, but those agile bandits had disappeared as if by magic. The soldiers then turned to aid the wounded and to bury the dead. As for the women, they reunited with the troops and continued the march alongside them, participating in all the setbacks and difficulties of a military campaign.

Well into the night, the Son of the Storm arrived at his cave followed by his two companions. Upon entering, one of them asked, "What will we tell our people when they see us return without our companions?"

"Say that they perished and that we have been defeated," answered the other.

"Liar!" interrupted their boss. "You lie, vile impostor, and for your punishment go to hell to greet the devil in my name!" As he said this he discharged a furious machete blow to the one who had spoken, but was deterred by the man who was now assuming a more insolent air toward his boss.

"You raise a hand at me, you traitor? At me?" shouted the son of darkness, gritting his teeth.

"You and a hundred more, Captain Pride. Son of the Storm, your star is fading."

"It could not be otherwise, when a vile traitor whom I saved from the gallows in other times dares to confront the Son of the Storm! My star is fading! My star is fading!"

There followed a profound silence and the three bandits entered the cave, their shapes disappearing into the darkness. The captain bathed the ground with the blood that gushed from his wound.

IV

In the darkest dungeon of those hideous catacombs in the hills, an ancient man with a heavy beard and silver hair moaned under the chains that held him. He was naked, save a coarse cloth that served to hide those parts that decorum and the nature of humanity wish to have covered. At his side suffered a young woman, beautiful though pale, with her hair loose and dressed in meager robes in the Phrygian style, with languid pleats that drew the shapely contours of her classic beauty. The young woman was nursing the old man, who drank with tenderness; in this way he sustained himself, suckling from that virgin breast. Her scarce milk was the only dish his palate had known for many years. A delicious dish it surely was, given that the young woman was the old man's daughter and together they were enduring one of the cruelest of imprisonments. The daughter's virtue and the father's heroism had thwarted the most savage impulses of the Son of the Storm. Born to suffer and educated in the school of chivalry, they preferred to suffer a thousand times all possible evils than submit to dishonor; and although prisoners, they rejected their tyrant with a serenity worthy of the heroic Roman era.

But how had they come to find themselves in such an unhappy state? How had destiny driven them to those labyrinths where human monsters more fearful than wild beasts made their nest? Listen then: in one of the rich villages of the kingdom the people had the custom of retreating every summer to the hills, and to this end they organized in bands of twenty, thirty, and up to fifty families. The object was to spend the hot season in a truly pastoral manner, resembling as much as life itself deserved the type of existence celebrated by the poets where the amaryllis flowers in abundance, and where sweet poetry and her sister, divine music, flourishes at the banks of a tranquil river. Well then, the noble people of that village in the kingdom made their exodus every summer, supplying themselves with provisions, servants, vihuelas, flutes, and various other instruments that befriend man during his idle hours. Participating in one of these excursions was the old man and his family, including the daughter who now kept him company in his enslavement. One night when their dance was at its height, beneath a pavilion with a roof of many broad-domed trees and a carpet of spongy grass, the Son of the Storm and his band fell like birds of prey upon the group, and those they did not kill they took as prisoners. Upon arriving at the cave to make the corresponding distribution, he delivered all the women to his bandits but one; he reserved the beautiful young woman for himself.

Supper was prepared, a splendorous scene worthy of kings. The wine flowed, spinning the heads of the thieves. The slaves that night and those who attended at the table were the ones who had been taken on that last foray. Among them, who was the most lovely? Who the least rapturous? Even the very pain that was painted on their faces seemed to make them more beautiful; anyone other than the bandits of that cursed cave would have been moved by that beauty, dejected as it was by such misfortune. But the orgy was not yet complete. For the satisfaction of the appetites of the stomach there was missing the complementary satisfaction of the ecstasies of the flesh. And what was there to impede those pleasures? Nothing: on the contrary, that constellation of enchanting slaves and the bouquet of the wine invited the most languid pleasures with the voluptuous harem of those underground passages.

The crowd of bandits arose, their eyes ablaze with desire. Having taken in their robust arms the victims of their lust, they led them to the dens of lechery, greater than any of the East, that each one had reserved for himself in that dense labyrinth of vaults and chambers. The Son of the Storm went to take his slave, but at that moment a dagger shone in her right hand as she exclaimed: "Back, wicked creature! Back, coward who ventures himself on the honor of a woman!"

"Ha! How beautiful you are when you're angry; this bravery becomes well the chosen woman of the Son of the Storm. Come, Sultaness beauty; come with me and we will share a languid swoon of the most supreme joy on earth," replied the bandit, as he advanced toward the young woman who was retreating, pallid but with a virile resolve drawn on her countenance.

"Didn't you hear me, you wild-haired ingrate? Don't you know that the fierce lion of the mountain who makes the jungles tremble, approaches you and, in the voice of a dove, asks for a loving caress?"

"This syrupy language," said the woman, "suits well the fierce lion you describe. Clever trickster, see the dagger that I have in my hand and know that I have the courage to plunge it into your chest if you intend to reduce me to dishonor by force. You are a crafty coward and you try flattery, believing me easy. Back, lion-eyed coward!"

"If the offended beauty who has tamed my heart calms herself a bit, perhaps we can reason. What use is it to oppose my desire? I am your master: I am the most powerful bandit in these mountains. From here you will never again see the light of day except to leave for your burial. If an exaggerated point of honor detains you, cast it aside. What does the world matter to you if it will never know that you have been a slave in the conjugal bed of the Son of the Storm? You are beautiful; your charms will favor you in my eyes."

"Infamy! Stop, be silent! The world, as you believe it to be, is such that if others do not know of your infamies the deeds are less contemptible. But there is another world where an omniscient eye watches over us. He penetrates every abyss and investigates the deeds of every one of us, even the offenders who steal the honor of a maiden in the dungeons of a hell like this one."

"Do you refuse me?"

"I despise you!"

"Well, you will regret it. Soon you will cry tears of bitterness. Hello, stepmother!" he shouted, directing himself toward the old gypsy who was exiting from an interior room. "Have them take this virgin Susana to the chamber where I have ordered them to bind her father in chains."

Taking long strides and chomping on his whiskers, he left for the den from which the old woman had exited. On crossing the threshold of the door, he found the monkey, which grunted and obstructed his passage. He gave it a furious kick, sending it to the middle of the corridor and, cursing, he closed himself in his compartment. That night he seemed more like a demon than a human being.

As for the old gypsy woman, she attended to the important task her stepson had entrusted to her. The heroic maiden was led to her father's cell and there they suffered and grieved together, the father feeding from the breast of his daughter, and the daughter from a bone that the old gypsy flung her every day as if to a dog.

Each night when the Son of the Storm returned from some incursion, voices and weeping could be heard in the prison of those pitiable beings. Later, curses and the noise of chains, the creaking of hinges, some footsteps, and then, nothing. The Son of the Storm continually pestered the maiden, but she would always refuse him. Finally, tired of suffering and seeing no change in their fate, father and daughter arrived at a conclusion.

"Daughter," her old father said, pulling her close against his heart, "I have little breath left me. In short, I am going to die and when I am no longer of this world, ay, the fate that awaits you!"

"My father, do not distress yourself."

"Ay, my poor little one," groaned the old man. "There is but one recourse left to save you from disgrace."

"What is it?"

"Marriage."

"With that monster?"

"With that monster. Perhaps heaven will touch his heart with the blessings of the spirit and transform him into another type of man, and you will have saved yourself from dishonor."

"Father, my father, what a great sacrifice. Do you demand it of me?"

"I wish to die in peace and not have to witness from the grave my daughter dishonored and sad."

"Father, if you wish it so, I will do it. Tonight when the tyrant comes, I will be his bride."

Father and daughter were speaking thus in the dungeon the day that the Son of the Storm relinquished his first battle. Two tears fought to well up from the eyelids of the old man, but he cut them off and closed his eyes. He was dead. That night they removed the body of the old man from the prison to give him burial, and brought before the leader a pale young woman, with her hair loosened, dressed in Phrygian robes draping her classic beauty.

V

What a different scene from the usual upon the return of a campaign! Such despondent faces! How silent the rooms! They were in the dining hall and around the table sat a hundred thieves, but the usual uproar was not heard, nor the happy clanking of goblets, the spicy stories, all the clamor that on similar occasions accompanied the lawless, vulgar people. In the caverns of the Son of the Storm a somber silence reigned, resembling the calm that precedes the arrival of a hurricane. At the head of the table sat the chief, as quiet as the night; he ate little, deep as he was in thought. A fatal presentiment gnawed at his heart. Raising at last his glance and passing it with somber dullness over his throng, he asked, "Are all my men here?"

"All of them, less eighteen," answered one who appeared to be second in command.

"Well then we shall drink to my health and to the health of her who is going to be my wife." The tops of one hundred bottles flew off and a frothy wine filled the goblets: glasses crashed together, one hundred arms rose into the air, and one hundred mouths sucked down with bitter relief the smooth liquid. "Bravo! Viva! Long live the Son of the Storm!" exclaimed the leader, and all answered, "Viva!"

"Now, mother," he added, directing himself toward the old gypsy, who had a place of honor at his left, "bring me the slave with the wavy tresses. Tonight is a night of happiness, my comrades. The Son of the Storm will shortly bend his neck to the yoke of love . . . music, slaves! Make our mansion moan with the sweetest chords."

At this order a torrent of harmony followed that seemed to come from very far away, and kept growing, growing, as the light became clearer and more beautiful; and shortly, led by a group of youths in white robes, appeared the orphan who was about to offer herself in sacrifice at the altar of filial love and obedience. Her paleness made her ethereal; her eyelids and her cheeks still carried fresh signs of her tears. Like Cordelia in the pathetic drama of *King Lear,* she was no less incorporeal, less intangible than that tender princess and benefactor to the delirious king in his moments of tremendous agony, when he entered the encampment at Douvres followed by two madmen and a blind man. Poor girl, poor disconsolate orphan! Firstly, heartbroken to find herself without her father, the only solace in her misfortune; and secondly, surrounded by brutal bandits from whose eyes appeared not one consoling gaze, nor from whose mouths escaped one tender word. Poor girl! Poor wretched girl! Nevertheless, pain had made her more arrogant, more entrancing; approaching the table where the bandits were drinking, stopping in front of the chief, she raised her voice and said: "Assassin of my father: I must finish at once with this sacrilegious farce. You have me now, prepared for sacrifice."

"Long live she who comes to be Sultaness of the mountains!" exclaimed the leader, standing up and walking over to receive the girl. The rest of the bandits repeated the "long live," but with what seemed more like a wail of anguish than an expression of pleasure.

The Son of the Storm took the hand of the one about to be his wife and, seating her at his right-hand side, made all fill their cups again and empty them in honor of his Sultaness. The music swelled, the scene grew lively, the faces of the crowd shone from the heat, and the young prisoner grew more and more pallid. What lamentation seemed to have arrived to disturb that well-constructed happiness? Was it the echo of a harmony among the crypts? The music and the hubbub ceased for a moment. The rustle of a footstep arrived at the leader's ear. Was it the clanking of battle gear? Perhaps it was nothing.

"Music, more music," the leader shouted again, and the sound started up among the chords of the band. The "long lives" and the toasts began to fly across the room again; the orgy proceeded; the girl was sad and pale. "Executioner!" she exclaimed, fixing her gaze on the chief. "Until when must I suffer this torment? End this for once and for all!"

"Wine, more wine!" shouted the bandits.

"Tyrant!"

"Wine!"

"Long live!"

"Long live the Sultaness of the Son of the Storm!"

"Long, long, long live!"

The voice started to grow unsure. The place seemed to spin in a rapid whirlwind; the din grew and reason lost its rule, objects began to assume grotesque and fantastic shapes. Have you ever heard by chance on the islets off the coast a flock of sea gulls stirring up the skies with a dark fluttering? Such is how the banquet sounded. But what noise began once again to sound among that commotion? Was it the ghostly throng of a troop of gnomes, who in the late hours of the night were coming to visit the robbers' feast? What visions seemed to pass for a moment there in the distance in the half-shadows? What movement without noise? What whispering like an autumn breeze among the yellow leaves of the forest? What horrible oppression so wearied the chief? What fear seized the gypsy? And what strange light shone from the eyes of the monkey? Powerful elements of the fragrant wine! How it snatches the souls from things replacing them with others, more capricious and chimerical!

The hour had arrived in which the spirits exit their tombs and pass through the world, and in which the will-o'-the-wisps serve as torches for the birds of the night as they take flight into the gloomy skies. One by one the robbers fell to the ground, overcome by the wine. They lay on the floor, inert with drowsiness from the narcotic, and only the girl, the old gypsy, the monkey, and the fearful leader remained alert. The music no longer played, and the slaves had retired to cry tears of desperation in the darkness of the underground passages. Rising from his seat, the leader took the girl's hand in his and smiling said: "Sultaness of the Son of the Storm, I take you for my wife."

"Then let us not delay; where is the priest who must give us the blessing?" asked the girl drily. "Where are the witnesses? Where is the altar and all the required accompaniment?"

The leader was about to respond, but another sound disturbed his ears. It was no longer the throng of gnomes, nor the echo of some harmony within the chambers; it was no creation of fantasy but, rather, walking toward him was a thick column of real soldiers, as truly determined as those who the day before had defeated him. In a word, it was the same men. Their daring plus a happy coincidence had led them to that cave. In the middle of their journey a strong storm had caught them and, roaming around, they had wandered into it by chance. The storm roared outside, but in the interior all was calm. Winding through those numerous labyrinths they had surprised the party and were only waiting for an opportune moment to make their sudden attack. When his view came across the battle-ready force, the Son of the Storm released the girl's hand and, drawing his sword, shouted with a voice that made the earth tremble. "What do you want?"

"That you hand me your sword, vile thief!" answered the captain.

"I am the one who never gave up his sword."

"Surrender, for God's sake!"

"I will kick out your tongue, you dirty hound of justice, and I will twist your heart out with my dagger!"

"Get him, men, get him!" shouted the captain, signaling the bandit with his finger.

There was a frightening crash, waking the men from their drunken stupor. Cursing and the clashing of swords was heard. The flustered drunks raised themselves up. A ferocious combat ensued with blood running on the ground, and broken heads flying off, separated from their bodies. The storm howled outside and inside, in the entrails of the earth, in the chambers of that cave, bellowed a battle like the tremor of a suppressed volcano. "God of mercy," the pale girl with wavy hair prayed on her knees, "let justice win and crime be punished."

"Let's go, let's go," the old gypsy cried. "Stop your foolishness, girl. Come. God no longer listens to us." And the monkey leaned on the old woman as she sighed.

The battle grew. Like a cloud caught up in a whirlwind that grows, then folds back on itself, flies, trails off, and disperses to once again recover, such is how that mass of warriors moved, hands brandishing terrible weapons, each instant discharging a blow and with each blow delivering a dead man.

The thieves succumbed after strenuous combat, and the troops dragged their loathsome cadavers along the ground. The chief had fallen, his body pierced through in various places; with a satanic blasphemy on his lips, he died.

Years later the peasants of neighboring regions would hear at the curfew hour each night strange noises and frightening cries that stole sleep from timid souls, women, and children. It was said that the bloodstained ghosts of warriors were passing on the edge of the precipice where the cursed cave rose up. It was said as well that on stormy nights an old stooped woman in the company of a fierce monkey came down from the mountain, steering themselves into the cemetery where she took her fill of human bones. A day came in which the old woman did not make her nocturnal excursion and was never seen again. What had happened to her? Listen to what the company captain said while he drained a pitcher of brandy one day: "You're interested in the old pimp, you rogues? Well, knoweth that the devil took her to the deepest pit of all hell, ha, ha! He has her there sweeping the chamber that should be occupied by certain petty politicians who keep our country in an upheaval. Ha, ha! Another round, for God's sake!"

The captain never told a lie. [1892]

Translation of *El hijo de la tempestad* by Amy Diane Prince

The Mexican corrido, also known as the border ballad, is a popular poem set to music. Corridos generally tell of the heroic exploits of one man who fights for his own rights or those of his people. The most famous of these is *The Ballad of Joaquín Murrieta*. Murrieta, a Robin Hood type who lived in California in the 1850s, furnished the central figure for Rodolfo "Corky" Gonzáles's *I Am Joaquín*.

The Ballad of Gregorio Cortez was written sometime after June 1901, when the events on which the poem is based took place. As the legend is related by the writer and scholar Américo Paredes in *With His Pistol in His Hand: A Border Ballad and Its Hero*, during a horse trade Cortez's brother Román outsmarted an Anglo who was trying to swindle him. When the Anglo came to the Cortez ranch a few hours after the alleged crime, he brought along the sheriff and a deputy, who interpreted for the sheriff — badly. When translation problems turned the discussion into a heated argument, the sheriff drew his gun and shot Román. Gregorio then killed the sheriff. For several weeks Cortez evaded the Texas Rangers, then finally gave himself up, fearing for the safety of his family. He was sentenced to ninety-nine years in jail but was later pardoned when his case was brought to the attention of Abraham Lincoln's daughter (Lincoln, of course, did not have a daughter). The story itself is an object lesson in miscommunication and racism; the questions it raises about the reliability of interlingual communication continue to this day.

There are at least a dozen versions of *El corrido de Gregorio Cortez,* including a film based on the story, which was released in 1984 and starred Edward James Olmos.

The Ballad of Gregorio Cortez

In the county of El Carmen
Look what has occurred,
The Major Sheriff is dead,
And Román lies gravely hurt.
The very next morning
When the people had arrived
They said to one another:
"No one knows who committed the crime."

They went about asking questions,
And after a three-hour quest,
They discovered that the wrongdoer
Had been Gregorio Cortez.

Now Cortez is outlawed,
In the whole state he is banned,
Let him be taken dead or alive,
Several have died at his hands.

Then said Gregorio Cortez,
With his pistol in his hand:
"I'm not sorry that I killed him,
My brother's death I would not stand."

Then said Gregorio Cortez,
With his soul all aflame:
"I'm not sorry that I killed him,
Self-defense is my rightful claim."

The Americans started coming,
Their horses seemed to soar,
Because they were all after
The three-thousand-dollar reward.

He set out for González,
Several sheriffs saw him go,
They decided not to follow
As they all feared him so.

The bloodhounds began coming,
His trail took them afar,
But tracking down Cortez
Was like following a star.

Then said Gregorio Cortez:
"Why bother scheming around,
When you can't even catch me
With all of your bloodhounds?"

Then said the Americans:
"If we catch him, what should we do?
If we fight him man to man,
The survivors will be few."

He left Brownsville for the ranch,
Some three hundred in that locale
Succeeded in surrounding him,
But he bolted their corral.

Over by El Encinal,
According to what is said,
They got into a gunfight,
And he shot another sheriff dead.

Then said Gregorio Cortez,
With his pistol in his hand:
"Don't run off, cowardly rangers,
From one sole Mexican man."

He struck out for Laredo,
With no fear in his breast:
"Follow me, spineless rangers,
For I am Gregorio Cortez."

Gregorio says to Juan
At the ranch they call Cypress:

"Tell me all the news,
For I am Gregorio Cortez."

Gregorio says to Juan:
"Now you just wait and see,
Go and call the sheriffs,
Tell them to arrest me."

When the sheriffs got there
Gregorio gave himself up to go:
"You can take me because I'm willing.
If you force me, the answer's no."

They've finally caught Cortez,
It's over now, they claim,
And his poor sad family
In their hearts must bear the pain.

With this I bid farewell
In the shade of a cypress,
And thus are sung the final notes
Of the ballad of Gregorio Cortez.

[ca. 1901]

Translation of "El corrido de Gregorio Cortez" by Margarite Fernández Olmos

Part III

LATINO UNITED STATES

Latino literature is generally regarded as a twentieth-century phenomenon; beginning in the 1960s, Chicano and Puerto Rican authors, then Cuban Americans and more recent Latino arrivals, have produced a substantial and impressive body of writing. While writers in Latin America were establishing what has been called the "boom" of Latin American narrative, their U.S. counterparts were forging a distinct tradition in poetry, drama, and fiction in their own voices. What this anthology hopes to demonstrate, however, is that the spectacular flowering of U.S. Latino letters from the 1960s onward grew from seeds carefully and painstakingly sown by earlier writers. Their lonely efforts often went unrecognized by mainstream critics as well as by younger Latino authors, who were frequently unaware of their existence.

A case in point is the novel *The Rebel* by Leonor Villegas de Magnón. The work is based on the author's fascinating experiences as the founder of a nursing corps that attended to the revolutionary forces in the Texas/Mexico border region during the Mexican Revolution. Frustrated in her attempts to have the novel published in Spanish in the 1920s, Villegas de Magnón later wrote a version in English in the 1940s, but it met a similar fate. Thanks to the efforts of contemporary scholars and the foresight of editors dedicated to promoting Latino literature, the novel was finally published in 1994. It stands as another challenge to the stereotypical misconceptions regarding Mexican Americans, particularly women, of that era. Similarly, for decades the poet William Carlos Williams was not included in the sphere of U.S. Latino culture due to the lack of appreciation of his profound Puerto Rican and Spanish-American roots. Recent scholarly research, however, has demonstrated that this important precursor of modern American poetry is truly worthy of the distinction; his poetic sensibilities have been shown to reflect a more hemispheric/New World application of the term "American."

The first decades of the twentieth century can be considered a period of ethnic consolidation, a steady process of validation and redefinition of U.S. Latino culture. The Cubans and Puerto Ricans who began to arrive in the United States in greater numbers after the Spanish Cuban American War and the native-born Mexican Americans, who were treated as outsiders, focused in these years on creating economic, educational, and political organizations to defend their communities against racial and ethnic oppression. As these groups became more settled, a type of invisible, Spanish-language parallel universe began to evolve that encompassed community organizations as well as the ongoing traditions of Spanish-language newspapers, local radio and television programming, cinema, and theater. This hidden culture met the needs of a people whose lives and experiences were not reflected in U.S. mainstream media.

The writing of this period also reflected a transitional stage. A number of authors, especially after the 1920s, wrote in English, which was for many their first language, while others maintained their native Spanish with occasional attempts at writing in the new language to accommodate their new cultural experiences within the United States. In addition, researchers like Arthur A. Schomburg and Arturo Campa explored and conserved African/Latin American and Mexican-American traditions, seeking out, recording, and preserving cultural legacies that had been ignored, frequently rescuing them from oblivion and laying the necessary groundwork for future artists and scholars.

The fruit of these efforts would emerge in the second half of the century. The eminent Chicano writer Tomás Rivera once referred to Chicano literature as "life in search of form." The often dramatic experiences and daily struggles of Latino people in general, who had long been invisible to the larger U.S. society, were vividly brought into national focus in the mid-1960s when Chicanos (as many younger, socially conscious Mexican Americans now preferred to be called) and U.S. Puerto Ricans (also referred to as "Nuyoricans") joined with African Americans, Native Americans, and other minority groups to demand that their voices be heard. Often in the vanguard of these political struggles, authors searched to find an aesthetic form, a literary fit to accommodate these historical realities.

The 1960s was an era of intense emotional and intellectual introspection and analysis, discontent and criticism, protest and dissent. It was also an era of intense optimism fueled by a dramatic impulse toward liberation. The era witnessed the decolonization of many Third World countries and the creation of international movements for peace and civil rights, which expanded in the 1970s and 1980s to encompass feminist, ecological, and gay rights movements. Conventional attitudes toward class, race, ethnicity, and gender were challenged. The rights to claim lost cultural identities and gain political power motivated the libertarian struggles of various minority communities, which often drew their inspiration from activist writers; the literary task was perceived as promoting political struggles and serving as a stimulus for action against social injustices.

The literature of this period that emerged from the Chicano and Nuyorican *barrios,* or neighborhoods, had a vital role in the affirmation of roots and the articulation of values in direct contrast and opposition to Anglo culture. In fiction, autobiographical narrative — memoirs and coming-of-age stories and novels with predominantly male protagonists — dominated thematically, to counterbalance mainstream images of youth, family life, and the evolution of personal identity. The conflict usually centered on the tensions between the drive toward assimilation, or becoming "Americanized," and loyalty to one's ethnic group. In asserting an identity not always condoned or accepted by the larger society, the writers attempted to create new standards and perspectives. The works reflect a conscious realization that the evolution of the individual is closely tied to sociohistoric and political circumstances. The articulation of countervalues also extended to the construction of countermyths, such as the promotion of the mythological Aztlán, ancestral home of the Aztecs or *mexicas,* in the U.S. Southwest. Aztlán was considered not only a territorial challenge but also a symbol of Chicano cultural origins, unity, and self-determination. Nuyorican writers likewise created myths of a lost island Eden, uncritically idealizing Puerto Rican culture as an assertion of national and cultural pride.

As opposed to the more nostalgic and romantic literary perceptions of earlier Latino writers, however, the authors of the 1960s by and large produced militant calls for social change, particularly in poetry and drama. No longer confined to the traditional forms of publication or concerned with critical recognition, writers delivered their works directly to an eager public at political rallies, union meetings, street performances, and myriad storefront coffeehouses. Although the combining of languages to form a new synthesis — often referred to deprecatingly as "Spanglish" — was not entirely a 1960s innovation, Chicano and Nuyorican artists embraced this mixing of cultural codes as a powerful technique to express their peripheral identities.

The defiant social and occasionally rhetorical public stance that characterizes much of the literature of this period has given way in the final decades of the twentieth century to a greater aesthetic flexibility and diversity. Latino writing has also become more inclusive, with women and gay and lesbian authors creating space for themselves after confronting their own double marginalization in the dominant society as well as in their own cultural groups. Held in low esteem or ignored by traditional patriarchal structures, Latina writers in particular have contested these limitations in their multidimensional works.

Although U.S. Latina writing has existed since at least the nineteenth century (earlier examples of Latina culture have thus far been found mainly in the oral tradition), Latinas did not begin to publish in substantial numbers until the 1980s. A central theme of Latina writing has been the debunking of stereotypes in favor of a plurality of experiences. Female growing-up narratives, for example, focus on the interaction between the protagonist and her environment but also allow for a critical examination of patriarchal values and traditions within her culture; gender is an important component in the definition of identity.

Female characters are now presented outside of their traditional archetypal modes; the usual images of the virginal, self-sacrificing mother, the sensual temptress, or the prophetic *curandera* or witch/healer are given alternative treatments. Latina authors have reformulated the traditional myths and archetypes: those that they judge valid and useful are retained, while those considered a limitation or obstacle to the realization of full human potential are redesigned in an ever-evolving process. Gender issues and questions of sexuality have increasingly broadened the thematic space of Latino writing; once perceived as an untenable position, "writing from the margins" is now revealed to be a liberating aspect of the creative process.

The expansion of a pan-Latino consciousness across ethnic and national lines in the 1990s has led many to claim that "crossing boundaries" is the dominant metaphor of contemporary Latino literature. Indeed, Latino authors are no longer circumscribed aesthetically, linguistically, or ideologically, and the resulting artistic creativity has enjoyed substantial critical and commercial success in the United States and abroad in recent years. With this increased recognition, however, new considerations have emerged. How, for example, will the Latino artist reconcile more open and unrestricted perceptions regarding ethnic identity with the commercial demands of a market that has a narrow, preconceived notion of "ethnic literature"? How will race, class, and gender intersect in this formulation? And success brings its own challenges: once thrust into the center from a sometimes uncomfortable but highly creative position on the periphery, Latino writers must avoid being engulfed by the mainstream. They must follow their own dynamic current, asserting their complex differences and commonalities as they strive to reach common ground.

Leonor Villegas de Magnón (1876–1955) was born in Nuevo Laredo into a wealthy and prominent family and raised in the Mexico/Texas border area. As we learn in her autobiographical novel *The Rebel* (1994), Villegas de Magnón spent a privileged but lonely youth in private American schools. The early years of her discouraging marriage were spent in the Mexican capital during the final years of Porfirio Díaz's dictatorship. The novel traces the author's evolution from bourgeois lady to conspirator and participant in the Mexican Revolution.

In contrast to the traditional role of women in her society, *The Rebel*'s female protagonist is willing to risk a comfortable marriage for her revolutionary ideals. The character referred to as "Rebel" supports the cause as a member of the Revolutionary Council, a journalist, and a founder of the White Cross, a corps of nurses active from the border region into Mexico. The excerpts here describe her birth near the Texas border and her later decision as a young woman to organize the nursing corps, demonstrating her fiery determination and total commitment to the revolutionary cause.

Unconventional in content and form, the work was written first in Spanish during the initial decades of the century, then in English in the 1940s. Despite Villegas's prolonged attempts to have it published, *The Rebel* was silenced and marginalized for more than half a century. It was rescued from oblivion through the persistence of the scholar Clara Lomas and the support of the Recovering the U.S. Hispanic Literary Heritage Project. Finally published in 1994, the novel attests to the important activist role of women and challenges misconceptions regarding Mexican-American women.

from **The Rebel**

The Rebel Is a Girl

The Río Bravo or Río Grande defines the dividing line between the two nations, Mexico and the United States. As the years pass, the river appears to be in a state of inactivity. Its waters seek a lower level, until it eventually leaves its banks exposed. In some places it becomes a thin stream that can be easily crossed on foot. The least cautious, or perhaps the most daring and hard-pressed, people take advantage of the fertile soil and, at their own risk, build huts, plant vegetables, raise chickens, cows, and a pig or two. The river maintains this happy mood for years, and the poor are hopeful that it will thus continue.

By some whim of nature, or it may be that Neptune, God of the Seas, wishes to amuse himself, the water awakens from its tranquil slumber and transforms itself into a gigantic serpent that crawls slowly, but gains a momentum of such menacing form that it carries with it everything that it contacts. Soon on its surface, floating with the torrent, cows, sheep, chickens, snakes, and huts struggle to keep above the waters until they are finally engulfed by the churning undercurrent. Nothing escapes the furious waters that rush on as if in answer to a challenge presenting a grotesque contrast to the many years of defiant lethargy.

On a night like this, the twelfth of June, 1876, the shrill whistle of the night guards gave the alarm. Civil guards on horses rode from town to town along the river, warning the inhabitants of the approaching peril. Shrill cries and terrifying screams filled the air, and the Laredos, two border towns across the river from each other, rose to the emergency. The darkness of the night became more terrifying as thunderclap after thunderclap intermingled with the cries of those in danger. The lightning illuminated their path momentarily only to leave it again and again in intense darkness.

The trees whipped by a gale of wind blew back and forth, beating against the walls of the big homes, while rampant waters gaining ground curled around the foundations, menacing homes and huts till they yielded to the mighty pressure of the water and fell like sugar toys.

The poor who lived on the edge of the river were making powerful efforts to save the little they possessed. They moved forward like beasts of burden, carrying as much as their strength allowed them. Women with children tied to their back in *rebozos* had their hands free to drag their animals. Men burdened with chattel also dragged their beasts, going ahead to find a safe foot path to scale the river banks. If they dared to halt, those behind gave a cry of warning.

"Go up higher! Higher! Higher!"

Again they redoubled their steps in an effort to gain safe ground; the waters were already flooding Nuevo Laredo on the Mexican side. The town was in darkness; only the lanterns carried by helpers provided the means to light the way of the refugees. The *mozos,* caretakers of the rich ones, were kept busy guarding the homes, and running back and forth with news of the rising water, its level, its perils, providing an excuse for wild excitement.

Emperor Maximilian had been dethroned, tried, and executed. Benito Juárez and Porfirio Díaz had dickered for power between themselves. After overthrowing the government of Lerdo de Tejada, General Porfirio Díaz had taken the Capital of Mexico, proclaiming his *Plan de Tuxtepec.* Slow means of communication and the rapid changes in governments left many guerrilla bands of either side scattered over the country. These groups, unaware of peace, continued to roam about attacking towns.

A band of these scattered rebels, taking advantage of the storm-frightened people of the little town of Nuevo Laredo, found it opportune to attack and loot the homes which had been temporarily abandoned or neglected, either from fear of the rising river or out of curiosity to view the damage. The terror of the night meant nothing to the rebel looters. They rode unchallenged to the heart of town, determined to break down the gates of a rich Spanish merchant to whom it was rumored a large consignment of fine wines had recently arrived by barge from the Gulf of Mexico.

Quickly they made their way through the darkness to the front of a strong gate, or *portón,* with the master's name, Don Joaquín, on the stone arch overhead.

"This is the place," they yelled, banging on the gate with the butts of their guns. "Open the gate! Open!"

Don Joaquín, a prudent man, ordered the gate opened. Pancho, the *mozo,* was accustomed to obeying orders, but he hesitated.

"Go, Pancho. Open the gate."

Slowly Pancho proceeded to accomplish the task which was always so easy, but tonight his trembling fingers refused to pull the heavy lock that held the door tight.

"Señor," he said, "they are bandits."

"You cannot do it, Pancho? I will do it myself." Don Joaquín, carrying a lantern in one hand, approached and opened the door that yielded softly.

Pancho hid behind the door. The Indian guessed the reason for this visit. Holding his lantern high, Don Joaquín got a quick view of the intruders. He saw the group of armed bandits and at once guessed their motive.

"Follow me," he said in a low voice, escorting them down the tile-paved courtyard.

Don Joaquín's establishment covered a long city block on the main plaza, a quarter of a mile from the river. Surrounded by a thick wall well over a man's height were the house, the *bodega* (warehouse), and the store. In the house lived the young master and his family. In rooms built along the side of the warehouse lived the young boys who had come from Spain to learn the merchandising business. Along the back wall was an open space behind the house and the *bodega,* where garlic was stored.

Entering the warehouse, Don Joaquín led the way down into the cellar where the big assortment of Spanish wines has been stowed away. The intruders at once became his guests, sitting around on the benches, but still holding their guns in a prominent position. Wine casks stacked on top of each other lined the sides of the room. The light from Don Joaquín's lantern on the rough wooden table was reflected in the tin wine cups. Where the wine had dripped from the spigots there were stains on the stone floor. The sweet smell of wine was heavy in the air.

Serving the wine Don Joaquín drew, Pancho faltered among the rough men. Grabbing a cup from Pancho, the leader held it up close to his eyes to see if it was full. Then flinging back his head he poured it down his throat. Putting his cup back on the table with a heavy thump he looked meaningfully at Pancho.

"His cup, Pancho. We do not want our friends to leave thirsty." Don Joaquín held out his hand for the empty cup.

"Ah, we are not leaving yet, Señor. Not until we have searched the house." The leader nodded to his men who forgot their wine and jumped up.

Don Joaquín pushed through the men and started toward the door near the gate, but the men were already attracted by a closed door across the patio, where voices were heard coming from within.

"Open this door, Señor," commanded the boldest one, making a sign to his companions to present arms. "Open this door."

Without hesitating, the master raised his lantern to throw a better light in the dimly lit room. At that moment cries of a newborn baby broke the silence.

Outside, the increasing fury of the stormy night threatened at any moment to demolish the house. The waters were slapping against the walls, slipping in through the low windows. Inside the bandit-held mansion, beaten by the wind, threatened by the water, a woman in majestic dignity had given birth to a child.

The rebels were touched by the familiar sacredness of the scene. Putting away their guns, some among them made the sign of the cross on their foreheads and on their hearts. They returned to the patio to resume their drinking.

"Pardon, señor," the leader murmured.

But before the band could descend to the wine cellar, loud knocks and threats of breaking in the gate were heard. A Federal commander in command of his own troops demanded entrance to search for bandits. Frightened by the Federals, the rebels scattered wildly over the courtyard, climbing the wall in back of the warehouse and escaping in the opposite direction.

Gripping his lantern, the master walked to the gate. He again held his light high. Opening the door, he signaled to the Federals to walk in and be quiet.

"Follow me," said Don Joaquín, starting toward the wine cellar.

The Federals in their anxiety to find some victim on whom to discharge their fury, pushed one another into the hall, some bouncing clear across the patio.

"The rebels are here," the commander said, seeing that Don Joaquín was leading them away from the direction of the house.

"Sí, señor," answered Don Joaquín quickly. "I am hiding one rebel." He walked toward the door, hesitated, then flung it open. The crying of the baby silenced the men.

"A man child, señor?" asked the commander.

Pancho shook his head at Don Joaquín.

"No, señor," the master answered. He drew himself up in pride. "My rebel is a girl."

"A girl!" one of the men said, and making excuses for their intrusion, turned away from the door.

"Pardon us, señor. We already knew that you were an honest man. But in these awful times, what about it? Anything may happen. All the people are alarmed with so many rumors of bandits."

Don Joaquín ushered the Federals to the same cellar where the bandits had just been. With their cups filled, the men held them high and offered a toast of welcome to the new arrival, the Rebel. They drank a second toast to the mother of the baby.

"This toast we offer," the commander said, "to the mother of this border town on the banks of the Río Bravo." He wished to appear in a good light before the eyes of the owner of such good wines.

"¡Viva! ¡Viva!" the men called out in high spirits because their bandit hunt had turned into a party.

Finally, Don Joaquín, who was impatiently awaiting their departure, began to show signs of restlessness. Pancho appeared with his lantern to lead the way out. As the Federals filed out of the gate, passersby reported that the river was now at a standstill and the storm had abated.

Pancho, lantern in hand, did not think it time to go to bed, but preferred walking the streets, telling the double good news of the baby and the dying storm. As he started out the gate, Don Joaquín called, "Pancho, go put on dry clothes while Julia makes coffee for us all."

Julia was considered part of the family. She was a young Indian girl whom Doña Valerianna, Don Joaquín's wife, had taken as a child and raised.

Meanwhile, Don Joaquín personally examined all the doors and windows; though the storm had ceased, the strong wind might blow them open. While he was walking about the place, his thoughts were filled with scenes from the year. He remembered that just one year before, his first son had been born in Corpus Christi.

"Strange coincidence," he recalled. On the night Leopoldo was born there had been a tempest and the waves had lashed his home on the bay.

"My son born on American soil. My daughter in Mexican territory, and I, a Spanish subject. Who will be more powerful, he or she?"

In bed, Doña Valerianna held her child in a warm embrace, whispering a benediction.

"A Mexican flag shall be yours. I will wrap it together with your brother's. His shall be an American flag, but they shall be like one to me."

Her eyes searched into the darkness for her husband's flag, murmuring in her semiconsciousness, "His country I shall never see; it is beyond the great ocean." . . .

General Aureliano Blanquet had become Minister of War, and all the army was being mobilized under his command. He was sending his best generals to the frontier. On March 17, 1913, in the early dawn the small garrison of Nuevo Laredo was attacked by General Jesús Carranza. Unexpectedly, a group of civilians took up arms and aided the unprepared Federals. The Carrancistas advanced to the city limits. After a brisk encounter, during which the outskirts of Nuevo Laredo were strewn with wounded, Jesús Carranza ordered his men to retreat. The Constitutionalists could have taken the town before the military train arrived bringing Federal reinforcements, but false news reached them that new aid was already arriving for the enemy.

Hearing the firing, the Rebel dressed quickly. She called her aunt's home in Nuevo Laredo. Getting no answer, she called several friends. There was no answer to any of her calls. Rushing out into the street, she stopped a big new car driven by a chauffeur. Directing him to drive to the offices of *El Progreso,* she told him to wait for her. She painted a red cross on a piece of paper and had it pasted on the windshield. Telephoning her friends, she told them her plans to go to Mexico and help take care of the wounded; she needed volunteers. With her faithful friend Jovita Idar, a writer for *El Progreso,* the Rebel encouraged four other young women to join them to offer immediate help.

Opening his pharmacy, Don Flavio Vargas gave her a basket of first-aid supplies. As she got in the car, he placed a towel-wrapped bundle behind her on the seat.

"You may need this," he said, patting her arm.

Told to drive to the international bridge, the chauffeur balked. He dared not take the car across the river into the battle-stricken town. Reaching behind her, the Rebel got the bundle. She felt the hard round object. Inside the towel was a long-necked bottle of whiskey. Unwrapping it, she pushed the hard bottle neck against the driver's back.

"Drive on," she ordered tersely.

As they neared the bridge at high speed, the Rebel leaned out of the car waving the white towel. The car was allowed to cross to the other side unhindered.

Leaving most of her girls at the hospital, the Rebel could be seen in the distance going south. The Rebel glanced toward a soldier. How she longed to run after him and give him the message to attack again quickly before Federal aid could arrive for the small garrison. She heard the captain's voice.

"So you are not one of us?" he said holding toward her the flag staff they had both advanced to get. "You may have this. It is yours to put your white flag on. Keep it." He handed it to her, gazing at the bronze eagle on the tip. It was not long afterward that the Rebel heard that the captain had joined the forces of Carranza.

The hospitalized Carrancistas were held prisoners in the hospital. The problem after a few days was to get them to their post at

Matamoros. All the men were in good shape to join the Constitutionalists that would soon attack the town of Matamoros. Aracelito, the Rebel's young secretary, seldom left her. She was well informed of all activities concerning the White Cross. The Rebel unfolded her plan for the prisoners' escape.

"As soon as we get news of the arrival of Federal reinforcements, we will take advantage of the excitement among the people," she said.

One morning soon afterward, Aracelito rushed to the Rebel.

"The troops arrive today. There will be a huge parade. Tonight there will be a big banquet and dance on the Main Plaza." The girl's eyes danced as she told the Rebel the news. The Rebel went about her duties and daily routine. Aracelito relayed the orders to the hospital corps to clean, disinfect, and prepare the hospital for inspection. Every bed was aired and clean linens put on. Only the Rebel and Aracelito changed the beds. As they did, they placed the prisoners' clothes beneath the mattresses. Each man was told to carefully dress himself at ten minutes before midnight. There was a big clock in the ward, and the men would be told when to start. Each bed had to be camouflaged after the soldiers fled. The nurses were told to entertain the guards at the right time. Jugs of pulque and tequila with tacos would be a banquet to the men while their *jefes* were gaily celebrating in the plaza.

The Rebel left the hospital to buy provisions, but instead crossed hurriedly to Laredo. She found Pancho eating. Together they shared the simple dinner. Their talk was full of reminiscing of the dead and absent ones.

"Mi ama," Pancho said sadly, "it is only you and your brother Leopold now. Do as your mother always prayed: be united."

"There is no fear about that, Pancho," she replied. "He and Inés, his wife, are my guardian angels, always taking care of my children and loving them as their own."

"I am old and useless," he sobbed. "I want to go back to Mexico when this war is over."

"You shall, Pancho," she comforted him. "I will take you with me. My husband is kind. You shall live with us. Now," she said lowering her voice, "I am going to entrust a very important mission to you."

Pancho straightened up, his eyes shone. He was ready to serve his country. He looked young again.

"Please tell me what you want me to do, Little Rebel," he said smiling fondly at her.

"First of all, you must sleep this afternoon and be rested. At twelve tonight you will hear the church bells and see the fireworks in Nuevo Laredo. The people will be celebrating. Take your skiff and row toward the cave that is at the foot of the road leading to the hospital. Soldiers will be there, hidden. Ask them if the Rebel sent them. Then row them quietly down the river on the Mexican side. As soon as you pass the last post of the Federals, land them near a *jacal.* Call the sentinel; he belongs to General Pablo González's people. Return quickly before morning, as you must not be seen." She spoke slowly so that Pancho would remember it all.

"My Julia will help me. Her spirit will protect me." Looking out over the waters of the river, he made the sign of the cross. The Rebel embraced him with the firm faith in him that he had always inspired in her in her childhood.

Buying a few things, she returned to the hospital. There was a strong smell of disinfectant; all quarters were clean, and nurses were rushing about ready for the federal inspection.

It was a little before midnight. The prisoners had dressed and were gone. Sleepy, well-fed guards looked over the wards, the dim lights helping to conceal the secret of the vacant beds. Laughingly, they returned to their posts. In a few minutes, there would be a changing of the guard. Hurriedly, the Rebel and Aracelito went past the great hospital portals and asked permission to go to the plaza for a little while. Most of the nurses had already left. The loyal nurses had taken a carriage to their homes across the river.

Aracelito and the Rebel walked to the bridge only two blocks from the plaza, which was ablaze with lights and crowded with newly arrived Federal troops celebrating with the townspeople. The hospital, eight blocks away, was in darkness and stillness. There were few people on the bridge. As the two women passed the monument in the middle of the bridge, the Rebel noticed that Aracelito was nervous and kept looking back. Someone was following them. The Rebel stopped as she heard the clock strike twelve. Anxiously looking toward the river bank, she thought she heard the rippling of water and the soft paddling of oars. She stood still and prayed. A young man had approached Aracelito and was speaking to her.

"Please believe me," he said earnestly, "ever since I first saw you, I have loved you. I am not a Federal. I am dressed as one, but I shall escape and go over to our people. Perhaps, tonight." He looked appealingly at the girl.

"I shall wait," she answered simply, unsmiling.

The young man disappeared in the darkness toward Mexico. The Rebel, anxious to be safely at Pancho's cabin, took Aracelito's trembling hand and pulled her toward the end of the bridge. Pushing open the door of Pancho's hut, they found a heavy dark blanket on the cot and on the dying coals a pot of coffee. They poured themselves coffee, then wrapping the blanket about them, walked to the edge of the river bank. They waited for Pancho's return.

"The young man who followed us," Aracelito began in a tremulous voice, "says he loves me, but I have not encouraged him. I thought he was a Federal. But he has told me that he will cross over to our people. I have promised to wait for him," she whispered, sobbing.

"Darling," the Rebel said, hugging her, "some night we will come here and Pancho will take a message for you to him."

They sat silently watching the lights across on the Mexican side go out, one by one. The hours of the clear moonlit night passed. Sometimes dozing, sometimes making plans, they kept vigil. Finally, they heard the soft ripple of water and drip of oars. They crouched down in the river weeds. The Rebel saw Pancho swiftly plying his oars. Behind him crumpled on the floor of the boat, her head on the seat, was a girl.

Lifting her gently in his arms, Pancho ran with his precious burden. The Rebel and Aracelito followed him to the cabin. Pancho placed her on his clean bed that Julia had always taken care of. Smoothing the pillow, he went for alcohol. The Rebel stood looking amazed at the beautiful girl, one hand hanging limp off the side of the bed, the other on her breast clutching something that was hidden under her blouse. There were blood stains on the other arm. They bandaged her arm, but did not try to move her hand. Whatever was there was sacred to her. She slept, exhausted. It was daylight when Pancho finished telling his part in the daring plot.

"I left here, *mi amita,*" he began as they sat drinking coffee, "just as you told me. Crossing the river, I rowed over toward the cave. I know it well; often Julia and I sat there after your mother died. I had only my skiff. I wondered what I would do if there were too many. Perhaps, I would have to make several trips. But as I was nearing the place, I noticed my *compadre*'s boat tied among the bushes at the river's edge. I tied it to my boat, saying all the time, '*Compadre,* I shall return it, God willing.'

"When I approached the cave, I was glad that I had taken the other boat. They all got in and helped me row. It was downstream; that made it easier. When we arrived at the hut past the last post, they left me. I rowed fast. Suddenly I heard a rustle of leaves in the shadows along the bank."

"Pancho, you are sure you took no enemy?" the Rebel asked clutching his hand.

"No, *mi amita,*" he said smiling at her fear. "I got the password from every one of them. They were quiet and kind."

"Well, go on," the Rebel insisted. "What was at the water's edge?"

"I heard a woman's voice, and out of the bushes a girl rushed to the water's edge toward me. '*¡Qué bonita!* Could it be the Virgin of Guadalupe herself coming to save me?' I thought to myself.

"Begging me to take her across the river she jumped into my *compadre*'s boat and helped me row. We rowed a little farther and then we heard a noise. It was Federals. They cried halt and fired a shot at us.

" 'It is Pancho, the *esquifero*. I am going home.' I called to them and they let us pass. We were nearing my *compadre*'s place. The girl had jumped into my boat as the shot had made its mark in the skiff she was in and was filling with water. We cut off the boat and I hid it where I had found it. After that, she must have fainted, as she did not speak again." Pancho finished his story and got up to put some mesquite on the low burning fire.

"Let her sleep," said the Rebel, also rising. "Do not disturb her. If she awakens and wants nourishment, prepare nice food like Julia made. I will come back as early as possible and bring you food and clothes. Tell no one of this; and let no one see her."

Making their way up the embankment silently, the two women parted, promising to meet again at mid-morning. People were beginning their usual daily routine, but there was excitement caused by the little newspaper vendors calling the news of the arrival of Federal reinforcements in Nuevo Laredo, and the daring escape of forty prisoners from the hospital.

Immediately, a meeting was called of all loyal nurses that had taken part in caring for the soldiers during the days after the combat. They sent a message to General Blanquet stating their displeasure regarding the Federal treatment of prisoners. While promising to care impartially for all wounded on the battlefield, they declared themselves strictly Constitutionalist sympathizers. Accordingly, the White Cross was no longer allowed to cross the frontier, and if so under penalty of death.

It was at the time of the Huerta outbreak that the Mexican National Red Cross, organized during the last years of the Díaz regime, failed in its principles of nonpartiality and nonpartisanship. In its cause destined to aid the wounded were spies and ammunition for the Federals. It was in protest and to counteract it that the Constitutionalist White Cross was established in Laredo, Texas, serving throughout the Carranza Revolution. The Red Cross served the Federals. It was pledged that the White Cross would go with the Carranza army, organizing hospitals and replacing Federal personnel with loyal doctors and nurses. The White Cross had stayed in the hospital until every wounded Constitutionalist had escaped.

The Constitutionalists repulsed, Federal reinforcements had arrived under the command of General Quintana. Nuevo Laredo bustled with preparations against attack. Trenches were built; search towers were erected with powerful searchlights; cannons were mounted on hill tops; brush and trees were cut down to clear the horizon for miles around the surrounding country.

At the time agreed, the Rebel went to Pancho's hut. A noise among the bushes and a rapid opening and closing of the door told of Aracelito's earlier arrival. Everything within Pancho's house was still. The visitor must have been asleep.

Aracelito came to the door to greet her silently. She dared not waken the sleeping girl. Pancho came in and started the fire. The girl awoke. Slowly getting herself together, she sat up on the side of the bed, stretching both her legs as if to assure herself of her identity. Then she stretched her arms. Suddenly becoming conscious of her mission, she searched in her blouse pocket.

"How well I feel," she said in a sweet voice. "I have had a perfect rest. I know that I am among friends who fight for the same cause." Looking at each of them, she spoke confidently. "Tell me please," the girl said, looking at Pancho, "who is the Rebel? It is urgent that I get in touch with her."

The Rebel grew pale, a strange thing for her, who knew not fear. Could it be a message from her husband? She had not heard from him since the tragic death of the President. Who was this violet-eyed girl?

"I am the Rebel," Leonor answered in a quiet voice.

"Yes," said Pancho, nodding emphatically. "She is our *jefe*."

"Who are you and where do you come from?" The Rebel spoke hoarsely, sitting on the bed beside her.

Aracelito pulled up a bench and looked earnestly at the newcomer.

"I am María de Jesús González, a teacher from Monterrey. I have a friend in the telegraph office; we are both telegraph operators and Constitutionalists. Here are telegrams that we held back. They will prove our loyalty. We heard of you and your brave companions and resolved to become allied with your work. One of these messages is from General Jerónimo Villarreal in Nuevo Laredo for Secretary Blanquet, asking for reinforcements; they were expecting the second attack by General Jesús Carranza. We also heard of the Constitutionalist retreat. Two days later we had another telegram that reinforcements would arrive in Matamoros at any moment. I traveled on horseback night and day until I found this good man at the river's edge." The girl spoke rapidly as if she feared something might happen to keep her from delivering her news.

"There are messages for you from Sonora," she continued. "A companion, Marie Bringas de Carturegli; the telegraph operator, Trinidad Blanco; and her sister will be here as soon as they can travel in Coahuila. Also, a teacher from there will join you, and in Tampico, Juanita Mancha, a brave girl. There are two more in Monterrey, the Blackaller sisters, teachers." She concluded her long recital of names with relief.

María de Jesús was having a cool bath. Pancho had stretched a sheet across the back of his hut for privacy. Standing in a big wash tub, the girl poured cool water over herself from a Mexican dried-gourd dipper that had been Julia's. Her long red hair hanging down, dressed in a cool summer kimono, she sat down to a humble repast that Pancho had prepared for her.

"María de Jesús," the Rebel said, "you are fully aware of the dangers we will encounter. Will you obey orders?"

"Yes, I am ready," she replied firmly.

"Then you must leave tonight," said the Rebel, "for the nearest Constitutionalist camp. Pancho will row you there. Rest now, and we will return tonight."

That night, Aracelito and the Rebel were stealing down the hill again with more clothes and food and a little money. María de Jesús was listening. She and Pancho had their supper while they were awaiting orders.

María put on her boots. She tucked a dagger that Pancho gave her in her blouse. She wore trousers that the Rebel had brought. Her hair was neatly braided and wound around her head.

"María," the Rebel said tensely, "you will take these telegrams to General Lucio Blanco, or any of his staff. They will probably attack Matamoros before reinforcements arrive. Come back quickly. This letter is for General Pablo González. Listen for any news."

The girl jumped in the skiff with Pancho. Soon they were lost in the shadows of the mesquites along the river banks. Aracelito and the Rebel sat again by the river, alone. Pancho was not to return until the next day. They did not know whether María would return or not.

"I wish," Aracelito sighed, "I wish I was as brave as our brave companion. I would go and look for Guillermo. Perhaps he is already with General Lucio Blanco's forces." [ca. 1920]

William Carlos Williams was born in 1883 in New Jersey into a Spanish-speaking household. His English-born Caribbean father, William George Williams, and Puerto Rican mother, Elena Hoheb, like so many other nineteenth-century Caribbean immigrants, had settled in the New York area. Their son, who became internationally famous as a poet, novelist, essayist, and playwright, was also a physician, who practiced for more than forty years in Rutherford, New Jersey. His numerous writings, ranging from his first poems in 1909 to works written before his death in 1963, are collected in several volumes.

Williams is recognized for his innovations in the language of poetry; he sought a "language modified by our environment, the American environment," as he searched to define "the American grain." His experimental poetry has been extensively studied from a variety of perspectives, including that of his distinctive relationship to his favorite subject, America. Explaining this attraction in a 1939 letter, Williams wrote, "Of mixed ancestry I felt from earliest childhood that America was the only home I could ever possibly call my own. I felt that it was expressedly founded for me, personally, and that it must be my first business in life to possess it."

What was not explored in any depth until Julio Marzán's groundbreaking study *The Spanish American Roots of William Carlos Williams* (1994) is the profoundly Latin American origin of Williams's poetry, which was influenced in great measure by his parents, particularly his mother. His American vision cannot be totally appreciated without an understanding of the wide variety of cultural sources that informed his work. His upbringing as a bilingual, bicultural child and his lifelong ambivalence toward his cultural origins reflect the feelings of many children of immigrants in the United States. Commenting on Williams's need to "possess" America due to his "mixed ancestry," Marzán observes the following: "Here Williams was discussing *In the American Grain* and, as in that book, the 'America' in question is not narrowly the United States, but the hemispheric America that Columbus stumbled onto. Elena's being from Puerto Rico, one of the sites where Columbus is believed to have actually set foot, and from a Spanish-speaking line that mingled its blood with the continent, made that 'America' Williams' legacy. He was an American and a 'pure product of America' because his mother was Puerto Rican."

The following poems, which date from the 1920s, reflect Williams's ideas on America and his origins.

To Elsie

The pure products of America
go crazy —
mountain folk from Kentucky

or the ribbed north end of
Jersey
with its isolate lakes and

valleys, its deaf-mutes, thieves
old names
and promiscuity between

devil-may-care men who have taken
to railroading
out of sheer lust of adventure —

and young slatterns, bathed
in filth
from Monday to Saturday

to be tricked out that night
with gauds
from imaginations which have no

peasant traditions to give them
character
but flutter and flaunt

sheer rags — succumbing without
emotion
save numbed terror

under some hedge of choke-cherry
or viburnum —
which they cannot express —

Unless it be that marriage
perhaps
with a dash of Indian blood

will throw up a girl so desolate
so hemmed round
with disease or murder

that she'll be rescued by an
agent —
reared by the state and

sent out at fifteen to work in
some hard-pressed
house in the suburbs —

some doctor's family, some Elsie —
voluptuous water
expressing with broken

brain the truth about us —
her great
ungainly hips and flopping breasts

addressed to cheap
jewelry
and rich young men with fine eyes

as if the earth under our feet
were
an excrement of some sky

and we degraded prisoners
destined
to hunger until we eat filth

while the imagination strains
after deer
going by fields of goldenrod in

the stifling heat of September
Somehow
it seems to destroy us

It is only in isolate flecks that
something
is given off

No one
to witness
and adjust, no one to drive the car [1923]

All the Fancy Things

music and painting and all that
That's all they thought of
in Puerto Rico in the old Spanish
days when she was a girl

So that now
she doesn't know what to do

with herself alone
and growing old up here —

Green is green
but the tag ends
of older things, *ma chère*

must withstand rebuffs
from that which returns
to the beginnings —

Or what? a
clean air, high up, unoffended
by gross odors [1927]

Arthur A. Schomburg (1874–1938) was born Arturo Alfonso Schomburg in Puerto Rico; his mother was a woman of African descent from the island of Saint Thomas, and his father was a merchant born in Germany. During his childhood, Schomburg lived for a time with his mother's family in the Virgin Islands, where he became interested in Caribbean political movements, especially those of Puerto Rico, Cuba, and Haiti. He arrived in New York City in 1891 and immediately involved himself in Cuban and Puerto Rican working-class communities, attending the inspiring lectures of José Martí and participating in Antillean political movements. Schomburg himself helped to organize the Las Dos Antillas (The Two Antilles) Club, which pledged to "actively assist in the independence of Cuba and Puerto Rico." On a visit related to club business in New Orleans in 1892, Schomburg came into contact with the African-American community there and, after the events of 1898, began to shift his allegiances from Puerto Rican liberation to the problems of African Americans in the United States.

Schomburg is best known for his extraordinary work as a bibliophile and as a curator of one of the world's largest collections of African-American books, prints, and artifacts. By 1926, through his travels and research he had amassed more than five thousand books, three thousand manuscripts, two thousand etchings, and several thousand pamphlets. His private collection eventually became the Schomburg Center for Research in Black Culture in New York City, a prestigious repository of material on African-American cultural life and a monument to Africanness as well as to a hemispheric appreciation of America.

Schomburg wrote numerous articles in journals and newspapers in the United States and elsewhere, including the following piece on the black Puerto Rican painter José Campeche. In it Schomburg reveals his dedication to recognizing the important role of African peoples in the Americas and unmasking the "conspiracy of silence" concerning the "lost black Hispanic heritage" he was dedicated to recovering.

José Campeche, 1752-1809: A Puerto Rico Negro Painter

Imagine a boy living in the city of his birth and not knowing who was the most noted native painter! It is true the fact was recorded on a marble tablet duly inscribed and placed on the wall of a building where it could easily be read. However, the inhabitants of San Juan knew but little of the man thus honored. The white Spaniards who knew, spoke not of the man's antecedents. A conspiracy of silence had been handed down through many decades and like a veil covered the canvases of this talented Puerto Rican. Today we understand the silence and know the meaning of it all. In Puerto Rico there lived an artist whose color prevented him from receiving the full recognition and enjoying the fame his genius merited.

On January 6, 1752, at San Juan, Puerto Rico, there was born a child to whom the parents gave the name of José. His father, Tomás Campeche, was a native; his mother, María Jordan, was from the Canary Islands. The early life of the father is mostly veiled in obscurity; little is known of him, except that he was a man of exemplary nature, who being a good painter and decorator found thereby a satisfactory means of supporting his family. The son was born on Cruz Street in the home of his parents. As boys wending our way to the schoolhouse located on the same street, we often noticed the large marble tablet some fifteen feet from the sidewalk, that to this day bespeaks with simplicity and dignity the great painter few other natives have excelled.

During his boyhood days, Campeche was known as excelling in clay modeling. His instinctive ability in design, his well-executed chalk and charcoal drawings on the city pavements near his home, were notable for their life-like fidelity. Clearly drawn in detail, animated with a vivid resemblance, each character depicted was easily recognized by the casual passerby.

Pencil in hand, José would trace on the pages of his notebook beautiful flowers, vivid shades of green grasses, lovely trees, and graceful rivers. It seemed as if he were carefully plucking from nature the secret forms and from the clouds and colors in their delicate tints, those indescribable, diaphanous shades that seem like revelry at dawn and at sunset. With these drawings from nature our artist devoted his thoughts to meditation; the evenings found him at home in further study of the day's work. His library was made up of a few works; the letter of Mengs,* the biography of the Spanish authority on paintings, Palomino,† and a few other books that could be borrowed in those early days.

In the year 1765, the population of Puerto Rico numbered about 44,833. Of this number 39,846 were free. In the capital, San Juan, there were only 3,562 of this class. Education on the island was almost sterile. The few schools which existed were all conducted by the Church.

In San Juan there were two classes of schools, distinguished as elementary and superior. In the latter, conducted in the Dominican Convent, our artist studied Latin, philosophy and grammar. A doctor taught him anatomy privately as an aid to the better study of the nude from life. Music came under the paternal discipline, and in time

* Antonio Rafael Mengs (1728–1779) was born in Bohemia. He was the portrait painter of August VI, Elector of Saxony and King of Poland. José Nicolás de Azara based his *Obras de Antonio Rafael Mengs* in Mengs' own notes on arts written in French, German, Italian and Spanish. Winckelman, the archaeologist, Mengs' friend, also based his *Historia del arte antiguo* on Mengs' aesthetic ideas, studies and advice. This work, which became a basic source on art, established the theory that beauty is the ultimate goal of art.

† Palomino de Castro y Velasco (Acisclo Antonio, c. 1653–1725), Spanish painter and art critic. His paintings were some of the best works produced in his epoch. He painted big frescoes in Valencia, Granada, Salamanca and El Paular. In *Museo pictórico y escala óptica* he expounded clearly and systematically all the elements involved in the art of painting. This work has two volumes of biographies of painters.

he became an adept oboe player and organ teacher. The flute was his favorite instrument for recreation. About 1780 Tomás Campeche died and José took command of the family ship and held the tiller until the end of his life, 1809. He succeeded his father as music teacher in the Carmelite Chapel, for which services he was paid from the public treasury until his death.

José Campeche rose by degrees in the scale of human achievement. It was by dint of hard work that he won recognition as an artist. He became known and admired, even beyond the shores of his own home. Campeche's paintings are recognized as excelling in correct drawing, coloring which distinguishes them from others, somewhat in the pleasant tones of Correggio. His delicate Virgins seem to float in the air; the exquisite graces and the exactness of the garments and mantles are much spoken of by his critics. Salvador Brau the historian, speaking at a celebration held in honor of another Negro, Rafael Cordero, the father of public instruction, mentions the evil effects of race distinction which prevented the Virgins of Campeche from enjoying a full measure of glory.

A marvelous likeness of Governor Ramón de Castro is in the City Hall of San Juan. All natives point with pride to this picture. In the convent of San Francisco de Asís is a painting known as "Nuestra Señora de los Angeles," a wonderful picture. A canvas, "La Virgen de los Dolores," owned by Juan C. Noa, was highly admired by Juan Fagundo, a native of Spain, who came to Puerto Rico in the year 1811, and taught drawing for painters in the Economic Society of the country.

Another visitor to Puerto Rico was the Spanish court painter, Luis Paredes, who having displeased his king, was expatriated. This eminent painter, like Cimabue, who discovered in the neighborhood of Florence a man who afterwards became the famous Giotti, helped Campeche to perfect his work and to attain a permanent place in the galaxy of great artists.

Paredes was so impressed with the native painter's brush that he engaged him to paint a portrait of him (Paredes) in native costume and forwarded the picture to his king, explaining the singular work of the man who had never seen a master painting. The Spanish king made inquiries of his talented subject and offered him, through Paredes, a handsome retainer and permanent position at his court. All these honors Campeche eventually refused.

There were other Europeans interested in the Puerto Rican painter. It is said an Englishman who saw and admired some of the canvases in the possession of James Daly, a resident of San Juan, invited Campeche to London at the princely salary of a thousand guineas. On this occasion, as well as others previously offered him, our artist consistently refused to accept any tender that would bring about separation from his country and from his sisters, for whom he always expressed great solicitude and love.

Rafael María de Labra y Cabrada, the most notable representative of the Spanish-American colonial possessions in the Cortes, or Spanish Parliament, was a man wholly devoted to the betterment of the proscribed people of Cuba and Puerto Rico. In 1870 there came from his pen a work entitled *La Brutalidad de los Negros* in which he asserted that the greatest painter of the island, one worthy of note, was the mulatto José Campeche of San Juan.

The funeral catafalques erected to render public honors to King Charles III and Pope Pius VI were the work of our artist. Many paintings of royalty, such as Charles IV, Fernando VII, Queen María Luisa, are in the Governor's House. Quite a number of paintings of former bishops can still be seen on the walls of the Bishop's Palace, and in many of the churches, chapels, and public institutions of the island may be found works by this artist. These include portraits of noted personages, historical and religious subjects, paintings of the Virgin and of the saints. Many are placed in inaccessible corners, others are so defaced by the action of the air and climate that it is almost impossible to procure copies of them.

In Puerto Rico there was little to excite the artist. Satisfied with his humble origin, he felt well taken care of. No entanglements such as are recorded of other great artists can be charged to José Campeche. It can be said that his life was clean and lovable. The testimony of the masses has presented him as a remarkable man "worthy as an artist, but priceless as an honest man." Posterity has preserved those words; Campeche lives in our mind as the embodiment of a moral man. It has been said his education was monachal and limited; however, it influenced his life greatly, making him feel less keenly the effect of subordination that existed in those days.

José Campeche lived as an example of virtue. His sisters loved him dearly, for he provided for all their necessities. Eventually they also passed away to the greater circle unknown to us, into that light which leads us to the Great Beyond.

José Campeche closed his eyes and was buried in the Convent of Santo Tomás de Aquino, for he was a faithful follower of the order of Predicadores and a professed brother of the third order of Santo Domingo. The Right Reverend Bishop of the diocese, in his eulogy delivered at the obsequies of the painter, printed in the official organ of the island, referring to his religious life said:

> His death, which took place on November 7th, has been deeply felt by all the inhabitants of this island, from the highest to the lowest, who admired his virtues and Christian example. Puerto Rico lost one of its illustrious sons and in the exercise of his faculties one of the most eminent. We cry for the lost one as an honored citizen and hope that in heaven he will receive the due and just recompense for his deeds and religious merits.

The Bishop concluded his panegyric with the following pregnant reflection:

> Happy is the man who lives for an ideal. This material life is so brief and worth so little when not employed in doing good. It is interesting to note, that the only occupation worthy of our thought and heart is that which is numbered doing good to others, as a source and occupation that will make us happy in the bosom of bitterness.

Campeche died poor and left his sisters in adversity. His home on Cruz Street was burdened with mortgages and in a dilapidated condition. A petition for a pension to Campeche's sisters Lucia and Maria was presented to His Catholic Majesty, the King, on February 28, 1810. The petition was granted.

The building with the marble tablet noted above, which many of us as children saw and read going to the primary school on Cruz Street, is still standing, a gift of the Sociedad Económica de Amigos del País, to commemorate a beautifully useful life devoted to art and morality. [1934]

Bernardo Vega was born in 1885 in Puerto Rico. He was a charter member of the Socialist Party and a *tabaquero;* the cigar workers were among the most politically advanced segments of the Puerto Rican working class. His early political involvement carried over to his experiences as a community leader in New York City, where he arrived in 1916. *Memoirs of Bernardo Vega* is an account of the following three decades of his life to the aftermath of World War II. At that time there began the huge diaspora of Puerto Rican emigrants to the United States and the ghettoization of that community in urban *barrios*.

The earlier period of the Puerto Rican community in New York, the era of the "pioneers," was virtually neglected until Vega's account — published in 1977, more than a decade after his death in 1965 — stimulated scholars to research the period. The book is considered an important resource for information concerning the late-nineteenth-century Caribbean, the political fervor of such Cuban and Puerto Rican leaders as José Martí and Eugenio María de Hostos, and the high level of political and worker organization among the Caribbean immigrant community in the United States.

Like other Caribbean immigrants of the period, Bernardo Vega envisioned independence not just for Puerto Rico but for Cuba and the rest of the Antilles. But after witnessing the great mix of nationalities who shared similar problems as workers in the New York metropolis, Vega's political perspective broadened even further. He was one of the first Latino writers to introduce the now familiar themes of unemployment, discrimination, social alienation, and similar experiences (Jesús Colón's *A Puerto Rican in New York*, 1961, is another example). Vega's *Memoirs* are written from a decentered perspective, stretching beyond narrow national identification to a larger Latino and minority solidarity. While his political consciousness may have distinguished Vega from the average immigrant of his time, his ideas have played an important role in the evolution of a Latino tradition.

Even as he was preparing to return to Puerto Rico in the late 1940s, Vega's attention was riveted by the "third party" being formed in the United States by Henry A. Wallace — "a man who enjoys the sympathies of Puerto Ricans, Chicanos, and of all the Hispanic and Latin American sectors of the population. It would be a real contribution to start organizing their support. It would be a great opportunity to help our people."

from **Memoirs of Bernardo Vega**

The Customs and Traditions of the Tabaqueros *and What It Was Like to Work in a Cigar Factory in New York City*

Since the day we had our street clothes stolen and had to come home from work in rags, Pepe and I started thinking of quitting work at the munitions plant. But we had no other job in mind, or time to look for one. One day I found Pepe gloomier than a rooster after a cockfight. I tried to console him, but he just broke down, crying his heart out. The job was even more unbearable for him than it was for me. He got sick and gave up.

I kept up that fierce daily battle for another few weeks. But one morning I caught sight of a bunch of rags on fire alongside a powder keg and, had I not grabbed an extinguisher and put out the fire just in time, right there and then I might have taken leave of the world of the living.

For fear of losing my skin, time had come to give notice. Payday was every two weeks, and I had worked only half that. I decided to leave that day no matter what, though I wanted to be sure of collecting what was due me. The only way I could see was to pick a fight with someone and force them to fire me. I chose as my victim the first co-worker who showed up. The foreman pulled us apart and took us to the office to fire us both. Once I got my pay, I assured the foreman that it was I who had started the trouble and that the other guy was innocent. The foreman shouted, "You son of a bitch!" That was the first time, though certainly not the last, that I was called by that name in the United States.

One day a few weeks later I picked up the morning newspaper and felt my heart skip a beat — that same plant had been blown to bits in an explosion!

With what savings I had I bought myself some clothes for winter. Having no notion yet what that season would demand, I made the sinful mistake of buying two loud colored suits and an equally flashy overcoat. Friends who had already spent a few winters in New York made fun of my new purchases. So there I was, after all that hardship, in the same old straits — flat broke and without the clothes I needed for winter.

It took El Salvaje, as Ramón Quiñones — another fellow townsman from Cayey and a first-rate *tabaquero* — was called, to get me out of my predicament. Though gentle and good-hearted, he would resort to his fists at the slightest provocation, and was always quick to seize the limelight. He never carried firearms, but tried to solve all his problems with his bare hands. That's how he got the nickname "Wild Man."

One day my friend El Salvaje took me down to Fuentes & Co., a cigar factory located on Pearl Street, near Fulton Street, in lower Manhattan. I started work immediately, but within a week they had marked down the price of my make of cigar, and I quit.* When El Salvaje found out, he went down to the shop in person and, as was his custom, had it out with the foreman with his bare fists. He had to pay a fine to stop them from locking him up.

As for me, I was actually lucky to leave that job. A few days later I found work at another cigar factory, El Morito ("The Little Moor"), on 86th Street off Third Avenue, a few steps from where I was living. At that wonderful place I struck up friendships with a lot of Cubans, Spaniards, and some fellow countrymen, all of whom awakened in me an eagerness to study. Among them, two Cubans remain prominently in my mind. One of them, Juan Bonilla, had been a close friend of José Martí. He was a noted orator and one of the editors of *Patria,* the newspaper founded in New York by the Apostle of the Cuban Revolution himself. The other was T. de Castro Palomino, a man of vast erudition, who had also gained renown for his role in the liberation struggles of the Antilles.

Of the Spaniards I remember fondly Maximiliano Olay, still hardly more than a boy in those years, who had had to flee Spain to escape charges of complicity in an anarchist assassination of a lead-

---

* Cigar prices varied according to the "make" or *vitola* — the quality of the tobacco and the cigarmakers' reputation. The *vitola* was indicated by the cigar ring.

Cigar factories ranged in size from the *chinchal* (workshop), which might include no more than the master cigarmaker and two or three apprentices, to *fábricas* (factories), which employed from fifty to four hundred workers. Some *fábricas* engaged in all phases of cigar production; in others, called *despalillados,* most of the workers were women, who separated the tobacco leaves from the stems. *Trans.*

ing political figure. He was a loyal friend of many Puerto Rican migrants; more than once I heard him claim that destiny had made him a brother of the Puerto Ricans, for one of them had once saved his life.

Maximiliano was born in Collota, a village in the Asturian mountains of Spain. Two of the Guardia Civil on duty in his town were from Puerto Rico. They were friends of his family, who had watched him grow up from early childhood. As a young man he got himself into serious trouble for political activities. He was arrested and the charges against him would have cost him his head. But one of the Guardia Civil hid him and arranged for his escape. He crossed the border into France and managed to get away to New York. "Now you see why all Puerto Ricans are my brothers," Maximiliano would say.

Another good Spaniard and dear friend of Puerto Ricans was Rufino Alonso, whom they used to call Primo Bruto ("Dumb Cousin"). Another of the Puerto Ricans I got to know there and still remember was Juan Hernández, the director of the workers' paper *El Internacional*. There was also the fine writer Enrique Rosario Ortiz, and J. Navas, Tomás Flores, Francisco Guevara, Ramón Rodríguez, Matías Nieves — known as El Cojo Ravelo ("Limping Ravelo") — all of whom were active in the cigarworkers' struggle and in the Hispanic community in general.

With workers of this caliber, El Morito seemed like a university. At the time the official "reader" was Fernando García. He would read to us for one hour in the morning and one in the afternoon. He dedicated the morning session to current news and events of the day, which he received from the latest wireless information bulletins. The afternoon sessions were devoted to more substantial readings of a political and literary nature. A Committee on Reading suggested the books to be read, and their recommendations were voted on by all the workers in the shop. The readings alternated between works of philosophical, political, or scientific interest, and novels, chosen from the writings of Zola, Dumas, Victor Hugo, Flaubert, Jules Verne, Pierre Loti, Vargas Vila, Pérez Galdós, Palacio Valdés, Dostoyevsky, Gogol, Gorky, or Tolstoy. All these authors were well known to the cigarworkers at the time.

It used to be that a factory reader would choose the texts himself, and they were mostly light reading, like the novels of Pérez Escrich, Luis Val, and the like. But as they developed politically, the workers had more and more to say in the selection. Their preference for works of social theory won out. From then on the readings were most often from books by Gustave LeBon, Ludwig Buchner, Darwin, Marx, Engels, Bakunin . . . And let me tell you, I never knew a single *tabaquero* who fell asleep.

The institution of factory readings made the *tabaqueros* into the most enlightened sector of the working class. The practice began in the factories of Viñas & Co., in Bejucal, Cuba, around 1864. Of course there were readings before then, but they weren't daily. Emigrants to Key West and Tampa introduced the practice into the United States around 1869 — at least, I was told that in that year the shop owned by Martínez Ibor in Key West had an official reader.

In Puerto Rico the practice spread with the development of cigar production, and it was Cubans and Puerto Ricans who brought it to New York. It is safe to say that there were no factories with Hispanic cigarworkers without a reader. Things were different in English-speaking shops where, as far as I know, no such readings took place.

During the readings at "El Morito" and other factories, silence reigned supreme — it was almost like being in church. Whenever we got excited about a certain passage we showed our appreciation by tapping our tobacco cutters on the work tables. Our applause resounded from one end of the shop to the other. Especially when it came to polemical matters no one wanted to miss a word. Whenever someone on the other side of the room had trouble hearing, he would let it be known and the reader would raise his voice and repeat the whole passage in question.

At the end of each session there would be a discussion of what had been read. Conversation went from one table to another without our interrupting our work. Though nobody was formally leading the discussion, everyone took turns speaking. When some controversy remained unresolved and each side would stick to a point of view, one of the more educated workers would act as arbiter. And should dates or questions of fact provoke discussion, there was always someone who insisted on going to the *mataburros* or "donkey-slayers" — that's what we called reference books.

It was not uncommon for one of the workers to have an encyclopedia right there on his worktable. That's how it was at El Morito, where Juan Hernández, Palomino, Bonilla, Rosario, and young Olay stood out as the arbiters of discussion. And when a point of contention escaped even their knowledge, the dogfight, as we used to call it, was laid to rest by appealing to the authority of the *mataburro*.

I remember times when a *tabaquero* would get so worked up defending his position that he didn't mind losing an hour's work — it was piecework — trying to prove his point. He would quote from the books at hand, and if there weren't any in the shop he'd come back the next day with books from home, or from the public library. The main issues in these discussions centered around different trends in the socialist and anarchist movements.

In those years of World War I, a central topic was imperialism and its relation to pacifism. In El Morito we had just been reading Henri Barbusse's *Le feu (Under Fire)*. The hair-raising depiction of life in the trenches gave rise to an endless discussion among the socialists, anarchists, and the handful of Germanophiles in the factory. Earlier we had read *La Hyene enragée (The Trial of the Barbarians)* by Pierre Loti, one of the writers often read to pass the time. But this particular book did a great deal to disarm the pacifists. The forceful description of the ruins of Rheims and Arras, the destructive avalanche of the Kaiser's soldiers, so graphically depicted, stirred us to thoughts of revenge and gained our deepest sympathy for the Allies. Just like so many of our comrades in both France and Germany, we fell prey to the call to "defend the fatherland," losing sight of the proletarian internationalism on which socialism is founded. Needless to say, Lenin and Bolshevism were still totally unknown in New York at the time.

When the Catholic newspapers in France took up their campaign against Marx and Marxism, we read the rigorous defense made by the socialist Jean Longuet. His articles kindled lively debates among the *tabaqueros*. For a while the sentiment in defense of France, inspired by Barbusse and Loti, began to lose support. The most militant pacifists among us struck back by arguing: "The French and the Germans both represent imperialist capitalism. We workers should not favor either one of them!" But this revolutionary position was again undermined by the reading of the Manifesto of March 1916, signed by the leaders of pacifist internationalism—Jean Grave, Carlo Malato, Paul Reclus, and Peter Kropotkin. This declaration struck a mortal blow to the worldwide anti-imperialist movement. "To talk of peace," it read, "is to play into the hands of the German government. . . . Teutonic aggression is a threat not only to our hopes for social emancipation but to human progress in general. For that reason we, who are antimilitarists, archenemies of war, and ardent partisans of peace and brotherhood among all nations, stand alongside of those who resist."

"Those who resist," of course, were the French. As a result, a growing current of Francophilia spread among socialists. A great majority of *tabaqueros* saw France as the standardbearer of democracy and progress, if not of socialism.

The dominant trend among North American socialists, however, and perhaps among the people of the United States in general, was neutrality. The leading pacifist and anarchist among the Spanish-speaking workers in New York was Pedro Esteves, who put out the paper *Cultura Proletaria*. As I mentioned before, most of the *tabaqueros* believed that the Germans had to be defeated. Many of them enlisted in the French army. Outstanding among them were Juan Sanz and Mario César Miranda, two leaders of the workers' movement who left Puerto Rico and were killed in combat in the first battle of Verdun. Florencio Lumbano, a Puerto Rican cigarworker in New York, also fell on the battlefields of France. Another *tabaquero* to take up arms was Justo Baerga. Years later I was told that he had been seen, old and sickly, in Marseilles.

Many, in fact, are the Puerto Ricans who have fought in defense of other countries. Perhaps for that reason, they have found themselves so alone in their own land. It was right there in El Morito that I first heard of the role of the *tabaqueros* in the Cuban wars of independence. There, too, I began to learn of the distinguished contribution our countrymen made to the Cuban revolution. I heard many true stories from the lips of Juan Bonilla and Castro Palomino, who had experienced them first hand. From then on, I was determined to write an account of the participation of Puerto Ricans in the Cuban independence struggle, which after all was a struggle for the independence of Puerto Rico as well.

But life among the *tabaqueros* was not all serious and sober.

There was a lot of fun too, especially on the part of the Cuban comrades. Many were the times that, after a stormy discussion, someone would take his turn by telling a hilarious joke. Right away tempers would cool down and the whole shop would burst out laughing.

None of the factories was without its happy-go-lucky fellow who would spend the whole time cracking jokes. In El Morito our man of good cheer was a Cuban named Angelito, who was known for how little work he did. He would get to the shop in the morning, take his place at his worktable, roll a cigar, light it, and then go change his clothes. When he returned to his table he would take the cigar from his mouth and tell his first joke. The co-workers nearest him would laugh, and after every cigar he'd tell another joke. He would announce when he had made enough cigars to cover that day's rent. Then he'd set out to roll enough to take care of his expenses. Once this goal was reached, he wouldn't make one more cigar, but would leave his workplace, wash up, get dressed, and head for the Broadway theaters.

A good-looking man, Angelito was tall and slender. He had a charming face and was an elegant dresser. He had arrived in the United States with a single, fixed idea in mind, which he admitted openly to anyone who would listen: he wanted to hook up with a rich woman. Pursuing his prey, he would walk up and down the streets, looking, as he himself would say, for his lottery prize. And the truth is that it didn't take him long to find it. A few months after I started at El Morito he landed a rich girl, who was beautiful and a violinist to boot. He married her and lived — in his own words — like a prince. But he never forgot us: time and again he would show up at the shop to tell us of his exploits and bless us with the latest addition to his vast repertoire of jokes.

Around that time news reached us at El Morito of a major strike in the sugar industry in Puerto Rico. A call went out for a rally in solidarity with the strikers. It took place on 85th Street near Lexington Avenue, and was attended by over a hundred *tabaqueros*, mostly Puerto Ricans. Santiago Rodríguez presided, and Juan Fonseca served as secretary. Many of those attending stood up to speak, including Ventura Mijón, Herminio Colón, Angel María Dieppa, Enrique Plaza, Pedro San Miguel, Miguel Rivera, Alfonso Dieppa, Rafael Correa, and Antonio Vega. The last mentioned immediately attracted my attention because of the way he spoke, and even more because of his appearance.

While I was listening to Antonio Vega I recalled how my father used to talk all the time about his lost brother, who had never been seen or heard from since he was very young. I'm not sure if it was the memory that did it, but I know I felt deeply moved by the man who bore my last name. He was a tall fellow, with a broad forehead, a full head of gray hair, a big handle-bar mustache, green eyes, and an oval-shaped face. . . . When I went up to him he jumped to his feet with the ease of an ex-soldier and responded very courteously when I congratulated him for his speech. We then struck up a conversation, at the end of which we hugged each other emotionally. He was none other than my father's long-lost brother. [ca. 1944]

Translation of *Las memorias de Bernardo Vega* by Juan Flores

Josephina Niggli was born in 1910 near Hidalgo, Nuevo León, Mexico, where her Texan father and Virginian mother had been living since 1893. Niggli wrote a book of poems, two novels, a collection of short fiction, plays, and screenplays. She was one of the foremost screenwriters and teachers of playwrighting of her day; her most famous play is perhaps *Sunday Costs Five Pesos,* which was included in *Best One-Act Plays of 1938*. Niggli collaborated on the screen adaptation for MGM of her story sequence *Mexican Village,* which starred Ricardo Montalban and Pier Angeli. From the 1930s until her retirement, Niggli taught writing in North Carolina. In 1948 she published the novel *Step Down, Elder Brother,* and in 1964 a collection of experimental novellas. She died in 1983.

Because of her Swiss, Alsatian, and Irish ancestry, Niggli is often omitted from discussions of U.S. Latino literature. Much of her work focuses on Mexicans and Mexican Americans, however, and she has recently been more widely accepted as a significant part of the canon.

The following story, "The Chicken Coop," is taken from *Mexican Village*. The main character in the book, Bob Webster — half-Mexican, half-Anglo, rejected by his father because of his resemblance to an Indian — has come to the small town of Hidalgo to earn enough money to start an airline with a friend he met during World War I. Most of the stories focus on the townspeople, but the finale returns to Webster, who now seems to have become a permanent resident.

from **Mexican Village**

The Chicken Coop

God gave me bread so I wouldn't long for cake. — *Mexican proverb*

"May this hand wither on my arm before I sign the marriage contract!" shrieked Nena Santos, her back tense against the door of her house.

The November moonlight spilled a silver mist over the two young people. Andrés Treviño flung out his hand in a helpless gesture, his round face darkly creased between the brows. "But the house has been built, Nena. The finest house in the Gallineros [the 'chicken coop']. All the world says so."

Nena tossed her head. "You build a fine house for the world to admire, but one little request from me, and it is a closing of the hand. That Porfirio has drugged your senses with love of money."

"That is a wicked untruth!" Andrés took a step toward her and pushed one clenched hand against the shack's wooden wall. "Twenty pesos I paid for your wedding gown. Of fine white satin it is, with waxen orange blossoms for your hair. With twenty pesos I could have bought a young goat, but did you hear a complaint from my mouth? I ask you!"

"A wedding dress!" Nena snapped her fingers. "Every girl in the Gallineros comes to her husband with a white satin gown. But when I ask you for one little thing — one little grander thing — you wail of money and the need to buy goats, while my heart — mine — the heart of your intended bride — breaks with longing for a thing of little size, a small thing, a thing no larger than your hand." Her eyes suddenly shone with tears, and the firm chin began to tremble.

"But, Nena," wailed Andrés, "of what good to you is a pair of shoes? You've never worn a pair in your life. You'll never wear them again. You say yourself they cost ten pesos — the same price as this lovely little goat I want to give you. And besides, a married man must be a man of property. Two stomachs hold more food than one stomach."

"Speak not to me of goats and stomachs and property. You yourself were at the wedding of Alma Orona. Are you less than Porfirio, the carver of wood? He bought her a pair of shoes. Shall all the world say that Alma Orona's wedding was grander than Nena Santos'?"

"In ten years," Andrés said stubbornly, "who will remember which wedding was the grander?"

"Indeed!" Nena buckled her hands on her hips and abandoned tears. "If I were as beautiful as María de las Garzas, you'd buy me a pair of shoes quickly enough."

"I'll hear no more of such stupidity," snapped Andrés. He, like all the men in the village, had learned from bitter experience that when María's name entered the conversation it was time to beat a hasty retreat. The fact that María lived alone in her house on the River Road and would have nothing to do with any individual from the five villages was of little importance. She was much too beautiful for the female population of the valley complacently to ignore.

Nena was not motivated by jealousy. She had merely introduced María's name as a flank attack. Now she struck straight to the center. Pulling her *rebozo* over her head, she opened the door of her house. "Hear my words, Andrés Treviño. No shoes to wear at my wedding, no wedding! My mouth has spoken!" Before the boy could answer, she retreated hastily into the house, slamming the door for emphasis.

Andrés pulled his straw hat over his eyes and stalked down the Avenue of Illustrious Men toward the Plaza of Independence. As he walked, his bare toes, strapped into flat brown sandals, scuffed at the powdery dust. Here he had been doing without sandals he really needed in order to buy that goat, while Nena calmly ordered shoes she would wear but once in her life. Perhaps he would be lucky and sell a young kid to the man from the shoe factory in Monterrey. In that case he could buy a pair of sandals from Abel, the next time the *árabe* trader passed through Hidalgo. Andrés lifted one foot and glared at it, then stamped it on the ground in punishment. His feet were so large, and Abel demanded two pesos for such a size in spite of fine bargaining. Porfirio was lucky. His feet were small. He had to pay only a peso and a half for his sandals. But then Porfirio was a wise man. He had chosen for himself a wife who knew the difference between a peso and a peso.

Perhaps the best thing to do was to go into the church and pray to the Blessed Lady for a miracle. Women understood women. The Sainted Mother might be able to convince Nena that shoes were of little importance where the buying of goats was concerned.

Andrés crossed the plaza and was just entering the churchyard when he saw Pablo, the goatherd, emerge from the pink-washed adobe temple. The round-faced boy frowned slightly and paused. Goatherds were necessary, of course, but Pablo had no right to come down from the hills and desecrate the church. A goatherd was the beloved of Grandfather Devil, and had no place in the churches of honest Christians.

Pablo waved his hand. "Eh, Andrés Treviño," he called, "Don Saturnino tells me your herd of goats increases by the month. Soon you will need a fine herder to care for them in the hills."

"That is true," said Andrés soberly. "I feed them along the river banks now, but the hot months will make them sicken for the hills."

"Add them to my flocks," said Pablo generously. "Don Timotéo won't mind. As for me, it is no trouble to watch yours as well as his."

"And the price?" asked Andrés suspiciously. One never knew when these lovers of the black-robed mountain witches would pull a fine trick on one.

Pablo rolled a corn-shuck cigarette between brown fingers. "The great ones are even now playing dominoes at Father Zacaya's. We could go to the priest's house and ask their opinion in the matter."

Andrés swung on one heel and started off toward the Residence. As a good Christian, it never occurred to him to allow this outcast to walk beside him. The wild men from the hills were cursed with a madness the townfolk could not understand. Father Zacaya said it was loneliness and pitied the herders, but the townfolk knew that the witches stole their souls for Grandfather Devil, and in exchange taught them the language of the goats.

There was, of course, a great social distinction between being an owner of goats and a herder. Fat complacent Timotéo Gonzalez, father to Pepe, the wild one, owned hundreds of goats. Andrés owned a very small flock that someday, he hoped, would develop into the finest herd between the Peak of the Ship's Prow and Saddle Mountain. But these men lived in the town, as proper Christians should. When Father Zacaya argued with the villagers about their attitudes toward the herders, they would merely shrug their shoulders and remind him of poor, insane John of God, the goatherd, whose soul the witches had stolen by forcing his blind sweetheart to fall over the river cliffs to her death.

But Andrés was not thinking of these things as he opened the Residence door and passed into the parlor with Pablo following at his heels like a brown shadow.

Seated around a small square table playing dominoes were the "great ones," the four rulers of Hidalgo. With his back toward the door sat Don Nacho, the mayor, his great stomach resting on his knees. To his right was Don Rosalío, his long, silky white beard flowing down over his narrow chest, and a sprig of orange blossoms from his beloved trees fastened on his lapel. Across from Don Rosalío sat the little Doctor, and the fourth man at the table was the white-haired Father Zacaya, spiritual head of the Sabinas Valley. He often said that the Devil had cursed him with a sense of humor. Lucky for him he possessed such a curse, or he could never have survived the eddying pool of village life.

These were the four men playing dominoes: science, the village government, the church, and the landed interest — absolute rulers of a town of one thousand inhabitants. With the exception of Don Nacho, they were not a part of the town's duly elected board of *regidores,* or administrators. Of these Don Nacho was the *alcalde primero,* that is, the municipal president. Meek little Don Ernesto, much bullied by Don Nacho, was the *alcalde segundo,* or secretary. The treasury was headed by Don Martiniano Cantú, whom no one liked very much, but he could add a column of figures without difficulty, and that was the important thing. Don Genaro was the civil judge. He had held this office for years, dealing out impartial but wise justice. He also performed all the civil marriages, for Mexican couples must be married twice: once according to the laws of the Republic, and once according to the laws of the church. Don Genaro had a full, rich voice, and he loved to read the marriage service, being careful to affect a lisping "z" and a rolled double "l" in the best Castilian tradition, so that the ceremony acquired a grandiloquent effect. The final member of the *regidores* was one-armed Don Ricardo, *inspector de policía,* a title in which he took much pride.

But these men were cold and aloof in their dignity of office. Only Don Nacho had been able to bridge the gap between the municipality and the individual. For he knew that a town has problems which the impersonal law can neither understand nor solve. And so it was arranged long ago that the administration should answer the needs of the state, but the four men around the domino table answered the needs of the people.

Here was not so much a capitalistic system as a patriarchy. When any villager was in trouble — from the dancing young Anita O'Malley to John of God, the goatherd — he came to one or all of these four men, perfectly confident that the problem would be taken off of his shoulders and solved to complete satisfaction. The only one who never came was María de las Garzas — the beautiful golden María of the River Road. But she was a lost wild creature whom not even these four wise men could save.

It was Father Zacaya who first noticed Andrés standing shyly just inside the room, his broad-brimmed straw hat clutched tightly between his hot, nervous hands.

"Eh, Andrés, how goes the world with you?"

"Sadly, Father, sadly."

"Are those proper words for an intended bridegroom to speak?" boomed Don Nacho, his great voice bounding back from the low-ceilinged walls.

"Who's that standing behind you?" demanded the little Doctor sharply. Then, recognizing Pablo, he smiled. Like Father Zacaya he had no fear of goatherds. "Come in, Pablo. Even a Devil's disciple can enter a priest's house, eh, Father?"

"Of course, Pablo. I didn't see you standing out there." Father Zacaya smiled gently at the two boys, thinking how much loneliness could age a man. Pablo was two years younger than Andrés, but he appeared at least five years older.

Pablo slipped past Andrés and paused at Don Rosalío's shoulder. "Good evening, my ancient ones. This young rooster has many goats. I thought I might take them up to the hills with Don Timotéo's herd in the spring, as this friend is a poor one and without money to hire a private herder."

The little Doctor looked gravely across the tops of his glasses at the round-faced boy. "Come into the circle of lamplight, Andrés. I do not like to speak with shadows."

Andrés moved slowly toward the table, his feet sliding reluctantly across the blue tiled floor. Sensing the boy's shyness, Father Zacaya poured a glass of wine from the decanter at his elbow and pushed it across the table.

"A bit of sherry will chase the November moonlight from your brain, my son."

"Thank you, Father." Andrés drank the wine and wiped his mouth politely on his sleeve. "This idea of the goats was Pablo's, not mine."

"And a good idea it is," Don Nacho boomed loudly. "Timotéo Gonzalez, that worthless man of many lies and magnificent cheeses, was telling me you are buying a goat from him every month now. He says you were looking at a fine new kid this morning."

"I was," acknowledged Andrés miserably, "but . . ." He paused and gravely replaced the wine glass on the table.

"But," prompted Don Rosalío, "the price was too high, eh?"

"That Timotéo Gonzalez is a robber," said the little Doctor sharply. "The mayor of El Carmen was telling me just today that Abel, the *árabe,* has more of a conscience than this same Timotéo Gonzalez."

"Oh, no, little Doctor," protested Andrés. "Don Timotéo asked a fair price — just ten pesos for a fine kid."

"A good price," agreed Don Rosalío, blowing out his full lips and sucking them in again. "What then is the difficulty in the sale?"

Thankful for an opportunity to recite his woes, Andrés poured forth the story of Nena and the shoes. "Women are strange creatures," he finished sadly. "She's never owned a pair of shoes. Why should she want them now? And shoes are items of expense. And the little goat of Don Timotéo . . . such a pretty creature." He sighed and rocked back on his heels. "It was in my mind to present it to Nena for her very own. But now — I am only a man. Who am I to understand the mind of a woman?"

For a moment after the question there was silence in the room. Into each man's mind sprang suddenly an individual image. Father Zacaya thought of the red-haired Anita O'Malley. What strange inheritance from Irish father and Mexican mother set her feet to dancing and her spirit to rebellion against all authority?

Don Nacho thought of his homely daughter Chela and her gift of seeing beyond the actions of men to the minds that controlled them. It would need a man of many mysteries to hold Chela's interest for very long. And Chela was too homely to attract many men.

Don Rosalío thought of his dead wife and the strange thing she had said to him just before she died: "Leave this Spain and return to your Mexican village. Hidalgo is your true wife." She was right, of course. But how had she understood the love of a Mexican for his land, and she Spanish born and bred? Of course, the death sight had been on her eyes . . .

The little Doctor thought of María de las Garzas, María of the River Road. Why did she stay in the valley? With her blond beauty she could command the Republic. Instead, she lived in the cliff caves and watched the people of the five villages travel back and forth — watched them not with the humility of an outcast, which she was, but with the arrogance of the great lady of the village, which she was not.

Pablo, the goatherd, the man from the hills, thought not of one woman but of all the village girls. He thought of the patient Alma Orona; of Chela, Don Nacho's homely daughter; of the plump, stubborn Nena Santos. He thought briefly of the red-haired, Irish-eyed Anita O'Malley, and all the rest of them, with their narrow, proscribed lives. Which one had hidden in her that love of wild freedom which would carry her out of the safety of the village to the thin, cool wind of the hills? None of them? All of them? Even Alma Orona had slanted a glance toward him from beneath demurely lowered lashes. Women were strange creatures, indeed, he thought, preferring the safety of the pen, yet peering always between the bars toward the dangerous open fields.

It was Father Zacaya who broke the silence. "Andrés, your problem involves its difficulties. On one side is a wedding plus ten pesos spent for foolishness. On the other is no wedding plus a goat."

"The question is," added Don Rosalío gravely, "which is most important: Nena or the goat?"

"But they are both important, Don Rosalío," insisted Andrés. "Surely you can understand my difficulty, Don Nacho."

"I understand this," said Don Nacho firmly. "I speak as a man possessed of both a wife and a daughter. If you give in to her now, there will be no stopping her. She will rule you into the narrow width of your coffin."

"But Nena is a stubborn one," said the little Doctor. "I once tried to vaccinate her. After she broke three needles, her mother had to tie her to a chair before I could apply the serum. If Nena says, 'No shoes, no wedding,' she means, 'No shoes, no wedding.' "

"If women were only creatures of logic," sighed Father Zacaya, recalling some of Anita O'Malley's comments when he was trying to teach her her catechism.

"That is the true difficulty," agreed Don Nacho, thinking of his daughter Chela.

"If you want to marry Nena," said Don Rosalío, passing his hand delicately down the length of his white beard, "you'll have to plan on buying the goat some other time."

"But ten pesos is a good price for a goat," protested Andrés. "Maybe two years will pass or three before I can buy another at such a price. And Don Timotéo is a man of business. If he can't sell it to me, he will offer it to the mayor of El Carmen, or the mayor of Mina."

"Wait a moment." Pablo bent forward, his broad shoulders heavy in the shadowy light. "To whom do you sell your goats to make your profit?"

"To the butcher."

"But the little ones — the kids?"

"To the shoe factory in Monterrey," answered Andrés, puzzled by the question. The four seated men turned their heads silently toward the wind-tanned, wiry goatherd.

"Precisely," said Pablo. "You say you want to buy a goat. Nena wants a pair of shoes. To buy her the shoes would be unmanly, for all the world would know that this Nena Santos could command you at her pleasure."

"True words," agreed Andrés. "But I love Nena. I want to marry her."

"Then buy her the shoes."

"But . . ." began Andrés.

"Not as shoes," said Pablo quickly, "but as a goat."

"What's that?" snorted Don Nacho. And Don Rosalío and Father Zacaya hastily covered their grinning mouths with their hands.

The little Doctor frowned in perplexity. Andrés' mouth opened slightly and his head dipped to one side as he tried to understand Pablo's words.

The goatherd pushed closer to the table as he warmed to his argument. "Don't you understand? Shoes are made out of kidskin. Therefore when you buy the shoes you are really buying a goat — a dead goat, that is true — but still a goat."

"Magnificent," breathed Don Nacho. The little Doctor abruptly turned in his chair and hid his face against his palm.

"Of what good," demanded Andrés angrily, "is a dead goat to me, and I am owner of live ones?"

"You want to marry Nena, don't you?"

"Naturally."

"Yet you want to appear a man in the eyes of the world?"

"Very true."

"Buy her the shoes, call them two dead goats, you will marry Nena, and all the world will applaud your cleverness." Pablo, having settled the question, squatted down against the wall.

Andrés thrust out his chin. "But the live goat of Timotéo Gonzalez — what about it?"

"A man fool enough to marry," said Pablo, the goatherd, "can not expect to own the world."

"Buy the shoes, Andrés," said Don Rosalío. "You are a boy of ambition. Foolish now and then, but the village is proud of you. We are all proud of you. And as for the goat — the little Doctor will give you this same one for a wedding present."

"I," sputtered the little Doctor. "I — ten pesos — a goat — I?"

"Certainly. Andrés will pay you enough in childbirths to make it up to you."

The men laughed loudly as the lamplight intensified the crimson of Andrés' face.

"Abel, the *árabe,* will be pleased to make such a fine sale of a pair of shoes," rumbled Don Nacho.

"Abel, the *árabe,* has gone to Torreón," said Pablo. "He told me this morning he would be gone a month."

"And my wedding ten days off!" gasped Andrés. "If he is gone — where can I buy the shoes?"

"In Monterrey," suggested Father Zacaya.

"And shoes from Monterrey would be a grand thing in Nena's eyes," slyly agreed Don Nacho.

"But Monterrey is a day's journey by horse. And a train ticket costs a peso." Andrés drew in a deep sobbing breath. "Is there no end to this spending of money?"

"Father Zacaya goes in to Monterrey on Wednesday," said the little Doctor softly.

As though pulled by one string, four faces swung around toward the white-haired priest. Father Zacaya hastily pushed back his chair and stood up. "One moment, my little ones. I have never bought a pair of woman's shoes in my life. I . . ."

"No arguments," rumbled Don Nacho. "All you have to do is tell the clerk the size you want and put down the money. It is of a sweet simplicity."

"The problem is finished," said Don Rosalío firmly. "Pablo, take Andrés away from here and arrange about the summer herding. I, myself, will speak with Timotéo Gonzalez about the inclusion of Andrés' herd with his."

"The price," began Andrés.

"The price will be two pesos. This also I will arrange."

Both knew that the two pesos meant nothing to Don Timotéo, but to Andrés they represented his position as a man of business.

"Now leave us," said the little Doctor. "We four are concerned with the importance of dominoes."

Pablo obediently put his hand under Andrés' elbow and guided the boy from the room. As they emerged from the house into the quiet starlit street, a girl hurried toward them down the Street of the Hidden Water and with a murmured greeting to the two boys, slipped through the dark entrance of the O'Malley house next door.

Andrés looked after her and shook his head in disapproval. "My Nena is trouble enough. I thank the Blessed Saints I'm not to marry Anita O'Malley — and she out alone at this hour of the night."

"Anita O'Malley," said Pablo thoughtfully. "The name makes a rhythm on the tongue."

"What's that you say?" Andrés peered suspiciously at him through the silvered darkness.

Pablo shrugged his shoulders. "Nothing," he said easily, "and a good night to you, Andrés Treviño. I will see you at your wedding." He had learned long ago that goatherds were not permitted to make comments about the town girls. Hooking his hands in his pockets, Pablo walked swiftly across the plaza and up the Avenue of Illustrious Men to the Street of the Cañon. In his own mind he repeated the name of Anita O'Malley. He was right. It did make a rhythm on the tongue.

On Wednesday morning Andrés hurried to the railroad station, a converted freight car near the blackened skeleton that was all the Revolution had left of Hidalgo's fine brick train platform. Near it was the water tank where the thirsty engines drank their fill before chugging southwest to Torreón in the evenings, or northeast to Monterrey in the mornings.

The passage of the slow-moving train was a social event. Girls with their hair rigidly set in water-wave combs, boys lounging loose-limbed on the saddles of restive horses, old men placidly chewing broom straws, old women balancing trays of chicken smothered in chili sauce, which they sold to the train's passengers, would begin to congregate at the first puff of approaching smoke in the distance. The single Pullman car was the focus of all attention. Eyes would peer curiously up at the wealthy tourists, who would as curiously stare back at the villagers. Most of the tourists were unaware of the first-, second-, and third-class coaches between the Pullman and the freight cars.

It was in the third-class coach that Father Zacaya thought, in all humility, he should ride. But Hidalgo, as the richest of the five valley towns, demanded that he should ride in elegance in the first class to uphold the village dignity. After much argument, the priest and the town compromised on second, and it was into this car that the white-haired man of God was climbing as Andrés caught up with him.

The usual village audience gaped like an audience in a theater as they watched Andrés, his hands moving in quick gesture, tell something to the priest. The train whistle was blowing too lustily for anyone to overhear the conversation, but Andrés' graphic hands and body were acting out the pantomime of buying something that was small. By afternoon the entire village knew of the meeting. Several friends had made a point of informing Nena about the morning's encounter. She smiled in secret satisfaction and went happily about the preparations for her wedding. When Nena met other girls from the Gallineros she would hold her head high with pride. She knew that she would be the only girl in the poor man's section to walk to her marriage in shoes. No girls from the wealthier districts — not even Evita Cantú or Anita O'Malley — would be any grander at their weddings than Nena Santos at hers in her white satin gown and her new white shoes.

And then an event occurred which drove all thought of Andrés Treviño's wedding and Nena Santos' shoes from the village mind. A telegram arrived at the railroad station which sent Don Nacho scurrying to Don Rosalío's. The two old friends read the words and both sat down to cry a little.

"After all these years," sighed Don Nacho. "Home again. Is it possible?"

"Candles in the church," said Don Rosalío. "Firecrackers on the plaza. And someone to open and air the great house."

"Tía Magdalena?"

"We could ask her."

They put on their hats and walked with slow dignity to Bob Webster's house, although their feet wanted to run. They found Bob standing in the street admiring his new door, which Porfirio had hung in place that morning. "Look," he said happily, "roses and lilies and intertwined vine leaves. Is it not a magnificent carving job? Porfirio has talent."

"Who cares for Porfirio?" Don Nacho boomed. "Friend Bob, we have news, great news. Where is Tía Magdalena?"

"Making sweet tamales and atole to celebrate the new door. What has happened?"

Instead of answering him, the old men pushed their way into the house. Tía was in the kitchen, punching raisins into a dough of mashed cornmeal, and expertly wrapping small chunks of the dough in corn-shucks. When she saw who her visitors were, she slid to her feet, and wiped her hands on her apron before folding them over her chest.

Don Nacho looked at Don Rosalío, who shrugged and stepped back. "You're the mayor. You ask her."

"But your tongue is smoother than mine, friend Rosalío."

"Nevertheless, you are the mayor."

Then, with one accord, their heads turned toward Bob. Each caught him by an arm and pulled him to the far side of the patio, while Tía watched them, her forehead creased in a frown. Their voices were only an indistinct mutter, but she saw Bob suddenly shake his head and try to pull away, while Don Rosalío and Don Nacho gripped him more firmly by the arms. Then Don Nacho made a sweeping gesture toward the southwest, and she suddenly realized what they wanted.

"So," she called out, "that black devil, Don Saturnino Castillo, returns to Hidalgo. Is that what you want to tell me?"

The men came toward her in relief.

"Precisely, Tía." Don Nacho mopped his forehead with a large red bandana. "And we thought — I mean Don Rosalío thought . . ."

"It was your idea, too," said the white-bearded man quickly. They both looked so pleadingly at Bob that he grinned.

"They want you to air out the house and see that there are servants and food waiting."

Tía's mouth shut in a straight line. Before she could answer, Don Rosalío said quickly, "The young Alejandro comes with him, grown now to man's size."

"Doña Elvira died in the birthing of Alejandro," said Tía slowly.

"Is that Alejandro's fault?" Don Nacho asked. "And Joaquín loved Alejandro."

"Yes," Tía said. "Joaquín loved him." She tapped her foot thoughtfully against the cement. "It is for Joaquín that I do this, you understand."

Don Nacho blew his nose with satisfaction. Bob promised to send women from the quarry to help clean, and by nightfall the news had spread from Mina to Topo Grande that Don Saturnino Castillo was coming home after eight years of exile.

On the morning of the arrival, people streamed into Hidalgo from River Road and Mina Road, some in carts, some riding on donkeys, on mules, on horses, and many on foot. Stands for eating were set up on the plaza, and Don Alonso's musicians played old melodies from the days before the Great Revolution, such as "Over the Waves" and "The Song of the Ripe Peach," and the ever beautiful "The River Lures Me."

When they heard this song, the people began to sing, the words seeming to shimmer in the air:

Shadow of our lord St. Peter,
The river lures me, the river lures me.

And thus does your great love
My love allure, my love allure.

Faintly in the distance came the sound of the train whistle, but no one moved toward the station. Eyes looked at eyes and turned away in delicacy. Don Saturnino was coming home, with Alejandro but without Joaquín. Better to let the proud old man weep in secret with sorrow for his lost oldest son, and with joy at being home again.

Don Nacho and Don Rosalío had gone to the great white house to welcome their old friend, whom Don Nacho, a good Revolutionist, had helped to escape the fury of Revolutionary soldiers.

Bob Webster, drawn to the plaza late that afternoon by the music and the crowd, found himself standing near Don Nacho's daughter Chela, who had mounted one of the benches and was looking about her with an intent air.

"Can I help you, Chela? Are you hunting your mother?"

She looked down at him. He was suddenly aware of her green eyes, startling under the thick black brows. She's not beautiful, he thought, but she has a strange, bone-drawn distinction. I wonder why I ever saw her as homely.

"Thank you, Don Bob," she murmured, jumping lightly to the ground. "I was hunting María of the River Road. I thought she might like to stand with me. She has few friends."

"You know," he said idly, "I've never seen María. Think of it. I'll have been here two years next March, and I've never seen the most beautiful woman in the Sabinas. I've even ridden past her house on the River Road, but I think she hides away in the cliff caves."

Chela shrugged. "She's very shy."

"What makes you think she'll be here today?"

"During the days of the Great Revolution she hid Don Saturnino and the young Alejandro, who was then, you understand, but thirteen years of age, on the Rancho Santo Tomás, until my father could make arrangements to pass them safely across the Río Bravo. I thought that in honor of this fiesta, she would come to the plaza, but . . ." She shrugged and laughed.

The little Doctor, pushing his way through the crowd, tapped

Bob on the shoulder. "The speaker's platform has been set up in front of the Boy's School. Come, friend Bob, let us take our places."

"But I'm not going to speak."

"Nor am I, thank the blessed saints. But we are important citizens." With a bow to Chela, he firmly led Bob across the plaza. "I want to ask you . . . As you know, I've bought a little goat for Andrés Treviño as a wedding present. Could you keep it in your patio until the wedding?"

"Me? Keep a goat?"

"I thought perhaps — I mean the village says — well, the village contends that it will not smell so bad if it stays near an eagle witch. Ay, don't laugh, friend Bob. As a man of science, I recognize your laughter. But as a man of the village, you comprehend, the goat does smell."

Bob bit down on his lower lip to control his merriment. "If Tía Magdalena can guarantee the lack of odor . . ."

"Good. I will speak to her this very . . ." He broke off and yelled, "Hurry, friend priest. Hurry! From the movement of the crowd, the procession must have started."

Father Zacaya collapsed on a platform chair, his black robes fluttering about his thin legs. "Such a morning," he groaned. "All the world wants to start cooking-fires inside the church. I've put Porfirio at the door to bar the entrance, and now he is furious with me because he wants to be in the procession. Why do people have to cook inside the church? Why can't they cook in the yard?"

"I don't know," the little Doctor answered moodily. "I've even seen them cooking inside the sainted Guadalupe Shrine outside the City. Don't ask me why village people do what they do."

Bob stood up. "Here they come."

The orchestra began to play the *Golondrina*. The crowd turned like a single entity to stare up the Street of the Forgotten Angel. Small boys in the churchyard set off strings of firecrackers that snapped into gray doughnuts of smoke.

First came Don Nacho, walking in stately dignity, the tall staff of his office in his left hand. Behind him, riding abreast, were Don Rosalío and Don Genaro, the civil judge. After them followed on foot a group of village men, Rubén, the candy-maker leading them as a general leads an army. Last of all was the Castillo victoria, the Castillo coat of arms on low curving doors, drawn by the proud Castillo blacks.

Bob stood on tiptoe, but even from the eminence of the platform it was difficult to see the carriage occupants because of the pressing crowd, which was shouting, "Long live the Castillos! Long live Hidalgo! Long live the Revolution! Long live the Republic!"

"I like that," sighed the little Doctor in Bob's ear. "The Castillos represent everything that the Revolution sought to destroy; so the people couple them in one long Hurrah! How wonderful is Mexico." The phrase came from his heart, and Bob smiled at him in sympathy.

The procession was coming down the Avenue of Independence. Small boys were clambering over the victoria's sides, and the candy-maker's regiment had dropped back to brush them off like flies.

Don Nacho climbed up on the platform, and bowed to the three men, and then turned and bowed to the people, who loudly applauded him. Don Rosalío and Don Genaro dismounted from their horses with a flourish, and also came up on the platform. Then the candy-maker's men linked arms to hold back the forward-rushing people as the victoria swung around the corner and came to a stop in front of the Boy's School.

Bob looked at the two occupants with curiosity. He realized that he was prejudiced against them by Tía Magdalena, and he tried to free his mind of resentment as he examined the courtly old man, with the closely clipped white hair and the delicate, finely chiseled features.

As Don Saturnino stepped to the platform and shook hands with all of them, Bob was surprised to notice that he and this Spanish gentleman had the same type of hand: narrow, flexible, with the little finger almost as long as the ring finger. He murmured his own name as the great man reached him, and once again, as on that morning when he first met Don Nacho, he had a feeling that the name of Webster, which he knew was his by right, should not be spoken in this clear Mexican air.

Then Don Saturnino was past him, and he found himself looking at Alejandro, who, since his older brother's disappearance, was now the young Castillo, and heir to all the valley lands. Bob had to look up at him, for Alejandro was tall, well over six feet, with the broad shoulders and narrow hips of a man who has lived much in the open. But his clear white skin lacked sun-warmth. His black hair, brushed back from a center part, had a soft wave in it, his eyes were a clear brown, and his Spanish nose was thin and finely cut. He, too, had the long narrow hands, and his grip on Bob's fingers was strong, lacking the loose Mexican formality.

His voice was rough and hoarse, but it had an oddly gentle timbre, as he said, "I hear that Tía Magdalena is your housekeeper." At Bob's nod, he smiled, and a light shone behind his eyes. "You will permit me to call upon her? I am very fond of her."

"Of course," Bob answered with surprise at this formality.

Don Saturnino's cold, remote tones sounded over his shoulders. "Be seated, Alejandro," and the young man sat down so quickly that Bob realized the reason for the request. Unspoken between them were the words: My father and Tía are enemies. Are you, too, an enemy of the House of Castillo?

Don Nacho opened the ceremony with a long speech on the glories of the Great Revolution, which he had made so often that when he paused for breath the people prompted him in a loud chant.

Then Don Genaro, the civil judge, stepped forward, and in his pure Castilian diction, harnessed to a Mexican accent, welcomed the great family home again.

As Don Saturnino advanced to the edge of the platform with many small bows, there was a shout of delight from the crowd. Chela, homely and awkward, but conscious of her dignity as daughter of the mayor, presented him with a large bouquet of white roses. The orchestra loudly played the applause music. Don Saturnino bowed again, but he was still not permitted to speak, for down the Avenue of Illustrious Men came the young Xavier riding on Bob's white horse.

Bob half rose from his chair in surprise, then shrugged and relaxed. Alejandro jumped to his feet. "A white horse! In this valley?"

A ripple of surprise passed over Don Saturnino's coldly perfect features. "A white horse," he murmured. "Is it possible?"

Don Nacho began a quick explanation, with many gestures toward Bob, but no one was paying him any attention. All eyes were focused on the young Xavier.

The boy raised his arm in signal, and the music swung into the greatest of Mexican waltzes, "Over the Waves." The horse lifted one dainty forefoot, replaced it delicately in the dust, and then began a rhythmic dance, advancing and retreating, swinging now to the right and now to the left.

The crowd yelled with pleasure, and Don Saturnino nodded his appreciation.

"I'll have that boy's ears," Bob muttered to the little Doctor. "Where did he get the courage to ride *El Blanco*?"

"He'd ride anything, even Satan's smoke-crowned dragon. There's horse's blood in that boy's veins, I'm sure of it."

The music came to a melodic close, and Xavier brought the horse to its knees in a deep curtsey. Don Saturnino gently applauded, and Alejandro bent forward to shake the boy's hand.

"They know how to honor the valley," Bob whispered. "Their technique is very interesting."

The little Doctor shrugged. "They should know how. They have three hundred years of training in their bones."

Don Rosalío leaned forward and tapped Bob's shoulder. "If Joaquín were here, he would show the young Xavier how to really ride a horse."

"You mean he was better than that boy?"

"Xavier has horse's blood in his veins, but Joaquín! . . . He grew out of a horse like a tree from the ground. And let me warn you. Never mention Joaquín to Don Saturnino. The loss of the oldest son, ay, that is always a sword in the heart."

As Don Rosalío sat back, Bob noticed that Xavier had dismounted and was proudly standing at the base of the platform, while Don Saturnino, his palm resting on Alejandro's arm, began to speak. The clear voice floated across the heads of the quiet crowd, and was returned to them in a faint echo from the western mountains.

After a moment, Bob was lulled into sleepiness by the monotonous tones. He realized that it was a perfection of oratory, delivered in the finest Spanish tradition, but the words meant nothing to him.

He glanced up and saw that Alejandro had turned his head, so that his profile was etched against the deep blue November sky.

One hand was plucking nervously at his throat as though he were trying to loosen something inside of it. He was frowning slightly, and he seemed to Bob to be a strangely solitary figure, a part of this valley, and yet not a part of it. He had been gone since he was thirteen, and now he was — Bob made swift calculations in his head — he must be twenty-one. But he looked older than that. He lacked the coltish youngness of his years, and had about him an aura of maturity, as though he had already completed a major part of his allotted span of life.

Bob caught a glimpse of Pablo, the goatherd, perched on the roof of the bandstand. Pablo, too, was just twenty-one, and he, too, had this quality of isolation. But Pablo's maturity was bred from loneliness, whereas Alejandro's . . .

But of course, Bob thought in quick sympathy, the boy is lonely. He's been snatched out of a glittering, sophisticated world, and plunged into this isolated valley, and he's too young to make a spiritual adjustment by himself. He needs help, and he needs it badly. It must have taken a good deal of courage for him to ask me that question about Tía Magdalena. I wonder if he would come home to supper with me?

After the ceremonies were over, Alejandro accepted the invitation with delight. "Don Rosalío is giving my father a little dinner. There will be many speeches, and much talk of days I can't remember. This will be a relief for them, and for me too."

He arrived at Bob's house with punctual courtesy, a long wooden box under his arm for Tía Magdalena. "All the way from Paris I brought it," he assured her, and was too excited to allow her to open it for herself, but tore at the wrappings with his nervous fingers.

The open box revealed a dress of green satin. Tía stared down at the fragrant softness with eyes that were misted with tears.

"For me?" she whispered, her hands hovering above the material and afraid to touch it.

"Put it on, Tía," Alejandro urged. "Show us how beautiful you are."

"Ay," she whispered, "if only Joaquín could know this, how pleased he would be."

She snatched up the box and fled with it to her room.

At mention of his brother's name, Alejandro's sensitive mouth trembled slightly. He looked quickly about him. "I remember when the Italian lived here. What a pigpen!" He patted the pomegranate bush, pulled an orange from its tree, and inhaled the skin's spicy perfume. "Now it is a house. Have you changed it inside?"

"No, not much. Tía complains about the furniture, but I'm too lazy to change it."

Alejandro nodded, and strolled to the dining room door. "The table is too big. If it were sawn in half and painted . . ." He stopped abruptly and color stained his too white skin. "I like to work with my hands," he said shyly. "My father tells me I have the mind of a carpenter."

"If it would interest you to play tricks with this furniture, you're welcome to the job." Bob began filling his pipe from a leather tobacco pouch stamped with his initials.

"Thank you," Alejandro said formally. "It would interest me very much." He looked at the pouch. "R.W. I did not hear your name on the platform."

"Bob Webster. Robert to my enemies."

"So? There is a family Webster in San Antonio. You are perhaps related?"

Bob could feel his face closing into Indian immobility. "There are many Websters," he said coolly. "It's a common name."

"Of course. And you are dark. This family I mentioned are all blond." He was talking quickly to prevent Bob's thinking him too curious of personal affairs.

An anguished yelp from the patio sent them running to Tía Magdalena, who was stretched out full length on her face, the dress a green wave about her. As Bob set her on her feet, she wailed, "I took a step, and zas! I was on the ground."

Alejandro began to howl with laughter, and Bob, after a desperate effort to control himself, laughed too. Tía had put the dress on backward, so that the train spread out like a pheasant's tail in front of her.

"You laugh at me! Ay, Alejandro, such grandeur is not for an old woman."

When Alejandro managed to explain what had happened, she looked down the length of green satin and shook her head. "But how else could I button it, save down the front? Am I creature with rubber arms, that I can reach to the back?"

With their help, the dress was reversed and fastened correctly,

Alejandro managing the buttons with many grunts while she moaned that he was cutting her breath into two sections. Then they stepped back to admire her.

The dress was cut low in front, and even lower in back, so for modesty's sake she had put on one of her long-sleeved pink blouses. From the tight basque waist, the skirt fell away in soft folds, and from ankle to knee large pansies of purple velvet were appliquéd, with trailing stems embroidered in gold.

"I remembered how small you were," Alejandro told her, "and I said to them, 'Make a dress for a child of twelve, who is really a hundred years old . . .' "

"You!" shrieked Tía with flashing anger. "A hundred years indeed! Is it in my grave you are putting me?" As she advanced toward him, her hand outstretched for a quick slap, there came a loud pounding at the door.

"I am now a lady," she snapped at Bob. "Go yourself."

Still convulsed with mirth, he opened the door. A white something flashed between his legs, catapulting him forward into the arms of the little Doctor, who yelled at him, "I've lost the goat. Don't let it get away!"

Both men jumped inside and slammed the door shut. In the patio there was pandemonium. The goat, attracted by the perfume of the dress, had dashed straight toward Tía, who leaped with agility to the top of the well. Alejandro was trying to drag the animal backward, while the little creature, a section of the train in its mouth, was kicking its four tiny legs in an effort to free itself.

Bob's hand closed on the small black muzzle. By cutting off its wind, he forced the goat to open its mouth, but Tía was not prepared for this sudden release of tension. Trying to protect her dress, she had been pulling backward, and now, with a high, shrill scream, she tumbled into the well.

It took the combined efforts of Bob and Alejandro, with the little Doctor clutching the goat and yelling instructions, to get her out.

They finally set her upright on the patio cement, her four feet eleven inches trembling with wrath. Water plastered her wispy gray hair to her face. The pink blouse clung to her bony shoulders, and the dress was now a lank twist of material, with the velvet spreading its purple dye over the green satin.

"That goat!" she shrieked, as soon as she had sputtered the water out of her mouth. "May it die in agony. May its feet sink in quicksand. May it cause tears and lamentations to its owner . . ."

"Ay, Tía," howled the little Doctor, "it is a wedding present for Andrés Treviño."

"The more fool he for wanting a goat as a wedding present. Look at me. Look at me!"

Bob had rushed into his bedroom for a blanket, and now he wrapped it around her, so that she was a small cocoon of striped wool, shading from dark brown to bright orange and back to brown again.

The little Doctor said firmly, "Light a fire some place," and while Alejandro started a blaze in the living room, Bob carried Tía in and settled her in a wicker rocker.

"Tell that little man to take his Devil's beast out of here!"

"Of course, Tía, at once," Bob said soothingly.

The little Doctor, still clutching the struggling goat, hovered in the doorway. "Such a pretty animal," he murmured temptingly. "Behold it, Tía. Its eyes are like two dark pools of innocence."

"Ha!" Tía glared at him. "For the first time in my life I have a magnificent dress, and what happens? That goat — that goat . . ."

"Yes, Tía, but look at it." He approached her cautiously, holding the goat upside down by its small hooves. "All white, with a little black moon on its forehead. Is it not a dainty thing?"

"Goats are the sons of Grandfather Devil . . ."

"But this is such a jewel of a creature." He swung it tantalizingly in front of her. The little animal began to baa piteously, and Tía's mouth softened.

"Well," she said grudgingly, "after all a goat is a goat . . ."

"Precisely. And with intelligence. Immediately it recognized the beauty of your dress. And with a goat, beauty is something to be eaten."

As he approached her, Bob and Alejandro drew closer together, admiration for him in their eyes.

Tía wriggled her shoulders inside the blanket, the wool scratching her through her thin clothes. "As you say, the entire world is an object for a goat's stomach."

"And if you could keep it for a few days — just until after the wedding, Andrés Treviño will bless you in his prayers, and I will bless you in my prayers."

Her lips covered her sparsely toothed gums, the chin rising to meet the nose. "The animal has a certain, a certain . . ."

"Personality," suggested the little Doctor.

"Ummm," said Tía. She opened the blanket and stretched out an arm to caress the small head. And then her eyes saw her dress. The pink blouse and green satin had absorbed the browns, yellows, and orange of the wool. Her mouth opened, and for a moment there was silence. Then a bursting shriek made Alejandro and Bob snap their hands over their ears, and tightly shut their eyes against the vision of the little Doctor being flayed alive. But hearing nothing more beyond that whip of sound, they cautiously opened their lids. Where the little Doctor had been was empty space. In the quiet they could hear the front door slam and the rapid patter of departing feet on the sidewalk outside. Then they looked at Tía, who was contemplating them with scorn.

"In this house," she said firmly, "no more goats!" She stalked through the patio to her own room, and that door also slammed.

Bob and Alejandro, choked with laughter, got their own supper. They timidly tried to persuade Tía to eat something, but silence was their only answer.

"Perhaps tomorrow I had better go to Monterrey and buy another dress," Alejandro suggested anxiously.

"Perhaps we'd better both go," Bob said gloomily. "I don't think Tía's really angry with either you or me, but I have a feeling that no man will be very popular in this house for the next few days."

"Men," said Alejandro, "and goats."

They stared at each other, and the memory of the goat eating Tía's train rose in their minds. They had to run out of the house to keep the old woman from hearing their mirth.

The days passed quickly, and on the evening of Andrés Treviño's wedding, the November moon rose brightly clear and full above the black jagged peaks of the western mountains. The village streets were dark and deserted, for most of the people were pressing through the wide gates that separated the cactus-enclosed Gallineros from the rest of the town. Why the poorest people of Hidalgo had chosen to enclose themselves within a cactus wall, no one knew. It was the same in Mina, in El Carmen, in Abasolo, in Topo Grande.

Tonight, Andrés and his good friends Porfirio and Pepe Gonzalez were in the patio of Nena's home, staring into the well where the wedding bouquet was being kept to preserve its freshness. Through the door of the house came a low hum as of angry bees around a hive. The guests, from the sound, were screaming at each other above the tuning of the orchestra. There would be no dancing, of course, until after Don Genaro, the civil judge, had married the young couple according to the laws of the state. Then the dancing would begin, lasting through the night until five in the morning, when the whole party would march through the town in the false dawn light to the pink-washed temple of Our Lady of the Miraculous Tear, there to attend the second wedding by Father Zacaya according to the laws of the church.

"Think of it," said Pepe Gonzalez, thrusting one long arm into the well and poking at the tightly bound bouquet of gardenias and tuberoses. "In the Republic a man must buy a house, furnish it, purchase the bride's trousseau, pay for the wedding festival, and provide the bouquet; but in the States all a man needs is two dollars and the girl."

"Me," said Porfirio, remembering with bitterness a certain ten-peso fine, "I should have been married in the States."

"You are a stingy man," said Andrés, hoping that the cold terror of the approaching ceremony was not apparent in his voice. "Me, I am generous. And what happens? Nena wears shoes and the little Doctor gives me a goat."

"It's a fine goat," said Pepe Gonzalez. "I raised it with these two hands from the day it slipped from its mother's womb . . ."

"You never did anything but get Andrés and me into trouble in all the years of your life," snorted Porfirio. "If it hadn't been for you, Andrés and I might have passed many a terror-filled night in sweet peace and comfort."

"Did I ask you to follow my lead?" retorted Pepe sharply. "But when I ring the bell, who is it comes running?"

Porfirio thrust out his chin. "Are you calling me a two-legged sheep?"

"Your nose grows flatter to your face every day!"

Andrés slipped quickly between the two quarreling men. "There'll be no fight at my wedding. There has been enough trouble, what with goats and shoes without fights being added.

May St. Andrew of the Crooked Cross protect me from any more difficulties."

Nena's shrill voice rose above the conversation hum in a clear, decisive scream of anger.

"Blessed Saints," gasped Andrés. "What has happened now?"

At that moment, Doña Fela, the town's great lady, surged through the door, something white and dainty clasped tightly between her hands.

"You, Andrés Treviño! Were you born entirely without brains?"

"What is wrong, auntie?" asked Pepe in as soothing a voice as he could muster. His mother was Doña Fela's sister, and he and Anita O'Malley were supposed to be the only two beings who were not secretly afraid of the old lady's anger.

"What is wrong, indeed, and this fool of an Andrés standing there as innocent as a bird freshly cracked from the egg."

"Why was Nena screaming?" Andrés stepped toward Doña Fela. "Was she hurt? Did someone wound her feelings?"

"Something wounded her feet!" snapped the old lady, and suddenly thrust what she was holding under Andrés' nose. By this time the patio was filled with people, and even Pablo the goatherd (invited as a gesture of good will toward Grandfather Devil), was listening with avid interest.

Slowly Andrés reached out and took the white slippers from Doña Fela. The brilliant green-silver moonlight threw their whiteness into strong relief against his dark hands. Those close enough to see the slippers caught their breath in admiration. These were not fashioned for a human being but for a delicate lady of fantasy. From heel to toe their length was no greater than a man's palm. They were dainty bits of leather belonging to the dancing useless feet of a fragile city girl, not the sturdy broad soles of a girl from the Gallineros.

"Nena thought them beautiful when I brought them to her this evening," said Andrés with a puzzled helplessness in his eyes. "What made her change her mind?"

"And what made you buy such trifles?" snorted Doña Fela. "Do you think a normal-sized woman can get her feet in those shoes?"

"Holy Mother of God, she can't get them on!" said Pepe Gonzalez with sudden illumination.

"Ah," breathed Doña Fela with heavy sarcasm. "A man of wisdom is amongst us. You are correct, my pretty nephew. Nena can't get even one toe inside of them. And as for you, my wise buyer of woman's goods . . ." her head snapped back to Andrés, "what evil devil suggested that you purchase these toys?"

"To save money," muttered Andrés, so low he could scarcely be heard.

"To save money?" shrieked the old woman. "Do you think women's shoes, then, are bought like your sandals, by the size?"

"But naturally. I went down to the station and asked Father Zacaya to purchase the smallest pair he could find. I never thought Nena's feet would be too large to wear them."

"Oh, didn't you!" There was a pushing aside of people as Nena advanced, her plump body sheathed in white satin, and her bare feet silvered bronze in the moonlight. "Are you saying now that I have the feet of a giantess?"

The low curve of the well prevented Andrés from retreating. "I swear such a thought was not in my mind."

"I told you, Andrés Treviño, with my own mouth I said it — that I would wear shoes at my wedding or there would be no wedding. And these shoes I cannot wear!"

As her voice died away into silence, the whole patio tensed, every eye on Andrés. The boy looked beseechingly at Porfirio, at Pepe Gonzalez, even at Pablo the goatherd for aid. But these three could offer him nothing. Over the heads of the quiet guests he could see Father Zacaya, Don Rosalío, Don Nacho, the little Doctor. But they, too, for once in their lives, had no advice to give him. Then, through the silence, came the soft baaing of a goat, the little Doctor's wedding present. Andrés felt bitterness flood through his entire body. He had heard that Tía Magdalena had cursed the goat, and she was an eagle witch. His hand went up to the small silver pin shaped in the figure of St. Peter, called the "Shadow of St. Peter," which was fastened under his coat lapel.

"A candle as long as my arm to break the curse," he whispered. If there was no wedding, the goat — in all honor — must be returned. It was bad enough to lose Nena, but to lose her and the goat, too, was not to be endured. He turned his back on the crowd and peered intently into the well to hide his misery from their curious eyes.

Suddenly his back stiffened, his head lifted with new authority.

He swung on his sandaled heel and faced the silent group. His voice rang clear and strong in the narrow patio.

"Tell the musicians to start the music. Nena, return to the kitchen. This wedding will be now. I have spoken."

"But the shoes," began Nena rebelliously.

"You will have your shoes. That, too, I have spoken."

At a nod from him, Pepe Gonzalez and Porfirio began to push the guests back into the house. Andrés, his mouth set in a straight, thin line, reached out and grasped Nena's arm firmly just above the elbow. In spite of her tugging and kicking out at him, he half carried, half led her into the kitchen where he shut the door with a bang, an inch from Doña Fela's startled nose.

A few moments later the long, narrow parlor, softly yellow in the glow of the hot, rancid oil lanterns, had a cleared space down the center from kitchen door to the far end, with the black cane sofa and the table behind which waited Don Genaro in all the dignity of his office as civil judge. To his right stood Don Rosalío, Don Nacho, and the little Doctor, ready to sign the book as witnesses for the groom. To his left stood Doña Fela, Doña Mariliria, and Doña Juanita Perez. They, too, would sign the book as witnesses for the bride.

There was tense expectancy in the crowd. What was Andrés saying to Nena behind that firmly shut kitchen door? Every head was turned at a polite angle toward that door. Tía Magdalena, encased in a new dress of bright red satin, clutched Bob's arm with one excited hand, and Alejandro's with the other. Like everyone else, their conversation was carried on automatically and in as low tones as possible, so that curiosity would not be too apparent, and yet in the hope that even a fragment of momentous dialogue could be heard. Once Nena's voice rose in a shrill, "No!" followed by something that sounded like the crashing of a chair. Again, Andrés gave a howling shout of rage, which quickly sank to a low, undistinguishable murmur.

The little Doctor whispered to Don Nacho. "I have a feeling that Nena is discovering Andrés intends to be master in his own house."

Suddenly Don Alonso's orchestra, at a signal from Pepe Gonzalez through the iron-barred patio window, began to play that favorite song of all northern frontier weddings: Tosti's "Good-bye Forever." The kitchen door opened and the bridal party marched in. First entered Nena's mother with Andrés' father; then Andrés' mother with Nena's father. Next, in couples, came Alma Orona, Pepe Gonzalez, Anita O'Malley, and Porfirio. And finally, Andrés and Nena.

Necks craned for a better view. People in the back stood on tiptoe. Softly at first, then gaining in volume, came the laughter. There was loud clapping in abrupt appreciation. The orchestra, catching the spirit of the occasion, swung out of the doleful Italian melody into the gay, jerky rhythm of the applause music. Nena, clutching Andrés' arm, bowed proudly to right and left. Had ever a girl from the Gallineros, from the whole Sabinas Valley for that matter, had such a wedding as this? Alma Orona had worn shoes at her wedding, true, but she had worn them on her feet. And as Andrés said when he broke the chair on the kitchen floor for emphasis, "You said you wanted to wear a pair of shoes. But you never mentioned wearing them on the feet. That was not in the bargain. Any fool can wear them on the feet. But the wife of Andrés Treviño is not a common bride. Why, then, should she wear elegance in a common manner? I said you would wear shoes and you shall — like gloves on your hands in place of a wedding bouquet!" [1945]

Mario Suárez was born in Tucson, Arizona, in 1925. During World War II he served in the U.S. Navy, after which he enrolled in the University of Arizona to study for a degree in liberal arts. During his first years at the university, his short stories came to notice and were published in the *Arizona Quarterly* between 1947 and 1950. These stories and articles depict thoughtful Chicanos (Suárez was one of the first writers to use this term in print) whose actions are motivated by friendship and family and who try to take joy in both.

Publication of these stories led to Suárez's moving to New York for a brief period to write novels, none of which have been published to date. He then returned to Arizona and to the university, from which he received a B.A. in 1952. For the past forty years, he has lived in the Southwest and has continued to write fiction. "Cuco Goes to a Party" was obviously influenced by John Steinbeck's *Tortilla Flat,* though Suárez's characters have more emotional depth and evince more personal responsibility than Steinbeck's ne'er-do-wells. His stories, though few in number, are an important link in the development of Chicano realism and presage such formidable contemporary talents as Dagoberto Gilb.

Cuco Goes to a Party

One night Cuco Martinez decided not to go home right away. Every night he hurried home from work because his two brothers-in-law did it and thought it right. The brothers-in-law believed that if a man got up very early in the morning and cooked his breakfast, it was right. The brothers-in-law believed that if a man came straight home from work, it was right. The brothers-in-law also believed that if a man worried about the price of household needs and discussed them with the wife, it was right. Maybe it was right. But only to his two brothers-in-law. To Cuco it was very boring. So tonight he would not go home right away. If his brothers-in-law wanted to be henpecked and do so, it was all right with him. Where he came from, men did as they pleased, and here, as long as his name was Cuco Martinez he would do the same thing. When Cuco walked out of Feldman's Furniture Store at six o'clock he did not direct his steps toward his home in El Hoyo as he usually did. He walked up the street to Garza's Barber Shop. It was already closed but Garza and his friends were inside. When Cuco was let in, Garza, who was shaving, said, "Happy are the eyes that greet you, Cuco."

"The feeling is mutual, Garza. And what is new with you?" asked Cuco as he sat down with two of Garza's friends on the long reception sofa and began thumbing through a magazine.

"Cuco," said Garza, "today is Lily-boy's birthday and I hope you will join Procuna, Lolo, and myself in honoring him."

"I will be glad to," said Cuco.

So when Garza was through shaving, when the lights were put out, and when the door was locked, Lily-boy, who was to be the honored one, Garza, Procuna, Lolo, and Cuco walked up the street to the Royal Inn. When they got there it was not yet very full of customers because it was at the time when most men were at home eating supper. The bartender was wiping glasses in anticipation of a good night. The juke box was still silent. Lolo, who walked in ahead of everybody, promptly found a good table and the five friends sat down and ordered beer. Cuco went to the juke box and soon the gay rhythm of *El Fandango* was filling the air. Garza ordered more beer and Lolo, who is sometimes very poetic, toasted to Lily-boy. Lily-boy was wished eternal happiness. Whether he deserved that kind of happiness was questionable. He was also wished a thousand happy years. Whether Lily-boy really wanted that many was also questionable. "Bottoms up," said Garza. The friends drank. And drank. After a few hours the table was so littered with bottles that Lolo began to wonder how much he could get for them should he decide to go into the bottle-collecting business. Lily-boy went to the phone booth to tell his wife that he would soon be home and that he would arrive sober. Lolo, who was the king of the jitter-bugs and an up-and-coming prize fighter as well, was thinking of challenging everybody. He looked across the table to see which one of his companions would make a good match. When Lolo realized that these were no fighters, he looked at a little group of drunks, and on seeing that they did not look like good potential foes, he shouted a few obscenities at them and continued drinking his beer. Garza was trying to brush off a little drunk who was sure that he had seen him somewhere and Garza was trying to convince him that it had probably been at Garza's Barber Shop. Cuco was saying to Procuna, "I think that if I had my way about most things I would go to Mexico City and see a full season of bullfights. I sure like them. I truthfully believe that there is nothing as full of emotion as a good bullfight. I remember having been at bullfights from the time I was about eight years old. I used to go with my father. But what I remember best is when I saw Silverio Perez make such a beautiful kill that that supreme moment has lived with me ever since."

"Why, Cuco?" asked Procuna.

"Well," continued Cuco, "Perez is not a good killer. He is a good bullfighter but he is not a good killer. But this bull, which was as big as a house, knocked him down. When Perez was on the ground the bull almost gored him but luckily, when he got up, only his pants were torn. Silverio was so mad that he picked up the *estoque* with which he would soon kill the bull and, in his rage, slapped the bull across the face. Silverio Perez was mad. Then he lined himself up with the left horn. He sighted the bull. The two met. Collided. For a second there was but a mass of enraged animal and embroidered silk. But in the end Silverio Perez was alive, though shaken, and the bull was dead. Yes, Procuna, Silverio Perez is great."

"How about Armillita, Cuco, is he any good?" asked Procuna.

"Is he any good? You ask me. Is he any good? Why — he is the *maestro* of *maestros*. He is the teacher of teachers. When Armillita wants to be good he can do the impossible. He is great. I saw him perform in the Mexico City arena. He was magnificent. Each time the bull passed by his body it seemed that the great Armillita would end up on the horns of the bull. Yet he was as much at ease in the midst of it all as we are here, drinking beer. There is no doubt. Like Armillita there are not two."

Soon Cuco got up to demonstrate, with the aid of his coat, how the bulls were passed. Procuna acted as a bull, and Cuco told his friends how the different passes were executed. He explained how in the art of bullfighting things must be done with delicacy and finesse. Cuco waved the coat and Procuna, the bull, charged. He charged true and straight and Cuco passed him with grace and charm. He charged again. And again. Each time Cuco passed him with all the known passes in the art of bullfighting. Each time Procuna, the bull, charged he came so close to Cuco that he almost bumped him. But he didn't. After a fine exhibition of cape work Cuco drank some more beer. Then he stood in front of the table of the companions and to Lily-boy, who was the guest of honor, dedicated as the *matadores* do in Mexico City, the death of the bull. Once again Cuco took the coat and Procuna, the bull, charged. The bull was getting tired. Soon Cuco realized this and went through the motions of killing him. By this time half of the people in the Royal Inn were crowded around Cuco. Procuna, who had been a good bull, got off the floor, dusted himself, and drank some more beer. Garza was proud of them. He hugged both of them. Lolo, who was very anxious for a bit of excitement, challenged Lily-boy to a fight. Lily-boy was very drunk. He, too, was willing to fight. He feared no man so he was willing. So Lolo and Lily-boy went out into the alley followed by a big crowd to fight it out. After a while Lily-boy and Lolo, who had shaken hands after their fight, came back to drink more beer. Lily-boy had merely sat on top of poor little Lolo. But still it had been a great fight. By this time, Garza, who has always been a good barber and better philosopher, was thinking of turning into an impresario. He was thinking of organizing a bullfight at the edge of the Santa Cruz River. He was also thinking of promoting a few boxing matches. Lily-boy once again went to the phone booth to tell his wife that he was about to start for home. Lolo was challenging Garza. Lolo was bribed into silence with another beer. Cuco was telling Procuna more about fighting bulls. Every now and then one of them would get up to execute a pass. Lily-boy was getting so drunk that he was looking for the phone booth in the men's room. After he came back to the table and had another beer he was looking for the men's room in the phone booth. Garza, in truth, was having a hell of a time keeping his friends on their feet. Lolo was insistent about fighting Lily-boy again. He wanted a re-match. Mike, the bartender, gave them a red drink on the house. After all, they had been very good customers. They had broken no chairs and upset no tables. Very soon Mike decided that they deserved another drink on the house. When the second drink went down the throats of the friends they began to drop. Soon the only ones left standing were Procuna, who was executing passes, and Garza. Garza realized that it was late so he bought Procuna another bottle of beer and told him to keep an eye on things while he went for the car to take the friends home. He well realized that if the authorities saw them in their present condition it would be taken for granted that they had been drinking. Garza went for the car and Procuna, who was left in charge, fell asleep on the shoulder of Lily-boy. When Garza came in for his friends he first woke Procuna. Together they carried Lolo, the king of the jitterbugs, feet first to the car. Then they carried out Cuco, a very nice young man, and put him in the car. Last but not least, they tried to awaken Lily-boy, who was very fat, and who had to hurry home to cut his birthday cake. Finally he had to be carried to the car, too. After the three friends were piled into the back seat and the doors closed, Procuna jumped into the front seat with Garza and the car started toward each of their respective homes. Lolo, the king of the jitterbugs, woke up long enough to say that he was hungry. Garza, who cannot stand anybody being hungry as long as they are with him, told Lolo to shut up and go to sleep. Garza turned toward the Hacienda Cafe. When they got there the only ones that were able to get out to eat were Procuna and Garza. Lolo did not wake up so Garza thought it best for him to sleep. After a hot meal and a singeing cup of coffee Garza and Procuna decided that they were still too sober so they went across the street to the

Gato Blanco Cafe. They drank a few beers. They shook hands with a few friends and then went back to the car. When they got going again Lolo was taken home first and put to bed because he was training for his next fight and needed rest. Cuco then decided that he did not want to go home right away. He wanted to get out of the car for a certain universal necessity. So Garza patiently stopped the car and Cuco remedied his need. Then he was taken home. Lily-boy was taken home. He was a little bit late to cut his birthday cake but at least he was home. After Procuna, who had to go to school the next day was dropped off at his house, Garza started for his own. After all, it had been a gay party. Lolo had fought Lily-boy. Cuco had fought many bulls. Procuna had executed passes and had consumed a lot of beer. Garza was happy that his friends had been happy and with a smile on his lips and very glassy, tired eyes, drove home. Tomorrow he had to go to work.

The next day, in the early afternoon, Procuna dropped around to Garza's Barber Shop with his schoolbooks under his arm. Garza was putting the finishing touches on a customer when he came in. When he saw him, he said, "My great Procuna, how are you?"

"Fine, Garza, and you?" asked Procuna with a tired voice. "I thought I was going to go to sleep in class today. But wow, I sure had a wonderful time last night."

"Yes. I guess we all did. When you and Cuco started you were fighting little bulls. By the time you got the free drink from the bartender you were fighting bulls from La Punta about five years old," said Garza.

"How about Cuco, has he been in?" inquired Procuna.

"Well, Procuna, I am going to tell you," said Garza.

"Tell me what," said Procuna.

"Well, Cuco was in here a little while ago and just went out to eat with Lily-boy. He is sad. In fact, he is very sad," said Garza.

"Why in the hell should he be sad today? He was very happy yesterday," said Procuna.

"Well, last night he lost his underwear," said Garza.

"And —?" inquired Procuna.

"Just that poor Cuco has been at odds with his in-laws and they found this as an excuse to turn his wife against him. Poor Emilia," said Garza, "but I think the damned in-laws are talking her into getting a divorce from Cuco." Garza brushed off the customer's neck and took off the linen apron. He rang up seventy-five cents in the cash register and continued, "Yes, that is the way it is. Cuco really loves his wife too. It is only that his in-laws do not give him a minute of peace."

At that moment Lily-boy and Cuco walked into the barber shop. Lily-boy put on his barber's apron and Cuco sat down on the reception sofa. He looked very sad. He did not want to talk about anything. He picked up a magazine and began to thumb through it. Looking up, Cuco said, "Yes, Garza, I guess it was all a mistake for me to get married in the first place. The only thing that worries me is that Emilia is going to have a child. I really planned to stay married to her. But I guess I will just wait until it is born and then go back to Mexico."

"And her?" asked Garza.

"She will keep the child and I will go back by myself."

Then Cuco once again began to look through the magazine for a little longer and then, without saying anything, got up and walked out of the barber shop. The friends, Procuna, Lily-boy, and Garza, felt sorry for him. He was a good young man. They felt somewhat guilty for having got him so drunk that he had to go and lose his underwear.

Cuco Martinez was not very gay after that. Every day he went home to hear the nagging ways of his in-laws. Cuco was not understood. At first he had been something new but now nobody seemed to like him any longer. The brothers-in-law told him that he was a no-good fancy storyteller that should have stayed working for the railroad. They told him that he would always be but a rest-room cleaner at Feldman's Furniture Store. That he was so stupid that he should not expect to ever make over thirty dollars a week. That he was nothing but a no-good drunk and that they did not see how Emilia had ever fallen in love and consented to marry him. Every day the same thing happened. Cuco got mad and said nothing. He knew that conditions would change. As soon as the child was born he would leave. Because he loved Emilia very much, he realized he could not stay long enough for her to dislike him for the same things his brothers-in-law did. He would return to Mexico. That is the way he would have it. [1947]

Julia de Burgos is one of Puerto Rico's most cherished poets; her passionate and often intimate verses reflect a keen identification with her country as well as an abiding quest for self-awareness and authenticity as a woman. Born in a rural area of Puerto Rico in 1914 to a large and needy family, she was nevertheless able, with great sacrifice, to obtain a teaching degree in 1933.

Burgos's biography is as well known as her works. The decade of the 1930s witnessed a surge in nationalist spirit on the island, and Julia de Burgos shared in this ideal, extending it in later years to a more pan-Caribbean and internationalist perspective. These were also intensely active years artistically for her: she published *Poemas exactos a mí misma* (Exact Poems to Myself) in 1937; several children's plays and *Poemas en veinte surcos* (Poems in Twenty Rows) in 1938; and *Canción de la verdad sencilla* (The Song of Simple Truth) in 1939. After the breakup of her first marriage, Burgos traveled to New York in 1940, then went on to Cuba to be reunited with a man she loved but who refused to acknowledge their relationship. The mystery surrounding this affair became part of the poet's mystique, as did her tragic years in New York City. She spent the last eleven years of her life there, struggling to come to terms with her disillusionment and yearning to find justice and meaning.

Burgos continued to write and participate in political causes in New York. Her final collection, *El mar y tú* (The Sea and You), published posthumously in 1954, contains many of the works written during the New York years, including the poem translated here, "Returning." Suffering from the effects of alcohol, Burgos was repeatedly hospitalized; "Farewell in Welfare Island" was written in English during one of those hospital stays. She wrote several prophetic poems about her anonymous death on an island of rock, and in July 1953 Burgos's body, with no identification, was discovered on a New York City street.

The letters she wrote during her final years reflect the love/hate relationship that many immigrants feel toward the huge metropolis. While it offered her the freedom to follow her unconventional ideas, it also represented, compared to her tropical island homeland, a "vast empire of solitude and darkness." Unlike other island writers who came to the United States during those years, Burgos seems to have attempted to integrate herself into her new environment, even creating poems in English to better express this reality. For many U.S. Puerto Rican poets, especially women, Julia de Burgos is considered an important precursor, an example of what should be emulated — her intense creativity, originality, and tenacity in the face of adversity — as much as what should be avoided. Her voice prefigured the Nuyorican poetic response yet to come.

Returning

Indefinitely,
extended like shadows and waves,
sunburnt in salt and foam and impossible skulls,
my sadness grows sadder;
this orbitless sadness which is mine
since the world became mine,
since darkness blazed my name,
since the first cause for all tears
came to be my own.

It's as if I'd like to love
and the wind doesn't let me.
It's as if I'd like to return
and yet can't discover why, now where to.
It's as if I'd like to follow the course of the waters
yet all thirst is gone.

Indefinitely . . .

A word so mine;
ghostly specter of my specter!

There's no longer a voice,
or tears,
or distant sprigs of grain.
No more shipwrecks,
or echoes,
not even anguish;
silence itself is dead!

What say you, my soul, should I flee?
Where could I go where I would not be
shadowing my own shadow? [1947]

Translation of "Retorno" by Dwight García
and Margarite Fernández Olmos

Farewell in Welfare Island

It has to be from here,
right this instance,
my cry into the world.

Life was somewhere forgotten
and sought refuge in depths of tears
and sorrows
over this vast empire of solitude
and darkness.

Where is the voice of freedom,
freedom to laugh,
to move
without the heavy phantom of despair?

Where is the form of beauty
unshaken in its veil simple and pure?
Where is the warmth of heaven
pouring its dreams of love in broken spirits?

It has to be from here,
right this instance,
my cry into the world.
My cry that is no more mine,
but hers and his forever,
the comrades of my silence,
the phantoms of my grave.

It has to be from here,
forgotten but unshaken,
among comrades of silence
deep into Welfare Island
my farewell to the world.

Goldwater Memorial Hospital
Welfare Island — N.Y.C.
February 1953

[1953]

Cleofas Jaramillo (1878–1956) was born in northern New Mexico into a wealthy family descended from the original *hispano* pioneers. She wrote as a means of preserving a culture that was gradually disappearing before her eyes, a culture that was also, she believed, being appropriated by outsiders who were forging a "New Mexican Mystique" from a fundamentally Anglo perspective. Jaramillo also founded the Folkloric Society of Santa Fe in 1935 to conserve Hispanic culture. Her vision of the past, however, was often nostalgic and idealized.

Jaramillo's literary career began as a reaction to an article in a 1935 magazine describing Mexican and Spanish cooking. She wrote, "It occurred to me that if we would look in our mothers' trunks we would find old costumes and jewelry which could be displayed at our Fiesta. I thought we who know the customs and styles of our region are letting them die out." Her response was to write *The Genuine New Mexico Tasty Recipes: Potajes sabrosos* (Delicious Stews, 1939); *Cuentos del hogar* (Family Tales, 1939), based on her mother's stories; *Shadows of the Past* (1941), which combines local folklore, customs, and personal experiences; and *Romance of a Little Village Girl* (1955) from which the excerpt below is taken.

Romance of a Little Village Girl is an autobiographical account, documenting almost seventy years of Jaramillo's life and the gradual loss of New Mexico's Hispanic culture. The author agonized over the decision to write in English; apologetic about writing in a language that was "foreign" to her, she nevertheless wished to reach a wider audience, even though her decision reflected the cultural loss she struggled against. The nostalgic perspective of Jaramillo's memoirs has led some critics to consider the work simplistic, for it focuses on the upper-class Hispanic perspective and obscures social, class, and racial differences. Feminist critics like Tey Diana Rebolledo, however, have commended the work for its defiance of the dominant Anglo culture. In her study of Fabiola Cabeza de Baca Gilbert, Nina Otero-Warren, and Cleofas Jaramillo, whom she considers ancestors of contemporary Chicana authors, Rebolledo notes the following:

"All three writers discussed here are remarkable for their concerns and their production at a time when most Hispanas/Mexicanas had little education, or if they were educated, little leisure or encouragement to write. They did so against the overwhelming dominance of Anglo culture and language, and against the patriarchal norms of their own culture. Their narratives are valuable not only because they preserve accounts of folk life but also because, in particular, they record the details women considered important, details rarely included in male narrative. Thus we are able to glimpse something of the female experience usually left out of history."

from **Romance of a Little Village Girl**

Pleasant Outings

The country had adjusted itself to the new changes, and prosperity had helped my father's business. His chief industries were sheep raising, farming and mercantile. But being so energetic, he touched on almost every kind of work.

Occasionally on Sundays father and mother sought relaxation from their heavy responsibilities and took the family out on the long rides and picnics. It was sheer delight to roll along in our horse-drawn buggy, gradually winding up fragrant, timbered hills, past remote villages silently drowsing on green carpet valleys. Or we rode across wide plains to the foot of high mountains and through Taos' scenic canyons.

I can still see myself, like a wild bird set free of a cage, running from one berry bush to another, filling my little play bucket, my heart beating with delight at the sight of beautiful mariposa lilies, blue bells, yellow daisies, feathery ferns — plucking some to trim the pretty sunbonnets mother made for me.

My brothers found these places a fisherman's and hunter's paradise. They caught long strings of speckled mountain trout in the streams. In lakes they found wild ducks, and on prairies they hunted wild rabbits, hen, quail and other game.

Even on these outing days, pleasure was combined with usefulness. Lupe, our cook, and Nieves, the nurse, filled flour sacks with wild hop blossoms, to be dried and kept for winter use. These were steeped in hot water and the water used to make the bread yeast. They picked berries and choke cherries for preserves.

Refreshed by the invigorating pine-fragrant air, my parents returned with renewed energy to take up their numerous tasks. Both were equally energetic. They had time for everything —

work, hospitality, religion and even politics. While my father lived at Arroyo Hondo, his political party never lost their election in that precinct. He ran his combined dry goods and grocery store without help. He directed the work on his farms, and his lands produced all kinds of grain, vegetables, fruit. He raised beef, sheep, pork and race horses. These were his chief industries, but there was no limit to his ambitions. He branched out into many others. He read his Bible and kept in it a record of the births and deaths of the members of his family.

In the backyard was the blacksmith shed, where wagons and farm implements were repaired and horses shod. In the carpenter shop was done all kinds of woodwork. My father, always keeping up with the times, took a notion to tear down the old-style porches and replace them with new white ones. The old ones had the best woodwork — thick round posts, carved lintels and scroll-cut corbels supported the round beams and the time-stained ceilings. The whole house was built in the best New Mexico architectural style of any old-style house I have ever seen. My grandfather, Vicente, had his wealthy father, Don José Manuel, to help him.

At nine years old, when I attended my Uncle Tobias's school, my father had José Manuel, the carpenter, make a little desk for me exactly like my teacher's, but painted the brightest red. He also ordered him to make a pew to be put in the old church, where there were no seats, for our family.

My mother did her share of the work, raising her large family of five boys and two girls. She kept three, and sometimes more, servants busy. If my father was out busy with the peons and someone came who wanted something at the store, mother dropped her work and went and waited on the customer. Our store supplied the simple needs of the people, from dry goods and groceries to patent medicines, which mother would tell the people how to use.

Change of work was their relaxation. My father found it in cool evenings directing Erineo in planting the vegetable garden, and mother in bringing the children out to pick currants and gooseberries for jellies, and for the pies we were so fond of. Lupe and Nieves found relaxation in going out to the green bean or green pea beds to pick large dishpans full. Then fat Lupe would sit on the kitchen porch, with her legs stretched out to rest her tired feet, and called us children to help her shell the peas.

The compensation for an everyday full day's work was not material, but rather the kind that is felt in the soul. The satisfaction of having accomplished something, of doing even the small things right. For the servants it was satisfaction of doing their duty well.

Harvest time was the busiest and the happiest. I loved the loud "gid-up" and the loud cracking of the long whip that kept the herd of wild horses running around the golden wheat and oat stacks until the stacks were trampled to the ground. Then came the rumble of heavy wagons loaded with the riches of the fields to fill granaries to the ceiling. On moonlit, Indian summer evenings, it was fun to sit around the corn pile, helping to husk the corn, while listening to the witty jokes and stories of our houseservants or of neighbors who came to help. Then, later, sitting in front of a warm fireplace to watch the shelling. The corn was roasted in the large adobe oven, or boiled in lime until it peeled, then spread to dry in the sun and sent down to our log, water-run mill, to be ground into meal, and brought back to the house to be sifted and sacked.

The beeves and porks were then butchered. Hundred-pound cans were filled with the rendered pork lard. From the residue, large kettles of hard soap were made. The fruit from the big orchard that father planted across the river was picked and brought in.

The abundance of those times now are past, even out in the country. The new generation doesn't like farming. Our home was so abundantly supplied, it was always ready to receive unexpected, uninvited guests, some just passing through. Even traveling men who came to take papa's orders for the store found some excuse for stopping overnight. With that old hospitality, they were always cheerfully received. After the harvesting was over came the general housecleaning. Mattresses, blankets and carpets were washed with amole root soap suds in a long trough by the river. The walls were whitewashed inside and on the porches. Floors were smoothly plastered.

The *capilla* was treated in the same way. Religious Grandpa Vicente had built this family private chapel by the house. After the whitewash on the walls dried, the many holy pictures were hung back in their places. There were two especially beautiful ones, one of the Holy Family painted by Manuel Maceda in 1852 at Guadalajara, Mexico, and the other, also an original, of the Madonna. In it, the Virgin's face was so beautiful that I used to climb up on the altar to get a closer view at it. I loved this picture, which looked to me like a very good copy of Raphael's "Madonna."

In those days the stores did not carry children's ready-made clothes. All items of clothing, from undervests to ruffled, sailor-collared blouses for my four younger brothers, and my laced and ruffled dresses, were made at home. Mother made her babies' layettes by hand from the sheerest nainsook. She never dressed her boys in overalls, and short pants were hard on long-stocking knees; her mending basket was never empty.

She cured all our ills, from measles to tonsilitis, without aid of a doctor. Herbs have medicinal virtue, and our mountains and fields are full of them. That was all she needed. My father brought vaccine from the doctor in Taos and vaccinated all the family and some of the village children. It took so well that we never had to have it done again.

With all this work to attend to, poor mother had time to visit even her sisters only once in several months. Then it always had to be on a Sunday, though they lived near. Too busy to develop boredom, she was always cheerful and happy. There seems to be no better tonic for happiness than work. Everyone was happy in those days. The peace that laid over the land imparted to its inhabitants satisfaction and contentment. How could people be otherwise, living according to God's laws and close to the good earth and the natural beauties of nature? Beauties were there that not even the most gifted artist can copy. The real tints of a glowing sunset, when the sky seems on fire or is suffused in delicate rose and gold. Those autumn colors on trees and shrubs covering mountains, and on wooded rivers. The crystal-like sheen on the river water, and the murmur as it splashes on its way. What sweeter music is there to soothe tired minds and nerves of hard-working people?

These good people made use of God's gifts and relaxed in their beauties, while living from the good earth's natural resources.

Children fed with simple food raised on their lands, and housed in neat little whitewashed houses with large sunny yards, were healthy and happy, too. But they were quiet and respectful, not spoiled by too much liberty and by the bold example they learn now from television and movies. Juvenile delinquency? — No one knew what it meant. People's lives radiated between church and home. Mothers stayed home taking care of their children, satisfied to live on their husbands' earnings. They were not buying new clothes all the time nor visiting beauty shops. No one was ever late for church, although some of them lived two and three miles distant and rode in slow wagons or even walked. How nice it would be if people now would live thus!

My parents were scrupulously strict in the performance of their duties, but always gentle and patient. I never heard them raise their voice to correct anyone. They lived with spiritual dignity and respect. Although never demonstrative in their affection toward their family, there was no need of display. We felt their love in everything they did for us. Mother was so refined. Once on the way to church she noticed my gloveless hands, saying: "Bare hands?" This was enough for me not to forget my gloves again.

She often quoted from her book of *Urbanidad y Buenas Maneras*. Her favorite proverb was *Nada quita al valiente lo cortez,* which meant that to be courteous even to the most humble never lowered anyone. She practiced what she preached by being kind to all. A friend said once to me: "You don't make enough distinction between yourselves and your servants." My parents were not the haughty kind of Dons; they never made their servants feel that they were inferior. There was no need, for our servants knew their places and kept it.

I loved to watch them at work. *"Comadrita,"* they called me, so kindly. I answered with a silent smile. Only with my mother or someone of my own age did my tongue ever loosen. It was that reverent respect we were taught to have for our elders, more by example than by word, that made us so quiet and restrained in our outer feelings, even among brothers and sisters. *"Hermanita"* — "Little Sister" — all my brothers and my sisters call me even to this day.

Harmony existed always. If father and mother had a different idea about something, they talked it over in a nice way. If mother could not convince my father as to how a thing should be done, she dropped the subject without arguing. When father built the new store extending into the courtyard, she said it would ruin the looks of the house, and it did. It shut out the light from the inside windows. We lost the east inside porch on the court, and with it went my swing that I enjoyed so much, the locust tree and elevated adobe garden around it, where mother grew her old-fashioned marigolds and larkspurs. Around it we had played *monita ciega,* blind man's buff. The porch posts we had used for bases in playing at "*las iglesias*."

The outside porch on the east side was also torn down and a new parlor and two bedrooms were built. The family was growing up and we must have more room, and father must have the store where it would be more handy, and not away between the house and the chapel, where my mother wanted it. She saw the attractive side rather than the convenient one. Although the change would save her all the work of having those long porches whitewashed and plastered every year, still she wanted it left in its lovely old style.

We children missed our outdoor sleep. Sometimes in very warm weather, mother allowed our maids to take our beds to the inside porch. What fun it was to find our beds by moonlight and to lie there looking up at the starlit heaven! We did not gaze long. After a full day of active work or play, there was no need of sleeping powders for anyone in the family. By nine o'clock every one was ready to drop into dreamland. . . .

The Territory Becomes a State

After decades of controversy between the two political parties — one favoring statehood, the other, territorial government — the statehood party won, and on January 6, 1912, President Howard Taft signed the proclamation of statehood in the presence of Congressman George Curry, and New Mexico became the forty-seventh star in the flag of the United States. A little later, one hundred elected members — my husband one of them — met at the capitol as members of the Constitutional Convention, to form the laws of the new state.

On January 15, Governor William McDonald, the first elected executive of New Mexico was inaugurated. On the eve of the inauguration, the governor and his family arrived from their Carrizoso ranch in a Santa Fe Railroad Pullman.

Elaborate preparations had been made. The dome of the capitol was illuminated with myriads of electric lights. At the entrance to the plaza blazed a welcoming arch. White and yellow bunting formed a background to the many rows of lights that lit the front of the Palace of the Governors; above glittered a star of lights and the name of Governor McDonald, together with the names of the first three governors, Oñate, De Vargas and Bent. The reception held in one of the large rooms in the Old Palace was a very formal affair, attended only by those holding tickets or invitations. At the end, the governor and guests passed into the National Guard Armory, which had been decorated for the dance. Governor and Mrs. McDonald led the grand march, followed by Governor Mills, Lieutenant Governor E. de Baca, Adjutant General Brooks, Democratic Chairman C. C. Jones and Republican Chairman Ven Jaramillo, accompanied by their wives.

At eleven o'clock, dinner was served in the assembly room, which had been decorated, and set with small tables. Many costly gowns were seen on the guests. Silk marquisette was in style. Mrs. McDonald's gold satin one was veiled with black marquisette. I had ordered mine from the Denver Dry Goods Company, and it came in yellow marquisette with a dresden-flowered border in colors, outlined in black, with a yellow satin foundation. I still have it as a souvenir of the last great function I attended with my husband. He was still in the governor's staff and was in his full colonel's uniform.

That following summer our Denver girl friends paid us an unexpected visit. The Rev. McMenemin, rector of the Denver cathedral and an eloquent orator, was with them. They had been visiting my cousins named Burns at Tierra Amarilla, and on their way back to Denver, stopped at our house overnight.

At the dinner table Ven told the priest that I still remembered the first sermon I had heard him preach, when he had fired out: "We will build the Denver cathedral in spite of the people of Denver." "Yes," he said. "I first ask them to do something, then I plead. When that does not work, I scold." He built it, costing over one million dollars. Some people thought his sermons too flowery. For myself, I like variation, a change from the common, everyday expressions.

Next morning I joined the party to show them the way through Taos. The road through the Rio Grande canyon was steep and rough, but our reverend friend proved to be an expert driver, and we passed through Taos late in the afternoon. A little ways out of town a shower met us, and Father, not being used to the Taos sticky mud, stopped to put on chains. In the meantime I sat in the car, enraptured, watching the undescribable panorama as the shower played on the beautiful Taos Mountains. A misty white fog was rising from the foot of the mountains. The top peaks were shrouded in dark clouds, now and then lit up by zigzag lightning. Shafts of golden sun rays shot from behind dark clouds and hit green spots on the mountains, and here and there around the valley sheets of rain poured down.

In about an hour we reached Arroyo Hondo. At my old home my three brothers were batching; but they had a good cook, and our flourishing appetites were soon quenched with the simple but nourishing menu served. The girls' father owned a cattle ranch; so they knew something about ranch life, and enjoyed the visit. Because of the lack of wine and hosts, the priest could not give us mass next morning in our private chapel before leaving.

> Let the old houses their secrets keep
> Leave them alone in their quiet sleep;
> They are like old folks who nod by the fire,
> Glad with their dreams of youth and desire.

My next trip to Taos was with my friend, Ruth Laughlin Barker, author of the popular book, *Caballeros*. She wanted to see an old Spanish-style house to describe in her new book. On the way, I described some of the big, attractive homes I knew when I was in school at Taos. It was during the rainy month of April, and a little shower met us as we were coming into town. Next morning, when I raised the window shade in my room at the Don Fernando Hotel, another enchanting sight met my eyes. Down in the valley, the peach and apricot trees covered with pink and white blossoms, and above, the high, snow-clad mountains blinded the eyes with their brilliancy in the brightest sunshine. No wonder Taos valley has always since my childhood fascinated me like a fairyland.

After breakfast, we rode to Ranchito, but where was Aunt Piedad's attractive old home, or the new one grandpa had built for her? It was hard to believe my eyes that what I was seeing were the melting remains of these once big, fine lively homes. A sob choked in my throat.

After lunch, I thought of the Valdez home at Placita. The round *torrion* always had marked this nice home for me; but now I could not find it; and we rode on to Arroyo Seco to see the fine Gonzales home. We were standing right before it, but I did not recognize it. "Where is Juanita Gonzales' home?" I asked a man in the yard.

"This is the house," he answered. The whitewashed porch with the blue railing posts was gone, and the whole house was in ruins. Juanita, whom her mother always had kept so well-dressed at school, came to the door with torn hose and shabby shoes. She asked us to come in. I asked her if she had some of her mother's fine jewelry or table silver. She brought out a silver set with an exquisite design and silver grape bunches on the lids. My friend became interested right away to buy it. Juanita asked $35.00. I am sure it was worth more, but my friend continued to bargain until finally she said, "I will give you a $15.00 check." I shook my hand at the side "no," but Juanita only smiled at me, showing her pretty dimples, and answered, "Alright." This is how our rich Spanish families have been stripped of their most precious belongings. "Why did you do it?" I whispered as I was going out the door. "I need the money to fix the house," she said.

At the Don Fernando (once the Barron Hotel), Mr. Gusdorf, the proprietor, kept introducing me to the hotel guests, telling them I had been married in this hotel. Oh, how I wished the old hotel had been as fine and attractive as this new one, to accommodate our wedding guests. [1955]

Pedro Juan Soto was born in Puerto Rico in 1928 and moved to the United States at the age of eighteen to complete his studies; he remained in New York City until his return to the island in 1955. A member of the well-known group of Puerto Rican authors referred to as the Generation of 1940, Soto is considered one of the island's most important narrators. He is acclaimed for works that reflect the harsh life of Puerto Ricans in New York, particularly in *Spiks,* his powerful collection of short stories published in 1956. Later works include *Usmail* (1958), *Ardiente suelo, fría estación* (Burning Ground, Cold Season, 1961), *El francotirador* (The Sniper, 1969), and *Un oscuro pueblo sonriente* (A Dark, Smiling People, 1982).

Juan Flores has described such authors as Pedro Juan Soto, René Marqués, José Luis González, and Emilio Díaz Valcárcel as exemplifying the "second stage" of U.S. Puerto Rican literature, coming after Bernardo Vega but before the Nuyorican writers of the 1960s;

these were island-born writers who wrote about the U.S. Puerto Rican community though not as members of that community. Among the best-known Puerto Rican writing in the United States, their works exhibit a heightened consciousness of the emigration experience but also have important ties to Latin American literature. According to Flores, the later Nuyorican writers are different from these authors principally in their use of extensive code-switching and bilingualism.

The following excerpt is one of the seven short stories and six vignettes in *Spiks,* which some critics feel is the best collection written thus far about the saga of the Puerto Rican diaspora.

God in Harlem

Her breasts were two painful mounds in the red sweater and her belly a passive volcano beneath the black taffeta skirt which only six months before had been her favorite party outfit. Leaning on the counter at El Iris Bar, she made circles with the wet glass, stopping from time to time to look at the clock above the mirrored shelf where the bottles were lined up.

"Hey, gimme another."

The waiter stopped mopping the floor and brought the bottle of Wilson's. He filled the shot glass and picked up the dollar the woman had been fingering distractedly. After bringing her change and wiping off the round stains on the counter, he went back to his mopping.

"Wachu up to, Nena?"

That thunderous voice reached her through the convulsions caused by the liquor. She put the empty glass on the bar, quickly blinked back her tears, and stood staring at the wall. She seemed to be demanding that the man project his image on the wall, so that she would not have to turn to see him put his foot on the rail. Then, as if she already saw his messy hair, his long sideburns, and his enormous double chin on the wall, she said:

"Bout time. I was gettin tired."

"Well, I almos didn' come," he said, smiling. He brought the slavered cigarette to his lips, then threw it away when he saw that it was out. "Since they tole me you was lookin for me to cut off my . . ."

She turned to look him up and down.

"I ain here to fool aroun, Microbio. You seem to think life's a joke."

"Nobody ain proved no different."

"Well, you got proof here," she said. "This is yours an you know it."

Moving away from the counter, she pointed to her body, a barrel without staves.

"Don' make me laugh, Nena, my lip's cut."

She tugged on her sweater to pull it over the deformed waistline and buttoned it, all the while looking at the man.

"One of these days somebody gonna cut it up for real," she said.

"Don' threaten me. You know what happens to me when people do that." Stiffening his neck in challenge, he almost looked as if he would bite her. But he immediately shrank back into disdain. "I start to shake, you see."

"You promised to help me," she cried. She lowered her voice when she realized that the few customers in the bar were listening. "After you got me when I was drunk an knocked me up, you said you'd . . ."

"What I tole you was I'd help you pay for the little job. But if you let all those months pass . . ."

He remained calm, not paying much attention to her, rapping his knuckles on the bar to call the bartender. As soon as he had ordered a beer she turned to him, her face distraught and shining like a new penny.

"Don' gimme that stuff cause it don' work all the time. Cause I don' wanna go aroun like Argelia with her ovaries an womb all outa place . . ."

"I could give a good shit about that," he said. He took his hand out of his pocket to toss a dime to the bartender.

"Coño, you know you did it in bad faith, Microbio. Pacache bet you couldn' knock me up an you . . ."

"Ah, Pacache tole you that? Well, let him take care of the kid. Anyhow, the five bucks I won off him didn' las long."

"Okay," she said. She raised her hand and moved it in a gesture of expectancy. "But jus remember that I'll get back at you."

"I tole you not to threaten."

Nena heard a violent click and felt a sharpness in her ribs. And before she dared look down, she knew it was a switchblade he had in his fingers.

"You better behave," said Microbio, hiding the weapon with the same sleight of hand he had used to take it out. He picked up the glass of beer and drank half of it down. "An if you gonna have a kid, you better look fer another job. If I knew how stupid you are, I wouldna bet."

For a moment he held the glass in the air as if he were demonstrating that the beer had evaporated and dared anyone to prove otherwise. Then he swallowed the rest, banged the glass down on the counter, winked at her as he wiped his mouth on the back of his hand, and walked out with his bow-legged swagger.

Nena remained, nervously rubbing the edge of the bar. She looked around for a glance of compassion, a gesture of understanding which would allow her to ask for help. But the painted women and the young men in baggy pants laughed and shouted without paying attention to her.

She asked for another whiskey and, fingers trembling, lit a cigarette. She was a stone rolling downhill. Not so, not even a stone, because her fear of abortion revealed her posture of imaginary strength. She was, simply, a clod of earth . . . rolling downhill. How could she get over the humps without crumbling to bits? The money she had saved for the trip to Puerto Rico — how many years since she had been there? five? — would hardly last until the delivery. Afterward she would have to get rid of the kid and put her life together again. But who would give it a home? The child of a whore. The only alternative was to abandon it on some stoop.

Easy to think it. She smiled with bitterness, once again making circles on the counter. To forget nine difficult months. To forget the somersaults in her belly. To forget that *that,* at least, had belonged to her. To forget that she could change paths. Be another woman: leave the dog's life of Harlem and devote herself to her child. Begin again, far from that devil Microbio.

She drank her whiskey deliberately. Fear still ran insane within her. The terror of a wound on her face. Involuntarily she remembered the tune and the words of that *plena:* "Cortaron a Elena, they cut up Elena . . ." She looked outside, fearing she would surprise Microbio hanging around. He was not there. Some men were leaning against the fenders of parked cars, watching for news of the lucky number in the clandestine Sunday drawing. On the opposite sidewalk people filed out of church, not crossing the avenue until they were far from the bar. Inside, the customers, realizing that eleven o'clock mass was over, began to play the jukebox.

She picked up her change, threw away her cigarette, and walked out the door, hiding her hands in the sleeves of her sweater. Once again she hated the city. She liked it in summer, when she could see it splashed with green. But not in autumn: not in the gray and cold enclosure smelling of dirty water. Not when it seemed to be the inside of an old metal washtub.

Two blocks down she heard the exclamations of the kids who walked toward her, and turned quickly, anticipating Microbio's attack. But behind her there were only surprised people looking and gesturing at the sheets of paper raining down. Some neighbors leaned out of the windows or went out onto the fire escapes trying to catch them.

Some reached her where she was standing. They were no more than white sheets, divided in half by a line of large, black letters which read in Spanish: AWAIT YE THE LORD. Looking at them indifferently, Nena raised her eyes toward the roofs where she expected to see people scattering them over the avenue. But she saw no one. And neither did she see the plane which could have been dropping them. The passersby had stopped to read and comment on the announcement. Curious, they looked around for the source of the sheets without finding it.

Turning the corner, Nena climbed the stoop of the first building she came to. The pane was cracked on the door she pushed open, and the walls of the hallway were peeling and chalk-scribbled: hearts and arrows, autographs and dirty words written in unschooled hand, deformed circles and lines and dots making the faces of unfinished figures. Behind the narrow and poorly lit staircase were piled dented garbage cans, varnished in grease, and a residue of bones and papers.

On the second floor, taking the key from between her breasts, she opened the door marked 2D and ran to stretch out on the bed to calm her panting. Although it was noon the room was dark. Little light entered through the only window, which gave onto the fire escape. The room's dilapidation was distributed among a moth-eaten bed, two fragile chairs, a small, ramshackle dresser, and the worn and dirty linoleum.

"I hope God comes down an strikes the world with his fist an buries us all," she said to the plaster crucifix hanging over the bed. She was already beginning to feel nausea and a pain in her ankles.

She heard laughter and the voices of a man and a woman on the stairs. The sound of a key in the lock next door made her expectant. Hands slapping a backside in the midst of whispering, and the groan of the mattress minutes later, made her forget her indisposition. Suddenly she remembered the teacher: the man (the first one) who five years before had decided to discover her bountifully seductive body. That afternoon, the room closed after class, he had pretended to tutor her for the coming exam. She had anticipated the deed. And she had waited for him to gather the courage to take her. She had wanted finally, at seventeen, to acquire the sexual consciousness and competence which she envied in her married friends. She had wanted to clarify once and for all her diffuse notions about sex, notions which were the product of an endless stream of licentious jokes heard at women's parties and of persistent reading of the novels of Pedro Mata. That afternoon she had been the spider and the teacher an insignificant insect. When he sent her for the books she entered the cabinet looking for the proper corner in which to await him. And then, in the embrace, she had whispered her string of dirty words in order to compensate for the inferiority she always felt in his presence, in order to mock her own ingenuous ploy, in order to offer herself to him however, whenever, and wherever he wanted. She herself had raised her skirt, had fumbled for his belt and between his legs, attacking him, trying to shame him with her fierceness. And, ears alert to any strange noise outside the cabinet, eyes closed and lips bitten, she had perceived the clarity of her eyelids and the moan and delirium and happy giddiness of orgasm. He had plotted to be the spider, and she had deprived him of that role.

Now once again she heard laughter outside and she heard the couple go downstairs. And she thought that the sex act had never again provoked in her, nor would it, the happy confusion of that far-off afternoon.

"Maybe with jus one man," she said, "who won' be ashamed and who'll help me to change."

And she covered her face with the pillow, wanting to suffocate herself along with her frustration.

~~~
~~~

Friday night, no longer able to resist the desire for a drink, she went into El Iris. Microbio was swaying at the bar and she tried to go unnoticed to an empty table. But Microbio stopped shouting to the group gathered around him and went to sit with her.

"How's my Nena? Hey, lissen, I'm more bombed than a fly in a pisspot. Well, I'm what they call loaded, and not with money."

He laughed without looking at her, and then, seeing her face still serious and anxious, he called the waiter.

"Two beers."

When the waiter moved away, Microbio took some coins from his pocket and put them on the table.

"Lissen, Nena, if you only knew that the fella you see servin there was a bum till a few days ago. But since he had a kid, or his wife had it, he's reformed. You don' believe the same thing can happen to me?"

"Yeah, sure. You real good for work."

"Come on, you don' believe I can go straight? Get this, that guy over there washes dishes in the daytime an waits on tables here at night. I can do the same thing. Don' tell me I can't."

Seeing that she didn't answer, that she merely stared at him, Microbio took out a pack of cigarettes and offered her one. She took it and waited for him to light it, trying at the same time to hide her nervousness. The musical din from the jukebox prevented her from hearing all of what he was saying, and for that reason she had to follow the jerky movements of his lips.

"Hey, Nena, how many more months you got?"

"Three."

"The kid better not turn out to be a pimp, cause the pimps' union here is full up."

She remained expressionless, not allowing Microbio's words or his laughter to move her, smoking in silence.

"An the hospital?"

Nena flicked the ashes onto the floor and shrugged.

"That ain a problem," she said. "I'll wait till the las minute an then go to emergency."

"An afterward, wha happens? Cause I tole you. If you gonna raise him like that, you screwin an . . ."

She drew on the cigarette and exhaled all at once into the mocking eyes, then changed the cigarette to the other hand so that he would not realize that she had done it on purpose.

"If I wanna I can work in a factory."

"I was gonna say the same thing," said Microbio, moving his head up and down forcefully, as if he wanted to shake it off his shoulders. "Cause if you don', wha kinda example you gonna be fer the kid?"

Nena straightened in her chair and watched the waiter leave the bottles and the glasses on the table and pick up the correct change.

"Wassa matter with you now? Like you was my father."

"Its that I been bad," said Microbio, filling both glasses. "Its a weight on my conscience that the kid's gonna live like that. Unnerstan? Though I'm gonna tell you, I figured you'd get rid of it. I swear I thought . . . No, I'm gonna help you. But the minute . . . eh? . . . I split. The minute you get to be too much, I split."

"Okay, man, okay."

Nena threw the cigarette down and crushed it vehemently, letting out some of the joy which overflowed from inside of her. She felt like running to hug all the customers. She looked at Microbio again. She wanted to be sure that this was not just another trick.

"Hey, you wouldn' be tryin to fool me?"

"No, vieja." Microbio's face contracted, took on a martyred expression. "You know that me, I . . . Any woman'd say yes to me, you know it. But us two can make a home fer that kid an . . ."

"Aw, don' come on with that. Take it slow, take it easy."

Seeing his face darken, Nena caressed the hand that twitched on the table.

"We'll do wha you wan, Microbio, but give it time."

"An ain I gonna see you?"

"Sure. But here."

"That all?"

"If you behave, then all you want," she said with a sly smile. "But I gotta try you out."

"Like we was engaged," he laughed.

"Like we was engaged," she laughed. And satisfaction flooded over her, and the world became a heap of dates and places and ordered acts.

~~~
~~~

Cheered by the clear sky which promised a warm Sunday, she settled down on a bench in Central Park to take the sun. She mistrusted Microbio's sudden transformation, but she relegated those thoughts to the farthest corner of her mind. Microbio wasn't bad. Microbio *wanted* to help her. And right now she needed more help, more advice, more support than ever. She was confused, fearful that she could not face the new life she was proposing to herself. Microbio *had* to be sincere. If not . . . what would become of her? A clod of earth rolling downhill . . . But with Microbio, all the problems of the future would be so much nonsense. And the moments of pleasant conversation and affection would be the smallest measure of a great happiness. God was watching over all three of them.

Seeing a group of boys approaching the lake, she thought of the children she would have one day. No doubt Microbio thought as she did: that in their children lay their own salvation. That they would have to work honorably for them. That they would have to change two lives in order to save others.

The boys were coming nearer now, following paper boats which, pushed by the wind, advanced toward her. When the boats bumped against the wall, their owners knelt by the water and put stones on the piles of papers they had under their arms. Then they gathered and lined up the boats for the next race. A foreboding made her look at the sheets of paper. They were identical, except for the text, to those of the previous Sunday. This time the line of large, black letters read in Spanish: THE LORD IS NIGH.

"Hey, where'd you get those papers?"

All of them looked up at the pregnant woman staring fearfully at the sheets.

"On Madison," said the oldest, raising his hand to give the go signal.

"Who from?"

The kid shrugged, gave the signal, and left with the others behind the boats.

Nena left the park hurriedly, and did not stop until she reached El Iris. The papers swirled madly on the corners.

"It's someone with nothin to do," she told herself.

Each time she thought of the inexplicable appearance of the papers, she felt her heart beat uncontrollably. They crawled along the pavement. They whipped against the entrance of the poolhall or danced on the stoops of the buildings. She almost started to run, looking back at every moment to watch them jumping in the distance.

At the next corner she bumped into Microbio. He was wearing his green shirt and yellow tie, looking like a carnival puppet in the wrong place at the wrong time. Shaved, combed, smelling of cologne, he seemed someone else.

"I was lookin fer you to go to the movies, Nena. At the Boricua there's a good one."

"I don' feel so good. I'm gonna go lay down."

"Ah . . . Yuh wan me to bring you somethin from the drugstore?"

"Its jus things you get when yer pregnant."

"Okay, go lay down. I figured you'd like to go to the movies, but if yer sick . . ."

"Wait," said Nena, when Microbio began to move away. She thought of the enormous loneliness of her small room, of her fear of the sheets of paper, of her need to chat with someone to forget them. "Come an les talk some."

In the room she motioned him to a chair and went to straighten the messy bed. Then she opened the window to evict the smell of dust and sleep. There were men kneeling on the stoop across the way, crowded around a pile of bills and coins. One of them was saying something unintelligible while he listened to the sound of the dice in the hollow of his hand. When he threw them against the wall, he closed his fist and cursed.

"I bet no one'll know how to pray when He comes."

"What?"

Turning, she faced Microbio, who was sitting astride the chair, his arms resting on its back.

"Those papers, I bet its true that God's about to come."

"Aw, cuddid out," he gesticulated. "You get fooled by any little thing. Watch out you don' pull a Mary Magdalen on me."

"Don' gimme Mary Magdalen!" Crossing the room, Nena went to stretch out on the bed, on her back, making a pillow of her arms. "I don' go to church, but I believe in God."

When she felt the movement in her belly, she began to rub it.

"Tha's like everybody," said Microbio. "I got my religion too."

He saw her bulging in the shadow, waving her legs in the air, her skirt moving with her hand and bit by bit uncovering her thighs.

"Ay, if I could only have this kid soon."

He got up, removing the chair from between his legs and putting it to one side.

"It hurt?"

"Naw, but I think I got gas. An then this kid kicks so much."

"You wan me to give you a rubdown?"

"If you do it careful, yeah. The witch hazel's on the dresser."

Microbio brought the bottle and settled down next to her. With one hand he unbuttoned her sweater and pulled her blouse from under the skirt. And then he pulled down her skirt and panties enough to expose the englobed flesh and the protruding navel. Nena shivered on feeling his damp hand on her belly. She closed her eyes and stretched her arms back, adding a slight sway to her body as it was rocked by Microbio's hand. She was scratching at the sheet and moving her hips more rhythmically when she heard the bottle fall to the floor. She thought of stopping Microbio, she thought of running out of the room, but she did nothing. He was settling his noisy breath against her eyelids and nothing else mattered.

She awoke to organ music and the patter of rain on the fire escape. She groped at her side for the naked body which was no longer there. Then she sat up in bed and waited for her eyes to adjust to the dark. The organ music was abruptly interrupted. Static and voices in English took its place randomly for a moment, until the hand which was turning the knob in a neighboring room stopped. Now a mambo played, got louder, and remained to shake and sway the atmosphere.

She finally made out the chairs. She lay back when she realized that Microbio's clothes were gone. Thinking about him, she remembered the past week: days and nights full of swaggering and moans and surprise attacks. She wanted life to go on like that, no more than one long, meaningful sex act. Only one man to bring an end to her loneliness. Only one body. Only one voice.

She wanted him on top of her again, listening to the sound of rain. In the midst of uninterrupted organ music, in the midst of radio sermons. In the midst of a rainy Sunday like this one, which needed only to see and hear them make love in order to clear up.

She stretched. For a moment she was distracted by the ticking of the alarm clock. She did not feel like getting up, yet she was hungry. If Microbio would only come back soon with coffee and a sandwich . . . She got out of bed listlessly and turned on the light. The clock said past eleven. No wonder she was hungry. She rolled up the window shade. If only it would stop raining. Still drowsy, she put on the red sweater and the taffeta skirt. She promised herself once again that that very afternoon she would fix up some dresses. The skirt no longer fastened, could not be let out anymore, and had lost its sheen.

In the bottom drawer of the dresser she looked for the olive jar where she kept her savings. Taking out a fifty-cent piece, she noticed that the contents had diminished considerably. She did not remember having spent that much. Unless . . . Microbio!

Taking an old newspaper to shield herself from the rain, she went out into the street.

"Seen Microbio?"

No one at the poolhall said he had. Some shook their heads disinterestedly. Others said no, but smiled, looking at her belly. They turned to chalk their cues or lean over the cue balls on the green felt, without saying any more.

"Seen Microbio?"

At El Iris, the few customers looked at her in silence.

"He ain been aroun here," said one. "What? You still ain dropped that kid?" He laughed, looking at the others.

She got the feeling that they were all plotting something against her, something that went beyond denying that Microbio had been with them some time before.

"Who'd Microbio bet with this time?"

The man feigned seriousness.

"What bet?"

"Don' worry," she said. "I'll fin out."

In the street once again, she stayed under the bar's awning, waiting for the rain to let up. People were coming out of church, clutching their missals like shields.

Suddenly the papers started to drop like slaps, beating on umbrellas and parked cars. People stopped without knowing what to do, without speaking, without even daring to look at the papers which were disintegrating in the rain.

The priest came out onto the sidewalk. His angry face looked out from under an umbrella and his chubby pink hand gestured with authority.

"Walk, walk," he said to the people. "I've already told you that this is the Devil's work."

A man with a broom followed him, on his orders hurriedly sweeping the papers toward the river which flowed down-gutter. The people moved into groups of three and four to share umbrellas and walked rapidly away.

Nena looked on the roofs to see who was scattering the papers. And did not find them. The papers had come as if from some catapult into the rectangular emptiness of the avenue. Heedless of the rain, she crouched slowly to pick one up. It was another large, black-lettered notice in Spanish, longer this time: THE LORD WILL BE AMONG US NEXT SUNDAY, 11 A.M. 114 ST. & MADISON AVE.

It was as if she had been pierced by an electric shock. She dropped the paper and started to run in the downpour, without seeking refuge under awnings, stopping for only a moment in the doorway of her building to catch her breath. Then she ran upstairs, through the door of her room, and fell to her knees on the bed in front of the crucifix. In her mind she was still running and closing doors and looking for a way out of the labyrinth through which Microbio was chasing her. She could never get away if God did not help her. Microbio's transformation, she now understood, was no more than a plot to kill the baby. God had to save her from his deceit.

"I won' sin no more," she said. "You can see me an you know I wanna change."

Praying, she had a vision of an old film she had seen so many times during Holy Week in her hometown: a shameless, half-naked woman passed through the village on a luxurious chair carried by some Negroes. Later, submissive and prematurely old, she kissed and washed with her tears the feet of Him who had pardoned her. And finally she was no more than a purified face, tearfully raised toward the cross on which hung the frail, slack body which would refuse to remain underground.

The banging on the door frightened her. Crossing herself quickly, she went to open it.

"Wa's goin on here?"

Before she could react, Microbio entered unsteadily, shouldering her aside, waving an almost empty bottle.

"A little drink, Nena."

She closed the door and went to sit on the bed, next to her fear.

"You began so early."

"You wanna little drink?"

"No."

"Here's to what I got an you aint," said Microbio. He tilted the bottle, swallowing noisily, and then threw it under the bed.

"Wachu come here for, Microbio, to steal sommore?"

"But I'll pay you back," he said, moving toward her. "I always pay what . . ."

Nena ran to the door when he tried to embrace her.

"Wassa matter with you?" asked Microbio. "Doncha like me no more?"

"I'm tired of yer shit. So, geddouda here!"

He was swaying next to the bed, smiling sloppily.

"An I'm gonna tell you somethin," said Nena. "I'm gonna have this kid fer better fer worse."

"An whose saying you can't have it?"

"I figured out yer little game, Microbio."

"You crazy," he said, throwing himself on the bed, face up.

"You better leave now."

"Who says, God?"

"From now on yer gonna see how things change."

"An if I go, how you gonna get yours then? Come on, you know yer religion's right between my legs."

Nena took off one shoe and hobbled to the bed.

"Geddouda here, you bastard, or yer gonna get it."

Microbio leaned on his elbow, seeing above him the fish mouth, the sharp mouth ending in a reddish point.

"You wouldn't dare, Nena."

"Geddout!"

"I betcha you won' do it!"

Nena raised the shoe and struck the head, which fell forward, shook itself, and raised again, opening angered eyes. Immediately she felt one hand gripping her throat and the other struggling with the hand which held the shoe.

The blood rushed to her face and her body wavered from a

drunken and enraged shove. When she stumbled and fell against the wall, her head became a bloody hammer in Microbio's hands. Again she struck the shapeless form which was almost on top of her, and then she felt the heel break, while her face still came and went with his slaps.

Once out of the vertigo, she found herself under the compassionate look of the neighbors who were trying to stop her endless scream. And only then did she stop beating against the floor with the useless sole, in order to cough and spit the phlegm that was choking her.

Through her crying she saw the men file out. She let herself be undressed by the women before she collapsed moaning on the bed. And while someone ripped the sheet to bandage her head, and others began to bathe her with witch hazel, she gripped her belly to make sure it had not caved in.

Brick dust was blowing from the abandoned buildings, and in a corner of an empty lot a pile of garbage burned. Kids in wide-brimmed hats and baggy pants kept their hands in their pockets and stamped on the ground to drive away the cold. In front of them, above the breath converted into little vapor clouds, they could see a man standing on a pile of broken bottles and rotted wood, and an anemic woman standing next to an American flag.

Nena joined the crowd, which continued to grow despite the cold and cloudy day. Her black fuzzy jacket, straining its buttons, was torn on both sides. And her eyes were no more than cracks in her bluish face.

Her credo of superstitions had convinced her that today there would be a catastrophe. Today she and the world which she hated so would collapse. Evil would disappear: this consoled her. Now she prayed in silence, thinking about the child who, since the beating, had stopped its movements in her belly. Thinking how different everything would have been if only she could have given birth.

"Listen, brother!" shouted a man in the crowd. "When does the Lord appear? Man, I'm gettin numb."

There, in front, the preacher whispered to one of his companions and she handed him a book with red edges.

"Aw, don' give us what we already know," said an old woman.

"Oh, you wretches!" bellowed the man in Spanish, after returning the book and raising his arms to the heavens.

"Carajo, if you gonna insult us . . ."

"Brothers!" said the man.

"Finish, chico, finish. We gonna be here all day."

"The Lord," said the man, "who sees everything and hears everything, won' come so long as there's so many sinners on Earth."

"What Earth? Doncha mean mud?"

As the laughter increased, the preacher stretched his arms toward them.

"Abandon the paths of perdition!" he warned.

"Aw, cuddid out!"

Nena understood now what was wrong with this spectacle. There would be no thunder, no lightning, no sound of harps, no celestial voices. The world would not crumble, nor would Evil disappear from amongst them. Like herself, everyone had come as to an empty cage where they hoped to see a freak. And it was stupid.

But *they* remained safe in their evil. Only she was losing a world: her hope. Because there was nothing more for her to do. Her child was lost, so she was lost. Tomorrow did not exist. Only the inferno of her loneliness, the continuation of an adventure begun five years before. For another woman it would have been no more than a risk, an impulsive adolescent act that with cunning could have remained a pleasant accident. She, however, had perpetuated the adventure, squandering and debilitating her impulsiveness. She had distorted risk itself.

"Hear the Lord's word, brothers, before it's too late!" said the man. "Don't insist on following Satan's path."

"Naw, wha happen is that nobody'd sell the Lord a plane ticket to come here!"

The guffaws became louder each time someone in the back let out a whinny. Then scattered voices began to intone a song:

"Manda fuego, Señor, manda fuueegoooo!"

The man stopped preaching and took the book to read from it. Perhaps to get strength from the passage itself. Perhaps to raise a wall between the mockery and himself.

"If I'd of known this, I would of stayed in bed," said one, leaving the crowd.

"Wait fer me," said his companion. "Les go to the bar an get some holy water."

They were followed by complete dispersion: children ran, pushing each other, and women followed behind them, admonishing them not to cross the street, while the men came last, imitating their screeching voices and their waddles.

Nena's voice stopped them for an instant.

"God is here!"

Tense, eyes closed, her face raised as if to sniff the dry air, she caressed her belly as she swayed.

"Jeezus, that one's gettin all hot an bothered," someone said. "Why, if what she got there's the holy ghost, then my wife's got a church!"

She heard neither laughter nor comments. All she heard was the voice coming from afar: "I am the door: he who passes through me will be saved . . ."

And feeling her belly, she murmured: "God-is-here God-is-here God-is-here . . ."

She knew neither pain, nor hate, nor bitterness. She was being born. [1956]

Translation of "Dios en Harlem" by Victoria Ortíz

José Antonio Villarreal was born in Los Angeles in 1924, served in the U.S. Navy from 1942 to 1946, and received a B.A. from the University of California at Berkeley in 1950. He has been a public relations writer for an insurance company, a technical editor and writer in the aerospace and defense industry, and a delivery-truck driver. Villarreal moved to Mexico in 1973. His three published novels are *Pocho* (1959), *The Fifth Horseman* (1974), and *Clemente Chacón* (1984).

Until the recent discoveries and publication of works by María Amparo Ruiz de Burton and Josephina Niggli, *Pocho* was thought to be the first novel published in English by a Latino. Though it no longer holds that stature, *Pocho* did introduce the American public to Chicano culture and its fiction.

Pocho is slang — usually used in a derogatory way — for an assimilated Mexican immigrant to the United States. The novel is the story of a veteran of the Mexican Revolution and his relationship with his son, Richard Rubio (Richard Blond), a bookish child who is not in tune with the field culture in which he lives. Critics have pointed out that the novel is "unbalanced," because the opening section on the Revolution has no followup and its characters are "unconvincing." Yet *Pocho* remains a landmark in Latino literature, opening the way for publication of work based on the history, politics, and culture of the Chicano community.

from Pocho

Richard Rubio, lost in thought, walked slowly into his front yard. He was relaxed, although his body was bruised and sore from football practice. They had scrimmaged that day, for there was a game on Friday, and although there was little chance that he, as a scrub, would get into the game at all, he played as much during practice as the first string did. It was with the reserves that the regulars conditioned themselves and perfected their timing. Richard had almost quit when he realized that he would never make the first team, but upon reflection he knew that he enjoyed the contact and that the practice sessions took up a great deal of his time, of which there was too much for him at the moment.

The Rubio front yard was a large one, and Juan Rubio had planted a vegetable garden. There were tomatoes there now, and chiles. The driveway and the back yard, where there was another garden, were neat and orderly. At the extreme end of the property was a chicken coop, newly whitewashed, and rabbit hutches.

He reached the end of the driveway and stepped onto the porch. Then he noticed that his sister Luz sat in a car in front of the house, talking to a boy from school whom he vaguely knew. Inside the house, he was suddenly filled with sorrow mingled with disgust, as he always was these days when he came home. Trash and garbage were on the floor; bedrooms were unkempt, with beds unmade. On the floor of the living room, where two of the girls slept, blankets and a mat still lay, reeking strongly of urine, because the girls still wet their beds at the ages of eight and ten. Only his bed was made up, because his mother could not neglect him. His clothes were pressed and in order in his closet, but elsewhere he saw a slip here, a brassière there; odds and ends of clothing lay wherever the wearer decided to undress. In the kitchen, the sink was full of dishes, dirty water nearly overflowing onto the littered floor. The stove was caked with grease, its burners barely allowing enough gas to permit a flame to live.

He threw his books on his bed, then went to his mother and kissed her. She sat with one of his younger sisters between her legs, going through her hair with a fine comb. A louse cracked loudly between her thumbnails.

"Go!" he said to the little girl. "Go and bring my sisters here — and Luz, too."

"But her head smells of coal oil," protested his mother. "She cannot go out among her neighbors smelling like that."

He was angry and impatient, and his voice was harsh. "Do you think that because our house is so filthy, we are the only ones in Santa Clara who have lice?" He turned to his little sister again and said, "Go!" She jumped to her feet and ran out the door.

The girls came into the house one by one. There was a frightened look in their faces, and they immediately began to clean the house. They knew what he wanted, for this was not the first time this had happened.

"Where is Luz?" he demanded.

"She won't come in," said one of the girls. "She said to tell you to go to hell."

He walked to the car very quickly, in a rage he had never known himself capable of feeling. He said calmly, however, and in Spanish, "Go inside and help your sisters, big lazy."

"Don't bother me," she answered.

"What does he want?" asked the boy, from behind the wheel.

"He don't want me to be out here with you," she lied.

"Go take a shit," said the boy to Richard.

Richard opened the door and pulled her out onto the sidewalk. He slapped her hard twice, and she ran into the house screaming. The boy got out of his car, and he was big, powerful. Richard backed away toward the yard next door and took a brick from an abandoned incinerator.

"Come on, you big son of a bitch," he said. "Come after me and I'll kill you!" The boy hesitated, then moved forward again. "That's it," said Richard, "come on and get your Goddamn head busted wide open."

The boy went back to his car. "You're crazy!" he shouted. "Crazier'n hell!"

That night, for the first time in months, they had dinner together in the old way. After dinner, his father sat on the rocker in the living room, listening to the Mexican station from Piedras Negras on short wave. When the kitchen was picked up, the girls sat around restlessly in the living room, and Richard knew they wanted to listen to something else, so he said to his father, "Let us go into the kitchen. I have a new novel in the Spanish I will read to you."

In the kitchen, around the table, his mother also sat down, and said, "It is a long time, little son, that you do not read to us."

How blind she must be, he thought. Aloud he said, "It is called 'Crime and Punishment,' and it is about the Rusos in another time." He read rapidly and they listened attentively, interrupting him only now and then with a surprised "Oh!" or "That is so true!" After two hours, he could not read fast enough for himself, and he wished that he could read all night to them, because it was a certainty that he would not get another opportunity to read to them like this. They would never get to know the book, and he knew they were to miss something great. He knew also that they would never be this close together again. How he knew this he could not even guess, and that was sad in itself, besides their having to do without the book.

"There are new Mexican people in town, Papá," he said. "In school today, there were two boys and a girl."

"Yes, I know," said Juan Rubio. "Every year, more and more of us decide to remain here in the valley."

"They are funny," said Luz, who, along with two or three of the girls, had come into the kitchen.

"They dress strangely," said Richard.

"In San Jose," said Juan Rubio, "on Saturday night during the summer, I have seen these youngsters in clown costumes. It is the fashion of Los Angeles."

"They are different from us," said Luz. "Even in their features they are different from us."

"They come from a different part of México, that is all," said Consuelo, who knew of such things, for she herself was different from all of them, except for her son, and this because her great-grandfather had come from Yucatán.

"Well, at any rate, they are a coarse people," said Luz.

Richard and his father exchanged looks and laughed. She flushed in anger, and said in English to Richard, "Well, they ain't got nuthin' and they don't even talk good English."

He laughed louder, and his father laughed even though he did not know what she had said.

It was not until the following year that Richard knew that his town was changing as much as his family was. It was 1940 in Santa Clara, and, among other things, the Conscription Act had done its part in bringing about a change. It was not unusual now to see soldiers walking downtown or to see someone of the town in uniform. He was aware that people liked soldiers now, and could still remember the old days, when a detachment of cavalry camped outside the town for a few days or a unit of field artillery stayed at the university, and the worst thing one's sister could do was associate with a soldier. Soldiers were common, were drunkards, thieves, and rapers of girls, or something, to the people of Santa Clara, and the only uniforms with prestige in the town had been those of the CCC boys or of the American Legion during the Fourth of July celebration and the Easter-egg hunt. But now everybody loved a soldier, and he wondered how this had come about.

There were the soldiers, and there were also the Mexicans in ever-increasing numbers. The Mexican people Richard had known until now were those he saw only during the summer, and they were migrant families who seldom remained in Santa Clara longer than a month or two. The orbit of his existence was limited to the town, and actually to his immediate neighborhood, thereby preventing his association with the Mexican family which lived on the other side of town, across the tracks. In his wanderings into San Jose, he began to see more of what he called "the race." Many of the migrant workers who came up from southern California in the late spring and early summer now settled down in the valley. They bought two hundred pounds of flour and a hundred pounds of beans, and if they weathered the first winter, which was the most difficult, because the rains stopped agricultural workers from earning a living, they were settled for good.

As the Mexican population increased, Richard began to attend their dances and fiestas, and, in general, sought their company as much as possible, for these people were a strange lot to him. He was obsessed with a hunger to learn about them and from them. They had a burning contempt for people of different ancestry, whom they called Americans, and a marked hauteur toward México and toward their parents for their old-country ways. The former feeling came from a sense of inferiority that is a prominent characteristic in any Mexican reared in southern California; and the latter was an inexplicable compensation for that feeling. They needed to feel superior to something, which is a natural thing. The result was that they attempted to segregate themselves from both their cultures, and became truly a lost race. In their frantic desire to become different, they adopted a new mode of dress, a new manner, and even a new language. They used a polyglot speech made up of English and Spanish syllables, words, and sounds. This they incorporated into phrases and words that were unintelligible to anyone but themselves. Their Spanish became limited and their English more so. Their dress was unique to the point of being ludicrous. The black motif was predominant. The tight-fitting cuffs on trouser legs that billowed at the knees made Richard think of some long-forgotten pasha in the faraway past, and the fingertip coat and highly lustrous shoes gave the wearer, when walking, the appearance of a strutting cock. Their hair was long and swept up to meet in the back, forming a ducktail. They spent hours training it to remain that way.

The girls were characterized by the extreme shortness of their skirts, which stopped well above the knees. Their jackets, too, were fingertip in length, coming to within an inch of the skirt hem. Their hair reached below the shoulder in the back, and it was usually worn piled in front to form a huge pompadour.

The pachuco was born in El Paso, had gone west to Los Angeles, and was now moving north. To society, these zootsuiters were a menace, and the name alone classified them as undesirables, but Richard learned that there was much more to it than a mere group with a name. That in spite of their behavior, which was sensational at times and violent at others, they were simply a portion of a confused humanity, employing their self-segregation as a means of expression. And because theirs was a spontaneous, and not a planned, retaliation, he saw it as a vicissitude of society, obvious only because of its nature and comparative suddenness.

From the leggy, short-skirted girls, he learned that their mores were no different from those of what he considered good girls. What was under the scant covering was as inaccessible as it would be under the more conventional dress. He felt, in fact, that these girls were more difficult to reach. And from the boys he learned that their bitterness and hostile attitude toward "whites" was not merely a lark. They had learned hate through actual experience, with everything the word implied. They had not been as lucky as he, and showed the scars to prove it. And, later on, Richard saw in retrospect that what happened to him in the city jail in San Jose was due more to the character of a handful of men than to the wide, almost organized attitude of a society, for just as the zootsuiters were blamed en masse for the actions of a few, they, in turn, blamed the other side for the very same reason.

As happens in most such groups, there were misunderstandings and disagreements over trivia. Pachucos fought among themselves, for the most part, and they fought hard. It was not unusual that a quarrel born on the streets or back alleys of a Los Angeles slum was settled in the Santa Clara Valley. Richard understood them and partly sympathized, but their way of life was not entirely justified in his mind, for he felt that they were somehow reneging on life; this was the easiest thing for them to do. They, like his father, were defeated — only more so, because they really never started to live. They, too, were but making a show of resistance.

Of the new friends Richard made, those who were native to San Jose were relegated to become casual acquaintances, for they were as Americanized as he, and did not interest him. The newcomers became the object of his explorations. He was avidly hungry to learn the ways of these people. It was not easy for him to approach them at first, because his clothes labeled him as an outsider, and, too, he had trouble understanding their speech. He must not ask questions, for fear of offending them; his deductions as to their character and makeup must come from close association. He was careful not to be patronizing or in any way act superior. And, most important, they must never suspect what he was doing. The most difficult moments for him were when he was doing the talking, for he was conscious that his Spanish was better than theirs. He learned enough of their vernacular to get along; he did not learn more, because he was always in a hurry about knowledge. Soon he counted a few boys as friends, but had a much harder time of it with the girls, because they considered him a traitor to his "race." Before he knew it, he found that he almost never spoke to them in English, and no longer defended the "whites," but, rather, spoke disparagingly of them whenever possible. He also bought a suit to wear when in their company, not with such an extreme cut as those they wore, but removed enough from the conservative so he would not be considered a square. And he found himself a girl, who refused to dance the faster pieces with him, because he still jittered in the American manner. So they danced only to soft music while they kissed in the dimmed light, and that was the extent of their lovemaking. Or he stood behind her at the bar, with his arms around her as she sipped a Nehi, and felt strange because she was a Mexican and everyone around them was also Mexican, and felt stranger still from the knowledge that he felt strange. When the dance was over, he took her to where her parents were sitting and said goodnight to the entire family.

Whenever his new friends saw him in the company of his school acquaintances, they were courteously polite, but they later chastised him for fraternizing with what they called the enemy. Then Richard had misgivings, because he knew that his desire to become one of them was not a sincere one in that respect, yet upon reflection he realized that in truth he enjoyed their company and valued their friendship, and his sense of guilt was gone. He went along with everything they did, being careful only to keep away from serious trouble with no loss of prestige. Twice he entered the dreamworld induced by marihuana, and after the effect of the drug was expended, he was surprised to discover that he did not crave it, and was glad, for he could not afford a kick like that. As it was, life was too short for him to be able to do the many things he knew he still must do. The youths understood that he did not want it, and never pressed him.

Now the time came to withdraw a little. He thought it would be a painful thing, but they liked him, and their friendliness made everything natural. He, in his gratefulness, loved them for it.

I can be a part of everything, he thought, because I am the only one capable of controlling my destiny . . . Never — no, never —

will I allow myself to become a part of a group — to become classified, to lose my individuality . . . I will not become a follower, nor will I allow myself to become a leader, because I must be myself and accept for myself only that which I value, and not what is being valued by everyone else these days . . . like a Goddamn suit of clothes they're wearing this season or Cuban heels . . . a style in ethics. What shall we do to liven up the season this year of Our Lord 1940, you from the North, and you from the South, and you from the East, and you from the West? Be original, and for Chrissake speak up! Shall we make it a vogue to sacrifice virgins — but, no, that's been done. . . . What do you think of matricide or mother rape? No? Well — wish we could deal with more personal things, such as prolonging the gestation period in the *Homo sapiens;* that would keep the married men hopping, no?

He thought this and other things, because the young are like that, and for them nothing is impossible; no, nothing is impossible, and this truism gives impetus to the impulse to laugh at abstract bonds. This night he thought this, and could laugh at the simplicity with which he could render powerless obstacles in his search for life, he had returned to the Mexican dancehall for the first time in weeks, and the dance was fast coming to a close. The orchestra had blared out a jazzed-up version of "Home, Sweet Home" and was going through it again at a much slower tempo, giving the couples on the dance floor one last chance for the sensual embraces that would have to last them a week. Richard was dancing with his girl, leading with his leg and holding her slight body close against his, when one of his friends tapped him on the shoulder.

"We need some help," he said. "Will you meet us by the door after the dance?" The question was more of a command, and the speaker did not wait for an answer. The dance was over, and Richard kissed the girl goodbye and joined the group that was gathering conspicuously as the people poured out through the only exit.

"What goes?" he asked.

"We're going to get some guys tonight," answered the youth who had spoken to him earlier. He was twenty years old and was called the Rooster.

The Mexican people have an affinity for incongruous nicknames. In this group, there was Tuerto, who was not blind; Cacarizo, who was not pockmarked; Zurdo, who was not left-handed; and a drab little fellow who was called Slick. Only Chango was appropriately named. There was indeed something anthropoidal about him.

The Rooster said, "They beat hell out of my brother last night, because he was jiving with one of their girls. I just got the word that they'll be around tonight if we want trouble."

"Man," said Chango, "we want a mess of trouble."

"Know who they are?" asked the Tuerto.

"Yeah. It was those bastards from Ontario," said the Rooster. "We had trouble with them before."

"Where they going to be?" asked Richard.

"That's what makes it good. Man, it's going to be real good," said the Rooster. "In the Orchard. No cops, no nothing. Only us."

"And the mud," said the Tuerto. The Orchard was a twelve-acre cherry grove in the new industrial district on the north side of the city.

"It'll be just as muddy for them," said the Rooster. "Let's go!"

They walked out and hurriedly got into the car. There were eight of them in Zurdo's sedan, and another three were to follow in a coupé. Richard sat in the back on Slick's lap. He was silent, afraid that they might discover the growing terror inside him. The Rooster took objects out of a gunnysack.

"Here, man, this is for you. Don't lose it," he said. It was a doubled-up bicycle chain, one end bound tightly with leather thongs to form a grip.

Richard held it in his hands and, for an unaccountable reason, said, "Thank you." Goddamn! he thought. What the hell did I get into? He wished they would get to their destination quickly, before his fear turned to panic. He had no idea who it was they were going to meet. Would there be three or thirty against them? He looked at the bludgeon in his hand and thought, Christ! Somebody could get killed!

The Tuerto passed a pint of whiskey back to them. Richard drank thirstily, then passed the bottle on.

"You want some, Chango?" asked the Rooster.

"That stuff's not for me, man. I stick to yesca," he answered. Four jerky rasps came from him as he inhaled, reluctant to allow the least bit of smoke to escape him, receiving the full force of the drug in a hurry. He offered the cigarette, but they all refused it. Then he carefully put it out, and placed the butt in a small matchbox.

It seemed to Richard that they had been riding for hours when finally they arrived at the Orchard. They backed the car under the trees, leaving the motor idling because they might have to leave in a hurry. The rest of the gang did not arrive; the Rooster said, "Those sons of bitches aren't coming!"

"Let's wait a few minutes," said the Tuerto. "Maybe they'll show up."

"No, they won't come," said the Rooster, in a calm voice now. He unzipped his pants legs and rolled them up to the knees. "Goddamn mud," he said, almost good-naturedly. "Come on!" They followed him into the Orchard. When they were approximately in the center of the tract, they stopped. "Here they come," whispered the Rooster.

Richard could not hear a thing. He was more afraid, but had stopped shaking. In spite of his fear, his mind was alert. He strained every sense, in order not to miss any part of this experience. He wanted to retain everything that was about to happen. He was surprised at the way the Rooster had taken command from the moment they left the dancehall. Richard had never thought of any one of the boys being considered a leader, and now they were all following the Rooster, and Richard fell naturally in line. The guy's like ice, he thought. Like a Goddamn piece of ice!

Suddenly forms took shape in the darkness before him.

And just as suddenly he was in the kaleidoscopic swirl of the fight. He felt blows on his face and body, as if from a distance, and he flayed viciously with the chain. There was a deadly quietness to the struggle. He was conscious that some of the fallen were moaning, and a voice screamed, "The son of a bitch broke my arm!" And that was all he heard for a while, because he was lying on the ground with his face in the mud.

They half-dragged, half-carried him to the car. It had bogged down in the mud, and they put him in the back while they tried to make it move. They could see headlights behind them, beyond the trees.

"We have to get the hell out of here," said the Rooster. "They got help. Push! Push!" Richard opened the door and fell out of the car. He got up and stumbled crazily in the darkness. He was grabbed and violently thrown in again. They could hear the sound of a large group coming toward them from the Orchard.

"Let's cut out!" shouted the Tuerto. "Leave it here!"

"No!" said the Rooster. "They'll tear it apart!" The car slithered onto the sidewalk and the wheels finally got traction. In a moment, they were moving down the street.

Richard held his hands to his head. "Jesus!" he exclaimed. "The cabrón threw me with the shithouse."

"It was a bat," said the Rooster.

"What?"

"He hit you with a Goddamn baseball bat!"

They took Richard home, and the Rooster helped him to his door. "Better rub some lard on your head," he told him.

"All right. Say, you were right, Rooster. Those other cats didn't show at all."

"You have to expect at least a couple of guys to chicken out on a deal like this," said the Rooster. "You did real good, man. I knew you'd do good."

Richard looked at his friend thoughtfully for a moment. In the dim light, his dark hair, Medusalike, curled from his collar in back almost to his eyebrows. He wondered what errant knight from Castile had traveled four thousand miles to mate with a daughter of Cuahtémoc to produce this strain. "How did you know?" he asked.

"Because I could tell it meant so much to you," said the Rooster.

"When I saw them coming, it looked like there were a hundred of them."

"There were only about fifteen. You're okay, Richard. Any time you want something, just let me know."

Richard felt humble in his gratification. He understood the friendship that was being offered. "I'll tell you, Rooster," he said. "I've never been afraid as much as I was tonight." He thought, If he knows this, perhaps he won't feel the sense of obligation.

"Hell, that's no news. We all were."

"Did we beat them?" asked Richard.

"Yeah, we beat them," answered the Rooster. "We beat them real good!"

And that, for Richard Rubio, was the finest moment of a most happy night. [1959]

Américo Paredes was born in 1915 on the Mexican border in Brownsville, Texas, and became interested in border traditions at an early age. In 1934 one of his early poems won first place in the Texas state contest sponsored by Trinity College in San Antonio. The following year he began publishing poetry in the newspaper *La Prensa* there. Paredes's interest in border folklore led to the 1958 publication of his doctoral thesis for the University of Texas at Austin, *With His Pistol in His Hand: A Border Ballad and Its Hero,* a book-length study of "The Ballad of Gregorio Cortez." Paredes is professor emeritus of English at the University of Texas at Austin. In 1989 he was awarded the Charles Frankel Prize by the National Endowment for the Humanities "for outstanding contributions to the public's understanding of the texts, themes, and ideas of the humanities." In 1990 Arte Público Press published Paredes's unfinished novel *George Washington Gomez;* in 1994 the same press brought out the collection *The Hammon and the Beans.*

"The Hammon and the Beans," one of Paredes's few published stories, focuses on the vast divide between the Anglo-dominated government of the United States and the private world of the Mexican American. That divide — of language, money, and world-view — is symbolized by the screen through which the young girl watches the American soldiers at their daily repast. The story's overall theme reflects a widely held view among Mexican Americans that the United States is an occupying power in the Southwest. For more information on this view, see Rudolfo Acuña's *Occupied America.*

The Hammon and the Beans

Once we lived in one of my grandfather's houses near Fort Jones. It was just a block from the parade grounds, a big frame house painted a dirty yellow. My mother hated it, especially because of the pigeons that cooed all day about the eaves. They had fleas, she said. But it was a quiet neighborhood at least, too far from the center of town for automobiles and too near for musical, night-roaming drunks.

At that time Jonesville-on-the-Grande was not the thriving little city that it is today. We told off our days by the routine on the post. At six sharp the flag was raised on the parade grounds to the cackling of the bugles, and a field piece thundered out a salute. The sound of the shot bounced away through the morning mist until its echoes worked their way into every corner of town. Jonesville-on-the-Grande woke to the cannon's roar, as if to battle, and the day began.

At eight the whistle from the post laundry sent us children off to school. The whole town stopped for lunch with the noon whistle, and after lunch everybody went back to work when the post laundry said that it was one o'clock, except for those who could afford to be old-fashioned and took the siesta. The post was the town's clock, you might have said, or like some insistent elder person who was always there to tell you it was time.

At six the flag came down, and we went to watch through the high wire fence that divided the post from the town. Sometimes we joined in the ceremony, standing at salute until the sound of the cannon made us jump. That must have been when we had just studied about George Washington in school, or recited "The Song of Marion's Men," about Marion the Fox and the British cavalry that chased him up and down the broad Santee. But at other times we stuck out our tongues and jeered at the soldiers. Perhaps the night before we had hung at the edges of a group of old men and listened to tales about Aniceto Pizaña and the "border troubles," as the local paper still called them when it referred to them gingerly in passing.

It was because of the border troubles, ten years or so before, that the soldiers had come back to old Fort Jones. But we did not hate them for that; we admired them even, at least sometimes. But when we were thinking about the border troubles instead of Marion the Fox, we hooted them and the flag they were lowering, which for the moment was theirs alone, just as we would have jeered an opposing ball team, in a friendly sort of way. On these occasions even Chonita would join in the mockery, though she usually ran home at the stroke of six. But whether we taunted or saluted, the distant men in khaki uniforms went about their motions without noticing us at all.

The last word from the post came in the night when a distant bugle blew. At nine it was all right because all the lights were on. But sometimes I heard it at eleven, when everything was dark and still, and it made me feel that I was all alone in the world. I would even doubt that I was me, and that put me in such a fright that I felt like yelling out just to make sure I was really there. But next morning the sun shone and life began all over again, with its whistles and cannon shots and bugles blowing. And so we lived, we and the post, side by side with the wire fence in between.

The wandering soldiers whom the bugle called home at night did not wander in our neighborhood, and none of us ever went into Fort Jones. None except Chonita. Every evening when the flag came down she would leave off playing and go down toward what was known as the lower gate of the post, the one that opened not on Main Street but against the poorest part of town. She went into the grounds and to the mess halls and pressed her nose against the screens and watched the soldiers eat. They sat at long tables calling to each other through food-stuffed mouths.

"Hey bud, pass the coffee!"

"Give me the ham!"

"Yeah, give me the beans!"

After the soldiers were through, the cooks came out and scolded Chonita, and then they gave her packages with things to eat.

Chonita's mother did our washing in gratefulness — as my mother put it — for the use of a vacant lot of my grandfather's which was a couple of blocks down the street. On the lot was an old one-room shack which had been a shed long ago, and this Chonita's father had patched up with flattened-out pieces of tin. He was a laborer. Ever since the end of the border troubles there had been a development boom in the Valley, and Chonita's father was getting his share of the good times. Clearing brush and building irrigation ditches, he sometimes pulled down as much as six dollars a week. He drank a good deal of it up, it was true. But corn was just a few cents a bushel in those days. He was the breadwinner, you might say, while Chonita furnished the luxuries.

Chonita was a poet, too. I had just moved into the neighborhood when a boy came up to me and said, "Come on! Let's go hear Chonita make a speech."

She was already on top of the alley fence when we got there, a scrawny little girl of about nine, her bare dirty feet clinging to the fence almost like hands. A dozen other kids were there below her, waiting. Some were boys I knew at school; five or six were her younger brothers and sisters.

"Speech! Speech!" they all cried. "Let Chonita make a speech! Talk in English, Chonita!"

They were grinning and nudging each other, except for her brothers and sisters, who looked up at her with proud, serious faces. She gazed out beyond us all with a grand, distant air and then she spoke.

"Give me the hammon and the beans!" she yelled. "Give me the hammon and the beans!"

She leaped off the fence and everybody cheered and told her how good it was and how she could talk English better than the teachers at the grammar school.

I thought it was a pretty poor joke. Every evening almost, they would make her get up on the fence and yell, "Give me the hammon and the beans!" And everybody would cheer and make her think she was talking English. As for me, I would wait there until she got it over with so we could play at something else. I wondered how long it would be before they got tired of it all. I never did find out, because just about that time I got the chills and fever, and when I got up and around, Chonita wasn't there anymore.

In later years I thought of her a lot, especially during the thirties when I was growing up. Those years would have been just made for her. Many's the time I have seen her in my mind's eye, on the picket lines demanding not bread, not cake, but the hammon and the beans. But it didn't work out that way.

One night Doctor Zapata came into our kitchen through the back door. He set his bag on the table and said to my father, who had opened the door for him, "Well, she is dead."

My father flinched. "What was it?" he asked.

The doctor had gone to the window and he stood with his back to us, looking out toward the light of Fort Jones. "Pneumonia, flu, malnutrition, worms, the evil eye," he said without turning around. "What the hell difference does it make?"

"I wish I had known how sick she was," my father said in a very mild tone. "Not that it's really my affair, but I wish I had."

The doctor snorted and shook his head.

My mother came in and I asked her who was dead. She told me. It made me feel strange but I did not cry. My mother put her arm around my shoulders. "She is in heaven now," she said. "She is happy."

I shrugged her arm away and sat down in one of the kitchen chairs.

"They're like animals," the doctor was saying. He turned around suddenly and his eyes glistened in the light. "Do you know what the brute of a father was doing when I left? He was laughing! Drinking and laughing with his friends."

"There's no telling what the poor man feels," my mother said.

My father made a deprecatory gesture. "It wasn't his daughter anyway."

"No?" the doctor said. He sounded interested.

"This is the woman's second husband," my father explained. "First one died before the girl was born, shot and hanged from a mesquite limb. He was working too close to the tracks the day the Olmito train was derailed."

"You know what?" the doctor said. "In classical times they did things better. Take Troy, for instance. After they stormed the city they grabbed the babies by the heels and dashed them against the wall. That was more humane."

My father smiled. "You sound very radical. You sound just like your relative down there in Morelos."

"No relative of mine," the doctor said. "I'm a conservative, the son of a conservative, and you know that I wouldn't be here except for that little detail."

"Habit," my father said. "Pure habit, pure tradition. You're a radical at heart."

"It depends on how you define radicalism," the doctor answered. "People tend to use words too loosely. A dentist could be called a radical, I suppose. He pulls up things by the roots."

My father chuckled.

"Any bandit in Mexico nowadays can give himself a political label," the doctor went on, "and that makes him respectable. He's a leader of the people."

"Take Villa, now —" my father began.

"Villa was a different type of man," the doctor broke in.

"I don't see any difference."

The doctor came over to the table and sat down. "Now look at it this way," he began, his finger in front of my father's face. My father threw back his head and laughed.

"You'd better go to bed and rest," my mother told me. "You're not completely well, you know."

So I went to bed, but I didn't go to sleep, not right away.

I lay there for a long time while behind my darkened eyelids Emiliano Zapata's cavalry charged down to the broad Santee, where there were grave men with hoary hairs. I was still awake at eleven when the cold voice of the bugle went gliding in and out of the dark like something that couldn't find its way back to wherever it had been. I thought of Chonita in heaven, and I saw her in her torn and dirty dress, with a pair of bright wings attached, flying round and round like a butterfly shouting, "Give me the hammon and the beans!"

Then I cried. And whether it was the bugle, or whether it was Chonita or what, to this day I do not know. But cry I did, and I felt much better after that. [1963]

John Rechy, who was born in El Paso, Texas, in 1934, is one of the most prolific Latino novelists of his generation. His first novel, *City of Night,* is a highly acclaimed and controversial work about a young man from an abusive El Paso home who drifts across the United States engaging in homosexual encounters for pay. Rechy has written seven other novels, including *The Miraculous Day of Amalia Gomez* (1992), which was his first to focus on Hispanic themes and situations.

City of Night's episodic structure has led some critics to call it "picaresque," in a reductive sense, opposing it to a "real novel." Others dispute this assessment, and such critics as Didier Jaén have noted that it has more structure and unity than most picaresque works.

Because Rechy's well-known works have focused more on the culture of homosexuality than on Latino life, he has usually been omitted from discussions of the Latino "canon" until recent, more inclusive assertions, especially by the scholar Juan Bruce-Novoa. (Sheila Ortiz Taylor, who writes about lesbians, suffered a similar fate.) But Rechy's work also made him a pioneer for later Latino writers who used homosexuals as principal characters, such as Arturo Islas, Elias Miguel Muñoz, and Jaime Manrique. Rechy lives in southern California; his most recent novel is *Babylon* (1996). Following is the first chapter of Rechy's landmark work, *City of Night*.

from City of Night

Later I would think of America as one vast City of Night stretching gaudily from Times Square to Hollywood Boulevard — jukebox-winking, rock-n-roll-moaning: America at night fusing its darkcities into the unmistakable shape of loneliness.

Remember Pershing Square and the apathetic palmtrees. Central Park and the frantic shadows. Movie theaters in the angry morning-hours. And wounded Chicago streets . . . Horrormovie courtyards in the French Quarter — tawdry Mardi Gras floats with clowns tossing out glass beads, passing dumbly like life itself . . . Remember rock-n-roll sexmusic blasting from jukeboxes leering obscenely, blinking manycolored along the streets of America strung like a cheap necklace from 42nd Street to Market Street, San Francisco . . .

One-night sex and cigarette smoke and rooms squashed in by loneliness . . .

And I would remember lives lived out darkly in that vast City of Night, from all-night movies to Beverly Hills mansions.

But it should begin in El Paso, that journey through the cities of night. Should begin in El Paso, in Texas. And it begins in the Wind . . . In a Southwest windstorm with the gray clouds like steel doors locking you in the world from Heaven.

I cant remember now how long that windstorm lasted — it might have been days — but perhaps it was only hours — because it was in that timeless time of my boyhood, ages six through eight.

My dog Winnie was dying. I would bring her water and food and place them near her, stand watching intently — but she doesnt move. The saliva kept coming from the edges of her mouth. She had always been fat, and she had a crazy crooked grin — but she was usually sick: Once her eyes turned over, so that they were almost completely white and she couldn't see — just lay down, and didnt try to get up for a day. Then she was well, briefly, smiling again, wobbling lopsidedly.

Now she was lying out there dying.

At first the day was beautiful, with the sky blue as it gets only in memories of Texas childhood. Nowhere else in the world, I will think later, is there a sky as clear, as blue, as Deep as that. I will remember other skies: like inverted cups, this shade of blue or gray or black, with limits, like painted rooms. But in the Southwest, the sky was millions and millions of miles deep of blue — clear, magic, electric blue. (I would stare at it sometimes, inexplicably racked with excitement, thinking: If I get a stick miles long and stand on a mountain, I'll puncture Heaven — which I thought of then as an island somewhere in the vast sky — and then Heaven will come tumbling down to earth . . .) Then, that day, standing watching Winnie, I see the gray clouds massing and rolling in the horizon, sweeping suddenly terrifyingly across the sky as if to battle, giant mushrooms exploding, blending into that steely blanket. *Now youre locked down here so Lonesome suddenly youre cold.* The wind sweeps up the dust, tumbleweeds claw their way across the dirt . . .

I moved Winnie against the wall of the house, to shelter her from the needlepointed dust. The clouds have shut out the sky completely, the wind is howling violently, and it is Awesomely dark. My mother keeps calling me to come in . . . From the porch, I look back at my dog. The water in the bowl beside her has turned into mud . . . Inside now, I rushed to the window. And the wind is shrieking into the house — the curtains thrashing at the furniture like giant lost birds, flapping against the walls, and my two brothers and two sisters are running about the beat-up house closing the windows, removing the sticks we propped them open with. I hear my father banging on the frames with a hammer, patching the broken panes with cardboard.

Inside, the house was suddenly serene, safe from the wind; but staring out the window in cold terror, I see boxes and weeds crashing against the walls outside, almost tumbling over my sick dog. I long for something miraculous to draw across the sky to stop the wind . . . I squeezed against the pane as close as I could get to Winnie: *If I keep looking at her, she cant possibly die!* A tumbleweed rolled over her.

I ran out. I stood over Winnie, shielding my eyes from the slashing wind, knelt over her to see if her stomach was still moving, breathing. And her eyes open looking at me. I listen to her heart (as I used to listen to my mother's heart when she was sick so often and I would think she had died, leaving me Alone — because my father for me then existed only as someone who was around somehow; taking furious shape later, fiercely).

Winnie is dead.

It seemed the windstorm lasted for days, weeks. But it must have been over, as usual, the next day, when I'm standing next to my mother in the kitchen. (Strangely, I loved to sit and look at her as she fixed the food — or did the laundry: She washed our clothes outside in an aluminum tub, and I would watch her hanging up the clean sheets flapping in the wind. Later I would empty the water for her, and I stared intrigued as it made unpredictable patterns on the dirt . . .) I said: "If Winnie dies —" (She had of course already died, but I didnt want to say it; her body was still outside, and I kept going to her to see if miraculously she is breathing again.) "— if she dies, I wont be sad because she'll go to Heaven and I'll see her there." My mother said: "Dogs dont go to Heaven, they havent got souls." She didnt say that brutally. There is nothing brutal about my mother: only a crushing tenderness, as powerful as the hatred I would discover later in my father. "What will happen to Winnie, then?" I asked. "Shes dead, thats all," my mother answers, "the body just disappears, becomes dirt."

I stand by the window, thinking: It isn't fair . . .

Then my brother, the younger of the two — I am the youngest in the family — had to bury Winnie.

I was very religious then. I went to Mass regularly, to Confession. I prayed nightly. And I prayed now for my dead dog: God would make an exception. He would let her into Heaven.

I stand watching my brother dig that hole in the backyard. He put the dead dog in and covered it. I made a cross and brought flowers. Knelt. Made the sign of the cross: "Let her into Heaven . . ."

In the days that followed — I dont know exactly how much later — we could smell the body rotting . . . The day was a ferocious Texas summerday with the threat of rain: thunder — but no rain. The sky lit up through the cracked clouds, and lightning snapped at the world like a whip. My older brother said we hadnt buried Winnie deep enough.

So he dug up the body, and I stand by him as he shovels the dirt in our backyard (littered with papers and bottles covering the weeds which occasionally we pulled, trying several times to grow grass — but it never grew). Finally the body appeared. I turned away quickly. I had seen the decaying face of death. My mother was right. Soon Winnie will blend into the dirt. There was no soul, the body would rot, and there would be Nothing left of Winnie.

~~~
~~~

That is the incident of my early childhood that I remember most often. And that is why I say it begins in the wind. Because somewhere in that plain of childhood time must have been planted the seeds of the restlessness.

Before the death of Winnie, there are other memories of loss.

We were going to plant flowers in the front of the house we lived in before we moved to the house where Winnie died. I was digging a ledge along the sidewalk, and my mother was at the store getting the seeds. A man came and asked for my father, but my father isnt home. "Youre going to have to move very soon," he tells me. I had heard the house was being sold, and we couldnt buy it, but it hadnt meant much to me. I continue shoveling the dirt. After my mother came and spoke to the man, she told me to stop making the holes. Almost snatching the seeds from her — and understanding now — I began burying them frantically as if that way we will have to stay to see them grow.

And so we moved. We moved from that clean house with the white walls and into the house where Winnie will die.

I stand looking at the house in child panic. It was the other half of a duplex, the wooden porch decayed, almost on the verge of toppling down; it slanted like a slide. A dried-up vine, dead from lack of water, still clung to the base of the porch like a skeleton, and the bricks were disintegrating in places into thin streaks of orangy powder. The sun was brazenly bright; it elongates each splinter on the wood, each broken twig on the skeleton vine . . . I rushed inside. Huge brown cockroaches scurried into the crevices. One fell from the wall, spreading its wings — almost two inches wide — as if to lunge at me — and it splashes like a miniature plane on the floor — *splut!* The paper was peeling off the walls over at least four more layers, all different graycolors. (We would put up the sixth, or begin to — and then stop, leaving the house even more patched as that layer peeled too: an unfinished jigsaw puzzle which would fascinate me at night: its ragged patterns making angryfaces, angry animalshapes — but I could quickly alter them into less angry figures by ripping off the jagged edges . . .) Where the ceiling had leaked, there are spidery brown outlines.

I flick the cockroaches off the walls, stamping angrily on them.

The house smells of Rot. I went to the bathroom. The tub was full of dirty water, and it had stagnated. It was brown, bubbly. In wild dreadful panic, I thrust my hand into the rancid water, found the stopper, pulled it out holding my breath, and looked at my arm, which is covered with the filthy brown crud.

Winters in El Paso for me later would never again seem as bitter cold as they were then. Then I thought of El Paso as the coldest place in the world. We had an old iron stove with a round belly which heated up the whole house; and when we opened the small door to feed it more coal or wood, the glowing pieces inside created a miniature of Hell: the cinders crushed against the edges, smoking . . . The metal flues that carried the smoke from the stove to the chimney collapsed occasionally and filled the house with soot. This happened especially during the windy days, and the wind would whoosh grimespecked down the chimney. At night my mother piled coats on us to keep us warm.

Later, I would be sent out to ask one of our neighbors for a dime — "until my father comes home from work." Being the youngest and most soulful looking in the family, then, I was the one who went . . .

Around that time my father plunged into my life with a vengeance.

To expiate some guilt now for what I'll tell you about him later, I'll say that that strange, moody, angry man — my father — had once experienced a flashy grandeur in music. At the age of eight he had played a piano concert before the President of Mexico. Years later, still a youngman, he directed a symphony orchestra. Unaccountably, since I never really knew that man, he sank quickly lower and lower, and when I came along, when he was almost 50 years old, he found himself Trapped in the memories of that grandeur and in the reality of a series of jobs teaching music to sadly untalented children; selling pianos, sheet music — and soon even that bastard relationship to the world of music he loved was gone, and he became a caretaker for public parks. Then he worked in a hospital cleaning out trash. *(I remember him, already a defeated old man, getting up before dawn to face the unmusical reality of soiled bloody dressings.)* He would cling to stacks and stacks of symphonic music which he had played, orchestrated — still working on them at night, drumming his fingers on the table feverishly: stacks of music now piled in the narrow hallway in that house, completely unwanted by anyone but himself, gathering dust which annoyed us, so that we wanted to put them outside in the leaky aluminum garage: but he clung to those precious dust-piling manuscripts — and to newspaper clippings of his once-glory — clung to them like a dream, now a nightmare . . . And somehow I became the reluctant inheritor of his hatred for the world that had coldly knocked him down without even glancing back.

Once, yes, there had been a warmth toward that strange red-faced man — and there were still the sudden flashes of tenderness which I will tell you about later: that man who alternately claimed French, English, Scottish descent — depending on his imaginative moods — that strange man who had traveled from Mexico to California spreading his seed — that turbulent man, married and divorced, who then married my Mother, a beautiful Mexican woman who loves me fiercely and never once understood about the terror between me and my father.

Even now in my mother's living room there is a glasscase which has been with us as long as I can remember. It is full of glass objects: figurines of angels, Virgins of Guadalupe, dolls; tissue-thin imitation flowers, swans; and a small glass, reverently covered with a rotting piece of silk, tied tightly with a faded-pink ribbon, containing some mysterious memento of one of my father's dead children . . . When I think of that glasscase, I think of my Mother . . . a ghost image that will haunt me — Always.

When I was about eight years old, my father taught me this:

He would say to me: "Give me a thousand," and I knew this meant I should hop on his lap and then he would fondle me — intimately — and he'd give me a penny, sometimes a nickel. At times when his friends — old gray men — came to our house, they would ask for "a thousand." And I would jump on their laps too. And I would get nickel after nickel, going around the table.

And later, a gift from my father would become a token of a truce from the soon-to-blaze hatred between us.

I loathed Christmas.

Each year, my father put up a Nacimiento — an elaborate Christmas scene, with houses, the wisemen on their way to the manger, angels on angelhair clouds. (On Christmas Eve, after my mother said a rosary while we knelt before the Nacimiento, we placed the

Christchild in the crib.) Weeks before Christmas my father began constructing it, and each day, when I came home from school, he would have me stand by him while he worked building the boxlike structure, the miniature houses, the artificial lake; hanging the angels from the elaborate simulated sky, replete with moon, clouds, stars. Sometimes hours passed before he would ask me to help him, but I had to remain there, not talking. Sometimes my mother would have to stand there too, sometimes my younger sister. When anything went wrong — if anything fell — he was in a rage, hurling hammers, cursing.

My father's violence erupted unpredictably over anything. In an instant he overturns the table — food and plates thrust to the floor. He would smash bottles, menacing us with the sharp-fanged edges. He had an old sword which he kept hidden threateningly about the house.

And even so there were those moments of tenderness — even more brutal because they didn't last: times in which, when he got paid, he would fill the house with presents — flowers for my mother (incongruous in that patched-up house, until they withered and blended with the drabness), toys for us. Even during the poorest Christmas we went through when we were kids — and after the fearful times of putting up the Nacimiento — he would make sure we all had presents — not clothes, which we needed but didnt want, but toys, which we wanted but didnt need. And Sundays he would take us to Juarez to dinner, leaving an exorbitant tip for the suddenly attentive waiter . . . But in the ocean of his hatred, those times of kindness were mere islands. He burned with an anger at life, which had chewed him up callously: an anger which blazed more fiercely as he sank further beneath the surface of his once almost-realized dream of musical glory.

One of the last touches on the Nacimiento was two pieces of craggy wood, which looked very heavy, like rocks (very much like the piece of petrified wood which my father kept on his desk, to warn us that once it had been the hand of a child who had struck his father, and God had turned the child's hand into stone). The pieces of rocklike wood were located on either side of the manger, like hills. On top of one, my father placed a small statue of a red-tailed, horned Devil, drinking out of a bottle.

Around that time I had a dream which still recurs (and later, in

New Orleans, I will experience it awake). We would get colds often in that drafty house, and fever, and during such times I dreamt this: Those pieces of rocklike wood on the sides of the manger are descending on me, to crush me. When I brace for the smashing terrible impact, they become soft, and instead of crushing me they envelop me like melted wax. Sometimes I will dream theyre draped with something like cheesecloth, a tenebrous, thin tissue touching my face like spiderwebs, gluing itself to me although I struggle to tear it away . . .

When my brothers and sisters all got married and left home — to Escape, I would think — I remained, and my father's anger was aimed even more savagely at me.

He sat playing solitaire for hours. He calls me over, begins to talk in a very low, deceptively friendly tone. When my mother and I fell asleep, he told me, he would set fire to the house and we would burn inside while he looked on. Then he would change that story: Instead of setting fire to the house, he will kill my mother in bed, and in the morning, when I go wake her, she'll be dead, and I'll be left alone with him.

Some nights I would change beds with my mother after he went to sleep — they didnt sleep in the same room — and I surrounded the bed with sticks, chairs. The slightest noise, and I would reach for a stick to beat him away. In the early morning, before he woke, my mother would change beds with me again.

Once — without him, because he was working on his music — we were going to take a trip to Carlsbad Caverns, in New Mexico: my mother, my sister and her husband, my older brother and his wife, and I. My mother prepared food that night.

In the morning, before dawn, I woke my mother and went to my sister's house to wake her. When I returned, I saw my mother in our backyard (under the paradoxically serene star-splashed sky). "Dont go in!" she yells at me. I ran inside, and my father is standing menacingly over the table where the food we were taking is. Swiftly I reached for the food, and he lunges at me with a knife, slicing past me only inches short of my stomach. By then, my sister's husband was there holding him back . . .

There was a wine-red ring my father wore. As a tie-pin, before being set into the gold ring-frame, it had belonged to his father, and before that to his father's father — and it was a ruby, my father told me — a ruby so precious that it was his most treasured possession, which he clung to. As he sat moodily staring at his music one particularly poor day, he called me over. Quickly, he gave me the ring. The red stone in the gold frame glowed for me more brilliantly than anything has ever since. A few days later he took it back.

During one of those rare, rare times when there was a kind of determined truce between us — an unspoken, smoldering hatred — I was crossing the street with him. He was quite old then, and he carried a cane. As we crossed, he stumbled on the cane, fell to the street. Without waiting an instant, I run to the opposite side, and I stand hoping for some miraculous avenging car to plunge over him.

But it didnt come.

I went back to him, helped him up, and we walked the rest of the way in thundering silence.

And then, when I was older, possibly 13 or 14, I was sitting one afternoon on the porch loathing him. My hatred for him by then had become a thing which overwhelmed me, which obsessed me the length of the day. He stood behind me, and he put his hand on me, softly, and said — gently: "Youre my son, and I love you." But those longed-for words, delayed until the waves of my hatred for him had smothered their meaning, made me pull away from him: "I hate you! — youre a failure — as a man, as a father!" And later those words would ring painfully in my mind when I remembered him as a slouched oldman getting up before dawn to face the hospital trash . . .

Soon, I stopped going to Mass. I stopped praying. The God that would allow this vast unhappiness was a God I would rebel against. The seeds of that rebellion — planted that ugly afternoon when I saw my dog's body beginning to decay, the soul shut out by Heaven — were beginning to germinate.

When my brother was a kid and I wasnt even born (but I'll hear the story often), he would stand moodily looking out the window; and when, once, my grandmother asked him, "Little boy, what are you doing by the window staring at so hard?" — he answered, "I am occupied with life." Im convinced that if my brother hadnt said that — or if I hadnt been told about it — I would have said it.

I liked to sit inside the house and look out the hall-window —

beyond the cactus garden in the vacant lot next door. I would sit by that window looking at the people that passed. I felt miraculously separated from the world outside: separated by the pane, the screen, through which, nevertheless — uninvolved — I could see that world.

I read many books, I saw many, many movies.

I watched other lives, only through a window.

Sundays during summer especially I would hike outside the city, along the usually waterless strait of sand called the Rio Grande, up the mountain of Cristo Rey, dominated at the top by the coarse, weed-surrounded statue of a primitive-faced Christ. I would lie on the dirt of that mountain staring at the breathtaking Texas sky.

I was usually alone. I had only one friend: a wild-eyed girl who sometimes would climb the mountain with me. We were both 17, and I felt in her the same wordless unhappiness I felt within myself. We would walk and climb for hours without speaking. For a brief time I liked her intensely — without ever telling her. Yet I was beginning to feel, too, a remoteness toward people — more and more a craving for attention which I could not reciprocate: one-sided, as if the need in me was so hungry that it couldnt share or give back in kind. Perhaps sensing this — one afternoon in a boarded-up cabin at the base of the mountain — she maneuvered, successfully, to make me. But the discovery of sex with her, releasing as it had been, merely turned me strangely further within myself.

Mutually, we withdrew from each other.

And it was somewhere about that time that the narcissistic pattern of my life began.

From my father's inexplicable hatred of me and my mother's blind carnivorous love, I fled to the Mirror. I would stand before it, thinking: I have only Me! . . . I became obsessed with age. At 17, I dreaded growing old. Old age is something that must never happen to me. The image of myself in the mirror must never fade into someone I cant look at.

And even after a series of after-school jobs, my feeling of isolation from others only increased.

Then the army came, and for months I hadnt spoken to my father. (We would sit at the table eating silently, ignoring each other.) And when I left, that terrible morning, I kissed my mother. And briefly I looked at my father. His eyes were watering. Mutely he held out the ruby-ring which once, long ago, he had given me and then taken back. And I took it wordlessly. And in that instant I wanted to hold him — *because he was crying,* because he did feel something for me, because, I was sure, he was overwhelmed at that moment by the Loss I felt too. I wanted to hold him then as I had wanted to so many, many times as a child, and if I could have spoken, I know I would have said at last: "I love you." But that sense of loss choked me — and I walked out without speaking to him . . . Only a few weeks later, in Camp Breckenridge, Kentucky, I received a telegram that he was very sick.

And I came back to El Paso.

I felt certain that this time it would be different.

I reached our house, in the government projects we had moved into from that house with the winged cockroaches, and I got in with the key I had kept. There is no one home. I called my brother. My father was dead.

I hang up the telephone and I know that now Forever I will have no father, that he had been unfound, that as long as he had been alive there was a chance, and that we would be, Always now, strangers, and that is when I knew what Death really is — not in the physical discovery of the Nothingness which the death of my dog Winnie had brought me (in the decayed body which would turn into dirt, rejected by Heaven) but in the knowledge that *my Father* was gone, *for me* — that there was no way to reach him now — that his Death would exist only for me, who am living.

And throughout the days that followed — and will follow forever — I will discover him in my memories, and hopelessly — through the infinite miles that separate life from death — try to understand his torture: in searching out the shape of my own.

The army passed like something unreal, and I returned to my Mother and her hungry love. And left her, standing that morning by the kitchen door crying, as she always would be in my mind, and I was on my way now to Chicago, briefly — from where I would go to freedom: New York! — embarking on that journey through nightcities and nightlives — looking for I dont know what — perhaps some substitute for salvation. [1963]

Rodolfo "Corky" Gonzáles was born in 1928 in Denver, Colorado, to a family of migrant workers. He graduated from high school at the age of sixteen, won a Golden Gloves boxing championship soon thereafter, and became the National Boxing Association's third-ranked featherweight. He was also a successful businessman and founded Los Voluntarios (the Volunteers), a grassroots youth organization that became the precursor to the Crusade for Justice. The Crusade was instrumental in helping develop El Plan Espiritual de Aztlán (the Spiritual Plan of Aztlán) in the 1960s, a manifesto for the awakening of cultural and political consciousness among Chicanos. The Plan led to a flowering of literature and art as well as political involvement; Gonzáles's poem *I Am Joaquín*, often published in a bilingual format, became a rallying point of the effort to create a Chicano consciousness.

I Am Joaquín telescopes all of Chicano history, from before the Spanish conquest to the present day, into the personal "I," using the self as a narrow entryway into a vast social, political, and artistic arena. The published poem was accompanied by a great deal of historical information, a time line, and photographs of Mexican Americans. In a sense *I Am Joaquín* is both a search for historic continuity, which was severed by the Spanish, and a blueprint for that search. In the introduction to the 1972 Bantam reprint, Gonzáles wrote, "Writing *I Am Joaquín* was a journey back through history, a painful self-evaluation, a wandering search for my peoples and, most of all, for my own identity."

In this Whitmanesque work the narrator shows an affinity with the 1850s pro-Mexican bandit Joaquín Murrieta, who was forced off his California gold-field claim and became a symbol of the Mexican American who fights the injustices levied against him. In the 1970s the Chilean poet Pablo Neruda wrote a play about Murrieta and, more recently, Richard Rodriguez wrote an essay on his search for Murrieta's severed head, which was lost and has still not been recovered.

In the past thirty years, tens of thousands of copies of the poem have been distributed free of charge at public meetings and rallies, and dramatic readings have been held across the West.

I Am Joaquín

I am Joaquín,
lost in a world of confusion,
caught up in the whirl of a
gringo society,
confused by the rules,
scorned by attitudes,
suppressed by manipulation,
and destroyed by modern society.
My fathers
have lost the economic battle
and won
the struggle of cultural survival.

And now!
I must choose
between
the paradox of
victory of the spirit,
despite physical hunger,
or
to exist in the grasp
of American social neurosis,
sterilization of the soul
and a full stomach.

Yes,
I have come a long way to nowhere,
unwillingly dragged by that
monstrous, technical,
industrial giant called
Progress
and Anglo success . . .
I look at myself.
I watch my brothers.
I shed tears of sorrow.
I sow seeds of hate.
I withdraw to the safety within the

circle of life —
MY OWN PEOPLE.

I am Cuauhtémoc,
proud and noble,
leader of men,
king of an empire
civilized beyond the dreams
of the gachupín Cortés,
who also is the blood,
the image of myself.
I am the Maya prince.
I am Nezahualcóyotl,
great leader of the Chichimecas.
I am the sword and flame of Cortés
the despot.
And
I am the eagle and serpent of
the Aztec civilization.

I owned the land as far as the eye
could see under the crown of Spain,
and I toiled on my earth
and gave my Indian sweat and blood
for the Spanish master
who ruled with tyranny over man and
beast and all that he could trample.
But . . .
THE GROUND WAS MINE.
I was both tyrant and slave.

As Christian church took its place
in God's good name,
to take and use my virgin strength and
trusting faith,
the priests,
both good and bad,
took —
but
gave a lasting truth that

Spaniard
Indian
Mestizo
were all God's children.
And
from these words grew men
who prayed and fought
for
their own worth as human beings,
for
that
GOLDEN MOMENT
of
FREEDOM.

I was part in blood and spirit
of that
courageous village priest
Hidalgo
who in the year eighteen hundred and ten
rang the bell of independence
and gave out that lasting cry —
el grito de Dolores:
"Que mueran los gachupines y que viva
la Virgen de Guadalupe . . ."

I sentenced him
who was me.
I excommunicated him, my blood.
I drove him from the pulpit to lead
a bloody revolution for him and me . . .
I killed him.
His head,
which is mine and of all those
who have come this way,
I placed on that fortress wall
to wait for independence.
Morelos!
Matamoros!

Guerrero!
all compañeros in the act,
STOOD AGAINST THAT WALL OF
INFAMY
to feel the hot gouge of lead
which my hands made.
I died with them . . .
I lived with them . . .
I lived to see our country free.
Free
from Spanish rule in
eighteen-hundred-twenty-one.
Mexico was free ? ?

The crown was gone
but
all its parasites remained
and ruled
and taught
with gun and flame and mystic power.
I worked
I sweated
I bled
I prayed
and waited silently for life
to begin again.
I fought and died
for
Don Benito Juárez,
guardian of the Constitution.
I was he
on dusty roads
on barren land
as he protected his archives
as Moses did his sacraments.

He held his Mexico
in his hand
on

the most desolate
and remote ground
which was his country.
And this giant
little Zapotec
gave
not one palm's breadth
of his country's land to
kings or monarchs or presidents
of foreign powers.

I am Joaquín.
I rode with Pancho Villa,
crude and warm,
a tornado at full strength,
nourished and inspired
by the passion and the fire
of all his earthy people.
I am Emiliano Zapata.
"This land,
this earth
is
OURS."

The villages
the mountains
the streams
belong to Zapatistas.
Our life
or yours
is the only trade for soft brown earth
and maize.
All of which is our reward,
a creed that formed a constitution
for all who dare live free!
"This land is ours . . .
Father, I give it back to you.
Mexico must be free . . ."

I ride with revolutionists
against myself.
I am the Rurales,
coarse and brutal,
I am the mountain Indian,
superior over all.
The thundering hoof beats are my horses.
The chattering machine guns
are death to all of me:
Yaqui
Tarahumara
Chamula
Zapotec
Mestizo
Español.

I have been the bloody revolution,
the victor,
the vanquished.
I have killed
and been killed.
I am the despots Díaz
and Huerta
and the apostle of democracy,
Francisco Madero.

I am
the black-shawled
faithful women
who die with me
or live
depending on the time and place.
I am
faithful
humble
Juan Diego,
the Virgin of Guadalupe,
Tonantzin, Aztec goddess, too.

I rode the mountains of San Joaquín.
I rode east and north
        as far as the Rocky Mountains,
                and
all men feared the guns of
                        Joaquín Murrieta.
I killed those men who dared
    to steal my mine,
        who raped and killed
                            my love
                            my wife.
Then
I killed to stay alive.
I was Elfego Baca,
    living my nine lives fully.
I was the Espinoza brothers
    of the Valle de San Luis.
All
were added to the number of heads
that
    in the name of civilization
were placed on the wall of independence,
heads of brave men
who died for cause or principle,
good or bad.

            Hidalgo! Zapata!
                Murrieta! Espinozas!
are but a few.
They
dared to face
the force of tyranny
                of men
                who rule
            by deception and hypocrisy.

I stand here looking back,
and now I see
                the present,
and still

I am the campesino,
I am the fat political coyote —
I,
of the same name,
Joaquín,
in a country that has wiped out
all my history,
stifled all my pride,
in a country that has placed a
different weight of indignity upon
my
age-
old
burdened back.
Inferiority
is the new load . . .

The Indian has endured and still
emerged the winner,
the Mestizo must yet overcome,
And the gachupín will just ignore.
I look at myself
and see part of me
who rejects my father and my mother
and dissolves into the melting pot
to disappear in shame.
I sometimes
sell my brother out
and reclaim him
for my own when society gives me
token leadership
in society's own name.

I am Joaquín,
who bleeds in many ways.
The altars of Moctezuma
I stained a bloody red.
My back of Indian slavery
was striped crimson
from the whips of masters

who would lose their blood so pure
when revolution made them pay,
standing against the walls of
retribution.

Blood
has flowed from
me
on every battlefield
between
campesino, hacendado,
slave and master
and
revolution.
I jumped from the tower of Chapultepec
into the sea of fame —
my country's flag
my burial shroud —
with Los Niños,
whose pride and courage
could not surrender
with indignity
their country's flag
to strangers . . . in their land.
Now
I bleed in some smelly cell
from club
or gun
or tyranny.

I bleed as the vicious gloves of hunger
cut my face and eyes,
as I fight my way from stinking barrios
to the glamour of the ring
and lights of fame
or mutilated sorrow.

My blood runs pure on the ice-caked
hills of the Alaskan isles,
on the corpse-strewn beach of Normandy,

the foreign land of Korea
and now
Vietnam.

Here I stand
before the court of justice,
guilty
for all the glory of my Raza
to be sentenced to despair.
Here I stand,
poor in money,
arrogant with pride,
bold with machismo,
rich in courage
and
wealthy in spirit and faith.

My knees are caked with mud.
My hands calloused from the hoe.
I have made the Anglo rich,
yet
equality is but a word —
the Treaty of Hidalgo has been broken
and is but another treacherous promise.
My land is lost
and stolen,
My culture has been raped.
I lengthen
the line at the welfare door
and fill the jails with crime.

These then
are the rewards
this society has
for sons of chiefs
and kings
and bloody revolutionists,
who
gave a foreign people
all their skills and ingenuity

to pave the way with brains and blood
for
those hordes of gold-starved
strangers,
who
changed our language
and plagiarized our deeds
as feats of valor
of their own.

They frowned upon our way of life
and took what they could use.
Our art,
our literature,
our music, they ignored —
so they left the real things of value
and grabbed at their own destruction
by their greed and avarice.
They overlooked that cleansing fountain of
nature and brotherhood
which is Joaquín.
The art of our great señores,
Diego Rivera,
Siqueiros,
Orozco, is but
another act of revolution for
the salvation of mankind.
Mariachi music, the
heart and soul
of the people of the earth,
the life of the child,
and the happiness of love.

The corridos tell the tales
of life and death,
of tradition,
legends old and new,
of joy
of passion and sorrow
of the people — who I am.

I am in the eyes of woman,
sheltered beneath
her shawl of black,
deep and sorrowful
eyes
that bear the pain of sons long buried
or dying,
dead
on the battlefield or on the barbed wire
of social strife.

Her rosary she prays and fingers
endlessly
like the family
working down a row of beets
to turn around
and work
and work.
There is no end.
Her eyes a mirror of all the warmth
and all the love for me,
and I am her
and she is me.
We face life together in sorrow,
anger, joy, faith and wishful
thoughts.

I shed the tears of anguish
as I see my children disappear
behind the shroud of mediocrity,
never to look back to remember me.
I am Joaquín.
I must fight
and win this struggle
for my sons, and they
must know from me
who I am.
Part of the blood that runs deep in me
could not be vanquished by the Moors.
I defeated them after five hundred years,

and I endured.
Part of the blood that is mine
has labored endlessly four hundred
years under the heel of lustful
Europeans.
I am still here!

I have endured in the rugged mountains
of our country.
I have survived the toils and slavery
of the fields.
I have existed
in the barrios of the city
in the suburbs of bigotry
in the mines of social snobbery
in the prisons of dejection
in the muck of exploitation
and
in the fierce heat of racial hatred.

And now the trumpet sounds,
the music of the people stirs the
revolution.
Like a sleeping giant it slowly
rears its head
to the sound of
tramping feet
clamoring voices
mariachi strains
fiery tequila explosions
the smell of chile verde and
soft brown eyes of expectation for a
better life.

And in all the fertile farmlands,
the barren plains,
the mountain villages,
smoke-smeared cities,
we start to MOVE.

La Raza!
Mejicano!
Español!
Latino!
Hispano!
Chicano!
or whatever I call myself,
I look the same
I feel the same
I cry
and
sing the same.

I am the masses of my people and
I refuse to be absorbed.
I am Joaquín.
The odds are great
but my spirit is strong,
my faith unbreakable,
my blood is pure.
I am Aztec prince and Christian Christ.
I SHALL ENDURE!
I WILL ENDURE!

[1967]

Piri Thomas was the first mainland-born Puerto Rican narrator to achieve national, mainstream recognition in the United States for his autobiographical work *Down These Mean Streets* (1967). A forceful portrait of lives affected by what Oscar Lewis described in *La Vida* (1965) as the "culture of poverty," *Down These Mean Streets* chronicles Thomas's difficult life in the streets of Spanish Harlem from the Depression era to the early 1960s.

Thomas was born in New York City in 1928 of a light-skinned Puerto Rican mother and a dark-skinned Cuban father. His experiences as a child in the barrio and as a teenager in an Italian section of East Harlem and later in Babylon, Long Island, forced him to confront issues of racial and ethnic identity. Thomas had to decide whether to consider himself a Puerto Rican based on language and family origin or to accept society's label of African American based on skin color.

The autobiography traces his early initiation into gangs, violence, drugs, and sex, as well as time spent in a maximum security prison after his conviction for armed robbery; the work ends with his reintegration into the community and ultimate personal redemption after his parole at the age of twenty-eight. In fact, Thomas began writing in prison. The popularity of the book, published in 1967, converted Piri Thomas into a spokesperson of the Puerto Rican community; he made frequent appearances on television and radio. Thomas's self-documentation continues in the sequel *Savior, Savior Hold My Hand* (1972) and *Seven Long Times* (1975).

The use of crude street language and Spanish words normally would have alienated the average American, but *Down These Mean Streets* emerged within a changing political climate, one that opened up new avenues for minority authors. There was a growing market for works that could help U.S. readers comprehend the social unrest taking place around them. The book has been compared to other testimonials of its time, such as *Manchild in the Promised Land* (1965), by Claude Brown, and *Soul on Ice* (1968), by Eldridge Cleaver. *Down These Mean Streets* remains as powerful and controversial today as it was when first published.

from **Down These Mean Streets**

Babylon for the Babylonians

In 1944 we moved to Long Island. Poppa was making good money at the airplane factory, and he had saved enough bread for a down payment on a small house.

As we got our belongings ready for the moving van, I stood by watching all the hustling with a mean feeling. My hands weren't with it; my fingers played with the top of a cardboard box full of dishes. My face tried hard not to show resentment at Poppa's decision to leave my streets forever. I felt that I belonged in Harlem; it was my kind of kick. I didn't want to move out to Long Island. My friend Crutch had told me there were a lot of paddies out there, and they didn't dig Negroes or Puerto Ricans.

"Piri," Momma said.

"Yeah, Moms." I looked up at Momma. She seemed tired and

beat. Still thinking about Paulie all the time and how she took him to the hospital just to get some simple-assed tonsils out. And Paulie died. I remember she used to keep repeating how Paulie kept crying, "Don't leave me, Mommie," and her saying, "Don't worry, *nene,* it's just for a day." Paulie — I pushed his name out of my mind.

"*Dios mío,* help a little, *hijo,*" Momma said.

"Moms, why do we gotta move outta Harlem? We don't know any other place better'n this."

"*Caramba!* What ideas," Momma said. "What for you talk like that? Your Poppa and I saved enough money. We want you kids to have good opportunities. It is a better life in the country. No like Puerto Rico, but it have trees and grass and nice schools."

"Yeah, Moms. Have they got Puerto Ricans out there?"

"*Sí,* I'm sure. Señora Rodriguez an' her family, an' Otelia — remember her? She lived upstairs."

"I mean a lotta *Latinos,* Moms. Like here in the *Barrio.* And how about *morenos?*"

"*Muchacho,* they got all kind." Momma laughed. "Fat and skinny, big and little. And —"

"Okay, Momma," I said. "You win. Give me a kiss."

So we moved to Babylon, a suburb on the south shore of Long Island. Momma was right about the grass and trees. And the school, too, was nice-looking. The desks were new, not all copped up like the ones in Harlem, and the teachers were kind of friendly and not so tough-looking as those in Patrick Henry.

I made some kind of friends with some paddy boys. I even tried out for the school baseball team. There were a lot of paddy boys and girls watching the tryouts and I felt like I was the only one trying out. I dropped a fly ball in the outfield to cries of "Get a basket," but at bat I shut everybody out of my mind and took a swing at the ball with all I had behind it and hit a home run. I heard the cheers and made believe I hadn't.

I played my role to the most, and the weeks turned into months. I still missed Harlem, but I didn't see it for six months. *Maybe,* I thought, *this squeeze livin' ain't as bad as Crutch said.* I decided to try the lunchtime swing session in the school gym. The Italian paddy, Angelo, had said they had hot music there. I dug the two-cents admission fee out of my pocket and made it up the walk that led to the gym.

"Two cents, please," said a little *muchacha blanca.*

"Here you are."

"Thank you," she smiled.

I returned her smile. Shit, man, Crutch was wrong.

The gym was whaling. The music was on wax, and it was a mambo. I let myself react. It felt good to give in to the natural rhythm. Maybe there were other worlds besides the mean streets, I thought. I looked around the big gym and saw some of the kids I knew a little. Some of them waved; I waved back. I noticed most of the paddy kids were dancing the mambo like stiff. Then I saw a girl I had heard called Marcia or something by the other kids. She was a pretty, well-stacked girl, with black hair and a white softness which set her hair off pretty cool. I walked over to her. "Hi," I said.

"Huh? Oh, hi."

"My first time here."

"But I've seen you before. You got Mrs. Sutton for English."

"Yeah, that's right. I meant this is my first time to the gym dance."

"I also was at the field when you smashed that ball a mile."

"That was *suerte,*" I said.

"What's that?" she asked.

"What?"

"What you said — 'swear-tay.' "

I laughed. "Man, that's Spanish."

"Are you Spanish? I didn't know. I mean, you don't look like what I thought a Spaniard looks like."

"I ain't a Spaniard from Spain," I explained. "I'm a Puerto Rican from Harlem."

"Oh — you talk English very well," she said.

"I told you I was born in Harlem. That's why I ain't got no Spanish accent."

"No-o, your accent is more like Jerry's."

What's she tryin' to put down? I wondered. Jerry was the colored kid who recently had moved to Bayshore.

"Did you know Jerry?" she asked. "Probably you didn't get to meet him. I heard he moved away somewhere."

"Yeah, I know Jerry," I said softly. "He moved away because he got some girl in trouble. I know Jerry is colored and I know I got his accent. Most of us in Harlem steal from each other's language or style or stick of living. And it's *suerte,* s-u-e-r-t-e. It means 'luck.' "

Jesus, Crutch, you got my mind messed up a little. I keep thinking this broad's tryin' to tell me something shitty in a nice dirty way. I'm gonna find out. "Your name is Marcia or something like that, eh?" I added.

"Ahuh."

"Mine's Piri. Wanna dance?"

"Well, this one is almost over."

"Next one?"

"Well, er — I, er — well, the truth is that my boyfriend is sort of jealous and — well, you know how —"

I looked at her and she was smiling. I said, "Jesus, I'm sorry. Sure, I know how it is. Man, I'd feel the same way."

She smiled and shrugged her shoulders pretty-like. I wanted to believe her. I did believe her. I had to believe her. "Some other time, eh?"

She smiled again, cocked her head to one side and crinkled her nose in answer.

"Well, take it easy," I said. "See you around."

She smiled again, and I walked away not liking what I was feeling, and thinking that Crutch was right. I fought against it. I told myself I was still feeling out of place here in the middle of all these strangers, that paddies weren't as bad as we made them out to be. I looked over my shoulder and saw Marcia looking at me funny-like. When she saw me looking, her face changed real fast. She smiled again. I smiled back. I felt like I was plucking a mental daisy:

> You're right, Crutch
> You're wrong, Crutch
> You're right, Crutch
> You're wrong, Crutch.

I wanted to get outside and cop some sun and I walked toward the door.

"Hi, Piri," Angelo called. "Where you going? It's just starting."

"Aw, it's a little stuffy," I lied. "Figured on making it over to El Viejo's — I mean, over to the soda fountain on Main Street."

"You mean the Greek's?"

"Yeah, that's the place."

"Wait a sec till I take a leak and I'll go over with you."

I nodded okay and followed Angelo to the john. I waited outside for him and watched the kids dancing. My feet tapped out time and I moved closer to the gym and I was almost inside again. Suddenly, over the steady beat of the music, I heard Marcia say, "Imagine the nerve of that black thing."

"Who?" someone asked.

"That new colored boy," said another voice.

They must have been standing just inside the gym. I couldn't see them, but I had that for-sure feeling that it was me they had in their mouths.

"Let's go, Piri," Angelo said. I barely heard him. "Hey fella," he said, "what's the matter?"

"Listen, Angelo. Jus' listen," I said stonily.

". . . do you mean just like that?" one of the kids asked.

"Ahuh," Marcia said. "Just as if I was a black girl. *Well!* He started to talk to me and what could I do except be polite and at the same time not encourage him?"

"Christ, first that Jerry bastard and now him. We're getting invaded by niggers," said a thin voice.

"You said it," said another guy. "They got some nerve. My dad says that you give them an inch them apes want to take a yard."

"He's not so bad," said a shy, timid voice. "He's a polite guy and seems to be a good athlete. And besides, I hear he's a Puerto Rican."

"Ha — he's probably passing for Puerto Rican because he can't make it for white," said the thin voice. "Ha, ha, ha."

I stood there thinking who I should hit first. *Marcia. I think I'll bust her jaw first.*

"Let's go, Piri," Angelo said. "Those creeps are so fuckin' snooty that nobody is good enough for them. Especially that bitch Marcia. Her and her clique think they got gold-plated assholes."

". . . no, *really!*" a girl was saying. "I heard he's a Puerto Rican, and they're not like Neg —"

"There's no difference," said the thin voice. "He's still black."

"Come on, Piri, let's go," Angelo said. "Don't pay no mind to them."

"I guess he thought he was another Jerry," someone said.

"He really asked me to dance with him," Marcia said indignantly. "I told him that my boyfriend . . ."

The rest of the mean sounds faded as I made it out into the sun. I walked faster and faster. I cut across the baseball field, then ran as fast as I could. I wanted to get away from the things running to mind. My lungs were hurting — not from running but from not being able to scream. After a while I sat down and looked up at the sky. How near it seemed. I heard a voice: "Piri! Holy hell, you tore up the ground running." I looked up and saw Angelo. He was huffing and out of wind. "Listen, you shouldn't let them get you down," he said, kneeling next to me. "I know how you feel."

I said to him very nicely and politely, "Do me a favor, you motherfuckin' paddy, get back with your people. I don't know why the fuck you're here, unless it's to ease your — oh, man, just get the fuck outta here. I hate them. I hate you. I hate all you white motherjumps."

"I'm sorry, Piri."

"Yeah, *blanco* boy, I know. You know how I feel, ain't that right? Go on, paddy, make it."

Angelo shook his head and slowly got up. He looked at me for a second, then walked away. I dug the sky again and said to it, "I ain't ever goin' back to that fuckin' school. They can shove it up their asses." I plucked the last mental daisy: *You was right, Crutch.* [1967]

Victor Hernández Cruz became the most acclaimed of the New York Puerto Rican poets. His works have been featured in respected journals and published by mainstream presses; despite his fusion of languages and cultures, his poems have managed to cross over into the larger U.S. literary scene. Hernández Cruz's collections of poetry include *Papo Got His Gun* (1960), *Snaps* (1969), *Mainland* (1973), *Tropicalization* (1976), *By Lingual Wholes* (1982), and *Rhythm, Content and Flavor* (1989); his poems have been reprinted in numerous anthologies.

Born in a rural area of Puerto Rico in 1949, Hernández Cruz emigrated to Spanish Harlem, "el barrio," as a young child. His memories of the blissful, traditional lifestyle of Aguas Buenas, Puerto Rico, in contrast with the cold, hard environment of New York City, had a major impact on this poet.

Hernández Cruz has described his poetry as Afro-Latin, although he touches on a broad range of multicultural and multiracial themes.

Critics have observed his delight in linguistic experimentation, the influence of music in the rhythm of his verses, and a tendency toward a broader world-view than is found in other poets of his generation. His works have been praised by Allen Ginsberg and Denise Levertov and proclaimed by others as "pure musical energy." Nicolás Kanellos describes Hernández Cruz's poetry as Puerto Rican "soul" music, emanating from "la salsa de Dios," and recording the "odyssey of the Rican in the twentieth century."

Today Is a Day of Great Joy

when they stop poems
in the mail & clap
their hands & dance to
them
when women become pregnant
by the side of poems
the strongest sounds   making
the river go along

it is a great day

as poems fall down to
movie crowds   in restaurants
in bars

when poems start to
knock down walls   to
choke politicians
when poems scream &
begin to break the air

that is the time of
true poets   that is
the time of greatness

a true poet   aiming
poems   & watching things
fall to the ground

it is a great day.   [1969]

African Things

o the wonder man   rides his space ship/
brings his power through
many moons
carries in soft blood   african spirits
dance & sing in my mother's house. in my cousin's house.
black as night can be/   what was Puerto Rican all about.
all about the
indios & you better believe it the african things
black & shiny
grandmother speak to me & tell me of african things
how do latin
boo-ga-loo sound   like you
conga drums in the islands   you know
the traveling through many moons
dance & tell me black african things
i know you know.

[1973]

Alurista is the pen name of Alberto Baltazar Urista Heredia, who was born in Mexico City in 1947 and migrated to California as an adolescent. There he pursued his studies in Spanish literature, completing a Ph.D. from the University of California, San Diego, in 1982. Poet, dramatist, and community organizer, Alurista had a profound impact on the emerging concept of Chicanismo in the late 1960s, particularly regarding the indigenous aspect of Chicano cultural heritage.

As in the case of many Chicano authors from this literary period, referred to as the Chicano Renaissance, Alurista was deeply inspired by the farmworkers' movement and its leader, César Chávez. He was immersed in the idealism of the era and, like Chávez, appreciated the value of organizing efforts to produce change. At San Diego State University in 1967, he helped establish the Chicano Student Movement of Aztlán (MECHA) and the Chicano Studies Program, and in 1969 he promulgated the concept and symbol of Aztlán — the mythological home of the Aztec peoples in the Southwest United States.

The poems reproduced here, "el maguey en su desierto" (the maguey cactus in its desert), "must be the season of the witch," and "to be fathers once again," were first published in *Floricanto en Aztlán* (1971), considered a landmark in Chicano poetics. While the poetic language and subject matter are direct and familiar, Alurista's use of bilingualism and Chicano Spanish, along with the cultural and intellectual diversity of his themes — pre-Columbian beliefs, pop culture, American rock, barrio experiences, and so on — present an original and provocative mix. The poems in *Floricanto* combine social protest with the quest for self-determination; indeed, all of Alurista's works affirm Chicano culture and the dignity of Chicano people; these include the later collections, *Nationchild Plumaroja* (1972), *Timespace Huracán* (1976), and *Spik in Glyph?* (1981). The style and sound of the poetry in *Floricanto* spawned numerous imitators.

el maguey en su desierto

el maguey en su desierto
   — even though arid —
produces tunas
   red tunas
let your seed turn fruit
allow the tuna of your humanity
to flourish
with the heritage of pirámides sagradas
and in the desert of this land
be humid
fertiliza with your fertility
and virility
allow yourself to be
the legacy of our ancestors
it is yours
to wear
and psychodelisize
to the inclinations
of your present
humanity
to dwell in free willed RAZA   [1971]

must be the season of the witch

must be the season of the witch
  la bruja
  la llorona
she lost her children
  and she cries
en las barrancas of industry
  her children
devoured by computers
and the gears
must be the season of the witch
  i hear huesos crack
in pain
  y lloros
la bruja pangs
  sus hijos han olvidado
la magia de durango
  y la de moctezuma
  — el ilhuicamina
must be the season of the witch
la bruja llora
sus hijos sufren; sin ella [1971]

to be fathers once again

to be fathers once again
  Chicanos have been born
to find
  a desert for an orchard
sepulcro de dolor
  flores en la tumba
  — to save love
yearning for years
  la criatura llora
  — en la tarde transparente

el patriarca de mi gente
  y sus hijos
(siembra de bronce)
   — perpetua Raza
fértil abono del desierto
   — crece,
reproduce
  protege los ojos
   — el infante llora
to grow
   — to father (once again) Chicanos

[1971]

Tomás Rivera was born in Crystal City, Texas, in 1935 and grew up in a Spanish-speaking household. He graduated from Southwest Texas Junior College and from Southwest Texas State University in 1958, earning an M.Ed. in administration in 1964. In 1969 Rivera received a Ph.D. in Romance languages and literatures from the University of Oklahoma. At the time of his death in 1984 he was chancellor of the University of California at Riverside.

Rivera was a poet, novelist, short-story writer, literary critic, college administrator, and educator. His novel *. . . y no se lo tragó la tierra,* written in 1971, has been translated three times, by Herminio Ríos-C. as *. . . And the Earth Did Not Part;* by Evangelina Vigil-Piñón as *. . . And the Earth Did Not Devour Him;* and by Rolando Hinojosa as *This Migrant Earth.*

The novel tells the story of a young man's coming of age; the boy's memories convey the migrant experience in the United States through vignettes and stories. To Rivera, memory brings together the people and the land in a heroic struggle for selfhood and identity against formidable odds. The title itself is intriguing, presented as if the reader has come upon the work in midsentence and must decide where in the book that sentiment might lie — the ending? *. . . And the Earth Did Not Devour Him,* a powerful literary work, is fragmented but highly structured, which may be the reason that until recently it has not been widely read outside Latino circles. The following excerpt furnished the title for the book.

. . . And the Earth Did Not Devour Him

The first time he felt hate and anger was when he saw his mother crying for his uncle and his aunt. They both had caught tuberculosis and had been sent to different sanitariums. So, between the brothers and sisters, they had split up the children among themselves and had taken care of them as best they could. Then the aunt died, and soon thereafter they brought the uncle back from the sanitarium, but he was already spitting blood. That was when he saw his mother crying every little while. He became angry because he was unable to do anything against anyone. Today he felt the same. Only today it was for his father.

"You all should've come home right away, m'ijo. Couldn't you see that your Daddy was sick? You should have known that he'd suffered a sunstroke. Why didn't you come home?"

"I don't know. Us being so soaked with sweat, we didn't feel so hot, but I guess that when you're sunstruck it's different. But I did tell him to sit down under the tree that's at the edge of the rows, but he didn't want to. And that was when he started throwing up. Then we saw he couldn't hoc anymore and we dragged him and put him under a tree. He didn't put up a fuss at that point. He just let us take him. He didn't even say a word."

"Poor viejo, my poor viejo. Last night he hardly slept. Didn't you hear him outside the house. He squirmed in bed all night with cramps. God willing, he'll get well. I've been giving him cool lemonade all day, but his eyes still look glassy. If I'd gone to the fields yesterday, I tell you, he wouldn't have gotten sick. My poor viejo, he's going to have cramps all over his body for three days and three nights at the least. Now, you all take care of yourselves. Don't overwork yourselves so much. Don't pay any mind to that boss if he tries to rush you. Just don't do it. He thinks it's so easy since he's not the one who's out there stooped."

He became even angrier when he heard his father moan outside the chicken coop. He wouldn't stay inside because he said it made him feel very anxious. Outside where he could feel the fresh air was where he got some relief. And also when the cramps came he could roll over on the grass. Then he thought about whether his father might die from the sunstroke. At times he heard his father start to pray and ask for God's help. At first he had faith that he would get well soon, but by the next day he felt the anger growing inside of him. And all the more when he heard his mother and his father clamoring for God's mercy. That night, well past midnight, he had been awakened by his father's groans. His mother got up and removed the scapularies from around his neck and washed them. Then she lit some candles. But nothing happened. It was like his aunt and uncle all over again.

"What's to be gained from doing all that, Mother? Don't tell me you think it helped my aunt and uncle any. How come we're like this, like we're buried alive? Either the germs eat us alive or the sun burns us up. Always some kind of sickness. And every day we work and work. For what? Poor Dad, always working so hard. I think he was born working. Like he says, barely five years old and already helping his father plant corn. All the time feeding the earth and the sun, only to one day, just like that, get struck down by the sun. And there you are, helpless. And them, begging for God's help . . . why, God doesn't care about us . . . I don't think there even is . . . No, better not say it, what if Dad gets worse. Poor Dad, I guess that at least gives him some hope."

His mother noticed how furious he was, and that morning she told him to calm down, that everything was in God's hands and that with God's help his father was going to get well.

"Oh, Mother, do you really believe that? I am certain that God has no concern for us. Now you tell me, is Dad evil or mean-hearted? You tell me if he has ever done any harm to anyone."

"Of course not."

"So there you have it. You see? And my aunt and uncle? You explain. And the poor kids, now orphans, never having known their parents. Why did God have to take them away? I tell you, God could care less about the poor. Tell me, why must we live here like this? What have we done to deserve this? You're so good and yet you have to suffer so much."

"Oh, please, m'ijo, don't talk that way. Don't speak against the will of God. Don't talk that way, please, m'ijo. You scare me. It's as if already the blood of Satan runs through your veins."

"Well, maybe. That way at least, I could get rid of this anger. I'm so tired of thinking about it. Why? Why you? Why Dad? Why my uncle? Why my aunt? Why their kids? Tell me, Mother, why? Why us, burrowed in the dirt like animals with no hope for anything? You know the only hope we have is coming out here every year. And like you yourself say, only death brings rest. I think that's the way my aunt and uncle felt and that's how Dad must feel too."

"That's how it is, m'ijo. Only death brings us rest."

"But why us?"

"Well, they say that . . ."

"Don't say it. I know what you're going to tell me — that the poor go to heaven."

That day started out cloudy and he could feel the morning coolness brushing his eyelashes as he and his brothers and sisters began the day's labor. Their mother had to stay home to care for her husband. Thus, he felt responsible for hurrying on his brothers and sisters. During the morning, at least for the first few hours, they endured the heat but by ten-thirty the sun had suddenly cleared the skies and pressed down against the world. They began working more slowly because of the weakness, dizziness and suffocation they felt when they worked too fast. Then they had to wipe the sweat from their eyes every little while because their vision would get blurred.

"If you start blacking out, stop working, you hear me? Or go a little slower. When we reach the edge we'll rest a bit to get our strength back. It's gonna be hot today. If only it'd stay just a bit cloudy like this morning, then nobody would complain. But no, once the sun bears down like this not even one little cloud dares to appear out of fear. And the worst of it is we'll finish up here by two and then we have to go over to that other field that's nothing but hills. It's okay at the top of the hill but down in the lower part of the slopes it gets to be real suffocating. There's no breeze there. Hardly any air goes through. Remember?"

"Yeah."

"That's where the hottest part of the day will catch us. Just drink plenty of water every little while. It don't matter if the boss gets mad. Just don't get sick. And if you can't go on, tell me right away, all right? We'll go home. Y'all saw what happened to Dad when he pushed himself too hard. The sun has no mercy, it can eat you alive."

Just as they had figured, they had moved on to the other field by early afternoon. By three o'clock they were all soaked with sweat. Not one part of their clothing was dry. Every little while they would stop. At times they could barely breathe, then they would black out and they would become fearful of getting sunstruck, but they kept on working.

"How do y'all feel?"

"Man, it's so hot! But we've got to keep on. 'Til six, at least. Except this water don't help our thirst any. Sure wish I had a bottle of cool water, real cool, fresh from the well, or a coke ice-cold."

"Are you crazy? That'd sure make you sunsick right now. Just don't work so fast. Let's see if we can make it until six. What do you think?"

At four o'clock the youngest became ill. He was only nine years old, but since he was paid the same as a grown-up he tried to keep up with the rest. He began vomiting. He sat down, then he lay down. Terrified, the other children ran to where he lay and looked at him. It appeared that he had fainted and when they opened his eyelids they saw his eyes were rolled back. The next youngest child started crying, but right away he told him to stop and help him carry his brother home. It seemed he was having cramps all over his little body. He lifted him and carried him by himself and, again, he began asking himself *why?*

"Why Dad and then my little brother? He's only nine years old. Why? He has to work like a mule buried in the earth. Dad, Mom, and my little brother here, what are they guilty of?"

Each step that he took toward the house resounded with the question, *why?* About halfway to the house he began to get furious. Then he started crying out of rage. His little brothers and sisters did not know what to do, and they, too, started crying, but out of fear. Then he started cursing. And without even realizing it, he said what he had been wanting to say for a long time. He cursed God. Upon doing this he felt that fear instilled in him by the years and by his parents. For a second he saw the earth opening up to devour him. Then he felt his footsteps against the earth, compact, more solid than ever. Then his anger swelled up again and he vented it by cursing God. He looked at his brother, he no longer looked sick. He didn't know whether his brothers and sisters had understood the graveness of his curse.

That night he did not fall asleep until very late. He felt at peace as never before. He felt as though he had become detached from everything. He no longer worried about his father nor his brother.

All that he awaited was the new day, the freshness of the morning. By daybreak his father was doing better. He was on his way to recovery. And his little brother, too; the cramps had almost completely subsided. Frequently he felt a sense of surprise upon recalling what he had done the previous afternoon. He thought of telling his mother, but he decided to keep it secret. All he told her was that the earth did not devour anyone, nor did the sun.

He left for work and encountered a very cool morning. There were clouds in the sky and for the first time he felt capable of doing and undoing anything that he pleased. He looked down at the earth and kicked it hard and said:

"Not yet, you can't swallow me up yet. Someday, yes. But I'll never know it." [1971]

Translation of . . . *y no se lo tragó la tierra* by Evangelina Vigil-Piñón

Rudolfo Anaya was born in Pastura, New Mexico, in 1937. He received his B.A. and M.A. in literature from the University of New Mexico. Among his literary awards are the Premio Quinto Sol for *Bless Me, Ultima* and the Before Columbus Foundation American Book Award for *Tortuga*. He has published eight novels, several collections of short stories, anthologies, poetry, and criticism. His most recent novels are *Zia Summer* (1995) and *Jalamanta* (1996).

Bless Me, Ultima represents a landmark in Latino fiction. It has sold more than 350,000 copies since its publication in 1972 and has been used in many courses in Latino literature. Anaya's story, focusing on a young boy's spiritual awakening, is set during his first years at public school. A sense of territorial culture pervades the book; the various Latino inhabitants of the town, which is predominantly Chicano, move easily in and out of Chicano and Anglo culture. The boy, Antonio, is guided through the choices he must make between male and female worlds, the influence of sea and moon, stasis and movement, by the *curandera* (healing woman) Ultima, whose death late in the book launches Antonio into the world of his future. The essence of Antonio's story is the redemptive power of writing, yet the striking aspect of the novel is its reaching into the roots of pre-Hispanic imagery, the Aztlanese world that survives in an oral folk tradition. Several critics have noted that the protagonist's feeling of personal completion contrasts with the emptiness expressed in much nonethnic American fiction and the discontinuity that engulfs many Latino works set in urban America. Others have felt that Anaya's insistent spirituality detracts from the story. Still, *Bless Me, Ultima* is remarkable for the magnetism of the culture Anaya portrays.

from Bless Me, Ultima

Ultima came to stay with us the summer I was almost seven. When she came the beauty of the llano unfolded before my eyes, and the gurgling waters of the river sang to the hum of the turning earth. The magical time of childhood stood still, and the pulse of the living earth pressed its mystery into my living blood. She took my hand, and the silent, magic powers she possessed made beauty from the raw, sun-baked llano, the green river valley, and the blue bowl which was the white sun's home. My bare feet felt the throbbing earth and my body trembled with excitement. Time stood still, and it shared with me all that had been, and all that was to come . . .

Let me begin at the beginning. I do not mean the beginning that was in my dreams and the stories they whispered to me about my birth, and the people of my father and mother, and my three brothers — but the beginning that came with Ultima.

The attic of our home was partitioned into two small rooms. My sisters, Deborah and Theresa, slept in one and I slept in the small cubicle by the door. The wooden steps creaked down into a small hallway that led into the kitchen. From the top of the stairs I had a vantage point into the heart of our home, my mother's kitchen. From there I was to see the terrified face of Chávez when he brought the terrible news of the murder of the sheriff; I was to see the rebellion of my brothers against my father; and many times late at night I was to see Ultima returning from the llano where she gathered the herbs that can be harvested only in the light of the full moon by the careful hands of a curandera.

That night I lay very quietly in my bed, and I heard my father and mother speak of Ultima.

"Está sola," my father said, "ya no queda gente en el pueblito de Las Pasturas —"

He spoke in Spanish, and the village he mentioned was his home.

My father had been a vaquero all his life, a calling as ancient as the coming of the Spaniard to Nuevo Méjico. Even after the big rancheros and the tejanos came and fenced the beautiful llano, he and those like him continued to work there, I guess because only in that wide expanse of land and sky could they feel the freedom their spirits needed.

"¡Qué lástima," my mother answered, and I knew her nimble fingers worked the pattern on the doily she crocheted for the big chair in the sala.

I heard her sigh, and she must have shuddered too when she thought of Ultima living alone in the loneliness of the wide llano. My mother was not a woman of the llano, she was the daughter of a farmer. She could not see beauty in the llano and she could not understand the coarse men who lived half their lifetimes on horseback. After I was born in Las Pasturas she persuaded my father to leave the llano and bring her family to the town of Guadalupe where she said there would be opportunity and school for us. The move lowered my father in the esteem of his compadres, the other vaqueros of the llano who clung tenaciously to their way of life and freedom. There was no room to keep animals in town so my father had to sell his small herd, but he would not sell his horse so he gave it to a good friend, Benito Campos. But Campos could not keep the animal penned up because somehow the horse was very close to the spirit of the man, and so the horse was allowed to roam free and no vaquero on that llano would throw a lazo on that horse. It was as if someone had died, and they turned their gaze from the spirit that walked the earth.

It hurt my father's pride. He saw less and less of his old compadres. He went to work on the highway and on Saturdays after they collected their pay he drank with his crew at the Longhorn, but he was never close to the men of the town. Some weekends the llaneros would come into town for supplies and old amigos like Bonney or Campos or the Gonzales brothers would come by to visit. Then my father's eyes lit up as they drank and talked of the old days and told the old stories. But when the western sun touched the clouds with orange and gold the vaqueros got in their trucks and headed home, and my father was left to drink alone in the long night. Sunday morning he would get up very crudo and complain about having to go to early mass.

"— She served the people all her life, and now the people are scattered, driven like tumbleweeds by the winds of war. The war sucks everything dry," my father said solemnly. "It takes the young boys overseas, and their families move to California where there is work —"

"Ave María Purísima," my mother made the sign of the cross for my three brothers who were away at war. "Gabriel," she said to my father, "it is not right that la Grande be alone in her old age —"

"No," my father agreed.

"When I married you and went to the llano to live with you and raise your family, I could not have survived without la Grande's help. Oh, those were hard years —"

"Those were good years," my father countered. But my mother would not argue.

"There isn't a family she did not help," she continued. "No road was too long for her to walk to its end to snatch somebody from the jaws of death, and not even the blizzards of the llano could keep her from the appointed place where a baby was to be delivered —"

"Es verdad," my father nodded.

"She tended me at the birth of my sons —" And then I knew her eyes glanced briefly at my father. "Gabriel, we cannot let her live her last days in loneliness —"

"No," my father agreed, "it is not the way of our people."

"It would be a great honor to provide a home for la Grande," my mother murmured. My mother called Ultima la Grande out of respect. It meant the woman was old and wise.

"I have already sent word with Campos that Ultima is to come and live with us," my father said with some satisfaction. He knew it would please my mother.

"I am grateful," my mother said tenderly. "Perhaps we can repay a little of the kindness la Grande has given to so many."

"And the children?" my father asked. I knew why he expressed concern for me and my sisters. It was because Ultima was a curandera, a woman who knew the herbs and remedies of the ancients, a miracle-worker who could heal the sick. And I had heard that Ultima could lift the curses laid by brujas, that she could exorcise the evil the witches planted in people to make them sick. And because a curandera had this power she was misunderstood and often suspected of practicing witchcraft herself.

I shuddered and my heart turned cold at the thought. The cuentos of the people were full of the tales of evil done by brujas.

"She helped bring them into the world, she cannot be but good for the children," my mother answered.

"Está bien," my father yawned, "I will go for her in the morning."

So it was decided that Ultima should come and live with us. I knew that my father and mother did good by providing a home for Ultima. It was the custom to provide for the old and the sick. There was always room in the safety and warmth of la familia for one more person, be that person stranger or friend.

It was warm in the attic, and as I lay quietly listening to the sounds of the house falling asleep and repeating a Hail Mary over and over in my thoughts, I drifted into the time of dreams. Once I had told my mother about my dreams and she said they were visions from God and she was happy, because her own dream was that I should grow up and become a priest. After that I did not tell her about my dreams, and they remained in me forever and ever . . .

In my dream I flew over the rolling hills of the llano. My soul wandered over the dark plain until it came to a cluster of adobe huts. I recognized the village of Las Pasturas and my heart grew happy. One mud hut had a lighted window, and the vision of my dream swept me towards it to be witness at the birth of a baby.

I could not make out the face of the mother who rested from the pains of birth, but I could see the old woman in black who tended the just-arrived, steaming baby. She nimbly tied a knot on the cord that had connected the baby to its mother's blood, then quickly she bent and with her teeth she bit off the loose end. She wrapped the squirming baby and laid it at the mother's side, then she returned to cleaning the bed. All linen was swept aside to be washed, but she carefully wrapped the useless cord and the afterbirth and laid the package at the feet of the Virgin on the small altar. I sensed that these things were yet to be delivered to someone.

Now the people who had waited patiently in the dark were allowed to come in and speak to the mother and deliver their gifts to the baby. I recognized my mother's brothers, my uncles from El Puerto de los Lunas. They entered ceremoniously. A patient hope stirred in their dark, brooding eyes.

This one will be a Luna, the old man said, he will be a farmer and keep our customs and traditions. Perhaps God will bless our family and make the baby a priest.

And to show their hope they rubbed the dark earth of the river valley on the baby's forehead, and they surrounded the bed with the fruits of their harvest so the small room smelled of fresh green chile and corn, ripe apples and peaches, pumpkins and green beans.

Then the silence was shattered with the thunder of hoofbeats; vaqueros surrounded the small house with shouts and gunshots, and when they entered the room they were laughing and singing and drinking.

Gabriel, they shouted, you have a fine son! He will make a fine vaquero! And they smashed the fruits and vegetables that surrounded the bed and replaced them with a saddle, horse blankets, bottles of whiskey, a new rope, bridles, chapas, and an old guitar. And they rubbed the stain of earth from the baby's forehead because man was not to be tied to the earth but free upon it.

These were the people of my father, the vaqueros of the llano. They were an exuberant, restless people, wandering across the ocean of the plain.

We must return to our valley, the old man who led the farmers spoke. We must take with us the blood that comes after the birth. We will bury it in our fields to renew their fertility and to assure that the baby will follow our ways. He nodded for the old woman to deliver the package at the altar.

No! the llaneros protested, it will stay here! We will burn it and let the winds of the llano scatter the ashes.

It is blasphemy to scatter a man's blood on unholy ground, the farmers chanted. The new son must fulfill his mother's dream. He must come to El Puerto and rule over the Lunas of the valley. The blood of the Lunas is strong in him.

He is a Márez, the vaqueros shouted. His forefathers were conquistadores, men as restless as the seas they sailed and as free as the land they conquered. He is his father's blood!

Curses and threats filled the air, pistols were drawn, and the opposing sides made ready for battle. But the clash was stopped by the old woman who delivered the baby.

Cease! she cried, and the men were quiet. I pulled this baby into the light of life, so I will bury the afterbirth and the cord that once linked him to eternity. Only I will know his destiny.

The dream began to dissolve. When I opened my eyes I heard my father cranking the truck outside. I wanted to go with him, I wanted to see Las Pasturas, I wanted to see Ultima. I dressed hurriedly, but I was too late. The truck was bouncing down the goat path that led to the bridge and the highway.

I turned, as I always did, and looked down the slope of our hill to the green of the river, and I raised my eyes and saw the town of Guadalupe. Towering above the housetops and the trees of the town was the church tower. I made the sign of the cross on my lips. The only other building that rose above the housetops to compete with the church tower was the yellow top of the schoolhouse. This fall I would be going to school.

My heart sank. When I thought of leaving my mother and going to school a warm, sick feeling came to my stomach. To get rid of it I ran to the pens we kept by the molino to feed the animals. I had fed the rabbits that night and they still had alfalfa and so I only changed their water. I scattered some grain for the hungry chickens and watched their mad scramble as the rooster called them to peck. I milked the cow and turned her loose. During the day she would forage along the highway where the grass was thick and green, then she would return at nightfall. She was a good cow and there were very few times when I had to run and bring her back in the evening. Then I dreaded it, because she might wander into the hills where the bats flew at dusk and there was only the sound of my heart beating as I ran and it made me sad and frightened to be alone.

I collected three eggs in the chicken house and returned for breakfast.

"Antonio," my mother smiled and took the eggs and milk, "come and eat your breakfast."

I sat across the table from Deborah and Theresa and ate my atole and the hot tortilla with butter. I said very little. I usually spoke very little to my two sisters. They were older than I and they were very close. They usually spent the entire day in the attic, playing dolls and giggling. I did not concern myself with those things.

"Your father has gone to Las Pasturas," my mother chattered, "he has gone to bring la Grande." Her hands were white with the flour of the dough. I watched carefully. "— And when he returns, I want you children to show your manners. You must not shame your father or your mother —"

"Isn't her real name Ultima?" Deborah asked. She was like that, always asking grown-up questions.

"You will address her as la Grande," my mother said flatly. I looked at her and wondered if this woman with the black hair and laughing eyes was the woman who gave birth in my dream.

"Grande," Theresa repeated.

"Is it true she is a witch?" Deborah asked. Oh, she was in for it. I saw my mother whirl then pause and control herself.

"No!" she scolded. "You must not speak of such things! Oh, I don't know where you learn such ways —" Her eyes flooded with tears. She always cried when she thought we were learning the ways of my father, the ways of the Márez. "She is a woman of learning," she went on and I knew she didn't have time to stop and cry, "she has worked hard for all the people of the village. Oh, I would never have survived those hard years if it had not been for her — so show her respect. We are honored that she comes to live with us, understand?"

"Sí, mamá," Deborah said half willingly.

"Sí, mamá," Theresa repeated.

"Now run and sweep the room at the end of the hall. Eugene's room —" I heard her voice choke. She breathed a prayer and crossed her forehead. The flour left white stains on her, the four points of the cross. I knew it was because my three brothers were at war that she was sad, and Eugene was the youngest.

"Mamá." I wanted to speak to her. I wanted to know who the old woman was who cut the baby's cord.

"Sí." She turned and looked at me.

"Was Ultima at my birth?" I asked.

"¡Ay Dios mío!" my mother cried. She came to where I sat and ran her hand through my hair. She smelled warm, like bread. "Where do you get such questions, my son? Yes," she smiled, "la Grande was there to help me. She was there to help at the birth of all of my children —"

"And my uncles from El Puerto were there?"

"Of course," she answered, "my brothers have always been at my side when I needed them. They have always prayed that I would bless them with a —"

I did not hear what she said because I was hearing the sounds of the dream, and I was seeing the dream again. The warm cereal in my stomach made me feel sick.

"And my father's brother was there, the Márez' and their friends, the vaqueros —"

"Ay!" she cried out. "Don't speak to me of those worthless Márez and their friends!"

"There was a fight?" I asked.

"No," she said, "a silly argument. They wanted to start a fight with my brothers — that is all they are good for. Vaqueros, they call themselves, they are worthless drunks! Thieves! Always on the move, like gypsies, always dragging their families around the country like vagabonds —"

As long as I could remember she always raged about the Márez family and their friends. She called the village of Las Pasturas beautiful; she had gotten used to the loneliness, but she had never accepted its people. She was the daughter of farmers.

But the dream was true. It was as I had seen it. Ultima knew.

"But you will not be like them." She caught her breath and stopped. She kissed my forehead. "You will be like my brothers. You will be a Luna, Antonio. You will be a man of the people, and perhaps a priest." She smiled.

A priest, I thought, that was her dream. I was to hold mass on Sundays like Father Byrnes did in the church in town. I was to hear the confessions of the silent people of the valley, and I was to administer the holy Sacrament to them.

"Perhaps," I said.

"Yes," my mother smiled. She held me tenderly. The fragrance of her body was sweet.

"But then," I whispered, "who will hear my confession?"

"What?"

"Nothing," I answered. I felt a cool sweat on my forehead and I knew I had to run, I had to clear my mind of the dream. "I am going to Jasón's house," I said hurriedly and slid past my mother. I ran out the kitchen door, past the animal pens, towards Jasón's house. The white sun and the fresh air cleansed me.

On this side of the river there were only three houses. The slope of the hill rose gradually into the hills of juniper and mesquite and cedar clumps. Jasón's house was farther away from the river than our house. On the path that led to the bridge lived huge, fat Fío and his beautiful wife. Fío and my father worked together on the highway. They were good drinking friends.

"¡Jasón!" I called at the kitchen door. I had run hard and was panting. His mother appeared at the door.

"Jasón no está aquí," she said. All of the older people spoke only in Spanish, and I myself understood only Spanish. It was only after one went to school that one learned English.

"¿Dónde está?" I asked.

She pointed towards the river, northwest, past the railroad tracks to the dark hills. The river came through those hills and there were old Indian grounds there, holy burial grounds, Jasón told me. There in an old cave lived his Indian. At least everybody called him Jasón's Indian. He was the only Indian of the town, and he talked only to Jasón. Jasón's father had forbidden Jasón to talk to the Indian, he had beaten him, he had tried in every way to keep Jasón from the Indian.

But Jasón persisted. Jasón was not a bad boy, he was just Jasón. He was quiet and moody, and sometimes for no reason at all wild, loud sounds came exploding from his throat and lungs. Sometimes I felt like Jasón, like I wanted to shout and cry, but I never did.

I looked at his mother's eyes and I saw they were sad. "Thank you," I said, and returned home. While I waited for my father to return with Ultima I worked in the garden. Every day I had to work in the garden. Every day I reclaimed from the rocky soil of the hill a few more feet of earth to cultivate. The land of the llano was not good for farming, the good land was along the river. But my mother wanted a garden and I worked to make her happy. Already we had a few chile and tomato plants growing. It was hard work. My fingers bled from scraping out the rocks and it seemed that a square yard of ground produced a wheelbarrow full of rocks which I had to push down to the retaining wall.

The sun was white in the bright blue sky. The shade of the clouds would not come until the afternoon. The sweat was sticky on my brown body. I heard the truck and turned to see it chugging up the dusty goat path. My father was returning with Ultima.

"¡Mamá!" I called. My mother came running out, Deborah and Theresa trailed after her.

"I'm afraid," I heard Theresa whimper.

"There's nothing to be afraid of," Deborah said confidently. My mother said there was too much Márez blood in Deborah. Her eyes and hair were very dark, and she was always running. She had been to school two years and she spoke only English. She was teaching Theresa and half the time I didn't understand what they were saying.

"Madre de Dios, but mind your manners!" my mother scolded. The truck stopped and she ran to greet Ultima. "Buenos días le de Dios, Grande," my mother cried. She smiled and hugged and kissed the old woman.

"Ay, María Luna," Ultima smiled, "Buenos días te de Dios, a ti y a tu familia." She wrapped the black shawl around her hair and shoulders. Her face was brown and very wrinkled. When she smiled her teeth were brown. I remembered the dream.

"Come, come!" my mother urged us forward. It was the custom to greet the old. "Deborah!" my mother urged. Deborah stepped forward and took Ultima's withered hand.

"Buenos días, Grande," she smiled. She even bowed slightly. Then she pulled Theresa forward and told her to greet la Grande. My mother beamed. Deborah's good manners surprised her, but they made her happy, because a family was judged by its manners.

"What beautiful daughters you have raised," Ultima nodded to my mother. Nothing could have pleased my mother more. She looked proudly at my father, who stood leaning against the truck, watching and judging the introductions.

"Antonio," he said simply. I stepped forward and took Ultima's hand. I looked up into her clear brown eyes and shivered. Her face was old and wrinkled, but her eyes were clear and sparkling, like the eyes of a young child.

"Antonio," she smiled. She took my hand and I felt the power of a whirlwind sweep around me. Her eyes swept the surrounding hills and through them I saw for the first time the wild beauty of our hills and the magic of the green river. My nostrils quivered as I felt the song of the mockingbirds and the drone of the grasshoppers mingle with the pulse of the earth. The four directions of the llano met in me, and the white sun shone on my soul. The granules of sand at my feet and the sun and sky above me seemed to dissolve into one strange, complete being.

A cry came to my throat, and I wanted to shout it and run in the beauty I had found.

"Antonio." I felt my mother prod me. Deborah giggled because she had made the right greeting, and I who was to be my mother's hope and joy stood voiceless.

"Buenos días le de Dios, Ultima," I muttered. I saw in her eyes my dream. I saw the old woman who had delivered me from my mother's womb. I knew she held the secret of my destiny.

"¡Antonio!" My mother was shocked I had used her name instead of calling her Grande. But Ultima held up her hand.

"Let it be," she smiled. "This was the last child I pulled from your womb, María. I knew there would be something between us."

My mother who had started to mumble apologies was quiet. "As you wish, Grande," she nodded.

"I have come to spend the last days of my life here, Antonio," Ultima said to me.

"You will never die, Ultima," I answered. "I will take care of you —" She let go of my hand and laughed. Then my father said, "Pase, Grande, pase. Nuestra casa es su casa. It is too hot to stand and visit in the sun —"

"Sí, sí," my mother urged. I watched them go in. My father carried on his shoulders the large blue-tin trunk which later I learned contained all of Ultima's earthly possessions, the black dresses and shawls she wore, and the magic of her sweet smelling herbs.

As Ultima walked past me I smelled for the first time a trace of the sweet fragrance of herbs that always lingered in her wake. Many years later, long after Ultima was gone and I had grown to be a man, I would awaken sometimes at night and think I caught a scent of her fragrance in the cool-night breeze.

And with Ultima came the owl. I heard it that night for the first time in the juniper tree outside of Ultima's window. I knew it was her owl because the other owls of the llano did not come that near the house. At first it disturbed me, and Deborah and Theresa too. I heard them whispering through the partition. I heard Deborah reassuring Theresa that she would take care of her, and then she took Theresa in her arms and rocked her until they were both asleep.

I waited. I was sure my father would get up and shoot the owl with the old rifle he kept on the kitchen wall. But he didn't, and I accepted his understanding. In many cuentos I had heard the owl was one of the disguises a bruja took, and so it struck a chord of fear in the heart to hear them hooting at night. But not Ultima's owl. Its soft hooting was like a song, and as it grew rhythmic it calmed the moonlit hills and lulled us to sleep. Its song seemed to say that it had come to watch over us.

I dreamed about the owl that night, and my dream was good. La Virgen de Guadalupe was the patron saint of our town. The town was named after her. In my dream I saw Ultima's owl lift la Virgen on her wide wings and fly her to heaven. Then the owl returned and gathered up all the babes of Limbo and flew them up to the clouds of heaven.

The Virgin smiled at the goodness of the owl. [1972]

Oscar "Zeta" Acosta was born in El Paso, Texas, in 1935, according to his application for the California Bar. After serving in the U.S. Air Force, he attended college and graduated from law school. He declared himself a candidate for sheriff of Los Angeles County in 1970 with La Raza Unida party. Acosta disappeared in Mazatlán, Mexico, in 1974, in a veil of darkness.

A larger-than-life, self-promoted character, Acosta was a friend of Hunter S. Thompson; he appears as Dr. Gonzo in *Fear and Loathing in Las Vegas*. His reputation has recently grown because of the republication of his two autobiographical fictions, *The Autobiography of a Brown Buffalo* (1972), in which he discusses his chaotic coming of age in California, and *The Revolt of the Cockroach People* (1973), a New Journalism insertion of self into a historical series of events. Recently the writer and critic Ilan Stavans has published *Bandido,* a book-length appreciation of Acosta, and his unpublished stories have been presented by Arte Público Press.

The Revolt of the Cockroach People begins with the takeover of St. Basil's Roman Catholic Church by Chicano activists in California, a historic act of defiance of both religion and state organized by members of El Movimiento (the Movement). Acosta, still in his guise of the Brown Buffalo and now an attorney, signs on to defend the protesters. But the book becomes less a discussion of the Movement than a disquisition on Acosta's life, the personal as the political. Acosta's writing, even the choice of his pen name ("Zeta" is the name of the letter Z in Spanish), is an exercise in self-mythmaking. He spent most of his adult life trying to define his own identity within the Mexican and Mexican-American worlds, but in the end he will most likely be remembered for his ethnic confusion, attempts at self-discovery, and startling, charming, self-made persona.

from The Revolt of the Cockroach People

It is Christmas Eve in the year of Huitzilopochtli, 1969. Three hundred Chicanos have gathered in front of St. Basil's Roman Catholic Church. Three hundred brown-eyed children of the sun have come to drive the money-changers out of the richest temple in Los Angeles. It is a dark moonless night and ice-cold wind meets us at the doorstep. We carry little white candles as weapons. In pairs on the sidewalk, we trickle and bump and sing with the candles in our hands, like a bunch of cockroaches gone crazy. I am walking around giving orders like a drill sergeant.

From the mansions of Beverly Hills, the Faithful have come in black shawls, in dead fur of beasts out of foreign jungles. Calling us savages, they have already gone into the church, pearls in hand, diamonds in their Colgate teeth. Now they and Cardinal James Francis McIntyre sit patiently on wooden benches inside, crossing themselves and waiting for the bell to strike twelve, while out in the night three hundred greasers from across town march and sing tribal songs in an ancient language.

St. Basil's is McIntyre's personal monstrosity. He recently built it for five million bucks: a harsh structure for puritanical worship, a simple solid excess of concrete, white marble and black steel. It is a tall building with a golden cross and jagged cuts of purple stained glass thirty feet in the air, where bleeding Christ bears down on the people of America below. Inside, the fantastic organ pumps out a spooky religious hymn to this Christ Child of Golden Locks and Blue Eyes overlooking the richest drag in town.

All around us, insurance companies with patriotic names are housed in gigantic towers of white plaster. Here prestigious law firms perform their business for rich people who live next to jaded movie stars. The Bank of America, Coast Federal Savings, and all those other money institutions that sit in judgment over our lives, keep the vaults across the street behind solid locks. But the personalized checkbooks now sit on the pews of St. Basil's, under siege by a gang of cockroaches from east of the Los Angeles River, from a "Mexican-American" barrio there called Tooner Flats.

It is dark out on the sidewalks. Cars pass along Wilshire Boulevard and slow down when they see us. Most of our crowd are kids. Most of them have never attacked a church before. One way or another, I've been doing it for years. And for this and other reasons, I have been designated *Vato Número Uno,* Number One Man for this gig.

The young wear clothes for battle, the old in thick woolen ponchos, gavans and serapes. College-age kids in long hair and combat garb: khaki pants, olive-drab field jackets and paratrooper boots spit-shined like those of the old *veteranos* who once went to war against America's enemies. Girls with long mascara-eyes, long black hair done up *chola* style, with tight asses and full blouses bursting out with song.

Three priests in black and brown shirts pass out the tortillas. Three hundred Chicanos and other forms of Cockroaches munch on the buttered body of Huitzilopochtli, on the land-baked pancake of corn, lime, lard and salt. Teetering over our heads are five gigantic papier-mâché figures with blank faces, front-lipped beaks, stone-head bishop dunce caps. A guitar gently plucks and sways *Las Posadas* to the memory of the White and Blue Hummingbird, the god of our fathers. We chew the tortillas softly. It is a night of miracles: never before have the sons of the conquered *Aztecas* worshipped their dead gods on the doorstep of the living Christ. While the priests offer red wine and the poor people up-tilt earthen pottery to their brown cold lips, there are tears here, quiet tears of history.

When the singing has ended and the prayers for the dead and the living are complete, I step forward and announce that we have been permitted to enter St. Basil's. A Chicano sergeant from Judd Davis' SOC Squad just told me we could enter if we left our "demonstration" outside.

"Do we need special passes?" I had baited him.

"This is a *church,* Brown. Just tell them to hold it down when they go in. It's being *televised.*"

I knew that, of course. We were at the home base of the holy man who encouraged presidents to drop fire on poor Cockroaches in far-off villages in Vietnam. From behind these stained glass windows, this man in the red frock and beanie, with the big blue ring on his knuckle, begs his god to give victory to the flames.

"Viva La Raza!" the crowd shouts at my announcement.

We turn and start walking up the cement steps. But at the top, the fifteen-foot doors of glass are shut in our faces. And when we try them, they are locked. Left out, once again; tricked into thinking we are welcome. An usher with a dark blue suit and red hair flaps his lips against the thick soundproof glass: *No More Room*.

There is a stirring. Pushing towards the front. What do they mean? No more room. Locked out. Period. Just like Jesus.

The wind is still cold. Everyone huddles together on the steps. Our leaders regroup in one corner. It's up to us. This is the nut, our test of strength. Are we men? Do we want freedom? Will we get laid tonight if we cop out now? And what would our children say?

"Fuck it, *ese*. Let's get in there!" Gilbert shouts at the student intellectuals who want to organize outside.

"Yeah, fuck these *putos*," Pelon puts in. Both are regular *vatos locos*, crazymen.

"But what will happen?"

"Oh, fuck that, *ese*. Let's go on in."

A dozen men and women trudge through the questioning crowd. We are going in to find out what's going on, we say. Wait for us. And with that we run around the side of the monster with steeples pointing to a star that no longer shines.

But whoops! Wait! What is this in the parking lot? Black and white and mostly blue. The SOC Squad desperados standing in formation. Clubs and pistols with dumdum bullets. Solid helmets with plastic visors from the moon of Mars. Ugly ants with transistor radios, walkie-talkies and tear gas canisters dangling from their hips. There are fifty pigs waiting for us to make the wrong move. But do they see us?

"Come on," our lawyer exhorts. I, strange fate, am this lawyer.

In the darkness we find a door leading to the basement. We are smiles again. Hah! We have a crack!

Yet caution: I peek into the basement. No mops. No brooms. It is a chapel, filled with the overflow of the Faithful. They are on their knees, clasping fingers and hands in front of their faces. Beads are being kissed, little black crosses dangled about in a cloud of incense. I see no room for us. Beside me is a stairway. We scramble up fast.

We enter a blue room, the vestibule inside the main entrance. There sits holy water in bowls beside the four huge doors. And through the glass we see the Cockroaches outside: faces in a sea of molasses. Teeth and bright colored clothes. The Chicanos are a beautiful people. Brown soft skin, purple lips and zoftig chests. Their fists are raised in victory, though all we may hear is the most reactionary voice in America sing "Joy to the World."

"Hey, what are you doing in here?" Again, the carrot-top usher with the dark blue suit. He looms before us out of nowhere.

"We are here to worship, sir," Risco, the *cubano* says.

"No more room, boys. You'll have to leave."

"How about up in the choir loft?" I say.

"Nope. We don't let *nobody* up there."

Outside, we see white teeth and feel fists banging on the doors. But we hear nothing. The glass is four inches thick. Mouths are moving and bodies are agitated. Things are tense.

"Hey, man. Why can't we just *stand* here?" Gilbert asks.

"In here? This isn't, uh . . . Sorry, boys. All the room is taken up. You'll just have to leave."

We all crowd around the usher. He is big but nervous; he keeps looking to his side. The vestibule is dark. The floors, walls and ceiling are all deep blue velvet. A soft room for worship. The light is dim and nearly yellow. Some of the women cross themselves. Some also dip their fingers in holy water and bless themselves.

Then Black Eagle says, "Hey, man. Why don't you just open up that door and we'll listen to the service from here?"

The usher looks up and down at Black Eagle's immense black beard and militant gear. I know he wants to say how that isn't dress for civilized worship.

"No, I just can't do that. All of you will have to leave right now. Or I'll be forced to call the police."

"Well, fuck it, *ese!*" Gilbert shouts at the man.

"Hey, come on, Gilbert," one of our law students reprimands.

"You'd better leave, boy!" The usher is now obviously worked up.

Gilbert reaches for the horizontal panic bar to one of the outside doors.

"Stop!" The usher screams but makes no move.

Gilbert stops. "You *said* to get out." But the door is somehow open a bit.

"Not that way! You'll have to leave the same way you got in." The man is sweating now. He is looking at the crowd of Chicanos banging away on the glass. With the door cracked open we can hear what they have been chanting all along:

LET THE POOR PEOPLE IN! LET THE POOR PEOPLE IN!

Just about then, the choir and the congregation begin to sing. The choir and the organ are in a loft right above the door leading to the main church. This loft overlooks the vestibule and, occasionally, the choir director, waving his baton madly, peers at us over the low wall.

"You leave right now!" he shouts.

So naturally, Gilbert and Black Eagle again reach for the panic bars. Out of desperation the usher grabs Gilbert by the back of his coat and swings him against the bucket of holy water. Black Eagle stops and turns. We all move into a circle with the usher in the middle.

"Touch me again, you *puto,* and I'll let you have it!" Gilbert shouts. Glroosh-flut! The usher has struck Gilbert, the black frog, in the kisser. We stare and wait for the fog to clear. We are in a church, remember.

Gilbert reaches for the door once again. Flluutt!! The usher has struck Gilbert Rodriguez, the poet laureate of East LA, right in the eye.

For two seconds no one moves. How in the fuck are you going to strike an usher? A *Catholic* usher. What would Gilbert's grandmother say? For two seconds time is suspended. And then it comes upon us in a wave: it isn't an usher. The police have tricked us again!

Boom! A solid uppercut to the pig's jaw. Then a scream. He hollers, "Sergeant Armas! Sergeant Armas!" Black Eagle finally opens the front door. Gilbert takes one in the stomach. *Vato Número Uno,* Warrior Number One, does not move. The lawyer stands and watches.

A wall curtain jumps and Sergeant Armas, the *real* boss of the

SOC Squad, bowls in with twenty men. The vestibule explodes as men in blue run in formation swinging two feet of solid mahogany. Five other "ushers" run out of nowhere pulling out badges from inside their coats and pinning them on their breast pockets. Then they pull out little canisters and systematically squirt stuff into the faces of Chicanos who are entering now, pushing in through the front doors. And there is swinging and screaming and shouting and we are into a full-scale riot in the blue vestibule of the richest church in town. But I am standing stock still. All around me bodies are falling. Terrified women and children are wailing while the choir sings above my head:

O come all ye faithful, joyful and triumphant,
O come ye, O come ye, to Bethlehem . . .

I see Gilbert, the fat Corsican pirate, grappling with a burly cop. Wearing his Humphrey Bogart raincoat, he's on the pig's back. His small brown hands are stuck in the eyes of the monster with the club. They pass me by.

Black Eagle has squared off with two ushers. One squirts Mace in his face while the other kicks him in the balls. Down and down he goes, crashing to the velvet floor. I watch it all serenely while the choir and congregation entertain. I wear a suit and tie. No one lays a hand on me. I take out my pipe and wade through the debris. Crash-crattle and krootle! A thirty-six-inch cement ash-tray flies through the plate glass door. Sticks to hold up posters fly over the crowd. Candles for the gods become missiles in the air. A religious war, a holy riot in full gear. Then, sirens screaming outside, the rest of the SOC squad bursts in to join its brothers. The choir never misses a beat:

Come and behold Him, born the king of angels . . .

I watch a red-haired girl with glasses and a mini-skirt rush through the door to the main church, which has opened momentarily. It is Duana Doherty, the street nun who once worshipped wearing black robes while her head was bald. Then she joined up with the Chicanos and became a Cockroach herself. I take a few steps to see what she is up to.

Inside another usher, a real one, sees us. I have on my pin-striped blue Edwardian and I've put my pipe back in my pocket. Duana has creamy peach skin. She has the face of an angel. The usher has no hair. The three of us make one of a kind.

"I think there's a seat up front," he says.

Duana doesn't stop for an answer. She runs down the length of the aisle. The Faithful in furs, in diamonds and hats of lace, are staring straight ahead at the altar where seven priests perform for TV.

"Just keep on, my children. Pay no attention to the rabble-rousers out there," Monsignor Hawkes is exhorting them, his red hands cupping the mike.

The usher can't keep up with Duana. She makes it to the front, turns and addresses the congregation: "People of St. Basil's, please, come and help us. They're killing the poor people out in the lobby! Please. Come and help!"

Two ushers finally grab her around the belly and carry her out. I stand aside and watch them pass. And almost at the same moment I see another woman running at full boat. It is Gloria Chavez, the fiery black-haired Chicano Militant. She charges down the aisle in a black satin dancing dress that shows her beautiful knockers and she carries a golf club in her pretty hands. I am aghast! The Faithful are petrified. No one makes a move for her. Her big zoftig ass shakes as she rushes up to the altar, turns to the pie-eyed man in the red cape, and shouts:

¡QUÉ VIVA LA RAZA!

Swoosh, swoosh, swoosh! With three deft strokes Gloria clears off the Holy of Holies from the altar of red and gold. The little white house with its cross falls. The little white wafers which stick to the roof of your mouth just before you swallow, the Body of Christ is on the red carpet.

It is too astounding a thing to believe. No one lifts a finger to stop this mad woman with her golf club as she hotfoots it down the aisle toward the vestibule. The ushers, the worshippers and myself simply stand and stare. The congregation has long since stopped singing. It is just the choir:

O come let us adore Him, O come let us adore Him . . .

The golden chalice, the cruets for the wine and water are scattered on the floor before the bleeding Christ and the Madonna with child in arm.

"CHICANO POWER!" Gloria shouts as she vanishes inside the battle zone.

I follow her. I stop in the doorway and see Gloria being taken by three huge pigs. The pigs have already backed the scum out into the streets.

"Just a minute, Officer . . . You don't have to hit her," I say.

"Get out of the way, Mr. Brown," Sergeant Armas says to me.

Gloria is kicking and cussing and slapping away. Her legs are shooting up at the three men who are hustling her to the floor.

"*¡Pinches, cabrones, hijos de la chingada!*" she screams.

I move. I grab the arm of one of the cops. He turns to slug me with his baton, but Armas stops him.

"Leave Brown alone! He's their lawyer," Armas tells the man.

When they have carried her away, I stand and scan the battlefield. The floor is covered with debris. Sand from the ash-trays, broken glass from the doors, papers listing our demands, a shoe, an umbrella, eyeglasses with gold frames, banners with *La Virgen de Guadalupe* drawn in color. Garbage galore litters the holy blue vestibule.

I walk carefully outside. It is the same on the steps. The street is lined with police vans, red lights glaring, sirens howling in the night. And on the other side, hundreds of Chicanos standing or walking around aimlessly.

I see Gilbert and Black Eagle being whacked over the head with batons as they are hauled into a car. I run down the steps, toward the street. Cops hold me back. I struggle, I shove, I kick away. For God's sake, I *want* to be arrested! "Don't touch the lawyer," they say to one another.

I run back toward St. Basil's which now has helmeted pigs standing in a skirmish line at the bottom of the steps. They are tense, their hands gnarled around the batons held before them at parade rest. Fear is in the eyes of black and Chicano cops. So I say to them, "Why don't you guys relax? You ought to see yourselves, you'd be ashamed." I see murder in their eyes. They *have* to take this shit. Armas, their tough Chicano sergeant, has told them to keep their bloody hands off me.

The St. Basil's side of Wilshire is filthy with cops and Wilshire itself is still clogged with police wagons. Beyond them the Chicanos are waiting for a call to regroup. I cup my hands to my mouth and shout, "Hey, *Raza* . . . Go home now. Go home and rest up. Tomorrow, during Christmas Mass, let's meet here again."

I walk up and down the street on the sidewalk. Nobody touches me as I shout at them to go home, shower up and regroup here tomorrow for another battle. To go home, bandage the wounded and heal the sick.

When it is done, the big pig, Sergeant Armas, comes up to thank me. "You're OK, Brown. Things got out of control here tonight. Thanks a lot."

"Ah, fuck you, you asshole!"

I returned alone to my office in downtown LA in the darkness of the first hours of Christmas. For more than a year now I have issued my orders, written my statements to the press and prepared for my daily work out of the tenth floor of a tall building in the middle of skid row.

At this moment, all my friends are bleeding in their cells, heads battered, arms hanging limp from the clubs of the pigs. And even now, as I sip my hot cup of coffee and prepare my newest statements to the press, to the reporters that I know will break down my door before the day is over, even now I sit and stare and ponder the havoc that has been unleashed. What to do?

I dial the phone and listen to the buzz and ring of Stonewall's telephone in Colorado, where the snow must be quietly falling upon massive aspen trees, upon green leaves and white trunks.

"Jesus, what the fuck?" a familiar groggy voice wants to know.

For nearly two years now I've called and written this bald-headed journalist who once told me during a volleyball game: "If you ever find a big story in your travels, call me. I'll put you in touch with the right man."

"Uh, sorry to wake you. But I've got us a big one."

"Brown? Jesus, Brown, it's Christmas! It's three o'clock in the morning. Are you loaded?"

"No, man. I just got back from . . . I just witnessed the first religious war in America. A full-blown riot inside a church."

"Just like I thought, you bastard! You're fucked up!"

I begin to explain the events of the past twelve hours. He mumbles and coughs his way through the first half of the story and I have to keep asking, "You still there?" Until I got to the part about the red-headed nun in a mini-skirt and Gloria with her golf club demolishing the tabernacle.

"Hold it! You said a *golf* club?"

"Yeah, a number seven wood, I think."

"You don't mind if I turn on my tape recorder, do you?"

"Jesus, I've been asking you to do that!"

I finish it out on tape. For fifteen minutes I dictate blood and songs and papier-mâché dolls.

"And, uh . . . they didn't arrest you?" he says finally.

"Shit, they didn't *touch* me."

Silence. A long pause. Does he believe it?

"And you were right there? You were inside?"

"Standing in the center of it all."

More silence. Another long pause. Could he afford not to believe it?

"And you want me to come out and write about this?"

"Well . . . either that or get someone of your caliber to do it."

"And you were one of the leaders?"

"In all modesty, yeah."

I can hear wheels grinding in his brain.

"Are you *serious*? Do you see what you've *done*?"

"Yeah, sure. I've upped the ante."

"You mean you've dumped it on your buddies," he says softly.

I don't remember hanging up the phone. When my mind finally thaws, I find myself alone in my tiny legal office on the tenth floor, high above the Cockroaches on the streets of spit and sin and foul air in downtown LA. [1973]

Nicholasa Mohr was born in New York City in 1935 and grew up in "el barrio" in the 1940s. A graphic artist as well as a writer, she was educated at the Art Students League, the Brooklyn Museum School, and the Pratt Center for Contemporary Printmaking. Her books have gained critical recognition: *Nilda* (1973) received the 1974 Jane Addams Children's Book Award and was selected as an Outstanding Children's Book of the Year 1973 by the editors of the *New York Times;* in 1976, *El Bronx Remembered* (1975) was a finalist for the National Book Award. Among her other literary works are *In Nueva York* (1977), *Felita* (1979), *Rituals of Survival: A Woman's Portfolio* (1985), and *Going Home* (1986).

Nilda is a bildungsroman, or novel of childhood formation, a genre often associated with the growing up of a young man. Mohr extended the genre to young Latinas, describing a young woman growing up in a specific historic context — the years from 1941 to 1945 — and a specific place — New York's oldest and largest Latino neighborhood. As in other works of this type, the protagonist confronts the universal problems of family life, sexuality, relationships with peers, friendships, school, and career goals. In this work, however, as in other U.S. Latino works, these problems are explored within the social reality of growing up as a member of a "minority" in the larger society; ethnicity and culture play an important role in the way the character deals with conflict. *Nilda* fits squarely in the tradition of U.S. Latino literature; at the same time, however, it makes a distinctly female statement regarding the quest for individuality and maturity within a New York Puerto Rican context.

from **Nilda**

July, 1942

From Grand Central Station, like the first time, along with many other children, Nilda went off to camp again. It was an all-girls camp, nonsectarian, taking children from all areas of the Eastern states. Her mother told her that it would be different this time. Reassuring her, she had said, "Look, Nilda, I had to pay something for the camp. It's not a free camp like the last time. I had to buy two pink jumpsuits for uniforms; everybody wears the same thing there. Everybody is the same. You see? Nobody is going to hit you, Nilda. There is not gonna be no nuns and none of that. I promise. O.K.?"

She was going for a whole month. That's like forever, she thought, feeling miserable. As the train sped out of New York City, leaving the Barrio and the tall buildings behind, Nilda became frightened, not knowing what was going to happen to her. Looking around her in the train car, she noticed that there were no dark children. Except for a couple of olive-skinned, dark-haired girls, she did not see any Puerto Rican or black children. She wondered if the two girls were Spanish.

Nilda thought about last summer and the nuns, and felt a sense of relief as she looked at one of the women counselors who was dressed in a light pink cotton suit. The woman caught Nilda's glance and smiled at her. Nilda quickly looked away, hoping that the woman would not ask her any questions. She did not want to speak to anyone. She began to think of home and her family, making an effort to keep from crying.

She knew her brothers had gone to camp. Paul was big enough to work at his camp and make some money. Lucky thing! she thought. She remembered Victor was not going to be at home any more. Determined, despite his mother's protests, he had joined the Army right after graduation. He had been gone two weeks already. She just couldn't imagine not having Victor at home any more. She had been very proud that her brother was going to be a soldier and had told Miss Langhorn all about it at school. "He is a good American," Miss Langhorn had said. "You and your family should be proud."

She remembered Victor's graduation party. Her mother had managed a small dinner for the family, and a cake. Aunt Rosario had come down from the Bronx with her husband, Willie, and her two children, Roberto and Claudia. Her mother and Aunt Rosario had been brought up together in Puerto Rico; they were first cousins. She was her mother's only relative in this country. Nilda saw Aunt Rosario and her cousins during holidays every year and on special occasions. She would travel with her family to the Bronx or Aunt Rosario would come to the Barrio to visit with them. Nilda didn't much like Roberto, but she enjoyed playing with Claudia.

Nilda smiled, thinking about all her family and Baby Jimmy. She remembered it had been a long time since she had seen him. He won't even know me any more when I see him again, she thought. Last winter they had received a card from Jimmy and Sophie postmarked somewhere in New York, not New Jersey, with no return address. She went on drifting into mental images.

A loud whistle sounded and the train began to slow down. "Bard Manor . . . Bard Manor . . . fifteen-minute stop," she heard a man's voice calling.

Outside they all lined up and marched over to several buses that were parked near the small railroad station. After a short ride, Nilda got off the bus with the rest of the girls. Nilda looked about her and saw no buildings; there were large areas of grass and trees. Off at a distance from the road she saw a group of cottages set among green hills.

They approached the cottages, which were made of unfinished logs with a dark rough bark. Nilda entered a cottage with her group; it was a large dormitory, simply furnished. There was a total of eight beds, four at either side of the room. A wooden bureau was placed next to each bed, with a small wooden bench at the foot. Each child automatically took a bunk.

"Hello, girls," said one counselor. "Let me introduce myself. I'm Miss Rachel Hammerman, and you can all call me Miss Rachel." Looking at the other counselor, she said, "Jeanette?"

"Yes," answered the other counselor. "Hi. I'm Miss Jeanette Pisacano. You can all call me Miss Jeanette."

Miss Rachel said, "Has everyone got a bunk? O.K. Then that will be your bunk for the rest of the time you are going to be here. In this section of Bard Manor Camp for Girls we have campers ages nine to twelve. The older girls live on the other side of the camp. We will visit them in time and they will visit us as well. In fact, we all eat together in the main house, which is about a ten-minute walk down the road. The pool is there with the tennis court, swings, and all the other goodies. Let's see . . ." she paused. "Oh yes. Miss Jeanette and I also sleep here; I don't know if you noticed, but there is another entrance to the cottage; that is our entrance only. O.K.?" She waited, then asked, "Now, Jeanette, you wanna say something?"

"Yes," Miss Jeanette smiled. "We hope to really have a good time here. You all might complain about our early bedtime . . . seven-thirty we get ready."

"Awww . . ." "Nawww," the girls complained.

"By eight o'clock we should be in bed," Miss Jeanette went on, smiling.

"Nooo . . . Awww." "Awwww," the girls responded.

"You will be so tired," Miss Jeanette went on talking, "that you will be glad to get to bed when we finish with you." She paused and smiled. "You'll see." She laughed. "Anyway —" The girls interrupted, giggling and protesting. "Shhhh . . . shhhh." She continued, "Now listen, you all have two pink jumpsuits. They will be what you are going to wear most of the time that you are here. Just put on a pair of clean panties and your jumpsuits. At the end of the day you can put them in the large laundry cart in the shower room. Now, they will be laundered; you will always have a clean jumpsuit to wear. In the morning someone will put all the suits and panties on one camper's bunk. She will look at the name tags and distribute them. Every day another camper will distribute the jumpsuits, so that everyone will take a turn, rotating . . . ummm . . . and . . ." Looking at Miss Rachel, she asked, "What else, Rachel?"

"Oh well, we will make a list of chores for everyone. Every day each camper has a special chore to do. We will alternate the work."

"Too bad." "Yeah." "Aw shucks," said some of the girls.

Miss Rachel smiled. "Never mind; everybody works. Here we make our own beds and keep our cottage clean, as well as help in the dining room at mealtime, and so on." Pausing, she asked, "Who's hungry?"

"Meeeee." "Me." "I'm starving," the girls yelled.

"O.K.," she said, "get your things put away and then wash up and make sure you all go to the toilet. Now, as soon as we finish, we go eat. All right? Make it snappy then," Miss Jeanette said.

"Wait, let's introduce ourselves."

"Oh, of course!" Miss Rachel looked around and said, "O.K., let's start." Pointing at Nilda, she said, "Your name is Nilda? Right? Tell us your full name."

"Nilda Ramírez," she said.

"Bernice White."

"Josie Forest."

"Evelyn Daniels."

"Stella Pappas." All the other girls called out their names.

Both women left the room and the girls started to put their things away. Nilda opened her suitcase and put her things away in the drawers. Then she set her bureau with her toothbrush, toothpaste, hairbrush, and comb. She picked up a pad of plain unlined paper and a small box of crayons, a present from Aunt Delia. She carefully wrote her name on them and placed them inside the top drawer. All finished, she looked around at the other girls. She smiled at the girl in the next bunk.

The girl, smiling back, said, "Hello."

"Hi," said Nilda. "What's your name again?"

"Josie. What's yours?"

"Nilda. You been here before?"

"No. I've never been to camp before at all. This is my first time."

"Oh well," said Nilda, "I been to camp before. Not here, in another place, but I didn't like it; they were too strict." Looking around at the room she added, "This looks nice, don't it?"

"Yes," said Josie smiling. Some of the other girls were going off to the bathroom. "I guess we'd better wash up if we wanna eat. You wanna come, Nilda?"

"O.K." Nilda walked along with Josie into a large bathroom with several sinks and toilets. There were clean towels and soap set out. Nilda saw that the toilets had doors. Good, she thought, I can make alone. She washed up and waited her turn to sit on the toilet.

Outside the sun was still out and the trees cast long shadows on the fields. She walked with the group, looking around her at the quiet woods. They walked along the road until they came to a large white two-story wood-frame house. A sign was over the entrance; gold letters trimmed in white on a black background read, BARD MANOR CAMP FOR GIRLS. Nilda saw a lot of outdoor equipment, swings, climbing bars, a tennis court, and a large swimming pool. There were also several small wood-framed buildings near the main house.

They went into a large dining room set with long tables and wooden folding chairs. Nilda saw that the chairs were exactly like the ones in Benji's church. Oh man, she thought. Turning to comment, she realized that there was no one who would know what she was talking about. Miss Rachel led them to a table set for ten persons and they sat down. The table was covered with a clean white tablecloth.

"Today we'll be served, but tomorrow we serve ourselves, as well as clear the table! So enjoy the service, ladies," she smiled.

They were served a vegetable soup, breaded chicken cutlets, carrots, hash brown potatoes, and a green salad. A large platter of bread with butter, dishes of jam, and pitchers of milk were on the table. Everyone passed them around. Dessert was an apple cake, which Nilda enjoyed. She ate everything.

The girls played outdoors for a little while after supper, running, and climbing on the equipment. Nilda began to play with a few of the girls in her group, chasing each other and tossing a large rubber ball around. Someone blew a whistle and the girls lined up.

As they walked back to their cottage, Nilda was feeling tired already. The counselors began to sing songs. At first, she barely opened her mouth, but then slowly she began to mouth a chorus, getting louder and louder. She heard herself singing clearly just like the rest of the girls.

That night in bed, Nilda pulled the covers around her, tucking in her feet. It was dark and quiet, except for the sound of the crickets. She could not fall asleep although she felt very tired. She thought of home again and the sounds and smells, so different. Sounds and smells she could understand. Footsteps on the hard sidewalk. A woman's high heels clicking, or a man's heavy shoes slapping the concrete as he ran to catch the bus late at night. Someone coughing. Someone whistling. All the traffic whizzing by. Summertime, everybody outside. The radios playing, people talking. Her mother making fresh coffee with boiled milk. The smell of the heat. Sometimes when it got unbearably hot, her mother let her sit on the fire escape with her pillow and blanket.

Suddenly the silence scared her and she wanted her mother; she wanted to go home. Nilda began to sob quietly and heard some of the other girls crying. She thought, They are crying too? Surprised, she listened to them cry for a little while, then remembered that tomorrow they were going to use the swimming pool. She had never been in a pool before. I wonder what that's gonna be like, she thought.

Everyone had stopped crying and she heard the heavy breathing of the girls fast asleep in the silent room. Outside the crickets continued chirping, occasionally changing their rhythm patterns slightly. Slowly Nilda became used to the new melody of sounds surrounding her.

July 14, 1942.

Dear Mami,

I am fine. I'm haveing a real good time. I passed my swimming test. I am now advance beginner insted of only beginner that is a higher thing to be. We do a lot of art and crafts I am makeing you something and something for Papa. I received you letter. I told everybody about Victor that he is in Fort Bragg North Carolina. We had a cook out that is where you make a fire and cook the food outside and it tasted real good. We ate hot dogs and hambergers and milk and juice. We also toasted marshmellos. I like Miss Jenete she is really nice to me she is my counselor. I seen a lot of flowers like you told me about when you live in Puerto Rico. I hope you are fine and haveing a good time. Tell Titi Delia I made some drawings of the camp so she could see what it looks like here. I learn some songs. we really have a lot of fun it is swell here.

Well that is it. Mami I love you and Papa and Aunt Delia and everybody. Bendicion Mama.

Love
Nilda xxxxxx

P.S. my friend Josie is
nice and so is Stella they
live in another state.

Nilda read the letter she had just written to her mother and, satisfied, folded it and put it inside an envelope. This was free time and she had finally decided that she had better answer her mother's letter. Most of the girls in her group were either writing, reading, or just sitting around. Getting up from her bunk, she decided to walk to the main house and put the letter in the mail basket. Looking for her two friends, she realized that they were probably at the main house anyway. Nilda started walking down the road; in the past two weeks she had gotten to know the camp quite well. She loved being able to recognize a large oak tree or a clump of bushes, a certain curve in the earth, a gentle slope in the horizon. All these familiar landmarks gave her a sense of security.

Nilda passed a trail off the side of the main road. They had all hiked through there one day; it was thick with trees and bushes. Stopping for a moment, she took the trail and started walking into the woods. She came to a fork in the trail. Taking the path on the right that seemed to climb, she continued along and came to a clearing where the landscape opened up into wide fields covered with wild flowers. The white Queen Anne's lace covered most of the fields, which were sprinkled with yellow goldenrod and clumps of tiny orange and purple flowers. The sky overhead was bright with the sun. Large white clouds glistened, rapidly moving across the horizon and out of sight.

Nilda remembered her mother's description of Puerto Rico's beautiful mountainous countryside covered with bright flowers and red flamboyant trees.

"There it was a different world from Central Park and New York City, Nilda," she could hear her mother saying. Looking ahead, she saw miles and miles of land and not a single sign promising to arrest her for any number of reasons. Signs had always been part of her life:

> DO NOT WALK ON THE GRASS . . .
>
> DO NOT PICK THE FLOWERS . . .
>
> NO SPITTING ALLOWED . . .
>
> NO BALL PLAYING ALLOWED . . .
>
> VIOLATORS WILL BE PROSECUTED.

No dog shit on my shoes, she laughed. And Mama always telling me to watch out for the broken pieces of whiskey bottles in the bushes. No matter where she was in Central Park, she could always see part of a tall building and hear the traffic.

Here there was not a building anywhere, she thought, no traffic and no streets to cross. She became aware of the silence again. The world of the Barrio and the crowds was someplace else far away, and it was all right. Miles and miles away someplace, but she could still be here at the same time; that could really happen. Yes, it's true, she smiled to herself. She felt the letter to her mother still in her pocket.

Nilda went back towards the main road, drinking in the sweet and pungent smells of the woods. She listened to the quiet buzzing of insects and the rustling of the bushes as small animals rushed through, sometimes appearing and disappearing within a split second. She noticed that off to the side of the trail a few feet away was a thick wall of bushes. Curious, Nilda went towards it and started to push her way through. Struggling, she pushed away the bushes with her arms and legs and stepped into an opening of yards and yards of roses delicately tinted with pink. The roses were scattered, growing wildly on the shrubs. The sun came through the leaves, stems, and petals, streaming down like rows of bright ribbons landing on the dark green earth.

Breathless, she stared at the flowers, almost unbelieving for a moment, thinking that she might be in a movie theater waiting for the hard, flat, blank screen to appear, putting an end to a manufactured fantasy which had engrossed and possessed her so completely. Nilda walked over to the flowers and touched them. Inhaling the sweet fragrance, she felt slightly dizzy, almost reeling. She sat down on the dark earth and felt the sun on her face, slipping down her body and over to the shrubs covered with roses. The bright sash of warm sunlight enveloped her and the flowers; she was part of them; they were part of her.

She took off her socks and sneakers, and dug her feet into the earth like the roots of the shrubs. Shutting her eyes, Nilda sat there for a long time, eyes closed, feeling a sense of pure happiness; no one had given her anything or spoken a word to her. The happiness was inside, a new feeling, and although it was intense, Nilda accepted it as part of a life that now belonged to her.

After supper that evening, Nilda's group received a visit from the older girls. They wore jumpsuits as well, yellow with a brown trim, styled differently. Nilda was sitting alone at the side of the hill opposite the cottages. She was barefoot, reading a book. A tall dark-haired girl approached her. She was about fourteen or fifteen years old. Smiling, she looked at Nilda and asked, "Are you Nilda?"

"Yes," Nilda said, returning her smile.

"What's your last name?"

"Ramírez, Nilda Ramírez."

"Hi," she said, sitting down comfortably next to Nilda. "I'm Olga. Olga Rodríguez. This is my third summer here." Nilda nodded, impressed with the older girl. "Somebody told me about you. They said you are Spanish. Do you speak it?"

"Yes!" said Nilda. "I speak it at home to my mother sometimes, and all the time to my aunt; she don't speak English at all."

"O.K. then," said Olga, "let's talk. How are you?" she asked in Spanish, and continued, "How do you like camp? Tell me, how long have you been here?"

"Oh," Nilda responded excitedly in Spanish. "I been here since like about two weeks already. But I will be here a whole month. I like it very much here."

"Where do you live? In New York City?" asked Olga.

"Yes. I live near Central Park right off Madison Avenue —"

"In the Barrio?" interrupted Olga.

"Yes! Do you know it? Do you live there too? Maybe you go to my brother Frankie's school."

"I don't live in the Barrio," Olga answered. "I live downtown, on 14th Street between Seventh and Eighth Avenues."

"Oh, my mother took me there once. Is that where there is a big church? Our Lady of Guadalupe, I think. My mother and me took a subway there. That is a great big church."

"Yes, that is our church," responded Olga. In English she asked Nilda, "You are Puerto Rican, ain't you?"

"Yes," Nilda answered, reverting to English.

"You know Puerto Ricans ain't really Spanish. You shouldn't say that. That you are Spanish. I can't even understand you when you talk." Surprised, Nilda realized the older girl was cross. "It's very hard to understand what you say . . . like when you say . . . say the number five in Spanish." Olga paused. "Go on, say it; say five in Spanish."

"Five," Nilda said clearly in Spanish.

"There, that's all wrong! You are saying it all wrong! What kind of accent is that? In Spain they talk Castilian. That's what my parents talk at home. You probably never even heard of that," Olga said angrily. Nilda did not know what to say and looked at Olga. "Say shoes," Olga went on. "Go ahead, I'll prove it again; say the word 'shoes.' "

Nilda wanted to say something. She thought, perhaps I should tell her about Papa. He speaks like that. He sounds like her and he comes from Spain, so he must speak like she says. But the older girl's angry face left Nilda mute. She said nothing.

"Go on," Olga insisted. "Say shoes. I'm waiting."

"Say shoes!" Nilda repeated in English.

"Very funny," Olga said. "Well that proves what you speak is a dialect." Getting up, she went on, "Don't let me hear you calling yourself Spanish around here when you can't even talk it properly, stupid."

"You're stupid," Nilda answered.

"I'm leaving," Olga said. "We don't bother with your kind. You give us all a bad name."

Nilda watched Olga turn away and disappear over the next mound of grass. Picking up a single green blade, she popped it in her mouth and began to chew. It had a bitter taste at first, then she got used to it and she chewed slowly, imitating some of the cows she had seen eating in the countryside. She lay back, digging her heels into the soft ground, thinking about the older girl and what had just happened. Nilda stuck out her tongue, then looked at the sky, the trees, and the small birds that flew overhead. At that moment she wanted to absorb all that was around her. Quickly, she began to let her body roll down the hill; faster and faster she went until her weight carried her to a full stop. Jumping up, she ran back to get her sneakers and her book. She didn't care about being Spanish; she didn't know exactly what that meant, except that it had nothing to do with her happiness. [1973]

Pedro Pietri (b. 1944) describes himself as a "native New Yorker born in Ponce," Puerto Rico. His first collection of poems, *Puerto Rican Obituary* (1973) remains his most popular work; the direct, nonconformist, performance-oriented style and the ironic and unconventional humor encompass the serious messages of working-class exploitation and the marginalization of people based on race and class. Imitated by many younger street poets, Pietri is strongly identified with the Nuyorican poets of the 1960s, although his subsequent books, *Lost in the Museum of Natural History* (1981), *Traffic Violations* (1983), and *The Masses Are Asses* (1984), are of several genres.

Pedro Pietri has assumed the persona of a public poet; an anarchic figure of mystery usually dressed in black, he can be seen carrying a briefcase full of his verses, combining poetry with a type of stand-up comic routine to question social mores and conventional behavior. His identification with the marginalized underclasses remains central to his subversive message which, as in the poetry of other U.S. Puerto Rican writers, is a critique of broken social promises and a more realistic counterbalance to the idealized, unfulfilled American Dream.

Sharing with other writings of the period the myth of the lost Puerto Rican island paradise as a cultural defense, "Puerto Rican Obituary" offers few alternatives beyond defiance, desperation, and an appeal to ethnic pride. However, Pietri raises the level of consciousness in his poetry by exposing the absurdities of emigrant life; this has led Alfredo Matilla in "Broken English Dream" to declare Pietri's poetry the first liberated Puerto Rican proletarian creation.

Puerto Rican Obituary

They worked
They were always on time
They were never late
They never spoke back
when they were insulted
They worked
They never took days off
that were not on the calendar
They never went on strike
without permission
They worked
ten days a week
and were only paid for five
They worked
They worked
They worked
and they died
They died broke
They died owing
They died never knowing
what the front entrance
of the first national city bank looks like

Juan
Miguel
Milagros
Olga
Manuel
All died yesterday today
and will die again tomorrow

passing their bill collectors
on to the next of kin
All died
waiting for the garden of eden
to open up again
under a new management
All died
dreaming about america
waking them up in the middle of the night
screaming: Mira Mira
your name is on the winning lottery ticket
for one hundred thousand dollars
All died
hating the grocery stores
that sold them make-believe steak
and bullet-proof rice and beans
All died waiting dreaming and hating

Dead Puerto Ricans
Who never knew they were Puerto Ricans
Who never took a coffee break
from the ten commandments
to KILL KILL KILL
the landlords of their cracked skulls
and communicate with their latino souls

Juan
Miguel
Milagros
Olga
Manuel
From the nervous breakdown streets
where the mice live like millionaires
and the people do not live at all
are dead and were never alive

Juan
died waiting for his number to hit
Miguel
died waiting for the welfare check

to come and go and come again
Milagros
died waiting for her ten children
to grow up and work
so she could quit working
Olga
died waiting for a five dollar raise
Manuel
died waiting for his supervisor to drop dead
so he could get a promotion

Is a long ride
from Spanish Harlem
to long island cemetery
where they were buried
First the train
and then the bus
and the cold cuts for lunch
and the flowers
that will be stolen
when visiting hours are over
Is very expensive
Is very expensive
But they understand
Their parents understood
Is a long non-profit ride
from Spanish Harlem
to long island cemetery

Juan
Miguel
Milagros
Olga
Manuel
All died yesterday today
and will die again tomorrow
Dreaming
Dreaming about queens
Clean-cut lily-white neighborhood
Puerto Ricanless scene

Thirty-thousand-dollar home
The first spics on the block
Proud to belong to a community
of gringos who want them lynched
Proud to be a long distance away
from the sacred phrase: Que Pasa

These dreams
These empty dreams
from the make-believe bedrooms
their parents left them
are the after-effects
of television programs
about the ideal
white american family
with black maids
and latino janitors
who are well train
to make everyone
and their bill collectors
laugh at them
and the people they represent

Juan
died dreaming about a new car
Miguel
died dreaming about new anti-poverty programs
Milagros
died dreaming about a trip to Puerto Rico
Olga
died dreaming about real jewelry
Manuel
died dreaming about the irish sweepstakes

They all died
like a hero sandwich dies
in the garment district
at twelve o'clock in the afternoon
social security number to ashes
union dues to dust

They knew
they were born to weep
and keep the morticians employed
as long as they pledge allegiance
to the flag that wants them destroyed
They saw their names listed
in the telephone directory of destruction
They were train to turn
the other cheek by newspapers
that misspelled mispronounced
and misunderstood their names
and celebrated when death came
and stole their final laundry ticket

They were born dead
and they died dead

Is time
to visit sister lopez again
the number one healer
and fortune card dealer
in Spanish Harlem
She can communicate
with your late relatives
for a reasonable fee
Good news is guaranteed

Rise Table Rise Table
death is not dumb and disable
Those who love you want to know
the correct number to play
Let them know this right away
Rise Table Rise Table
death is not dumb and disable
Now that your problems are over
and the world is off your shoulders
help those who you left behind
find financial peace of mind

Rise Table Rise Table
death is not dumb and disable

If the right number we hit
all our problems will split
and we will visit your grave
on every legal holiday
Those who love you want to know
the correct number to play
Let them know this right away
We know your spirit is able
Death is not dumb and disable
RISE TABLE RISE TABLE

Juan
Miguel
Milagros
Olga
Manuel
All died yesterday today
and will die again tomorrow
Hating fighting and stealing
broken windows from each other
Practicing a religion without a roof
The old testament
The new testament
according to the gospel
of the internal revenue
the judge and jury and executioner
protector and eternal bill collector

Secondhand shit for sale
Learn how to say Como Esta Usted
and you will make a fortune

They are dead
They are dead
and will not return from the dead
until they stop neglecting
the art of their dialogue
for broken english lessons
to impress the mister goldsteins

who keep them employed
as lavaplatos porters messenger boys
factory workers maids stock clerks
shipping clerks assistant mailroom
assistant, assistant assistant
to the assistant's assistant
assistant lavaplatos and automatic
artificial smiling doormen
for the lowest wages of the ages
and rages when you demand a raise
because is against the company policy
to promote SPICS SPICS SPICS

Juan
died hating Miguel because Miguel's
used car was in better running condition
than his used car
Miguel
died hating Milagros because Milagros
had a color television set
and he could not afford one yet
Milagros
died hating Olga because Olga
made five dollars more on the same job
Olga
died hating Manuel because Manuel
had hit the numbers more times
than she had hit the numbers
Manuel
died hating all of them
Juan
Miguel
Milagros
and Olga
because they all spoke broken english
more fluently than he did

And now they are together
in the main lobby of the void

Addicted to silence
Off limits to the wind
Confine to worm supremacy
in long island cemetery
This is the groovy hereafter
the protestant collection box
was talking so loud and proud about

Here lies Juan
Here lies Miguel
Here lies Milagros
Here lies Olga
Here lies Manuel
who died yesterday today
and will die again tomorrow
Always broke
Always owing
Never knowing
that they are beautiful people
Never knowing
the geography of their complexion

PUERTO RICO IS A BEAUTIFUL PLACE
PUERTORRIQUENOS ARE A BEAUTIFUL RACE

If only they
had turned off the television
and tune into their own imaginations
If only they
had used the white supremacy bibles
for toilet paper purpose
and make their latino souls
the only religion of their race
If only they
had return to the definition of the sun
after the first mental snowstorm
on the summer of their senses
If only they
had kept their eyes open
at the funeral of their fellow employees

who came to this country to make a fortune
and were buried without underwears

Juan
Miguel
Milagros
Olga
Manuel
will right now be doing their own thing
where beautiful people sing
and dance and work together
where the wind is a stranger
to miserable weather conditions
where you do not need a dictionary
to communicate with your people
Aqui Se Habla Espanol all the time
Aqui you salute your flag first
Aqui there are no dial soap commercials
Aqui everybody smells good
Aqui tv dinners do not have a future
Aqui the men and women admire desire
and never get tired of each other
Aqui Que Pasa Power is what's happening
Aqui to be called negrito
means to be called LOVE [1973]

Miguel Piñero's writings reflect the harsh, dehumanizing environment in which many Puerto Rican emigrants are forced to live and which ultimately claimed his own life in 1988. Born in 1946 in Puerto Rico, Piñero came to the United States as a young boy and was raised on New York's Lower East Side, an area with a long and varied immigrant history as well as a reputation for poverty, drug abuse, and social violence. His own problems with the authorities began early: by the age of fifteen he had already been arrested for truancy, shoplifting, and drug possession; at age twenty-four the self-educated high school dropout was sent to Sing Sing prison for armed robbery.

While in prison, Piñero participated in theater workshops, where he caught the attention of a *New York Times* reporter. As a result his play *Short Eyes* (1974) was produced first with a cast of convicts and ex-convicts at New York's Riverside Church and later at the New York Shakespeare Festival's Public Theater. The play has been performed on Broadway and throughout the United States and abroad; a film version was also produced. The play received the New York Drama Critics' Circle Award and the Obie for best off-Broadway play of 1973–74.

Piñero once claimed, "When you're in prison, you're nowhere being nobody. [I write] to survive." Prison violence and the multiple forms of subjugation and domination in a repressive environment are several of the themes in this complex play. A young Puerto Rican prisoner, Juan, attempts to come to terms with another prisoner's need for sex with young children; "short eyes" is prison slang for a child molester, considered to be at the very bottom of the prison hierarchy. The violence of the prisoners toward the alleged molester is ironically revealed at the end to have been a tragic mistake.

In addition to writing several other plays, Piñero coedited an important collection of poems, *Nuyorican Poetry* (1975), with Miguel Algarín, introducing Nuyorican poets to a larger readership for the first time. His own collection of poems, *La Bodega Sold Dreams,* an angry view of those who are marginalized in city life, was published in 1980; in it Piñero expressed his wish to have his ashes scattered throughout the Lower East Side, a wish that was eventually fulfilled.

from **Short Eyes**

THE PEOPLE

JUAN *A Puerto Rican in his early thirties*

CUPCAKES *A Puerto Rican pretty boy of twenty-one who looks younger*

PACO *A Puerto Rican in his early thirties with the look of a dope fiend*

ICE *A black man in his late twenties who looks older*

OMAR *A black amateur boxer in his mid-twenties, virile*

EL RAHEEM *A black man in his mid-twenties with regal look and militant bearing*

LONGSHOE *A hip, tough Irishman in his mid-twenties*

CLARK DAVIS *A handsome, frightened white man in his early twenties*
MR. NETT *An old-line white prison guard in his late forties*
CAPTAIN ALLARD *Officer in House of Detention. Straight and gung-ho*
MR. BROWN *An officer in the House of Detention*
SERGEANT MORRISON *Another officer*
BLANCA AND GYPSY *Walk-on, nonspeaking parts*

MORRISON: *(Whistle — dayroom lights come on)* All right, on the lockout.

(Enter OMAR, LONGSHOE, EL RAHEEM, PACO, and ICE. *Each runs toward his respective position. Ad-libs.*

Then JUAN *walks slowly toward his position.*

CUPCAKES *is the last to come in. The* MEN *accompany him with simple scat singing to the tune of "The Stripper." Ad-libs)*

JUAN: Why don't you cut that loose? Man, don't you think that kid get tired of hearing that every morning?

PACO: Oh, man, we just jiving.

ICE: Hey, Cupcake, you ain't got no plexes behind that, do you?

CUPCAKES: I mean . . . like no . . . but . . .

PACO: You see, Juan, Cupcake don't mind.

CUPCAKES: No, really, Juan. Like I don't mind . . . But that doesn't mean that I like to listen to it. I mean . . . like . . . hey . . . I call you guys by your name. Why don't you call me by mine? My name ain't Cupcakes, it's Julio.

EL RAHEEM: If you would acknowledge that you are God, your name wouldn't be Cupcake or Julio or anything else. You would be Dahoo.

LONGSHOE: Already! Can't you spare us that shit early in the a.m.?

EL RAHEEM: No . . . one . . . is . . . talking . . . to . . . you . . . Yacoub.

LONGSHOE: The name is Longshoe Charlie Murphy . . . *Mister* Murphy to you.

EL RAHEEM: Yacoub . . . maker and creator of the devil . . . swine merchant. Your time is near at hand. Fuck around and your time will be now. Soon all devils' heads will roll and now rivers shall flow through the city — created by the blood of Whitey . . . Devil . . . beast.

OMAR: Salaam Alaikum.

PACO: Salami with bacons.

ICE: Power to the people.

LONGSHOE: Free the Watergate 500.

JUAN: Pa'lante.

CUPCAKES: Tippecanoe and Tyler too.

PACO *(On table, overly feminine)*: A la lucha . . . a la lucha . . . que somo mucha . . .

OMAR: Hey! Hey . . . you know the Panthers say "Power to the people."

MR. NETT: On the gate.

OMAR: *(Strong voice)* Power to the people. And gay liberators say . . . *(High voice, limp wrist in fist)* Power to the people.

(Enter NETT*)*

MR. NETT: How about police power?

JUAN: How about it? Oink, oink.

MR. NETT: Wise guy. Paco, you got a counsel visit.

PACO: Vaya.

OMAR: Mr. Nett?

MR. NETT: Yeah, what is it?

OMAR: Mr. Nett, you know like I've been here over ten months — and I'd like to know why I can't get on the help. Like I've asked a dozen times . . . and guys that just come in are shot over me . . . and I get shot down . . . Like why? Have I done something to you? Is there something about me that you don't like?

MR. NETT: Why, no. I don't have anything against you. But since you ask me I'll tell you. One is that when you first came in here you had the clap.

OMAR: But I don't have it any more. That was ten months ago.

MR. NETT: How many fights have you had since the first day you came on the floor?

OMAR: But I haven't had a fight in a long time.

MR. NETT: How many?

OMAR: Seven.

MR. NETT: Seven? Close to ten would be my estimation. No, if I put you on the help, there would be trouble in no time. Now if you give me your word that you won't fight and stay cool, I'll give it some deep consideration.

OMAR: I can't give you my word on something like that. You know I don't stand for no lame coming out the side of his neck with me. Not my word . . . My word is bond.

EL RAHEEM: Bond is life.

OMAR: That's why I can't give you my word. My word is my bond. Man in prison ain't got nothing but his word, and he's got to be careful who and how and for what he give it for. But I'll tell you this, I'll try to be cool.

MR. NETT: Well, you're honest about it anyway. I'll think it over.

(PACO and MR. NETT exit)

EL RAHEEM: Try is a failure.

OMAR: Fuck you.

EL RAHEEM: Try is a failure. Do.

OMAR: Fuck you.

EL RAHEEM: Fuck yourself, it's cheaper.

CUPCAKES: Hey, Mr. Nett — put on the power.

MR. NETT: *(From outside the gate)* The power is on.

CUPCAKES: The box ain't on.

MR. NETT: Might be broken. I'll call the repairman.

JUAN: Might as well listen to the radio.

ICE: The radio ain't workin' either, Juan. I tried to get BLS a little while ago and got nothin' but static, Jack.

CUPCAKES: Anyone wants to play Dirty Hearts? I ain't got no money, but I'll have cigarettes later on this week.

OMAR: Money on the wood makes bettin' good.

ICE: Right on.

(LONGSHOE gives CUPCAKES cigarettes)

JUAN: Hey, Julio.

(Throws CUPCAKES cigarettes. BROWN appears outside entrance gate)

BROWN: On the gate.

(Gate opens and PACO enters. Gate closes and BROWN exits)

CUPCAKES: Shit. That was a real fast visit.

PACO: Not fast enough.

LONGSHOE: What the man say about your case?

PACO: The bitch wants me to cop out to a D — she must think my dick is made of sponge rubber. I told her to tell the D.A. to rub the offer on his chest. Not to come to court on my behalf — shit, the bitch must have made a deal with the D.A. on one of her paying customers. Man, if I wait I could get a misdemeanor by my motherfucking self. What the fuck I need with a Legal Aid? Guess who's on the bench?

ICE: Who they got out there?

PACO: Cop-out Levine.

ICE: Wow! He give me a pound for a frown.

PACO: First they give me a student, and now a double-crossin' bitch.

LONGSHOE: We all got to make a living.

PACO: On my expense? No fucking good.

EL RAHEEM: You still expect the white man to give you a fair trial in his court? Don't you know what justice really means? Justice . . . "just us" . . . white folks.

PACO: Look here, man. I don't expect nothing from nobody — especially the Yankees. Man, this ain't my first time before them people behind these walls, cause I ain't got the money for bail. And you can bet that it won't be my last time — not as long as I'm poor and Puerto Rican.

CUPCAKES: Come on, let's play . . . for push-ups.

JUAN: How many?

CUPCAKES: Ten if you got just one book, fifteen if you got two.

PACO: I ain't playing for no goddamn push-ups.

ICE: Hey — come on, don't be like that.

PACO: Said ain't playing for no push-ups. Tell you what, let's play for coochie-coochies.

ICE: What the hell is coochie-coochies?

JUAN: It's a game they play in Puerto Rico. You ever see a flick about Hawaii? Them girls with the grass skirts moving their butts dancing? That's coochie-coochies.

ICE: I thought that was the hula-jack.

PACO: Put your shirt on your hips like this and move your ass. Coochie-coochie-coochie . . .

CUPCAKES: That's out.

PACO: You got a plexes?

CUPCAKES: Told you before that I don't have no complexes.

JUAN: You got no plexes at all?

CUPCAKES: No.

JUAN: Then why not let me fuck you?

CUPCAKES: That's definitely out.

JUAN: People without complexes might as well turn stuff.

OMAR: Thinking of joining the ranks? Cruising the tearooms?

EL RAHEEM: What kind of black original man talk is that? Cupcakes puts the wisdom before the knowledge because that's his nature. He can't help that. But you are deliberately acting and thinking out of your nature . . . thinking like the white devil, Yacoub. Your presence infects the minds of my people like a fever. You, Yacoub, are the bearer of three thousand nine hundred and ninety-nine diseases . . . corrupt . . . evil . . . pork-chop-eating brain . . .

LONGSHOE: Look.

EL RAHEEM: Where?

LONGSHOE: I'm sick and . . .

EL RAHEEM: See, brothers, he admits he is sick with corruption.

LONGSHOE: Who?

EL RAHEEM: You're not only the devil, you're also an owl?

LONGSHOE: Why?

EL RAHEEM: "Y" — why? Why is "Y" the twenty-fifth letter of the alphabet?

LONGSHOE: You . . . son of . . .

EL RAHEEM: You . . . me . . . they . . . them. This . . . those . . . that . . . "U" for the unknown.

LONGSHOE: I . . . I . . .

EL RAHEEM: Eye . . . I . . . Aye . . . Aye . . . Aiiii . . . hi . . .

LONGSHOE: Games, huh?

EL RAHEEM: The way of life is no game. Lame.

LONGSHOE: G . . . O . . . D . . . D . . . O . . . G . . . God spelled backward is dog . . . dog spelled backward is God . . . If Allah is God, Allah is a dog.

EL RAHEEM: Allah Akbar. *(Screams, jumps on him)* Allah Akbar.

*(*MR. NETT *and* BROWN *appear outside entrance gate)*

MR. NETT: On the gate.

*(*BROWN *opens gate.* MR. NETT *and* BROWN *enter.* MR. NETT *breaks them apart)*

MR. NETT: What the hell is going on here?

OMAR: Mr. Nett, let these two git it off, else we's gonna have mucho static around here.

ICE: Yeah . . . Mr. Nett . . . they got a personality thing going on for weeks.

MR. NETT: Fair fight, Murphy?

LONGSHOE: That's what I want.

MR. NETT: Johnson?

EL RAHEEM: El Raheem. Johnson is a slave name. *(Nods)* May your Christian God have mercy on your soul, Yacoub.

*(*BROWN *closes gate.* EL RAHEEM *and* LONGSHOE *square off and begin to fight . . . boxing . . . some wrestling.* LONGSHOE *is knocked clean across the room)*

LONGSHOE: Guess you say that left hook is Whitey trickology?

EL RAHEEM: No, honky, you knocked me down. My sister hits harder than that. She's only eight.

(They wrestle until EL RAHEEM *is on top. Then* NETT *breaks them apart)*

OMAR: Why didn't you break it up while Whitey was on top?

MR. NETT: Listen, why don't you two guys call it quits — ain't none of you really gonna end up the winner . . . Give it up . . . be friends . . . shake hands . . . Come, break it up, you both got your shit off . . . break it up. Go out and clean yourselves up. Make this the last time I see either of you fighting. On the gate. Next time I turn on the water.

*(*BROWN *and* NETT *exit, gate closes. The* RICANS *go to their table and begin to play on the table as if it were bongos)*

ICE: You two got it together.

EL RAHEEM: I am God . . . master and ruler of my universe . . . I am always together.

OMAR: Let me ask you one question, God.

EL RAHEEM: You have permission to ask two.

OMAR: Thank you . . . If you're God, why are you in jail? God can do anything, right? Melt these walls down, then create a stairway of light to the streets below . . . God. If you're God, then you can do these things. If you can't, tell me why God can't do a simple thing like that.

EL RAHEEM: I am God . . . I am a poor righteous teacher of almighty Allah and by his will I am here to awaken the original lost in these prisons . . . Black original man is asleep . . . This is your school of self-awareness. Wake up, black man, melt these walls? You ask me, a tangible god, to do an intangible feat? Mysterious intangible gods do mysterious intangible deeds. There is nothing mysterious about me. Tangible gods do tangible deeds.

*(*PUERTO RICAN GROUP *goes back to playing "Toca, si, va, tocar")*

CUPCAKES: *(On table, M.C.-style)* That's right, ladies and gentlemen . . . damas y caballeros . . . every night is Latin night at the House of Detention. Tonight for the first time . . . direct from his record-breaking counsel visit . . . on congas is Paco Pasqual . . .

yeaaaaaaa. With a all-star band . . . for your listening enjoyment . . . Juan Bobo Otero on timbales . . . On mouth organ Charles Murphy . . . To show you the latest dancing are Iceman, John Wicker . . . and his equally talented partner, Omar Blinker . . . yeaaaaaaa. While tapping his toes for you all . . . moving his head to the rhythm of the band is the mighty El Raheem, yeaaaaaa. Boooooooo. Yes, brothers and sisters, especially you sisters, don't miss this musical extravaganza. I'll be there, too . . . to say hello to all my friends . . . So be there . . . Don't be the one to say "Gee, I missed it" . . . This is your cha-cha jockey, Julio . . .

ALL: Cupcakes . . .

CUPCAKES: Mercado . . . Be sure to be there . . . Catch this act . . . this show of shows before they leave on a long extended touring engagement with state . . . *(*PACO *pinches* CUPCAKES*'s ass)* Keep your hands off my ass, man.

*(*CUPCAKES *moves stage left, sits pouting. Ad-libs)*

PACO: Hey, kid, do one of those prison toasts . . .

(They urge him on with various ad-libs)

CUPCAKES: All right, dig . . . You guys gotta give me background . . . Clap your hands and say . . . Mambo tu le pop . . . It was the night before Christmas . . . and all through the pad . . . cocaine and heroin was all the cats had. One cat in the corner . . . copping a nod . . . Another scratching thought he was God . . . I jumps on the phone . . . and dial with care . . . hoping my reefer . . . would soon be there . . . After a while . . . crowding my style . . . I ran to the door . . . see what's the matter . . . And to my surprise . . . I saw five police badges . . . staring . . . glaring in my eyes . . . A couple of studs . . . starts to get tough, so I ran to the bathroom . . . get rid of the stuff . . . narc bang . . . bang . . . but they banged in vain . . . cause you see . . . what didn't go in my veins went down the drain . . . Broke down the door . . . knock me to the floor . . . and took me away, that's the way I spent my last Christmas Day . . . like a dirty dog . . . in a dark and dingy cell . . . But I didn't care cause I was high as hell . . . But I was cool . . . I was cool . . . I was cool . . . You people are the fools . . . cream of the top . . . cause I got you say something as stupid as Mambo tu le pop.

*(*GROUP *chases* CUPCAKES *around stage.* BROWN *and* CLARK DAVIS *appear outside entrance gate)*

BROWN: On the gate.

(Gate opens and CLARK DAVIS *enters, goes to stage center.* BROWN *closes gate and exits)*

CUPCAKES: Hey, Longshoe . . . one of your kin . . . look-a-like sin just walked in . . .

EL RAHEEM: Another devil.

LONGSHOE: Hey . . . hey, whatdayasay . . . My name's Longshoe Charlie Murphy. Call me Longshoe. What's your name?

CLARK: Davis . . . Clark . . . Ah . . . Clark Davis . . . Clark is my first name.

PACO: Clark Kent.

CUPCAKES: Mild-mannered, too.

OMAR: No, no, Superman.

(*Other ad-libs: "Faster than a speeding bullet," etc.*)

PACO: Oye . . . Shoe . . . Está bueno . . . Pa'rajalo . . .

LONGSHOE: Back . . . back . . . boy . . . no está bueno . . . anyway, no mucho . . . como Cupcake.

PACO: Vaya.

LONGSHOE: Pay them no mind . . . crazy spics . . . where you locking?

CLARK: Upper D 15.

LONGSHOE: Siberia, huh? . . . Tough.

CLARK: First time in the joint.

LONGSHOE: Yeah? Well, I better hip you to what's happening fast.

ICE: Look out for your homey, Shoe.

OMAR: Second.

LONGSHOE: Look here, this is our section . . . white . . . dig? That's the Rican table, you can sit there if they give you permission . . . Same goes with the black section.

ICE: Say it loud.

OMAR: I'm black and proud.

ICE: Vaya!

LONGSHOE: Most of the fellas are in court. I'm the Don Gee here. You know what that mean, right? Good . . . Niggers and the spics don't give us honkies much trouble. We're cool half ass. This is a good floor. Dynamite hack on all shifts. Stay away from the black gods . . .

(NETT *appears outside gate)*

NETT: On the gate.

LONGSHOE: You know them when you see them.

(NETT opens gate and enters)

NETT: On the chow.

ICE: What we got, Mr. Nett?

NETT: Baloney à la carte.

ICE: Shit, welfare steaks again.

(All exit except CLARK and LONGSHOE. Gate stays open. The men reenter with sandwiches and return to their respective places. NETT closes gate and exits)

LONGSHOE: Black go on the front of the line, we stay in the back . . . It's okay to rap with the blacks, but don't get too close with any of them. Ricans too. We're the minority here, so be cool. If you hate yams, keep it to yourself. Don't show it. But also don't let them run over you. Ricans are funny people. Took me a long time to figure them out, and you know something, I found out that I still have a lot to learn about them. I rap spic talk. They get a big-brother attitude about the whites in jail. But they also back the niggers to the T.

ICE: *(Throws LONGSHOE a sandwich)* Hey, Shoe.

LONGSHOE: If a spic pulls a razor blade on you and you don't have a mop wringer in your hands . . . run . . . If you have static with a nigger and they ain't no white people around . . . get a spic to watch your back, you may have a chance . . . That ain't no guarantee . . . If you have static with a spic, don't get no nigger to watch your back cause you ain't gonna have none.

OMAR: You can say that again.

ICE: Two times.

LONGSHOE: You're a good-looking kid . . . You ain't stuff and you don't want to be stuff. Stay away from the bandidos. Paco is one of them . . . Take no gifts from no one.

(NETT appears outside entrance gate)

NETT: Clark Davis . . . Davis.

CLARK: Yes, that's me.

NETT: On the gate. *(NETT opens gate, enters with CLARK's belongings, leaves gate open)* Come here . . . come here . . . white trash . . . filth . . . Let me tell you something and you better listen good cause I'm only going to say it one time . . . and one time only. This is a nice floor . . . a quiet floor . . . There has never been too much trouble on this floor . . . With you, I smell trouble . . . I don't question the warden's or the captain's motive for putting you on this floor . . . But for once I'm gonna ask why they put a sick fucking degenerate like you on my floor . . . If you just talk out the side of your mouth one time . . . if you look at me sideways one time . . . if you mispronounce my name once, if you pick up more food than you can eat . . . if you call me for something I think is unnecessary . . . if you oversleep, undersleep . . . if . . . if . . . if . . . you give me just one little reason . . . I'm gonna break your face up so bad your own mother won't know you . . .

LONGSHOE: Mr. Nett is being kinda hard . . .

NETT: Shut up . . . I got a eight-year-old daughter who was molested by one of those bastards . . . stinking sons of bitches and I just as well pretend that he was you, Davis, do you understand that . . .

PACO: Short eyes.

LONGSHOE: Short eyes? Short eyes . . . Clark, are you one of those short-eyes freaks . . . are you a short-eyes freak?

NETT: Sit down, Murphy . . . I'm talking to this . . . this scumbag . . . yeah, he's a child rapist . . . a baby rapist, how old was she? How old? . . . Eight . . . seven . . . Disgusting bastard . . . Stay out of my sight . . . cause if you get in my face just one time . . . don't forget what I told you . . . I'll take a night stick and ram it clean up your asshole . . . I hope to God that they take you off this floor, or send you to Sing Sing . . . The men up there know what to do with degenerates like you.

CLARK: I . . . I . . .

NETT: All right, let's go . . . Lock in . . . lock in . . . for the count . . . Clark, the captain outside on the bridge wants to see you. I hope he takes you off this floor . . .

LONGSHOE: Hey, Davis . . .

(Walks up to him and spits in his face. Men exit) [1974]

A Lower East Side Poem

Just once before I die
I want to climb up on a
tenement sky
to dream my lungs out till
I cry
then scatter my ashes thru
the Lower East Side.

So let me sing my song tonight
let me feel out of sight
and let all eyes be dry
when they scatter my ashes thru
the Lower East Side.

From Houston to 14th Street
from Second Avenue to the mighty D
here the hustlers & suckers meet
the faggots & freaks will all get
high
on the ashes that have been scattered
thru the Lower East Side.

There's no other place for me to be
there's no other place that I can see
there's no other town around that
brings you up or keeps you down
no food little heat sweeps by
fancy cars & pimps' bars & juke saloons
& greasy spoons make my spirits fly
with my ashes scattered thru the
Lower East Side . . .

A thief, a junkie I've been
committed every known sin
Jews and Gentiles . . . Bums and Men
of style . . . run away child
police shooting wild . . .
mother's futile wails . . . pushers

making sales . . . dope wheelers
& cocaine dealers . . . smoking pot
streets are hot & feed off those who bleed to death . . .
all that's true
all that's true
all that is true
but this ain't no lie
when I ask that my ashes be scattered thru
the Lower East Side.

So here I am, look at me
I stand proud as you can see
pleased to be from the Lower East
a street fighting man
a problem of this land
I am the Philosopher of the Criminal Mind
a dweller of prison time
a cancer of Rockefeller's ghettocide
this concrete tomb is my home
to belong to survive you gotta be strong
you can't be shy less without request
someone will scatter your ashes thru
the Lower East Side.

I don't wanna be buried in Puerto Rico
I don't wanna rest in long island cemetery
I wanna be near the stabbing shooting
gambling fighting & unnatural dying
& new birth crying
so please when I die . . .
don't take me far away
keep me near by
take my ashes and scatter them thru out
the Lower East Side . . . [1980]

Dolores Prida, poet, dramatist, journalist, scriptwriter, and magazine editor, was born in Cuba in 1943 and immigrated to the United States in 1961, where she studied Latin American literature. Her varied pursuits have been recognized with awards and fellowships, including a doctor of humane letters degree from Mount Holyoke College.

Prida, best known for her work in theater, is considered one of the most important playwrights of the contemporary Hispanic theater in the United States. She skillfully blends humor and farce with popular culture in plays that experiment with a range of themes, usually including the numerous problems facing Latina women. The ambiguity of U.S. Latino identity, the ambivalence about assimilation, and the centuries-old repression of Latinas, expressed bilingually and biculturally, are among Prida's powerful themes.

Five of her most popular works, which have been presented internationally and are regularly staged in New York theaters, are gathered in *Beautiful Señoritas and Other Plays* (1991). *Beautiful Señoritas* (1977) incorporates music, Spanish sayings, songs, and dance numbers within the motif of a beauty contest, creating a spirited call for female liberation. *Coser y cantar* (Sewing and Singing, 1981), "A One-Act Bilingual Fantasy for Two Women," presents Ella and She — Ella in Spanish and She in English — two aspects of a Cuban emigrant's culture-clashing split personality. *Pantallas* (1986) is a sardonic examination of the ever-popular Spanish-language television "novelas" (soap operas); *Savings* (1985) is a musical fable on the theme of gentrification; and *Botánica* (1990) is a tender and humorous glimpse into the gaps between three generations of New York Latina women.

For Judith A. Weiss, Dolores Prida's plays "underscore the Latino paradox of a strong identity born of ambiguity. The works included in this collection trace a continuing struggle for self-definition. The evolution parallels Prida's growth into maturity as a Latina writer and her broadened and strengthened self-definition as a Caribbean New Yorker."

from Beautiful Señoritas

CHARACTERS

Four BEAUTIFUL SEÑORITAS *who also play assorted characters: Catch Women, Martyrs, Saints and just women.*

The MIDWIFE *who also plays the Mother*

The MAN *who plays all the male roles*

The GIRL *who grows up before our eyes*

SET

The set is an open space or a series of platforms and a ramp, which become the various playing areas as each scene flows into the next.

ACT I

As lights go up DON JOSÉ *paces nervously back and forth. He smokes a big cigar, talking to himself.*

DON JOSÉ: Come on, woman. Hurry up. I have waited long enough for this child. Come on, a son. Give me a son . . . I will start training him right away. To ride horses. To shoot. To drink. As soon as he is old enough I'll take him to La Casa de Luisa. There they'll teach him what to do to women. Ha, ha, ha! If he's anything like his father, in twenty years everyone in this town will be related to each other! Ha, ha, ha! My name will never die. My son will see to that . . .

MIDWIFE: *(*MIDWIFE *enters running, excited.)* Don José! Don José!

DON JOSÉ: ¡Al fin! ¿Qué? Dígame, ¿todo está bien?

MIDWIFE: Yes, everything is fine, Don José. Your wife just gave birth to a healthy . . .

DON JOSÉ: *(Interrupting excitedly).* Ha, ha, I knew it! A healthy son!

MIDWIFE: . . . It is a girl, Don José . . .

DON JOSÉ: *(Disappointment and disbelief creep onto his face. Then anger. He throws the cigar on the floor with force, then steps on it.)* A girl! ¡No puede ser! ¡Imposible! What do you mean a girl! ¡Cómo puede pasarme esto a mí? The first child that will bear my name and it is a . . . girl! ¡Una chancleta! ¡Carajo! *(He storms away, muttering under his breath.)*

MIDWIFE: *(Looks at* DON JOSÉ *as he exits, then addresses the audience. At some point during the following monologue the* GIRL *will appear. She looks at everything as if seeing the world for the first time.)* He's off to drown his disappointment in rum, because another woman is born into this world. The same woman another man's son will covet and pursue and try to rape at the first opportunity. The same woman whose virginity he will protect with a gun. Another woman is born into this world. In Managua, in San Juan, in an Andes mountain town. She'll be put on a pedestal and trampled upon at the same time. She will be made a saint and a whore, crowned queen and exploited and adored. No, she's not just any woman. She will be called upon to . . . *(The* MIDWIFE *is interrupted by offstage voices.)*

BEAUTIFUL SEÑORITA 1: ¡Cuchi cuchi chi-a-boom!

BEAUTIFUL SEÑORITA 2: ¡Mira caramba oye!

BEAUTIFUL SEÑORITA 3: ¡Rumba pachanga mambo!

BEAUTIFUL SEÑORITA 4: ¡Oye papito, ay ayayaiiii!

Immediately a rumba is heard. The four BEAUTIFUL SEÑORITAS *enter dancing. They dress as* CARMEN MIRANDA, IRIS CHACÓN, CHARO *and* MARÍA LA O. *They sing:*

"THE BEAUTIFUL SEÑORITAS' SONG"

We beautiful señoritas
With maracas in our souls
Mira papi ay cariño
Always ready for amor

We beautiful señoritas
Mucha salsa and sabor
Cuchi cuchi Latin bombas
Always ready for amor

Ay caramba mira oye
Dance the tango all night long
Guacamole Latin lover
Always ready for amor

One papaya one banana
Ay sí sí sí sí señor
Simpáticas muchachitas
Always ready for amor

Piña plátanos chiquitas
Of the rainbow el color
Cucarachas muy bonitas
Always ready for amor

We beautiful señoritas
With maracas in our souls
Mira papi ay cariño
Always ready for amor

Ay sí sí sí sí señor
Always ready for amor
Ay sí sí sí sí señor
Always ready for amor
¡Ay sí sí sí sí señor!

The SEÑORITAS *bow and exit.* MARÍA LA O *returns and takes more bows.* MARÍA LA O *bows for the last time. Goes to her dressing room. Sits down and removes her shoes.*

MARÍA LA O: My feet are killing me. These juanetes get worse by the minute. *(She rubs her feet. She appears older and tired, all the glamour gone out of her. She takes her false eyelashes off, examines her face carefully in the mirror, begins to remove makeup.)* Forty lousy bucks a week for all that tit-shaking. But I need the extra money. What am I going to do? A job is a job. And with my artistic inclinations . . . well . . . But look at this joint! A dressing room! They have the nerve to call this a dressing room. I have to be careful not to step on a rat. They squeak too loud. The patrons out there may hear, you know. Anyway, I sort of liked dancing since I was a kid. But this! I meant dancing like Alicia Alonso, Margot Fonteyn . . . and I end up as a cheap Iris Chacón. At least she shook her behind in Radio City Music Hall. Ha! That's one up the Rockettes!

BEAUTY QUEEN: *(She enters, wearing a beauty contest bathing suit.)* María la O, you still here. I thought everyone was gone. You always run out after the show.

MARÍA LA O: No, not tonight. Somebody is taking care of the kid. I'm so tired that I don't feel like moving from here. Estoy muerta, m'ija. *(Looks* BEAUTY QUEEN *up and down.)* And where are *you* going?

BEAUTY QUEEN: To a beauty contest, of course.

MARÍA LA O: Don't you get tired of that, mujer!

BEAUTY QUEEN: Never. I was born to be a beauty queen. I have been a beauty queen ever since I was born. "La reinecita," they used to call me. My mother entered me in my first contest at the age of two. Then, it was one contest after the other. I have been in a bathing suit ever since. I save a lot in clothes . . . Anyway, my mother used to read all those women's magazines —*Vanidades, Cosmopolitan, Claudia, Buenhogar* — where everyone is so beautiful and happy. She, of course, wanted me to be like them . . . *(Examines herself in the mirror.)* I have won hundreds of contests, you know. I have been Queen of Los Hijos Ausentes Club; Reina El Diario-La Prensa; Queen of Plátano Chips; Queen of the Hispanic Hairdressers Association; Reina de la Alcapurria; Miss Caribbean Sunshine; Señorita Turismo de Staten Island; Queen of the Texas Enchilada . . . and now of course, I am Miss Banana Republic!

MARÍA LA O: Muchacha, I bet you don't have time for anything else!

BEAUTY QUEEN: Oh, I sure do. I wax my legs every day. I keep in shape. I practice my smile. Because one day, in one of those beauty contests, someone will come up to me and say . . .

MARÍA LA O: You're on Candid Camera?

BEAUTY QUEEN: . . . Where have you been all my life! I'll be discovered, become a movie star, a millionaire, appear on the cover of *People* magazine . . . and anyway, even if I don't win, I still make some money.

MARÍA LA O: Money? How much money?

BEAUTY QUEEN: Five hundred. A thousand. A trip here. A trip there. Depends on the contest.

MARÍA LA O: I could sure use some extra chavos . . . Hey, do you think I could win, be discovered by a movie producer or something . . .

BEAUTY QUEEN: Weeell . . . I don't know. They've just re-made "King Kong" . . . ha, ha!

MARÍA LA O: *(*MARÍA LA O *doesn't pay attention. She's busily thinking about the money.* BEAUTY QUEEN *turns to go.)* Even if I am only third, I still make some extra money. I can send Johnny home for the summer. He's never seen his grandparents. Ya ni habla español. *(*MARÍA LA O *quickly tries to put eyelashes back on. Grabs her shoes and runs after* BEAUTY QUEEN.*)* Wait, wait for me! ¡Espérame! I'll go with you to the beauty contest! *(She exits. The* MIDWIFE *enters immediately. She calls after* MARÍA LA O.*)*

MIDWIFE: And don't forget to smile! Give them your brightest smile! As if your life depended on it!

The GIRL *enters and sits at* MARÍA LA O*'s dressing table. During the following monologue, the girl will play with the makeup, slowly applying lipstick, mascara, and eye shadow in a very serious, concentrated manner.*

MIDWIFE: Yes. You have to smile to win. A girl with a serious face has no future. But what can you do when a butterfly is trapped in your insides and you cannot smile? How can you smile with a butterfly condemned to beat its ever-changing wings in the pit of your stomach? There it is. Now a flutter. Now a storm. Carried by the winds of emotion, this butterfly transforms the shape, the color, the texture of its wings; the speed and range of its flight. Now it becomes a stained glass butterfly, light shining through its yellow-colored wings, which move ever so slowly, up and down, up and down, sometimes remaining still for a second too long. Then the world stops and takes a plunge, becoming a brief black hole in space. A burned-out star wandering through the galaxies is like a smile meant, but not delivered. And I am so full of undelivered smiles! So pregnant with undetected laughter! Sonrisas, sonrisas, who would exchange a butterfly for a permanent smile! Hear, hear, this butterfly will keep you alive and running, awake and on your toes, speeding along the herd of wild horses stampeding through the heart! This butterfly is magic. It changes its size. It becomes big and small. Who will take this wondrous butterfly and give me a simple, lasting smile! A smile for day and night, winter and fall. A smile for all occasions. A smile to survive . . . *(With the last line, the* MIDWIFE *turns to the* GIRL, *who by now has her face made up like a clown. They look at each other. The* GIRL *faces the audience. She is not smiling. They freeze. Blackout.)*

In the dark we hear a fanfare. Lights go up on the MC. *He wears a velvet tuxedo with a pink ruffled shirt. He combs his hair, twirls his moustache, adjusts his bow tie and smiles. He wields a microphone with a flourish.*

MC: Ladies and gentlemen. Señoras y señores. Tonight. Esta noche. Right here. Aquí mismo. You will have the opportunity to see the most exquisite, sexy, exotic, sandungueras, jacarandosas and most beautiful señoritas of all. You will be the judge of the contest, where beauty will compete with belleza; where women of the tropical Caribbean will battle the señoritas of South America. Ladies and gentlemen, the poets have said it. The composers of boleros have said it. Latin women are the most beautiful, the most passionate, the most virtuous, the best housewives and cooks. And they all know how to dance to salsa, and do the hustle, the mambo, the guaguancó . . . And they are always ready for amor, señores! What treasures! See for yourselves! . . . Ladies and gentlemen, señoras y señores . . . from the sandy beaches of Florida, esbelta as a palm tree, please welcome Miss Little Havana! *(Music from "Cuando salí de Cuba" is heard.* MISS LITTLE HAVANA *enters. She wears a bathing suit, sunglasses and a string of pearls. She sings.)*

Cuando salí de Cuba
Dejé mi casa, dejé mi avión
Cuando salí de Cuba
Dejé enterrado medio millón

MC: Oye, chica, what's your name?

MISS LITTLE HAVANA: Fina de la Garza del Vedado y Miramar. From the best families of the Cuba de Ayer.

MC: *(To the audience.)* As you can see, ladies and gentlemen, Fina es muy fina. Really fine, he, he, he. Tell the judges, Fina, what are your best assets?

MISS LITTLE HAVANA: Well, back in the Cuba of Yesterday, I had a house with ten rooms and fifty maids, two cars, un avión and a sugar mill. But Fidel took everything away. So, here in the U.S. of A. my only assets are 36-28-42.

MC: Hmmm! That's what I call a positive attitude. Miss Fina, some day you'll get it all back. Un aplauso for Fina, ladies and gentlemen! *(*MISS LITTLE HAVANA *steps back and freezes into a doll-like posture, with a fixed smiled on her face.)*

MC: Now, from South of the Border, ladies and gentlemen — hold on to your tacos, because here she is . . . Miss Chili Tamale! *(Music begins: "Allá en el Rancho Grande.")* Please, un aplauso!

Welcome, welcome chaparrita! *(*MISS CHILI TAMALE *enters. She also wears a bathing suit and a serape over her shoulder. She sings.)*

Allá en el rancho grande
Alla donde vivía
Yo era una flaca morenita
Que triste se quejaba
Que triste se quejaabaaa
No tengo ni un par de calzones
Ni sin remiendos de cuero
Ni dos huevos rancheros
Y las tortillas quemadas

MC: Your name, beautiful señorita?
MISS CHILI TAMALE: Lupe Lupita Guadalupe Viva Zapata y Enchilada, para servirle.
MC: What good manners! Tell us, what's your most fervent desire?
MISS CHILI TAMALE: My most fervent desire is to marry a big, handsome, very rich americano.
MC: Aha! What have we here! You mean you prefer gringos instead of Latin men?
MISS CHILI TAMALE: Oh no, no no. But, you see, I need my green card. La migra is after me.
MC: *(Nervously, the* MC *looks around, then pushes* MISS TAMALE *back. She joins* MISS LITTLE HAVANA *in her doll-like pose.)* Ahem, ahem. Now, ladies and gentlemen, the dream girl of every American male, the most beautiful señorita of all. Created by Madison Avenue exclusively for the United Fruit Company . . . ladies and gentlemen, please welcome Miss Conchita Banana! *("Chiquita Banana" music begins.* MISS CONCHITA BANANA *enters. She wears plastic bananas on her head and holds two real ones in her hands. She sings.)*

I'm Conchita Banana
And I'm here to say
That bananas taste the best
In a certain way
You can put 'em in your hum hum
You can slice 'em in your ha ha
Any way you want to eat 'em
It's impossible to beat 'em

But never, never, never
Put bananas in the refrigerator
No, no, no no!

(She throws the two real bananas to the audience.)

MC: Brava, bravissima, Miss Banana! Do you realize you have made our humble fruit, el plátano, very very famous all over the world?

MISS CONCHITA BANANA: Yes, I know. That has been the goal of my whole life.

MC: And we are proud of you, Conchita. But, come here, just between the two of us . . . tell me the truth, do you really like bananas?

MISS CONCHITA BANANA: Of course, I do! I eat them all the time. My motto is: a banana a day keeps the doctor away!

MC: *(Motioning to audience to applaud.)* What intelligence! What insight! Un aplauso, ladies and gentlemen . . . *(*MISS CONCHITA BANANA *bows and steps back, joining the other doll-like contestants. As each woman says the following lines she becomes human again. The* MC *moves to one side and freezes.)*

WOMAN 1: *(Previously* MISS LITTLE HAVANA.*)* No one knows me. They see me passing by, but they don't know me. They don't see me. They hear my accent but not my words. If anyone wants to find me, I'll be sitting by the beach.

WOMAN 2: *(Previously* MISS CHILI TAMALE.*)* My mother, my grandmother, and her mother before her walked the land with bare feet, as I have done too. We have given birth to our daughters on the bare soil. We have seen them grow and go to market. Now we need permits to walk the land — our land.

WOMAN 3: *(Previously* MISS CONCHITA BANANA.*)* I have been invented for a photograph. Sometimes I wish to be a person, to exist for my own sake, to stop dancing, to stop smiling. One day I think I will want to cry.

MC: *(We hear a fanfare. The* MC *unfreezes. The contestants become dolls again.)* Ladies and gentlemen . . . don't go away, because we still have more for you! Now, señoras y señores, from la Isla del Encanto, please welcome Miss Commonwealth! Un aplauso, please! *(We hear music from "Cortaron a Elena."* MISS COMMONWEALTH *enters, giggling and waving. She sings.)*

Cortaron el budget
Cortaron el budget
Cortaron el budget
Y nos quedamos
Sin food stamps
Cortaron a Elena
Cortaron a Juana
Cortaron a Lola
Y nos quedamos
Sin na' pa' na'

MC: ¡Qué sabor! Tell us your name, beautiful jibarita . . .

MISS COMMONWEALTH: Lucy Wisteria Rivera *(Giggles.)*

MC: Let me ask you, what do you think of the political status of the island?

MISS COMMONWEALTH: *(Giggles.)* Oh, I don't know about that. La belleza y la política no se mezclan. Beauty and politics do not mix. *(Giggles.)*

MC: True, true, preciosa-por-ser-un-encanto-por-ser-un-edén. Tell me, what is your goal in life?

MISS COMMONWEALTH: I want to find a boyfriend and get married. I will be a great housewife, cook and mother. I will only live for my husband and my children. *(Giggles.)*

MC: Ave María, nena! You are a tesoro! Well, Miss Commonwealth, finding a boyfriend should not be difficult for you. You have everything a man wants right there up front. *(Points to her breasts with the microphone.)* I am sure you already have several novios, no?

MISS COMMONWEALTH: Oh no, I don't have a boyfriend yet. My father doesn't let me. And besides, it isn't as easy as you think. To catch a man you must know the rules of the game, the technique, the tricks, the know-how, the how-to, the expertise, the go-get-it, the . . . works! Let me show you. *(The* MC *stands to one side and freezes. The doll-like contestants in the back exit.* MISS COMMONWEALTH *begins to exit. She runs into the* GIRL *as she enters.* MISS COMMONWEALTH*'s crown falls to the floor. She looks at the* GIRL*, who seems to remind her of something far away.)*

WOMAN 4: *(Previously* MISS COMMONWEALTH.*)* The girl who had never seen the ocean decided one day to see it. Just one startled footprint on the sand and the sea came roaring at her. A thousand waves, an infinite horizon, a storm of salt and two diving birds thrusted themselves furiously into her eyes. Today she walks blindly through the smog and the dust of cities and villages. But she travels with a smile, because she carries the ocean in her eyes. *(*WOMAN 4 *exits. Spot on the* GIRL. *She picks up the crown from the floor and places it on her head. Spot closes in on the crown.)*

As lights go up, the MAN *enters with a chair and places it center stage. He sits on it. The* GIRL *sits on the floor with her back to the audience. The* CATCH WOMEN *enter and take their places around the* MAN. *Each* WOMAN *addresses the* GIRL, *as a teacher would.*

CATCH WOMAN 1: There are many ways to catch a man. Watch . . . *(Walks over to the* MAN.*)* Hypnotize him. Be a good listener. *(She sits on his knees.)* Laugh at his jokes, even if you heard them before. *(To* MAN.*)* Honey, tell them the one about the two bartenders . . . *(The* MAN *mouths words as if telling a joke. She listens and laughs loudly. Gets up.)* Cuá, cuá, cuá! Isn't he a riot! *(She begins to walk away, turns and addresses the* GIRL.*)* Ah, and don't forget to move your hips.

CATCH WOMAN 2: *(*CATCH WOMAN 1 *walks moving her hips back to her place.* CATCH WOMAN 2 *steps forward and addresses the* GIRL.*)* Women can't be too intellectual. He will get bored. *(To* MAN, *in earnest.)* Honey, don't you think nuclear disarmament is our only hope for survival? *(The* MAN *yawns. To* GIRL.*)* See? When a man goes out with a woman he wants to relax, to have fun, to feel good. He doesn't want to talk about heavy stuff, know what I mean? *(*CATCH WOMAN 2 *walks back to her place. She flirts with her boa, wrapping it around the* MAN*'s head. Teasing.)* Toro, toro, torito!

CATCH WOMAN 3: *(The* MAN *charges after* CATCH WOMAN 2. CATCH WOMAN 3 *stops him with a hypnotic look. He sits down again.* CATCH WOMAN 3 *addresses the* GIRL.*)* Looks are a very powerful weapon. Use your eyes, honey. Look at him now and then. Directly. Sideways. Through your eyelashes. From the corner of your eyes. Over your sunglasses. Look at him up and down. But not with too much insistence. And never ever look directly at his crotch. *(She walks away dropping a handkerchief. The* MAN *stops to pick it up.* CATCH WOMAN 4 *places her foot on it. Pushes the* MAN *away.)* Make him suffer. Make him jealous. *(Waves to someone offstage, flirting.)* Hi Johnny! *(To* GIRL.*)* They like it. It gives them a good excuse to get drunk. Tease him. Find out what he likes. *(To* MAN.*)* Un masajito, papi? I'll make you a burrito de machaca con huevo, sí? *(She massages his neck.)* Keep him in suspense. *(To* MAN.*)* I love you. I don't love you. Te quiero. No te quiero. I love you. I don't love you . . . *(She walks away.)*

ALL: *(All four* CATCH WOMEN *come forward.)* We do it all for him!

MAN: They do it all for me! *(*MAN *raps the song, while the* CATCH WOMEN *parade around him.)*

"THEY DO IT ALL FOR ME"
(Wolf whistles.)
Mira Mami, psst, cosa linda!
Oye muñeca, dame un poquito
Ay, miren eso
Lo que dios ha hecho
Para nosotros los pecadores
Ay mamá, don't walk like that
Don't move like that
Don't look like that
'Cause you gonna give me
A heart attack
They do it all for me
What they learn in a magazine
They do it all for me
'Cause you know what they want
Ay mamá, tan preciosa tan hermosa
Give me a piece of this
And a piece of that
'Cause I know you do it all for me
Don't you don't you
Don't you do it all for me

*(*CATCH WOMAN 2 *throws her boa around his neck, ropes in the* MAN *and exits with him in tow.)*

CATCH WOMAN 1: ¡Mira, esa mosquita muerta ya agarró uno!

CATCH WOMAN 3: Look at that, she caught him!

CATCH WOMAN 4: Pero, ¡qué tiene ella que no tenga yo! *(All exit.)* *The* GIRL *stands up, picks up the handkerchief from the floor. Mimes imitations of some of the* WOMEN*'s moves, flirting, listening to jokes, giggling, moving her hips, etc. Church music comes on.*

The NUN *enters carrying a bouquet of roses cradled in her arms. She stands in the back and looks up bathed in a sacred light. Her lips move as if praying. She lowers her eyes and sees the* GIRL *imitating more sexy moves. The* NUN*'s eyes widen in disbelief.*

NUN: What are you doing, creature? That is sinful! A woman must be recatada, saintly. Thoughts of the flesh must be banished from your head and your heart. Close your eyes and your pores to desire. The only love there is is the love of the Lord. The Lord is the only lover!

NUN: *(The* GIRL *stops, thoroughly confused. The* NUN *strikes her with the bouquet of roses.)* ¡Arrodíllate! Kneel down on these roses! Let your blood erase your sinful thoughts! You may still be saved. Pray, pray! *(The* GIRL *kneels on the roses, grimacing with pain. The* PRIEST *enters, makes the sign of the cross on the scene. The* NUN *kneels in front of the* PRIEST.*)* Father, forgive me for I have sinned . . . *(The* SEÑORITAS *enter with her lines. They wear mantillas and peinetas, holding Spanish fans in their hands, a red carnation between their teeth.)*

SEÑORITA 1: Me too, father!

SEÑORITA 2: ¡Y yo también!

SEÑORITA 3: And me!

SEÑORITA 4: Me too! *(A tango begins. The following lines are integrated into the choreography.)*

SEÑORITA 1: Father, it has been two weeks since my last confession . . .

PRIEST: Speak, hija mia.

SEÑORITA 2: Padre, my boyfriend used to kiss me on the lips . . . but it's all over now . . .

PRIEST: Lord, oh Lord!

SEÑORITA 3: Forgive me father, but I have masturbated three times. Twice mentally, once physically.

PRIEST: Ave María Purísima sin pecado concebida . . .

SEÑORITA 4: I have sinned, santo padre. Last night I had wet dreams.

PRIEST: Socorro espiritual, Dios mío. Help these lost souls!

SEÑORITA 1: He said, fellatio . . . I said, cunnilingus!

PRIEST: No, not in a beautiful señorita's mouth! Such evil words, Señor, oh Lord!

SEÑORITA 2: Father, listen. I have sinned. I have really really sinned. I did it, I did it! All the way I did it! *(All the* SEÑORITAS *and the* NUN *turn to* SEÑORITA 2 *and make the sign of the cross. They point at her with the fans.)*

SEÑORITAS 1, 3, 4: She's done it, Dios mío, she's done it! Santísima Virgen, she's done it!

PRIEST: She's done it! She's done it!

SEÑORITA 2: *(Tangoing backwards.)* I did it, yes. Lo hice. I did it, father. Forgive me, for I have fornicated!

PRIEST: She's done it! She's done it! *(The* NUN *faints in the* PRIEST*'s arms.)*

SEÑORITAS 1, 3, 4: Fornication! Copulation! Indigestion! ¡Qué pecado y que horror! ¡Culpable! ¡Culpable! ¡Culpable! *(They exit tangoing. The* PRIEST, *with the fainted* NUN *in his arms, looks at the audience bewildered.)*

PRIEST: *(To audience.)* Intermission! *(Blackout)* [1977]

Luis Valdez was born in 1940 to a family of migrant farmworkers living in Delano, California. Working among César Chávez's United Farm Workers, he founded El Teatro Campesino (Theater of the Farmhand), a mixture of art and politics that received acclaim around the country for its grassroots activism. He has written, produced, or directed twenty dramas, beginning with *The Shrunken Head of Pancho Villa* (1963), produced while he was still a student at San Jose State College, and including *I Don't Have to Show You No Stinking Badges,* produced in Los Angeles in 1986. He is also a television and film director (the films *Zoot Suit,* 1982, and *La Bamba,* 1987), an actor (*Which Way Is Up?* 1972), and anthologist (*Aztlán: An Anthology of Mexican American Literature,* 1987, coedited with Stan Steiner).

Zoot Suit focuses on a group of pachucos, the inner-city Mexican-American youth of the prewar and wartime generation in Los Angeles, who were famous for their clash with U.S. sailors in 1942, which became known as the zoot suit riots (chronicled in fiction by Thomas Sánchez), and for the Sleepy Lagoon murder case. As the first Chicano drama to reach beyond the Chicano community, *Zoot Suit* was a breakthrough production; it played to sold-out houses for ten months, won the Los Angeles Critics Circle Award for distinguished production, and was nominated for a Golden Globe Award.

from **Zoot Suit**

SETTING

The giant facsimile of a newspaper front page serves as a drop curtain.

The huge masthead reads: LOS ANGELES HERALD EXPRESS *Thursday, June 3, 1943.*

A headline cries out: ZOOT-SUITER HORDES INVADE LOS ANGELES. US NAVY AND MARINES ARE CALLED IN.

Behind this are black drapes creating a place of haunting shadows larger than life. The somber shapes and outlines of pachuco images hang subtly, black on black, against a background of heavy fabric evoking memories and feelings like an old suit hanging forgotten in the depths of a closet somewhere, sometime . . . Below this is a sweeping, curving place of levels and rounded corners with the hard, ingrained brilliance of countless spit shines, like the memory of a dance hall.

ACT ONE

Prologue

A switchblade plunges through the newspaper. It slowly cuts a rip to the bottom of the drop. To the sounds of "Perdido" by Duke Ellington, EL PACHUCO *emerges from the slit.* HE *adjusts his clothing, meticulously fussing with his collar, suspenders, cuffs.* HE *tends to his hair, combing back every strand into a long luxurious ducktail, with infinite loving pains. Then* HE *reaches into the slit and pulls out his coat and hat.* HE *dons them. His fantastic costume is complete. It is a zoot suit.* HE *is transformed into the very image of the pachuco myth, from his pork-pie hat to the tip of his four-foot watch chain. Now* HE *turns to the audience. His three-soled shoes with metal taps click-clack as* HE *proudly, slovenly, defiantly makes his way downstage.* HE *stops and assumes a pachuco stance.*

PACHUCO:

¿Que le watcha a mis trapos, ese?
¿Sabe qué, carnal?
Estas garras me las planté porque
Vamos a dejarnos caer un play, ¿sabe?
(HE *crosses to center stage, models his clothes.)*

Watcha mi tacuche, ese. Aliviánese con mis calcos, tando, lisa, tramos, y carlango, ese.
(Pause.)
Nel, sabe qué, usted está muy verdolaga. Como se me hace que es puro square.
*(*EL PACHUCO *breaks character and addresses the audience in perfect English.)*
Ladies and gentlemen
the play you are about to see
is a construct of fact and fantasy.
The Pachuco Style was an act in Life
and his language a new creation.
His will to be was an awesome force
eluding all documentation . . .
A mythical, quizzical, frightening being
precursor of revolution
Or a piteous, hideous heroic joke
deserving of absolution?
I speak as an actor on the stage.
The Pachuco was existential
for he was an Actor in the streets
both profane and reverential.
It was the secret fantasy of every bato
in or out of the Chicanada
to put on a Zoot Suit and play the Myth
más chucote que la chingada.
(Puts hat back on and turns.)
¡Pos órale!
(Music. The newspaper drop flies. EL PACHUCO *begins his chuco stroll upstage, swinging his watch chain.)*

1. *Zoot Suit*

The scene is a barrio dance in the forties. PACHUCOS *and* PACHUCAS *in zoot suits and pompadours.*

They are members of the 38TH STREET GANG, *led by* HENRY REYNA, 21, *dark, Indian-looking, older than his years, and* DELLA BARRIOS, 20, *his girlfriend in miniskirt and fingertip coat. A* SAILOR *called*

SWABBIE *dances with his girlfriend* MANCHUKA *among the* COUPLES. *Movement. Animation.* EL PACHUCO *sings.*

PACHUCO:

Put on a zoot suit, makes you feel real root
Look like a diamond, sparkling, shining
Ready for dancing
Ready for the boogie tonight!
(The COUPLES, *dancing, join the* PACHUCO *in exclaiming the last term of each line in the next verse.)*
The hepcats up in Harlem wear that drape shape
Como los Pachucones down in L.A.
Where huisas in their pompadours look real keen
On the dance floor of the ballrooms
Donde bailan swing.

You better get hep tonight
And put on that zoot suit!

(The DOWNEY GANG, *a rival group of pachucos, enters upstage left. Their quick dance step becomes a challenge to* 38TH STREET.*)*

DOWNEY GANG: Downey . . . ¡Rifa!

HENRY: *(Gesturing back.)* ¡Toma! *(The music is hot.* EL PACHUCO *slides across the floor and momentarily breaks the tension.* HENRY *warns* RAFAS, *the leader of the* DOWNEY GANG, *when* HE *sees him push his brother* RUDY.*)* ¡Rafas!

PACHUCO: *(Sings.)*

Trucha, ese loco, vamos al borlo
Wear that carlango, tramos y tando
Dance with your huisa
Dance to the boogie tonight!

'Cause the Zoot Suit is the style in California
También en Colorado y Arizona
They're wearing that tachuche en El Paso
Y en todos los salones de Chicago

You better get hep tonight
And put on that zoot suit!

2. The Mass Arrests

We hear a siren, then another, and another. It sounds like gangbusters. The dance is interrupted. COUPLES *pause on the dance floor.*

PACHUCO: Trucha, la jura. ¡Pélenle! *(Pachucos start to run out, but* DETECTIVES *leap onstage with drawn guns. A* CUB REPORTER *takes flash pictures.)*

SGT. SMITH: Hold it right there, kids!

LT. EDWARDS: Everybody get your hands up!

RUDY: Watcha! This way! *(*RUDY *escapes with some others.)*

LT. EDWARDS: Stop or I'll shoot! *(*EDWARDS *fires his revolver into the air. A number of pachucos and their girlfriends freeze. The cops round them up.* SWABBIE*, an American sailor, and* MANCHUKA*, a Japanese-American dancer, are among them.)*

SGT. SMITH: ¡Ándale! *(Sees* SWABBIE*.)* You! Get out of here.

SWABBIE: What about my girl?

SGT. SMITH: Take her with you. *(*SWABBIE *and* MANCHUKA *exit.)*

HENRY: What about my girl?

LT. EDWARDS: No dice, Henry. Not this time. Back in line.

SGT. SMITH: Close it up!

LT. EDWARDS: Spread! *(The* PACHUCOS *turn upstage in a line with their hands up. The sirens fade and give way to the sound of a teletype. The* PACHUCOS *turn and form a lineup, and the* PRESS *starts shooting pictures as* HE *speaks.)*

PRESS: The City of the Angels, Monday, August 2, 1942. The Los Angeles Examiner, Headline:

THE LINEUP: *(In chorus.)* Death Awakens Sleepy Lagoon. *(Breath.)* LA Shaken by Lurid "Kid" Murder.

PRESS: The City of the Angels, Monday, August 2, 1942. The Los Angeles Times, Headline:

THE LINEUP: One Killed, Ten Hurt in Boy Wars. *(Breath.)* Mexican Boy Gangs Operating Within City.

PRESS: The City of the Angels, August 2, 1942. Los Angeles Herald Express, Headline:

THE LINEUP: Police Arrest Mexican Youths. Black Widow Girls in Boy Gangs.

PRESS: The City of the Angels . . .

PACHUCO: *(Sharply.)* El Pueblo de Nuestra Señora la Reina de los Angeles de Porciúncula, pendejo.

PRESS: *(Eyeing the* PACHUCO *cautiously.)* The Los Angeles Daily News, Headline:

BOYS IN THE LINEUP: Police Nab 300 in Roundup.

GIRLS IN THE LINEUP: Mexican Girls Picked Up in Arrests.

LT. EDWARDS: Press Release, Los Angeles Police Department: A huge showup of nearly 300 boys and girls rounded up by the police and sheriff's deputies will be held tonight at eight o'clock in Central Jail at First and Hill Street. Victims of assault, robbery, purse snatching, and similar crimes are asked to be present for the identification of suspects.

PRESS: Lieutenant . . . ? *(*EDWARDS *poses as the* PRESS *snaps a picture.)*

LT. EDWARDS: Thank you.

PRESS: Thank you. *(*SMITH *gives a signal, and the lineup moves back, forming a straight line in the rear, leaving* HENRY *up front by himself.)*

LT. EDWARDS: Move! Turn! Out! *(As the rear line moves off to the left following* EDWARDS, SMITH *takes* HENRY *by the arm and pulls him downstage, shoving him to the floor.)*

3. *Pachuco Yo*

SGT. SMITH: Okay, kid, you wait here till I get back. Think you can do that? Sure you can. You pachucos are regular tough guys. *(*SMITH *exits.* HENRY *sits up on the floor.* EL PACHUCO *comes forward.)*

HENRY: Bastards. *(*HE *gets up and paces nervously. Pause.)* ¿Ese? ¿Ese?

PACHUCO: *(Behind him.)* ¿Qué pues, nuez?

HENRY: *(Turning.)* Where the hell you been, ese?

PACHUCO: Checking out the barrio. Qué desmadre, ¿no?

HENRY: What's going on, ese? This thing is big.

PACHUCO: The city's cracking down on pachucos, carnal. Don't you read the newspapers? They're screaming for blood.

HENRY: All I know is they got nothing on me. I didn't do anything.

PACHUCO: You're Henry Reyna, ese — Hank Reyna! The snarling juvenile delinquent. The zootsuiter. The bitter young pachuco gang leader of 38th Street. That's what they got on you.

HENRY: I don't like this, ese. *(Suddenly intense.)* I DON'T LIKE BEING LOCKED UP!

PACHUCO: Calmantes montes, chicas patas. Haven't I taught you to survive? Play it cool.

HENRY: They're going to do it again, ese! They're going to charge me with some phony rap and keep me until they make something stick.

PACHUCO: So what's new?

HENRY: *(Pause.)* I'm supposed to report for the Navy tomorrow. *(*THE PACHUCO *looks at him with silent disdain.)* You don't want me to go, do you?

PACHUCO: Stupid move, carnal.

HENRY: *(Hurt and angered by* PACHUCO*'s disapproval.)* I've got to do something.

PACHUCO: Then hang tough. Nobody's forcing you to do shit.

HENRY: I'm forcing me, ese — ME, you understand?

PACHUCO: Muy patriotic, eh?

HENRY: Yeah.

PACHUCO: Off to fight for your country.

HENRY: Why not?

PACHUCO: Because this ain't your country. Look what's happening all around you. The Japs have sewed up the Pacific. Rommel is kicking ass in Egypt but the Mayor of L.A. has declared all-out war on Chicanos. On you! ¿Te curas?

HENRY: Órale.

PACHUCO: Qué mamada, ¿no? Is that what you want to go out and die for? Wise up. These bastard paddy cops have it in for you. You're a marked man. They think you're the enemy.

HENRY: *(Refusing to accept it.)* Screw them bastard cops!

PACHUCO: And as soon as the Navy finds out you're in jail again, ya estuvo, carnal. Unfit for military duty because of your record. Think about it.

HENRY: *(Pause.)* You got a frajo?

PACHUCO: Simón. *(*HE *pulls out a cigarette, hands it to* HENRY*, lights it for him.* HENRY *is pensive.)*

HENRY: *(Smokes, laughs ironically.)* I was all set to come back a hero, see? Me la rayo. For the first time in my life I really thought Hank Reyna was going someplace.

PACHUCO: Forget the war overseas, carnal. Your war is on the homefront.

HENRY: *(With new resolve.)* What do you mean?

PACHUCO: The barrio needs you, carnal. Fight back! Stand up to them with some style. Show the world a Chicano has balls. Hang tough. You can take it. Remember, Pachuco Yo!

HENRY: *(Assuming the style.)* Con safos, carnal.

4. *The Interrogation*

The PRESS *enters, followed by* EDWARDS *and* SMITH.

PRESS: *(To the audience.)* Final Edition, The Los Angeles Daily News. The police have arrested twenty-two members of the 38th Street Gang, pending further investigation of various charges.

LT. EDWARDS: Well, son, I was hoping I wouldn't see you in here again.

HENRY: Then why did you arrest me?

LT. EDWARDS: Come on, Hank, you know why you're here.

HENRY: Yeah. I'm a Mexican.

LT. EDWARDS: Don't give me that. How long have I known you? Since '39?

HENRY: Yeah, when you got me for stealing a car, remember?

LT. EDWARDS: All right. That was a mistake. I didn't know it was your father's car. I tried to make it up to you. Didn't I help you set up the youth club?

SGT. SMITH: They turned it into a gang, Lieutenant. Everything they touch turns to shit.

LT. EDWARDS: I remember a kid just a couple of years back. Head boy at the Catholic Youth Center. His idea of fun was going to the movies. What happened to that nice kid, Henry?

PRESS: He's "Gone with the Wind," trying to look like Clark Gable.

SGT. SMITH: Now he thinks he's Humphrey Bogart.

PACHUCO: So who are you, puto? Pat O'Brien?

LT. EDWARDS: This is the wrong time to be anti-social, son. This country's at war, and we're under strict orders to crack down on all malcontents.

SGT. SMITH: Starting with all pachucos and draft dodgers.

HENRY: I ain't no draft dodger.

LT. EDWARDS: I know you're not. I heard you got accepted by the Navy. Congratulations. When do you report?

HENRY: Tomorrow?

SGT. SMITH: Tough break!

LT. EDWARDS: It's still not too late, you know. I could still release you in time to get sworn in.

HENRY: If I do what?

LT. EDWARDS: Tell me, Henry, what do you know about a big gang fight last Saturday night, out at Sleepy Lagoon?

PACHUCO: Don't tell 'em shit.

HENRY: Which Sleepy Lagoon?

LT. EDWARDS: You mean there's more than one? Come on, Hank, I know you were out there. I've got a statement from your friends that says you were beaten up. Is that true? Were you and your girl attacked?

HENRY: I don't know anything about it. Nobody's ever beat me up.

SGT. SMITH: That's a lie and you know it. Thanks to your squealer friends, we've got enough dope on you to indict for murder right now.

HENRY: Murder?

SGT. SMITH: Yeah, murder. Another greaser named José Williams.

HENRY: I never heard of the bato.

SGT. SMITH: Yeah, sure.

LT. EDWARDS: I've been looking at your record, Hank. Petty theft, assault, burglary, and now murder. Is that what you want? The gas chamber? Play square with me. Give me a statement as to what happened at the Lagoon, and I'll go to bat for you with the Navy. I promise you.

PACHUCO: If that ain't a line of gabacho bullshit, I don't know what is.

LT. EDWARDS: Well?

PACHUCO: Spit in his pinche face.

SGT. SMITH: Forget it, Lieutenant. You can't treat these animals like people.

LT. EDWARDS: Shut up! I'm thinking of your family, Hank. Your old man would be proud to see you in the Navy. One last chance, son. What do you say?

HENRY: I ain't your son, cop.

LT. EDWARDS: All right, Reyna, have it your way. (EDWARDS *and* PRESS *exit.*)

PACHUCO: You don't deserve it, ese, but you're going to get it anyway.

SGT. SMITH: All right, muchacho, it's just me and you now. I hear tell you pachucos wear these monkey suits as a kind of armor. Is that right? How's it work? This is what you zooters need — a little old-fashioned discipline.

HENRY: Screw you, flatfoot.

SGT. SMITH: You greasy son of a bitch. What happened at the Sleepy Lagoon? Talk! Talk! Talk! *(*SMITH *beats* HENRY *with a rubber sap.* HENRY *passes out and falls to the floor, with his hands still handcuffed behind his back.* DOLORES *his mother appears in a spot upstage, as he falls.)*

DOLORES: Henry! *(Lights change. Four* PACHUCO COUPLES *enter, dancing a* '40s *pasodoble* (two-step) *around* HENRY *on the floor, as they swing in a clothesline of newspaper sheets. Music.)*

PACHUCO:

Get up and escape, Henry . . .
leave reality behind
with your buenas garras
muy chamberlain
escape through the barrio streets of your mind
through a neighborhood of memories
all chuckhole lined
and the love
and the pain
as fine as wine . . .

*(*HENRY *sits up, seeing his mother* DOLORES *folding newspaper sheets like clothes on a clothesline.)*

DOLORES: Henry?

PACHUCO: It's a lifetime ago, last Saturday night . . . before Sleepy Lagoon and the big bad fight.

DOLORES: Henry!

PACHUCO: Tu mamá, carnal. *(*HE *recedes into the background.)*

DOLORES: *(At the clothesline.)* Henry, ¿hijo? Ven a cenar.

HENRY: *(Gets up off the floor.)* Sorry, jefita, I'm not hungry. Besides, I got to pick up Della. We're late for the dance.

DOLORES: Dance? In this heat? Don't you muchachos ever think of anything else? God knows I suffer la pena negra seeing you go out every night.

HENRY: This isn't just any night, jefa. It's my last chance to use my tacuche.

DOLORES: Tacuche? Pero tu padre . . .

HENRY: *(Revealing a stubborn streak.)* I know what mi 'apá said, 'amá. I'm going to wear it anyway.

DOLORES: *(Sighs, resigns herself.)* Mira, hijo. I know you work hard for your clothes. And I know how much they mean to you. Pero por diosito santo, I just don't know what you see en esa cochinada de "soot zoot."

HENRY: *(Smiling.)* Drapes, 'amá, we call them drapes.

DOLORES: *(Scolding playfully.)* Ay sí, drapes, muy funny, ¿verdad? And what do the police call them, eh? They've put you in jail so many times. ¿Sabes qué? I'm going to send them all your clothes!

HENRY: A qué mi 'amá. Don't worry. By this time next week, I'll be wearing my Navy blues. Okay?

DOLORES: Bendito sea Dios. I still can't believe you're going off to war. I almost wish you were going back to jail.

HENRY: ¡Órale! *(*LUPE REYNA, *16, enters dressed in a short skirt and baggy coat. She is followed by* DELLA BARRIOS, *17, dressed more modestly.* LUPE *hides behind a newspaper sheet on the line.)*

LUPE: Hank! Let's go, carnal. Della's here.

HENRY: Della . . . Órale, esa. What are you doing here? I told you I was going to pick you up at your house.

DELLA: You know how my father gets.

HENRY: What happened?

DELLA: I'll tell you later.

DOLORES: Della, hija, buenas noches. How pretty you look.

DELLA: Buenas noches. *(*DOLORES *hugs* DELLA, *then spots* LUPE *hiding behind the clothesline.)*

DOLORES: *(To* LUPE.*)* ¿Oye y tú? What's wrong with you? What are you doing back there?

LUPE: Nothing, 'amá.

DOLORES: Well, come out then.

LUPE: We're late, 'amá.

DOLORES: Come out, te digo. *(*LUPE *comes out exposing her extremely short shirt.* DOLORES *gasps.)* ¡Válgame Dios! Guadalupe, are you crazy? Why bother to wear anything?

LUPE: Ay, 'amá, it's the style. Short skirt and fingertip coat. Huh, Hank?

HENRY: Uh, yeah, 'amá.

DOLORES: ¿Oh sí? And how come Della doesn't get to wear the same style?

HENRY: No . . . that's different. No, chale.

ENRIQUE: *(Off.)* ¡VIEJA!

DOLORES: Ándale. Go change before your father sees you.

ENRIQUE: I'm home. *(Coming into the scene.)* Buenas noches, everybody. *(All respond.* ENRIQUE *sees* LUPE.*)* ¡Ay, jijo! Where's the skirt?!

LUPE: It's here.

ENRIQUE: Where's the rest of it?

DOLORES: She's going to the dance.

ENRIQUE: ¿Y a mí qué me importa? Go and change those clothes. Ándale.

LUPE: Please, 'apá?

ENRIQUE: No, señorita.

LUPE: Chihuahua, I don't want to look like a square.

ENRIQUE: ¡Te digo que no! I will not have my daughter looking like a . . .

DOLORES: Like a puta . . . I mean, a pachuca.

LUPE: *(Pleading for help.)* Hank . . .

HENRY: Do what they say, sis.

LUPE: But you let Henry wear his drapes.

ENRIQUE: That's different. He's a man. Es hombre.

DOLORES: Sí, that's different. You men are all alike. From such a stick, such a splinter. De tal palo, tal astillota.

ENRIQUE: Natural, muy natural, and look how he came out. ¡Bien macho! Like his father. ¿Verdad, m'ijo?

HENRY: If you say so, jefito.

ENRIQUE: *(To* DELLA.*)* Buenas noches.

DELLA: Buenas noches.

HENRY: 'Apá, this is Della Barrios.

ENRIQUE: Mira, mira . . . So this is your new girlfriend, eh? Muy bonita. Quite a change from the last one.

DOLORES: Ay, señor.

ENRIQUE: It's true. What was her name?

DELLA: Bertha?

ENRIQUE: That's the one. The one with the tattoo.

DOLORES: Este hombre. We have company.

ENRIQUE: That reminds me. I invited the compadres to the house mañana.

DOLORES: ¿Que qué?

ENRIQUE: I'm buying a big keg of cerveza to go along with the menudo.

DOLORES: Oye, ¿cuál menudo?

ENRIQUE: *(Cutting her off.)* ¡Qué caray, mujer! It isn't every day a man's son goes off to fight for his country. I should know. Della, m'ija, when I was in the Mexican Revolution, I was not even as old as my son is.

DOLORES: N'ombre, don't start with your revolution. We'll be here all night.

HENRY: Yeah, jefe, we've got to go.

LUPE: *(Comes forward. She has rolled down her skirt.)* 'Apá, is this better?

ENRIQUE: Bueno. And you leave it that way.

HENRY: Órale, pues. It's getting late. Where's Rudy?

LUPE: He's still getting ready. Rudy! *(*RUDY REYNA, *19, comes downstage in an old suit made into a tachuche.)*

RUDY: Let's go everybody. I'm ready.

ENRIQUE: Oye, oye, ¿y tú? What are you doing with my coat?

RUDY: It's my tachuche, 'apá.

ENRIQUE: ¡Me lleva la chingada!

DOLORES: Enrique . . . ¡por el amor de Dios!

ENRIQUE: *(To* HENRY.*)* You see what you're doing? First that one and now this one. *(To* RUDY.*)* Hijo, don't go out like that. Por favor. You look like an idiot, pendejo.

RUDY: Órale, Hank. Don't I look all right?

HENRY: Nel, ese, you look fine. Watcha. Once I leave for the service, you can have my tachuche. Then you can really be in style. ¿Cómo la ves?

RUDY: Chale. Thanks, carnal, but if I don't join the service myself, I'm gonna get my own tachuche.

HENRY: You sure? I'm not going to need it where I'm going. ¿Tú sabes?

RUDY: Are you serious?

HENRY: Simón.

RUDY: I'll think about it.

HENRY: Pos, no hay pedo, ese.

ENRIQUE: ¿Cómo que pedo? Nel, ¿Simón? Since when did we stop speaking Spanish in this house? Have you no respect?

DOLORES: Muchachos, muchachos, go to your dance. (HENRY *starts upstage.)*

HENRY: Buenas noches . . . (ENRIQUE *holds out his hand.* HENRY *stops, looks, and then returns to kiss his father's hand. Then* HE *moves to kiss his* MOTHER *and* RUDY *in turn kisses* ENRIQUE*'s hand.* ENRIQUE *says "Buenas Noches" to each of his sons.)*

HENRY: Órale, we'd better get going . . . *(General "goodbyes" from everybody.)*

ENRIQUE: *(As* RUDY *goes past him.)* Henry! Don't let your brother drink beer.

RUDY: Ay, 'apá. I can take care of myself.

DOLORES: I'll believe that when I see it. (SHE *kisses him on the nose.)*

LUPE: Ahí te watcho, 'amá.

ENRIQUE: ¿Que qué?

LUPE: I mean, I'll see you later. (HENRY, DELLA, LUPE *and* RUDY *turn upstage. Music starts.)*

ENRIQUE: Mujer, why didn't you let me talk?

DOLORES: *(Sighing.)* Talk, señor, talk all you want. I'm listening. (ENRIQUE *and* DOLORES *exit up right.* RUDY *and* LUPE *exit up left. Lights change. We hear hot dance music.* HENRY *and* DELLA *dance at center stage.* EL PACHUCO *sings.)*

PACHUCO:

Cada sábado en la noche
Yo me voy a borlotear
Con mi linda pachucona
Las caderas a menear

Ella le hace muy de aquellas
Cuando empieza a guarachar
Al compás de los timbales
Yo me siento petatear

(From upstage right, three pachucos now enter in a line, moving to the beat. They are JOEY CASTRO, *17;* SMILEY TORRES, *23; and* TOMMY ROBERTS, *19, Anglo. They all come downstage left in a diagonal.)*

Los chucos suaves bailan rumba
Bailan la rumba y le zumban
Bailan guaracha sabrosón
El botecito y el danzón!

(Chorus repeats, the music fades. HENRY *laughs and happily embraces* DELLA.*)* [1978]

Tato Laviera is a varied artist — poet, musician, dramatist, and songwriter — whose works and performances reflect what has been called the Nuyorican modality. Born in Puerto Rico in 1950, he migrated with his family in 1960 to New York's Lower East Side. Like many Nuyorican poets, Laviera had little academic training. Nevertheless he has produced a substantial body of work and has received critical recognition, including an invitation by President Carter in 1980 to read at a White House gathering of American poets.

Laviera's poetry has been promoted by such scholarly critics as Juan Flores, who compares his work to that of Pedro Pietri for its defiant tone and open expression of ethnic pride. His first collection, *La Carreta Made a U-Turn* (1979), is a U.S. Puerto Rican's response to René Marqués's classic drama *La carreta (The Oxcart,* 1953), in which the famous Puerto Rican author traces the archetypical emigrant's journey from the rural areas of the island to the slums of San Juan and the ghettos of the South Bronx. *La carreta* has been widely perceived as an emblematic depiction of the Puerto Rican diaspora; corrupted by foreign values, the emigrant family deteriorates morally and culturally. The play closes with the vision of a return to the mythified island and its traditional values as a form of personal and national redemption.

Laviera's book gives voice to the millions of Puerto Ricans for whom a permanent return to the island is impossible; nevertheless, in Laviera's poetry, those emigrants can still legitimately claim to be a valuable part of Puerto Rican culture. His skillful use of code-switching, or "Spanglish," reveals the linguistic dilemma of this population, as in his oft-quoted, subversively ironic poem "My Graduation Speech."

The influence of music, particularly African rhythms, combined with a keen ear for street talk, double talk, and barrio dialect, make Laviera's works best appreciated in public presentations. His third collection, *AmeRícan* (1986), is a tribute to multiethnicity and to Laviera's ongoing efforts to redefine Americanness apart from the mythological melting pot.

My Graduation Speech

i think in spanish
i write in english

i want to go back to puerto rico,
but i wonder if my kink could live
in ponce, mayagüez and carolina

tengo las venas aculturadas
escribo en spanglish
abraham in español
abraham in english
tato in spanish
"taro" in english
tonto in both languages

how are you?
¿cómo estás?
i don't know if i'm coming
or si me fui ya

si me dicen barranquitas, yo reply,
"¿con qué se come eso?"
si me dicen caviar, i digo,
"a new pair of converse sneakers."

ahí supe que estoy jodío
ahí supe que estamos jodíos

english or spanish
spanish or english
spanenglish
now, dig this:

...matao
...ol matao
...guno bien

...glish to matao
...)
¡ay, ...gen, yo no sé hablar!

[1979]

AmeRícan

we gave birth to a new generation,
AmeRícan, broader than lost gold
never touched, hidden inside the
puerto rican mountains.

we gave birth to a new generation,
AmeRícan, it includes everything
imaginable you-name-it-we-got-it
society.

we gave birth to a new generation,
AmeRícan salutes all folklores,
european, indian, black, spanish,
and anything else compatible:

AmeRícan, singing to composer pedro flores' palm
trees high up in the universal sky!

AmeRícan, sweet soft spanish danzas gypsies
moving lyrics la española cascabelling
presence always singing at our side!

AmeRícan, beating jíbaro modern troubadours
crying guitars romantic continental
bolero love songs!

AmeRícan, across forth and across back
back across and forth back
forth across and back and forth
our trips are walking bridges!

it all dissolved into itself, the attempt

was truly made, the attempt was truly
absorbed, digested, we spit out
the poison, we spit out the malice,
we stand, affirmative in action,
to reproduce a broader answer to the
marginality that gobbled us up abruptly!

AmeRícan, walking plena-rhythms in new york,
strutting beautifully alert, alive,
many turning eyes wondering,
admiring!

AmeRícan, defining myself my own way any way many
ways Am e Rícan, with the big R and the
accent on the í!

AmeRícan, like the soul gliding talk of gospel
boogie music!

AmeRícan, speaking new words in spanglish tenements,
fast tongue moving street corner "que
corta" talk being invented at the insistence
of a smile!

AmeRícan, abounding inside so many ethnic english
people, and out of humanity, we blend
and mix all that is good!

AmeRícan, integrating in new york and defining our
own destino, our own way of life,

AmeRícan, defining the new america, humane america,
admired america, loved america, harmonious
america, the world in peace, our energies
collectively invested to find other civilizations, to touch God, further and further,
to dwell in the spirit of divinity!

AmeRícan, yes, for now, for i love this, my second
land, and i dream to take the accent from
the altercation, and be proud to call
myself american, in the u.s. sense of the
word, AmeRícan, America! [1985]

Sandra María Esteves is the exceptional female voice among the Nuyorican poets of the 1970s. Born in 1948 in the Bronx, New York, "a community inhabited by immigrants which has since been abandoned," she was the child of a Dominican mother and a Puerto Rican father. Raised by a single, Spanish-speaking, working-class mother and educated in the English-speaking environment of a Catholic boarding school, she was attracted to the ethnic and racial consciousness movements taking place around her in the 1960s and 1970s. It was the era of militant demands for civil rights and peace, and in the Puerto Rican barrios the Young Lords, like the African-American Black Panthers, were organizing efforts for social and political change.

Nuyoricans were also discovering their own poetic voices, distinct from those of the island-educated poets who had come before and continued to arrive during those years. Sandra María Esteves began to read her works in public, along with other Nuyorican writers, in poetry cafés and university workshops. Her first collection, *Yerba Buena* (Good Herb), was published in 1980, followed by *Tropical Rains: A Bilingual Downpour* (1984) and *Bluestown Mockingbird Mambo* (1990). Her ethnic awareness expanded in later works to encompass the struggles of Native Americans, African Americans, and Chicanos, and her approach became more woman-centered.

A general theme of Esteves's poetry is the search for harmony and for reconciliation of her Afro-Caribbean roots with her experiences in this country. Her poetry is strongly oral, best appreciated when heard. "A la Mujer Borrinqueña" (To the Woman of Borinquen —the indigenous name for Puerto Rico), typical of her work, is influenced in style and tone by Afro-American poets. The incorrect spelling of "borinqueña" in the title is probably deliberate, as it has appeared in subsequent reprintings of the poem. Like other U.S. Puerto Rican poetry of the era, Esteves's verses occasionally include ungrammatical words in Spanish or English, perhaps to reflect the lack of formal education in the community; it also mirrors the language skills of an untrained second-generation Spanish speaker. Esteves claims among her mentors Julia de Burgos, Pablo Neruda, and Nicolás Guillén, "whose works are a leading source of education for guiding one through the darkness."

Her occasionally uncritical defense of Latino culture has been criticized by other women poets; nevertheless, Esteves's poetry reveals the attempt of Latina authors to achieve the delicate balance between defending one's culture and traditions and analyzing them with a critical eye.

From the Commonwealth

So you want me to be your mistress
and find dignity in a closed room
because you say your first real love is music
even though I too am music
the sum total of contrary chords and dissonant notes
occasionally surviving in mutilated harmony
even though I could fill you so full
to grow outside yourself
and walk with you thru opalescent gardens

But you only want me to be your Sunday afternoon mistress
and I have to recycle this flow of ebony tailored ambition
limit the mother in me that wants to intoxicate herself
in the center of your soul
not watch alien wives trade you off for multi colored trinkets
flashing against the real you

Understanding what a whore sophistication really is
I reject a service role
a position I've truly hated whenever it was forced upon me

And it's true that I am a drifter, a wanderer
a gypsy whose objective in life is to travel in whole circles
that resemble the path of Venus around the Sun

I never reveled in washing clothes
or reached orgasms from dirty dishes
but I didn't mind being part of someone
who could help me to be me
with all my transcient contradictions

And I am a woman, not a mistress or a whore
or some anonymous cunt whose initials barely left an impression
on the foreskin of your nationhood
Y si la patria es una Mujer
then I am also a rebel and a lover of free people
and will continue looking for friction in empty spaces
which is the only music I know how to play. [1979]

A la Mujer Borrinqueña

My name is Maria Christina
I am a Puerto Rican woman born in el barrio

Our men . . . they call me negra because they love me
and in turn I teach them to be strong

I respect their ways
inherited from our proud ancestors
I do not tease them with eye catching clothes
I do not sleep with their brothers and cousins
although I've been told that this is a liberal society
I do not poison their bellies with instant chemical foods
our table holds food from earth and sun

My name is Maria Christina
I speak two languages broken into each other
but my heart speaks the language of people
born in oppression

I do not complain about cooking for my family
because abuela taught me that woman is the master of fire
I do not complain about nursing my children
because I determine the direction of their values

I am the mother of a new age of warriors
I am the child of a race of slaves
I teach my children how to respect their bodies
so they will not o.d. under the stairway's shadow of shame
I teach my children to read and develop their minds
so they will understand the reality of oppression
I teach them with discipline . . . and love
so they will become strong and full of life

My eyes reflect the pain
of that which has shamelessly raped me
                    but my soul reflects the strength of my culture
My name is Maria Christina
I am a Puerto Rican woman born in el barrio
Our men . . . they call me negra because they love me
and in turn I teach them to be strong.   [1980]

Lourdes Casal was born in Cuba in 1938 into a middle-class professional family. During her years at the university in Havana, Casal fought against the dictatorship of Fulgencio Batista, later joining the Student Revolutionary Directorate after the victory of the Cuban Revolution in 1959. She became critical of the revolution's ideology, however, and moved to the United States in 1961, living in New York City from 1962 until 1979.

Casal is best known for her attempts to promote improved cultural relations between Cuba and the United States; her participation in the U.S. civil rights movement in the 1960s led her to rethink her political position regarding Cuba. Among her numerous contributions to the preservation of Cuban culture in exile was the founding in 1974 of the magazine *Areíto,* which aspired to provide an alternative vision of U.S. Cuban culture.

Casal published extensively in her chosen field, psychology, as well as in politics and social themes. Her literary activity was confined to short stories and poetry; her poems were collected posthumously in *Palabras juntan revolución* (Words Join Revolution, 1981), which won the Casa de las Américas prize in Havana. Seriously ill, Casal returned to Cuba in 1979 and died there in 1981.

The following well-known poem, "For Ana Veldford," reflects the ambivalence of exile, which Casal once defined poetically as: "Exile / is to live where no house exists / in which we were children."

For Ana Veldford

Never the summer in Provincetown
and even on this afternoon so clear
(so unusual for New York)
it's from the bus window that I contemplate
the serenity of the grass in the park along Riverside
and the inactivity of all the summer people who lie on frayed
blankets
of those who play on bikes along the narrow paths.
I remain so foreign behind that protective window
like in that winter
— unanticipated weekend —
when for the first time I came face to face with Vermont snow

and nevertheless New York is my home.
I am fiercely loyal to this acquired homeland.
Because of New York I am a foreigner now in any other part,
terrible pride in the smells that assault us on any street of the West
Side,
marijuana and the odor of beer
and the stink of dog urine
and the wild lyrics of Santana
descending on us
from a speaker that thunders improbably balanced on a fire escape,
the raucous glory of New York in summer,
Central Park and us,
the poor,
who have inherited the side of the north side,
and Harlem labors in the laxness of this sluggish afternoon.
The bus glides lazily
downtown, down Fifth Avenue;
and in front of me, the bearded youth
who's loaded down with an enormous pile of books from the
Public Library
and it seems as if it were possible to touch the summer on the
sweaty forehead of the bicyclist
who rides hanging on to my window.
But New York was not the city of my infancy,
it wasn't here that I came by my first certainties,
it isn't here that corner of my first fall
or the lacerating whistle that marked the nights.
That's why I'll always remain on the margin,
a stranger among the stones,
even under the friendly sun of this summer day,
as now forever I'll remain a foreigner,
I carry this marginality immune to all returns,
too Havanan to be newyorkina,
too newyorkina to be
— even to be again —
anything else. [1981]

Translation of "Para Ana Veldford" by Rod Lauren

Lorna Dee Cervantes was born in 1954 in the Mission District of San Francisco, and later moved to San Jose with her mother and brother. Cervantes began writing poetry at a young age. She edited, published, and printed a small-press journal, *Mango,* which successfully promoted other Chicano poets and helped establish her own reputation. She began to receive national attention in the late 1970s. After spending nine months at the Fine Arts Workshop in Provincetown, Massachusetts, she completed *Emplumada* (1981), the title of which is an amalgam of the participle "emplumado" (feathered or in plumage) and the nouns "pluma" (pen) and "plumada" (a pen stroke).

Emplumada is divided into three sections dealing with the social environment, the class status of women, the poet's harmonious relationship with the world of nature, and the act of writing, among other things. "Poem for the Young White Man Who Asked Me How I, an Intelligent, Well-Read Person, Could Believe in the War Between the Races" attempts to understand her world through the act of writing. Her full realization as a Chicana is articulated in "Visions of Mexico While at a Writing Symposium in Port Townsend, Washington."

Cervantes has come to terms with her multiple and complex identities. About her 1981 collection, Roberta Fernández says: "Written in a controlled language and with brilliant imagery, *Emplumada* is the work of a poet who is on her way to becoming a major voice in American literature." Cervantes's later collection, *From the Cables of Genocide: Poems on Love and Hunger* (1991), validates Fernández's sentiments.

Poem for the Young White Man Who Asked Me How I, an Intelligent, Well-Read Person, Could Believe in the War Between the Races

In my land there are no distinctions.
The barbed wire politics of oppression
have been torn down long ago. The only reminder
of past battles, lost or won, is a slight
rutting in the fertile fields.

In my land
people write poems about love,
full of nothing but contented childlike syllables.
Everyone reads Russian short stories and weeps.
There are no boundaries.
There is no hunger, no
complicated famine or greed.

I am not a revolutionary.
I don't even like political poems.
Do you think I can believe in a war between races?
I can deny it. I can forget about it
when I'm safe
living in my own continent of harmony
and home, but I am not
there.

I believe in revolution
because everywhere the crosses are burning,
sharp-shooting goose-steppers round every corner,
there are snipers in the school . . .
(I know you don't believe this.
You think this is nothing
but faddish exaggeration. But they
are not shooting at you.)

I'm marked by the color of my skin.
The bullets are discrete and designed to kill slowly.
They are aiming at my children.
These are facts.
Let me show you my wounds: my stumbling mind, my
"excuse me" tongue, and this
nagging preoccupation
with the feeling of not being good enough.

These bullets bury deeper than logic.
Racism is not intellectual.
I can not reason these scars away.

Outside my door
there is a real enemy
who hates me.

I am a poet
who yearns to dance on rooftops,
to whisper delicate lines about joy
and the blessings of human understanding.
I try. I go to my land, my tower of words and
bolt the door, but the typewriter doesn't fade out
the sounds of blasting and muffled outrage.
My own days bring me slaps on the face.
Everyday I am deluged with reminders
that this is not
my land
and this is my land.

I do not believe in the war between the races

but in this country
there is war. [1981]

Visions of Mexico While at a Writing Symposium in Port Townsend, Washington

Mexico

When I'm that far south, the old words
molt off my skin, the feathers
of all my nervousness.
My own words somersault naturally as my name,
joyous among all those meadows: Michoacan,
Vera Cruz, Tenochtitlán, Oaxaca . . .
Pueblos green on the low hills
where men slap handballs below acres of maiz.
I watch and understand.
My frail body has never packed mud
or gathered in the full weight of the harvest.

Alone with the women in the adobe, I watch men,
their taut faces holding in all their youth.
This far south we are governed by the law
of the next whole meal.
We work and watch seabirds elbow their wings
in migratory ways, those mispronouncing gulls
coming south
to refuge or gameland.

I don't want to pretend I know more
and can speak all the names. I can't.
My sense of this land can only ripple through my veins
like the chant of an epic corrido.
I come from a long line of eloquent illiterates
whose history reveals what words don't say.
Our anger is our way of speaking,
the gesture is an utterance more pure than word.
We are not animals
but our senses are keen and our reflexes,
accurate punctuation.
All the knifings in a single night, low-voiced
scufflings, sirens, gunnings . . .
We hear them
and the poet within us bays.

Washington

I don't belong this far north.
The uncomfortable birds gawk at me.
They hem and haw from their borders in the sky.
I heard them say: Mexico is a stumbling comedy.
A loose-legged Cantinflas woman
acting with Pancho Villa drunkenness.
Last night at the tavern
this was all confirmed
in a painting of a woman: her glowing
silk skin, a halo
extending from her golden coiffure
while around her, dark-skinned men with Jap slant eyes

were drooling in a caricature of machismo.
Below it, at the bar, two Chicanas
hung at their beers. They had painted black
birds that dipped beneath their eyelids.
They were still as foam while the men
fiddled with their asses, absently;
the bubbles of their teased hair snapped
open in the forced wind of the beating fan.

there are songs in my head I could sing you
songs that could drone away
all the Mariachi bands you thought you ever heard
songs that could tell you what I know
or have learned from my people
but for that   I need words
simple black nymphs between white sheets of paper
obedient words   obligatory words   words I steal
in the dark when no one can hear me.

as pain sends seabirds south from the cold
I come north
to gather my feathers
for quills   [1981]

Richard Rodriguez, who was born in 1946, is considered one of the foremost essayists in the United States. He appears regularly on Public Broadcasting Service's *Jim Lehrer NewsHour*.

Rodriguez's first book, *Hunger of Memory: The Education of Richard Rodriguez* (1982), a landmark collection of autobiographical essays, is one of the most debated texts in U.S. Latino letters. In this aesthetically beautiful book he discusses significant social and political issues, using incidents from his own life to illustrate his points, including the change of language upon beginning school, his alienation from his family, and a confrontation with affirmative action programs. His points are often well taken, but he omits some important aspects of his life — feelings of homosexuality and self-loathing, for example — that may have affected his choice to separate himself from Mexican-American culture as a child and young adult. The effectiveness of the essays suffers from these limitations. Rodriguez's second collection of essays, *Days of Obligation: Conversations with My Mexican Father* (1992), is a much more mature work, similarly heartfelt but more nuanced and less prone to broad pronouncements on the success or failure of U.S. institutions. Still, *Hunger of Memory* remains a touchstone in discussions of bilingual education, affirmative action, and ethnocentrism.

The essays in *Hunger of Memory* were written and published separately over a period of years, from 1973 to 1981. The following excerpt is taken from the final, collected version.

from Hunger of Memory: The Education of Richard Rodriguez

Aria

I

I remember to start with that day in Sacramento — a California now nearly thirty years past — when I first entered a classroom, able to understand some fifty stray English words.

The third of four children, I had been preceded to a neighborhood Roman Catholic school by an older brother and sister. But neither of them had revealed very much about their classroom experiences. Each afternoon they returned, as they left in the morning, always together, speaking in Spanish as they climbed the five steps of the porch. And their mysterious books, wrapped in shopping-bag paper, remained on the table next to the door, closed firmly behind them.

An accident of geography sent me to a school where all my classmates were white, many the children of doctors and lawyers and business executives. All my classmates certainly must have been uneasy on that first day of school — as most children are uneasy — to find themselves apart from their families in the first institution of their lives. But I was astonished.

The nun said, in a friendly but oddly impersonal voice, "Boys and girls, this is Richard Rodriguez." (I heard her sound out: *Rich-heard Road-ree-guess.*) It was the first time I had heard anyone name me in English. "Richard," the nun repeated more slowly, writing my name down in her black leather book. Quickly I turned to see my mother's face dissolve in a watery blur behind the pebbled glass door.

Many years later there is something called bilingual education — a scheme proposed in the late 1960s by Hispanic-American social activists, later endorsed by a congressional vote. It is a program that seeks to permit non-English-speaking children, many from lower-class homes, to use their family language as the language of school. (Such is the goal its supporters announce.) I hear them and am forced to say no: it is not possible for a child — any child — ever to use his family's language in school. Not to understand this is to misunderstand the public uses of schooling and to trivialize the nature of intimate life — a family's "language."

Memory teaches me what I know of these matters; the boy reminds the adult. I was a bilingual child, a certain kind — socially disadvantaged — the son of working-class parents, both Mexican immigrants.

In the early years of my boyhood, my parents coped very well in America. My father had steady work. My mother managed at home. They were nobody's victims. Optimism and ambition led them to a house (our home) many blocks from the Mexican south side of town. We lived among *gringos* and only a block from the biggest, whitest houses. It never occurred to my parents that they couldn't live wherever they chose. Nor was the Sacramento of the fifties bent on teaching them a contrary lesson. My mother and father were more annoyed than intimidated by those two or three neighbors who tried initially to make us unwelcome. ("Keep your brats away from my sidewalk!") But despite all they achieved, perhaps because they had so much to achieve, any deep feeling of ease, the confidence of "belonging" in public, was withheld from them both. They regarded the people at work, the faces in crowds, as very distant from us. They were the others, *los gringos*. That term was interchangeable in their speech with another, even more telling, *los americanos*.

I grew up in a house where the only regular guests were my relations. For one day, enormous families of relatives would visit, and there would be so many people that the noise and the bodies would spill out to the backyard and front porch. Then, for weeks, no one came by. (It was usually a salesman who rang the doorbell.) Our house stood apart. A gaudy yellow in a row of white bungalows. We were the people with the noisy dog. The people who raised pigeons and chickens. We were the foreigners on the block. A few neighbors smiled and waved. We waved back. But no one in the family knew the names of the old couple who lived next door; until I was seven years old, I did not know the names of the kids who lived across the street.

In public, my father and mother spoke a hesitant, accented, not always grammatical English. And they would have to strain — their bodies tense — to catch the sense of what was rapidly said by *los gringos*. At home they spoke Spanish. The language of their Mexican past sounded in counterpoint to the English of public society. The words would come quickly, with ease. Conveyed through those sounds was the pleasing, soothing, consoling reminder of being at home.

During those years when I was first conscious of hearing, my mother and father addressed me only in Spanish; in Spanish I learned to reply. By contrast, English (*inglés*), rarely heard in the house, was the language I came to associate with *gringos*. I learned my first words of English overhearing my parents speak to strangers. At five years of age, I knew just enough English for my mother to trust me on errands to stores one block away. No more.

I was a listening child, careful to hear the very different sounds of Spanish and English. Wide-eyed with hearing, I'd listen to sounds more than words. First, there were English (*gringo*) sounds. So many words were still unknown that when the butcher or the lady at the drugstore said something to me, exotic polysyllabic sounds would bloom in the midst of their sentences. Often, the speech of people in public seemed to me very loud, booming with confidence. The man behind the counter would literally ask, 'What can I do for you?' But by being so firm and so clear, the sound of his voice said that he was a *gringo;* he belonged in public society.

I would also hear then the high nasal notes of middle-class American speech. The air stirred with sound. Sometimes, even now, when I have been traveling abroad for several weeks, I will hear what I heard as a boy. In hotel lobbies or airports, in Turkey or Brazil, some Americans will pass, and suddenly I will hear it again — the high sound of American voices. For a few seconds I will hear it with pleasure, for it is now the sound of *my* society — a reminder of home. But inevitably — already on the flight headed for home — the sound fades with repetition. I will be unable to hear it anymore.

When I was a boy, things were different. The accent of *los gringos* was never pleasing nor was it hard to hear. Crowds at Safeway or at bus stops would be noisy with sound. And I would be forced to edge away from the chirping chatter above me.

I was unable to hear my own sounds, but I knew very well that I spoke English poorly. My words could not stretch far enough to form complete thoughts. And the words I did speak I didn't know well enough to make into distinct sounds. (Listeners would usually lower their heads, better to hear what I was trying to say.) But it was one thing for *me* to speak English with difficulty. It was more troubling for me to hear my parents speak in public: their high-whining vowels and guttural consonants; their sentences that got stuck with *eh* and *ah* sounds; the confused syntax; the hesitant rhythm of sounds so different from the way *gringos* spoke. I'd notice, moreover, that my parents' voices were softer than those of *gringos* we'd meet.

I am tempted now to say that none of this mattered. In adulthood I am embarrassed by childhood fears. And, in a way, it didn't matter very much that my parents could not speak English with ease. Their linguistic difficulties had no serious consequences. My mother and father made themselves understood at the county hospital clinic and at government offices. And yet, in another way, it mattered very much — it was unsettling to hear my parents struggle with English. Hearing them, I'd grow nervous, my clutching trust in their protection and power weakened.

There were many times like the night at a brightly lit gasoline station (a blaring white memory) when I stood uneasily, hearing my father. He was talking to a teenage attendant. I do not recall what they were saying, but I cannot forget the sounds my father made as he spoke. At one point his words slid together to form one word — sounds as confused as the threads of blue and green oil in the puddle next to my shoes. His voice rushed through what he had left to say. And, toward the end, reached falsetto notes, appealing to his listener's understanding. I looked away to the lights of passing automobiles. I tried not to hear any more. But I heard only too well the calm, easy tones in the attendant's reply. Shortly afterward, walking toward home with my father, I shivered when he put his hand on my shoulder. The very first chance that I got, I evaded his grasp and ran on ahead into the dark, skipping with feigned boyish exuberance.

But then there was Spanish. *Español:* my family's language. *Español:* the language that seemed to me a private language. I'd hear strangers on the radio and in the Mexican Catholic church across town speaking in Spanish, but I couldn't really believe that Spanish was a public language, like English. Spanish speakers, rather, seemed related to me, for I sensed that we shared — through our language — the experience of feeling apart from *los gringos.* It was thus a ghetto Spanish that I heard and I spoke. Like those whose lives are bound by a barrio, I was reminded by Spanish of my separateness from *los otros, los gringos* in power. But more intensely than for most barrio children — because I did not live in a barrio — Spanish seemed to me the language of home. (Most days it was only at home that I'd hear it.) It became the language of joyful return.

A family member would say something to me and I would feel myself specially recognized. My parents would say something to me and I would feel embraced by the sounds of their words. Those sounds said: *I am speaking with ease in Spanish. I am addressing you in words I never use with* los gringos. *I recognize you as someone special, close, like no one outside. You belong with us. In the family.*

(*Ricardo.*)

At the age of five, six, well past the time when most other children no longer easily notice the difference between sounds uttered at home and words spoken in public, I had a different experience. I lived in a world magically compounded of sounds. I remained a child longer than most; I lingered too long, poised at the edge of language — often frightened by the sounds of *los gringos,* delighted by the sounds of Spanish at home. I shared with my family a language that was startlingly different from that used in the great city around us.

For me there were none of the graduations between public and private society so normal to a maturing child. Outside the house was public society; inside the house was private. Just opening or closing the screen door behind me was an important experience. I'd rarely leave home all alone or without reluctance. Walking down the sidewalk, under the canopy of tall trees, I'd warily notice the — suddenly — silent neighborhood kids who stood warily watching me. Nervously, I'd arrive at the grocery store to hear there the sounds of the *gringo* — foreign to me — reminding me that in this world so big, I was a foreigner. But then I'd return. Walking back toward our house, climbing the steps from the sidewalk, when the front door was open in summer, I'd hear voices beyond the screen door talking in Spanish. For a second or two I'd stay, linger there, listening. Smiling, I'd hear my mother call out, saying in Spanish (words): "Is that you, Richard?" All the while her sounds would assure me: *You are home now; come closer; inside. With us.*

"Sí," I'd reply.

Once more inside the house I would resume (assume) my place in the family. The sounds would dim, grow harder to hear. Once more at home, I would grow less aware of that fact. It required, however, no more than the blurt of the doorbell to alert me to listen to sounds all over again. The house would turn instantly still while my mother went to the door. I'd hear her hard English sounds. I'd wait to hear her voice return to soft-sounding Spanish, which assured me, as surely as did the clicking tongue of the lock on the door, that the stranger was gone.

Plainly, it is not healthy to hear such sounds so often. It is not healthy to distinguish public words from private sounds so easily. I remained cloistered by sounds, timid and shy in public, too dependent on voices at home. And yet it needs to be emphasized: I was an extremely happy child at home. I remember many nights when my father would come back from work, and I'd hear him call out to my mother in Spanish, sounding relieved. In Spanish, he'd sound light and free notes he never could manage in English. Some nights I'd jump up just at hearing his voice. With *mis hermanos* I would come running into the room where he was with my mother. Our laughing (so deep was the pleasure!) became screaming. Like others who know the pain of public alienation, we transformed the knowledge of our public separateness and made it consoling — the reminder of intimacy. Excited, we joined our voices in a celebration of sounds. *We are speaking now the way we never speak out in public. We are alone — together,* voices sounded, surrounded to tell me. Some nights, no one seemed willing to loosen the hold sounds had on us. At dinner, we invented new words. (Ours sounded Spanish, but made sense only to us.) We pieced together new words by taking, say, an English verb and giving it Spanish endings. My mother's instructions at bedtime would be lacquered with mock-urgent tones. Or a word like *sí* would become, in several notes, able to convey added measures of feeling. Tongues explored the edges of words, especially the fat vowels. And we happily sounded that military drum roll, the twirling roar of the Spanish *r*. Family language: my family's sounds. The voices of my parents and sisters and brother. Their voices insisting: *You belong here. We are family members. Related. Special to one another. Listen!* Voices singing and sighing, rising, straining, then surging, teeming with pleasure that burst syllables into fragments of laughter. At times it seemed there was steady quiet only when, from another room, the rustling whispers of my parents faded and I moved closer to sleep.

II

Supporters of bilingual education today imply that students like me miss a great deal by not being taught in their family's language. What they seem not to recognize is that, as a socially disadvantaged child, I considered Spanish to be a private language. What I needed to learn in school was that I had the right — and the obligation — to speak the public language of *los gringos*. The odd truth is that my first-grade classmates could have become bilingual, in the conventional sense of that word, more easily than I. Had they been taught (as upper-middle-class children are often taught early) a second language like Spanish or French, they could have regarded it simply as that: another public language. In my case such bilingualism could not have been so quickly achieved. What I did not believe was that I could speak a single public language.

Without question, it would have pleased me to hear my teachers address me in Spanish when I entered the classroom. I would have felt much less afraid. I would have trusted them and responded with ease. But I would have delayed — for how long postponed? — having to learn the language of public society. I would have evaded — and for how long could I have afforded to delay? — learning the great lesson of school, that I had a public identity.

Fortunately, my teachers were unsentimental about their responsibility. What they understood was that I needed to speak a public language. So their voices would search me out, asking me questions. Each time I'd hear them, I'd look up in surprise to see a nun's face frowning at me. I'd mumble, not really meaning to answer. The nun would persist, "Richard, stand up. Don't look at the floor: Speak up. Speak to the entire class, not just to me!" But I couldn't believe that the English language was mine to use. (In part, I did not want to believe it.) I continued to mumble. I resisted the teacher's demands. (Did I somehow suspect that once I learned public language, my pleasing family life would be changed?) Silent, waiting for the bell to sound, I remained dazed, diffident, afraid.

Because I wrongly imagined that English was intrinsically a public language and Spanish an intrinsically private one, I easily noted the difference between classroom language and the language of home. At school, words were directed to a general audience of listeners. ("Boys and girls.") Words were meaningfully ordered. And the point was not self-expression alone but to make oneself understood by many others. The teacher quizzed: "Boys and girls, why do we use that word in this sentence? Could we think of a better word to use there? Would the sentence change its meaning if the words were differently arranged? And wasn't there a better way of saying much the same things?" (I couldn't say. I wouldn't try to say.)

Three months. Five. Half a year passed. Unsmiling, ever watchful, my teachers noted my silence. They began to connect my behavior with the difficult progress my older sister and brother were making. Until one Saturday morning three nuns arrived at the house to talk to our parents. Stiffly, they sat on the blue living room sofa. From the doorway of another room, spying the visitors, I noted the incongruity — the clash of two worlds, the faces and voices of school intruding upon the familiar setting of home. I overheard one voice gently wondering, "Do your children speak only Spanish at home, Mrs. Rodriguez?" While another voice added, "That Richard especially seems so timid and shy."

That Rich-heard!

With great tact the visitors continued, "Is it possible for you and your husband to encourage your children to practice their English when they are home?" Of course, my parents complied. What would they not do for their children's well-being? And how could they have questioned the Church's authority which those women represented? In an instant, they agreed to give up the language (the sounds) that had revealed and accentuated our family's closeness. The moment after the visitors left, the change was observed. "Ahora, speak to us en inglés," my father and mother united to tell us.

At first, it seemed a kind of game. After dinner each night, the family gathered to practice "our" English. (It was still then *inglés,* a language foreign to us, so we felt drawn as strangers to it.) Laughing, we would try to define words we could not pronounce. We played with strange English sounds, often over-anglicizing our pronunciations. And we filled the smiling gaps of our sentences with familiar Spanish sounds. But that was cheating, somebody shouted. Everyone laughed. In school, meanwhile, like my brother and sister, I was required to attend a daily tutoring session. I needed a full year of special attention. I also needed my teachers to keep my attention from straying in class by calling out, *Rich-heard* — their English voices slowly prying loose my ties to my other name, its three notes, *Ri-car-do.* Most of all I needed to hear my mother and father speak to me in a moment of seriousness in broken — suddenly heartbreaking — English. The scene was inevitable: one Saturday morning I entered the kitchen where my parents were talking in Spanish. I did not realize that they were talking in Spanish, however, until, at the moment they saw me, I heard their voices change to speak English. Those *gringo* sounds they uttered startled me. Pushed me away. In that moment of trivial misunderstanding and profound insight, I felt my throat twisted by unsounded grief. I turned quickly and left the room. But I had no place to escape to with Spanish. (The spell was broken.) My brother and sisters were speaking English in another part of the house.

Again and again in the days following, increasingly angry, I was obliged to hear my mother and father: "Speak to us en inglés." (*Speak.*) Only then did I determine to learn classroom English. Weeks after, it happened: one day in school I raised my hand to volunteer an answer. I spoke out in a loud voice. And I did not think it remarkable when the entire class understood. That day, I moved very far from the disadvantaged child I had been only days earlier. The belief, the calming assurance that I belonged in public, had at last taken hold.

Shortly after, I stopped hearing the high and loud sounds of *los gringos*. A more and more confident speaker of English, I didn't trouble to listen to *how* strangers sounded, speaking to me. And there simply were too many English-speaking people in my day for me to hear American accents anymore. Conversations quickened. Listening to persons who sounded eccentrically pitched voices, I usually noted their sounds for an initial few seconds before I concentrated on *what* they were saying. Conversations became content-full. Transparent. Hearing someone's *tone* of voice — angry or questioning or sarcastic or happy or sad — I didn't distinguish it from the words it expressed. Sound and word were thus tightly wedded. At the end of a day, I was often bemused, always relieved, to realize how "silent," though crowded with words, my day in public had been. (This public silence measured and quickened the change in my life.)

At last, seven years old, I came to believe what had been technically true since my birth: I was an American citizen.

But the special feeling of closeness at home was diminished by then. Gone was the desperate, urgent, intense feeling of being at home; rare was the experience of feeling myself individualized by family intimates. We remained a loving family, but one greatly changed. No longer so close; no longer bound tight by the pleasing and troubling knowledge of our public separateness. Neither my older brother nor sister rushed home after school anymore. Nor did I. When I arrived home there would often be neighborhood kids in the house. Or the house would be empty of sounds.

Following the dramatic Americanization of their children, even my parents grew more publicly confident. Especially my mother. She learned the names of all the people on our block. And she decided we needed to have a telephone installed in the house. My father continued to use the word *gringo*. But it was no longer charged with the old bitterness or distrust. (Stripped of any emotional content, the word simply became a name for those Americans not of Hispanic descent.) Hearing him, sometimes, I wasn't sure if he was pronouncing the Spanish word *gringo* or saying gringo in English.

Matching the silence I started hearing in public was a new quiet at home. The family's quiet was partly due to the fact that, as we children learned more and more English, we shared fewer and fewer words with our parents. Sentences needed to be spoken slowly when a child addressed his mother or father. (Often the parent wouldn't understand.) The child would need to repeat himself. (Still the parent misunderstood.) The young voice, frustrated, would end up saying, "Never mind" — the subject was closed. Dinners would be noisy with the clinking of knives and forks against dishes. My mother would smile softly between her remarks; my father at the other end of the table would chew and chew at his food while he stared over the heads of his children.

My *mother!* My *father!* After English became my primary language, I no longer knew what words to use in addressing my parents. The old Spanish words (those tender accents of sound) I had used earlier — *Mamá* and *Papá* — I couldn't use anymore. They would have been too painful reminders of how much had changed in my life. On the other hand, the words I heard neighborhood kids call *their* parents seemed equally unsatisfactory. *Mother* and *Father; Ma, Papa, Pa, Dad, Pop* (how I hated the all-American sound of that last word especially) — all these terms I felt were unsuitable, not really terms of address for *my* parents. As a result, I never used them at home. Whenever I'd speak to my parents, I would try to get their attention with eye contact alone. In public conversations, I'd refer to "my parents" or "my mother and father."

My mother and father, for their part, responded differently, as their children spoke to them less. She grew restless, seemed troubled and anxious at the scarcity of words exchanged in the house. It was she who would question me about my day when I came home from school. She smiled at small talk. She pried at the edges of my sentences to get me to say something more. (What?) She'd join conversations she overheard, but her intrusions often stopped her children's talking. By contrast, my father seemed reconciled to the new quiet. Though his English improved somewhat, he retired into silence. At dinner he spoke very little. One night his children and even his wife helplessly giggled at his garbled English pronunciation of the Catholic grace before meals. Thereafter he made his wife recite the prayer at the start of each meal, even on formal occasions, when there were guests in the house. Hers became the public voice of the family. On official business, it was she, not my father, one would usually hear on the phone or in stores, talking to strangers. His children grew so accustomed to his silence that, years later, they would speak routinely of his shyness. (My mother would often try to explain: both his parents died when he was eight. He was raised by an uncle who treated him like little more than a menial servant. He was never encouraged to speak. He grew up alone. A man of few words.) But my father was not shy, I realized, when I'd watch him speaking Spanish with relatives. Using Spanish, he was quickly effusive. Especially when talking with other men, his voice would spark, flicker, flare alive with sounds. In Spanish, he expressed ideas and feelings he rarely revealed in English. With firm Spanish sounds, he conveyed confidence and authority English would never allow him.

The silence at home, however, was finally more than a literal silence. Fewer words passed between parent and child, but more profound was the silence that resulted from my inattention to sounds. At about the time I no longer bothered to listen with care to the sounds of English in public, I grew careless about listening to the sounds family members made when they spoke. Most of the time I heard someone speaking at home and didn't distinguish his sounds from the words people uttered in public. I didn't even pay much attention to my parents' accented and ungrammatical speech. At least not at home. Only when I was with them in public would I grow alert to their accents. Though, even then, their sounds caused me less and less concern. For I was increasingly confident of my own public identity.

I would have been happier about my public success had I not sometimes recalled what it had been like earlier, when my family had conveyed its intimacy through a set of conveniently private sounds. Sometimes in public, hearing a stranger, I'd hark back to my past. A Mexican farm worker approached me downtown to ask directions to somewhere. "Hijito . . . ?" he said. And his voice summoned deep longing. Another time, standing beside my mother in the visiting room of a Carmelite convent, before the dense screen which rendered the nuns shadowy figures, I heard several Spanish-speaking nuns — their busy, singsong overlapping voices — assure us that yes, yes, we were remembered, all our family was remembered in their prayers. (Their voices echoed faraway family sounds.) Another day, a dark-faced old woman — her hand light on my shoulder — steadied herself against me as she boarded a bus. She murmured something I couldn't quite comprehend. Her Spanish voice came near, like the face of a never-before-seen relative in the instant before I was kissed. Her voice, like so many of the Spanish voices I'd hear in public, recalled the golden age of my youth. Hearing Spanish then, I continued to be a careful, if sad, listener to sounds. Hearing a Spanish-speaking family walking behind me, I turned to look. I smiled for an instant, before my glance found the Hispanic-looking faces of strangers in the crowd going by.

Today I hear bilingual educators say that children lose a degree of "individuality" by becoming assimilated into public society. (Bilingual schooling was popularized in the seventies, that decade when middle-class ethnics began to resist the process of assimilation — the American melting pot.) But the bilingualists simplistically scorn the value and necessity of assimilation. They do not seem to realize that there are *two* ways a person is individualized. So they do not realize that while one suffers a diminished sense of *private* individuality by becoming assimilated into public society, such assimilation makes possible the achievement of *public* individuality.

The bilingualists insist that a student should be reminded of his difference from others in mass society, his heritage. But they equate mere separateness with individuality. The fact is that only in private — with intimates — is separateness from the crowd a prerequisite for individuality. (An intimate draws me apart, tells me that I am unique, unlike all others.) In public, by contrast, full individuality is achieved, paradoxically, by those who are able to consider themselves members of the crowd. Thus it happened for me: only when I was able to think of myself as an American, no longer an alien in *gringo* society, could I seek the rights and opportunities necessary for full public individuality. The social and political advantages I enjoy as a man result from the day that I came to believe that my name, indeed, is *Rich-heard Road-ree-guess*. It is true that my public society today is often impersonal. (My public society is usually mass society.) Yet despite the anonymity of the crowd and despite the fact that the individuality I achieve in public is often tenuous — because it depends on my being one in a crowd — I celebrate the day I acquired my new name. Those middle-class ethnics who scorn assimilation seem to me filled with decadent self-pity, obsessed by the burden of public life. Dangerously, they romanticize public separateness and they trivialize the dilemma of the socially disadvantaged.

My awkward childhood does not prove the necessity of bilingual education. My story discloses instead an essential myth of childhood — inevitable pain. If I rehearse here the changes in my private life after my Americanization, it is finally to emphasize the public gain. The loss implies the gain: the house I returned to each afternoon was quiet. Intimate sounds no longer rushed to the door to greet me. There were other noises inside. The telephone rang. Neighborhood kids ran past the door of the bedroom where I was reading my schoolbooks — covered with shopping-bag paper. Once I learned public language, it would never again be easy for me to hear intimate family voices. More and more of my day was spent hearing words. But that may only be a way of saying that the day I raised my hand in class and spoke loudly to an entire roomful of faces, my childhood started to end. [1982]

Edward Rivera was born in Orocovis, Puerto Rico, in 1944 and moved to New York at the age of seven. He graduated from the City College of New York and received an M.F.A. from Columbia University. Rivera lives in New York and teaches English at City College.

Rivera's *Family Installments: Memories of Growing Up Hispanic* (1982) is a series of hilarious, bitingly satirical stories of growing up in New York City. They are also thoughtful literary examinations of the culture into which Puerto Ricans were thrown upon their arrival in New York: Irish-dominated Catholicism, multiethnic neighborhoods, and cold working-class urban environments. The main character in *Family Installments,* Santos Malánguez, spent his first few years in Puerto Rico. The abruptness of his transition to New York is conveyed by a jump cut, a cinematic device that brings him from a classroom with a beloved teacher to a confusing but similar environment in New York. In the following excerpt, originally published in 1974, he plays with literature and literary tradition while satirizing the teaching of that literature by someone who has little understanding of the language in which he is teaching.

from Family Installments: Memories of Growing Up Hispanic

Caesar and the Brutuses: A Tradegy

A couple of days before Christmas, I locked myself up in the cold last room of the house, our family eating room, and Papi's study, and opened up *The Tragedy of Julius Caesar.* "Gayest Orange Julius Caesar," I mangled his name in my notebook, already getting off on what Bro'Leary would have called a bad foot. The book, full of misprints ("It's a slightly corrupted text, boys," Brother had warned us. Slightly corrupted nothing. Colossally corrupted, he meant.) — the text was brand-new, which meant Bro'Leary must have put in a special order for thirty-one copies, one for himself. A first for Saint Misery's, and probably a last first, too, a perfect waste of poor-parish money. It was a bright-green copy (our school's color, that and gold, some Irish symbol, I figured), with the school's name stamped (by Bro'Leary himself) in bold green caps at the top of the title page. On another page there was an ink drawing of "Wm. Shakespeare, Bard of Avon," which I mutilated into "Bar of Soap." He was wearing tight-fitting pantaloons — Elizabethan pantyhose — and striped pantalettes, and reading a book, waiting for somebody to come along and goose him.

The school name was also stamped inside the back cover; and I even discovered it at the top of page 22. Twenty-two was the number of our school building. Several times Bro'Leary had told us: "Boys, the best way to find your books if somebody steals them is to put your name where the thief won't think to find it." He had ordered us to print our full names on a page that matched our birthdays, or the number of the building one lived in, whichever came closest to the center of the book. "A demonic device," I thought I'd heard him call it.

Number 22 also happened to be the day of the month Saint Misericordia, our patron saint, had been martyred for refusing to surrender her teenage virginity to a platoon of Roman legionnaires. Angered by what Bro'Leary had described as her "standfast stance on chastity," the horny foot soldiers had banged her unconscious with their tortoise-shell shields, torn off her "vestal vestments," gang-banged her, and then finished her off with their six-foot spears. All that mess would have been in vain for Miss Misericordia if she hadn't regained consciousness when the last of the foot soldiers was giving it to her, and renounced her parents' paganism. Brother Kotrba in the fifth grade had said, "She expired with Our Lord's name on her lips, boys." Moral: it's never too late to embrace the True Faith; it's never too late to repent; it's never too late to lose your chastity.

"But they weren't done with her yet, boys," Bro'Leary told us three years later. "After Trajan's thugs martyred the poor dame, they tied her to a Roman stallion and dragged her all over the Seven Hills and filthy streets of Rome, the way movie Indians dragged cowboys around in Yuma and Dodge City. Only at least the Indians had the decency to not strip the unfortunate cowboys naked when they pulled their stunt."

But the Roman lechers had done it merely to intimidate and seduce young Christian beauties. And for that — their cruel pagan lechery — God had destroyed their vast, evil empire. He had let the blond *alemánes* from the north inside the great gates of Rome, and they had sacked, looted, burned, pillaged, raped, and plundered the place. Not the Christians: the Christians, being nonviolent and unarmed, and "Catholic," couldn't possibly shed blood themselves. Then, as everyone knew, the bad-and-bold blondies had converted to the True Faith, and everything had ended happily for Christianity. "It was all part of a great, secret scheme, boys. Read St. Augustine." No hurry.

Julius Caesar, I decided, was also part of a great big scheme Bro'Leary, whose wits were slipping, had dreamed up for us between sheets and mattress: He wanted to fail the entire class. For some secret reason he didn't want us to graduate that June. Maybe he *was* queer and didn't want to lose us, his thirty "boys," to the "outside world" or some other planet where he couldn't play First Mate with us. I came to that conclusion halfway through the opening scene of Act I, and I slammed the book shut, for good, I thought, on page 22, where Brutus the butterfly tells his simple-minded "gentle" wife not to kneel, and she says:

I should not need, if you were gentle, Brutus. . . .

There was a spelling error there: "need" should have been "kneel," and the rest of it was antique crap. "Kneel not, gentle Portia," my foot! If I ever saw Mami kneeling for a favor from Papi — she'd never do that, but just suppose — I'd denounce them both in straight language, right on the spot, and walk out of the house. The boathouse in the black and Puerto Rican section of Central Park was better than a house where that kind of shit took place. And that wasn't all. There was also the big faggot talk and the big Roman vocabulary: words like *Lupercal, appertain, suburbs, harlot, plebeians, betimes, carrion, cautelous, cognizance, countenance, Erebus,* and a quarter-million others just as bad. The only English dictionary in our house was my brother Tego's "technical" one, and he didn't like me "playing" with it; he kept it locked up in a cardboard closet Papi had bought him for his graduation from Saint Misericordia's. But a dictionary could only mess up even more my Christmas vacation. Without having to calculate (I wasn't much good at that either), I concluded that it would take me a full year, from Christmas to Christmas, to look up all those Old World words that nobody in my neighborhood had any use for. Besides, what good was a dictionary for things like "But, as it were, in sort of limitation, to keep up with you at meals"? Aside from correcting the grammatical mistake (as it *was,* or *is,* not *were!* I thought), there was nothing I could do with this — no sense to the nonsense.

If this was good English, it was going against the "straightforward English" Bro'Leary and the other ACBs and nuns had been encouraging, ordering us to use for years. I could also forget about "mastering" my adopted language, what Papi, with good intentions, had been telling me and Tego to do for our own good, our "futures." But had he ever tried reading this syrupy garbage? I preferred to stick to the blunt, no-shit English I traded with my friends on the block, and to my shrinking Spanish, which Saint Misery's was helping me lose fast for good.

Back in my bedroom, furious with the *Caesar* assignment, and the crackpot who'd assigned it, I hurled the bald-headed, pagan Romans against the wall and watched them topple spread-eagled behind the bed. They were going to spend the rest of my Christmas vacation there, too, gathering dust motes, feeding roaches, and sucking up dank and biting vapors till putrefaction set in. I wasn't going to read another line, screw the coming quiz and Bro'Leary's threats and fits of foam.

A couple of days later, though, Mami was sweeping under the bed and found the green "Bar of Soap." She held it under my nose.

"What's this, Santos?"

"A green book."

"It's yours, isn't it?"

It couldn't have been Tego's; he was attending Chelsea Vocational High School and learning a useful trade, not wasting his time on fat Romans in drag. I nodded, though, to keep her calm. "I don't know how it got there, Mami."

"*Pues,* and who do you think is going to pay for it if it gets lost or broken?"

"Papi. I forgot."

I tried to walk around her; the subject wasn't worth going into, especially since she had rescued Caesar and his hoods from the limbo I'd dispatched them to, and saved Papi a dollar and change. She accused me of being disrespectful to books; she didn't care whose books they were, mine, the school's, or the street-corner shoeshine man's. Books, she said, turning eloquent, were so important for so many things that —

"That what, Mami?"

"You know what. I don't have to tell you."

"But I don't know, Mami."

"Don't play dumb with me, *malagradecido*."

I didn't know. I knew some books, like Tego's radio-TV manual, were good for jobs, money, and girls, but this green book she had rescued from dust and roaches who could use a nibble now and then — what good was this Bird of Soap except as an excuse for poet-crazy lunatics like Bro'Leary to lord it over us with quizzes, grade averages, and threats? If they didn't tell me, why should I take their word for it?

"When," she asked me, "do you think you'll start doing your Christmas homework?"

"I still have time. There's four days left."

"That's nothing, *bobo*. Start now."

She and Papi had a conspiracy to keep me and Tego off the "dangerous" streets. Tego and I thought the streets were more like playgrounds where you learned all kinds of useful things, from sports to sex. You could get hurt down there now and then, but that was true of all playgrounds and gyms. In our church, one of the neighborhood's all-around athletes had slipped one Sunday and sprained his ankle on his way to receiving the Eucharist. When The Almighty had it in for you, He didn't care where you were hiding; He'd get your ankle indoors or out.

But Mami and Papi disagreed, and our homework, homework, homework, was their trump pretext. They had solid-ranks backing from the ACBs, Sisters of Misery, and Holy Mother Church —all the way back to the New Testament, where, in my confused head, Mary had taken her only begotten Kid to task for farting around with a bunch of bearded old men in their smelly clubhouse. He should have been home learning a useful trade with his flesh-and-blood old man, Joe the Carpenter. Instead He had come on like a wise-ass punk, telling her He was doing His other Old Man's work. For embarrassing her in public, she should have snatched a whip and laid it on His calves and ankles. But He might sic the Holy Ghost on her. That was some fix she was in. Fanatics like her Son would have read *Julius Caesar* front and back once a day for two weeks in preparation for the Big Post–Christmas Quiz.

While I was off stabbing the New Testament, she was busy telling me that she knew the powers of Saint Misery's always gave out extra homework for the holy days (especially Christmas), that she was sure this one was no exception, and that four days of steady studying would just about suffice for me to squeeze in all the work I had to do for *el* Brother. *"Inmediatamente, oyes?"*

I heard her all right, but I didn't heed. I shut the bedroom door, put *Caesar* to sleep inside Tego's tiny desk, and dropped onto the bed for a long snooze. Then it was Tego's turn to start in on me. He came inside the room, shook me awake, and said, "Get your ass off of my side of the bed, Santos."

I put my head where my outstretched feet had been and said, "That's bad English," as a way of retaliating.

"What's bad English?"

"Off of."

He ignored me and picked up the green book. "What's this shit?"

"My homework. Wanna read it?"

"That's what I came in here for, Santos."

"No, it's not. You came in here to make me miserable."

"Who's this Shakes Pear?"

"A faggot. He wrote strategies."

He flipped through the book, blinked, shut it, and threw it at my feet. "Mami told me to come in here and make sure you was studying."

"I been studying. Four hours."

"Well, you ain't studying now. She said to wake you up."

"So mind your business."

"It is my business. I'm your brother. And just watch yourself."

"Why don't *you* study?"

"I studied already. Two days ago."

"Yeah, down on the stoop. Stud poker."

"Watch your mouth, Santos."

"Wash yours." I liked to practice puns on him.

"You got a bunch of lousy grades last time. Remember what Papi said." Papi had threatened me with a month's worth of house arrest if I didn't start acting like a true scholar, instead of like someone who was going to spend his life opening doors and walking dogs for rich slobs.

"It's my ass, Tego. Whatchu worried about?"

"I tole you. I'm your brother."

"You don't act like it." The real reason, I was sure, was that he had it in for me because I'd attacked one of his friends with a broken bottle two weeks back. His one-eyed friend had snatched a basketball away from me and one of my friends so he could play with his own boys. I had succeeded only in slashing the back of his leather jacket with the bottle, when Tego came along and pounced on me. It had taken him a while to convince his buddy that I was crazy and didn't know what the hell I was doing. He used that line whenever I got into trouble and he felt forced to defend me. But he had it in for me for making his life hard, "for giving me the nightmares, Santos."

"Listen, Santos, don't do like me, man. I made a big mistake not working harder when I was in Saint Miseria's. I wouldn't be in the dump I'm in now."

He had failed the entrance exams to five Catholic high schools, and Papi hadn't talked to him for a week.

"What the hell's wrong with that dump?"

"It sucks. I ain't learning a goddam thing. TV-radio's not a real trade, anyway."

"I'll trade places with you."

"Bowlshit."

"Go somewheres else, then."

He couldn't go somewhere else. He was out of their districts. And no parochial school would touch him; he was outside their pale, damned, deported.

"And I still can't put a radio together," he went on. "All I do is get my hands dirty with crap."

"So maybe you're stupid."

"Yeah, Santos, me and you got some things in common. Just remember what Mami said to tell you."

"I'm too stupid to remember, you slob!" I yelled, jumping to my feet. He slammed the door instead of me.

I could do without that kind of pressure; there was something mean and phony in it. Secretly I wanted to enter a vocational high school after Saint Misery's signed me out, but I was afraid to come out and confess it to anyone, except Virgilio. It was bad enough that Tego had failed to "make it" to a priests-and-brothers school. Two failures in a row in our family could lead to a Malánguez tragedy: Papi might leave us, vanish out of our lives with his shamed head drooping like a sunflower on a trampled stem. Mami might take an old idle threat seriously for once and fly back to Puerto Rico, leaving me and Tego, who could take care of himself by himself, back in New York. All that because one overambitious teacher had shot his arrow over his students' heads and assigned us Caesar's assassination for Christmas. Some Christmas. Some teacher.

So once again I sat down to *Don Julio César and the Mariposas,* as I nicknamed them the second time around. This time I read as slowly as if the tyrant himself had ordered me to under pain of swallowing fire or a twelve-ounce can of Papi's rat poison. My knowledge of Spanish helped me out with a lot of Spanish-sounding words, but most of what I read was like Cicero's "Greek" to Casca; and like "Don Cascabel," I didn't see anything to smile about. I also made a half-assed attempt to commit a few of the big speeches to memory — "key speeches," Bro'Leary had called them, and he had written down the "key acts," "key scenes," and "key lines" on the board, which meant we'd have no excuse for not getting them right on his colossal quiz. I memorized a few lines of Brutus's and Antony's funeral speeches, then forgot them quickly, all but the first line of Antony's big ears speech. Maybe it was because I kept thinking that people who talked like that didn't even know how to screw.

Then I got tired of the "honourable man" gibberish and went back to bed. I'd done as much as I could with nothing. And I pitied myself to sleep. I was the kind of student my seventh-grade brother, looking for a witty put-down label, had called a member of the "Limbo Gang," the middle state. Not even "middle"; "middle" was Purgatory, a temporary burn. Limbo was nothing, and I adjusted my ambitions to nothing, *nada, mierda,* the lavatory. "The best thing about that state," my seventh-grade teacher went on, patting his cinctured paunch, "is that most people belong to it. So at least it's not a lonely situation; it's just dull is all." Bro'Leary had never discussed his philosophy of the middle state — oratory unnerved him — but since he was one of them, even if he was an oddball, I assumed he shared those feelings about people like me. They were all in on it: honorable, venerable, chaste men and women.

The day after the Christmas break Bro'Leary hit us with a test that he must have spent two weeks hatching under his blanket:

> *Part I (30 pts.): Identify fifteen (15) of the ff. characters in one or two sentences (and keep it simple!):*
>
> 1. M. Aemilius Lepidus (hint: triumph-man)
> 2. Popilius Lena and Soothsayer (counts as one)
> 3. Trebonius
> 4. Caius Ligarius
> 5. Metellus Cimber
> 6. Flavius and Marullus (counts as one)
> 7. Cinna the senator
>   (Hint for the last four: their own mothers wouldn't trust them)
> 8. The other Cinna (hint: mistaken identity can be fatal)
> 9. Artemidorus (hint: "The mighty gods defend thee! Thy lover . . .")
> 10. Lucilius
> 11. Titinius
> 12. Messala
> 13. Volumnius
>   (Hint for the last four: Tell me who your friends are, and I'll tell you who you are.)

14. Varro, Clitus, Claudious, Straito, Luscious, Dardaneous (counts as one. Hint: Brutus was full of them.)
15. Pindarious (hint: Cassius was poorer than Brutus)
16. Caliphurnia (hint: every great man has a great dame behind him)
17. Portia (hint: "Knell not, gentle Portia.")
    Nota Bene: Try not to get these mixed up. I know they all sound alike, but that's no excuse.)

Part II — short essay (70 pts.). Answer nine (9) fully: (and try to keep it down to one or two paragraphs, you haven't got all day for this):

18. Why does Cassious want Brutus to pluck Casca's sleeve? How is *pluck* used here? For example, would Brutus *pluck* a chicken the same way?
19. Why does Caesar only want fat types around him? (Is he on a diet?)
20. Why does Caesar tell Caliphurnia to block off Antony "when he doth run his course"? What course? Ex.: a full-course meal? a race track? an English course?
21. Why does Caesar say *"Et tu, Brutes"*? Are they a bunch of fatheads, or what? (Note: this was explained in a footnote on p. 46, but don't open your books up during the exam. It's too late.)
22. a. Why does Mark Antony say to the Plaeibians that all he wants to do up there is bury Caesar? Does he really mean it, or is he just playing a trick on their ignorance?
    b. Why does he keep calling Brutus and the other thugs honorable men? Be careful with this, it's tricky.
23. Explain the terms of Caesar's will. For ex., how much does he leave to the Playbeans? Is this generous or cheap, considering all he must have owned. (Remember: in those days when you won a battle, you ransacked and looted the enemy's towns and villages and kept everything for yourself. It was Christianity that changed all this barbarism.)
24. Name at least five (5) examples of Pagan superstition in the play, and explain what makes them Pagan. (Note: don't say it was because these characters weren't Christians. I *know* that.)
25. Father Stanislaus O'MacMahon, a very renowned and respected Jesuit scholar, once wrote that this play we're dealing with illustrates the unquestionable fact that ". . . in Pagan times, especially among the Romans who collitis with Christianity, friendships — and there were very few exceptions

— were as slimy and slippery as a school of eels in the River Liffey . . ." and that this is a very crucial difference between the Pagan Romans and the Christian Catholics. If you agree with this statement, take a stand pro-and-con and explain your position But you haven't got all morning.

26. Could this tragedy have taken place in a Catholic country? E.G., Ireland? Italy? Porto Rico? Poland? Why not?
27. If for the sake of argument the play *had* been possible in a Catholic country like the ones above (but you can pick your own country if you like), how would Mother Church have reacted to Caesar's murder?
28. If Brutus and Cassious had been Catholics, would they have been buried in consecrated ground with full (or partial) rites? How about Brutus' wife and Caesar?
29. This and the next one are for extra credit, but don't rush the other questions just to get to these two. Is there anything strange about a) the clock going off when Brutus and his fellow hoodlums are plotting to knife Caesar in the back? b) about Cassius and his hired killers coming to Bruteses' house in the middle of the night with "their *hats pluck'd* about their ears / And half their faces buried in their *cloaks* . . ."? (II,i,191 and II,i,73–74: keep your books *closed* at all times) (Hint: my italics.) (Note how the word *pluck'd* is used this time. Could these be feather hats he's talking about? *Who?* if you remember.)
30. This is another clock question. Compare the striking of the clock in (II,i,191) with the crowing of the cock in a very famous scene that takes place in the New Testament. (Mt. 26:57–58, 69–75; Mk. 14:53–54, 66–72; Lk. 22:31–34; Jn. 18:12–18, 25–27)
31. What do the two scenes and their chief protagonists have in common? Is the second one a *tragedy?* (We talked about this in class.)

Final Note: Don't rush this. Double-check all answers. Points will be taken off for bad grammar, bad spelling, and bad punctuation, also for slopy handwritting. You have 2½ hours. Good luck.)

Before letting us start, he warned us about looking around during the quiz, and about making funny noises which could be "secret answer signals." Same for gestures of hands, face, and feet. Even the throat: "Don't start a fit of coughing or blowing your noses. This room is well-heated. If you have a cold or hoarse throat, go sit in the stern." About ten guys got up at this point and shuffled off to the back seats, faking a fit of coughs. He let them. "But seat two sits apart. I don't want any fishy business back there." Then he read every question out loud to us, correcting what he called a couple of "typos" as he went along, and then finally asking if we had any questions before he looked at his watch and brought his right hand down as a starting signal. Sudano raised his fat hand, but Bro'Leary didn't let him open his mouth. "Just sit still, Sudano. I'll handle your question in private." The rest of us were too nervous and confused to come up with intelligent questions.

In the seat behind me, Virgilio began acting up. "This is the worstest *mamotreto* I ever seen in my whole life, man! This focken four-hand wallball bastard is crazy! I can't do this shit! Take a look at Number twenty-three, Santos. What the hell is this shit? What's a 'Playbean,' man? Some kinda jelly bean? Eh? Tell me, man!"

I shook my head quickly while Bro'Leary was bent over Sudano's desk, shaking his own head and shutting his eyes for patience.

"Don't shake your head, man, just tell me! Fuck that Four-Hands."

"It's the mob," I whispered, cupping my mouth and twisting my face in his direction.

"The what?"

"The people, you dumb fuck!"

"It don't look like no people to me, Santos. It says 'playbeans'; you blind?"

"He misspelled it," I hissed, just as Bro'Leary's head shot up like a mammoth porcupine sensing danger.

"Who's talking?"

A startled pause, then:

First Student: "Not me, Brother."

Second Student: "Me neither, Brother."

Third Student: "Me too, Brother."

Fourth Student: "I didn't say a thing, Brother."

Fifth Student: "Me neither, Brother."

Me: "Me two, Brother."

Virgilio: "Me three, Brother."

Bro'Leary: "All right, shut up and start writing or I'll tear up your papers, all-a youse!"

But Virgilio wasn't done with his whining. A minute later, while I was still trying to make out the hint for M. Aemilius Lepidus, he began fuming comments at the back of my neck: "Mother hopper! Did you look at Number twenty-five already? What's that, a mountain cleef or something? Who's that Father O'Mojón? What the hell's an 'ells in the River Leafy'?" I jerked my head once to shut him up, but he was out of control. "I'm gonna quit this school before this fock kills me, mother hopper. Who's Number One, Santos? Some kind of leopard? Emilio the Leopard. Some focken faggot. They're all faggots. Brother Four-Hands is the biggest *maricón* in this city. Right?"

I ignored him. There was no time to listen to his whining. If I got caught looking as if I was listening to him, Bro'Leary would stomp up to us and tear up our papers. He'd ball them up and play foul-shots with the wastebasket. He'd done just that to cheaters' papers on other tests. I didn't like this test any more than Virgilio, but I didn't want to fail it either. It was bad enough that there was still another semester left us at Saint Misery's.

Virgilio finally cooled off. I figured that, like me, he hadn't finished the play, if he even got beyond the Bird of Soap's portrait. So I wasn't surprised that his pencil wasn't making the labored scratching sounds I was used to hearing whenever Bro'Leary set us to scribbling. In spite of his whining that the work was too hard for someone like him who'd only been in the city two years, he was a hard worker and had inched his way up to the Limbo state. In math he was my better, and helped me out with that part of the homework in exchange for my help with his English grammar and hopeless English spelling. English was his big weakness, and like Papi, and me for that matter, he took it as a tenet that nothing else was any good — no subject, no vocation, no romance, no marriage, and no future — if your English was inferior or even deficient.

I think Bro'Leary believed that too: he was always fishing for the right words (and the more he fished, the more meager his catches), the right grammar and punctuation, the correct pronunciation. And, though as a rule he avoided embarrassing his students in public, he wouldn't hesitate to correct their English errors openly. Some flaws, he felt, should be pointed out and squashed in the open. And of those, English errors were second only to religious ones. It was for our own good, he said. We didn't always doubt it, but liking all this finicky English finesse was something else.

Virgilio started snoring behind me, so loudly that I thought it was coming out of my ears. I woke him up with a cough, which drew Bro'Leary's attention and an apology from my eyes. Virgilio started, and gave off a grunt that distracted others around us. They were probably looking for distractions; maybe Bro'Leary was, too.

"Whatsa matter, Silver?" he asked.

Virgilio began an answer: "Nothing, Bro —"

And Bro'Leary cut him off: "Don't talk in class."

Virgilio let out a fat sigh and began tapping the back of my desk with his pencil. I stretched my leg behind me and kicked his foot. He told me to go fuck myself, and I thought, I'll get you later for that, you lame. A minute later he was snoring again, and this time I let him. Hell with him. In no time Bro'Leary was breathing down on him.

"Whatsa matter, Silver? Staying up late on your vacation?"

"Yeah, Brother," Virgilio began, without any conviction, "I had to take my little brother to the 'mergency clinic last night. I was up till four amen."

"Since when do you have a little brother?" Bro'Leary asked. They knew all about our family backgrounds in that school.

"He's an adopted brother, Brother. His father and mother died in a fire."

"Let me see your paper."

Virgilio handed it to him silently. Brother handled it for a few seconds; he seemed to be turning it back and forth from Side A to Side B, and was breathing hot and hotter on it, and on my head. "There's nothing here," he said finally.

"I know, Brother. My mind is in a very big blank this morning."

"Your mind's always in a big blank, Silver. You think you're gonna get out of this school with a Zero in all your papers?"

"I want to be excuséd, Brother. I think I am not too preparéd."

A long pause full of heavy breathing from the two antagonists. And in no time everyone in that stuffy classroom was expelling heavy breath and sucking in what little oxygen remained. Virgilio had some qualities I envied, although I never told him as much, and tried not to show it; open admiration for someone your own age, especially a friend, was a flaw and could earn you a punk's reputation. His lack of finesse was one of the traits I liked. He didn't like the *Caesar* exam, and he was saying as much to the toughest man in that school — outside of Principal Moriarty, Old Testicles himself.

At that moment nobody else in the class even had the nerve to ask permission for a quick trip to the john. Virgilio was asking to be excused from the entire quiz, which the look on his face just then must have been describing as pure crap, or as a trap Bro'Leary had set to turn us all into little fags. And Bro'Leary must have understood his feelings just then, because all he said was, "Go ahead, then, Silver. Leave the room. Give me your paper. I'll see you at one." Virgilio picked himself up, swiped my shoulder, and marched out. Nobody looked up from *Julius Caesar*. Bro'Leary lumbered back to his desk and sat there silently throughout the rest of the quiz, except to let us know every fifteen minutes how much time we had left. Whenever I looked up momentarily from my paper, I spotted him staring at his hairy wrists and big knuckles, as if he'd never really noticed them before. When our time was up, he collected our quizzes in low whispers. Before letting us go he wished us one and all a good hot lunch.

I wasn't surprised to find Virgilio's cafeteria spot empty that afternoon. I knew he'd go around foraging for empty soda and beer bottles in backyards and alleys and exchanging them for movie and lunch money. He could take care of himself, but I was afraid he might take Brother's *Caesar* threats seriously and disappear from Saint Misery's. The other students spent the lunch hour grumbling about Bro'Leary's "lunatic quiz" and swearing to their mothers, their God, and their interred loved ones that they'd flunked it, "and fuckit." I didn't like discussing my failures, so I stuffed my mouth with baked beans and bread, and refused to join the diatribes.

Virgilio didn't come back that afternoon, and Bro'Leary didn't mention his absence or the *Caesar* test. He stuck strictly to religion and the other afternoon topics.

Virgilio showed up at Mass next morning, grinning, and five minutes late. (Bro'Leary didn't write his name down in his church-attendance pad.) In our class's last pew, where we always sat, he told me during the *Introibo ad altare* that he had spent his hooky afternoon in the Third Avenue Eagle, a three-feature flick frequented by truants, that he had sat through two "boss" flicks — *Key Largo* and "Alan Ladd" — and slept through the third, "some chit with Fred Stair and that dame he chove around the balls room."

During the *Introit* he wanted to know how come I hadn't walked out with him in the middle of the test. I didn't answer that one; it was none of his business.

"The Big Hulk."

"Who?"

"Four-Hands."

"He ain't that bad. He gets carried away is all."

"He always fucking up."

"He ain't the only one, Virgilio. You didn't even read the play."

"I could not figure it."

In class an hour later Bro'Leary, in a sour, lip-biting mood, read out the test results. Virgilio got his expected Zero, no comment; I received a 50, twenty points short of a D; Sudano scored a 58, Saccaffidi a 64, and Díez the genius a 69, one point short of D. Bro'Leary, lumbering back and forth between his desk and the closed classroom door, chewed us out for fifteen minutes.

"I gave youse guys two weeks to bone up on that test, so don't come crying to me when you fail the Diocesans. Overall, thisn't the most brilliant class I ever taught, but even so" — foam began bubbling from his mouth — "this is a total disgrace even for a bunch of fatheads. What were youse guys doing for the holy days — wasting your mothers' money in that cheap movie house out on Third Avenue?" Most of us went to the Star on Lexington, where the price was cheaper and you didn't have to double up, two to a seat, on crowded afternoons. "Youse don't have to graduate from this school, you know. This ain't — this isn't public school, where they have to move you up to the next grade. Unnerstand?"

His spit sprayed every student in the first row. Their arms kept shooting up to their faces, as if expecting him to lay them out with chops and uppercuts. It looked as if that was what he had in mind, too: he kept going into a crouch, hands clenched at chest level, quilled head bobbing, and his barely visible feet shuffling in a clumsy flat-footed dance.

He asked us (and we'd better not answer) how in the name of Saint John Bosco ("Apostle of Youth") we expected to do well on, "let alone pass, the real tough entrances to choice schools like Bishop Tully, and Power Memorial and Carnal Hays. Not even a place like Lily of the Valley High's gonna admit a bunch of fathead delinquents like youse, not with those type grades youse got. What you guys think's gonna happen when they hit you with Latin and logger rhythms?" (Pause: heads drooping in disgrace.) "Whatsa matter with youse, anyway? You wanna end up selling those shaved-ice snowballs off the streets like your fath — you guys wanna disgrace me or something? After the way I sacrifice my spare time working up some real good litrachur and other useful stuff into your heads! Youse know where you're gonna end up?" (Pause.) "Huh? Huh? In *public school*. The buncha youse. That's a promise. And don't come blaming Brother O'Leary." He was close to purple now, close to tears. He should have stayed in the Navy. We kept our eyes fixed on our desks, our hands holding up our heavy heads; every now and then a chorus of coughs broke out.

Before releasing us for lunch, he had two more warnings to foam out: that if our disgrace repeated itself, he was going to write a note to all our parents asking them to come in so he could chew them out for being too easy on us. "And second, I'm gonna hit you blubbers with another tough classic book very soon, just as soon as I get it ordered." "Homer's Old Essay," I thought I heard him call it. "If youse think Shakespeare's tough, wait'll you get a load of this Greek genius, Homer. You're gonna get three quizzes on him, and I dare youse to fail them. Now get out! Go stuff your bellies with hot food."

He waved us off to our hot lunches, reminding us, as we were dragging our feet toward the door, that at one o'clock he was going to quiz us orally on our religion homework. We knew that; it was what he put us through every afternoon.

Down in the green cafeteria, Virgilio told me he was definitely going to a "plumbing school" when he graduated from Saint Misery's. He said he'd rather not go to *any* school than ruin the rest of his school life reading lames like Julius Caesar and Homer the Greek. And that kind of shit, he assured me, was just what we were going to suffer with in "the other high schools that set you up for the lame college." His father and uncle were both plumbers' assistants, which meant he'd be tracking their footsteps, not breaking out on his own and moving beyond papá and tío; but that didn't faze him now. Besides, he swore, he was going to become a real, "good-money" plumber, not a toilet engineer's assistant. "The plommers, they get good *pega,*" he said. "Five bucks an hour. And they don't have to estudy this Chekspier chit."

He wanted to know what I was going to do with myself, where I was going. "I don't know," I said, sulking. "Maybe I'll go to Chelsea Vocational. That's where my brother goes." If I told him the truth, he'd probably call me a "lame punk," which was what I felt like just then.

"You know what I hate with the holy days, Santos?"

"What?"

"They always fock you up."

"Ain't that the truth. And we still got Easter too."

"Let's go steal some chocolate kisses in the Fives and Tens."

Kresge's was out of kisses that afternoon, so we settled for balloons with sand inside them. We snatched about five each. And what we ended up doing with them was, for once, my bright idea: "Let's fill 'em up with water and bomb Bro'Leary with 'em."

"You getting smart, Santos."

Next day we skipped the baked-beans lunch (we skulked out of the cafeteria before a clock alarm went off signaling the official end of chow time), and filled our ten balloons from a leaky hydrant on the corner of Second Avenue. In a plastic shopping bag I'd brought along, we carried our water-and-sand bombs to the roof of a tenement connected to the school building. Then, lying stomachs down on the parapet, we waited for the lunch mob to emerge. Principal Moriarty posted himself at the boys' entrance; Principal Scholastica paced back and forth in front of the girls' entrance, keeping an eye on her underlings, who, along with Moriarty's Brothers, patrolled the sidewalk from Morris' Toys and Stationery to the far end of the Hell Gate Post Office. Bro'Leary, who wasn't sympathetic to patrol duty, parked himself on a car fender and craned his wrestler's neck to kibitz the noontime handball game.

At my signal, we let go the water bombs. The school crowd split and scattered like ants in a downpour. Bro'Leary, confused at first, swiveled his crewcut head in every direction, like a periscope scanning an enemy destroyer. We hurled the other balloons at him and the two principals, who ducked inside the building. But he stood his ground under enemy attack. One balloon splattered inches from his feet; another hit the top of the car he was leaning on and sprayed his face, neck, and chest; a third caught him between the shoulder blades as he turned to retreat. He didn't run or duck or double-time it like the others; he walked off slowly, soaked from head to foot, looking over his shoulder before vanishing inside the school.

At one o'clock he came to class looking as though he'd given in to a childhood impulse and jumped into a shower with his cassock on. His shoes squeaked, but his face and head at least were dry. Usually he sat down at his desk before beginning the first afternoon lesson; this time he stayed on his feet and marched, hands behind his back, from the room door to the window opposite it. Nobody said a thing, not even Virgilio, who usually used words like "bear" and "elerfount" to describe Bro'Leary's back-and-forth rolling gait. I stared at his wet uniform and figured that was nothing for a man who had dived into the Pacific to save a shipmate from sharks, who had spent years floating around in typhoons and tidal waves all over the world's oceans, and who was probably indifferent to umbrellas, galoshes, and raincoats, which he was probably too poor to own anyway. He looked less angry than shaken, shocked by the suspicion that someone, or a group of hooligans, was out to get him, or like those Doomsday Protestants who get baptized in polluted Orchard Beach and come up looking stunned and nauseated after the third dunking. His silent-moving lips seemed to be searching for something to say, but nothing came out. He had to say something on the balloon bombardment, though; he knew we expected him to. At that moment every other Brother and nun in the school must have been disgorging monologues on the souls of heathens and hoodlums who did such immoral things, and maybe pumping their students for clues to the scoundrels' identities.

"I don't know who dropped those things on us," Bro'Leary said finally, in a low voice, "but whoever did is most likely the kind of saps that end up taking drugs and selling numbers. Yeah, that kind." Then, after a long pause during which he eyed me and Virgilio a little too long, I thought, he said, "If any thugs from this school did it, they should transfer out to public school. We don't want their kind here. . . . Anyway, I don't think any boys from this school would pull something like that — do youse?"

We all agreed: "No, Brother!"

"I thought so. This ain't — is not — that kind of reform school. It must have been a bunch of brutes from public school did it." And that was all he said on the balloon incident: no Shakespeare. I didn't think he'd meant a word of it, either.

So we turned our minds and mouths to religion: a long, lifeless discussion of the *Nobis Quoque Peccatoribus* part of the Mass. At five minutes to three, he told us he was going to cross our *Julius Caesar* grades "off of" his grade book. "We're not ready for that stuff yet. Wait till high school."

We weren't ready for "Homer's Old Essay" either, it looked like, because it never arrived. He said Principal Moriarty had canceled the order: too expensive for a school like Saint Misery's.

"*We* canceled the order, Santos," Virgilio told me on the way home. "Me and you."

"Moriarty canceled it."

"Bull. The balloons."

We got a new teacher the following semester, red-faced, heavyset Brother Fish, fresh from Brooklyn. He told us Bro'Leary had been transferred to a high school on the Hudson. "He said he likes it there," said Fish. "He goes fishing every weekend. He said he misses this place, but moving around is part of the Order's rules. You never know where they're going to send you next. Happens all the time, boys."

Maybe, but none of us had ever heard of a brother getting transferred before the end of the school year.

Virgilio: "Maybe they sended him to the crazy house, Santos."

Me: "Nah. They send 'em to monasteries or something when they flip."

Virgilio: "You think he really flip?"

Me: "Him? Nah. He wasn't all that crazy."

Virgilio: "He was better than this big Fish. Fish smell like the Communion bread. Too clean for my taste, Santos."

Me: "Ten times better than Fish. Maybe he went back to the Navy."

Virgilio: "You never can know , but he look to me too old for the ocean. Maybe they lock him up."

Me: "Shut up, man. Jesus!"

Maybe they *had* put him away. Except for Fish, none of the Brothers ever mentioned his whereabouts. And none of us took Fish's word for it. Nobody we knew had ever heard of that high school up the Hudson. Not even, I suspected, Cassian O'Leary, A.C.B. [1982]

Cherríe Moraga, poet, essayist, and playwright, has given a voice to the Latina lesbian experience in the groundbreaking anthology she coedited with Gloria Anzaldúa, *This Bridge Called My Back: Writings by Radical Women of Color* (1981), as well as in her book *Loving in the War Years: lo que nunca pasó por sus labios* (what never passed her lips, 1983). Born in California in 1952, the daughter of a Chicana mother and an Anglo father, Moraga moved from Los Angeles to the San Francisco Bay area in 1977 after completing her studies in English. In San Francisco she participated in a women's writing group and immersed herself in the increasingly political atmosphere of the late 1970s.

This Bridge Called My Back, which consists of stories, poetry, and essays, was Moraga's master's thesis from San Francisco State University. The book helped to define a perspective on feminism that incorporates issues of race, culture, and class as well as those of gender and sexuality. It provided a counterbalance to white Anglo feminist perspectives by bringing together writings by Latina, African-American, Native American, and Asian-American women. Though highly controversial, *This Bridge Called My Back* has won such critical acclaim as the Before Columbus Foundation American Book Award in 1986; it has been translated into Spanish and is frequently assigned in courses in women's studies and Third World studies.

In 1983 Moraga published her collection of essays and poems *Loving in the War Years*. The essay "A Long Line of Vendidas" (sellouts) is an important piece that analyzes the influences of certain cultural myths on the definition of male and female gender roles. One such myth is that of "La Malinche," the Aztec mistress of Mexican conqueror Hernán Cortés, who served as his interpreter and is considered a traitor by the Mexican people. The subservient position of Chicanas vis-à-vis their male counterparts is explored in the essay presented here. Moraga connects the personal to the political in trying to make sense of what it means to be a Chicana woman.

from **Loving in the War Years: lo que nunca pasó por sus labios**

A Long Line of Vendidas

para Gloria Anzaldúa, in gratitude

Sueño: 15 de julio 1982
During the long difficult night that sent my lover and I to separate beds, I dreamed of church and cunt. I put it this way because that is how it came to me. The suffering and the thick musty mysticism of the catholic church fused with the sensation of entering the vagina — like that of a colored woman's — dark, rica, full-bodied. The heavy sensations of complexity. A journey I must unravel, work out for myself.

I long to enter you like a temple.

MY BROTHER'S SEX WAS WHITE. MINE, BROWN

If somebody would have asked me when I was a teenager what it means to be Chicana, I would probably have listed the grievances done me. When my sister and I were fifteen and fourteen, respectively, and my brother a few years older, we were still waiting on him. I write "were" as if now, nearly two decades later, it were over. But that would be a lie. To this day in my mother's home, my brother and father are waited on, including by me. I do this now out of respect for my mother and her wishes. In those early years, however, it was mainly in relation to my brother that I resented providing such service. For unlike my father, who sometimes worked as much as seventy hours a week to feed my face every day, the only thing that earned my brother my servitude was his maleness.

It was Saturday afternoon. My brother, then seventeen-years-old, came into the house with a pile of friends. I remember Fernie, the two Steves, and Roberto. They were hot, sweaty, and exhausted from an afternoon's basketball and plopped themselves down in the front room, my brother demanding, "Girls, bring us something to drink."

"Get it yourself, pig," I thought, but held those words from ever forming inside my mouth. My brother had the disgusting habit on these occasions of collapsing my sister JoAnn's and my name when referring to us as a unit: his sisters. "Cher'ann," he would say. "We're really thirsty." I'm sure it took everything in his power *not* to snap his fingers. But my mother was out in the yard working and to refuse him would have brought her into the house with a scene before these boys' eyes which would have made it impossible for us to show our faces at school that following Monday. We had been through that before.

When my mother had been our age, over forty years earlier, she had waited on her brothers and their friends. And it was no mere lemonade. They'd come in from work or a day's drinking. And las mujeres, often just in from the fields themselves, would already be in the kitchen making tortillas, warming frijoles or pigs feet, albondigas soup, what-have-you. And the men would get a clean white tablecloth and a spread of food laid out before their eyes and not a word of resentment from the women.

The men watched the women — my aunts and mother moving with the grace and speed of girls who were cooking before they could barely see over the top of the stove. Elvira, my mother, knew she was being watched by the men and loved it. Her slim hips moved patiently beneath the apron. Her deep thick-lidded eyes never caught theirs as she was swept back into the kitchen by my abuelita's call of "Elvirita," her brown hands deepening in color as they dropped back into the pan of flour.

~~~
~~~

I suppose my mother imagined that Joe's friends watched us like that, too. But we knew different. We were not blonde or particularly long-legged or "available" because we were "Joe's sisters." This meant no boy could "make" us, which meant no boy would bother asking us out. Roberto, the Guatemalan, was the only one among my brother's friends who seemed at all sensitive to how awkward JoAnn and I felt in our role. He would smile at us nervously, taking the lemonade, feeling embarrassed being waited on by people he considered peers. He knew the anglo girls they visited would never have succumbed to such a task. Roberto was the only recompense.

As I stopped to wait on their yearning throats, "jock itch" was all that came to my mind. Their cocks became animated in my head, for that was all that seemed to arbitrarily set us apart from each other and put me in the position of the servant and they, the served.

I wanted to machine-gun them all down, but swallowed that fantasy as I swallowed making the boy's bed every day, cleaning his room each week, shining his shoes and ironing his shirts before dates with girls, some of whom *I* had crushes on. I would lend him the money I had earned house-cleaning for twelve hours, so he could blow it on one night with a girl because he seldom had enough money because he seldom had a job because there was always some kind of ball practice to go to. As I pressed the bills into his hand, the car honking outside in the driveway, his double-date waiting, I knew I would never see that money again.

Years later, after I began to make political the fact of my being a Chicana, I remember my brother saying to me, "*I've* never felt 'culturally deprived,' " which I guess is the term "white" people use to describe Third World people being denied access to *their* culture. At the time, I wasn't exactly sure what he meant, but I remember in retelling the story to my sister, she responded, "Of course, he didn't. He grew up male in our house. He got the best of both worlds." And yes, I can see now that that's true. *Male in a man's world. Light-skinned in a white world. Why change?*

The pull to identify with the oppressor was never as great in me as it was in my brother. For unlike him, I could never have *become* the white man, only the white man's *woman*.

The first time I began to recognize clearly my alliances on the basis of race and sex was when my mother was in the hospital, extremely ill. I was eight years old. During my mother's stay in the hospital, my tía Eva took my sister and me into her care; my brother stayed with my abuela; and my father stayed by himself in our home. During this time, my father came to visit me and my sister only once. (I don't know if he ever visited my brother.) The strange thing was I didn't really miss his visits, although I sometimes fantasized some imaginary father, dark and benevolent, who might come and remind us that we still *were* a family.

I have always had a talent for seeing things I don't particularly want to see and the one day my father did come to visit us with his wife/our mother physically dying in a hospital some ten miles away, I saw that he couldn't love us — not in the way we so desperately needed. I saw that he didn't know how and he came into my tía's house like a large lumbering child — awkward and embarrassed out of his league — trying to play a parent when he needed our mother back as much as we did just to keep him eating and protected. I hated and pitied him that day. I knew how he was letting us all down, visiting my mother daily, like a dead man, unable to say, "The children, honey, I held them. They love you. They think of you." Giving my mother *something.*

Years later, my mother spoke of his visits to the hospital. How from behind the bars of her bed and through the tubes in her nose, she watched this timid man come and go daily — going through the "motions" of being a husband. "I knew I had to live," she told us. "I knew he could never take care of you."

In contrast to the seeming lack of feeling I held for my father, my longings for my mother and fear of her dying were the most passionate feelings that had ever lived inside my young heart.

We are riding the elevator. My sister and I pressed up against one wall, holding hands. After months of separation, we are going to visit my mamá in the hospital. Mi tía me dice, "Whatever you do, no llores Cherríe. It's too hard on your mother when you cry." I nod, taking long deep breaths, trying to control my quivering lip.

As we travel up floor by floor, all I can think about is not crying, breathing, holding my breath. "¿Me prometes?" she asks. I nod again, afraid to speak, fearing my voice will crack into tears. My sister's nervous hand around mine, sweating too. We are going to see my mamá, mamá, after so long. She didn't die after all. She didn't die.

The elevator doors open. We walk down the corridor, my heart pounding. My eyes are darting in and out of each room as we pass them, fearing/anticipating my mamá's face. Then as we turn around the corner into a kind of lobby, I hear my tía say to an older woman — skin and bones. An Indian, *I think, straight black and grey hair pulled back. I hear my tía say, "Elvira."*

I don't recognize her. This is not the woman I knew, so round and made-up with her hair always a wavy jet black! I stay back until she opens her arms to me — this strange and familiar woman — her voice hoarse, "¡Ay mi'jita!" Instinctively, I run into her arms, still holding back my insides — "Don't cry. Don't cry." I remember. "Whatever you do, no llores." But my tía had not warned me about the smell, the unmistakable smell of the woman, mi mamá — el olor de aceite y jabón and comfort and home. "Mi mamá." And when I catch the smell I am lost in tears, deep long tears that come when you have held your breath for centuries.

There was something I knew at that eight-year-old moment that I vowed never to forget — the smell of a woman who is life and home to me at once. The woman in whose arms I am uplifted, sustained. Since then, it is as if I have spent the rest of my years driven by this scent toward la mujer.

when her india makes love
it is with the greatest reverence
to color, texture, smell

by now she knew the scent of earth
could call it up
even between the cracks
in sidewalks
steaming dry
from midday summer
rain

With this knowledge so deeply emblazed upon my heart, how then was I supposed to turn away from La Madre, La Chicana? If I were to build my womanhood on this self-evident truth, it is the love of the Chicana, the love of myself as a Chicana I had to embrace, no white man. Maybe this ultimately was the cutting difference between my brother and me. To be a woman fully necessitated my claiming the race of my mother. My brother's sex was white. Mine, brown. [1983]

Loving in the War Years

Loving you is like living
in the war years.
I *do* think of Bogart & Bergman
not clear who's who
but still singin a long smoky
mood into the piano bar
drinks straight up
the last bottle in the house
while bombs split
outside, a broken
world.

A world war going on
but you and I still insisting
in each our own heads
still thinkin how
if I could only make some contact
with that woman across the keyboard
we size each other up
    yes . . .

Loving you has this kind of desperation
to it, like do or die, I
having eyed you from the first
time you made the decision to move
from your stool
to live dangerously.

All on the hunch
that in our exchange of photos
of old girlfriends, names
of cities and memories
back in the states
the fronts we've manned
out here on the continent
all this on the hunch
that *this* time there'll be
no need for resistance.

Loving in the war years
calls for this kind of risking
without a home to call our own
I've got to take you as you come
to me, each time like a stranger
all over again. Not knowing
what deaths you saw today
I've got to take you
as you come, battle bruised
refusing our enemy, fear.

We're all we've got. You and I

maintaining
this war time morality
where being queer
and female is as rude
as we can get. [1983]

Helena María Viramontes was born in East Los Angeles in 1954, one of a family of nine children. She received a B.A. in English literature from Immaculate Heart College in 1975. She currently lives in Ithaca, New York. Viramontes published her first collection of fiction, *The Moths and Other Stories,* in 1985; in 1995 she published her first novel, *Under the Feet of Jesus*. Also a literary critic, Viramontes coedited an issue of the journal *The Americas Review* with María Herrera-Sobek titled *Chicana Creativity and Criticism: Charting New Frontiers in American Literature* (1987).

In many works of Chicana narrative the voices are those of young girls; *The Moths* contains powerful stories that focus on girls and women and attack the patriarchal values that pervade Latino culture. The title story, one of the most anthologized pieces of prose fiction by a Chicana author, mixes realist and magic realist styles, developing the secret, sacred connection between a dying grandmother and the impressionable young woman in opposition to male dominance.

The Moths

I was fourteen years old when Abuelita requested my help. And it seemed only fair. Abuelita had pulled me through the rages of scarlet fever by placing, removing, and replacing potato slices on my temples; she had seen me through several whippings, an arm broken by a dare jump off Tío Enrique's toolshed, puberty, and my first lie. Really, I told Amá, it was only fair.

Not that I was her favorite granddaughter or anything special. I wasn't even pretty or nice like my older sisters and I just couldn't do the girl things they could do. My hands were too big to handle the fineries of crocheting or embroidery and I always pricked my fingers or knotted my colored threads time and time again while my sisters laughed and called me Bull Hands with their cute water-like voices. So I began keeping a piece of jagged brick in my sock to bash my sisters or anyone who called me Bull Hands. Once, while we all sat in the bedroom, I hit Teresa on the forehead, right above her eyebrow, and she ran to Amá with her mouth open, her hand over her eye while blood seeped between her fingers. I was used to the whippings by then.

I wasn't respectful either. I even went so far as to doubt the power of Abuelita's slices, the slices she said absorbed my fever. "You're still alive, aren't you?" Abuelita snapped back, her pasty gray eye beaming at me and burning holes in my suspicions. Regretful that I had let secret questions drop out of my mouth, I couldn't look into her eyes. My hands began to fan out, grow like a liar's nose until they hung by my side like low weights. Abuelita made a balm out of dried moth wings and Vicks and rubbed my hands, shaped them back to size, and it was the strangest feeling. Like bones melting. Like sun shining through the darkness of your eyelids. I didn't mind helping Abuelita after that, so Amá would always send me over to her.

In the early afternoon Amá would push her hair back, hand me my sweater and shoes, and tell me to go to Mama Luna's. This was to avoid another fight and another whipping, I knew. I would deliver one last direct shot on Marisela's arm and jump out of our house, the slam of the screen door burying her cries of anger, and I'd gladly go help Abuelita plant her wild lilies or jasmine or heliotrope or cilantro or hierbabuena in red Hills Brothers coffee cans. Abuelita would wait for me at the top step of her porch, holding a hammer and nail and empty coffee cans. And although we hardly spoke, hardly looked at each other as we worked over root transplants, I always felt her gray eye on me. It made me feel, in a strange sort of way, safe and guarded and not alone. Like God was supposed to make you feel.

On Abuelita's porch, I would puncture holes in the bottom of the coffee cans with a nail and a precise hit of a hammer. This completed, my job was to fill them with red clay mud from beneath her rosebushes, packing it softly, then making a perfect hole, four fingers round, to nest a sprouting avocado pit, or the spidery sweet potatoes that Abuelita rooted in mayonnaise jars with toothpicks and daily water, or prickly chayotes that produced vines that twisted and wound all over her porch pillars, crawling to the roof, up and over the roof, and down the other side, making her small brick house look like it was cradled within the vines that grew pear-shaped squashes ready for the pick, ready to be steamed with onions and cheese and butter. The roots would burst out of the rusted coffee cans and search for a place to connect. I would then feed the seedlings with water.

But this was a different kind of help, Amá said, because Abuelita was dying. Looking into her gray eye, then into her brown one, the doctor said it was just a matter of days. And so it seemed only fair that these hands she had melted and formed found use in rubbing her caving body with alcohol and marijuana, rubbing her arms and legs, turning her face to the window so that she could watch the bird of paradise blooming or smell the scent of clove in the air. I toweled her face frequently and held her hand for hours. Her gray wiry hair hung over the mattress. For as long as I could remember, she'd kept her long hair in braids. Her mouth was vacant, and when she slept her eyelids never closed all the way. Up close, you could see her gray eye beaming out the window, staring hard as if to remember everything. I never kissed her. I left the window open when I went to the market.

Across the street from Jay's Market there was a chapel. I never knew its denomination, but I went in just the same to search for candles. There were none, so I sat down on one of the pews. After I cleaned my fingernails, I looked up at the high ceiling. I had forgotten the vastness of these places, the coolness of the marble pillars and the frozen statues with blank eyes. I was alone. I knew why I had never returned.

That was one of Apá's biggest complaints. He would pound his hands on the table, rocking the sugar dish or spilling a cup of coffee, and scream that if I didn't go to mass every Sunday to save my goddamn sinning soul, then I had no reason to go out of the house, period. *Punto final.* He would grab my arm and dig his nails into me to make sure I understood the importance of catechism. Did he make himself clear? Then he strategically directed his anger at Amá for her lousy ways of bringing up daughters, being disrespectful and unbelieving, and my older sisters would pull me aside and tell me if I didn't get to mass right this minute, they were all going to kick the holy shit out of me. Why am I so selfish? Can't you see what it's doing to Amá, you idiot? So I would wash my feet and stuff them in my black Easter shoes that shone with Vaseline, grab a missal and veil, and wave goodbye to Amá.

I would walk slowly down Lorena to First to Evergreen, counting the cracks on the cement. On Evergreen I would turn left and walk to Abuelita's. I liked her porch because it was shielded by the vines of the chayotes and I could get a good look at the people and car traffic on Evergreen without them knowing. I would jump up the porch steps, knock on the screen door as I wiped my feet, and call, Abuelita? Mi Abuelita? As I opened the door and stuck my head in, I would catch the gagging scent of toasting chile on the *placa*. When I entered the *sala*, she would greet me from the kitchen, wringing her hands in her apron. I'd sit at the corner of the table to keep from being in her way. The chiles made my eyes water. Am I crying? No, Mama Luna, I'm sure not crying. I don't like going to mass, but my eyes watered anyway, the tears dropping on the tablecloth like candle wax. Abuelita lifted the burnt chiles from the fire and sprinkled water on them until the skins began to separate. Placing them in front of me, she turned to check the menudo. I peeled the skins off and put the flimsy, limp-looking green and yellow chiles in the *molcajete* and began to crush and crush and twist and crush the heart out of the tomato, the clove of garlic, the stupid chiles that made me cry, crushed them until they turned into liquid under my bull hand. With a wooden spoon, I scraped hard to destroy the guilt, and my tears were gone. I put the bowl of chile next to a vase filled with freshly cut roses. Abuelita touched my hand and pointed to the bowl of menudo that steamed in front of me. I spooned some chile into the menudo and rolled a corn tortilla thin with the palms of my hands. As I ate, a fine Sunday breeze entered the kitchen and a rose petal calmly feathered down to the table.

I left the chapel without blessing myself and walked to Jay's. Most of the time Jay didn't have much of anything. The tomatoes were always soft and the cans of Campbell soup had rust spots on them. There was dust on the tops of cereal boxes. I picked up what I needed: rubbing alcohol, five cans of chicken broth, a big bottle of Pine Sol. At first Jay got mad because I thought I had forgotten the money. But it was there all the time, in my back pocket.

When I returned from the market, I heard Amá crying in Abuelita's kitchen. She looked up at me with puffy eyes. I placed the bags of groceries on the table and began putting the cans of soup away. Amá sobbed quietly. I never kissed her. After a while, I patted her on the back for comfort. Finally: "¿Y mi Amá?" she asked in a whisper, then choked again and cried into her apron.

Abuelita fell off the bed twice yesterday, I said, knowing that I shouldn't have said it and wondering why I wanted to say it because it only made Amá cry harder. I guess I became angry and just so tired of the quarrels and beatings and unanswered prayers and my hands just there hanging helplessly by my side. Amá looked at me again, confused, angry, and her eyes were filled with sorrow. I went outside and sat on the porch swing and watched the people pass. I sat there until she left. I dozed off repeating the words to myself like rosary prayers: when do you stop giving when do you start giving when do you . . . and when my hands fell from my lap, I awoke to catch them. The sun was setting, an orange glow, and I knew Abuelita was hungry.

There comes a time when the sun is defiant. Just about the time when moods change, inevitable seasons of a day, transitions from one color to another, that hour or minute or second when the sun is finally defeated, finally sinks into the realization that it cannot, with all it power to heal or burn, exist forever, there comes an illumination where the sun and earth meet, a final burst of burning red-orange fury reminding us that although endings are inevitable, they are necessary for rebirths, and when that time came, just when I switched on the light in the kitchen to open Abuelita's can of soup, it was probably then that she died.

The room smelled of Pine Sol and vomit, and Abuelita had defecated the remains of her cancerous stomach. She had turned to the window and tried to speak, but her mouth remained open and speechless. I heard you, Abuelita, I said, stroking her cheek, I heard you. I opened the windows of the house and let the soup simmer and overboil on the stove. I turned the stove off and poured the soup down the sink. From the cabinet I got a tin basin, filled it with lukewarm water, and carried it carefully to the room. I went to the linen closet and took out some modest bleached white towels. With the sacredness of a priest preparing his vestments, I unfolded the towels one by one on my shoulders. I removed the sheets and blankets from her bed and peeled off her thick flannel nightgown. I toweled her puzzled face, stretching out the wrinkles, removing the coils of her neck, toweled her shoulders and breasts. Then I changed the water. I returned to towel the creases of her stretch-marked stomach, her sporadic vaginal hairs, and her sagging thighs. I removed the lint from between her toes and noticed a mapped birthmark on the fold of her buttock. The scars on her back, which were as thin as the lifelines on the palms of her hands, made me realize how little I really knew of Abuelita. I covered her with a thin blanket and went into the bathroom. I washed my hands, turned on the tub faucets, and watched the water pour into the tub with vitality and steam. When it was full, I turned off the water and undressed. Then, I went to get Abuelita.

She was not as heavy as I thought, and when I carried her in my arms, her body fell into a V, and yet my legs were tired, shaky, and I felt as if the distance between the bedroom and bathroom was miles and years away. Amá, where are you?

I stepped into the bathtub, one leg first, then the other. I bent my knees to descend into the water, slowly, so I wouldn't scald her skin. There, there, Abuelita, I said, cradling her, smoothing her as we descended, I heard you. Her hair fell back and spread across the water like eagle's wings. The water in the tub overflowed and poured onto the tile of the floor. Then the moths came. Small, gray ones that came from her soul and out through her mouth fluttering to light, circling the single dull light bulb of the bathroom. Dying is lonely and I wanted to go to where the moths were, stay with her and plant chayotes whose vines would crawl up her fingers and into the clouds; I wanted to rest my head on her chest with her stroking my hair, telling me about the moths that lay within the soul and slowly eat the spirit up; I wanted to return to the waters of the womb with her so that we would never be alone again. I wanted. I wanted my Amá. I removed a few strands of hair from Abuelita's face and held her small light head within the hollow of my neck. The bathroom was filled with moths, and for the first time in a long time I cried, rocking us, crying for her, for me, for Amá, the sobs emerging from the depths of anguish, the misery of feeling half born, sobbing until finally the sobs rippled into circles and circles of sadness and relief. There, there, I said to Abuelita, rocking us gently, there, there. [1985]

Rosario Morales and **Aurora Levins Morales** coauthored *Getting Home Alive* in 1986. Rosario Morales (b. 1930) moved to Puerto Rico after her marriage; there in 1954 her daughter, Aurora, was born, as she says, "of a U.S. Jewish father and a New York Puerto Rican mother." The family returned to live in the United States when Aurora was a young girl, and both authors have continued to publish separately and in collaboration. The writings of both mother and daughter appeared in *This Bridge Called My Back: Writings by Radical Women of Color* (1981) and *Cuentos: Stories by Latinas* (1983).

Getting Home Alive is a collection of poetry, stories, and vignettes of women who share the similarities of being Puerto Rican, mother and daughter, but who are divided by generational differences and differing viewpoints regarding assimilation and cultural heritage. The book has been widely used in courses and included in anthologies because of its fresh and original perspectives.

Ending Poem

I am what I am.
A child of the Americas.
A light-skinned mestiza of the Caribbean.

A child of many diaspora, born into this continent at a crossroads.
I am Puerto Rican. I am U.S. American.
I am New York Manhattan and the Bronx.
A mountain-born, country-bred, homegrown jíbara child,
up from the shtetl, a California Puerto Rican Jew
A product of the New York ghettos I have never known.
I am an immigrant
and the daughter and granddaughter of immigrants.
We didn't know our forebears' names with a certainty.
They aren't written anywhere.
First names only or mija, negra, ne, honey, sugar, dear.

I come from the dirt where the cane was grown.
My people didn't go to dinner parties. They weren't invited.
I am caribeña, island grown.
Spanish is in my flesh, ripples from my tongue, lodges in my hips,
the language of garlic and mangoes.
Boricua. As Boricuas come from the isle of Manhattan.
I am of latinoamerica, rooted in the history of my continent.
I speak from that body. Just brown and pink and full of drums inside.

I am not African.
Africa waters the roots of my tree, but I cannot return.

I am not Taína.
I am a late leaf of that ancient tree,
and my roots reach into the soil of two Americas.
Taíno is in me, but there is no way back.

I am not European, though I have dreamt of those cities.
Each plate is different.
wood, clay, papier mâché, metals, basketry, a leaf, a coconut shell
Europe lives in me but I have no home there.

The table has a cloth woven by one, dyed by another,
embroidered by another still.
I am a child of many mothers.
They have kept it all going.

All the civilizations erected on their backs.
All the dinner parties given with their labor.

We are new.
They gave us life, kept us going,
brought us to where we are.
Born at a crossroads.
Come, lay that dishcloth down. Eat, dear, eat.
History made us.
We will not eat ourselves up inside anymore.

And we are whole. [1986]

Rolando Hinojosa Smith was born in the border town of Mercedes, Texas, in 1929 to a Mexican-American father and an Anglo mother. He grew up in a bilingual household. He holds a doctorate in Spanish from the University of Illinois and is currently Ellen Clayton Garwood Professor at the University of Texas at Austin. His major work is the Klail City Death Trip series of novels, which began in 1973 with the publication of *Estampas del valle y otras obras* (*Sketches of the Valley*). The series follows the lives of the inhabitants of Belken County as told in their own voices through anecdotes, dialogue, and interviews. In 1973 Hinojosa was awarded the Premio Quinto Sol for *Estampas del valle,* and in 1976 the Casa de las Americas Prize for *Klail City y sus alrededores* (*Klail City*).

Hinojosa writes in both Spanish and English but does not translate his work. Instead he rewrites each piece for the other language, as if the choice of language itself determined the tone. His portraits of the inhabitants of the Texas border region, the narrow strip of land along the Rio Grande where Mexicans and Anglos live in close proximity, have led many critics to compare him to William Faulkner, and the region he writes about to Faulkner's Yoknapatawpha County. Because Hinojosa has chosen to write nontraditional narrative and has published with small presses that will keep his work in print, his fiction is little known outside a relatively small group of devotees. The following selection from *Klail City* can only hint at the structure and wit of his novels.

Doña Sóstenes

(About the time I returned from Korea) Doña Sóstenes Jasso, widow to Capt. Carmona, must have been about sixty-five-years old and widowed for some forty-odd of those sixty-five years.

The widowhood was the handiwork of José Isabel Chávez, a baby-faced, freebooting guerrilla leader who lined up Mexican Army regular Jacinto Carmona (Capt., Cav.) against a wall in Parangaracutiro, Michoacán, and ordered him shot along with eleven others in Carmona's mounted patrol. Doña Sóstenes and her sister Herminia came to Klail City in 1915; Herminia, the younger of the two, became my Uncle Julián's first wife. Me, I was bartending during the summers at Lucas Barrón's place, the *Aquí me quedo,** when one day doña Sóstenes walked by, grandson in tow, as I was serving Esteban Echevarría a cold Falstaff.

A beer, Rafe; just the one more I need to get going here. I've got a good head of steam, boys, so step aside . . . Sóstenes, Sóstenes, I'm one of the ones who knew you when, yes I am, and I can say it again: *I knew you when . . .*

Ours is an old generation, boys, even though I got her beat by some twenty years there; I first saw her and that sister of hers back in '17 or '18, I think it was; at any rate, it was right before they paved the streets here in Klail, and she wasn't skinny then, boys, and she wasn't dried up either. No sir. That widow of Cavalry Captain Carmona was a traffic stopper; yes, those were the days, Sóstenes girl, and I knew you when, didn't I?

Well, sir, it just so happens that when Jacinto Carmona together with his horses and men fell into that trap laid out by the guerrilla Chávez, Carmona's wife was living in the Carmona family homestead in Doctor Cos, Nuevo León. That telegram giving her the terrible news was sent out two months later, and then, she didn't get the wire itself until three weeks after it got to town. In short, Sóstenes, times being what they were, had been a widow the whole of the summer of '14, without her knowing it. News, good or bad, just didn't travel fast in those days; it was another time, boys . . .

Well, as I was saying, she and her sister got to Klail in '15 or so, and they were first helped out by don Manuel Guzmán's wife;

---

*Lucas Barrón is also known as Dirty Luke.

didn't know 'em, of course, just saw 'em and took 'em in. The sisters needed help, and that was enough for Josefa Guzmán. And they stayed there, too, least ways until Herminia married don Julián Buenrostro . . . Did you know that, Rafe?

"Yes."

Now, where was I? Oh, yeah. Anyway, in those days when women started wearing shorter skirts and dresses, the Jasso women kept the long ones, but shave my hair and call me Baldy: long skirts or no, we're talking of first-class goods here, top-a-the-line merchandise. Yessir!

Now, when some of the gang here learned that the oldest one was a widow, some of 'em started getting all sort-a ideas. But they couldn't have been more out of true if they tried. Nothing.

Not even the faintest angel's breath of hope, no sir. Then, a year or so later, Herminia marries up with don Julián at the Carmen Ranch and Sóstenes moves right in. Now, had she — just by chance let's say — had she stayed here in Klail, maybe nothing would've happened; no way to tell now, of course, and maybe . . . well, lemme just back up a bit here . . .

"Echevarría! Stay on course!"

Right where I'm at, Turnio; just checkin' the riggin' and the sails, is all . . . Well, sir, Sóstenes went off to the Carmen Ranch, and it was there that Melesio Parra, the eldest of Melesio Senior's bunch — the ones that still run that dairy farm there — and Antonio Cruz, a short little old runt raised by the Archuletas, remember those New Mexicans who moved in here? Well, it was at the Carmen Ranch where those two youngsters shot and killed each other right to death and all for Sóstenes. Damfools.

That's right, just-like-that . . . shot themselves full-a holes, they did. And for what, I ask you? Ah, for Sóstenes's love . . . Ha! For Sóstenes's love . . . And will you look at 'er now . . . old, gray-haired, wrinkly, bent over by all those years, and to think — like the tango says — and to think that life's a puff of breath and little else . . . ha!

But that was it . . . they just shot and killed each other, and the widow didn't know a thing about it. It's enough to make you laugh or cry, one . . . She didn't even *know* them, hadn't laid *eyes* on 'em. Ever. They were the ones who got it into their heads that they were rivals. I mean, she had absolutely no idea . . .

Ahhhh, but you know how it always is: the crowd said that fault and blame had to be placed on a woman. Yeah. Convenient, even if I say so. But hang on to this: they died, they stayed dead, and they're not coming back. Uh-uh . . .

Shoot! Sóstenes wasn't a dishrag to be picked up and rubbed and squeezed and laid out by just anyone who happened to come along. No sir. She wasn't even at the dance when those two went at it. And you know *what?* The dance was being held right at the Carmen Ranch itself, but she didn't go to 'em. Anywhere. Period.

Young Parra and the Cruz boy killed themselves, and that was it. That other people came by later on and said *she* was to blame, well, that was someone's tongue working back and forth, and that was it, because as far as she was concerned: nothing. Right, Maistro?

"God's truth and no one else's, Echevarría. It was one of those dances organized by María Lara . . ."

"María Lara? That old sack fulla-bones?"

"You youngsters don't know what you're talking about."

"Echevarría's had too much to drink!"

"Yeah? Well, he pays his own way."

"Keep it down . . . go on, Echevarría."

Nothing to it, boys . . . I saw Sóstenes go by, and I thought about the old days; when she was young. That's all.

"See what you guys've done now?"

"Don't mind 'em, Echevarría. Can I buy you a beer?"

"Go on, Echevarría; don't pay 'em no mind."

Well, lemme ask Rafe here. You think I'm drunk?

"No."

And would you sell me a beer right now?

"Anytime."

Let's hear it for the Buenrostros, goddammit. Rafe, make this one a Falstaff.

"Oh, I remember it, all right . . . Young Parra's gun was one-a them Ivory-Johnson's, the kind you break open in the middle. But it wasn't his. The damn thing belonged to his brother-in-law, Tomás Arreola."

"And the other guy?"

"No, that gun was his, all right. A .38. And, it was just like Esteban Echevarría said it was: face to face, pistol in hand."

"And like real men, and all that old stuff, right?"

"Yeah, it was a damfool thing to do."

"And Echevarría was there? He saw it all?"

"Oh, yeah; we both did. We must've gone there together that night . . . As for Sóstenes, well, she received — and she still may, you know — a smallish pension from the Mexican government on account of her husband's being a regular army officer."

"I can't imagine the pension's all that much; do you?"

"No, probably not."

"But regular as the sunset, I bet."

"So then what happened between the two families, the Parras and the Cruz bunch?"

"Oh, it worked out all right. It started and ended there, with those two."

"That was a stroke of luck."

"But to kill each other for someone like that . . ."

"Well, she wasn't like *that,* then . . ."

"Yeah, I know, but still 'n all, it was a damfool thing to do."

Ho! Rafe, I gotta be going.

"See you tomorrow, Echevarría."

God hear you. [1987]

Gloria Anzaldúa was born on the ranch settlement Jesus Maria of the Valley in South Texas in 1942. At the age of eleven her family moved to Hargill, Texas, which Anzaldúa has described as a town with "one signal light and thirteen bars and thirteen churches and maybe two mini-marts." At the age of fifteen, after her father's death, the author and her family experienced the hardships of migrant farmworkers; nevertheless, with unusual determination, she managed to become "not just the only woman, but the only person from the area who ever went to college." She attended Pan American University in Texas and received an M.A. from the University of Texas at Austin.

Anzaldúa's early experiences helped shape her creative and critical writings. She is the coeditor, with Cherríe Moraga, of *This Bridge Called My Back: Radical Writings by Women of Color* (see the entry for Moraga), which received the Before Columbus Foundation American Book Award. She also edited *Haciendo Caras / Making Face, Making Soul: Creative and Critical Perspectives by Women of Color* (1990).

Anzaldúa's major work to date is *Borderlands / La frontera: The New Mestiza* (1987), a bilingual book combining several genres. The work is a sort of literary *mestizaje* (racial mixing); the structure itself represents Anzaldúa's ideas of mixing historiography with poetry in a broad thematic range, from philosophy to poetry. Her ideas relate directly to the hemispherics of José Martí; she has stated that the most descriptive term for those of Hispanic descent in the United States is neither Hispanic nor Latino but Mestizo, since all Latinos are of mixed blood. But perhaps her most important goal is one she has worked toward from an early age: to overturn Chicano patriarchal family traditions. Feminism, lesbianism, an intense ethnic identity, and a highly personal emphasis (including the use of her own family in her writing) characterize her work.

The following essay, "How to Tame a Wild Tongue," from *Borderlands / La frontera* is characteristically ironic.

from Borderlands / La frontera: The New Mestiza

How to Tame a Wild Tongue

"We're going to have to control your tongue," the dentist says, pulling out all the metal from my mouth. Silver bits plop and tinkle into the basin. My mouth is a motherlode.

The dentist is cleaning out my roots. I get a whiff of the stench when I gasp. "I can't cap that tooth yet, you're still draining," he says.

"We're going to have to do something about your tongue," I hear the anger rising in his voice. My tongue keeps pushing out the wads of cotton, pushing back the drills, the long thin needles. "I've never seen anything as strong or as stubborn," he says. And I think, how do you tame a wild tongue, train it to be quiet, how do you bridle and saddle it? How do you make it lie down?

> Who is to say that robbing a people of its language is less violent than war? — *Ray Gwyn Smith*, Moorland Is Cold Country

I remember being caught speaking Spanish at recess — that was good for three licks on the knuckles with a sharp ruler. I remember being sent to the corner of the classroom for "talking back" to the Anglo teacher when all I was trying to do was tell her how to pronounce my name. "If you want to be American, speak 'American.' If you don't like it, go back to Mexico where you belong."

"I want you to speak English. *Pa' hallar buen trabajo tienes que saber hablar el inglés bien. Qué vale toda tu educación si todavía hablas inglés con un* 'accent,'" my mother would say, mortified that I spoke English like a Mexican. At Pan American University, I and all Chicano students were required to take two speech classes. Their purpose: to get rid of our accents.

Attacks on one's form of expression with the intent to censor are a violation of the First Amendment. *El Anglo con cara de inocente nos arrancó la lengua.* Wild tongues can't be tamed, they can only be cut out.

OVERCOMING THE TRADITION OF SILENCE

Ahogadas, escupimos el oscuro.
Peleando con nuestra propia sombra
el silencio nos sepulta.

En boca cerrada no entran moscas. "Flies don't enter a closed mouth" is a saying I kept hearing when I was a child. *Ser habladora* was to be a gossip and a liar, to talk too much. *Muchachitas bien criadas,* well-bred girls don't answer back. *Es una falta de respeto* to talk back to one's mother or father. I remember one of the sins I'd recite to the priest in the confession box the few times I went to confession: talking back to my mother, *hablar pa' 'tras, repelar. Hocicona, repelona, chismosa,* having a big mouth, questioning, carrying tales are all signs of being *mal criada*. In my culture they are all words that are derogatory if applied to women — I've never heard them applied to men.

The first time I heard two women, a Puerto Rican and a Cuban, say the word "*nosotras,*" I was shocked. I had not known the word existed. Chicanas use *nosotros* whether we're male or female. We are robbed of our female being by the masculine plural. Language is a male discourse.

And our tongues have become
dry   the wilderness has

dried out our tongues   and
we have forgotten speech.
— *Irene Klepfisz*, "Di rayze aheyme/The Journey Home"

Even our own people, other Spanish speakers *nos quieren poner candados en la boca*. They would hold us back with their bag of *reglas de academia*.

OYÉ COMO LADRA: EL LENGUAJE DE LA FRONTERA

Quien tiene boca se equivoca. — Mexican saying

"*Pocho*, cultural traitor, you're speaking the oppressor's language by speaking English, you're ruining the Spanish language," I have been accused by various Latinos and Latinas. Chicano Spanish is considered by the purist and by most Latinos deficient, a mutilation of Spanish.

But Chicano Spanish is a border tongue which developed naturally. Change, *evolución, enriquecimiento de palabras nuevas por invención o adopción* have created variants of Chicano Spanish, *un nuevo lenguaje. Un lenguaje que corresponde a un modo de vivir.* Chicano Spanish is not incorrect, it is a living language.

For a people who are neither Spanish nor live in a country in which Spanish is the first language; for a people who live in a country in which English is the reigning tongue but who are not Anglo; for a people who cannot entirely identify with either standard (formal, Castillian) Spanish nor standard English, what recourse is left to them but to create their own language? A language which they can connect their identity to, one capable of communicating the realities and values true to themselves — a language with terms that are neither *español ni inglés*, but both. We speak a patois, a forked tongue, a variation of two languages.

Chicano Spanish sprang out of Chicanos' need to identify ourselves as a distinct people. We needed a language with which we could communicate with ourselves, a secret language. For some of us, language is a homeland closer than the Southwest — for many Chicanos today live in the Midwest and the East. And because we are a complex, heterogeneous people, we speak many languages. Some of the languages we speak are:

1. Standard English
2. Working-class and slang English
3. Standard Spanish
4. Standard Mexican Spanish
5. North Mexican Spanish dialect
6. Chicano Spanish (Texas, New Mexico, Arizona and California have regional variations)
7. Tex-Mex
8. *Pachuco* (called *caló*)

My "home" tongues are the languages I speak with my sister and brothers, with my friends. They are the last five listed, with 6 and 7 being closest to my heart. From school, the media and job situations, I've picked up standard and working-class English. From Mamagrande Locha and from reading Spanish and Mexican literature, I've picked up Standard Spanish and Standard Mexican Spanish. From *los recién llegados,* Mexican immigrants, and *braceros,* I learned the North Mexican dialect. With Mexicans I'll try to speak either Standard Mexican Spanish or the North Mexican dialect. From my parents and Chicanos living in the Valley, I picked up Chicano Texas Spanish, and I speak it with my mom, younger brother (who married a Mexican and who rarely mixes Spanish with English), aunts and older relatives.

With Chicanas from *Nuevo México* or *Arizona* I will speak Chicano Spanish a little, but often they don't understand what I'm saying. With most California Chicanas I speak entirely in English (unless I forget). When I first moved to San Francisco, I'd rattle off something in Spanish, unintentionally embarrassing them. Often it is only with another Chicana *tejana* that I can talk freely.

Words distorted by English are known as anglicisms or *pochismos.* The *pocho* is an anglicized Mexican or American of Mexican origin who speaks Spanish with an accent characteristic of North Americans and who distorts and reconstructs the language according to the influence of English.* Tex-Mex, or Spanglish, comes most naturally to me. I may switch back and forth from English to Spanish in the same sentence or in the same word. With my sister and my

* R. C. Ortega, *Dialectología Del Barrio,* trans. Hortencia S. Alwan (Los Angeles: R. C. Ortega, 1977), 132.

brother Nune and with Chicano *tejano* contemporaries I speak in Tex-Mex.

From kids and people my own age I picked up *Pachuco*. *Pachuco* (the language of the zoot suiters) is a language of rebellion, both against Standard Spanish and Standard English. It is a secret language. Adults of the culture and outsiders cannot understand it. It is made up of slang words from both English and Spanish. *Ruca* means girl or woman, *vato* means guy or dude, *chale* means no, *simón* means yes, *churro* is sure, talk is *periquiar, pigionear* means petting, *que gacho* means how nerdy, *ponte águila* means watch out, death is called *la pelona*. Through lack of practice and not having others who can speak it, I've lost most of the *Pachuco* tongue.

CHICANO SPANISH

Chicanos, after 250 years of Spanish/Anglo colonization, have developed significant differences in the Spanish we speak. We collapse two adjacent vowels into a single syllable and sometimes shift the stress in certain words such as *maíz/maiz, cohete/cuete*. We leave out certain consonants when they appear between vowels: *lado/lao, mojado/mojao*. Chicanos from South Texas pronounce *f* as *j* as in *jue* (*fue*). Chicanos use "archaisms," words that are no longer in the Spanish language, words that have been evolved out. We say *semos, truje, haiga, ansina,* and *naiden*. We retain the "archaic" *j*, as in *jalar*, that derives from an earlier *h* (the French *halar* or the Germanic *halon* which was lost to Standard Spanish in the sixteenth century), but which is still found in several regional dialects such as the one spoken in South Texas. (Due to geography, Chicanos from the Valley of South Texas were cut off linguistically from other Spanish speakers. We tend to use words that the Spaniards brought over from medieval Spain. The majority of the Spanish colonizers in Mexico and the Southwest came from Extremadura — Hernán Cortés was one of them — and Andalucía. Andalucians pronounce *ll* like a *y*, and their *d*'s tend to be absorbed by adjacent vowels: *tirado* becomes *tirao*. They brought *el lenguaje popular, dialectos y regionalismos*.)*

---

* Eduardo Hernandez-Chávez, Andrew D. Cohen, and Anthony F. Beltramo, *El lenguaje de los Chicanos: Regional and Social Characteristics of Language Used by Mexican Americans* (Arlington, Va.: Center for Applied Linguistics, 1975), 39.

Chicanos and other Spanish speakers also shift *ll* to *y* and *z* to *s*.* We leave out initial syllables, saying *tar* for *estar, toy* for *estoy, hora* for *ahora* (*cubanos* and *puertorriqueños* also leave out initial letters of some words). We also leave out the final syllable such as *pa* for *para*. The intervocalic *y*, the *ll* as in *tortilla, ella, botella,* gets replaced by *tortia* or *tortiya, ea, botea*. We add an additional syllable at the beginning of certain words: *atocar* for *tocar, agastar* for *gastar*. Sometimes we'll say *lavaste las vacijas,* other times *lavates* (substituting the *ates* verb endings for the *aste*).

We use anglicisms, words borrowed from English: *bola* from ball, *carpeta* from carpet, *máchina de lavar* (instead of *lavadora*) from washing machine. Tex-Mex argot, created by adding a Spanish sound at the beginning or end of an English word such as *cookiar* for cook, *watchar* for watch, *parkiar* for park, and *rapiar* for rape, is the result of the pressures on Spanish speakers to adapt to English.

We don't use the word *vosotros/as* or its accompanying verb form. We don't say *claro* (to mean yes), *imagínate,* or *me emociona,* unless we picked up Spanish from Latinas, out of a book, or in a classroom. Other Spanish-speaking groups are going through the same, or similar, development in their Spanish.

LINGUISTIC TERRORISM

> *Deslenguadas. Somos los del español deficiente.* We are your linguistic nightmare, your linguistic aberration, your linguistic *mestisaje,* the subject of your *burla*. Because we speak with tongues of fire we are culturally crucified. Racially, culturally and linguistically *somos huérfanos* — we speak an orphan tongue.

Chicanas who grew up speaking Chicano Spanish have internalized the belief that we speak poor Spanish. It is illegitimate, a bastard language. And because we internalize how our language has been used against us by the dominant culture, we use our language differences against each other.

Chicana feminists often skirt around each other with suspicion and hesitation. For the longest time I couldn't figure it out. Then it dawned on me. To be close to another Chicana is like looking into

---

* Hernandez-Chávez, xvii.

the mirror. We are afraid of what we'll see there. *Pena.* Shame. Low estimation of self. In childhood we are told that our language is wrong. Repeated attacks on our native tongue diminish our sense of self. The attacks continue throughout our lives.

Chicanas feel uncomfortable talking in Spanish to Latinas, afraid of their censure. Their language was not outlawed in their countries. They had a whole lifetime of being immersed in their native tongue; generations, centuries in which Spanish was a first language, taught in school, heard on radio and TV, and read in the newspaper.

If a person, Chicana or Latina, has a low estimation of my native tongue, she also has a low estimation of me. Often with *mexicanas y latinas* we'll speak English as a neutral language. Even among Chicanas we tend to speak English at parties or conferences. Yet, at the same time, we're afraid the other will think we're *agringadas* because we don't speak Chicano Spanish. We oppress each other trying to out-Chicano each other, vying to be the "real" Chicanas, to speak like Chicanos. There is no one Chicano language just as there is no one Chicano experience. A monolingual Chicana whose first language is English or Spanish is just as much a Chicana as one who speaks several variants of Spanish. A Chicana from Michigan or Chicago or Detroit is just as much a Chicana as one from the Southwest. Chicano Spanish is as diverse linguistically as it is regionally.

By the end of this century, Spanish speakers will comprise the biggest minority group in the U.S., a country where students in high schools and colleges are encouraged to take French classes because French is considered more "cultured." But for a language to remain alive it must be used.* By the end of this century English, and not Spanish, will be the mother tongue of most Chicanos and Latinos.

So, if you want to really hurt me, talk badly about my language. Ethnic identity is twin skin to linguistic identity — I am my language. Until I can take pride in my language, I cannot take pride in myself. Until I can accept as legitimate Chicano Texas Spanish, Tex-Mex and all the other languages I speak, I cannot accept the legiti-

---

* Irena Klepfisz, "Secular Jewish Identity; Yiddishkayt in America," in *The Tribe of Dina: A Jewish Women's Anthology,* Melanie Kaye/Kantrowitz and Irena Klepfisz, eds. (Montpelier, Vt.: Sinister Wisdom Books, 1986), 43.

macy of myself. Until I am free to write bilingually and to switch codes without having always to translate, while I still have to speak English or Spanish when I would rather speak Spanglish, and as long as I have to accommodate the English speakers rather than having them accommodate me, my tongue will be illegitimate.

I will no longer be made to feel ashamed of existing. I will have my voice: Indian, Spanish, white. I will have my serpent's tongue — my woman's voice, my sexual voice, my poet's voice. I will overcome the tradition of silence.

> My fingers
> move sly against your palm
> Like women everywhere, we speak in code . . .
>
> — *Melanie Kaye/Kantrowitz*, "Sign"

"VISTAS," CORRIDOS, Y COMIDA: MY NATIVE TONGUE

In the 1960s, I read my first Chicano novel. It was *City of Night* by John Rechy, a gay Texan, son of a Scottish father and a Mexican mother. For days I walked around in stunned amazement that a Chicano could write and could get published. When I read *I Am Joaquín** I was surprised to see a bilingual book by a Chicano in print. When I saw poetry written in Tex-Mex for the first time, a feeling of pure joy flashed through me. I felt like we really existed as a people. In 1971, when I started teaching high school English to Chicano students, I tried to supplement the required texts with works by Chicanos, only to be reprimanded and forbidden to do so by the principal. He claimed that I was supposed to teach "American" and English literature. At the risk of being fired, I swore my students to secrecy and slipped in Chicano short stories, poems, a play. In graduate school, while working toward a Ph.D., I had to "argue" with one advisor after the other, semester after semester, before I was allowed to make Chicano literature an area of focus.

Even before I read books by Chicanos or Mexicans, it was the Mexican movies I saw at the drive-in — the Thursday night special of $1.00 a carload — that gave me a sense of belonging. *"Vámonos a las vistas,"* my mother would call out and we'd all — grandmother, brothers, sister and cousins — squeeze into the car. We'd wolf

* Rodolfo Gonzales, *I Am Joaquín/Yo Soy Joaquín* (New York: Bantam Books, 1972).

down cheese and bologna white bread sandwiches while watching Pedro Infante in melodramatic tear-jerkers like *Nostros los pobres,* the first "real" Mexican movie (that was not an imitation of European movies). I remember seeing *Cuando los hijos se van* and surmising that all Mexican movies played up the love a mother has for her children and what ungrateful sons and daughters suffer when they are not devoted to their mothers. I remember the singing-type "westerns" of Jorge Negrete and Miguel Aceves Mejía. When watching Mexican movies, I felt a sense of homecoming as well as alienation. People who were to amount to something didn't go to Mexican movies, or *bailes* or tune their radios to *bolero, rancherita,* and *corrido* music.

The whole time I was growing up, there was *norteño* music, sometimes called North Mexican border music, or Tex-Mex music, or Chicano music, or *cantina* (bar) music. I grew up listening to *conjuntos,* three- or four-piece bands made up of folk musicians playing guitar, *bajo sexto,* drums and button accordion, which Chicanos had borrowed from the German immigrants who had come to Central Texas and Mexico to farm and build breweries. In the Rio Grande Valley, Steve Jordan and Little Joe Hernández were popular, and Flaco Jiménez was the accordion king. The rhythms of Tex-Mex music are those of the polka, also adapted from the Germans, who in turn had borrowed the polka from the Czechs and Bohemians.

I remember the hot, sultry evenings when *corridos* — songs of love and death on the Texas-Mexican borderlands — reverberated out of cheap amplifiers from the local *cantinas* and wafted in through my bedroom window.

Corridos first became widely used along the South Texas/Mexican border during the early conflict between Chicanos and Anglos. The *corridos* are usually about Mexican heroes who do valiant deeds against the Anglo oppressors. Pancho Villa's song, *"La cucaracha,"* is the most famous one. *Corridos* of John F. Kennedy and his death are still very popular in the Valley. Older Chicanos remember Lydia Mendoza, one of the great border *corrido* singers who was called *la Gloria de Tejas*. Her *"El tango negro,"* sung during the Great Depression, made her a singer of the people. The ever-present *corridos* narrated one hundred years of border history, bringing news of events as well as entertaining. These folk musicians and folk songs are our chief cultural mythmakers, and they made our hard lives seem bearable.

I grew up feeling ambivalent about our music. Country-western and rock-and-roll had more status. In the '50s and '60s, for the slightly educated and *agringado* Chicanos, there existed a sense of shame at being caught listening to our music. Yet I couldn't stop my feet from thumping to the music, could not stop humming the words, nor hide from myself the exhilaration I felt when I heard it.

There are more subtle ways that we internalize identification, especially in the forms of images and emotions. For me food and certain smells are tied to my identity, to my homeland. Woodsmoke curling up to an immense blue sky; woodsmoke perfuming my grandmother's clothes, her skin. The stench of cow manure and the yellow patches on the ground; the crack of a .22 rifle and the reek of cordite. Homemade white cheese sizzling in a pan, melting inside a folded *tortilla*. My sister Hilda's hot, spicy *menudo, chile colorado* making it deep red, pieces of *panza* and hominy floating on top. My brother Carito barbequing *fajitas* in the backyard. Even now and 3,000 miles away, I can see my mother spicing the ground beef, pork and venison with *chile*. My mouth salivates at the thought of the hot steaming *tamales* I would be eating if I were home.

SI LE PREGUNTAS A MI MAMÁ, "¿QUÉ ERES?"

> Identity is the essential core of who we are as individuals, the conscious experience of the self inside. — *Gershen Kaufman*, Shame: The Power of Caring

Nosotros los Chicanos straddle the borderlands. On one side of us, we are constantly exposed to the Spanish of the Mexicans, on the other side we hear the Anglos' incessant clamoring so that we forget our language. Among ourselves we don't say *nosotros los americanos, o nosotros los españoles, o nosotros los hispanos*. We say *nosotros los mexicanos* (by *mexicanos* we do not mean citizens of Mexico; we do not mean a national identity, but a racial one). We distinguish between *mexicanos del otro lado* and *mexicanos de este lado*. Deep in our hearts we believe that being Mexican has nothing to do with which country one lives in. Being Mexican is a state of soul — not one of mind, not one of citizenship. Neither eagle nor serpent, but both. And like the ocean, neither animal respects borders.

> *Dime con quien andas y te diré quien eres.* (Tell me who your friends are and I'll tell you who you are.) — *Mexican saying*

Si le preguntas a mi mamá, "¿Qué eres?" te dirá, "Soy mexicana." My brothers and sister say the same. I sometimes will answer *"soy mexicana"* and at others will say *"soy Chicana" o "soy tejana."* But I identified as *"Raza"* before I ever identified as *"mexicana"* or *"Chicana."*

As a culture, we call ourselves Spanish when referring to ourselves as a linguistic group and when copping out. It is then that we forget our predominant Indian genes. We are 70–80% Indian.* We call ourselves Hispanic† or Spanish-American or Latin American or Latin when linking ourselves to other Spanish-speaking peoples of the Western hemisphere and when copping out. We call ourselves Mexican-American‡ to signify we are neither Mexican nor American, but more the noun "American" than the adjective "Mexican" (and when copping out).

Chicanos and other people of color suffer economically for not acculturating. This voluntary (yet forced) alienation makes for psychological conflict, a kind of dual identity — we don't identify with the Anglo-American cultural values and we don't totally identify with the Mexican cultural values. We are a synergy of two cultures with various degrees of Mexicanness or Angloness. I have so internalized the borderland conflict that sometimes I feel like one cancels out the other and we are zero, nothing, no one. *A veces no soy nada ni nadie. Pero hasta cuando no lo soy, lo soy.*

When not copping out, when we know we are more than nothing, we call ourselves Mexican, referring to race and ancestry; *mestizo* when affirming both our Indian and Spanish (but we hardly ever own our Black ancestory); Chicano when referring to a politically aware people born and/or raised in the U.S.; *Raza* when referring to Chicanos; *tejanos* when we are Chicanos from Texas.

---

* John R. Chávez, *The Lost Land: The Chicano Images of the Southwest* (Albuquerque: University of New Mexico Press, 1984), 88–90.

† "Hispanic" is derived from *Hispania* (*España,* a name given to the Iberian Peninsula in ancient times when it was part of the Roman Empire) and is a term used by the U.S. government to make it easier to handle us on paper.

‡ The Treaty of Guadalupe Hidalgo created the Mexican-American in 1848.

Chicanos did not know we were a people until 1965 when César Chávez and the farmworkers united and *I Am Joaquín* was published and *la Raza Unida* party was formed in Texas. With that recognition, we became a distinct people. Something momentous happened to the Chicano soul — we became aware of our reality and acquired a name and a language (Chicano Spanish) that reflected that reality. Now that we had a name, some of the fragmented pieces began to fall together — who we were, what we were, how we had evolved. We began to get glimpses of what we might eventually become.

Yet the struggle of identities continues, the struggle of borders is our reality still. One day the inner struggle will cease and a true integration take place. In the meantime, *tenémos que hacer la lucha. ¿Quién está protegiendo los ranchos de mi gente? ¿Quién está tratando de cerrar la fisura entre la india y el blanco en nuestra sangre? El Chicano, si, el Chicano que anda como un ladrón en su propia casa.*

Los Chicanos, how patient we seem, how very patient. There is the quiet of the Indian about us.* We know how to survive. When other races have given up their tongue, we've kept ours. We know what it is to live under the hammer blow of the dominant *norteamericano* culture. But more than we count the blows, we count the days the weeks the years the centuries the eons until the white laws and commerce and customs will rot in the deserts they've created, lie bleached. *Humildes* yet proud, *quietos* yet wild, *nosotros los mexicanos-Chicanos* will walk by the crumbling ashes as we go about our business. Stubborn, persevering, impenetrable as stone, yet possessing a malleability that renders us unbreakable, we, the *mestizas* and *mestizos,* will remain. [1987]

* Anglos, in order to alleviate their guilt for dispossessing the Chicano, stressed the Spanish part of us and perpetrated the myth of the Spanish Southwest. We have accepted the fiction that we are Hispanic, that is, Spanish, in order to accommodate ourselves to the dominant culture and its abhorrence of Indians. Chávez, 88–91.

Sandra Cisneros was born in Chicago in 1954 and graduated from Loyola University with a B.A. in English. Her poetry books include *Bad Boys* (1980), set in a Chicago childhood; *My Wicked, Wicked Ways* (1987), featuring Cisneros, provocatively dressed and posed, on the cover and poems of sensuality and eroticism; and *Loose Woman* (1995). Her two published books of prose are *The House on Mango Street* (1983), an exploration of the consciousness of a young girl told through finely crafted vignettes, which won the Before Columbus Foundation American Book Award, and *Woman Hollering Creek and Other Stories* (1991), a stylistically powerful collection that brought Cisneros national attention, won several awards, and put her into the first rank of American fiction writers.

Woman Hollering Creek is marked by insistently powerful language and a heightened political consciousness. Sacred cows, legends, and myths are questioned, and in some cases revised, if the patriarchal values are found unacceptable to women. About *Woman Hollering Creek* the author Ann Beattie wrote, "My prediction is that Sandra Cisneros will stride right into the spotlight — though an aura already surrounds her. These stories about how and why we mythologize love are revelations about the constant, small sadnesses that erode our facades, as well as those unpredictably epiphanic moments that lift our hearts from despair. A truly wonderful book." The title story is emblematic of a "demythologizing," as Cisneros recasts the traditional legend of La Llorona, the Weeping Woman, who is traditionally believed to prey on young children. Instead of a victim, La Llorona finds her voice and, in Cisneros's story, "hollers."

The publication of *Woman Hollering Creek and Other Stories* by Random House, a major New York publisher, and Vintage, its paperback imprint, and selection by the national book clubs helped open doors for other Chicana writers.

Woman Hollering Creek

The day Don Serafín gave Juan Pedro Martínez Sánchez permission to take Cleófilas Enriqueta DeLeón Hernández as his bride, across her father's threshold, over several miles of dirt road and several miles of paved, over one border and beyond to a town *en el otro lado* — on the other side — already did he divine the morning his daughter would raise her hand over her eyes, look south, and dream of returning to the chores that never ended, six good-for-nothing brothers, and one old man's complaints.

He had said, after all, in the hubbub of parting: I am your father, I will never abandon you. He *had* said that, hadn't he, when he hugged and then let her go. But at the moment Cleófilas was busy looking for Chela, her maid of honor, to fulfill their bouquet conspiracy. She would not remember her father's parting words until later. *I am your father, I will never abandon you.*

Only now as a mother did she remember. Now, when she and Juan Pedrito sat by the creek's edge. How when a man and a woman love each other, sometimes that love sours. But a parent's love for a child, a child's for its parents, is another thing entirely.

This is what Cleófilas thought evenings when Juan Pedro did not come home, and she lay on her side of the bed listening to the hollow roar of the interstate, a distant dog barking, the pecan trees rustling like ladies in stiff petticoats — *shh-shh-shh, shh-shh-shh* — soothing her to sleep.

In the town where she grew up, there isn't very much to do except accompany the aunts and godmothers to the house of one or the other to play cards. Or walk to the cinema to see this week's film again, speckled and with one hair quivering annoyingly on the screen. Or to the center of town to order a milk shake that will appear in a day and a half as a pimple on her backside. Or to the girlfriend's house to watch the latest *telenovela* episode and try to copy the way the women comb their hair, wear their makeup.

But what Cleófilas has been waiting for, has been whispering and sighing and giggling for, has been anticipating since she was old enough to lean against the window displays of gauze and butterflies and lace, is passion. Not the kind on the cover of the *¡Alarma!* magazines, mind you, where the lover is photographed with the bloody fork she used to salvage her good name. But passion in its purest crystalline essence. The kind the books and songs and *telenovelas* describe when one finds, finally, the great love of one's life, and does whatever one can, must do, at whatever the cost.

Tú o Nadie. "You or No One." The title of the current favorite *telenovela*. The beautiful Lucía Méndez having to put up with all kinds of hardships of the heart, separation and betrayal, and loving, always loving no matter what, because *that* is the most important thing, and did you see Lucía Méndez on the Bayer aspirin commercials — wasn't she lovely? Does she dye her hair do you think? Cleófilas is going to go to the *farmacia* and buy a hair rinse; her girlfriend Chela will apply it — it's not that difficult at all.

Because you didn't watch last night's episode when Lucía confessed she loved him more than anyone in her life. In her life! And she sings the song "You or No One" in the beginning and end of the show. *Tú o Nadie.* Somehow one ought to live one's life like that, don't you think? You or no one. Because to suffer for love is good. The pain all sweet somehow. In the end.

Seguín. She had liked the sound of it. Far away and lovely. Not like *Monclova. Coahuia.* Ugly.

Seguín, Tejas. A nice sterling ring to it. The tinkle of money. She would get to wear outfits like the women on the *tele,* like Lucía Méndez. And have a lovely house, and wouldn't Chela be jealous.

And yes, they will drive all the way to Laredo to get her wedding dress. That's what they say. Because Juan Pedro wants to get married right away, without a long engagement since he can't take off too much time from work. He has a very important position in Seguin with, with . . . a beer company, I think. Or was it tires? Yes, he has to be back. So they will get married in the spring when he can take off work, and then they will drive off in his new pickup — did you see it? — to their new home in Seguin. Well, not exactly new, but they're going to repaint the house. You know newlyweds. New paint and new furniture. Why not? He can afford it. And later on add maybe a room or two for the children. May they be blessed with many.

Well, you'll see. Cleófilas has always been so good with her sewing machine. A little *rrrr, rrrr, rrrr* of the machine and *¡zas!* Miracles. She's always been so clever, that girl. Poor thing. And without even a mama to advise her on things like her wedding night. Well, may God help her. What with a father with a head like a burro, and those six clumsy brothers. Well, what do you think! Yes, I'm going to the wedding. Of course! The dress I want to wear just needs to be altered a teensy bit to bring it up to date. See, I saw a new style last night that I thought would suit me. Did you watch last night's episode of *The Rich Also Cry*? Well, did you notice the dress the mother was wearing?

La Gritona. Such a funny name for such a lovely *arroyo*. But that's what they called the creek that ran behind the house. Though no one could say whether the woman had hollered from anger or pain. The natives only knew the *arroyo* one crossed on the way to San Antonio, and then once again on the way back, was called Woman Hollering, a name no one from these parts questioned, little less understood. *Pues, allá de los indios, quién sabe* — who knows, the townspeople shrugged, because it was of no concern to their lives how this trickle of water received its curious name.

"What do you want to know for?" Trini the laundromat attendant asked in the same gruff Spanish she always used whenever she gave Cleófilas change or yelled at her for something. First for putting too much soap in the machines. Later, for sitting on a washer. And still later, after Juan Pedrito was born, for not understanding that in this country you cannot let your baby walk around with no diaper and his pee-pee hanging out, it wasn't nice, *¿entiendes? Pues.*

How could Cleófilas explain to a woman like this why the name Woman Hollering fascinated her. Well, there was no sense talking to Trini.

On the other hand there were the neighbor ladies, one on either side of the house they rented near the *arroyo*. The woman Soledad on the left, the woman Dolores on the right.

The neighbor lady Soledad liked to call herself a widow, though how she came to be one was a mystery. Her husband had either died, or run away with an ice-house floozie, or simply gone out for cigarettes one afternoon and never came back. It was hard to say which since Soledad, as a rule, didn't mention him.

In the other house lived *la señora* Dolores, kind and very sweet, but her house smelled too much of incense and candles from the altars that burned continuously in memory of two sons who had died in the last war and one husband who had died shortly after from grief. The neighbor lady Dolores divided her time between the memory of these men and her garden, famous for its sunflowers — so tall they had to be supported with broom handles and old boards; red red cockscombs, fringed and bleeding a thick menstrual color;

and, especially, roses whose sad scent reminded Cleófilas of the dead. Each Sunday *la señora* Dolores clipped the most beautiful of these flowers and arranged them on three modest headstones at the Seguin cemetery.

The neighbor ladies, Soledad, Dolores, they might've known once the name of the *arroyo* before it turned English but they did not know now. They were too busy remembering the men who had left through either choice or circumstance and would never come back.

Pain or rage, Cleófilas wondered when she drove over the bridge the first time as a newlywed and Juan Pedro had pointed it out. *La Gritona,* he had said, and she had laughed. Such a funny name for a creek so pretty and full of happily ever after.

The first time she had been so surprised she didn't cry out or try to defend herself. She had always said she would strike back if a man, any man, were to strike her.

But when the moment came, and he slapped her once, and then again, and again, until the lip split and bled an orchid of blood, she didn't fight back, she didn't break into tears, she didn't run away as she imagined she might when she saw such things in the *telenovelas*.

In her own home her parents had never raised a hand to each other or to their children. Although she admitted she may have been brought up a little leniently as an only daughter — *la consentida,* the princess — there were some things she would never tolerate. Ever.

Instead, when it happened the first time, when they were barely man and wife, she had been so stunned, it left her speechless, motionless, numb. She had done nothing but reach up to the heat on her mouth and stare at the blood on her hand as if even then she didn't understand.

She could think of nothing to say, said nothing. Just stroked the dark curls of the man who wept and would weep like a child, his tears of repentance and shame, this time and each.

The men at the ice house. From what she can tell, from the times during her first year when still a newlywed she is invited and accompanies her husband, sits mute beside their conversation, waits and sips a beer until it grows warm, twists a paper napkin into a knot, then another into a fan, one into a rose, nods her head, smiles, yawns, politely grins, laughs at the appropriate moments, leans against her husband's sleeve, tugs at his elbow, and finally becomes good at predicting where the talk will lead, from this Cleófilas concludes each is nightly trying to find the truth lying at the bottom of the bottle like a gold doubloon on the sea floor.

They want to tell each other what they want to tell themselves. But what is bumping like a helium balloon at the ceiling of the brain never finds its way out. It bubbles and rises, it gurgles in the throat, it rolls across the surface of the tongue, and erupts from the lips — a belch.

If they are lucky, there are tears at the end of the long night. At any given moment, the fists try to speak. They are dogs chasing their own tails before lying down to sleep, trying to find a way, a route, an out, and — finally — get some peace.

In the morning sometimes before he opens his eyes. Or after they have finished loving. Or at times when he is simply across from her at the table putting pieces of food into his mouth and chewing. Cleófilas thinks, This is the man I have waited my whole life for.

Not that he isn't a good man. She has to remind herself why she loves him when she changes the baby's Pampers, or when she mops the bathroom floor, or tries to make the curtains for the doorways without doors, or whiten the linen. Or wonder a little when he kicks the refrigerator and says he hates this shitty house and is going out where he won't be bothered with the baby's howling and her suspicious questions, and her requests to fix this and this and this because if she had any brains in her head she'd realize he's been up before the rooster earning his living to pay for the food in her belly and the roof over her head and would have to wake up again early the next day so why can't you just leave me in peace, woman.

He is not very tall, no, and he doesn't look like the men on the *telenovelas*. His face still scarred from acne. And he has a bit of a belly from all the beer he drinks. Well, he's always been husky.

This man who farts and belches and snores as well as laughs and kisses and holds her. Somehow this husband whose whiskers she finds each morning in the sink, whose shoes she must air each evening on the porch, this husband who cuts his fingernails in public, laughs loudly, curses like a man, and demands each course of dinner be served on a separate plate like at his mother's, as soon as he gets home, on time or late, and who doesn't care at all for music or *telenovelas* or romance or roses or the moon floating pearly over the *arroyo,* or through the bedroom window for that matter, shut the blinds and go back to sleep, this man, this father, this rival, this keeper, this lord, this master, this husband till kingdom come.

A doubt. Slender as a hair. A washed cup set back on the shelf wrong-side-up. Her lipstick, and body talc, and hairbrush all arranged in the bathroom a different way.

No. Her imagination. The house the same as always. Nothing.

Coming home from the hospital with her new son, her husband. Something comforting in discovering her house slippers beneath the bed, the faded housecoat where she left it on the bathroom hook. Her pillow. Their bed.

Sweet sweet homecoming. Sweet as the scent of face powder in the air, jasmine, sticky liquor.

Smudged fingerprint on the door. Crushed cigarette in a glass. Wrinkle in the brain crumpling to a crease.

Sometimes she thinks of her father's house. But how could she go back there? What a disgrace. What would the neighbors say? Coming home like that with one baby on her hip and one in the oven. Where's your husband?

The town of gossips. The town of dust and despair. Which she has traded for this town of gossips. This town of dust, despair. Houses farther apart perhaps, though no more privacy because of it. No leafy *zócalo* in the center of the town, though the murmur of talk is clear enough all the same. No huddled whispering on the church steps each Sunday. Because here the whispering begins at sunset at the ice house instead.

This town with its silly pride for a bronze pecan the size of a baby carriage in front of the city hall. TV repair shop, drugstore, hardware, dry cleaner's, chiropractor's, liquor store, bail bonds, empty storefront, and nothing, nothing, nothing of interest. Nothing one could walk to, at any rate. Because the towns here are built so that you have to depend on husbands. Or you stay home. Or you drive. If you're rich enough to own, allowed to drive, your own car.

There is no place to go. Unless one counts the neighbor ladies. Soledad on one side, Dolores on the other. Or the creek.

Don't go out there after dark, *mi'jita*. Stay near the house. *No es bueno para la salud. Mala suerte.* Bad luck. *Mal aire.* You'll get sick and the baby too. You'll catch a fright wandering about in the dark, and then you'll see how right we were.

The stream sometimes only a muddy puddle in the summer, though now in the springtime, because of the rains, a good-size alive thing, a thing with a voice all its own, all day and all night calling in its high, silver voice. Is it La Llorona, the weeping woman? La Llorona, who drowned her own children. Perhaps La Llorona is the one they named the creek after, she thinks, remembering all the stories she learned as a child.

La Llorona calling to her. She is sure of it. Cleófilas sets the baby's Donald Duck blanket on the grass. Listens. The day sky turning to night. The baby pulling up fistfuls of grass and laughing. La Llorona. Wonders if something as quiet as this drives a woman to the darkness under the trees.

What she needs is . . . and made a gesture as if to yank a woman's buttocks to his groin. Maximiliano, the foul-smelling fool from across the road, said this and set the men laughing, but Cleófilas just muttered. *Grosera,* and went on washing dishes.

She knew he said it not because it was true, but more because it was he who needed to sleep with a woman, instead of drinking each night at the ice house and stumbling home alone.

Maximiliano who was said to have killed his wife in an ice-house brawl when she came at him with a mop. I had to shoot, he had said — she was armed.

Their laughter outside the kitchen window. Her husband's, his friends'. Manolo, Beto, Efraín, el Perico. Maximiliano.

Was Cleófilas just exaggerating as her husband always said? It seemed the newspapers were full of such stories. This woman found on the side of the interstate. This one pushed from a moving car. This one's cadaver, this one unconscious, this one beaten blue. Her ex-husband, her husband, her lover, her father, her brother, her uncle, her friend, her co-worker. Always. The same grisly news in the pages of the dailies. She dunked a glass under the soapy water for a moment — shivered.

~~~
~~~

He had thrown a book. Hers. From across the room. A hot welt across the cheek. She could forgive that. But what stung more was the fact it was *her* book, a love story by Corín Tellado, what she loved most now that she lived in the U.S., without a television set, without the *telenovelas*.

Except now and again when her husband was away and she could manage it, the few episodes glimpsed at the neighbor lady Soledad's house because Dolores didn't care for that sort of thing, though Soledad was often kind enough to retell what had happened on what episode of *María de Nadie,* the poor Argentine country girl who had the ill fortune of falling in love with the beautiful son of the Arrocha family, the very family she worked for, whose roof she slept under and whose floors she vacuumed, while in that same house, with the dust brooms and floor cleaners as witnesses, the square-jawed Juan Carlos Arrocha had uttered words of love, I love you, María, listen to me, *mi querida,* but it was she who had to say No, no, we are not of the same class, and remind him it was not his place nor hers to fall in love, while all the while her heart was breaking, can you imagine.

Cleófilas thought her life would have to be like that, like a *telenovela,* only now the episodes got sadder and sadder. And there were no commercials in between for comic relief. And no happy ending in sight. She thought this when she sat with the baby out by the creek behind the house. Cleófilas de . . . ? But somehow she would have to change her name to Topazio, or Yesenia, Cristal, Adriana, Stefania, Andrea, something more poetic than Cleófilas. Everything happened to women with names like jewels. But what happened to a Cleófilas? Nothing. But a crack in the face.

Because the doctor has said so. She has to go. To make sure the new baby is all right, so there won't be any problems when he's born, and the appointment card says next Tuesday. Could he please take her. And that's all.

No, she won't mention it. She promises. If the doctor asks she can say she fell down the front steps or slipped when she was out in the backyard, slipped out back, she could tell him that. She has to go back next Tuesday, Juan Pedro, please, for the new baby. For their child.

She could write to her father and ask maybe for money, just a loan, for the new baby's medical expenses. Well then if he'd rather she didn't. All right, she won't. Please don't anymore. Please don't. She knows it's difficult saving money with all the bills they have, but how else are they going to get out of debt with the truck payments? And after the rent and the food and the electricity and the gas and the water and the who-knows-what, well, there's hardly anything left. But please, at least for the doctor visit. She won't ask for anything else. She has to. Why is she so anxious? Because.

Because she is going to make sure the baby is not turned around backward this time to split her down the center. Yes. Next Tuesday at five-thirty. I'll have Juan Pedrito dressed and ready. But those are the only shoes he has. I'll polish them, and we'll be ready. As soon as you come from work. We won't make you ashamed.

Felice? It's me, Graciela.

No, I can't talk louder. I'm at work.

Look, I need kind of a favor. There's a patient, a lady here who's got a problem.

Well, wait a minute. Are you listening to me or what?

I can't talk real loud 'cause her husband's in the next room.

Well, would you just listen?

I was going to do this sonogram on her — she's pregnant, right? — and she just starts crying on me. *Híjole,* Felice! This poor lady's got black-and-blue marks all over. I'm not kidding.

From her husband. Who else? Another one of those brides from across the border. And her family's all in Mexico.

Shit. You think they're going to help her? Give me a break. This lady doesn't even speak English. She hasn't been allowed to call home or write or nothing. That's why I'm calling you.

She needs a ride.

Not to Mexico, you goof. Just to the Greyhound. In San Anto.

No, just a ride. She's got her own money. All you'd have to do is drop her off in San Antonio on your way home. Come on, Felice. Please? If we don't help her, who will? I'd drive her myself, but she needs to be on that bus before her husband gets home from work. What do you say?

I don't know. Wait.

Right away, tomorrow even.

Well, if tomorrow's no good for you . . .

It's a date, Felice. Thursday. At the Cash N Carry off I-10. Noon. She'll be ready.

Oh, and her name's Cleófilas.

I don't know. One of those Mexican saints, I guess. A martyr or something.

Cleófilas. C-L-E-O-F-I-L-A-S. Cle. O. Fi. Las. Write it down.

Thanks, Felice. When her kid's born she'll have to name her after us, right?

Yeah, you got it. A regular soap opera sometimes. *Qué vida, comadre. Bueno* bye.

All morning that flutter of half-fear, half-doubt. At any moment Juan Pedro might appear in the doorway. On the street. At the Cash N Carry. Like in the dreams she dreamed.

There was that to think about, yes, until the woman in the pickup drove up. Then there wasn't time to think about anything but the pickup pointed toward San Antonio. Put your bags in the back and get in.

But when they drove across the *arroyo,* the driver opened her mouth and let out a yell as loud as any mariachi. Which startled not only Cleófilas, but Juan Pedrito as well.

Pues, look how cute. I scared you two, right? Sorry. Should've warned you. Every time I cross that bridge I do that. Because of the name, you know. Woman Hollering. *Pues,* I holler. She said this in a Spanish pocked with English and laughed. Did you ever notice, Felice continued, how nothing around here is named after a woman? Really. Unless she's the Virgin. I guess you're only famous if you're a virgin. She was laughing again.

That's why I like the name of that *arroyo*. Makes you want to holler like Tarzan, right?

Everything about this woman, this Felice, amazed Cleófilas. The fact that she drove a pickup. A pickup, mind you, but when Cleófilas asked if it was her husband's, she said she didn't have a husband. The pickup was hers. She herself had chosen it. She herself was paying for it.

I used to have a Pontiac Sunbird. But those cars are for *viejas*. Pussy cars. Now this here is a *real* car.

What kind of talk was that coming from a woman? Cleófilas thought. But then again, Felice was like no woman she'd ever met.

Can you imagine, when we crossed the *arroyo* she just started yelling like a crazy, she would say later to her father and brothers. Just like that. Who would've thought?

Who would've? Pain or rage, perhaps, but not a hoot like the one Felice had just let go. Makes you want to holler like Tarzan, Felice had said.

Then Felice began laughing again, but it wasn't Felice laughing. It was gurgling out of her own throat, a long ribbon of laughter, like water. [1991]

Cristina Garcia has won critical and popular acclaim, including a nomination for a National Book Award, for her spirited first novel, *Dreaming in Cuban* (1992). Born in Cuba in 1958, Garcia immigrated with her family to the United States in 1960. She studied at Barnard College and Johns Hopkins University and later worked as a reporter and correspondent for *Time* magazine. *Dreaming in Cuban* is an original and compelling novel inspired by her Cuban heritage. A lyrical work that blends realism with dreamlike sequences, the story chronicles three generations of the del Pino family from the 1930s to the early 1980s.

The novel focuses on the women of the family and the Cuban Revolution's irrevocable effect on their lives. The matriarch, Celia, disillusioned with her unhappy marriage, is enamored of the revolution and its leader, Fidel Castro; her daughter Lourdes strongly rejects communism and moves with her family to New York, where she achieves success with her enterprising Yankee Doodle Bakery. Celia's other daughter, Felicia, remains in Cuba and meets a tragic end. Pilar Puente del Pino, Lourdes's daughter, rejecting her mother's quest for the American Dream, creates her own dreams that bridge the distance between herself and her lost past.

Michiko Kakutani praised the book in her *New York Times* review: "Fierce, visionary, and at the same time oddly beguiling and funny, *Dreaming in Cuban* is a completely original novel. It announces the debut of a writer, blessed with a poet's ear for language, a historian's fascination with the past, and a musician's intuitive understanding of the ebb and flow of emotion."

from **Dreaming in Cuban**

Pilar Puente

I'm trying on French-style garters and push-up brassières in the dressing room of Abraham & Straus when I think I hear his voice. I stick my head out and see them. My father looks like a kid, laughing and animated and whispering in this woman's ear. The woman is huge and blond and puffy like a 1950s beauty queen gone to seed. She has a cloud of bleached hair and high-muscled calves as if she's been walking in those heels since birth. "Shit!" I think. "Shit! I can't believe this!" I get dressed and follow them, hiding behind racks of hats and on-sale sweaters. At the candy counter, my father holds a toffee crunch above her flicking, disgusting tongue. She's a head taller than he is so it's not easy. It makes me sick to my stomach.

They walk down Fulton Street arm in arm, pretending to window-shop. It's just a run-down stretch of outdated stores with merchandise that's been there since the Bay of Pigs. I guess my father figures that nobody he knows will see him in this neighborhood. The beauty queen leans into him outside a stereo place that's blasting, incredibly, "Stop in the Name of Love." I see that flycatcher tongue of hers go into his mouth. Then my father holds her waxy, bloated face in his hands, as if it were a small sun.

That's it. My mind's made up. I'm going back to Cuba. I'm fed up with everything around here. I take all my money out of the bank, $120, money I earned slaving away at my mother's bakery, and buy a one-way bus ticket to Miami. I figure if I can just get there, I'll be able to make my way to Cuba, maybe rent a boat or get a fisherman to take me. I imagine Abuela Celia's surprise as I sneak up behind her. She'll be sitting in her wicker swing overlooking the sea and she'll smell of salt and violet water. There'll be gulls and crabs along the shore. She'll stroke my cheek with her cool hands, sing quietly in my ear.

I was only two years old when I left Cuba but I remember everything that's happened to me since I was a baby, even word-for-word conversations. I was sitting in my grandmother's lap, playing with her drop pearl earrings, when my mother told her we were leaving the country. Abuela Celia called her a traitor to the revolution.

Mom tried to pull me away but I clung to Abuela and screamed at the top of my lungs. My grandfather came running and said, "Celia, let the girl go. She belongs with Lourdes." That was the last time I saw her.

My mother says that Abuela Celia's had plenty of chances to leave Cuba but that she's stubborn and got her head turned around by El Líder. Mom says "Communist" the way some people say "cancer," low and fierce. She reads the newspapers page by page for leftist conspiracies, jams her finger against imagined evidence and says, "See. What did I tell you?" Last year when El Líder jailed a famous Cuban poet, she sneered at "those leftist intellectual hypocrites" for trying to free him. "They created those prisons, so now they should rot in them!" she shouted, not making much sense at all. "They're dangerous subversives, red to the bone!" Mom's views are strictly black-and-white. It's how she survives.

My mother reads my diary, tracks it down under the mattress, or to the lining of my winter coat. She says it's her responsibility to know my private thoughts, that I'll understand when I have my own kids. That's how she knows about me in the tub. I like to lie on my back and let the shower rain down on me full force. If I move my hips to just the right position, it feels great, like little explosions on a string. Now, whenever I'm in the bathroom, my mother knocks on the door like President Nixon's here and needs to use the john. Meanwhile, I hear her jumping my father night after night until he begs her to leave him alone. You never would have guessed it by looking at her.

When Mom first found out about me in the tub, she beat me in the face and pulled my hair out in big clumps. She called me a *desgraciada* and ground her knuckles into my temples. Then she forced me to work in her bakery every day after school for twenty-five cents an hour. She leaves me nasty notes on the kitchen table reminding me to show up, or else. She thinks working with her will teach me responsibility, clear my head of filthy thoughts. Like I'll get pure pushing her donuts around. It's not like it's done wonders for her, either. She's as fat as a Macy's Thanksgiving Day float from all the pecan sticky buns she eats. I'm convinced they're doing something to her brain.

~~~
~~~

The bus ride down isn't too bad. After New Jersey, it's a straight shot down I-95. I'm sitting next to this skinny woman who got on in Richmond. Her name is Minnie French but she's weirdly old-looking for a young person. Maybe it's her name or the three shopping bags of food she's got under her seat. Fried chicken, potato salad, ham sandwiches, chocolate cupcakes, even a jumbo can of peaches in heavy syrup. Minnie takes dainty bites of everything, chewing it fast like a squirrel. She offers me a chicken thigh but I'm not hungry. Minnie tells me she was born in Toledo, Ohio, the last of thirteen children, and that her mother died giving birth to her. The family split up and Minnie was raised by a grandmother who can quote the Bible chapter and verse and drives a beat-up Cadillac with a CB radio in it. Minnie says her grandma likes talking to other born-again motorists on her way to Chicago to visit relatives.

I tell her how back in Cuba the nannies used to think I was possessed. They rubbed me with blood and leaves when my mother wasn't looking and rattled beads over my forehead. They called me *brujita,* little witch. I stared at them, tried to make them go away. I remember thinking, Okay, I'll start with their hair, make it fall out strand by strand. They always left wearing kerchiefs to cover their bald patches.

I don't really want to talk about my father but I end up telling Minnie how he used to take me horseback riding on our ranch, strapping me in his saddle with a leather seat belt he designed just for me. Dad's family owned casinos in Cuba, and had one of the largest ranches on the island. There were beef cattle and dairy cows, horses, pigs, goats, and lambs. Dad fed them molasses to fatten them, and gave the chickens corn and sorghum until they laid vermilion eggs, rich with vitamins. He took me on an overnight inspection once. We camped out under a sapodilla tree and listened to the pygmy owls with their old women's voices. My father knew I understood more than I could say. He told me stories about Cuba after Columbus came. He said that the Spaniards wiped out more Indians with smallpox than with muskets.

"Why don't we read about this in history books?" I ask Minnie. "It's always one damn battle after another. We only know about Charlemagne and Napoleon because they *fought* their way into posterity." Minnie just shakes her head and looks out the window. She's starting to fall asleep. Her head is lolling about on her shoulders and her mouth is half open.

If it were up to me, I'd record other things. Like the time there was a freak hailstorm in the Congo and the women took it as a sign that they should rule. Or the life stories of prostitutes in Bombay. Why don't I know anything about them? Who chooses what we should know or what's important? I know I have to decide these things for myself. Most of what I've learned that's important I've learned on my own, or from my grandmother.

Abuela Celia and I write to each other sometimes, but mostly I hear her speaking to me at night just before I fall asleep. She tells me stories about her life and what the sea was like that day. She seems to know everything that's happened to me and tells me not to mind my mother too much. Abuela Celia says she wants to see me again. She tells me she loves me.

My grandmother is the one who encouraged me to go to painting classes at Mitzi Kellner's. She's a lady down the block who used to hang out in Greenwich Village with the beatniks. Her house stinks of turpentine and urine from all her cats. She gave an art class Friday afternoons for the neighborhood kids. We started off doing blind contour drawings of our hands, then of lettuce leaves, gourds, anything wrinkly. Mitzi told us not to worry about copying objects exactly, that it was the strength of our lines that counted.

My paintings have been getting more and more abstract lately, violent-looking with clotted swirls of red. Mom thinks they're morbid. Last year, she refused to let me accept the scholarship I won to art school in Manhattan. She said that artists are a bad element, a profligate bunch who shoot heroin. "I won't allow it, Rufino!" she cried with her usual drama. "She'll have to kill me first!" Not that the thought hadn't crossed my mind. But Dad, in his unobtrusive way, finally persuaded her to let me go.

After I started art school last fall, Dad fixed up a studio for me in the back of the warehouse where we live. He bought the warehouse from the city for a hundred dollars when I was in third grade. It had lots of great junk in it until Mom made him move it out. There were a vintage subway turnstile and an antique telephone, the shell of a Bluebird radio, even the nose fin of a locomotive. Where my mother saw junk, Dad saw the clean lines of the machine age.

Dad tells me the place was built in the 1920s as temporary housing for out-of-town public-school teachers. Then it was a dormitory for soldiers during World War II, and later the Transit Authority used it for storage.

A cinder-block wall divides the warehouse in two. Mom wanted a real home up front, so Dad built a couple of bedrooms and a kitchen with a double sink. Mom bought love seats and lace doilies and hung up a tacky watercolor landscape she had brought with her from Cuba. She installed window boxes with geraniums.

My father likes to sift through street castoffs and industrial junk heaps for treasures. Like a proud tomcat showing off the spoils of his hunt, he leaves what he finds for my mother in the kitchen. Mostly she doesn't appreciate it. Dad likes raising things, too. It's in his blood from his days on the farm. Last summer he left a lone bee in a jar on the kitchen counter for my mother.

"What does this mean?" Mom asked suspiciously.

"Apiculture, Lourdes. I've got a nest out back. We're going to grow our own honey, maybe supply all of Brooklyn."

The bees lasted exactly one week. Mom wrapped herself in beach towels and released them all one afternoon when Dad and I were at the movies. They stung her arms and face so badly she could hardly open her eyes. Now she never goes to the back of the warehouse, which is better for us.

Dad has his workshop next to mine and tinkers with his projects there. His latest idea is a voice-command typewriter he says will do away with secretaries.

To get hold of us, Mom rings a huge bell that Dad found in the abandoned shipyard next door. When she's upset, she pulls on the damn thing like the hunchback of Notre Dame.

Our house is on a cement plot near the East River. At night, especially in the summer when the sound carries, I hear the low whistles of the ships as they leave New York harbor. They travel south past the Wall Street skyscrapers, past Ellis Island and the Statue of Liberty, past Bayonne, New Jersey, and the Bay Ridge Channel and under the Verrazano Bridge. Then they make a left at Coney Island and head out to the Atlantic. When I hear those whistles, I want to go with them.

When Minnie wakes up, she says she knows she shouldn't be telling me this, that I'm too young to hear it, but I swear I'm thirteen and that seems to satisfy her. She's seventeen and a half. Minnie says she's going down to Florida to see a doctor her boyfriend knows and get herself an abortion. She doesn't have any children and she doesn't want any either, she tells me. Her voice is flat and even and I hold her hand until she falls asleep again.

I think about how the New Guinea islanders didn't connect sex with pregnancy. They believed that children float on logs in the heavens until the spirits of pregnant women claim them. I'm not too tired so I stay up reading the neon signs off the highway. The missing letters make for weird messages. There's a Shell station missing the "S."

-HELL
OPEN 24 HOURS

My favorite, though, is one, I swear it, in North Carolina that says Cock----s, with an electric martini minus the olive.

No matter how hard I try, though, I keep seeing the bloated face of that aging beauty queen bouncing off the lights into my father's outstretched hands. I guess my parents don't see all that much of each other anymore except when Mom rings for Dad. He always looks real worried, too. Dad used to help Mom in the bakery but she lost patience with him. As handy as he is for some things, he couldn't get the hang of the pastry business, at least not the way my mother runs it.

These days, Mom goes through her employees like those damn pecan sticky buns she eats. Nobody ever lasts more than a day or two. She hires the real down-and-outs, immigrants from Russia or Pakistan, people who don't speak any English, figuring she can get them cheap. Then she screams at them half the day because they don't understand what she's saying. Mom thinks they're all out to steal from her so she rifles through their coats and shopping bags when they're working. Like what are they going to steal? A butter cookie? A French bread? She told me to check someone's purse once and I said no fucking way. She believes she's doing them a favor by giving them a job and breaking them in to American life. Hell, if she's the welcome wagon, they'd better hitch a ride with someone else.

I remember when we first came to New York. We lived in a hotel in Manhattan for five months while my parents waited for the revolution to fail or for the Americans to intervene in Cuba. My mother used to take me for walks in Central Park. Once, an agent from the Art Linkletter show stopped us at the Children's Zoo and asked my mother if I could be on the show. But I didn't speak English yet so he passed.

Mom used to dress me in a little maroon woolen coat with a black velveteen collar and cuffs. The air was different from Cuba's. It had a cold, smoked smell that chilled my lungs. The skies looked newly washed, streaked with light. And the trees were different, too. They looked on fire. I'd run through great heaps of leaves just to hear them rustle like the palm trees during hurricanes in Cuba. But then I'd feel sad looking up at the bare branches and thinking about Abuela Celia. I wonder how my life would have been if I'd stayed with her.

I saw my grandfather, Abuela Celia's husband, when he came to New York to get treated for his stomach cancer. They took him off the plane in a wheelchair. Abuelo Jorge's face was dry and brittle like old parchment. He slept in my bed, which my mother fixed up with a new nubby beige bedspread, and I slept on a cot next to him. Mom bought him a black-and-white television and Abuelo watched the fights and the Spanish *novelas* on Channel 47. No matter how much my mother bathed him, he always smelled of burnt eggs and oranges.

My grandfather was so weak that he'd usually fall asleep by eight o'clock. I'd take his teeth out for him and put them in a glass of water fizzing with denture tablets. He'd whistle softly through his gums all night. Sometimes he'd have nightmares and box the air with his fists. "Come here, you good-for-nothing Spaniard!" he'd shout. "Come and fight like a man!" But then he'd settle down, muttering a few curses.

When Mom first started taking him for cobalt treatments I imagined sharp blue beams aimed at his stomach. A strange color for healing, I thought. Nothing we eat is blue, not *blue* blue like my grandfather's eyes, so why didn't the doctors change the color of those damn beams to green? We eat green, it's healthy. If only they had changed those lights to green, I thought, a nice jade green, he'd have gotten better.

My grandfather told me once that I reminded him of Abuela

Celia. I took that as a compliment. He used to write her letters every day, when he still had the strength, long letters in an old-fashioned script with flourishes and curlicues. You wouldn't expect him to have such fine handwriting. They were romantic letters, too. He read one out loud to me. He called Abuela Celia his "dove in the desert." Now he can't write to her much. And he's too proud to ask any of us to do it for him. Abuela Celia writes back to him every once in a while, but her letters are full of facts, about this meeting or that, nothing more. They make my grandfather sad.

Minnie rides as far as Jacksonville. I'm curious so I look out the window to see who's come to pick her up. But by the time the bus pulls away she's still waiting.

The scenery gets so dull in Florida that I finally fall asleep. I remember one dream. It's midnight and there are people around me praying on the beach. I'm wearing a white dress and turban and I can hear the ocean nearby, only I can't see it. I'm sitting on a chair, a kind of throne, with antlers fastened to the back. The people lift me up high and walk with me in a slow procession toward the sea. They're chanting in a language I don't understand. I don't feel scared, though. I can see the stars and the moon and the black sky revolving overhead. I can see my grandmother's face. . . .

Pilar (1978)

My mother told me that Abuela Celia was an atheist before I even understood what the word meant. I liked the sound of it, the derision with which my mother pronounced it, and knew immediately it was what I wanted to become. I don't know exactly when I stopped believing in God. It wasn't as deliberate as deciding, at age six, to become an atheist, but more like an imperceptible sloughing of layers. One day I noticed there was no more skin to absently peel, just air where there'd been artifice.

A few weeks ago, I found photographs of Abuela Celia in my mother's hosiery drawer. There was a picture of Abuela in 1931, standing under a tree in her T-strap shoes and wearing a flouncy dress with a polka-dotted bow and puffed sleeves. Abuela Celia's fingers were tapered and delicate and rested on her hips. Her hair was parted on the right and came down to her shoulders, accentuating the mole by her lips. There was a tension at the corners of her mouth that could have veered toward sadness or joy. Her eyes told of experience she did not yet possess.

There were other photographs. Abuela Celia in Soroa with an orchid in her hair. In a cream linen suit descending from a train. At the beach with my mother and my aunt. Tía Felicia is in Abuela's arms, a plump, pink-lozenge baby. My mother, unsmiling, skinny and dark from the sun, stands a distance away.

I have a trick to tell someone's public face from their private one. If the person is left-handed, like Abuela Celia, the right side of her face betrays her true feelings. I placed a finger over the left side of my grandmother's face, and in photograph after photograph I saw the truth.

I feel much more connected to Abuela Celia than to Mom, even though I haven't seen my grandmother in seventeen years. We don't speak at night anymore, but she's left me her legacy nonetheless — a love for the sea and the smoothness of pearls, an appreciation of music and words, sympathy for the underdog, and a disregard for boundaries. Even in silence, she gives me the confidence to do what I believe is right, to trust my own perceptions.

This is a constant struggle around my mother, who systematically rewrites history to suit her views of the world. This reshaping of events happens in a dozen ways every day, contesting reality. It's not a matter of premeditated deception. Mom truly believes that her version of events is correct, down to details that I know, for a fact, are wrong. To this day, my mother insists that I ran away from her at the Miami airport after we first left Cuba. But it was *she* who turned and ran when she thought she heard my father's voice. I wandered around lost until a pilot took me to his airline's office and gave me a lollipop.

It's not just our personal history that gets mangled. Mom filters other people's lives through her distorting lens. Maybe it's that wandering eye of hers. It makes her see only what she wants to see instead of what's really there. Like Mr. Paresi, a pimpy Brooklyn lawyer who my mother claims is the number-one criminal defense attorney in New York, complete with an impressive roster of Mafia clients. And this because he comes to her shop every morning and buys two chocolate-frosted donuts for his breakfast.

Mom's embellishments and half-truths usually equip her to tell a good story, though. And her English, her immigrant English, has a touch of otherness that makes it unintentionally precise. Maybe in the end the facts are not as important as the underlying truth she wants to convey. Telling her own truth is *the* truth to her, even if it's at the expense of chipping away our past.

I suppose I'm guilty in my own way of a creative transformation or two. Like my painting of the Statue of Liberty that caused such a commotion at the Yankee Doodle Bakery. It's funny but last year the Sex Pistols ended up doing the same thing with a photograph of Queen Elizabeth on the cover of their *God Save the Queen* single. They put a safety pin through the Queen's nose and the entire country was up in arms. Anarchy in the U.K., I love it.

Mom is fomenting her own brand of anarchy closer to home. Her Yankee Doodle bakeries have become gathering places for these shady Cuban extremists who come all the way from New Jersey and the Bronx to talk their dinosaur politics and drink her killer espressos. Last month they started a cablegram campaign against El Líder. They set up a toll-free hot line so that Cuban exiles could call in and choose from three scathing messages to send directly to the National Palace, demanding El Líder's resignation.

I heard one of my mother's cohorts boasting how last year he'd called in a bomb threat to the Metropolitan Opera House, where Alicia Alonso, the prima ballerina of the National Ballet of Cuba and a supporter of El Líder, was scheduled to dance. "I delayed *Giselle* for seventy-five minutes!" he bragged. If I'd known about it then, I would have sicked the FBI on him.

Just last week, the lot of them were celebrating — with cigars and sparkling cider — the murder of a journalist in Miami who advocated reestablishing ties with Cuba. Those creeps passed around the Spanish newspaper and clapped each other on the back, as if they themselves had struck a big blow against the forces of evil. The front-page photograph showed the reporter's arm dangling from a poinciana tree on Key Biscayne after the bomb in his car had exploded.

I wonder how Mom could be Abuela Celia's daughter. And what I'm doing as my mother's daughter. Something got horribly scrambled along the way. [1992]

Judith Ortiz Cofer was born in 1952 in Hormigueros, Puerto Rico. She spent much of her childhood in Paterson, New Jersey, where her love of comics led people to call her "the Comic Book Kid." She received an M.A. in English from Florida Atlantic University, and she teaches at the University of Georgia. Ortiz Cofer is a poet (*Terms of Survival,* 1987), fiction writer, and memoirist (*Silent Dancing,* 1990). Her novel *The Line of the Sun* (1990) was the first new work of fiction ever published by the University of Georgia Press.

Ortiz Cofer is one of the few Puerto Rican writers on the mainland whose writing does not express the New York experience. In her lyrical, often bittersweet work the individual is terrifyingly sensitive to personal slight and loss and forced to adapt to forces beyond his or her control. "American History" and "Guard Duty" are excerpted from *The Latin Deli* (1993), a collection of prose and poetry.

American History

I once read in a *Ripley's Believe It or Not* column that Paterson, New Jersey, is the place where the Straight and Narrow (streets) intersect. The Puerto Rican tenement known as El Building was one block up from Straight. It was, in fact, the corner of Straight and Market; not "at" the corner, but *the* corner. At almost any hour of the day, El Building was like a monstrous jukebox, blasting out *salsas* from open windows as the residents, mostly new immigrants just up from the island, tried to drown out whatever they were currently enduring with loud music. But the day President Kennedy was shot, there was a profound silence in El Building, even the abusive tongues of viragoes, the cursing of the unemployed, and the screeching of small children had been somehow muted. President Kennedy was a saint to these people. In fact, soon his photograph would be hung alongside the Sacred Heart and over the spiritist altars that many women kept in their apartments. He would become part of the hierarchy of martyrs they prayed to for favors that only one who had died for a cause would understand.

On the day that President Kennedy was shot, my ninth grade

class had been out in the fenced playground of Public School Number 13. We had been given "free" exercise time and had been ordered by our P.E. teacher, Mr. DePalma, to "keep moving." That meant that the girls should jump rope and the boys toss basketballs through a hoop at the far end of the yard. He in the meantime would "keep an eye" on us from just inside the building.

It was a cold gray day in Paterson. The kind that warns of early snow. I was miserable, since I had forgotten my gloves and my knuckles were turning red and raw from the jump rope. I was also taking a lot of abuse from the black girls for not turning the rope hard and fast enough for them.

"Hey, Skinny Bones, pump it, girl. Ain't you got no energy today?" Gail, the biggest of the black girls, who had the other end of the rope, yelled, "Didn't you eat your rice and beans and pork chops for breakfast today?"

The other girls picked up the "pork chop" and made it into a refrain: "Pork chop, pork chop, did you eat your pork chop?" They entered the double ropes in pairs and exited without tripping or missing a beat. I felt a burning on my cheeks, and then my glasses fogged up so that I could not manage to coordinate the jump rope with Gail. The chill was doing to me what it always did, entering my bones, making me cry, humiliating me. I hated the city, especially in winter. I hated Public School Number 13. I hated my skinny flat-chested body, and I envied the black girls who could jump rope so fast that their legs became a blur. They always seemed to be warm while I froze.

There was only one source of beauty and light for me that school year. The only thing I had anticipated at the start of the semester. That was seeing Eugene. In August, Eugene and his family had moved into the only house on the block that had a yard and trees. I could see his place from my window in El Building. In fact, if I sat on the fire escape I was literally suspended above Eugene's backyard. It was my favorite spot to read my library books in the summer. Until that August the house had been occupied by an old Jewish couple. Over the years I had become part of their family, without their knowing it, of course. I had a view of their kitchen and their backyard, and though I could not hear what they said, I knew when they were arguing, when one of them was sick, and many other things. I knew all this by watching them at mealtimes. I could see their kitchen table, the sink and the stove. During good times, he sat at the table and read his newspapers while she fixed the meals. If they argued, he would leave and the old woman would sit and stare at nothing for a long time. When one of them was sick, the other would come and get things from the kitchen and carry them out on a tray. The old man had died in June. The last week of school I had not seen him at the table at all. Then one day I saw that there was a crowd in the kitchen. The old woman had finally emerged from the house on the arm of a stocky middle-aged woman whom I had seen there a few times before, maybe her daughter. Then a man had carried out suitcases. The house had stood empty for weeks. I had had to resist the temptation to climb down into the yard and water the flowers the old lady had taken such good care of.

By the time Eugene's family moved in, the yard was a tangled mass of weeds. The father had spent several days mowing, and when he finished, I didn't see the red, yellow, and purple clusters that meant flowers to me from where I sat. I didn't see this family sit down at the kitchen table together. It was just the mother, a red-headed tall woman who wore a white uniform — a nurse's, I guessed it was; the father was gone before I got up in the morning and was never there at dinner time. I only saw him on weekends when they sometimes sat on lawn chairs under the oak tree, each hidden behind a section of the newspaper; and there was Eugene. He was tall and blond, and he wore glasses. I liked him right away because he sat at the kitchen table and read books for hours. That summer, before we had even spoken one word to each other, I kept him company on my fire escape.

Once school started I looked for him in all my classes, but P.S. 13 was a huge, overpopulated place and it took me days and many discreet questions to discover that Eugene was in honors classes for all his subjects; classes that were not open to me because English was not my first language, though I was a straight A student. After much maneuvering I managed "to run into him" in the hallway where his locker was — on the other side of the building from mine — and in study hall at the library, where he first seemed to notice me but did not speak; and finally, on the way home after school one day when I decided to approach him directly, though my stomach was doing somersaults.

I was ready for rejection, snobbery, the worst. But when I came up to him, practically panting in my nervousness, and blurted out "You're Eugene. Right?" he smiled, pushed his glasses up on his nose, and nodded. I saw then that he was blushing deeply. Eugene liked me, but he was shy. I did most of the talking that day. He nodded and smiled a lot. In the weeks that followed, we walked home together. He would linger at the corner of El Building for a few minutes then walk down to his two-story house. It was not until Eugene moved into that house that I noticed that El Building blocked most of the sun and that the only spot that got a little sunlight during the day was the tiny square of earth the old woman had planted with flowers.

I did not tell Eugene that I could see inside his kitchen from my bedroom. I felt dishonest, but I liked my secret sharing of his evenings, especially now that I knew what he was reading, since we chose our books together at the school library.

One day my mother came into my room as I was sitting on the windowsill staring out. In her abrupt way she said: "Elena, you are acting 'moony.'" *Enamorada* was what she really said — that is, like a girl stupidly infatuated. Since I had turned fourteen and started menstruating my mother had been more vigilant than ever. She acted as if I was going to go crazy or explode or something if she didn't watch me and nag me all the time about being a señorita now. She kept talking about virtue, morality, and other subjects that did not interest me in the least. My mother was unhappy in Paterson, but my father had a good job at the blue jeans factory in Passaic, and soon, he kept assuring us, we would be moving to our own house there. Every Sunday we drove out to the suburbs of Paterson, Clifton, and Passaic, out to where people mowed grass on Sundays in the summer and where children made snowmen in the winter from pure white snow, not like the gray slush of Paterson, which seemed to fall from the sky in that hue. I had learned to listen to my parents' dreams, which were spoken in Spanish, as fairy tales, like the stories about life in the island paradise of Puerto Rico before I was born. I had been to the Island once as a little girl, to grandmother's funeral, and all I remembered was wailing women in black, my mother becoming hysterical and being given a pill that made her sleep two days, and me feeling lost in a crowd of strangers all claiming to be my aunts, uncles, and cousins. I had actually been glad to return to the city. We had not been back there since then, though my parents talked constantly about buying a house on the beach someday, retiring on the island — that was a common topic among the residents of El Building. As for me, I was going to go to college and become a teacher.

But after meeting Eugene I began to think of the present more than of the future. What I wanted now was to enter that house I had watched for so many years. I wanted to see the other rooms where the old people had lived and where the boy I liked spent his time. Most of all, I wanted to sit at the kitchen table with Eugene like two adults, like the old man and his wife had done, maybe drink some coffee and talk about books. I had started reading *Gone with the Wind*. I was enthralled by it, with the daring and the passion of the beautiful girl living in a mansion, and with her devoted parents and the slaves who did everything for them. I didn't believe such a world had ever really existed, and I wanted to ask Eugene some questions, since he and his parents, he had told me, had come up from Georgia, the same place where the novel was set. His father worked for a company that had transferred him to Paterson. His mother was very unhappy, Eugene said, in his beautiful voice that rose and fell over words in a strange, lilting way. The kids at school called him the Hick and made fun of the way he talked. I knew I was his only friend so far, and I liked that, though I felt sad for him sometimes. Skinny Bones and the Hick was what they called us at school when we were seen together.

The day Mr. DePalma came out into the cold and asked us to line up in front of him was the day that President Kennedy was shot. Mr. DePalma, a short, muscular man with slicked-down black hair, was the science teacher, P.E. coach, and disciplinarian at P.S. 13. He was the teacher to whose homeroom you got assigned if you were a troublemaker, and the man called out to break up playground fights, and to escort violently angry teenagers to the office. And Mr. DePalma was the man who called your parents in for "a conference."

That day, he stood in front of two rows of mostly black and Puerto Rican kids, brittle from their efforts to "keep moving" on a November day that was turning bitter cold. Mr. DePalma, to our complete shock, was crying. Not just adult tears, but really sobbing. There were a few titters from the back of the line where I stood, shivering.

"Listen," Mr. DePalma raised his arms over his head as if he were about to conduct an orchestra. His voice broke, and he covered his face with his hands. His barrel chest was heaving. Someone giggled behind me.

"Listen," he repeated, "something awful has happened." A strange gurgling came from his throat, and he turned around and spit on the cement behind him.

"Gross," someone said, and there was a lot of laughter.

"The president is dead, you idiots. I should have known that wouldn't mean anything to a bunch of losers like you kids. Go home." He was shrieking now. No one moved for a minute or two, but then a big girl let out a "yeah!" and ran to get her books piled up with the others against the brick wall of the school building. The others followed in a mad scramble to get to their things before somebody caught on. It was still an hour to the dismissal bell.

A little scared, I headed for El Building. There was an eerie feeling on the streets. I looked into Mario's drugstore, a favorite hangout for the high school crowd, but there were only a couple of old Jewish men at the soda bar, talking with the short order cook in tones that sounded almost angry, but they were keeping their voices low. Even the traffic on one of the busiest intersections in Paterson — Straight Street and Park Avenue — seemed to be moving slower. There were no horns blasting that day. At El Building, the usual little group of unemployed men were not hanging out on the front stoop, making it difficult for women to enter the front door. No music spilled out from open doors in the hallway. When I walked into our apartment, I found my mother sitting in front of the grainy picture of the television set.

She looked up at me with a tear-streaked face and just said: "Dios mío," turning back to the set as if it were pulling at her eyes. I went into my room.

Though I wanted to feel the right thing about President Kennedy's death, I could not fight the feeling of elation that stirred in my chest. Today was the day I was to visit Eugene in his house. He had asked me to come over after school to study for an American history test with him. We had also planned to walk to the public library together. I looked down into his yard. The oak tree was bare of leaves, and the ground looked gray with ice. The light through the large kitchen window of his house told me that El Building blocked the sun to such an extent that they had to turn lights on in the middle of the day. I felt ashamed about it. But the white kitchen table with the lamp hanging just above it looked cozy and inviting. I would soon sit there, across from Eugene, and I would tell him about my perch just above his house. Maybe I would.

In the next thirty minutes I changed clothes, put on a little pink lipstick, and got my books together. Then I went in to tell my mother that I was going to a friend's house to study. I did not expect her reaction.

"You are going out *today?*" The way she said "today" sounded as if a storm warning had been issued. It was said in utter disbelief. Before I could answer, she came toward me and held my elbows as I clutched my books.

"*Hija,* the president has been killed. We must show respect. He was a great man. Come to church with me tonight."

She tried to embrace me, but my books were in the way. My first impulse was to comfort her, she seemed so distraught, but I had to meet Eugene in fifteen minutes.

"I have a test to study for, Mama. I will be home by eight."

"You are forgetting who you are, *Niña*. I have seen you staring down at that boy's house. You are heading for humiliation and pain." My mother said this in Spanish and in a resigned tone that surprised me, as if she had no intention of stopping me from "heading for humiliation and pain." I started for the door. She sat in front of the TV, holding a white handkerchief to her face.

I walked out to the street and around the chain-link fence that separated El Building from Eugene's house. The yard was neatly edged around the little walk that led to the door. It always amazed me how Paterson, the inner core of the city, had no apparent logic to its architecture. Small, neat, single residences like this one could be found right next to huge, dilapidated apartment buildings like El Building. My guess was that the little houses had been there first, then the immigrants had come in droves, and the monstrosities had been raised for them — the Italians, the Irish, the Jews, and now us, the Puerto Ricans, and the blacks. The door was painted a deep green: *verde,* the color of hope. I had heard my mother say it: *Verde-Esperanza*.

I knocked softly. A few suspenseful moments later the door opened just a crack. The red, swollen face of a woman appeared. She had a halo of red hair floating over a delicate ivory face —

the face of a doll — with freckles on the nose. Her smudged eye makeup made her look unreal to me, like a mannequin seen through a warped store window.

"What do you want?" Her voice was tiny and sweet-sounding, like a little girl's, but her tone was not friendly.

"I'm Eugene's friend. He asked me over. To study." I thrust out my books, a silly gesture that embarrassed me almost immediately.

"You live there?" She pointed up to El Building, which looked particularly ugly, like a gray prison with its many dirty windows and rusty fire escapes. The woman had stepped halfway out, and I could see that she wore a white nurse's uniform with "St. Joseph's Hospital" on the name tag.

"Yes. I do."

She looked intently at me for a couple of heartbeats, then said as if to herself. "I don't know how you people do it." Then directly to me: "Listen. Honey. Eugene doesn't want to study with you. He is a smart boy. Doesn't need help. You understand me. I am truly sorry if he told you you could come over. He cannot study with you. It's nothing personal. You understand? We won't be in this place much longer, no need for him to get close to people — it'll just make it harder for him later. Run back home now."

I couldn't move. I just stood there in shock at hearing these things said to me in such a honey-drenched voice. I had never heard an accent like hers except for Eugene's softer version. It was as if she were singing me a little song.

"What's wrong? Didn't you hear what I said?" She seemed very angry, and I finally snapped out of my trance. I turned away from the green door and heard her close it gently.

Our apartment was empty when I got home. My mother was in someone else's kitchen, seeking the solace she needed. Father would come in from his late shift at midnight. I would hear them talking softly in the kitchen for hours that night. They would not discuss their dreams for the future, or life in Puerto Rico, as they often did; that night they would talk sadly about the young widow and her two children, as if they were family. For the next few days, we would observe *luto* in our apartment; that is, we would practice restraint and silence — no loud music or laughter. Some of the women of El Building would wear black for weeks.

That night, I lay in my bed, trying to feel the right thing for our dead president. But the tears that came up from a deep source inside me were strictly for me. When my mother came to the door, I pretended to be sleeping. Sometime during the night, I saw from my bed the streetlight come on. It had a pink halo around it. I went to my window and pressed my face to the cool glass. Looking up at the light I could see the white snow falling like a lace veil over its face. I did not look down to see it turning gray as it touched the ground below. [1993]

Guard Duty

In my Spanish-language childhood
I was put under the care
of *El Ángel de la Guarda*,

my Guardian Angel, the military guard
who required a nightly salute, a plea
on my knees for protection
against the dangers hidden in dreams,
and from night-prowling demons.

In the print framed over my bed,
he was portrayed as a feathered androgyny
hovering above two barefoot children
whose features were set in pastel horror —

and no wonder — under the bridge
they were crossing yawned
a sulfurous abyss — their only light being
the glow of the thing with wings
otherwise invisible to them.

I could take no comfort in this dark
nursery myth, as some nights
I lay awake listening to the murmur
of my parents' voices

sharing their incomprehensible plans
in a well-lit kitchen, while I brooded
over the cruel indifference of adults
who abandoned children to the night,
and about that *Comandante* in the sky
who knew everything I did, or thought of doing,
whose soldier could so calmly smile
while innocent children crossed over darkness,
alone, afraid, night after night.

[1993]

Oscar Hijuelos was born in New York City in 1951 and received his bachelor of arts and master's degrees from City College of New York. His first novel was *Our House in the Last World* (1983), one of the best novels about immigration to the urban United States, unique in its portrayal of a family arriving in the years preceding the Cuban Revolution. His second, *The Mambo Kings Play Songs of Love* (1989), won the Pulitzer Prize for Fiction in 1990, the only such prize ever awarded to a U.S. Latino, and was made into a film starring Armand Assante. The work reinvents the mambo and cha-cha era in New York, and explores frustrated crossover dreams; according to Marc Zimmerman, the novel is a "literary transposition of a music culture in a prose that uncovers the love songs all but buried in the blur of sex, drink, and U.S. commodification." *The Fourteen Sisters of Emilio Montez O'Brien* (1993), Hijuelos's third novel, is a beautifully composed pastorale about the family of an Irish photographer and his Cuban wife. His most recent work, the acclaimed *Mr. Ives' Christmas* (1995), explores the possibility of spiritual life in America.

Hijuelos is an ambitious writer, bold in his choice of themes and his use of language. *The Fourteen Sisters of Emilio Montez O'Brien* contains some of the stylistically most beautiful prose in American fiction. Though the book meanders somewhat, and its ending dissolves into a nonending, the portrayal of the Irish-Cuban family is outstanding. Following are the opening pages of *The Fourteen Sisters*. Note the erotic awareness of the omniscient narrator, who seems to be drawn to his own creations as much as the auspicious aviator is.

from The Fourteen Sisters of Emilio Montez O'Brien

The Handsome Man from Heaven

The house in which the fourteen sisters of Emilio Montez O'Brien lived radiated femininity. Men who passed by the white picket fence — the postman, the rag seller, the iceman — were sometimes startled by a strong scent of flowers, as if perfume had been poured onto the floorboards and ground. And when the door to the house — a rickety, many-roomed Victorian affair some few miles outside the small Pennsylvania town of Cobbleton, with teetering beams and rain-soaked clapboard façade (with gables, rusted hinges, and a fetid outhouse on a foundation that tended to creak during heavy rains, a roof that leaked, and with splintering surfaces everywhere) — when their door opened on the world, the power of these females, even the smallest infants, nearly molecular in its adamancy, slipped out and had its transforming effect upon men. Over the years a thick maple tree, standing out in the yard, had been the scene of numerous accidents: men were thrown from their horses or, begoggled and yet blinded by what they may have taken as the sun, skidded their Model Ts, their Packards, their sporty sedans off the road into a ditch, axles bent and crankcases hissing steam.

Even their Irish father, Nelson O'Brien, photographer and the owner of the Jewel Box Movie Theater in town, sometimes noticed the effects of their feminine influence on himself: this gentleman would move through the rooms of the house feeling a sense of elation and love that sometimes startled him; on other days, he had the air of a lost sailor looking out toward the edges of the sea. Struggling with his thoughts, he'd try to understand just what his pretty girls were thinking, and he, a brooding man, aware of life's troubles, did not know what to make of their gaiety. Sometimes, when his daughters were gathered in the parlor, he would walk by them slowly, as if passing through a corridor thick with silk curtains that had been warmed in the sun. And he would find himself sitting on the couch with one of his little daughters on his lap, playing a silly game like "smack-your-Poppy-on-the-nose," or easily spend a half hour trying to teach baby a single word like "apple," repeating it until he would pull from his jacket pocket a watch on a chain and, noticing the time, make his way out into the world to work, leaving his quivering, exuberant daughters behind. And they would call out to him or follow him to the door, and when he got into his Model T to drive into town or along the country roads to some job, they would gather on the porch, waving goodbye to their father, who at such moments would experience a pleasant befuddlement.

Once, around 1921, when Margarita Montez O'Brien, the oldest of the sisters, was nineteen, an aviator brought down his biplane, a Sopwith Camel, in a hayfield about a quarter of a mile west of the house, a dizziness having come over him just as his plane was passing overhead, a half mile above, as if caught in a sirenic beam of influence that flowed upward from the parlor, where the sisters happened to have gathered in chaotic preparation for a midday meal. He had been flying west over the fields of grazing cattle and sheep, silos, barns, and farmhouses, a banner advertising the Daredevils' Flying Circus trailing behind him, when they heard his engine sputtering, the propeller jamming in the distance, and out their window they watched him drop down through the clouds, his craft much like a falling and sometimes spinning cross. And because they hadn't seen very many airplanes in their lives, they had rushed outside to their porch, along with everybody else in that part of the countryside.

At that time of the day, some of them were sitting around on couches, studying their schoolbooks, yawning, laughing, sewing, while others were stretched out on the rug before the fireplace, trying to contact the spirits with a Ouija board or playing rummy or Go Fish, good American card games. Still others were in the kitchen helping their mother (hers was the voice that, sighing, one heard every now and then as she would cross a room). And the twins were practicing — Olga playing the piano, Jacqueline the violin, and the third of the musical sisters, Maria, singing, everything from "I'd Rather Love What I Cannot Have Than Have What I Cannot Love" to "The Sheik of Araby" (or, as a joke, to announce the arrival of their father, "Ta-Ra-Ra-Boom-Dee-Ay"). And others were scavenging for chairs, preparing the children's table for the toddlers and pulling the long oak table, with animal feet and lion knobs with brass rings through their noses, away from the wall and setting each place with its proper utensils, plates, and glasses — all this work for a single meal, momentous.

There were thirteen sisters then — counting little Violeta, four months old, who had been born in February of that year, colicky and quite adept at waking the house up in the middle of the night, when she'd scream out for her tired Cuban mother's milk; and excluding the fourteenth sister, Gloria, who would be born in 1923. The oldest of the sisters, Margarita — or Meg, as her Irish father called her — had been born aboard a ship bound from Cuba to the United States in 1902. Then Isabel had been born in 1904, in that very house, like the others, and had come into the world with a scowl and was named after the queen who had ruled Spain at the time of Columbus. And then Maria, the third of the sisters, was born in 1906, Maria whose birth had been weightless and effortless, a birth that made Mariela filled up with light and the yellow, candle-like warmth of grace, so that she named this little girl after her mother, Maria, in Cuba, as she was a beautiful and graceful presence that could bring no harm to others and could be blessed with a nearly divine singing voice — years later she would be able to break glass bells and plates with a high-C note, and reach the next A — and with so good a disposition and such humility as to have the air of a saint or an angel culled from the choirs of the Lord. Then came the birth (and death) of Ebe, who lived for five days and passed away in 1907 because of a draft from the window, coming down with a fever which she, poor thing, could not overcome. Because of that trial, Mariela wanted to name the next daughter Dolores, but the following year, perhaps because of a curious conjunction of the planetary spheres, melodious with astral harmonies, the twins Olga and Jacqueline arrived, among the sisters the two who loved each other the most in their cribs and wailed and cooed in harmony, banged and kicked in time, and were most aware of the musical nature of things. Olga was named after a Russian ballerina whose picture had once appeared in a local advertisement for a ballet company that was to perform in Philadelphia during the weeks of her impending conception, and who was shown pirouetting on a point of light, impressing their mother. Jacqueline was so named simply because their mother had liked the ring of the word, sounding Parisian and worldly and auguring, to her mind, a good life. These were the mellifluously cooing daughters whose presence, with Maria's, would inspire music in the household, for their father, Nelson O'Brien, would one day buy them a weighty upright piano, an accordion, and a violin and they would learn to play and sing, their first teacher a Miss Redbreast, for piano and violin, and the elegant and most Parisian Mrs. Vidal for voice, so that the house would fill with lieder and popular songs — "If Money Is Friendly, It Ain't on Speaking Terms with Me!" They would hum as babies and later sing, these two sisters, along with Maria, one day forming the musical trio that would be known as the Three Nightingales, the Chanteuses, and finally, and more simply, as Olga, Maria, and Jacqueline. The following year their mother rested, but in 1910 she brought Helen into the world, the little female, or *"hembrita,"* as her mother called all the babies, naming her after the glittery label on a facial ointment, The Helen of Troy Beauty Pomade, said to eradicate wrinkles, to soften and add a youthful glow to the user's skin — a fortuitous choice because, of all the sisters, she would be the most beautiful and, never growing old, would always possess the face of a winsome adolescent beauty. Then in 1911 the ever-plump, from the cradle into life, Irene was born, and then Sarah in 1912, pensive and a little angry, the first of the fourteen sisters to feel as though her older sisters were aunts. She was the first of the daughters whom their mother relegated to the care of the others, and she spoke fewer words of Spanish than her older sisters and tended to feel lost in the house when they started chitchatting in the parlor. Then came another girl, who strangled on her umbilical cord, and she was called Patricia, and that name passed on to the next girl, born in 1914, Patricia, the ninth living sister, who because of her namesake's misfortune came in the wake of grief and seemed terribly aware of shadows and fleeting spirits — sometimes spying them in the hall, in the windowpanes, and in the mirrors. She'd hope for a glimpse of that other Patricia, who frightened and castigated her and who would over the years bring her to the edge of an affable, spiritist eccentricity, so that one day she would live in a nondescript house in northern New York State, in a community of spiritists, and hang in her window a little sign reading, "Fortunes Told." Then in 1916 Veronica was born and she was named after the saint who had covered Christ's bloodied face with a veil. She was the sister who would perceive the suffering and torment of men in this world and who would like a strong man to protect her, even if she would confuse harshness and abruptness of action with strength, as if it would be her destiny to wipe the bloodied face of a husband who was to bring unnecessary pain into her life and the lives of others. Then Marta was born in 1917, then Carmen in 1919, and poor Violeta in 1921 — pleasure-bound and promiscuous, happy and delighted with the pleasing complexities of her body, the sister who liked to linger the longest in the bathtub, touching herself and pinching her breasts so much that they grew the largest, whose nipples would become famous with her lovers for being so cherry-red, and whose left labia had a mole, which intensified the pleasure of love.

These were calamitous sisters, ambitious sisters, sisters who stood by the windows at night weeping over the moon; they were sisters who cut out advertisements from the newspapers for pretty dresses and sat in front of an old foot-pedaled Singer sewing machine making lace bonnets and lace-trimmed dresses. They were sisters who had once sat dreaming about the Great War; sisters with arched eyebrows, who undressed quietly, their skirts and undergarments falling softly to the floor, whose toes turned red and breasts taut-tipped, nipples puckering when they bathed, sinking into the water; sisters who played the piano, stoically practicing their scales and daydreaming about a world in which music gushed and every blossom sang. They were small-boned or buxom sisters, sisters with moles and sisters whose infantile nakedness revealed the featureless beauty of angels, sisters whose bodies began to quiver voluptuously, some with the high and wide cheekbones of their father, those who would be tall, those with blue or hazel eyes or the dark eyes of their mother, and some who were petite and elegant, some whose eyes would suggest mischief and mirth: vibrant, sad, funny, and powerful sisters.

Their presence was so intense that, even at night, when slipping off into dreams, Margarita, the oldest, sometimes could not escape them. Not that they were always physically there, but while sleeping she'd come across them in other manifestations: as wiry ivy, entangled and dense on a wall, as a piece of rope knotted many times into itself, or as a spool of yarn being pummeled and drawn through the legs of chairs and tables by a playful cat. She sometimes found herself imagining the night sky and counting out the stars over the horizon, and two planets: Jupiter, her father, the Irishman Nelson O'Brien; and Venus, the morning star, her Cuban mother (as, in life itself, her mother had an affinity for looking up and watching for heavenly motions from the porch of their house). And she often dreamed about flocks of birds and schools of fish, and buzzing hives, herds of cattle and sheep. Weather vanes spun, porch chimes rang, flower petals fell from the clouds, a dozen (or more) moons rose. Sometimes she dreamed of roaming through a house much like the one in which they lived but with an endless number of rooms whose doors opened to another succession of rooms, each dense and crowded with the rudimentary objects of Margarita's and her sisters' lives. (Some rooms, she would remember years later, were cluttered with dolls — china dolls, bisque-headed dolls, rag dolls, Marie Antoinette dolls — and sometimes, just when she would begin to feel queasy, knowing that in fact her sisters were still all around her, the dolls simply hopped to their feet, turned into figures of flesh, bone, and blood, and, as in a fairy tale, became, quite simply, her sisters.)

Even while innocently attending to their business, the Montez O'Brien sisters were able, whether in a crib or in the bud of their troubling, alluring femininity, to produce such disturbances as to make even an experienced pilot (a veteran of the campaigns of France during the Great War) grow lachrymose and, without knowing why, lose control of his aircraft. As farmers stopped before their plows, kids climbed trees, and housewives with aprons on and plates in hand gazed up at the sky, the aircraft's shadow passed over the quilted earth, a jagged, wobbly, T-shaped phantasm breaking up and subdividing each time it passed over a fence or sloping rooftop. Then the engine stopped altogether and the Sopwith Camel dropped down in a blunt glide toward the ground, where its tires blew out from the impact and its wings clipped a haystack, the craft rolling along a field, scaring away the grazing animals and sending the crows and blackbirds out of the trees, before it tumbled over on its side.

When the sisters, among others, arrived at the wreck, the pilot had already made his way out of the plane, zigzagging like a drunkard around hay mounds and limping past the most docile cows with sad beetle-brown eyes and fly-wracking tails. He was wearing a brown, wind-worn leather jacket, a helmet, and aviator's goggles, his handsome brow smeared with engine grease. Overwhelmed by delirium and a desire to sleep, he found the sight of the sisters, who'd surrounded him, too much to resist. Soon the powerful Isabel and the rotund and ever-hungry Irene were helping him back to the house. There he collapsed on the parlor sofa and fell asleep.

Later, opening his eyes (he'd dreamed about swimming through a dense, nearly gelatinous water thick with wavery plants and blossoms), the aviator, weary and a little startled, suddenly found himself in the center of this household. Female molecules, the perfume of their bodies, the carbon dioxide of their breath, left him light-headed, and the excitement of the landing and subsequent sleep made him voraciously hungry. It did not help that Irene and Maria, two of the most natural cooks in the world, were in the kitchen preparing fattening and delicious food, inexpensive but enlarging, as these sisters were fond of using heavy cream and butter and liked to fry potatoes and onions and chicken and had become specialists when it came to making big pots of Irish-style beef stew, which was really like a Cuban concoction called *caldo gallego* with a broth base. And even though their mother had never been one to dwell on the finer details of cuisine, often daydreaming and burning the bottoms of pots, as she'd leave them on the stove too long, these sisters displayed great natural talents in this regard, knowing their sweets and fats and herb-spiced sauces. As a result, there was always great industry in their kitchen. They made applesauce with boiled raisins, pancakes with sugar, flour, and butter. Muffins and cookies, long loaves of the hardiest breads, all came from their oven — foods which, like the sisters' collective personalities, had a pleasant effect on those who passed into the house, so that even their father, who tended to think women "fat," especially when they were wide of hip and heavy in the chest, could not resist picking around in the kitchen cupboards and pantry boxes. The foods he ate, despite his reservations, were so flavorful that he would often astound himself by the servings he wolfed down, as if the naturalness of such consumption seemed to contradict the steely aloofness of being a man. These meals were not only delicious and fattening but they were rich in affection, as the sisters poured not only butter and sugar and blueberry and blackberry sauces over the pancakes they served, but they inculcated the very substance of this fare with such natural tenderness and love that one arose from their meals filled with a sunny optimism, a desire to laugh, and a generally cheerier outlook on life.

This the pilot felt when, swarming around him, the sisters served him a piquant lemonade and some leftover beef stew and potato salad, their eyes on each movement of his knife and fork, impressed by his knee-high leather boots, the half-moons of dust and oil on his brow, the boniness of his hands.

In something like an Arkansas accent, he remarked, "I don't recall having eaten anythin' quite so tasty in a long, long time, ladies. I thank you."

He noticed, too, a pretty young woman across the room in an indigo dress with a red bow, and long black hair to her waist, Italian or in any case Mediterranean-looking — Margarita, with her blue Irish eyes, intently watching the pilot's handsome face. When he looked at her, she smiled and seemed aglow, as she was sitting by the window, a book in hand, she would one day recall. In the natural light, form radiant, her quite beautiful gypsy-looking face was marred only by a slightly crooked row of teeth — her father Nelson's other physical legacy to her — so that her smile was tight-lipped but pleasing just the same.

Margarita had been reading one of L. Frank Baum's Oz tales to two-year-old Carmen when the plane had started buzzing downward, and by then she was immersed in a crumpled-page edition of Sir Walter Scott's *Ivanhoe,* which she had taken from one of the cluttered bookshelves to be found here and there around the house. This, ladies and gentlemen, was the great stash of books that Margarita and her sisters, on her behalf, had collected after a fierce storm in 1915, when the old public library roof was torn away and such books as its humble collection held were carried aloft and scattered over the countryside and left for dead, as it were, their covers buckled, pages swollen and torn or lost, ink running, and text sometimes indecipherable. The sisters headed out with a wheelbarrow and baskets, picking the books out of puddles and fields and out of treetops and down wells and off barn roofs, in the end returning the best-preserved to the library, for which they were paid a penny apiece, and coming away with those books in too bad a condition for the library to keep — a hardship for the collection, but a boon for the household, and especially for Margarita, who loved books and thought that there had never been enough in the house. Suddenly they had gone from owning a dozen books — photography manuals, two Bibles (one in English, another in Spanish), an atlas, a

Catechism (wonderful with its evocation of dark little devils and luminescent angels with burning swords and souls that, as in *The Picture of Dorian Gray,* turned black with sin), and a few other books in Spanish which their mother brought with her in 1902 on her journey from Cuba, one of them entitled *La vida en el planeta marte,* or *Life on the Planet Mars* — to possessing several hundred warped, water-stained, mildewed volumes unsavory in appearance but whose presence, despite their flaws, had made Margarita quite happy in her youth. And there were also the books she would pick out from a barrel in front of Collins' General Store in town, which sold for five cents apiece, obscure stories for the most part, written by retired schoolteachers and New England high-society matrons, with titles like *The President of Quex: A Woman's Club Story* or *The Life of Mary Zenith Hill, Explorer of the Heart,* books in whose pages she would often find pressed flowers and old valentines — *"For my love, thou art the dearest blessing, dearer than the sun"* — and sometimes more well-known books inscribed by their famous authors — *"With best wishes for a jolly Christmas, Rudy Kipling, London 1906."*

Perhaps the docile way Margarita wiped his face with a lemon-scented handkerchief and looked him deep in the eyes, doting upon him, inspired the aviator to call her "kid," as in "Thank you much, kid." And while she being the oldest of the sisters, felt complimented, at the same time it made her feel a little angry — a second-classness anger, a skin-darker-than-what-people-were-used-to-in-these-parts anger, a female-wanting-to-be-taken-seriously anger. And yet, because she liked him so, she thought of his daring exploits and how he had nice full lips, a hard jaw, a curly head of hair, all manly, like in those old army recruitment posters in the town hall, and she blushed.

That was when the twins, Olga and Jacqueline, hoping to impress the handsome young man, stood by the upright piano performing "Come, Josephine, in My Flying Machine." [1993]

SELECTED ADDITIONAL READING

Since a list of primary sources of texts written and published by Latinos during the past 450 years would be absurdly long, we have chosen to recommend here books that have their own bibliographies. We also recommend reading other works by authors represented in this book, including those noted in the introductions to the individual entries, and those listed in the section introductions.

Although no existing scholarly books take a broad overview of literature by Latinos in what is now the United States from its beginnings to the present day, integrating the national groups and time periods, there are some very good books on specific eras, themes, and the national literatures, especially Chicano literature. Ramón Gutiérrez and Genaro Padilla, eds., *Recovering the U.S. Hispanic Literary Heritage* (Arte Público Press, 1993), is an excellent collection of articles that describe the period from 1542 to 1940, with particular emphasis on the nineteenth century. The sources of information listed for each article are helpful, though one hopes that future editions will include a general index and bibliography for the book as a whole. Ilan Stavans's highly personal, extraordinary work, *The Hispanic Condition: Reflections on Culture & Identity in America* (HarperCollins, 1995), is invaluable for the late nineteenth and twentieth centuries because it integrates thematically the cultures of the various groups and their relationship to Latin America. Earl Shorris, *Latinos: A Biography of the People* (Norton, 1992), takes a casebook approach to Latino cultures, with some information on literature.

For Spanish colonial literature, the Quivira Society, under the general editorship of George P. Hammond, in the 1920s and '30s published translations of many colonial works, including those of Garcilaso de la Vega and Pérez de Villagrá. Among these books is an extraordinary two-volume, annotated bibliography of the literature of the colonial period, compiled and edited by Henry Raup Wagner, *The Spanish Southwest, 1542–1794* (Quivira Society, 1937). For a good narrative introduction to the era, Herbert E. Bolton, *The Spanish Borderlands: A Chronicle of Old Florida and the Southwest* (Yale University Press, 1921), is still very readable, as are other titles by Bolton. Frederick W. Hodge, *Spanish Explorers in the Southern United States 1528–1543* (Scribner's, 1907), provides edited versions of the early chronicles, including that of the de Soto expedition by the Hidalgo de Elvas (compare this version to that of Garcilaso de la Vega).

Background on the colonial period in New Mexico is included in the first section of Erlinda Gonzáles-Berry, *Pasó por Aquí: Critical Essays on the New Mexican Literary Tradition 1542–1988* (University of New Mexico Press, 1989), and in María Herrera-Sobek, *Reconstructing a Chicano/a Literary Heritage: Hispanic Colonial Literature of the Southwest* (University of Arizona Press, 1993). For more specific information on Cabeza de Vaca, see the introduction and bibliography in the Martin A. Favata and José B. Fernández edition of *The Account* (Arte Público Press, 1993). The Quivira Society's edition of *The Florida of the Inca* (1931) provides interesting biographical background on the Inca, as does John Grier Varner and Jeannette Johnson Varner's translation of *La florida* (University of Texas Press, 1951). An excellent introduction to Gaspar Pérez de Villagrá can be found in Miguel Encinias, Alfred Rodríguez, and Joseph P. Sánchez, *Introduction to the History of New Mexico* (University of New Mexico Press, 1992). Information on Fray Mathias Sáenz de San Antonio and the Franciscan settlement of Texas can be found in Thomas P. O'Rourke, *The Franciscan Missions in Texas 1690–1793* (Catholic University of America Press, 1927). For information on *Los comanches,* see Aurelio Espinosa's introduction to the play in *The University of New Mexico Bulletin,* Language Series 1, no. 1, 1907, and Arthur L. Campa's commentary in that *Bulletin,* Language Series 7, no. 17, 1942, as well as Reed Anderson's article in the aforementioned *Pasó por Aquí.* For biographical information on Francisco Palóu, see Herbert Bolton's introduction to Palóu, *Historical Memoir of California* (C. L. James, 1927). There are several biographies of Junípero Serra himself, of which Donald Demarest, *The First Californian: The Story of Fray Junípero Serra* (Hawthorn, 1963), presents a good narrative, even though it is a bit too adulatory. A good counterpoint to discussions on the impact of Spanish colonial literature is Ramón Gutiérrez's controversial *When Jesus Came, the Cornmothers Went Away* (Stanford University Press, 1991).

Nineteenth-century scholarship presents a different problem, since much of the literature is only now being recovered from magazines and newspapers of the era. Rodolfo J. Cortina's article "Cuban Literature of the United States 1824–1959" in Gutiérrez and Padilla, *Recovering the U.S. Hispanic Literary Heritage,* gives a good overview of Caribbean literature in the Northeast. Luis Leal's classic "Mexican American Literature: A Historical Perspective," *Revista Chicano-Riqueña* 1, no. 1, 1973, initiated the debate on what constitutes Mexican-American letters. Charles Tatum, *Chicano Literature* (Twayne, 1982), is perhaps still the best overview of the subject, while Ramón Saldívar, *Chicano Narrative: The Dialectics of Difference* (University of Wisconsin Press, 1990), takes a distinctly political view. Julian Olivares, *U.S. Hispanic Autobiography* (Arte Público Press, 1988), is a good introduction to that aspect of Chicano culture. María Herrera-Sobek, *Beyond Stereotypes: The Critical Analysis of Chicana Literature* (Bilingual Press, 1985), has some information on personal narratives of the period; Rosaura Sánchez, *Telling Identities: The Californio testimonios* (University of Minnesota Press, 1995), is an in-depth study of the narratives commissioned by Hubert Howe Bancroft in the late nineteenth century. Américo Paredes, *With His Pistol in His Hand: A Border Ballad and Its Hero* (University of Texas Press, 1958); María Herrera-Sobek, *The Mexican Corrido: A Feminist Analysis* (Indiana University Press, 1990); and José E. Limón, *Mexican Ballads, Chicano Poems* (University of California Press, 1992) are good sources of information on the *corrido.*

Thematic books on the contemporary period abound. In addition to the aforementioned works on Mexican-American literature, many of which include information on the twentieth century, Juan Bruce-Novoa, *Retrospace: Collected Essays on Chicano Literature* (Arte Público Press, 1990), brings together the works of an influential scholar. Joseph Sommers and Tomás Ybarra-Frausto, *Modern Chicano Writers: A Collection of Critical Essays* (Prentice Hall, 1979); Ramón Saldívar, *Chicano Narrative* (mentioned above); José David

Saldívar, *The Dialectics of Our America* (Duke University Press, 1991); and Héctor Calderón and José David Saldívar, *Criticism in the Borderlands: Studies in Chicano Literature, Culture, and Ideology* (Duke University Press, 1991) contain a great deal of interesting ideological analysis and information. Eugene Mohr, *The Nuyorican Experience: Literature of the Puerto Rican Minority* (Greenwood Press, 1982); Asela Rodríguez de Laguna, *Images and Identities: The Puerto Rican in Two World Contexts* (Transaction Books, 1987), and Juan Flores, *Divided Borders: Essays on Puerto Rican Identity* (Arte Público Press, 1993), are valuable. Julio Marzán, *The Spanish American Roots of William Carlos Williams* (University of Texas Press, 1994), is a fascinating study of a poet who has only recently been considered part of the Latino canon.

The growth of literature by Latinas has also spawned critical works. Apart from Herrera-Sobek's work, Norma Alarcón, *Chicana Critical Issues* (Third Woman Press, 1993), and Asunción Horno-Delgado et al., *Breaking Boundaries: Latina Writings and Critical Readings* (University of Massachusetts Press, 1989), are excellent. Good introductory essays also appear in Tey Diana Rebolledo and Eliana S. Rivero, eds., *Infinite Divisions: An Anthology of Chicana Literature* (University of Arizona Press, 1993); Bryce Milligan, Mary Guerrero Milligan, and Angela de Hoyos, eds., *Daughters of the Fifth Sun* (Norton, 1995); and Tey Diana Rebolledo, *Women Singing in the Snow* (University of Arizona Press, 1995).

Sources of biographical information include Francisco A. Lomelí and Carl R. Shirley, *Dictionary of Literary Biography,* volume 82: *Chicano Writers*, First Series (Gale, 1989), and volume 122: *Chicano Writers*, Second Series (Gale, 1992); Lomelí and Julio A. Martínez, *Chicano Literature: A Reference Guide* (Greenwood Press, 1985), and Nicolas Kanellos, *Biographical Dictionary of Hispanic Literature in the United States: The Literature of Puerto Ricans, Cuban Americans, and Other Hispanic Writers* (Greenwood Press, 1989). Readable bibliographies on Latino literature in the United States include Marc Zimmerman, *U.S. Latino Literature: An Essay and Annotated Bibliography* (MARCH/Abrazo Press, 1992), which includes an excellent introduction, and Harold Augenbraum, *Latinos in English: A Selected Bibliography of Latino Fiction Writers of the United States* (Mercantile Library of New York Press, 1992).

ABOUT THE EDITORS

Harold Augenbraum is director of the Mercantile Library of New York and of its Center for World Literature. Among his books are *Latinos in English: A Selected Bibliography of Latino Fiction Writers of the United States* (1992) and *Growing Up Latino* (1993), coedited with Ilan Stavans.

Margarite Fernández Olmos is professor of Spanish at Brooklyn College of the City University of New York. She is the author of *La cuentística de Juan Bosch: un análisis crítico cultural* (1982) and *Sobre la literatura puertorriqueña de aquí y de allá* (1989), and coeditor with Doris Meyer of *Contemporary Women Authors of Latin America:* vol. 1, *Introductory Essays*, and vol. 2, *New Translations* (1983). Her most recent books are *Pleasure in the Word: Erotic Writing by Latin American Women* (1993), *Remaking a Lost Harmony: Stories from the Hispanic Caribbean* (1995), and the forth-coming *Sacred Possessions: Vodou, Santería and Obeah in the Caribbean,* all coedited with Lizabeth Paravisini-Gebert.

CREDITS

Chapters 1, 8, 19, and 22 of *The Account: Álvar Núñez Cabeza de Vaca's Relación,* translated by Martin Favata and José B. Fernández. Reprinted by permission of Arte Público Press, University of Houston.

"Florida," from *The Florida of the Inca* by Garcilaso de la Vega, translated and edited by John Grier Varner and Jeannette Johnson Varner. Copyright © 1951 by John Grier Varner and Jeannette Johnson Varner. Reprinted by permission of the University of Texas Press.

"The History of New Mexico," from *The History of New Mexico* by Gaspar Pérez de Villagrá, translated by Miguel Encinias, Alfred Rodríguez, and Joseph P. Sanchez. Copyright © 1992 by Miguel Encinias, Alfred Rodríguez, and Joseph P. Sanchez. Reprinted by permission of the University of New Mexico Press.

"Lord, If the Shepherd Does Not Hear," by Fray Mathias Sáenz de San Antonio, translated by Harold Augenbraum. Reprinted by permission of Arte Público Press, University of Houston.

"Niagara," by José María Heredia, translated by Harold Augenbraum. Reprinted by permission of Arte Público Press.

"An Old Woman Remembers," by Eulalia Pérez, translated by Vivian C. Fisher, from *Three Memoirs of Mexican California.* Copyright © 1988 by the Friends of the Bancroft Library. Reprinted by permission of the Bancroft Library, University of California.

"Simple Verses," by José Martí, from *José Martí: Major Poems,* translated by Elinor Randall, edited by Philip S. Foner. Copyright © 1982 by Holmes & Meier. Reprinted by permission of Holmes & Meier.

"New York from Within: One Phase of Its Bohemian Life," by Pachín Marín, translated by Lizabeth Paravisini-Gebert. Reprinted by permission of Arte Público Press, University of Houston.

"In the Album of an Unknown Woman" and "Improvisation," by Pachín Marín, translated by Theresa Ortiz de Hadjopoulos. Reprinted by permission of Arte Público Press, University of Houston.

"The Son of the Storm," by Eusebio Chacón, translated by Amy Diane Prince. Reprinted by permission of Arte Público Press, University of Houston.

"The Ballad of Gregorio Cortez," translated by Margarite Fernández Olmos. Reprinted by permission of Arte Público Press, University of Houston.

"The Rebel Is a Girl," from *The Rebel* by Leonor Villegas de Magnón. Reprinted by permission of Arte Público Press, University of Houston.

"To Elsie" and "All the Fancy Things," by William Carlos Williams, from *The Collected Poems of William Carlos Williams,* vol. 1: *1909–1939.* Copyright © 1938 by New Directions Publishing Corp. Reprinted by permission of New Directions Publishing Corp.

"José Campeche, 1752–1809," by Arthur A. Schomburg. Reprinted by permission of the Manuscripts, Archives and Rare Books Division, Schomburg Center for Research in Black Culture, the New York Public Library, Astor, Lenox and Tilden Foundations.

"Memoirs of Bernardo Vega," from *Memoirs of Bernardo Vega,* translated by Juan Flores. Copyright © 1984 by Monthly Review Press. Reprinted by permission of Monthly Review Foundation.

"The Chicken Coop," from *Mexican Village* by Josephina Niggli. Copyright © 1945 by Josephina Niggli. Reprinted by permission of the University of North Carolina Press.

"Returning," by Julia de Burgos, translated by Dwight García and Margarite Fernández Olmos. Reprinted by permission of Arte Público Press, University of Houston.

"Romance of a Little Village Girl," from *Romance of a Little Village Girl* by Cleofas Jaramillo. Reprinted by permission of Virginia M. Smith Rogers.

"God in Harlem," from *Spiks* by Pedro Juan Soto, translated by Victoria Ortiz. Copyright © 1973 by Monthly Review Press. Reprinted by permission of Monthly Review Foundation.

"Pocho," from *Pocho* by José Antonio Villarreal. Copyright © 1959 by José Antonio Villarreal. Reprinted by permission of Doubleday, a division of Bantam Doubleday Dell Publishing Group, Inc.

"The Hammon and the Beans," from *The Hammon and the Beans and Other Stories* by Américo Paredes. Reprinted by permission of Arte Público Press, University of Houston.

"City of Night," from *City of Night* by John Rechy. Copyright © 1963 by John Rechy. Reprinted by permission of Grove/Atlantic, Inc.

"Babylon for the Babylonians," from *Down These Mean Streets* by Piri Thomas. Copyright © 1967 by Piri Thomas. Reprinted by permission of Alfred A. Knopf, Inc.

"Today Is a Day of Great Joy," by Victor Hernández Cruz. Copyright © 1969 by Victor Hernández Cruz. "African Dreams," by Victor Hernández Cruz. Copyright © 1973 by Victor Hernández Cruz. Reprinted by permission of the author.

"el maguey en su desierto," "must be the season of the witch," and "to be fathers once again," from *Floricanto en Aztlán* by Alurista. Copyright © 1971 by Alurista. Reprinted by permission of the Regents of the University of California from *Aztlán: A Journal of Chicano Studies,* vol. 20, nos. 1–2, UCLA Chicano Studies Research Center.

". . . And the Earth Did Not Devour Him," from *. . . y no se lo tragó la tierra / . . . And the Earth Did Not Devour Him* by Tomás Rivera, translated by Evangelina Vigil-Piñón. Reprinted by permission of Arte Público Press, University of Houston.

"Bless Me, Ultima," from *Bless Me, Ultima* by Rudolfo Anaya. Copyright © 1972 by Rudolfo Anaya. Reprinted by permission of Susan Bergholz Literary Services, New York.

"The Revolt of the Cockroach People," from The *Revolt of the Cockroach People* by Oscar "Zeta" Acosta. Copyright © 1973 by Oscar "Zeta" Acosta. Reprinted by permission of Alfred A. Knopf Inc.

"July, 1942," from *Nilda* by Nicholasa Mohr. Reprinted by permission of Arte Público Press, University of Houston.

"Puerto Rican Obituary," by Pedro Pietri. Copyright © 1973 by Pedro Pietri. Reprinted by permission of Monthly Review Foundation.

"Short Eyes," from *Short Eyes* by Miguel Piñero. Copyright © 1974, 1975 by Miguel Piñero. Reprinted by permission of Hill and Wang, a division of Farrar, Straus & Giroux, Inc.

"A Lower East Side Poem," from *La Bodega Sold Dreams* by Miguel Piñero. Reprinted by permission of Arte Público Press, University of Houston.

"Beautiful Señoritas," from *Beautiful Señoritas and Other Plays* by Dolores Prida. Reprinted by permission of Arte Público Press, University of Houston.

"Zoot Suit," from *Zoot Suit and Other Plays* by Luis Valdez. Reprinted by permission of Arte Público Press, University of Houston.

"My Graduation Speech," from *La Carreta Made a U-Turn* by Tato Laviera. Reprinted by permission of Arte Público Press, University of Houston.

"AmeRícan," from *AmeRícan* by Tato Laviera. Reprinted by permission of Arte Público Press, University of Houston.

"A la Mujer Borrinqueña" by Sandra María Esteves. Copyright © 1979 by Sandra María Esteves. "From the Commonwealth," by Sandra María Esteves. Copyright © 1980 by Sandra María Esteves. Reprinted by permission of the author.

"Poem for the Young White Man Who Asked Me How I, an Intelligent, Well-Read Person, Could Believe in the War Between the Races" and "Visions of Mexico While at a Writing Symposium in Port Townsend, Washington," from *Emplumada* by Lorna Dee Cervantes. Copyright © 1981 by Lorna Dee Cervantes. Reprinted by permission of the University of Pittsburgh Press.

"Aria," from *Hunger of Memory: The Education of Richard Rodriguez* by Richard Rodriguez. Copyright © 1982 by Richard Rodriguez. Reprinted by permission of David R. Godine, Publisher, Inc.

"Caesar and the Brutuses: A Tradegy," from *Family Installments: Memories of Growing Up Hispanic* by Edward Rivera. Copyright © 1982 by Edward Rivera. Reprinted by permission of William Morrow & Company.

"A Long Line of Vendidas" and "Loving in the War Years," from *Loving in the War Years: lo que nunca pasó por sus labios* by Cherrie Moraga. Copyright © 1983 by Cherrie Moraga. Reprinted by permission of South End Press.

"The Moths," from *The Moths and Other Stories* by Helena María Viramontes. Reprinted by permission of Arte Público Press, University of Houston.

"Ending Poem," from *Getting Home Alive* by Aurora Levins Morales and Rosario Morales. Copyright © 1983 by Aurora Levins Morales and Rosario Morales. Reprinted by permission of Firebrand Books, Ithaca, New York.

"Doña Sóstenes, from *Klail City* by Rolando Hinojosa-Smith. Reprinted by permission of Arte Público Press, University of Houston.

"How to Tame a Wild Tongue," from *Borderlands/La Frontera: The New Mestiza* by Gloria Anzaldúa. Copyright © 1987 by Gloria Anzaldúa. Reprinted by permission of Aunt Lute Books.

"Woman Hollering Creek," from *Woman Hollering Creek and Other Stories* by Sandra Cisneros. Copyright © 1991 by Sandra Cisneros. Reprinted by permission of Susan Bergholz Literary Services, New York.

"Dreaming in Cuban," from *Dreaming in Cuban* by Cristina Garcia. Copyright © 1992 by Cristina Garcia. Reprinted by permission of Alfred A. Knopf, Inc.

"American History" and "Guard Duty," from *The Latin Deli: Prose and Poetry* by Judith Ortiz Cofer. Copyright © 1993 by Judith Ortiz Cofer. Reprinted by permission of the University of Georgia Press.

"The Handsome Man from Heaven," from *The Fourteen Sisters of Emilio Montez O'Brien* by Oscar Hijuelos. Copyright © 1993 by Oscar Hijuelos. Reprinted by permission of Farrar, Straus & Giroux, Inc.